# BURNED

## A Daughters of Salem Novel

Kellie O'Neill

For mom, miss you.

# A Spell for Grief

*(For those whose hearts need mending)*

## Ingredients:

Amethyst                White Virgin Candle*
Votive                  Lavender Oil
Moon Water

## Instructions:

Using your thumb and forefinger, grace the candle with lavender oil. Place the candle in votive in three inches of moon water, then place the amethyst at the midnight position of your candle. Whisper the incantation to the flame, then blow out the candle.

## Incantation:

*Blessed be the sacred fell,*
*The candles glow, the heart will tell,*
*Quit the flame and soul be free,*
*Gone be grief, blessed be.*

*a candle that has never been lit

# Chapter One
## The Funeral

"As we walk through the valley of the shadow of death…"

The priest, robed in black polyester, towers over my father's closed casket in reverence, reading scripture to the church over-flowing with strangers.

My grandmother Lydia, clad in black Chanel, is draped over my father's casket like a veil. She brays, vying for the same attention sought by my father's siblings strategically in the center pew as if grief is somehow a contest. This tactical game for the congregation's sympathy is more transparent than they realize.

The only genuine emotion in the room comes from the actual mourners: my two sisters, my mother, and myself. They've never been ones for such performances. Neither have I.

My mother, standing at my side, gives my hand a small squeeze. My younger sister, Margaret, burrows her face into our mother's slender shoulder. Beside her is our older sister, Shannyn, home from Harvard for the funeral, standing resolute and determined not to show weakness in front of the extended family. She gently brushes away a few stubborn tears and bites down hard to silence her trembling lower lip. For her benefit, I pretend not to notice when her shoulders shudder and crumble, giving way to her grief.

"Seriously, Eleanor? Not a single tear for your dead dad?" my cousin Allegra hisses at me from behind.

My chest tightens and I peer down, letting my long dark hair hide my face.

She doesn't need to see my eyes to know there are no tears to be found.

I can't cry. It's not because of any lack of love for my dad, that isn't it at all. I just can't cry. It's as if my tear ducts choose not to cooperate. They'll perform the other duties of a tear duct, glossing and clearing out my eyes, but full-on tears, beautiful emotion-filled tears have, for some reason, always eluded me. I don't know why. But my parents never seemed to worry, so they never sought treatment for my tearless "condition".

Although I don't show it, my pain is very real, too real. My entire body aches with misery, my limbs feel intolerably heavy to the point that even breathing is an impossible chore. If I focus too much on the fact that my father is gone, my heart races with each piercing thought. *I won't see him tomorrow. Dad won't see me graduate. Dad won't be at my wedding one day. We'll never snorkel again. He'll never again deliver one of his cringe-inducing jokes. He'll never put his arm around me again. Oh, Dad...*

I clutch my chest. My heart withers, aching to quell the pain. But despite the screaming inside, my exterior is silent, calm, and cold.

After my father's service, everyone congregates at our house for a light buffet, as if eating eases all human pain. I watch them, like moths to the flame they gather. Everyone eats as if they have been deprived of food their entire lives. I guess I can't blame them; my mom is an incredible cook. She insisted on cooking — I think to keep herself busy. Though her hands have always worked miracles in the kitchen.

My dad used to say that everything flourishes around my mother. If she isn't adding some secret touch to an old family recipe, she is restoring life to the most wilted of plants. Her green thumb isn't limited to the garden, either. Even her patients at the hospital just seem to heal faster when she's around.

I sit on our over-stuffed sofa, hoping the "mourners" will leave soon, but no one obliges my silent wish. My stomach twists and churns as I watch them desecrate our family pictures. They pick them up, discuss them, pass them between each other, and then put them back on the shelf out of place. I'm failing to ignore their catty, meaningless chatter.

"I don't know what William saw in her," spits one of my mother's "friends".

Another woman chimes in. "Did you notice none of Helen's family is here? I wonder what the story is behind that. You never hear about them..."

"Poor Lydia. Everyone knows William was her favorite."

"That won't matter in the end. He isn't a Brandt. He's from the first marriage, so when Lydia kicks, William's family won't get anything. Robert made sure of that before he passed. Iron clad will, and Lydia wouldn't even bother trying to change that now..."

Someone mumbles my name nearby, and my ears perk.

My cousin Leah leans over to Allegra, whispering just low enough to pretend they are attempting to gossip in private. "Pretty sure I cried more than Eleanor today. I mean, the way she acts; I'd be freaking out. But she's like, 'hey, NBD, I still have a trust fund.'"

Allegra grunts. "Not anymore. Daddy said they lost almost everything in the market."

Leah chuckles gleefully. "That's hilarious." They both glance over at me sitting on the sofa. I'm quick to look away as to not make it obvious I can hear their cruel judgements.

"But damn, if losing your platinum card isn't enough to make you cry, you'd think getting your dad killed would," Allegra snaps before whipping out her phone, taking a picture of something in the living room. "Okay Leah, selfie!" They flash duck lips in front of my parent's wedding photo. "Hashtag: mourning. Hashtag: Uncle Will forever."

*They seriously need to leave.*

I ball my fists, my nails sinking deeply into my palms, creating little crescent moons in the skin. I want to keep squeezing, tighter and tighter until my bones shatter.

Instead, I desperately scan the room for my younger sister, Margaret, or Maggie, as we call her. I hope she hasn't heard the poisonous remarks the guests are pouring all over our father's memory. I fight the urge to run to her, cover her ears and whisk her from the room to protect her despite the fact that she's fourteen.

My eyes find her, but we don't connect. I slump back on the sofa. She's sitting on a stool by the dining room, her copper curls pulled up into a bun on the crown of her head. Her freckled hands clutch her soccer ball. My dad used to practice with her for hours and hours in the yard, until the sun went down, and they couldn't see the goal posts any longer.

My heart clenches. *I miss him so much...*

I glance at my older sister perched on the edge of the leather armchair. Shannyn is either determined to ignore the barbarous cracks made at our family's expense or is completely oblivious to them. She smiles graciously as there is a line of attractive men waiting to press or impress their condolences upon her. Shannyn tilts her soft chin, acknowledging the gentle words being said. She is always so poised, so elegant and graceful. Everything I'm not. She tucks her long hair behind her dainty ears, unintentionally bringing attention to her delicate neckline. The men (some of whom are relatives) gaze at her glowing locks. Dad used to tease that her hair is as light as mine is dark.

"Helen can cook, but decorating is not her forte..."

I quietly slip out of the living room, hoping to find a moment's peace elsewhere. The kitchen and dining room are overcrowded with hungry guests going for seconds and thirds at the buffet. Grandma Lydia is holding an assembly at the dining room table, dabbing her puffy eyes with her mono-grammed handkerchief.

I stop as I come to the sliding glass doors of the kitchen. My eyes sweep over the patio and backyard, past the pool towards my mother's garden, to an old, weathered whicker bench. Sitting on its faded cushion is my mother. Her head is cradled in her hands, collecting her sorrow. I feel a lump gather in my throat. My hand slides down the glass, resting on the handle, ready to pull the door open to go be a comforting shoulder for my mom, or maybe a comforting hug, a comforting something.

As I flip the lock and move to open the door, my temples begin to pound like a bass drum. I squeeze my eyes shut as an electrical storm brews behind my forehead. I turn away from the sun, which has just begun to set on the early spring horizon. When the light hits my eyes, I am momentarily blinded. My desire to be a warm embrace for my mom is sadly overshadowed by the tempest in my head violently demanding attention.

I sprint past inquiring looks and insulting glances by family as I rush upstairs to my bedroom, looking for a reprieve from the storm. This type of headache has become a nearly constant companion since my seventeenth birthday five days ago.

I throw myself onto my bed and prepare for the pain to worsen. Before my birthday, I had never experienced headaches like these. I massage my temples, hoping the pain will stop. I have yet to tell my mother of the phys-ical agony I am in; my physical discomfort is very much outweighed by her emotional pain. A headache, no matter how intolerable, is inconsequential when compared to losing your soulmate.

I want to scream. The physical anguish is staggering. I could swear some kind of pickaxe-wielding creatures are trying to crack their way through my skull. I roll to my side. The pain is so intense I feel like vomiting. Clutching my waist, I feel a deep, roiling burn brewing more and more intensely in my stomach. I think about shrieking for help as it spreads to my limbs, causing my joints to tighten as if being screwed into torturous immobility.

My entire body stiffens as if rigor mortis is setting in. My pores smolder like magma is running through my veins. If I could move, I would peer down just to see if steam was rising from me.

Finally, my body begins to cool. It starts on my skin, then slowly sinks down to my marrow. I let out a deep breath, the evil little miners in my head tiptoe back into oblivion. Relief floods through me while my body relaxes. The pain is tapering out, fading into a prickling white noise at the fringe of my consciousness. *What the hell is happening to me?*

There's a soft rap on my door and before I can answer, Shannyn steps into my room. Her light brown eyes appraise me. "Are you okay?" she questions, sounding genuinely concerned.

I can barely squeak out a yes, so I limply nod, not moving from a prone position.

She lightly sits on the corner of the bed. "Has Mom talked to you yet?"

I close my eyes, resting against my pillows. "Talked to me about what?" I can feel her adjust herself on my bed before standing up and walking about my room, as if looking for something.

She irons out the creases of her black satin dress. "You guys are moving. Mom doesn't want to stay in Florida anymore, so she's moving with you and Margaret to live in Salem with Aunt Marie and Aunt Sally. Mom needs to be near her family now." She sounds dry and rehearsed, like she's reading off some script.

I'm suddenly drenched by a bucket of ice water. We don't even know our aunts. I've only met them once, when I was very little; I'll be living with complete strangers. My heart throbs at the prospect of leaving Coral Gables. This is where my friends are, the junior orchestra, the place where we were a family. Dad loved this house and now we are just going to up and abandon it? Abandon our lives? Abandon Dad?

I'm too exhausted to protest. Despite the resentment I feel, I know in my heart it is what is best for Mom. She doesn't have a lot of friends here. My father's family never liked her, and she isn't emotionally tied to the little clinic where she works. Maybe this will be good for Maggie, too.

Tears well in my eyes, but as always, nothing falls. "Okay," I mumble.

My sister nods ever so slightly with a relieved and satisfied smile. She turns to leave, opening the door only to swivel on her heel. "Ell?"

I roll onto my side, curling up into a ball. "What?" I sniff, not looking at my sister. Waiting for her reply, I spot a small black spider in the corner of the ceiling near my closet. I watch as it slowly repels down its silky, and translucent web. This is the third spider I've found in my room this week. Not to mention the nightmare I had on my birthday where I was covered in them.

My sister takes a tentative step closer to my bed. "Don't fight against it…"

I roll my eyes at her cryptic comment. "What are you talking about, the move?"

She lowers her voice, her brow knitted in concern. "The pain."

# Chapter Two
## Salem

Time is a *very* relative thing. The flight to Boston was only three hours and seventeen minutes, technically, but it felt like an eternity. I never got Shannyn alone again to ask her what she meant about not fighting the pain. Somehow, her ticket got randomly upgraded to first class, leaving Mom, Maggie, and me in coach. Whenever I tried to pull Shannyn aside, either my mother would call for one of us or Shannyn's phone would go off with her boyfriend Lennox trying to reach her. Maybe Shannyn was just experiencing grief-induced migraines like me. But mine started before I had any reason to grieve…

I stare at Shannyn from my seat several rows behind her. *Why is she avoiding me?* I quickly avert my eyes while the Italian tourist next to her prattles on about her brown eyes being boundless or endless. Something cheesy like that.

I give into an eye roll and lean my head back. No hot tourist would ever call my eyes a creamy chocolate that melts. *Gag. Talk about laying it on thick.* No, instead I have a *slight* genetic albinism. Not full albinism, not enough to make my hair white or lose all pigmentation in my skin. Just *very* purple eyes and *very* pale skin. I'm the only one in my family with the trait. I used to come home sobbing (without tears) when I was in grade school after having been teased, but my mother reassured me they were just jealous. *Yeah, right…* Now when I go out with friends, people ask how in the world I have such violet eyes. I would tell them about my albinism, and they'd try to not seem grossed out by it. My parents had always tried to make me feel better about my eyes. My dad would bring up the likes of Elizabeth Taylor, but right before we booked our flight to Boston, my mom suggested wearing colored contacts.

"Hey, these are for you," my mom said, standing in the doorway as she tosses me a small white box.

"What are these?" I asked, sitting in my bedroom surrounded by stacked cardboard boxes. I examine the package in my hand featuring pictures of teenagers with large doe eyes staring out. *Eyes Perfected,* the box reads. "Mom?" I question, turning it over. *Achieve Those Beautiful Brown Eyes You've Always Desired.*

"Just try them, please. It's really not that big of a deal," she said dismissively.

I frowned. "If it's not a big deal, then why do I have to cover up my eyes?"

Mom exhaled irritably. "Please don't argue with me, Eleanor. Just try them."

The plane shudders slightly. I take out my compact, my elbow accidentally poking the passenger next to me. I quickly apologize and duck my head, glancing at my reflection in the round mirror. I peer down at the contacts in my purse. *Maybe I can tone it down with make-up?* Gently, as to not bother either sleeping gentlemen at my sides, I fish out my dark blue eyeliner and do a quick sweep. The blue makes my violet irises look a more vibrant bluish-lavender than a too-strange-to-be-cool purple.

I peer around the portly man on my left to spy at my mom across the aisle with Margaret tucked in close to her, fast asleep.

I'm jittery with nerves. I keep chewing away at what's left of my thumbnail. My eyes drift back to my phone, as if I'm expecting some text or notification from a friend. But I know in my gut there won't be one when we land. Saying goodbye to my friends wasn't as messy as I had thought it would be. I actually expected an influx of love and sadness accompanied by unwanted attention and sympathies for my father. Instead, I was met with cold, unfeeling indifference. The one person who was kind to me was the only male in the orchestra, which somehow turned into a long, awkwardly tender embrace. I don't think he had ever spoken to me before that.

After the flight, it is just a forty-five-minute drive to Salem. The sky is a clear baby blue with puffy cartoon-like clouds. Margaret and my dad would have played the 'What Do You See in the Clouds' game. Of course, she would have objected first, claiming she was too old, only to quickly spot the first object. But he isn't here. He won't be at our aunts'. He won't see us off for school tomorrow. I swallow a whimper and lean my head against the window. My insides are twisted, like I am about to be sick. *I miss you so much, Dad. No. No. I can't fall apart right now. No.* I quickly straighten up in my seat, desperate to distract myself.

As we wind through the streets of Salem, my mom refusing to admit we're lost, a white building to the right catches my eye. It's a two-story

Georgian Colonial mansion with blue shutters. Surrounding the home is a mostly dead garden only just showing the first signs that a spring bloom is near, and the entire scene is actually… quite beautiful.

I'm amazed to find beauty while I am in such a sour mood. I'm used to the spicy Cuban air of tropical south Florida, with Art Deco architecture and the city with its majestic skyline filled to the brim with glass and chrome skyscrapers. The teaming Miami streets trapped in the salty smell of the ocean and the lush tropical humidity. But Salem is like a portal into the History Channel. A beautiful, quaint city plucked from Europe and dropped on our eastern shores.

It feels like we've gone back in time as we speed past old brick and clapboard buildings, the kind you'd see in history books. Dead vines of ivy spider across the building walls in a twisted, spindly mass. Crusty snow scabs up the gutters and small piles of it battle the sun while they melt, reluctantly watering the lawns.

The harbor with all its greys and blues is, for all intents and purposes, nice. Still, it can't compare to Biscayne Bay back home with its eternal summer of tropical heat.

We pass some rather scruffy characters who walk around the harbor in thick wool coats with fishing nets slung over their shoulders.

"Hey, Ell," Maggie calls. "Didn't we see those guys on a box of fish sticks?"

I can't help but chuckle. They do look like the quintessential fishermen with their lumbering rubber boots, their yellow water repellent hats and mangy facial hair. But unlike the fishermen from Herman Melville, these men have iPhones in their chapped, worn hands.

My mother stops the car to get directions to my aunts' home. Out the window, sitting by the dock, is a couple about my age wearing heavy, thick sweatshirts. The boy is in hiking boots and the girl in Hunter rubber boots. Now if this was back home, she would be in a bikini top and shorts and he would probably be shirtless, showing off his golden-brown tan. I doubt my wardrobe will work here; I'm going to stick out like a frozen thumb. Fortunately, I don't have to worry about what to wear to school; Mom said my new school has uniforms. If I have to wear a costume, at least I won't be the only one.

Mom puts the car in drive, arguing with Shannyn about Google Maps not working and how the men were no help either, much to my mother's chagrin.

"Mom, just turn here, seriously. How are you this directionally challenged?" Shannyn says. Her voice is part teasing, part exasperated.

We drive away from town and into a thick forest, passing incredible trees the likes of which I've never seen. They're tall, skeletal giants with moss and bracken covering every bit of bark. From the sharp, sprawling branches emerge the first green buds of spring's renewal, existing in contrast to the last dregs of winter lingering in shadowy corners.

"Mom, see? I told you, that's why it wasn't coming up on the map. When Sal called, she told you the road wasn't marked," Shannyn says.

We drive down a gravel road parting thick birch and dense pine like Moses through the red sea. The sky is completely blotted out by the tree's canopy, leaving us in a midday shadow. I adjust in my seat and gaze out the back window of the rental car. The gravel road disappears in the foliage behind us as if swallowed by some ancient serpent.

Margaret slings her arm around my shoulders as she whispers, "and that's the last anyone ever saw of them." Her smirk gives way into a snorty laugh and even I have to smile.

We approach a clearing, gradually making our way out of the forest tunnel. Sunlight paints patterns across an immense lawn framed by a broken wooden fence with peeling paint. The disjointed fence looks more like mangled, withered hands reaching up from the grave than a white picket "American dream" enclosure. A once-grand Victorian home comes into view. My mother coasts to a stop where the picket fence crumbles into complete disarray. All that's missing from this horror-film-waiting-to-happen is a dirty old harbinger warning us to go no further and to turn back now. *If only we would.*

Mom never talked about our aunts, or really anything about her family, for that matter. They never once paid us a visit in the past ten years. But neither did we. I've always had hurt feelings toward this side of my family, never even considering until now that it might be the other way around.

Mom stares at the house, and for a moment her teeth clench behind sneering lips. She quickly amends with a smile and says weakly, "Well, we're here."

I can't pinpoint it, but there's something eerie about the house that goes well beyond its obvious "Haunted Mansion" theme. It makes the hair on my neck stand on end. Everything just seems out of place or not quite fitting in. It's beautiful but brooding, stunning yet spooky. Like blood smeared across a priceless Monet.

"This… is… awesome!" Margaret says. "Ten bucks I see a ghost by midnight."

"Ten bucks you become a ghost by midnight," I mumble.

Shannyn twists in her seat to face me. "Eleanor, you love those gross scary movies. I'd think you'd be in heaven living in a place like this."

I roll my eyes. "I like them. No interest in actually being in one."

"Enough," my mom cuts in. "This isn't a haunted house. There's nothing freaky going on. So please, just stop with the ghost talk. It might be a bit of a fixer-upper, but that's it."

We all turn and gaze back at the house. The clapboard Victorian has strange early-colonial touches with a gothic ambience. It's a dingy white, as if someone had sprinkled it with soot and then unsuccessfully tried to wash it off, repeating the entire process over and over again. It has a weird, angular shape with a wraparound porch and a sinister-looking tower at the top. A broken porch swing by the front door suggests a lonely sadness to the otherwise edgy feel of the house. A few windows in the front look out onto the road. The blue shutters next to them hang by a thread, but somehow look like they have been hung crooked on purpose.

An ancient oak nearly blocks the entire left side of the house, screaming for its own haunted attention. The branches twist and unfurl, like a primordial giant reaching out from his grave. *It looks so… morbid.*

We all sit in the car staring, not moving. Shannyn glances around from the passenger's seat gaging our reactions, completely unaffected by the Aunts' home. *Is this not her first time here? She lives in Boston for school, but why would she ever reach out to our estranged aunts?*

"I don't see the moving truck, so let's just go inside and try to be polite," my mom instructs in her best no-nonsense tone. She releases a sigh and unclips her seatbelt. "And Margaret, no ball in the house."

Margaret scowls. "Seriously? Like what the hell, Mom. I'm not five years old."

"And don't swear, I mean it. They like clean mouths, not trashy mouths." No longer gazing at Maggie and I in the back seat, instead my mom's hyperventilating and carrying on her lecture to seemingly no one in particular. "And don't mention Marie's ex-husband Howard, or his son Marcus. And please don't listen to either of their nonsense, and none of their holistic medicines or fixes or anything!"

Maggie giggles. "Really, Mom? You shoved herbs up Shannyn's nose when she broke it."

Shannyn, unfazed by our panicking mother, glances over her shoulder. "It worked, didn't it?"

Mom ignores us completely and closes her eyes, thinking. I can just see on her face she is searching for anything else she may have missed in our prep. Her eyes pop open. "Don't slag off. This isn't a holiday we're on, so watch yourself! I'm in charge and you're still my wains and what I say is law!"

Mom screeches the last part in a thick Irish brogue reminiscent of before she immigrated to the States. It only creeps out when she's most agitated.

*What in the actual hell is happening to her?*

Shannyn and Margaret snicker.

"Um...Mom, your Irish is really coming out," Shannyn teases with a grin, trying to ease the tension.

Mom peeks at us from the rearview mirror and a reluctant smile forms. Then she squints at me. "Eleanor, you aren't wearing the contacts I bought you?"

I bite my lower lip and turn away.

"Are we allowed to get out or...?" Maggie asks.

Mom lets out a heavy sigh through her nostrils, then takes off her sunglasses and tosses them onto the dashboard.

Margaret is the first to jump out the door and nods her head toward the house; Shannyn follows suit. As I slide out of the seat, I can hear my mom grumble, "this was a mistake."

By the time we reach the veranda, Maggie's already knocked on the front door. Mom and I arrive last, neither of us in a rush to start this lesser life without Dad. However, Mom's arms are tightly folded; she seems to dread this even more than I expected.

There are no neighbors on either side, not for miles. A chilled wind breathes through the trees, causing the branches to bend and bow like fingers ominously waving.

I grip my maroon zip-up hoodie around me tighter as goosebumps prickle across my skin. The broken fence, the twisted oak, the branches of the forest, we're surrounded by all manner of claws beckoning us closer, unable to disguise their malevolence beneath.

"Who the hell is it?" barks a coarse, coughing voice from inside. "Damnit, where's my drink?"

I raise one eyebrow and smirk at my mom. "Clean mouths, eh?" I say cleverly.

My mom ignores my wisecrack and knocks once more. "Sally, Marie? It's Helen."

"Who?" the voice asks again.

I nod my head and roll back on my heels. *Well, this looks promising.*

Shannyn shoves her cell into the back pocket of her tight jeans with an exaggerated roll of her eyes. She lifts her hand, about to grip the brass door knocker shaped like a hare, its body impaled by a tarnished golden ring.

"Shut up, Sally!" a second voice scolds. "It's our baby sister, Helen, and her daughters! They were coming today, remember?"

Shannyn drops her hand and turns to hide a small, impish smile.

Somewhere behind the door, feet shuffle quickly, accompanied by the sound of sharp nails dragging across the wood.

"Oohh, oh, oh come in! Come in! It's not locked!" the first woman calls. I peer through the spacious front windows, startled to see six or more curious cats glaring back at us.

I jump in front of the door. "Mom! You didn't say they had cats!" I spread my hands out, blocking the door.

Mom looks confused. Then she spots the cats in the window and hears them clawing at the door behind me. She sighs and lets her mask slip, showing a moment of relief. "Eleanor, it's time you get over your phobia of cats."

I cross my arms across my chest. "It's not a phobia. I'm like, deathly allergic. They're going to kill me," I lie.

"Not from allergies," Shannyn mumbles under her breath.

Margaret tries to stifle a laugh without success.

"Ell, it's time," Mom says. She gives my shoulder a condescending squeeze.

"What in the hell is happening? Are they coming in or?" the second voice says, disgruntled from behind the front door.

Margaret groans. "Oh my gosh, seriously, let's go in already!" She pushes me aside and swings open the door; immediately the cats creep and crawl over to us. I cringe and swallow, with difficulty, as they rub against my legs. *Why cats? Why not dogs? Why not hamsters? Hell, I'd take freaking pigeons.* I'm so focused on the cats I don't even notice the long arms wrapping around me like boa constrictors.

"Eleanor, babe! It has been way too damn long!" My aunt exclaims.

I think of my mother's clean mouth comment again. I can tell from the short, spiky black hair, with way too much hair gel, it's my Aunt Sally. I haven't seen her since I was seven, but she is still rocking the Morticia Addams wardrobe and Halle Berry pixie. She pushes me aside, nearly sending me stumbling to the floor, and hugs Shannyn. Then Marie grabs me and smothers me in her arms. Her frizzy grayish-red hair is everywhere, as if fashioned by a whirlwind, poking me in the eye as she pulls me close.

"Ellie, how are you, dearie?" she calls into my ear. Her thick wool sweater is like a Brillo pad against my cheek.

Marie doesn't wait for an answer and releases me from her vice-like grip. "Eleanor, you need to eat something; you feel a little too thin," she says. She pokes me in the ribs and tugs on my cheeks and arms. Sally nods in agreement, but she is hardly one to point fingers. She looks like a toothpick on a diet.

Sally claps her boney hands together, causing her many gold bangles to jingle and clang. "Oh Helen, we missed you so much! We still can't believe you girls are really here!" She squeals. "Though we've already gotten the chance to get acquainted with this beauty!" Sally snakes her thin arm around Shannyn's waist.

The color drains from my mother's face. "How nice," she says through a mechanical, locked-in smile.

I turn, letting my eyes drift to the front door directly behind me, as if any minute now my dad will come in carrying our luggage, and "thank us" for helping with the bags.

Marie grips my mom's shoulders. "Not to worry, Helen. We just had some clever chit chats over tea. Nothing too alarming."

We all stay huddled in the dim entryway with all the cats. To our right is a wide-open living room with walls papered in a faded, mustard yellow floral pattern. Though the pattern is mostly obscured by dozens of antique framed photographs, all black and white and sepia toned. Some are of people I don't recognize, and others are of random objects, such as an apple resting on a stool in the yard, a cat laying in a bed of squashed flowers, and the large dead oak tree outside while it was raining.

Of course, this antique home would have no television, just gigantic windows that let in a small amount of sunlight through the heavy velvet curtains that are only halfway open. The room basks in a yellow glow coming from a high hanging crystal chandelier. I squint, looking closer. Hanging from one of the crystal strands is a—I frown—a rubber spider? *They are either decorating for Halloween very late or very early.*

Once Maggie is done with her welcome hugs, she bends down and begins stroking the cats.

The pernicious cats all circle around Maggie. "What are all your cats' names?" she asks, making sure to pet each one of them. She grins as an orange tabby cat purrs and rubs its skinny body up her leg, leaving a trail of orange hair.

*Gross.*

Marie kneels at her side with a proud look and says, "the Siamese one Sally is holding is Pyre, she and Sal are very close. See that grey one right there, with the white patch above her nose? That is Freya. The smokey grey cat is Gunther, that little dwarf cat scratching at the door is Newton, and the orange tabby that you are petting, Margaret sweetie, is Phoenix, and his identical sister there is Persephone."

Marie's eyes practically glisten as she turns toward the sun-bleached, fainting couch in front of the window. "And that beautifully full-bodied white princess on the couch is Miss Priss, her lover is the miserable-looking thing near the window named Neptune" — miserable doesn't even cover it, he looks like someone had bashed his face in with a shovel — "and the Bengal cat, you know, the one laying near Shannyn's foot is named Cat." She pauses, producing a ball of string from, well I'm not sure where, and rolls it across the floor for the cats. Only two even pay attention.

Margaret seems excited to be living in a house that I'm sure under a black light looks like a Jackson Pollock from all the cat urine. My mother is still worried for some reason. Her somewhat bloodshot eyes stray to my face, then dart away when we make contact.

Marie claps, watching the short, squatty Newton bat at some yarn with Gunther. My curvaceous aunt shoves one hand into the pocket of her long open knit sweater that drags on the floor, and motions to the enormous spiral staircase behind her. "And that black cat with the deep blue eyes, sitting up on the staircase behind you, my dear, is Blue-Eyes. Be very careful with him."

"Ten cats? Wow," Maggie says, petting Phoenix affectionately.

Shannyn lovingly scoops up Cat and snuggles its face against her cheek. The cat is a strange mishmash of tiger stripes and cheetah spots.

I try to conceal the disgust on my face. This place is essentially one big litter box. I don't care how big this house is; ten cats are more than terrifying, they're disgusting. I can't help but glance over at the thin black cat perched on the stairs. Blue-Eyes stares at me, right into my eyes like he's challenging me. *Cats are the only vermin that look people in the eye like they're equals.* My thought is immediately followed by a distinct scoff, like an amused huff that sends a chill up my spine.

Marie shrugs at Maggie's ten cat comment. "Well, they aren't all ours. I mean, Cat belongs to Shannyn but lives here because cats aren't allowed at her apartment building. Gunther is her boyfriend's cat, and Persephone is actually your mother's cat she left in our care years ago."

Sally glances over at Blue-Eyes, then back to me, then back to the damn cat.

"How old are you now, Eleanor?" Sally asks innocently.

Marie straightens up and looks over at Sally in surprise. She then takes a closer look, staring at my eyes. "Eleanor, those eyes, are…interesting. Have they always been that way, dear?"

I open my mouth to answer my age and hopefully sidestep the circus-freak thing; then I remember my mother wanted me to wear contacts. She didn't want her sisters to see my eyes. *Why not?* My heart skips a beat.

My mom interjects before I can answer. "Sally, Marie, why don't you come with me into the kitchen? We need to talk. Girls, why don't you take a look around." Mom snatches Marie's arm and shepherds Sally towards the kitchen.

"Yes, yes, um, the rooms upstairs are labeled where you will be staying!" Marie calls over my mother's shoulder as she is pushed down the hall. The curvy woman nearly trips on her long peasant skirt.

Blue-Eyes, as if annoyed at the sudden new company, leaps lithely off the staircase and lands without so much as a creak on the floor and curls up on the couch.

Shannyn sighs. "Well, I would love to stay and watch Mom freak out, but I have a class tomorrow and a paper to write… Plus I agreed to meet Lennox—so have fun, girls." She hugs Maggie and I. Perfect timing as her boyfriend, Lennox, pulls up in his silver Audi. I can tell by the look on her face she knows exactly what Mom and her sisters are whispering about. Shannyn skips out the door and off the veranda.

Maggie and I stare out the front window, watching our older sister leave. Shannyn is in her third year at Harvard. She chose the Ivy League school to study Art History because her high school sweetheart Lennox Burroughs was attending the school. With every Sunday night phone call, she would go on and on about the seasons, the snowfall, the autumn colors, the history, the people, blah, blah, blah, blah, blah. Give me the Florida sun and beaches over snow and sleet any day. But she never ever mentioned Sally, Marie, or Cat.

"I'm so jealous," Margaret mumbles, still staring after our sister.

"Of…?"

She rolls her eyes at me. "Hello?! Lennox, he's so hot!"

"You think so?" I ask in surprise. I never really thought about it myself. He'd been essentially dating our older since they were both twelve years old. And yes, I've heard girls, Shannyn included, describe him as 'chiseled', but to me he was already another family member, an older brother.

"Ah yeah, he looks like Michael B. Jordan," she says longingly, then releases a sigh.

"Who?" I ask, squinting out the window as if I could see through the trees and still spot them.

Maggie's head drops back dramatically. "Oh, my gosh, Ell! Creed movies? He played Erik Killmonger, Marvel? Really? I mean, you can watch that stupid silent film Nosfa-ru-too a million times, but you can't make time for something made this century?"

Now it was my time to roll my eyes. "It's Nosferatu, and it's an amazing movie. One of Dad's favorites," I say, ending in a near whisper. My heart gives a weak stab, as if it can no longer conjure up a sharp, blade-like response. It's too broken and bloody for much more than that.

Maggie's lower lip trembles. Fresh tears gloss over her dark green eyes. "He liked anything in black and white." Her eyes, downcast, look haplessly lost.

I need to do something. A distraction. I wordlessly tug on Maggie's olive-green coat and motion towards the large spiral staircase left of the entryway. She nods and turns her head, trying to conceal the tears she anxiously wipes away.

Phoenix stays close to her as we climb. I clench the rail, feeling the stairs bow as if the shiny veneer surface hides the rotten core beneath it. Each step makes its own unique cry of pain from the weight. Maggie releases a laugh, before glancing down at the steep fall we would make if the wood collapsed.

She stops and scoops up Phoenix, snuggling his small head to her chest. "Well, we didn't crash through and shatter our bones," she jokes when we reach the top.

The landing is shaped like a pentagram with an enormous grandfather clock ticking between two doors ahead of us. In the middle of the landing, stands a round table sheathed with a moss-colored cloth and a ceramic vase. The vase is filled with pussy willow branches, cattails, and... *holy crap, is that hemlock?*

"Don't touch the vase, okay?" I instruct Margaret.

"You're looking at the weeds? Ell, look at this place!" Maggie says. She spins around the table. "Look at the ceiling. It's painted like that chapel... ugh, I forget the name." She racks her brain, searching for the answer.

"Sistine," I retort.

"Ugh, I was about to say it!" she exclaims. I watch as she twirls, arms out as if she's using every ounce of energy she possesses to conjure up some excitement. "This place is awesome!"

For as long as I've known my sister, Maggie was never glass half-empty; her cup was always overflowing. Every rain cloud, a silver lining. Margaret was that good girl you couldn't keep down.

"More like an asylum," I mumble to myself.

On each side of the pentagram, there is a dark chestnut brown door identical to the flooring (minus the dust and scuff marks). The antique brass doorknobs are the kind you see turning without hands in haunted house movies. Another Phantom of the Opera-esque chandelier hangs from the ceiling with one of the lights burned out. The house is like House-on-Haunted-Hill- meets-1920s Hollywood.

Maggie and I gaze at the five foreboding wooden doors ahead. The first door on the left has a sign that reads: Helen. The second reads: Margaret, the third reads: Bathroom, the fourth door: Sally and the last door reads: Marie.

Maggie chuckles. "I guess you'll be sleeping outside!" She punches me on the arm. I don't want to admit that it hurt a little, both the blow to the arm and to the ego.

I roll my eyes. "Yeah thanks, Maggie," I mutter. I notice behind me a smaller spiral staircase. It's tucked away in a corner, shrouded in shadow. *Maybe my room is up there?* I climb the stairs as Margaret goes into her new bedroom.

"Holy cow, my room is enormous!" she squeals in celebration. Her door swings shut with a heavy thump. "I have a projector! I'm never leaving!"

When I get to the top of the stairs, there are two doors. One says: Eleanor. The other reads: Do not enter under any circumstances. I open the door labeled 'Eleanor'.

My assigned room is not only huge but has a vaulted ceiling and a slanted sky light. It's at the very least twice—no, three times the size of my old bedroom. In the middle of the room is a magnificent queen-sized canopy bed. It looks fairly old, but beautiful, hauntingly so. The canopy is a deep midnight blue. The mahogany bed posts have suns, moons, and stars carved into the dark grained wood. There are also Gaelic words intricately carved into the headboard and inlaid with what looks like rose quartz and amethyst. I stare at the carved words. I recognize the language, but not what it says.

Growing up, my mom had shown me books, poems, and Irish proverbs written in Gaelic, even though I couldn't quite read it. The dead language seemed very much alive in this house. There is Gaelic writing sprawled across books, picture frames, and etched in the woodwork inside the house.

In front of my bed is an enormous, battered trunk with a rusty lock and heavy chains wrapped around it. There are also several cardboard boxes strewn about. *I guess they must have used this room for storage.*

Out of the little pentagram-shaped window, I can see the moving truck pull up to the house and Maggie running out to claim her things.

I fling myself onto the bed, suddenly feeling the exhaustion of travel, grief, moving, all of it flooding throughout my body. I release a breath from deep within my lungs, letting it pass out of my parted lips till I'm nearly winded.

Then something else inside the room takes a deep breath…

# Chapter Three
## Graves and Dead Things

I freeze. Something in the room just took a breath. My skin prickles with fear. I sit up slowly and hesitate. "Hello...?"

Delicate pinpricks of dust gently drift through the shaft of light impaling the room through the skylight. My eyes fall to the Persian rug that covers most of the floor. "Here kitty, kitty," I say, although I'm not sure what could possibly be worse than a cat.

Slowly, I slide off my bed onto the floor. My hand quivers a little, grasping for the blue velvet bed skirt. Before I can lift it, something scuttles across the floor. It bounds out from under the bed and scrapes against the opposite wall.

I leap to my feet. "What the fu—!" I cut my shriek short. I tiptoe around the bed, hearing soft, deliberate scratching. *Rats maybe? How can this place have rats with so many cats around? What the good are they?* My eyes frantically scan the floor. No droppings, no evidence of vermin, nothing. The scratching stops. My heart is a bass drum thumping in my chest; my ribcage threatens to burst at any second. My ears perk up, my face goes flush. The scratching resumes and I hold my breath, leaning closer to the wall. It gets a little louder, so I place my ear against the lavender wall, my palm pressing against the cold plaster. The scratching slows and speeds up at an irregular pace. *Seriously, what the hell?* I squeeze my eyes shut, focusing on the noise. It becomes a little clearer, and I realize it's not scratching at all—it's whispering. The air catches in my throat and my mouth goes dry.

"Get them, get them, get them, get them, get them, get them, get them now, now, now, now, now, NOW!"

*Boom!* Something smacks the wall with such force it rattles my skull. I jump back with a yelp and sprint down the stairs, taking them two at a time.

"Mom! Mom!" I scream. I frantically peer over my shoulder, convinced something is following behind me. I race down the spiral stairs, nearly reaching the bottom now. My hands quake, gripping the rail. I'm desperate to catch my breath, but I can't stop panting.

"Whoa! Be careful, Eleanor," my mom says, as she uses her only open hand to steady me. "What is going on with you?" Her eyes are red from crying, or maybe that's just how her eyes look now.

My eyes shift several times from her to the landing and back. "Mom, we have to go. There is someone in the room next to mine. Something was, like, inside the wall! I heard it!"

My mother squeezes the bridge of her nose, sucking in an annoyed breath. "I just can't."

I take hold of her small, curled in shoulders. "Mom, please. I can see you're about to tell me I'm hearing things. But can we skip the horror movie bull crap where the parents don't believe their kid, please?" I'm exasperated, and it shows, but holding onto my mother feels like a slow-moving anchor pulling me back to reality.

"Ella," she says through clenched teeth.

I drop my hands from her shoulders. "Don't. Please don't call me that." *Only Dad called me that.*

Her face softens; I can see she's recognized her mistake. Mom adjusts the purse on her shoulder and slips on her shoes. "Eleanor, this is a very, *very* old house. You're going to hear all kinds of things; it creaks, it moans, it sighs, and the pipes alone make this place sound like—"

"Mom," I interrupt, "these weren't pipes. It wasn't the house. It was a voice. I could hear it. It said, 'get them, get them,' over and over again, and then it hit the wall."

My mother shakes her head. "Sweetheart, you probably heard a TV in one of the bedrooms. Maybe Sally was playing a prank because she has the maturity of a seventh grader." Mom's voice is tired. She reaches up and gently squeezes my shoulder. "You'll get used to your aunts, the house, *and* the noises." Her shoulders sag, exhaustion emanates from her thin frame. Mom's collarbone juts out under her skin like a rickety bridge extending over deep valleys.

She looks so fragile wrapped in her ivory cashmere sweater. Mom didn't collapse on the floor like Margaret and I did when the call came. She didn't scream and cry like Shannyn when she called her with the news. Mom has been our pillar, but now she's got little left to give.

I sigh, holding the back of my neck. *Maybe she's right, maybe it is just the house.* "You're probably right, and I'm sure I'm just exhausted from the move." I nod, my eyes fixed on the floor. Only then do I notice the black leather travel bag in her hand, then piece it together with the purse on her shoulder and the "mom shoes" back on her feet.

"Mom?" I question. My eyes dart nervously from her bag to her body positioned towards the front door.

Another sigh and a shrug of her shoulders. "I just got off the phone with the realtor," she says, too drained to be frustrated. "We have a buyer, but someone broke in and if I don't return now and deal with the damage, we could lose the sale. We need to sell the house. And the fact that we have someone interested in this market is incredible."

Sally hollers from the kitchen, "Marie, did you finish up the schnapps?"

Mom sucks in an unsteady breath. "I have no choice. It shouldn't take more than a couple of days, a week at the most, and then we will be done with all of this. Please take care of Maggie for me, okay? And hey, don't worry, it's just the house." She slips on a forced smile and gives me a small nudge with her hip.

"Wait, so you're heading back to Florida right now?" I ask, still muddled in the sudden change of events. *She came, she saw, she abandons?* "Can I come, Mom? *Please?* Mom, please put me to work. You know I can help."

My mother shakes her head. "Eleanor, you're starting school tomorrow. Besides, I need you to look out for Maggie, okay? It kills me to be leaving you girls. I haven't even helped you settle in yet. But I'm catching the last direct flight tonight."

"You finished it yesterday! Just use whiskey. My bottle is under the bathroom sink!" Marie shouts back.

"Nope! I finished that too!"

I hitch my thumb out towards the back of the house where the kitchen is. "You're really leaving us with them?"

My mom chuckles. Not a real one, just an attempt to defuse the tension. She tucks her platinum blonde hair behind her small, dainty ears, a feature my father adored. "You'll be fine. They're in recovery—,"

"Vodka's in the freezer, Sal!"

I scoff. "Does that sound like recovery?"

"Ell, please just support me with this. I've already spoken to Margaret. She knows you're in charge, lights out by ten. Oh, and your aunts picked up your uniforms for school, ask them where they put them." She glances down at her cellphone. "I already organized Margaret into a carpool for St. Catherine's, but the aunts will take you to school tomorrow, okay?"

I can't believe this is happening. We shouldn't even be here. I peer down at my socks, noticing how stupid they are with little dinosaurs on them. They were a joke gift from my dad. "I guess just text when you land," I mumble.

My mom sniffs. Tears gather in her eyes. She pulls me into a hug, squeezing me with shaking arms. "Please be careful, Eleanor. I love you girls so much." She kisses the side of my head. "And please wear those contacts." She reluctantly let's go and dashes for the door.

I linger at the door to watch her pull out and drive down the dirt road until she's swallowed up by the encroaching forest. I know it isn't her fault; she wasn't responsible for the break-in, and with our financial situation we certainly need to sell the house, but again with the contacts?

I close the door and warily turn for the stairs. I'm not going back into that bedroom, but I can at least see how Maggie is coming along. I stop; a blockade of cats stands at the foot of the stairs. I glare at each of them in turn. *Okay, you don't scare me, assholes.* Sucking in a jagged breath, I take a defiant step forward. Gunther lets out a low hiss, arching his back and baring his fangs.

*Nope. Nope. I'm done!*

I snatch my shoes and sprint outside, slamming the door behind me. *This is my nightmare, but maybe with Mom gone I can convince the aunts I really am allergic, then off to the shelter they go!*

I pull on my sneakers and amble over to the old wooden swing covered in bracken swinging gently in the breeze. Carefully, I sit down. The rusted chains shriek in protest. *Okay, not so bad.* I push off with my feet and sway back. The chains tremble as I swing forward, and I hear a screw come loose. *Well, that's a lawsuit waiting to happen.*

I hop off and leave the covered veranda, then peer up at the tall looming tower that's been designated for me. *Like hell I'm going back up there, even if my mom is probably right about stupid old houses.* I brush off the bracken and rust from my bottom.

A few yards away is an old dead oak. The twisted, gnarled branches look like it's — I don't know — silently screaming. Taking a step closer, I feel something cold prick my scalp. I gaze up and run my hand through my hair. Greyish black clouds unfurl across the formerly welcoming blue sky, casting a gloomy pall.

"That seems about right." I hold my hand out, waiting for another drop-let, but nothing falls. I shove my hands into my pockets and turn away from the tree, making my way around to the back of the house. The ground is soft and mossy beneath my feet.

I follow the forged path, passing a pottery shed with half painted bowls and erotic vases strewn about on stacked shelves with a few larger pots litter-ing the ground. I stop at a lone wrought-iron gate with no attaching fence. With a raised brow, I sidestep the gate and continue into the backyard.

My eyes lift to the bizarre disaster that is their landscaped lawn. You don't have to be an expert to know my aunts do not know what they are doing. On one end, they have what might have once been a vegetable garden. A large granite fountain occupies the far edge like it fell out of the sky. Overgrown shrubs and flowering bushes are scattered randomly about. I try to follow a stone path around the large water barrels, but there are several sizeable gaps in the path. Absolute chaos.

I run my finger under the blossomed bleeding-heart planted in the farthest corner of the yard from the house. Despite my mother's best efforts to educate me, most of the plants in this anarchic garden are a mystery to me; I'm just not that into gardening. I circle about, stalling my return inside the house.

A light breeze ruffles my hair and tickles my neck. The gentle wind belies an indescribable chill that seizes my bones. I pull my hood over my head, wishing I had a thicker jacket.

I sense something big is coming. The feeling had crept in with the change in the wind, an eerie sense that I'm being watched. My eyes dart about. I can't see much beyond the yard and the ominous woods that wait patiently ahead. My pulse quickens as the wind blows through the branches like giants whispering around me or about me. I peer over my shoulder and look side to side; it appears I'm still alone in the garden. I take a cautious step forward. A loud snap calls out as if I had stepped on a branch, but there's nothing beneath my foot. That snap didn't come from me.

*Grow up.* I cross my arms, shivering and annoyed at my stupid paranoia. *I'm going to lose my mind in this place.*

Straightening up, I continue to wander aimlessly through their spacious and sprawling garden until I notice a small, oddly shaped stone near a bed of randomly placed ruffled tulips that are somehow in full bloom. It's a headstone, shorter yet thicker than my forearm, and the dirt in front of the marker is fresh and wet. Kneeling, I brush aside the grass and read the name.

My brow furrows at the inscription. It reads: "Blue-Eyes. May he return to his rest and may it be here." *Is this a future grave for the black cat inside the house? Or did they adopt another blue-eyed cat after the original died?* The hair on the nape of my neck stands on end as I feel something standing behind me. *Had something crawled out of the woods?* I slowly turn…

It's just Marie. Her head is cocked, staring at me. "Blue-Eyes is a great cat. I know you two will be bosom friends," she assures, with a tight little smile.

I nod, unsure of my poker face. "Yeah, maybe. So… are you preparing for his death or is this like his parent or something?" I ask, not knowing what else to say.

Marie's eyes crinkle as she gives me a bemused look. "No, there is only one Blue-Eyes," she says, "and he's in the house—it's only his body that's out here. He just appeared in the house seventeen years ago. Technically, I believe he lived here first, hence his grave in our backyard. He's such a sad dearie, but he must fulfill his purpose," Marie says mournfully.

I stare at her, unsure I heard her correctly. Does she deserve my pity or a slap of harsh reality? *My mother did say they were full of "nonsense". Was that code for mental illness?*

"But alas, as his body decays, so does his spirit inside the house. I think it's because he wasn't supposed to die in the first place or perhaps wasn't meant to come back. But either way, he's stuck, wedged in the in-between. Horrible place to be. Not to mention it's been a bit of a nuisance, I've personally sown his ear back on four times now," she complains. " And don't even get me started with the smell. We've shoved so much rose potpourri up his you-know-where, you'd think it'd last longer."

I glance at the fresh soil, then back to my aunt. "Are you saying you come out here and bury potpourri in this… grave?" I motion to the ground.

Marie giggles. "Of course not. What good would that do? We put it inside the corpse, of course!"

I try to think of a rebuttal, but I have none. My aunt is utterly insane. I open my mouth to say something, but nothing comes out.

"Cat got your tongue, dear?" Marie jokes and elbows me in the ribs.

I peer over at the grave once more. "Aunt Marie—" my phone dings in my pocket and I fish it out. It's a text from my mom. "Never mind," I mutter.

Made it through security. I miss you girls already.
Spoke to Shannyn. She'll be checking in. Love you.

I slide my phone back into my pocket, deflated.

Marie shrugs her shoulders and looks to the churning grey sky. "Well, come inside. It's getting dark." Her eyes flicker toward the woods. "We can't protect you from what lurks beyond our borders," she warns with a soft wink. Marie takes my hand in hers, but not before giving my hand a curious peek. "Eleanor," she begins as she pulls my fingertips close to her eyes, "does my sight deceive me, my dear, or are you missing something vital?" she asks, scrutinizing the tips of my fingers.

My face flushes. "Uh, yeah. I have a dumb condition called adermatoglyphia." I tire of answering questions about my hands; hopefully that explained why I have no fingerprints. Supposedly it's genetic, but I'm the only one in my family who has it. Albinism, adermatoglyphia, I have won the genetic lottery.

Marie nods and smiles lovingly at me. "It's so interesting the things "doctors"," she says with air quotes, "come up with nowadays, isn't it?"

I frown. My parents never took me to a doctor. My mom looked up the condition online, showed my dad and that was that. My mother often said doctors were superfluous, interesting coming from a nurse who began in a trauma unit.

Marie pulls my fingers up closer to her face, skeptically studying the lack of ridges and grooves. "I'm sure it's nothing to worry about, sweetie-pie. There's probably a simple explanation. So not to worry!" she lightly pats the top of my hand as if that should comfort me.

I take back my hand and shove both into my pockets. "It's not. I know. I just don't have fingerprints."

She purses her lips, completely ignoring my answer. "Well, perhaps some moon bathed water, a dove's feather, a droplet of rose seed oil, mint leaves, and robin's eggshell would help?" I frown at the absolutely ridiculous remedy to a condition that is merely annoying and not at all life threatening.

Marie hurries us along the path toward the house. "Come, perhaps we have some," she says, frowning. "Or Sally might have used it all when she thought she saw a few warts sprouting on her feet. She's as stupid as she is pretty. She should know that recipe won't do a thing for warts. You need crushed garlic, tea tree oil, green tea, apple cider vinegar, and urine from a spring lamb. And we have plenty of urine left over from the last batch." She links arms with me, her frizzy unkempt hair tousling in the light breeze, poking me in the eye.

"Totally," I say, hoping she doesn't see the roll of my eyes. "Wait…you guys are stock piling urine?"

Marie's mouth crinkles in a saccharine smile. "Don't you worry, we have plenty if you need it."

Quietly, I let Marie tow me into the house just as rain trickles down.

"Sally?" Marie calls before bending over and scooping up a cat in the entryway. "Miss Priss, are you excited for tonight, huh my sweet, huh?" she coos and kisses her plump cat.

I slip my hood off my head, expecting to feel enveloped in the warmth of the house, but instead it's drafty and tepid. I breathe into my hands, warming them. I've never done well in the cold. We once took a family vacation to Sundance as my dad loved to ski. I was twelve and never left the fireplace in the chalet.

"Ouch! What the—" I exclaim. A cat dashing from the living room smacks into my leg. An oval serving tray is strapped to its back. I whip around, watching it scamper off.

As I step into the living room, the temperature rises significantly with the hundreds of lit candles occupying every shelf and table. Crimson streamers spider out from the crystal chandelier. Silver trays overflowing with finger foods are placed about the room.

Sally comes bounding down the hall from the dining room. She's dressed in a ridiculous hot pink cocktail dress with vertical mesh strips running down the sides and center, leaving little to the imagination. Sally's Siamese cat lounges around her shoulders and neck, glaring at me. Sally towers over us both in her metallic spike heels. "What is she doing out of bed?" she demands, staring pointedly at Marie.

My eyes slide from aunt to aunt. "Sally, it's only seven thirty," I point out.

My aunts gaze at each other for a moment. Some unspoken agreement seems to flow through them. Several of their cats meow in chorus at their feet. The calico cat reaches up, about to claw and paw at Sally's fishnet stockings, then stops, thinking better of it.

"Okay, I guess you can stay up for the swing-a-ding-ding party," Sally says casually, with a simple shrug of her boney shoulders. Her cat lithely jumps down.

Marie frowns. "Sal, I don't like it when you call it that. That name is complete rubbish."

Sally cocks her thin, penciled-on eyebrow. "I thought I couldn't call it swing-a-ding-dong?" She then leans closer to me, whispering behind her bejeweled hand, "Aren't we both looking for a little dong?" she mumbles indiscreetly with a wicked wink. "Well, not *little*."

"Sally!" Marie scolds. "And it's not a swingers' party! It's just a party. That's all, just a few friends dropping in."

Sally cackles, slinging her lanky arm around my shoulder like I'm in on the joke.

I gently shake off her arm and ignore the show of comradery. "A party? Isn't it a school night? Where's Margaret?" I ask, suddenly feeling like the only adult in the room. "And shouldn't we have dinner?" I pale, imagining what they would consider edible.

*Venus in Furs* blasts from a crackling gramophone in the corner of the living room.

Sally shrugs, "Oh, she's in her room playing with the cats and getting settled in. She has school tomorrow, you know. Plus, we ordered her a pineapple, pepperoni, and mushroom pizza. She has it now," she informs, having supplied Maggie with her favorite pizza. "As for the party, we have parties almost every other night. You'll get used to it!" She grins and giggles.

*Okay, now that she's covered, what am I supposed to eat?*

A shrill ring fills the air. I spin my attention to the front door.

"Oh, dear me. I'm not even dressed yet!" Marie waddles anxiously to answer the door. A parade of tacky and exotically dressed men and women fill the entryway.

There's a nudge at my side. "Now come with me, I have a great idea!" Sally tugs me through a candlelit dining room and the revolving doors of a kitchen. The room catches me completely off guard. The kitchen is what you would expect from any normal kitchen. Nothing special. It's decorated simply in shades of soft white and transparent glass. The walls are adorned in white cabinets with glass windows displaying what is inside. Even the wooden island in the center of the room is an eggshell white with a pearly bowl of fruit resting in the middle.

Sally hands me a tray filled with strange drinks of assorted colors, all in delicate stemware. A red glass billows steam like a mini volcano—but somehow is *cool* to the touch. In another glass is a liquid filled with small, yellow, spherical particles that hiss before popping inside the glass like tiny fireworks.

The other drinks are equally bizarre. There is a green liquid that is thicker than shampoo, slimy and quivering as if the cup were vibrating. The black and purple drink is constantly swirling like they are emptying down a drain. I have no clue what sort of concoctions they are. They are the strangest and most vividly colored drinks I have ever seen. I can't even begin to speculate on what is happening inside the glass flutes. Mesmerized, I whisper, "Are these...edible?"

Sally ignores my question. "Okay, can you handle being a waitress tonight? Usually Phoenix does it, but he seems to have taken a shine towards Margaret and would rather be with her than play butler tonight. So...?" Sally asks with a hopeful expression.

I straighten up. "Well, that's very nice of you to take the cat's feelings into consideration," I reply sarcastically. *No wonder my mother asks me to keep an eye on Margaret. I'm starting to think my mom was adopted.*

Sally stares at me deadpan, her hands on her narrow hips. She raises one of her black, pencil thin eyebrows. "Ellie babe, circulate 'til the tray is empty, then switch to gin. It's cheaper. Now go on, make friends, and have some fun." She sounds bored with the conversation. She snatches a martini glass from the counter, filled with red liquid, and downs it.

"Sally, get that boney little hinny out here!" some male calls from the living room.

Sally pulls her dress down a little and lifts her A-Cup breasts up.

"Coming!" She hollers back before plowing through the revolving door of the kitchen. She peeks her head back in. "Just walk around and try to be friendly. You know, be like Shannyn!"

I roll my eyes as she tacks on that last part. I carefully pick up the trays. *I suppose why not? It's not like I want to head up to that room right now, anyway.*

I'm only a few steps into the living room before I'm surrounded, like bees buzzing around a hive. My tray quickly empties. One glass is left on the tray completely empty. *What the hell?*

As I turn back to the kitchen, a heavy hand lands on my shoulder. I turn to see a paunchy, middle-aged man with a bushy mustache coated with wax and the ends curled up. He is dressed in a tweed four-button coat with flared pants like he just stepped out of some grand equestrian competition. Sticking out of one of his breast pockets is a tarot card and a dandelion. He tries to balance himself by holding onto me with his pudgy fingers and a surprisingly vice-like grip.

*Did he come already drunk?*

His round nose brushes against my shoulder before he straightens his head up, his back still hunched over. "So, what kind of witch are you?" he questions before releasing a drunken hiccup.

I'm not sure if I should be offended by that. I continue to stare, half-expecting him to have a soothing British accent to fit the dusty, oxford professor vibe. But alas, he has the accent of a well-spoken native.

"A witch, witch. You're Helen's daughter, aren't you? Your mom is a powerful witch. Have you started your training yet?" His eyes seem to be in a drunken fog. They flutter several times before meeting my curious gaze. "The entire coven has been abuzz with your family's arrival."

*What are in those drinks?*

"It's okay, sir. I think you're just on a bad trip. Maybe you should sit down and take it easy." I coax him towards the couch, which is almost empty since most people are mingling about. Several are clasping one another's hand and dashing upstairs.

*Oh crap!*

"Karaoke time!" Sally shouts from somewhere in a far-off corner of the living room.

The mustachioed man stumbles along beside me, putting most of his weight on me. "Sally and Marie have been so excited for your family's return to Salem. You're Eleanor, right?" he slurs. His white-haired head lulls from side to side. He falls back onto the sofa in a whoosh.

"Yep," I answer while fishing my phone out. I perch on the arm of the couch next to him and quickly shoot Maggie a text to lock her door.

He hiccups and pounds his chest with a closed, thumping fist. "My name is Winston Balthazar Leopold Edwards, but you can call me Winston. Not Winnie. Never Winnie. I'll hang you myself if you ever utter *Winnie*," he warns with a smile and a pudgy finger in my face. He tilts his head to the side, examining me.

My phone buzzes in my pocket. It's Maggie. She lets me know that her room is locked, but people are jumping on a bed in either Sally or Marie's room.

"So how old are you, Eleanor?" he asks while patting his slick forehead with a handkerchief.

A cat with an eyepatch slinks towards us, rubbing up and down Winston's legs.

*Damn, how many cats do my aunts have?* "I'm seventeen," I answer simply. I'm slightly put off by the cat glaring up at me while snuggling with Winston.

He straightens up. "Ah, then you must have started your training?" he asks with a rhetorical wink.

"My what?" I squeak, confused.

His wide eyes meet mine. "Why your witch's training, of course!" he huffs.

I shake my head. "I have no idea what you're talking about." I have that sick feeling in my stomach again. A twisting, churning sensation deep inside me, and I don't know why.

He peers at me through a tipsy haze of condescension and knitted brow, unamused by my perceived ignorance.

"Witches," he says, as if that word is supposed to clear everything up.

I say nothing.

He throws his hands up in the air theatrically. "Witches, my dear Eleanor! Witches! If you take after your mother, you must be powerful indeed. What are your gifts? To what branch do you lean? Have you discovered it yet? My dear, I realized my gift a week after my seventeenth birthday. It was pretty obvious!" He chuckles with a slight twinkle in his eye.

I exhale sharply. I feel like I'm being messed with. I don't like feeling like the butt of some joke. "I have no clue what you are talking about."

He giggles to himself like I'm the one being ridiculous. "Come, child. You can be open with me. I'm sure you were told to keep your true nature a secret, but you have to remember, I'm *in* on the secret. So come on, let me in."

I roll my eyes at his apparent drunken state. "Yeah," I say dryly, "I mean, you all live in Salem. Why not be a wiccan, I guess."

He continues his rant, as if he didn't hear my retort. "Have you performed any good shenanigans? Oh goodness gracious, the rollicking high jinks I would commit alongside my fellow witches. It was just a good dose of tomfoolery, mind you…" he babbles on about witches, magic, and old tricks he pulled in his youth, laughing at lurid jokes I don't understand.

Why does my stomach turn as he speaks? I turn my eyes away, peering over at my aunts. Marie is devouring a star cut sandwich and Sally is dancing on the coffee table. I peer down at my smooth fingertips. Dad used to call me a "daughter of science". We would argue about destiny vs. probability, statistics vs. fate. I'm not sure if my dad actually believed his argument. He typically chose the devil's advocate to make the debate interesting. I watch as a squatty brunette takes out tarot cards. All this hippie nonsense isn't just ridiculous, it's dangerous. Instead of staking on facts and logic, they dwindle away in mysticism and, well, nonsense.

I quietly excuse myself and slip from the living room. He's so enthralled by his own rambling he doesn't even notice I've left. He has gained a small audience of admirers laughing and jesting about his pranks. Among his admirers sits Marie, hanging doe-eyed on every word. I snag a few sandwiches before heading upstairs.

The second story is as silent as the grave. Whoever occupied my aunts' room has apparently finished and found their way back to the party. I tiptoe to my sister's door and place my ear against it. Maggie giggles on the phone with one of her friends back home. I lean against the door, peering up the tower stairs. I swallow nervously, squeezing my eyes closed. *There's no such thing as ghosts. It can't be haunted. You heard air in the pipes. Marie playing the radio. Maybe Sally played a stupid prank.* Righting my shoulders, I force myself to trudge up the spiral stairs to the tower room.

I hesitate with my hand on the brass knob and think about the voice I heard earlier. *Maybe Margaret was playing with her speakers. Maybe Marie was talking to somebody.* I gnaw on my lip, unsure if I want to bother with going in at all. *My mom isn't here. I could sleep in her room next to Margaret's. Nope. Daughter of science. There's a logic explanation and thus I shouldn't be afraid.*

I turn from my door and stop before climbing back down. The stupid black cat with sapphire eyes is resting on the bottom step, gazing up at me like he's challenging me.

*Freaking cats…*

My throat goes dry. I take a step down and he releases a high-pitched hiss, fangs barred, his back arched… *Hell no.* I spin around and race into the room, slamming my door shut and twisting the lock.

# Chapter Four
## Darkness Follows

Throughout the night and well into the morning, I could hear the raucous crowd below shouting things like "pants," "shirt," and then "drop 'em!" I didn't want to imagine what they were doing. I groaned as I took a spare pillow and pressed it against my exposed ear, hoping it would at least muffle the noise. I finally fell asleep around three.

The yellow haze of dawn peeks through my blinds and spills across my bed. I try to roll on my side, but *some* force keeps me from turning over. There's an unmistakable weight on my chest. I weakly open my eyes to see Blue-Eyes sitting on my chest, his tail dusting back and forth over my stomach. My eyes bulge. I smack my head back into the pillow, my heart racing. *I seriously hate cats.*

His eyes search mine. He even lowers his head to get a better look at them while I lay against my feather down pillow.

"Go," I order. I lift my arms, about to push him off, then think better of it. I hold my hands in the air when he takes a step forward, his sharp paw landing on my sternum.

"Shoo!" I shout at him. The closer he gets, the worse he smells. The aroma wafting off him is sulfuric, with a strong current of vanilla and lilac. *Potpourri.* My stomach sinks. My heart is doing wind sprints in my chest. *Don't be stupid.*

The bedroom door flies open. "Blue-Eyes, you pest! You were supposed to wake her, not scare her!" Marie scolds, popping her head in. "Okay, Ellie sweetheart, let's get a move on it. You don't want to be late on your first day now, do you?" She disappears down the stairs. To my relief, Blue-Eyes leaps off my chest and follows her out.

"Ugh," I groan. I roll over and gaze at my phone. My alarm is set to go off in two minutes. "Instead of going late, could I just skip all together?"

My new uniform is hanging on the glass knob of the wardrobe. *Was that there last night?* I roll out of bed and shuffle over. My yawn brings tears to my eyes, but nothing falls.

I pull the short-sleeved oxford button-up off the hanger. Its shape is boxy and the material stiff. I grab the navy blue and grey pleated skirt and hold it up to myself. A Britney Spears music video this is not. There's a pair of khaki pants with a pleated front resting on a hanger as a second option. And for accessories, it seems I can choose between a matching striped tie or I can wear the school pin, a "G" framed by a sprig of leaves. "G" for Griggs Academy. *Oh, and look, it comes with a bulky blue blazer with a sewn-on patch of the school's emblem.* I toss the skirt, top, and knee-high socks onto my bed and dig into my suitcase, searching for some shoes.

"Eleanor, don't make me get the hose. Up and at 'em, your mother gave strict instructions you aren't allowed to skip!" Marie hollers.

I snatch the top pair, my battered black Converses that I've had to glue back together on three separate occasions. "Coming!"

Running down the tower stairs to the second landing, I can hear Maggie blow drying her hair in her bedroom and singing some old emo-pop song.

My eyes take in the bathroom décor while I throw off my pajamas and hop into the porcelain claw foot-tub. There's a faded photograph on the wall of a woman in the nude dancing around an enormous bonfire. Her long light-colored hair is braided up with flowers. Her face looks so familiar, but it's obscured by the flames. Next to it are framed tarot cards, greatly worn and clearly antique. The items in their house give the air that they had been collected over centuries. Perhaps they are all family heirlooms passed down, and down, and down.

I wisp the dark plum-colored shower curtain closed. Naked and shivering, I turn the silver handles of the faucet, but nothing happens. I brace myself for a blast, hoping a quick spray of cold water might help jolt me awake. And I wait some more. I peek one eye open and peer up at the shower head. Dry as a bone. I shake the pipes that jut out of the wall, then twist and jiggle the knobs, but still nothing is coming.

"Aunt Sally or Marie?" I shout. "The shower won't turn on!"

Sally creeks the door open. "Oh, sorry Ell, babe. It's not my specialty, but this should do the trick," Sally says. She whispers something under her breath. "Enjoy! Should last about eleven minutes," she says cryptically before closing the door behind her.

Immediately, the shower is blasting hot water with just the perfect pressure to both wake me up and ease away the tension. I hang my head forward and let the hot water iron out my muscles as it streams down my body. *This must be a smart shower or something. Hopefully, they can show me how it works before tomorrow.*

My hands keep shaking nervously as I apply my makeup. There's a hurricane of butterflies furiously fluttering around in the pit of my stomach. I roll my lips in, clenching them between my teeth. *I'm going to hiccup. I just know it.* I can feel my diaphragm start to spasm. *Deep breaths, Ella,* I can hear my dad say in the back of my mind. *In through the nose, out through the nose. Do you see the ocean, sand beneath your feet, calm, another breath now?* It's not enough to help me now.

*Hic!*

For as long as I can remember, anytime I'm nervous, I hiccup. Sometimes it would interrupt my speech, nearly giving me a stutter. Speech therapists, pediatricians, and a school counselor, who all thought very highly of themselves, had all tried and failed to cure me. Only my dad could help me keep them at bay, at least some of the time, which was better than none.

*Hic!* another one escapes.

*Calm down, it's just school. You're good at school.* I pull on my white-collar shirt and pleated skirt. I step in front of the body length oval mirror next to the large pentagon window and blanch at my reflection.

*Hic!*

The shirt hangs awkwardly as I drown in the fabric. Tucking the top into my skirt gives me accordion wrinkles. An entire second person could fit inside the shirt. The buttons stop below the neck, intending to make a "flattering" V; however, without boobs, it falls too far down. And yet the skirt is somehow worse. Far from the sexy catholic schoolgirl fantasy, I resemble a drabby, shapeless field hockey player.

My sisters and I attended a private school back in Florida, but we didn't have to wear uniforms. The school was considered progressive, wanting to allow kids to express themselves through fashion, so in a constant humid buzz and perpetual heat wave, kids wore threadbare crop tops that made the male teachers blush and shorts so short underwear need not apply. Outside the uniform, I'm not even sure what's fashionable in Salem. A parka?

This outfit doesn't feel right. But the day itself doesn't seem right. I'm a Florida native starting a new school, second semester of my junior year; no outfit can fix that.

My phone chimes from the dresser. I rush over to it, hoping it's Mom texting that the house is just fine and that she's on her way back to us.

Eleanor, have a great first day. I wish I were there to see you girls off. Call me later and please don't forget to wear your contacts.

I sigh as I go to my luggage and take out the small white box. *I guess, what's the harm? Maybe Mom is worried about me fitting in.* I carefully place a brown tinted contact in each eye.

Snatching my ugly blazer and my school satchel, I run to the kitchen, desperate for some kind of breakfast.

"Sorry!" I call after accidentally stepping on a cat's tail. I sprint faster out of fear the cat will retaliate. I dodge cats, causing me to knock into book-shelves and stumble into the dining room.

A heavenly smell wafts up my nostrils. Margaret sits at the very end of the long dark wooden table, shoveling pancakes into her mouth.

"Oh my gosh, Ell! Seriously need to try these! They're amazing! White chocolate macadamia nut pancakes with butter cream syrup," Margaret says between bites.

It takes my eyes a moment to comprehend what I'm seeing. Pancakes of various flavors: strawberry, banana, blueberry, chocolate, chocolate chip, and several more were spread across the table on gold plates. Baskets of every kind of muffin, from dark chocolate to blueberry cream, are squeezed between the heaping piles of pancakes and eggs of every variety imaginable. On the far side, closest to me, are platters with slabs of ham, salmon, steak, country fried steak, bacon, and sausage links. Towering in the middle of the obscene feast is a juice fountain.

"Eat up, baby-cakes!" Sally calls, strolling in from the kitchen and select-ing a strip of bacon. Marie follows, sipping from a floral teacup.

"Just, wow! There's no way you guys eat like this every day." Margaret side-eyes Sally's toothpick waistline. She reaches for the tabasco and pours it over her tower of scrambled eggs. The food must be amazing if Maggie is willing to veer from her strict diet for soccer season.

I pull out a chair next to Margaret and pick at the lemon poppyseed muffin top. I doubt my nerves will let me eat much more than that. My eyes scan the table in amazement. *Did they have our first day of school breakfast catered?* Even my grandmother Lydia would be impressed, which would mean Hell had finally frozen over.

My aunts keep gazing over at me. Sally winks while Marie bunches up her face in a smile.

I swallow, my stomach in knots. "Um, thanks for turning the water on for me. That might have been the best shower I've ever had."

There's a wicked twinkle in Sally's dark brown eyes. "No prob, babe, but we won't be able to do it for you every morning. Marie has no choice but to show you how," she says with a knowing smile.

Marie shoots her sister a steely look. "No. Now that the girls are here, we will have to get the shower fixed."

A car horn honks.

Sally ignores her sister. "In fact, there's actually a lot to show you, err, teach you rather—ouch!" Sally cries out. Someone kicked her under the table. From the glare Sally is giving Marie, the culprit is obvious. "I don't care what Helen said, Marie."

Another honk.

Marie turns her death glare away from her sister and screws her lips into a sickly saccharine smile. "Oh, sweets, your ride is here. Oh, and don't forget your lunch!" Aunt Marie says as she hands Margaret a large brown paper sack. Maggie sprints to the door, complaining that she'll be too out of shape for soccer soon.

I cock an eyebrow. "It's okay. You guys can show me how to program it. It's not a big deal," I say, eyeing the sparkling cider resting in an icy bucket next to the poached eggs. "Did you guys have chefs come and prepare breakfast?" I pour myself a glass.

Marie giggles and loads her plate full of sausage and chocolate-marsh-mallow pancakes before drowning everything in viscous, dark chocolate syrup. "Oh sweetheart, of course not. We eat like this all the time. You'll get used to it," Marie assures. Her smile vanishes. "Sally, where are the brownie bits for the pancakes?" a disgruntled Marie questions. Marie scrutinizes the table until she spots them right next to the erotically sculpted salt and pepper shakers to her left. Marie's phone buzzes against her plate. She quickly snatches it. "This is early," she complains under her breath. She frowns, staring at her screen.

"What is it?" Sally questions while she salts some eggs.

Marie shakes her head, placing her phone face down. "It's probably nothing. Do you remember Doris Calloway? She's part of the Greenwich Connecticut cov—club."

Two cats claim open chairs and eye the table.

"Yes, yes, I remember her. Didn't Winnie date her for a bit?" Sally recalls, tapping her chin with her finger.

Marie rolls her eyes, waving her off. "Well, she didn't return from her retreat in Maine."

"Sounds like Doris, if you ask me." Sally lifts a silver flask with her initials etched onto the side with rhinestones. "So, Elly-belly babe, do you want us to take you to school or do you want to drive?" Her eyes roll back as she takes a swig.

I force a smile. "Um, I'll drive. I think I know where it is. We passed it on our way to your house," I answer. I can only imagine what old jalopy they must have.

Sally nods, assuming that would be my answer. She examines her blood-red nails. "Take the Mercedes, you'll look cooler," Sally suggests.

My eyes almost pop out of their sockets. "A *Mercedes*? Are you serious? I mean, a *real* Mercedes?" I ask, dubiously.

"Would you rather take the Tesla, sweetie? It's a rather fun drive. Or do we still have the Rolls? We gave the Jaguar to Shannyn for her birthday last year, so you won't be able to take that one. Oh, honey bun, you take whatever car you fancy," Marie says, with a little chocolate dribbling down her chin. "The garage door is just down the hall next to the greenhouse door across from the bookshelf." Marie points a finger painted in whipped cream. "If you walk into the broom closet, you've gone too far."

"Marie, you rat! I wanted whipped cream last night and you said we were out!" Sally yells indignantly. "J'Accuse!"

I slip my bag back over my shoulder and slowly inch away from the table. Once I'm out of sight, I hurry past the greenhouse and rush into the garage. The white walls have the smell of fresh paint and the floor shines like new with black-and-white checkered tile. It's the line of cars, however, that captures my attention. There are five cars in a row: the Tesla, the Mercedes, an old-fashioned truck, a tan soccer mom mini-van, and a teal Jeep Wrangler. *How loaded are these women!?*

The Mercedes is a sleek red, like a bullet with smooth curves and a sharp design. I find the keys on the driver's seat. I slide onto the soft leather interior. My knuckles turn white, gripping the wheel. I imagine my long hair blowing out the window, racing down to Coral Gables to see my friends, the beach, my old orchestra, my dad… My grip on the wheel loosens as my excitement wains. I can feel it circling the drain, leaving me empty. Still, I turn the key. The engine roars, then settles into a soft seductive purr, but I feel nothing.

Now lethargic, I search the glove compartment for a remote to open the garage door. Instead, I find Golden Elite condoms, ruby red lipsticks, and a broken spike belonging to a high heel. *Maybe "witch" is code for hooker?*

The garage door groans as it lifts, filling the space with natural sunlight. *The aunts must have done it from inside or something.*

I fly in reverse and skid to a halt, kicking up dirt in the driveway. Luckily for me, my father taught me how to drive a stick. Before shifting gears, I see that stupid black cat Blue-Eyes slink into the yard, stretching out beneath the leafless tree, staring at me. My eyes flick to the branches above; there has to be at least a hundred crows perched on the gnarled tree branches. Or are they ravens? I'm not up on my ornithology. Maybe I'm just being paranoid, but it seems they're all staring at me.

# Chapter Five
## First Impressions

With the help of the Mercedes's navigation system, it's an eighteen-minute drive from the aunts' house to school. My heart speeds up about fifty notches as I turn onto Wilson Street and William Grigg's Academy comes into view. The school looks more like a castle in the United Kingdom than a mere private high school with tuition my mom can afford. Ivy creeps up the building's brown brick walls and around the spiked wrought-iron gate that surrounds it. In fact, the moss-colored ivy seems to cover half the town. The arch of the gate with the WGA crest, however, seems impervious to the local vegetation.

I follow the flow of traffic into the student parking lot across the street from the school. I quickly notice that although my aunt's Mercedes is the nicest and newest model here, it's far from being the only sports car. That doesn't stop boys from gawking, their eyes following while I search for a spot.

Hiccups erupt from my throat, causing my chest to ache. "I can—" *hic* "do this." *Hic.* I glance at my phone; I still have twelve minutes until I need to go in. *Why did the aunts say I was going to be late?* I sit in the car and listen to music. I get through Rob Zombie's "Dragula", Salt-N-Pepa's "Shoop", and "Pretty Little Head" by Eliza Rickman before I feel my heart beating in proper rhythm and the hiccups subside. The darkly tinted windows make it easy to ignore the kids walking past. Resting my forehead against the steering wheel, I know I can't stall any longer. I must enter Dante's Inferno.

My hands shake as I grip the strap of my messenger bag while passing under the arched gateway. All around me are the clicking and clacking of high-heeled boots and stilettos against the cobblestone. A breeze ruffles my hair and a damp chill settles into my bones. I grip my polyester blazer tight around me, then notice I'm the only one not wearing a coat over it. The icy breeze penetrates the blazer like tissue paper.

On the manicured lawn is a man with a newsboy cap snug on his head, dressed in dirty overalls with thick thermals underneath. He's muttering something as he gets down on his hands and knees, setting up some cages. "Rabbit traps", is the only clear thing I hear from him. Another man, leaner and younger, perhaps in his mid-forties, harangues him while clutching closed his tweed dress coat.

"Move!" orders a girl in a navy cape coat. She has flaxen hair pulled up in a tight chignon, and I nearly topple over as she marches up the path and stone steps into the school.

*What the hell?*

Several girls in similar coats flank her sides, clearly the blonde's acolytes. I wait till they enter the building before I continue up the stone steps.

"Oh, let me get that for you," says a tall, boxy guy wearing a shearling lambskin coat. He sweeps open the heavy front door of the school and holds it for me, then quickly follows in close behind me.

"Thanks." I peek over at him, wondering if he's a student teacher, then see he's wearing the standard issue chinos like all the other guys. He has dark brown, nearly black hair pulled back into a man bun at the back of his head, with shaved sides and dark stubble.

"You look new. Do you need any help?" he asks, flashing his ultra white teeth.

Looking up at him makes me feel oddly short. "Yeah, I need to get to the administration office to pick up my schedule," I say in a sheepish mumble, fighting a hiccup battle once again. Several kids glance at us but continue on although most are clutching Starbucks Styrofoam cups, and their eyes glued to their phones.

He continues grinning at me. "Down that hall," he says, pointing to the left of us. "Do you want me to take you there? The halls can be quite treacherous this early in the morning," he says with a wink.

I smile despite myself. "No, thank you, it's okay, I'll find it." I duck my head and stride down the hall. I roll my lips in and bite down. My chest reverberates with hiccups. Nervously, I peer over my shoulder to see him greeting some other guys, pounding fists. He glances back at me with a nod, but I glance away.

There's a line outside the office doors, so I take a seat in an available chair across from the ornate high school trophy case. The shelves are crowded with bright blue ribbons and gilded statues. Some are for wrestling, lacrosse, tennis, crew, and — I squint — debate, apparently. Surrounding the case, the school brazenly displays its illustrious history with framed pictures of esteemed alumni, like ranking politicians, Rhodes Scholars, and Ivy League professors. Poised between the bombastic achievements is their school mascot, a knight in shining armor, sword unsheathed, leading a charge.

A bell rings just as I reach the front of the line.

A curvy middle-aged woman flicks through folders in her filing cabinet. I step up to the front desk.

"Hi."

I wait for a response.

Nothing.

I cough.

Annoyed by my presence, with her eyes fixed on her files, she asks, "Can I help you, honey?"

I nod as I tuck my hair behind my ears. "Um, yeah. I'm Eleanor O'Reilly, I'm new… I guess," I mumble, staring down at my shoes.

She spins her chair around and digs through a metal filing cabinet. "Transferred from Brenton?" she questions drolly.

"Yeah, my credits should be good," I say anxiously.

She sighs. "They are. Here's the schedule your parents put together for you. You're allowed three tardies before your first demerit, your first demerit will result in detention, three demerits will result in suspension. Anything beyond that and you've reached expulsion. Welcome to Grigg." She glances at her Apple Watch. "You have seven minutes to get to your first class before you're late." She shoves a class schedule in my hand. Before I even have a good grip on the paper, she's already buried her nose back into her files, making herself unavailable for questions.

"Thanks so much for your help," I muttered under my breath. I march out into the hallway and read the schedule:

1st hour: Edwards, AP English, room 123 East
2nd hour: Andersen, AP American History, 134 West
3rd hour: Sewall, Orchestra, Auditorium South
First break Period: Lunch A
4th hour: Albert, Adv. Anatomy 117 East
5th hour: Smith, Calculus, 205 North
6th hour: Robertson, Physics II, 303 North
7th hour: Garner, French III, room 222 West

*East, west, and north wings? But no gym class? Well, I guess it won't be too bad.*

I glance around the halls and back at the paper in my hand, looking for room numbers. Nearly every girl passing me wears a uniform skirt that's been tailored to have a little more flow and bounce. Not everyone dons the blazer, and if they have, they once again have it tailored. Some girls added brooches or piping. I spot the blonde chignon from outside. She's wearing the coveted double C logo of a Chanel pin dotted with pearls. Other girls have added shoulder pads to their blazers for that extra flair. *What was out is now back in, I guess.*

Everyone looks so polished and posh. Several boys carry leather attaché cases embossed with initials; girls tote Prada backpacks, although it seems the highest-ranking girls carry nothing with them at all. Those girls didn't wear the issued oxford short-sleeve button downs; no, they wore pearly button blouses more akin to Barneys New York than Dickie's outlet. The students here hold the same egotistical air as my old high school royalty, but instead of the beachy decadence of South Beach, they have the aristocratic snobbery of the Eastern Seaboard.

I glare back down at my schedule as I walk. I'm never finding my classes at this rate. I feel a sudden smack, like I've walked into a brick wall. I'm flat on my back in the blink of an eye. My tail bone is going to have a nasty bruise, it's already beginning to throb. The wind knocked out of me, my eyes flutter open, only to be blinded by the fluorescent light hanging from the ceiling. *I couldn't have walked into a wall, could I?* My skirt is suddenly cold and wet. Next to me on the ground is a bottle of lemonade spilling out onto the floor and onto me.

"I'm so sorry!"

I squint up towards the voice as I prop myself up onto my elbows. The locker encrusted hallway fades away. There's a bizarre "click" deep in my gut, like a lock sliding into place. My breathing staggers, getting caught in my throat. Whoever this stranger is, he's exceptionally tall, not quite as tall as the other boy from earlier, but he can't be less than six feet. He's lean but not lanky; his shoulders are broad and powerful. His hair is molten gold, wavy and tousled, giving him a rakish air. He could have been a Calvin Klein model from the early two-thousands with his sculpted jaw and cheekbones and "All American" good looks. His green eyes are soft yet fierce somehow, and they pierce mine when he looks at me. Those eyes go wide, like he recognizes me.

I can hear my heart pounding in my ears. The seat of my skirt is now completely soaked. My boy short underwear clings to me as they are now seeped with liquid.

He continues to stare at me. His expression has gone from shock and surprise to unsettled and anxious. He swallows, teetering on the edge of discomfort. His lips part as if he's about to say something, only to then shut tight with absolution. His jaw flexes.

His grey and navy-blue striped tie hangs askew from his neck. Only this boy could take the dorky uniforms and make them appear worthy of the runway.

Shaking off his intense gaze, he bends down. "Are you okay? I'm really sorry." He takes another breath, as if to steady himself. He frowns, glancing down at the floor for an unmeasurable moment, then back at me almost quizzically. He stares into my eyes before he shakes his head.

I can't even feel my bruised tailbone anymore. Suddenly I have the feeling I'm free falling, a fast-sinking anchor not yet reaching the ocean floor. When the falling stops, I become hyperaware of my body. Every molecule, every cell, tingles as if awaking from a deep sleep.

"Hello?" He waves his hand in front of me. "How hard did you fall?" He questions with a light, almost uncomfortable chuckle. There's something about him that tells me he's too confident and gorgeous to have ever felt uncomfortable.

I continue to gawk like an idiot until I realize there is still a bottle of lemonade emptying onto the floor, and me.

His full lips pull back in an almost sarcastic, crooked smile. "Um, are you okay? I'm really sorry," he says. He offers his hand. "You should really watch where you're going," he teases as he hoists me up. "I'm Jack Woods. I don't believe I've seen you before. The student body here is fairly small."

My stupid stomach flips nervously at the word "body". My head feels pathetically light and my skin is enveloped in goosebumps. From the cold drink or the boy, I'm not sure which.

He peers at me concerningly. "Do you need the nurse? I'm worried you might have conked your head."

I shake my head, snapping myself out of the trance his obnoxious, not-so-great green eyes have me under. I'm an ardent student of Susan B. Anthony, Anne Brontë, and Marie Curie. No boy puts me under a spell. "I'm fine. And now, thanks to *you*, I'm sticky and wet," I growl, suddenly finding my spine that usually evades me. I brush my wet shirt and skirt. My jaw drops, horrified as I survey my legs. My knee-high socks are not only wet but yellowed too; his drink made it appear like the new girl has bladder control issues.

Someone snickers as they walk by. "We don't have Depends here, sweetie," he mocks over his shoulder. "Poor thing, that skirt is doing her no favors."

Jack leans in a little closer. "Well, it's nice to meet you, Ms. Sticky-Wet," he jokes with a slight bow of his head.

"That isn't even clever," I snap. More students walk around us, pouring into their first hour class that's mere seconds from starting.

He softens his face, all teasing set aside. "I am really sorry. Can I help you get cleaned up or something? I'm sure we can get a note from the office."

"I'm not going back there." *I hate this place. I hate you. I hate these stupid kids. I effing hate Salem!*

Jack nods laconically at students passing by. He smiles at some girl who calls his name and walks into the open door to our right.

I grind my teeth, now even more livid. His eyes turn back to me.

I examine my shoulder bag; apparently it had not escaped the splatter either. *Great, this is just perfect!* The brown leather is speckled with his drink. *I mean, who drinks lemonade at eight AM!?*

The hall is mostly vacant; just a few teachers and one or two students hustle on by.

Jack takes a step closer to me. "I think I have an extra sweatshirt in my car. I could go get it for you," he offers. "You can tie it around your waist," his eyes go down my body, "Or as long as the collar is showing you can wear it over your shirt to cover up the…" he trails off, motioning to the yellow splash down my front.

"Just stay away from me," I mumble before stomping away in a huff. I can feel my slick skirt sticking to my butt and legs.

It's bad enough being new at this stupid, outdated school with its labyrinth like building, but now I'm soaking wet and sticky as a movie theater floor.

The second bell rings, warning students still in the hall they were now late to class. A few couples stayed huddled against their lockers, more focused on making out than getting to class. I wander through the hall like a moron before finally finding my classroom.

Creaking open the classroom door, I pray I can inconspicuously slip in and find a seat. Everyone turns in unison. A scorching heat ignites in my cheeks.

*Hic*

I hurry to the teacher standing in front of the whiteboard. I hand the teacher my schedule as whispers from the front row burn my ears. I distinctly hear the word "lemons" being uttered.

I look back at the teacher, then do a double take. I stare at his thick walrus mustache and white comb-over. *Winston Edwards! From last night! Great, just where you want to have spotted your AP English teacher… at a boozy house party… that your aunts hosted…*

"Winston?" I whisper. He looks at me as if he'd never seen me in his life. He straightens up, his bowtie bobbed on his Adam's apple. "It's Mr.

Edwards, Miss O'Reilly. Now take your seat in front of Mr. Woods."

I stifle a groan and spy the kid smiling at me. I stay rooted in my spot next to Winston. "Are you serious? Win—Mr. Edwards, isn't there somewhere, anywhere else I can sit?"

He answers me with a steely look. He crosses his arms, leaning his shoulder against the chalkboard. "Tell me, Ms. O'Reilly, is it customary to hold up your class where you come from? Please be assured, it shall not be tolerated here, young lady. Now take your seat or you can sit in the headmaster's office!" Once again, he points to the empty desk in the front row, right in front of Jack. I drop into the uncomfortable desk seat, wishing I didn't exist.

Jack Woods leans forward and quietly whispers, "So Ms. Sticky-Wet has a last name: O'Reilly."

I seethe with anger and embarrassment. It feels like steam will soon jet from my ears. I sulk for a few moments, staring down at my desk as heads slowly swivel from me back to the whiteboard, scribbled with discussion topics. Mr. Edwards resumes his lecture on Shakespeare's *Macbeth*. When the hour ends, I race out of the room as fast as I can.

After English is American History with Mr. Andersen. He seems friendly, and I have a feeling we'll get along well. He's an animated teacher, using his hands enthusiastically describing the civil war, and the blood that was shed. He captivated the entire classroom with his theater in the round antics. But, as great as his class seems, I'm eager to get to orchestra.

"Excuse me, do you know where the auditorium is?" I ask the girl to the right of my desk. She's doodling in her notebook.

Mr. Andersen makes his hand in the shape of a gun, acting out a scene. "He pulled out his revolver. Now, the Colt Navy revolver is the most iconic handgun of the civil war…"

"Of course. I'm in orchestra, that's where we meet," she says matter-of-factly. She never looks up from her notebook.

My shoulders settle with relief. "Oh good. This school is a maze. Could I walk with you?"

She looks up at me. "No," she states. Her eyes do a quick once over before turning back to the lecture.

I shrink back into my seat, my eyes darting side to side to see if anyone noticed the cold rejection. Thankfully, the class is totally engrossed by Mr. Andersen pantomiming a dramatic death.

After class, I silently follow the girl to the auditorium. We have to take two different stairwells to get there. Once I figure out where the auditorium was, I dart back to my car to get my violin.

I sprint down the sloped walkway up the stage where Ms. Sewall is standing at her conductor's stand. My violin case keeps banging into my leg as I run.

I hand Ms. Sewall my schedule, and she approves of me with a thin smile. She motions a girl out of the first chair seat and tells me to take it. The miffed girl mouths some profanity at me as she walks to the back of the orchestra. My stomach clenches.

Ms. Sewall is a thin, severe looking woman with black hair streaked with grey. "Alright, class. Relax, pay attention. We will now let Eleanor O'Reilly, our newest pupil, hear how a real orchestra sounds. Eleanor, please do not play, just listen and observe. Okay?" She adjusts her red cat glasses before giving me a sharp side eye.

I nod and put my violin to rest on my lap.

Ms. Sewall smiles. "Jupiter, Bringer of Jollity." She taps her baton and raises it high.

I cringe as they play.

The out-of-pitch, out-of-tune, out-of-time shrieking makes my teeth hurt. The undisciplined bow-strokes are nearly comical. One of the violinists didn't even bother to play. She is far too busy texting someone. I try to hide my disgust when a bassist drops his bow.

*Okay, they've got to be joking... Right?* Then I think of the trophy case, absent of any musical accolades. Now I know why.

I scan the nearly empty auditorium. Jack and a few other students are in the audience. By their shadowed facial expressions, they are enjoying the sour, gut-wrenching performance. Not the music but the lack thereof, and the ammo it will supply them with later. I can just imagine the grenade of insults Jack now has in his arsenal after he hears a performance like this...

In glowering at him, I don't realize the music has stopped.

"Ms. O'Reilly, it is your turn to play for the class," Ms. Sewall repeats in a slow, deliberate voice.

Once again, for the fifteen hundredth time today, my face feels like it's going to melt off. I gulp, certain that my face matches a juicy ripe tomato. "You want," hic, 'me to," hic "play for the," hic, "class?" I ask. Sweat beads across my brow. Hic.

Ms. Sewall nods at me, her evil eyes glinting. "Yes, I even have the piece picked out. 'The Last Rose of Summer', Ernst's variation, of course." She retrieves two sheets of music from a folder on her stand and places them in front of me.

My jaw drops. "Are," hic, "are you s-s-serious?" Hic. It's only considered one of the most difficult violin solos of all time. I stare, petrified, at the sheets of music. My hands tremble. "Ms. S-S-Sewall," hic, "I c-c-c," hic, "can't possibly play."

Back home, my beloved conductor would ask the first chair to give the solo performance, so I *always* made sure I *never* made it to first chair. I silently consider evoking the "dead father" card to see if sympathy could get me out of playing.

Ms. Sewall's brown beady eyes narrowed on me, her long slender nose twitches in disproval. The point of her chin and length of her nose makes her face resemble a feral rat. "If you would like to stay in this orchestra, you better get up and start playing—NOW!"

The hiccups pour out of me faster than my body can handle.

My hands shake while rising from my seat. My diaphragm aches. Someone is clapping from their seat in the dark auditorium. Nervously, and with great effort, I swallow back my embarrassment and put my bow to my violin. My eyes stay on the music sheets as I pull my bow downward. My left hand is fluid up and down the strings, my bowing smooth and aggressive. I deliver vibrato with such elegance I can't be more thrilled. I flow with such composure and skill that I wish my dad could see me…

I finish my solo effort with a surprised, small smile. I scan the rest of the orchestra as I slowly lower my violin. Some look stunned, others agree with Ms. Sewall's disgruntled look. I don't understand Ms. Sewall's premature and obvious disdain for me. Jack's applause breaks the uncomfortable silence. He continues to cheer and hoot loudly as my face shows a brighter red than before. I fall to my chair, wishing it was the jaws of some enormous monster waiting to swallow me whole.

Ms. Sewall could break the world record for how long a glare could be held. I try to ignore it, look away and stare at my shoes, but that woman's eyes feel like tiny lasers blazing narrow holes in my skull.

"Class, you are dismissed. Early, enjoy it. It won't happen again. Leave your music and stands here. Miss O'Reilly, I would like to speak to you."

Ms. Sewall towers over me. She reminds me of one of my aunt's cats, perhaps Miss Priss, if you tightly pulled the fat back from her face. Her gaze intensifies, but she holds her tongue until she hears the door close. We're alone.

"Proud of yourself?" she spits. She's tapping her shoe on the stage floor.

*Actually, I kind of am.* I stay silent, unsure of what I'm supposed to say.

She exhales sharply. "Eleanor, I do not like cocky little show-offs. And from that little stunt you just pulled, you're obviously going to be more than I can handle this year."

"You asked me to play," I mumble.

"Are you talking back to your conductor?" She takes a step closer.

"Because if you are, you will be kicked out without a second thought!"

My heart hammers. *What is happening here? Did I walk into the Twilight Zone? Is this some kind of new girl hazing?* I try to backpedal. "No, I'm sorry. I thought you wanted me to play. Maybe I was wrong…"

Ms. Sewall shakes her head dramatically from side to side. "You're just as vapid and vainglorious as your whorish mother. She was a troublemaker too."

My head snaps up.

She tries to stand a little taller, as if insulting me is supporting her spine. "I'm sure you think you'll rule this academy like she did." She leans over, trying to level me with her gaze. "We didn't like *her* and they won't like *you.*"

*So that's why she hates me.* She knew my mom in high school. I've heard very little of my mother's adolescent years, what I did, however, painted my beautiful blonde mother in a popular and incandescent light: class president, volleyball captain, track star, some poetry club. But I hadn't known she attended this school with this woman.

"Tell me, *Eleanor,*" she sneers my name, "is your mother still a voracious slut like she was in school? Do you even know who your father is? You don't, do you?"

My bottom lip trembles. My violin and bow fall to the floor in an ugly clatter. A fury deep within me builds, at first like a little spark deep in my gut, then turns into a vicious knave ascending a staircase. The burning fury is rising, rising, rising inside me. The stage lights flicker and there's a rumble beneath my feet, like the stage itself is quivering. I've never felt such anger or hatred in my life. The lights brighten to a blinding light. POP. POP. POP. Three stage light bulbs burst.

Ms. Sewall jumps back, startled.

"I told him to get those fixed," she curses under her breath. Her eyes flash back to me with pursed lips that cause the little black hairs above her top lip to stand at attention. "You will stay here and pick up everyone's music and stands," she orders with a spiteful smile. "Place the stands on the cart, and I expect the music to be placed in every folder behind the stage." She parades off the stage and heads toward the back office.

*I hate this place! Why did Mom bring us here? Dad, why did you have to go?* I want to scream. I want to break something. My hands shake. This anger, this hate, stews deep within, just like earlier. I honestly thought I might smack her ugly rat face right there. Before I realize what's happening, I kick a music stand across the stage, knocking down an entire section in its wake. Sheet music flies into the air like confetti and gently flutters back down, snowing the stage in crinkled white sheets.

My legs buckle beneath me. A knot forms in my throat and tears well up before sinking back down. Blinking several times, I can feel the contacts gliding over my eyes. *I want to go home.* I cup my face into my hands, releasing my emotion in a dry sob. *I can't do this, Dad. I quit, I just quit.*

The auditorium door opens.

Startled, I amble to my knees and pick up my violin. Thankfully no damage was done. I delicately place my instrument back into its case. Footsteps pad down an aisle. I squint against the remaining stage lights but see nothing. I continue rounding up the scattered sheet music. I reach for another piece, but a different hand lands before mine.

It's Jack.

The fire inside me settles and annoyance takes its place. "What do you think you're doing?" I snatch a nearby sheet of music and shuffle it in with the rest. I just wanted to be left alone.

"What does it look like I'm doing? I'm helping you so you don't have to miss lunch." He picks up a music stand and stacks it on the beige pull cart.

"You don't have to do this," I mumble.

"You're right. I don't have to help you. But I want to." He flashes me his boyish grin. "So…how's your shirt?"

"Sticky," I answer, sardonic. "But dry now. Did you enjoy the show?" I motion to the velvet seats in the audience.

He continues to stack papers. "Not particularly, but I enjoyed the solo."

"Why do you come at all?" I look up at him from the floor. He hesitates, glancing at me over his shoulder.

He gives a slight shrug. "My friend Hale Von Kessler is dating Poppy Simonsen. I believe you dethroned her in first chair," he says with a little wince like he knows a revenge plot was simmering. "He invites me to come on days we don't have senior seminar. Today, I decided to join him." He quietly places another stand on the cart. "So, Miss O'Reilly, do you have a first name?"

He apparently didn't hear Ms. Sewall sneer my name. I bite my lower lip. At my last school, I was known as weird, socially awkward, and my personal favorite: "no-boobs". But I was never mysterious or elusive. Maybe here in Salem I can be someone different. I could be known as a curious specter, the girl you want to get to know but never really get the chance. The girl with no first name…

I match his impish, flirtatious attitude, or at least I try to. "You can call me Miss O'Reilly, Jack," I say, fighting back a grin. I turn on my knee to pick up more music on the floor.

"Would you tell me if I guess it?" he teases, wheeling the cart to the back of the stage.

I tuck my hair behind my ear and pray my hiccups won't come. I can feel one bubbling up. "Probably not."

The lights turn off one by one, slowly cloaking us in darkness. Only a solitary spotlight shines down where I'm kneeling. Jack steps out from behind the curtain. "You're probably right—," he pauses as he circles around me like a predator, ready to pounce on its prey, "I could never guess, but I have other ways of finding out." He slowly steps into the light. A soft, crooked smile on his impish face keeps me in place.

My mouth is firmly sealed, ready to stutter and hiccup the moment I try to speak.

He kneels down beside me. "Well, since you won't tell me your first name, will you answer something else for me?"

I shrug.

"How did you get that stand to fly across the stage like that? Kickboxing? BJJ? Karate?"

I blush as he had seen me "Hulk-Out". "I don't know…I just kicked it. I didn't mean to kick it that hard," I admit sheepishly.

He frowns, looking surprised, maybe even skeptical. "You were really fast; I mean, I didn't even see your leg move."

I shrug again, looking away, abashed. "I don't know. Maybe I tossed it. I was kind of… upset."

He nods, as if losing interest. "I'll go put them back for you." Jack takes the music from my hands and heads behind the stage once more. The dim auditorium lights flick on, illuminating the vacant audience.

My eyes drift over the Baroque auditorium. The walls are painted in pastoral scenes of muskets and preachers, judges and courtrooms, barns, and rabbits dangling from racks. It has the austere remnants of an old cathedral. You could easily replace the red velvet seats with wooden pews and still be on theme. I squint, looking closer to the sea of plush, folded chairs. One is curiously occupied. In the very last row, closest to the exit, a dark figure sits and watches. Its face is in dark silhouette. The head cocks to the side, staring down at me.

Footsteps come up from behind the stage. "I've never been grateful that we have a small orchestra. I put the music back in the correlating cubbies. That's what your conductor wanted, right?" Jack asks, returning to my side.

I peer back at him. "Um, yeah. Thank you for your help. That would have taken me forever," I say. I quickly glance back at the corner seat. I don't know why, but my heart quickens. The seat is now empty.

# Chapter Six
## A Bathroom Confessional

My eyes linger on the open chair, unsure why I'm suddenly so unnerved.

Jack returns to my side. "No problem," he says as he helps me to my feet. "Ready?"

We saunter down the aisle together. I glance around, waiting for some person to jump out and admit they were the one spying. *But spying on what? What was there to see?*

Jack smoothly places his hand on my lower back, tucking me close as we duck through a crowd of freshmen exiting into the hall.

He sweeps back the stained-glass door before ushering me in.

Even if high school cafeterias weren't already a joke, this place would still put them to shame; it would more accurately be called a banquet hall than a cafeteria. The grey stone walls are akin to the halls of a medieval castle. Round wooden tables are scattered about the center of the room where student hierarchies are clearly defined. Leather armchairs and settee benches are pushed up against the walls where teachers perch, chatting and watching students eat. In the corner grotto, lunch ladies ladle hot food onto plastic trays, anathema to the rest of the room.

"How steep is tuition in this place?" I mutter, far too quiet for Jack to actually hear me. My sneakers make a weird, hollow sound against the flagstone floor. Adorning the walls are large photographs of previously graduating classes. The men wear bespoke white ties and coattails, and the girls are dressed in white tea-length gowns with lace gloves that end at the wrist and a single strand of pearls around their necks. *I wonder if my mother's face is staring at me from behind the glass right now…?*

"You must have generous boosters," I comment.

Jack smiles. "The money ends with architecture and upkeep. The food is closer to "Soylent Green" than Eleven Madison Park," he teases.

My stomach wobbles inside me after I smell what I'm guessing is burnt macaroni and cheese.

"Jack! Jack! Hello? Aren't you coming?"

At the table closest to the ample stone fireplace, a skinny, corn-silk blonde in a navy tweed coat waves him over. Her hair is pulled up in the hairstyle I recognize from earlier, complete with iconic pearls donning each ear and around her neck. Her eyes don't stray from Jack, as if I don't exist. *Fine by me.*

Jack steps closer to me. "There's another spot open. Want to come?" he asks, nodding his head to the table. His emerald eyes scan my face like he's searching for something.

I shake my head. "Um, no, it's okay. Thanks for your help earlier," I mumble.

Jack's mouth pulls up in a crooked smile, the light catching the blonde in his thick lashes. "I believe I owed you one."

I shake my head, my eyes falling to his square hands. "I probably overreacted a little. It was an accident, after all." My insides are fluttering.

His cheeks turn a hint of pink. He gives me a nod before sauntering over to his usual table. The blonde's eyes slide to me as soon as Jack sits down. Her arctic stare snaps me out of my daze, and I quickly turn away.

Limp lettuce soaked with what smells like cleaning vinegar attempting to pass off as salad is dropped on my brown tray. I hold back a grimace. *I should have eaten more than a muffin top for breakfast.* I grab a water and the least bruised banana available.

I scan the tables, doing my best not to look at Jack as I look for an open spot. There's a cluster of students at the table closest to me on laptops, dedicatedly working on Excel spreadsheets. Adjacent to them is a table of girls pouring over chem textbooks, sifting through notecards, and snapping quips at each other. I sigh, spotting the various cliques, none of which seem all that welcoming. Kids from orchestra, students making cellphone videos, and couples practically chewing each other's faces off.

In the far back corner, under the framed black-and-white photograph of the school, is a nearly empty table. A lone girl with sandy blonde waves cascading over her shoulders has her head bent over a jewel toned book, completely engrossed. Her doe-eyes never veer from the page, even when she leans back, laughing at something she just read. Her tawny skin glows against the garish uniform. A sprig of lavender peeks out of a handsewn pocket on her blazer coat.

I frown. *Why is this supermodel sitting alone?* At my old school, she would have been worshipped, idols would have been erected in her honor. Boys' lockers would have a treasure trove of print out pictures from her social media accounts. But despite her celebrity good looks and her salon-envy hair, there's something unnerving about her. She seems familiar somehow and yet completely foreign all at once.

Her azure eyes leave her book and meet my curious gaze. I want to look away and rush in the opposite direction—but to my surprise—she seems pleased at my gawking. She mouths some words. All I can make out is the word "come".

I point to myself, checking if she is talking to me. She scrunches her nose, laughing, but nods in confirmation. I step toward the table. *Maybe she has a relative in Florida or something that would have crossed our paths.* I feel a weird tractor beam sensation as I'm only a few feet from her table, pulling me towards her, but then a heavy arm slinks around my shoulders and steers me away.

"I see you got to the office okay, I was wondering if I should have walked you," the boy with the enormous arms and man bun says. "You're Elsie O'Reilly, right? You're in my history class. I'm Nick," he stops, glancing over my head, "I couldn't help but notice you were about to sit with Trixie Caldwell," he says as if something vile crept across his tongue. "But no worries. I saved you. C'mon, you can sit with my friends and me." He doesn't wait for any kind of reply.

"It's Eleanor," I correct. I glance back over my shoulder that's weighed down by his gigantic paw. Her table is vacant. I sit down at Nick's table, resigning myself to stifle my objections. Instead, I peer over at my "savior" Nick, who plops down next to me. My eyes fall to his shoulders and chest. To call him excessively muscular would be an understatement. His uniform ripples as it strains to cover his cut physique. Even John Cena would tell him to lay off the protein shakes.

I instinctually lean away, feeling a twinge of fear given he could snap me like a twig if he wanted to. Despite sitting on level seats, he *towers* over me by a foot and a half. Which doesn't happen all that often with my 5'7" height. *I mean, how does this kid sit at normal desks? Did his parents hold him back by five years before sending their ten-year-old to kindergarten?*

He peers down at me before glancing back at his friends. "This is Tripp, Alden, Pete, and Noah," he introduces, going clockwise around the table. I feel like a small child sitting at a table of linebackers. They all smile at me like grizzly bears staring at a succulent pink salmon. I recognize some of them from my morning classes. They continue eating meals they had brought from off campus. As busy as their mouths are, their eyes perpetually look up from their fast-food burgers to gawk, starting with my eyes and moving downward.

My stomach is doing back flips. I can't decide if all this unaccustomed attention is good or bad. I had always dreamed about being admired; however, I think I'm getting buyer's remorse.

They quickly delve into helpful tips for the new girl, like the teachers I need to watch out for, the classes that were an easy A and the people to avoid. Trixie Caldwell was at the top of his list; Jack was second or third. They even invite me to a party. Nick skims his arm across my back. His hands caress my ribs while his fingers stretch out before finding purchase on my hip.

*Is this normal? Is this what guys do? They just casually touch you?*

"Don't worry, I'll keep an eye out for you," he whispers into my ear. His breath tickles my ear lobe. All I can do in reply is cinch a smile across my face, feeling truly puzzled. Back home, I couldn't even get a guy to look at me, let alone someone to "watch out for me". I hadn't changed the way I looked, the way I behaved, other than with Jack. *Perhaps it's just new girl's luck?*

I spot Jack gazing at me from across the room. Everything around me gently falls back into darkness and silence. He smiles at me before turning back to his friends.

The blonde chignon sends me an evil glare, then picks up her chopsticks and turns back to her raw fish in an ebony box.

"Hey Nick," I say, interrupting his eating. "Who is that pretty blonde sitting across from Jack?"

Pete chuckles. "You mean Frost Bitch?"

I frown, confused.

Nick rolls his eyes at his friend's reply. "Pete's just bitter. She's rejected everyone at this table at some point, except *me*. But that's Vivienne Mather. She's a senior, student body president, head of the climate change coalition, co-chairs junior league, and captain of the knighting gales. Does she still do field hockey, Noah?" he asks. "Noah manages the girl's field hockey team."

Noah grins. "Gotta rub out all those sore muscles." He then shakes his head. "But nah, not this year. She got that modeling contract with Burberry, so she quit, couldn't risk the bruises," he says, ending in a mocking tone.

Pete laughs. "Yeah, like she ever got bruised. Didn't she send that St. Ambrose girl to the hospital?"

Alden laughs, his mouth full of French fries. "Bro, that was awesome."

Noah nods. "Yeah, after that game was when we got drunk and made out."

"That never happened, bro." Nick crumples up his greasy paper and tosses it perfectly into the trash can. "Boom!"

The lunch bell rings.

"I better go," I say, picking up my tray of uneaten food. "I don't want to be late."

Nick slides his chair out. "Here, let me walk you. I've got German next, and Frau Hoffman loves me. She won't care if I'm a little zu spät, *late*."

I shake my head. "No, don't worry about it. If I don't find my own way, I'll be completely lost tomorrow. But I'll see you later." I give my new male acquaintances a quick wave and dash. I sigh in great relief, having easily found my next class, anatomy with Mrs. Albert.

I open the classroom door just as the second bell rings. Perfect timing!

I hand the teacher my schedule. She signs it, smudging it with chocolate that drips off her left hand from the cream filled doughnut she's devouring.

Trixie, the golden goddess, strolls into the classroom behind me and gracefully takes her seat. Everyone acts like she doesn't exist.

"You can sit with—" Mrs. Albert glances around the room for an open seat. "Ah, you can sit next to Trixie, right there," Mrs. Albert says, pointing the way.

I walk up to the second row of black top tables and politely smile at her. She is beaming up at me as I take my seat next to her.

"Hi! I'm Trixie, Trixie Caldwell!" She extends her hand in a formal greeting.

Her hand is soft, like it's crafted from the richest satin, and smells of daffodils and sweet pea blossoms. My hand probably feels clammy and gross from how nervous I am.

"Eleanor," I quietly return while other students chatter and quickly take their seats.

She giggles, her smile nearly bursting from her sun-shinny face. "Oh, I know," she states. She's so bubbly she's nearly bouncing in her seat. I notice she has a daisy tucked behind her ear.

*I guess word travels fast. I'm sure Jack knows my name too now. That was fun while it lasted.*

The classroom lights flick off.

"You're Helen's daughter. Get ready," Trixie utters playfully under her breath.

"How do you know my mom?" I ask.

She grins wickedly at me. "While we're in school, let's just say we're family friends. My mom is on the committee with your Aunt Marie."

"Oh," I frown. "Is that like Junior league or something?" I ask, thinking of Vivienne.

Trixie releases a twinkling giggle, almost like wind chimes. "Oh no.

Nothing like that, what the posh girls in school do with their mothers is completely different. They organize different charity events and do weekends in Manhattan. The committee my mom is on and your aunt is well…much… older…and better. It's an honor to be chosen to work on the committee. And unlike Junior league, you don't buy your way in."

Mrs. Albert settles down in her chair and points a small black remote at the flat screen TV fixed to the wall. She coughs, clearing her throat. "Okay class, today we will observe doctors in a complex hospital setting! You can just sit and listen. No need to bother with taking notes." Mrs. Albert tosses the remote on her desk just before she hungrily snags a romance novel from her desk drawer.

The opening credits to "Grey's Anatomy" play across the large screen. *This was advanced anatomy and biology?* I rest my head in my hand, ready to bunker down for the long class period. Orchestra was a major letdown, but I thought my favorite subject would make up for it. *Nope.*

"Do you guys do this a lot?" I mumble to Trixie.

Trixie flips open her notebook. Each page is filled with pressed flora. "Only lately, she's recovering from some unknown illness. She's probably milking it, but she's nice."

I turn back to the saccharine voice over. *Life can be like a layer cake; each layer comes with secrets.* The screen shows two doctors making out in a closet, *the sweet,* a baby is being held by a new parent, *and sometimes, the bitter…*

I want to bang my head on the table.

"Hey," Trixie elbows me gently, "Do you want to get out of here?" she whispers.

I quickly scan the room. A few kids' heads rest on the tabletop sleeping, some page through magazines, but most sit with their cellphones out, including Noah from lunch sitting in the back. He moves his phone slowly, deliberately; he adjusts it to point towards Trixie and me.

I duck my head closer to Trixie. "Won't we get in trouble?"

She shrugs with a careless roll of her eyes. "Yeah, unless you have a pass," she says as she pulls out two yellow slips of paper from her notebook. At the top of the paper read in official lettering: HALL PASS, under read her name, on the other read mine.

I frowned. "How did you—."

Trixie rolled her deep blue eyes. "Let's just go. I'll explain later." She casually strolls up to Mrs. Albert, turns back and nods for me to come. I tiptoe up the aisle to Trixie's side and she hands Mrs. Albert our hall passes for approval.

Mrs. Albert put her finger to the sentence she left off in her book before looking over our passes. "Uh huh, okay. See you two in a bit." She nods us off and we abscond from the room.

Trixie saunters down the hall as breezily as if she is wandering through a sprawling garden on a summer day. I speed walk to catch up. *What are they feeding kids here?*

"How was that possible?" I ask, bewildered by her parlor trick. "How did you have a pass with my name on it? Did you take that from the office? They never gave me one." My name hadn't been handwritten; it was an official pass printed by the school.

"Come with me into the bathroom." Trixie takes hold of my hand and quickly tows me to the nearest restroom, which is about the size of a closet.

She locks the door behind us and whips around to face me. "That was fun," she says impishly.

I bob my head along with her. "Yeah, that was really cool. Did you get my pass from the office?"

She shakes her head no. "No need. So, what do you think of Griggs?" she turns to the mirror and adjusts the flower in her hair. She pulls a four-leaf clover out of her breast pocket, kisses it, whispers something against the lush green, and drops it into my coat pocket.

"Um, thanks," I say awkwardly. "Uh, it's okay. I really hate the uniforms." I motion to my oversized and itchy outfit. The skirt seems short on Trixie's toned legs.

"I saw you met Jack Woods," she says with wiggling brows.

I blush. "Yeah, he's okay." I peer down at my scuffed-up shoes.

Trixie giggles. "I think he's dreamy. He looks like a blonder version of that one guy in those dirty movies. I called him Christian for like a month after they came out. I'm not sure he understood it, but I thought it was funny."

I blink against my contacts, feeling one drift across my eyeball. I exhale, annoyed, continuing to blink.

"You okay?" she asks, her voice sweet with concern.

"Yeah, it's these stupid contacts." I turn to the mirror, holding my lid open and move the contact around until I've got a good grip and I pluck them out, one by one. I pull out the lens case from my satchel and drop them in.

Trixie gasps and falls back into the tiled bathroom wall. "Oh, my goodness!"

I resist rolling my eyes. "They're *barely* purple. Most days they look blue," I mutter, slightly annoyed by her over the top reaction.

She pushes herself off the wall and grips my shoulders tightly. "I know what you are now, Eleanor O'Reilly. Are you scared?" she questions in a harsh tone.

I swallow, positive I've solved the mystery of why Trixie has no friends. "Do you bring all the new girls in here and ask them that?" I try to tease. Anxiety fills my voice, making me sound more sheepish than jesting. "Seriously, let go. You're hurting me." I try shaking off her grip.

She continues to search my eyes. "Your eyes shouldn't be lavender. You're all wrong."

I feel the full sting of her comment. I suddenly feel like I'm back in the schoolyard with little kids pointing and laughing at me.

"Demon?" she ventures with an eyebrow raised.

"Is that a question or a statement?"

She shakes her gorgeous head, sending her silken waves to flutter out from her, dropping her arms to her side. "Nah, too innocent. I feel it, you're not wearing a glamor. You're one of us but…your eyes don't make sense." she cocks her head to the side, examining me like a bug through a microscope. "How old are you?"

"What is your damage? I'm seventeen." I look away from her intense stare and peer at the terrazzo tiling.

"You're oblivious, but your eyes don't lie. No one has told you, have they?" Her face seems disbelieving, then shifts to sympathetic, only to end overly pitying. "How is that possible? How could anyone keep that a secret?"

"Know what?" I snap. I feel trapped as her super model body blocks the only exit.

She leans closer to me. "This shouldn't come from me, but you have to know. As your best friend, I think I need to."

*Best friend? That was fast.*

"I'm always here for you, Eleanor. Can you keep a secret?" Her nose is almost touching mine.

"Yes," I whisper. *At my old school, given the right bathroom stall, we could probably have scored her some much-needed valium.*

She straightens up, pulling her chin up proudly. "I'm a witch," she states haughtily. "And the powerful essence you are giving off tells me you're a witch too," she says with complete confidence.

*Oh great, another one. It's Salem, sis. I'm sure every third person thinks they're a witch.*

"Perfect. Let's get piercings and a pentagram tat after we hit a shop for some ganja," I murmur.

Trixie giggles, cupping her mouth like a child. Although she looks more like a fairy or a sprite than a little kid. "You're super funny. But that's not what

I'm talking about. I'm talking about actual witches, not wannabes," she says between angelic giggles.

"Great," I mutter sarcastically. I move my hand towards the doorknob only to have Trixie cut me off.

"Seriously though, Eleanor, have you gotten the headaches yet? If not, they'll come. They always come when you turn seventeen and your magic grows inside you. They'll get worse too. Don't fight against it. I've heard horror stories, so be careful. You don't want to go crazy." She sounds sincerely worried, giving me the same advice my sister Shannyn gave. She reaches over, tucking my hair behind my ears and placing a daisy in there too.

*Seriously, where is she getting all these flowers?*

I feel a heavy knot forming in my throat. "I have to get back to class." I nearly push her out of my way and run out of the bathroom.

Thankfully, Trixie never comes back to class.

# Chapter Seven
## The Birthday

The rest of the day went by in a blur. It turns out I'm behind in calculus and I have a test in physics tomorrow. Being new is no excuse apparently, not to mention I have an entire chapter of French translations due tomorrow. Though Nick's friend, Alden, did offer to do all my translations if I wanted. He humbly informed me that his father did a visiting professorship last year at the Sorbonne and he is now practically fluent.

I didn't feel better until I heard the last bell. I was so exhausted both mentally and emotionally that I had to practically drag my feet to get to my locker. The hum of the fluorescent lights is grating on my nerves due to my raging, pulsating headache, which I know is from lack of sleep and stress, not whatever Trixie was going on about in the bathroom.

I turn the combination on my locker, but the lock is jammed. I try it three more times before it finally pops open.

Jack is coming down the hall to my left. Our eyes meet. My stomach twitches. His lips hold a smile, then falters. He stops walking as his face drains of color and turns ashen. He tears his eyes away, looking down at the floor. He takes a deep breath and releases it before he adjusts his backpack on his shoulders and strides past me, not giving me a second glance.

*What was that about?*

I grab my things from my locker and duck my head, hoping to escape without being noticed. The drive home didn't make me feel any better. I wasn't driving to *my* home, nor would either of my parents be there. *Who cares about Jack's stupid and sudden indifference? I've got worse things going on.* My heart aches in my chest, like it's choking from lack of blood flow, but I know it's all in my head. I know that. I had thought I was having a heart attack when Mom told me about Dad. My mom later explained it had been a panic attack caused by grief. Maybe when she returns, she can explain my headaches. When I turned sixteen, I got my driver's license. The following March first, my seventeenth birthday, I got migraines and a dead dad. *Maybe it's all downhill from here.* If my dad was here, he'd have laughed at my melodrama.

Cats scatter and ravens take flight when I pull into the driveway. *Since when do cats and birds get along?* I rest my chin on the steering wheel, watching Maggie kick around a soccer ball in the front yard. The orange tabby cat, Phoenix I think his name is, sits on the branches of the old, dead, twisted oak tree, watching her closely. *That didn't take long for her to get settled in.*

My gaze slowly tightens into an unintentional glare. She shouldn't settle in and get comfortable here. Resentment fills my body. Maggie is fitting in like a seasoned local, like she has completely forgotten the reason we are stuck here in the first place.

Phoenix seems riveted, watching the redheaded elfin girl chasing a checkered ball up and down the lawn.

She spots me and gives a limp wave with a somewhat glum smile. I fall back against my leather seat. Margaret isn't happy, but she's making do. But that's not reassuring either.

"Hey, Maggie," I call, trying to sound light and nonchalant while heading into the house. Slipping my shoes off in the entry cluttered with cat toys, I practically choke on the smell of patchouli and cinnamon.

Aunt Marie comes bounding out of the kitchen carrying a teak wood tray with antique teacups simmering next to a plate of cookies. "How was your first day?" she questions, excitedly. Marie can barely put the tray down fast enough before she gathers me in a smothering hug. "I made Lavender cookies and chamomile tea." She motions proudly to her tray.

Sally clomps down the stairs, her wedge shoes thump with each step. "Ell, babe! Enjoy school?" My aunt links our arms and pulls me to the fainting couch in their stuffy living room. Sally plops down on the floor in front of me, resting on a round chenille pillow. "Go on, tell us about the boys! Margaret was no fun," Sal says before snagging a cookie.

I shrug, feeling my sticky, stiff fabric. "Um, yeah, I met some guys. It's not an all-girl school," I point out.

Sally snorts, "An all-girl school? We aren't sadists, Ell. We would never send you to an all-girl gulag. Helen enrolled Maggie before we had a chance to save her." She sinks her teeth into her cookie that has a real flower pressed into it.

Marie rolls her eyes while spooning several scoops of sugar into her cup. "Ignore my sister, that's what I do, dearie," she says, glancing at Sally lounging lazily from the corner of her eye. "What did you think of your teachers? Is Winston one of them? Did you make any new friends? Did you even see Winston today? Winston is an excellent teacher."

I wonder if Maggie endured the same interrogation process when she came home.

Marie takes a long-drawn sip from her teacup. "Winston is a fantastic teacher, not *only* in the classroom. I sure hope you have him. He has such a vivacious appetite for literature!" Marie claps her hands together, then clasps them together as if star struck. "Oh, Ellie dear, I sure hope you become Winnie's pupil."

Sally raises a brow, looking at Marie's dreamy, faraway look.

I frown, recalling Mr. Edwards's death glare. "Yeah, I think he hates me. He pretended he didn't remember me from last night. In fact, I thought he might punch me when I brought it up."

Marie shakes her head, causing her cheeks to jiggle. "Oh no, dearie, he's a lover, not a fighter." She takes another sip of her tea before dipping a cookie in. "You know, he was probably worried you would let it slip he's a witch. It's not a good thing to let your students know. Or anyone outside our coven know," Marie says. She reaches up and strokes my hair.

Sally tosses a pillow at Marie's head, but Marie deflects it with her arm. "I thought we weren't allowed to talk to Eleanor about that. Remember miss witchy-bitchy this morning? You kicked me so hard under the table I can't go pantless tonight," she snaps.

Marie shimmies her shoulders, folding her arms across her chest, and points her chin up, looking away from her sister. "You brought it up. Winston confessed last night, and Helen won't be back now for another week. So, I've reconsidered, we need to talk to her about witchcraft," she says indignantly. "Besides, I told you to use the iced arnica on your shin and drink your thistle tea, so any bruising at this point is on you, sister."

Sally blanched. "You know I can't drink the thistle! It makes me smell funny…"

I close my eyes and take a deep breath. *I can't take this anymore.* "You guys seriously believe that? Like magic, cauldrons, spell books, and demons?" I ask, dry and unamused. I couldn't help but notice Sally wince at the word "demon" and Marie practically jump at the word.

Sally loudly slurps from her teacup. "Baby-cakes, do you want us to prove it? We can show you what we mean," she offers, adjusting herself on her cushion.

Marie shakes her head. "No, no Sal. We can tell her about the coven and our family, but her introduction into spells should be with Helen. It's her right," she insists while nervously stirring even more sugar into her tea. "We need to tell her the truth, but instruction and demonstration are a mother's right."

Sally narrows her eyes on her sister. "She lost that right. She's hurt her girls. We shouldn't have stood by all these years! We shouldn't have stayed away." The room percolates with energy. A prickling sharpness, like static shock. "Besides," she mumbles under her breath, "we broke that rule with Shannyn."

Cats slink and crawl into the room. Miss Priss rests on Marie's feet, not even bothering to try and leap up onto the couch. She purrs and brushes her bushy white tail up Marie's leg, gazing at her as if trying to communicate.

The pressure keeps building; the tension is impenetrable, making me anxious. It's like sitting in a full bathtub with a running blow dryer resting precariously on the porcelain edge.

I exhale, needing to get out of here. "Well, if you don't mind, I think I'm going to go upstairs and see if I have an extra suitcase tucked away with my stuff." I amble out of the living room.

Blue-Eyes sits at the top of the stairs, gazing at me. It gives me the shivers the way that stupid cat stares. Blue-Eyes tilts his curious head to the side, his eyes still gazing deeply into mine. I hiccup. Like a child losing interest in a toy, Blue-Eyes saunters past me down the stairs. When he reaches the landing, he stretches out his paws next to me, then slinks away.

I hurry up the spiral staircase, then halt on the landing, taken aback by the center table. No longer is there a vase filled with poisonous flora and cattails, now it's replaced by an ornate box, about the size of a shoe box. But what made me stop isn't the absence of the bizarre floral arrangement but the writing, etched in scarlet scrawled across the surface. I step closer to get a better look; the floor creaks beneath me. I reach over, flicking on the chandelier as there are no windows to allow natural light.

The box is ebony with gold filigree on all corners. I dip my head lower, examining the crudely written script. It appears it was carved by hand… literally. Like someone had scratched words onto the sides. I bend till I'm on my knees, my eyes searching the words. I recognize the Gaelic language but not what is inscribed, although there is one word I understand: rith. It means "run." I drag my finger over the h's arch. My finger snags on something, and I carefully pull out the object from the engraved letter. It's a bent, slightly split fingernail. *What in the actual hell?*

My hands recoil as I drop it onto the rug and spring to my feet. The box slowly creaks open, the lid raising upright. My heart pounds in my ears as the blood drains from my face. Instead of a poised, pink ballerina there's a small white rabbit, crouched. I watch it rotate gradually on a spring in the center of the box, in front of a round mirror, fastened to the lid's red felt interior. Tinkling music delicately plays a sad plucking tune. I squint, unsure of what I'm seeing. The rabbit quivers and unfolds to reveal a woman standing with a broom and a witch's hat on top of her head. I can't look away as she makes a full circle and crinkles like paper back into the shape of the rabbit. The rotating rabbit stops, its red eyes looking forward.

I slam the box close. *What the effing hell was that? Did someone scratch run in Gaelic on that music box? Why? And why do my aunts have that?*

My heart is still fluttering in my chest when I rush up to the towering bedroom. I fall back against my door the moment I slam it close. *How did that rabbit turn into a witch? It was like—no, don't you dare say it.* I squeeze my eyes shut, drinking in the smell of lemon and jasmine permeating my bedroom. *Why does it smell so good in here?* My nerves *slowly* iron themselves out, the throbbing that was building beneath my flesh eases ever so slightly until it's a soft, barely there pulse.

When I open my eyes, I see the shelf above my bed is littered with different colored candles, some thin and long, some short and fat. The light cream and gentle yellow candles are lit and glowing. *Were those here yesterday?*

I toss my satchel on the ground and throw my blazer onto a velvet cushioned chair resting next to the pentagon window. All my belongings that had been packed away in cardboard boxes just this morning are now organized about the room. My books fill a whicker bookshelf. My record player and records occupy a small wooden dresser. Playbills from Broadway productions kept from family trips, polaroids of friends, concert tickets, and my small vision board are all pinned to a newly hung corkboard. *The aunts must have been busy.* My heart gives a grateful squeeze. *I should have been more gracious downstairs.*

I peel off my uniform and toss it into the bamboo hamper. I pull on some grey leggings and a salmon-colored sweatshirt, tuck my hands into the cuffs, and crawl onto the bed. I'm starving from skipping lunch but too exhausted to do much about it. *I wonder if they have any leftovers from breakfast.*

I suddenly notice a cat bed underneath the corkboard. *Yeah… that's not happening.* Tears fill my eyes as I surrender to a jaw-popping yawn. My lids feel impossibly heavy and drift to sleep.

My bedroom door creaks open with an eerie slowness. I lift my head off my pillow. "Hello?" I ask, groggy from the impromptu nap.

Blue-Eyes slinks into my bedroom. His confident blue eyes survey the room before finding purchase at the edge of my bed mere inches from my feet.

I swallow back my fear, my eyes squeezed shut. "Leave," I order. I peek my eyes open to see him still resting near me.

*Did that thing just smile at me?*

I inch farther up the bed until my back is pinned against the headboard. "Go! Shoo!" I flick out my foot, showing him I mean business. It doesn't work. "Please, go?" I plea.

Blue-Eyes rolls his eyes before springing gingerly off the bed and landing without a sound. A tuft of hair is missing from the tip of his long, black tail revealing bone as he struts out the door.

*A rotting dead cat?* I ball my hands into fists. *No, no, that's stupid. He's a disgusting cat with some feline disease.*

I glance out my bedroom window; it's pitch-black outside. The oak's serpentine branches tremble with the howling wind that rattles the window-panes. *How long did I nap for?*

A sweet scent of food wafts through the open bedroom door. My stomach growls.

I descend the tower stairs, then pause. The ebony box sits on the table, awaiting in the darkened landing, like Pandora waiting to be once again opened. Averting my eyes, I tiptoe on by. *It's just a box, don't be stupid.*

I take the steps two by two, nearly racing to the dining room table. My stomach rumbles at the sight of the feast filling every inch of their table.

Steak tartar, crab and shrimp-stuffed lobster tails, roasted duck, chicken marsala, stuffed mushroom caps, a chilled pea soup, mashed potatoes with rosemary and garlic, fried potatoes, baked potatoes, beans, grilled corn on the cob slathered in creamy butter, and caramelized carrots. Then there were rolls, breadsticks, a bread pinwheel, and a spinach salad resting in a crystal bowl filled with different veggies carved like roses. There is no way that all this food is intended just for the four of us women.

Marie sits at the table near the array of potatoes. Maggie is on the opposite side, giggling at me, just as amused by the fantastical spread as I am. Sally can be heard singing at the top of her lungs in the kitchen.

Marie fills her flute with champagne. "Eleanor, sit wherever you like, but you might want to sit next to Blue," she says, tipping her glass to him.

Blue-Eyes sits at the head of the table in a high back quilted chair, patiently sitting as if he were invited to dinner as an honored guest. They even gave him a booster seat so he can see over the table. His judgmental cat eyes look me over, assessing me.

Declining Marie's invitation to sit next to the putrid cat, I pull out a chair next to Margaret. "You guys seriously out do yourselves."

Sally breezes through the kitchen doors carrying a four-tier birthday cake with unlit candles. The cake has ice blue frosting with yellow flowers and white icing. "Yes, well, it's Blue-Eyes' birthday, so it's a perfect night to out-do oneself." Sally pats Blue-Eyes on the head.

I pray the aunts don't see my eye roll. I'm about to speak when I hear tinkling music. The soft chime is so soft a breath would blot it out. The music box is open.

Sally coos at Blue-Eyes, rubbing his frayed ear.

I lift my fork, pretending to nonchalantly study the silverware. "So, what's with the music box upstairs?"

Maggie snorts. "Yeah, I opened that earlier. It's super creepy. Is it from like Halloween or something? I swear the words were bleeding earlier." She picks up her flute and takes a swig of some sparkling beverage.

I momentarily forget the box. "Margaret Rose, are you drinking champagne?" I accuse, aghast. *Ugh, I sounded just like Mom.*

She does a long-exaggerated eye roll at me. "No Eleanor Elizabeth, it's cider. They have like an unlimited supply."

"Do you want champagne?" Sally offers.

"Nope. Neither of us are twenty-one, you know, the legal drinking age," I say pointedly.

Sally cackles. "Pish posh, those rules don't apply to us."

Marie, unconcerned with the alcohol tangent, turns to Margaret and me. "That box was a gift from the Committee. It's very important this time of year to remember," she says, then glances about the table. "Sally, we don't have enough glasses. Why can't you ever set a proper table?" The aunts bicker amongst themselves, counting the glasses on the table.

"They need reminding to, what, scare the hell out of us?" Margaret whispers to me under her breath.

"You shouldn't swear," I mumble back.

Maggie balks at me. "What the hell is your problem?"

I shake my head, squeezing my eyes shut. "I don't know, I'm sorry. With Mom being gone and everything, it's really messing with my head."

"I already have two parents, I don't need a thir—" Margaret stops, she pales, realizing she might have made a mistake, unsure if Dad still counts anymore. She peers down at her plate. Her lips tremble. Bowing her head her red hair spills over her shoulders.

I reach over and squeeze her hand under the table. Margaret brushes away tears, clears her throat, and shakes her hair out, pointing her chin up.

"When was Blue-Eyes born, like how old is he?" Maggie asks, interrupting the aunts. I can tell she's desperate to change the subject. She and I both glance to our right at Blue-Eyes, who is eyeing the food.

*I couldn't care less about the stupid cat's birthday. It's more than ridiculous to have a feast of this magnitude for a dumb, ugly cat.*

*"Excuse me?"*

"Well, let's see, he appeared seventeen years ago?" Sally scratches her pointed chin and claims a seat next to Marie. "I'm not sure. I'll be honest, he doesn't make much sense. And technically, it's not his *actual* birthday, but we were detained and couldn't throw him a bash on the actual day," Sally explains. "But he's been loyal to our family ever since he ascended."

Marie smiles lovingly at the ugly black cat with striking pale blue eyes. "He more than deserves this party!"

Margaret looks around the table. "When was his actual birthday?"

"March first," Sally retorts. "Though that was when he rose, his actual day of birth is unknown. He's a very, *very* old cat."

Maggie grins. "Hey Ell, you and Blue-Eyes have the same birthday! Maybe we should make this a joint party," she teases with a wink and a nudge to my ribs.

I glower at her, which only further entertains her. "I'm fine. I wouldn't dream of taking away Blue's thunder," I say, mockingly.

*"As if I'd allow it."*

I glance around the dining room, unsure if I just heard someone speak.

"Are we the only ones invited to this birthday bash?" Maggie motions to the empty plates and excessive stemware.

*If it weren't for the food, I'd rather not be invited.*

*"Likewise."*

My eyes dart about for that same voice that seems to belong to no one. *What the hell?*

Marie leaps from her seat, despite having just sat down. "I must go change, my goodness, look at what I'm wearing," she shrieks. I give her a sideways glance. She's wearing a long black skirt with a frumpy black sweater accessorized with endless strands of silver necklaces.

Maggie looks longingly at the table. "Would it be okay if we started eating? I skipped lunch to hang with some girls in the library."

"Yes please," I second. I ravenously survey the table, unsure where to begin. "Wait, you made friends?"

Maggie shrugs casually. "Yeah, didn't you?"

I think back on Nick and the lot, then Trixie, and Jack… "I actually don't know. It was a weird day," I conclude.

Marie nods, sending her chins a flutter. "Oh girls, of course, of course. Winnie is running unusually late."

Maggie loads up her plate as my head falls back. *Does Mr. Edwards really have to come?* I swallow back my annoyance. *Whatever, he can come, but that doesn't mean I have to talk to him.* I reach for the serving bowl of chicken marsala and dish out a generous portion before moving onto the dragon fruit and horned melon fruit salad.

"Okay, I'm trying that lemonade," Maggie says, reaching for a glass pitcher after polishing off the rest of her cider.

Drool nearly dribbles out my mouth as I devour the succulent chicken in less than thirty seconds. An embarrassing moan escapes me when a sauteed mushroom slides over my tongue. My irritation with Mr. Edwards dissipates with every bite of the heavenly food. *What do they put in their food?* I grab a lobster tail and an ear of corn, then I nearly drop the cob into my lap as Marie comes bursting through the dining room entry.

Her wardrobe change was not an improvement. Her white party dress is tighter than Saran Wrap. But the worst part is the obnoxious red spots splattered across the frock. She looks like she fought a tommy gun and lost.

Margaret chokes on her blueberry mint lemonade and she pounds her chest to open her airway. "Oh Marie, you look—great!"

Marie's face colors. "Thank you, dear. Winnie loved it the last time I wore it. He should be here in a few minutes. He just rang from his broom."

Maggie frowns, cocking her head to the side.

I ignore the broom comment; it's probably just a nickname for his Cadillac, anyway. My fork shakes in my hand while I shovel in a mouthful of seafood, chomping down hard. *Why does this bother me so much?* I realize it's not my English teacher's attendance tonight that is grating me. It's the insanity my aunts and Winston want to indulge in. *But who cares if they want to larp in a fantasy world? All the power to them, pun definitely intended.* But every time they try to drag us into their delusions, my skin crawls, and my insides twist like the crank of a torture device. They're trying to force my hand, and I refuse to oblige them.

*"Oh, capitulate child, there's no need for a tantrum..."*
*Who the hell is that!?*
"Ell?" Margaret says.

With my mouth still stuffed, I breathe deeply through my nostrils. I spear a mushroom and shove it in, eating my food like I'm trying to punish it.

"Sweetie, are you alright? Do you not like Winnie?" Marie asks.

I swallow and draw in a proper breath before speaking. "No," I dab my mouth with a napkin, "like I said before, he hates—" I stop as Mr. Edwards saunters into the room from behind Marie. He's draped in black dress robes. The fabric is of the finest looking silk, shiny and smooth. On his head rests a limp witch's hat, the point lays bent and flaccid on the brim. I could swear he has an ethereal glow about him.

"Good evening, Marie, Sally," he says, holding his lapels. "It's Margaret, is it not?" he questions with an affable smile. His top lip is completely sheathed beneath his meticulously groomed mustache. His cheeks and nose are rosy with an almost wind-whipped appearance.

Maggie delivers a halfhearted nod, skeptically appraising him. She leans over and whispers, "Was this supposed to be a costume party?"

Winston gives both my aunts a double take. "You two aren't wearing your formal robes tonight?" He seems put out that he went to all that trouble dressing up, despite that he appears like he's merely wearing formal pajamas.

Marie blushes. "I left mine at the dry cleaners." Her eyes sweep her shoes apologetically.

Sally frowns. "Let me think, where are my robes? Oh, that's right, I accidentally set mine on fire. I'll have to replace them."

"Tsk, tsk, ladies!" He only now realizes I'm seated just in front of him. "And Eleanor! How was your first day of school?" He slides out a chair next to the "birthday boy" right across from me.

"Oh, the cocktails! Where is my head today? Sally, help me make them! " Marie waddles out of the room to fetch drinks; Sally slumps behind her to assist.

I lift and drop one shoulder in a lazy half shrug. Recalling his embarrassing rudeness, I mumble, "It was fine." I push some sweet potato around with my fork.

His shoulders slump, his eyes downcast. "I was quite abrupt with you today, my sincerest apologies," he says giving me a small sympathetic smile. "You see, at school, it is the highest imperative that we keep a strictly professional student/teacher relationship. But outside of school, I should like to be a confidant, perhaps in time, a cohort." A honey biscuit levitates from across the table to his plate.

I drop my jaw and my fork. Maggie freezes at my side, and a look of panic and excitement washes over her.

I shake my head slowly, wrapping myself in a nice fuzzy blanket of denial. *I had to be seeing things. I had to. I'm just having a psychotic break.*

Completely unencumbered by hands, a butter knife independently butters the biscuit. The bottle of wine pours into the goblet before him. "Sally, Marie, hurry with those cocktails. A fellow could die of thirst." He gives us girls a playful wink. "This pinot will have to do for now." He shakes his head at the label, turning it in the air to give him a better look. "Terrible year."

"No. Freaking. Way!" Margaret squeals.

Blue-Eyes stares at me.

My mouth is arid. I can't swallow. My eyes just lied to my brain. The room spins around me. *Am I going to pass out? Die? What the hell is happening?* My stomach clenches nervously. *I'm crazy. This is it. They're going to lock me up.*

Winston stares at me, confused by my reaction to the impossible phenomena I had just witnessed. "Pray tell, what is wrong with you, child? Please tell me you've embarked on your training." He frowns, disparagingly. "My goodness, you look as if you've seen a ghost."

I can't move or speak. I feel sick and mystified at the same time. My mind can't handle this. *Am I just mistaken? Did he just reach, and I didn't see?*

"Eleanor?" he questions as a knife slices up the prime rib. The cut of meat then floats over to his plate.

I feel a wave of nausea ripple over me. "Mr.—" hic "Edwards," I start without knowing what to say next. My eyes flash to Margaret's for confirmation. Her eyes, now the size of saucers, confirm she saw it too. My safety blanket of denial and self-imposed ignorance has viciously been ripped away. There is *no* denying it. This is happening. Things are moving on their own. Magic exists, or at least it does here. The world as I knew it was just a mirage. My nerves go on full throttle. Hic!

Mr. Edwards raises a bushy eyebrow, appraising both my sister and I. "Ladies, was this your first demonstration of magic?"

My mind still whirls. *Was Trixie right? My Aunts? Winston? They really are witches? Had they made a deal with the devil? Is this why my mother tried to keep us away from them? Did my mother escape a cult?* My mind spins out of control as fear penetrates every fiber of my being. *Why did my mother bring us here!? Do they have spell books? Shackles for princesses? Where did they keep their bats? Warts? How did they cover up their green skin? Was their black cauldron in the kitchen under the sink?*

*"It's kept in the greenhouse and there is a spare in the garage."*

*WHO IS SPEAKING IN MY HEAD!!??*

I grip the table, feeling lightheaded.

Winston bangs his fist on the table. "Sally! Marie!"

Their heads peek out of the kitchen like they've been eavesdropping the entire time, just waiting for their cue to enter the dining room.

"What's going on?" Sally asks, feigning innocence.

Marie laces her fingers together, letting them rest on her stomach. She stares at Winston in earnest concern.

"Eleanor is seventeen! Seventeen! Not only has she not started her training, she doesn't even know what she is!" Winston's voice thunders through the house. "This is preposterous! I mean, the girls watched me do a simple levitation spell and now they're staring like wide-eyed simpletons!"

Marie peers down at one of her bullet wound polka-dots as she speaks. "Well, Winnie, Helen doesn't want her to practice witchcraft." Her eyes dart to me for the briefest second. This feels like a set-up, like Marie's little repentant act is completely bogus. She wants Winston to get fired up.

Winston continues to storm. The long wax candles on the shelves shake and tremble. A few of them spontaneously ignite with such power the wax bleeds into little puddles within seconds. "Is Helen insane!?" he bellows.

Margaret and I flinch at his rage.

He pounds the table, causing one of the glasses to tumble and smash onto the floor. "That Helen! How could she? I heard the rumors about her, but I refused to believe them!" Winston's chest is bloated with self-righteous gas. He points a finger at my aunts. "And don't for one second think I don't notice her eyes. Those silly little browns she adorned today didn't fool me. I wasn't so lost to the drink last night I had forgotten those irises."

Sally's eyes fall to the shattered glass on the floor. Suddenly there's a strange sucking noise and in a blink of an eye the glass is reformed and back on the tabletop. I jump back. Sally's eyes meet mine, then slide back to Winston while he continues to rant.

"The Byrnes are immensely powerful! They don't have the luxury of turning their backs on their destiny! So, Eleanor knows *nothing* of her heritage? She knows nothing of our path in life!" Winston wails. "We all took a vow! That includes Eleanor! Is Helen trying to damn her family!? How dare she!? How dare *you*! You are her aunts! Her kin! You could have prevented this!" His face deepens to a purplish crimson while he raves. "It is our *only* purpose. If we turn our back on it, we might as well just perish back into the dust whence we came!"

Slowly, silently, Maggie and I leave the table, hoping no one will notice. Once we're out of eyesight, we sprint up the stairs. We don't slow down until we reach Margaret's room and slam the door shut behind us. I flip the brass lock, as if that will stop a witch from entering.

Her walls are sea foam green, accented with cream. Her bedroom is as large as the one I sleep in, if not bigger. She has a mini fridge in the corner, a snow-colored leather love seat, and a recliner against the far end of her bedroom. I just realized this is my first time visiting her room.

Maggie sits on the plush stool in front of her Hollywood-inspired vanity. She stares at her feet as she flexes her toes and releases. She does this a few times before speaking. "So, Mom was like in some kind of cult?" she asks within the safety of her room.

I collapse on her bed, deflated, knowing I'll never go back to life before. I can't lie my way out of this. My present and future continue to spiral into an unknown, murky existence, one that doesn't resemble life with my father whatsoever. "I honestly don't know." I exhale, trying to think. "We just need to call Shannyn to see if she can take us to the airport. We can't stay in this freak show another minute." I whip out my cell phone and dial my sister.

"It *was* cool though, how he made that roll float across the table like that," Maggie mumbles to herself.

*Oh no! She drank the Kool-Aid. I have to get her out of here.*

"Hello?" Shannyn calls into the phone loudly.

There's heavy thumping music and a myriad of people in the background. A few partiers are calling to my sister, trying to get her attention.

"Shannyn?" I shout into the phone. "You have to come and pick us up right now! It's an emergency! Please."

"Wait, what? I can't hear you, ugh, just wait a minute, okay?" she yells back. The pulsating music and voices fade away as I hear a door close. "Okay," she breathes, "what do you want?"

"Come get Maggie and me!" I holler. Shannyn has always been her own little island, her secrets best shared with only herself. But when my father died, Shannyn went from an acquaintance to a stranger. It wasn't personal. She wasn't really talking to anyone. Her boyfriend Lennox even let it slip that she's been struggling to get through. Her Harvard apartment is now her Fortress of Solitude.

"Why, where are you?" she asks, confused. "You're not with the aunts? What's going on Eleanor?"

I take a shaky breath, trying to steady the crumbling foundations of my fractured reality. "We're at the aunts' house. Shannyn, they're completely insane. And they also might be possessed. They honestly believe they're witches! I mean, Shannyn, I know this is going to sound crazy, but Margaret saw it, too. We saw a bread roll fly across the table, not thrown, not tossed, *fly* like a little airplane. Then Sally fixed a shattered glass with a snap of her fingers! Please, Shannyn, get us out of here!" My head pounds, my eyes need to cry, to have that emotional crescendo and release.

I wait for Shannyn to reply, maybe freak out, or maybe try to rationalize what really happened. She continues to stay distant, cutting our conversation in piercing silence.

*Did she hang up?*

I glanced at my phone; I'm still connected.

"And?" she asks, anticipating another revelation.

My frustration flames within me. "What are you saying 'and' for? Do you not believe me!? Shannyn, I'm telling you the *truth*! Margaret can vouch for me! Please, Shannyn, you've got to trust me!"

"Look, you've got to keep this a secret. Don't you dare say anything to Mom!" She sounds like her old self again. Then she sighs, finding her composure. "Eleanor, you're a witch, so is Mom, so are they, and so am I. One day, when Margaret turns seventeen, she'll join us."

*Us? There is no us! I'm not a witch! I would know. I'm not a part of this!*

"You're supposed to start training at seventeen. I didn't start till I was eighteen. Mom didn't even plan on telling me about our family, let alone do witchcraft. But I kept having these strange dreams, making things happen, and the headaches were killer. I went to a doctor, a shrink, to my friends, but no one could help me. Then one day Lennox advised me to reach out to our aunts. He must have reached out first, because one day out of the blue, I got a call from Sally. She and I had a lunch date, and suddenly *everything* made sense. I mean, *everything* became clear, Ell. Mom's hostility towards her family, the miracle medications, everything. Mom used magic every day and none of us noticed a thing." She pauses, giving me a chance to take it all in, but a simple pause wouldn't be enough. A year in therapy wouldn't be enough. "Eleanor, take it from me. Let the aunts train you…"

This can't be my sister. How could she have kept this from me? I mean, she kept everything from everyone—but *this*? How could she? This is bigger than some little secret. "Was…was Dad…was he a witch too?" I manage to ask. *Did he lie to me too?*

"No, he wasn't. I'm not sure how much he knew about Mom. But the aunts said he wasn't a witch."

I press "End" without another word. There's a void inside me. It's like losing my dad all over again. I feel slight guilt about hanging up but I couldn't hear anymore.

Maggie stares at me before a small smile blooms across her face. "What did Shannyn say?" she asks, already knowing the answer.

I fall back on the bed, the fluffy comforter whooshing beneath me. "Shannyn says it's all true." I feel utterly hopeless. My heart pounds in my ears. I decide not to tell her what Shannyn said about Dad.

"So… we're witches?" She couldn't hide her excitement if she tried. "Like the real deal, not the whole goth or hippie crap?"

"Apparently."

"You know…it's kind of cool," she says to rouse my spirits.

I sit up and look at her with total disbelief. "Just stop. Okay. Just stop, Margaret. This is awful."

Maggie rolls her green eyes at me like I'm the silly one. "Oh, come on, Eleanor. It'll be like that book *Matilda*. She could make things move just like us, or like *The Wizard of Oz*! And we're the good witches!" She nearly squeals with excitement.

"Yeah, but you've got to be seventeen, apparently," I say, dead-pan.

Margaret's face falls in utter disappointment. "Ugh, man! I don't even turn fifteen until June! This totally sucks! You don't even want to be a witch and you get your powers before me!"

"I've got to do some homework..." Retreat is the best idea I can come up with. "And I've got a test I need to study for."

Margaret hangs her head back dramatically. "Oh, my gosh, Eleanor! You're such a nerd! How can you think about school at a time like this? Just learn magic and have it do it for you! Oh, man. School is going to be such a breeze when I'm a witch."

I trudge to my bedroom and throw myself onto my bed. My phone buzzes in my pocket. I glance at the screen. I have several missed calls from Shannyn, a voicemail from her, and a text from my mom.

Hey Ell, how was your first day? I feel horrible I couldn't be there.
A plumber is coming tomorrow to fix the broken pipe
and the carpets in the office and Maggie's room are being replaced.
Call me tonight, I want to hear all about your classes.
XX, Mom

*Who are you, Mom? Can I still call you that?* My entire life has been a lie. Not just a lie to me, but to Dad, too. A tremor goes down my spine. *And if I'm a witch, if I'm truly one of them, why do my eyes scare them?*

# Chapter Eight
## Sprinklers and Macbeth

I sneak out of the house during breakfast. Margaret kept the aunts engaged in twenty witchy questions, giving me the opportunity to slip out unnoticed.

"Eleanor!" someone calls out behind me as I amble across the street from the student parking lot.

I yawn and slow down my already lethargic pace for him to catch up. I stayed up *way* too late trying to study', which, after calling my mom, was almost impossible. We both pretended it was business as usual, which it wasn't. After we hung up, I considered throwing my phone but thought better of it.

I force a smile. "Hey Nick, what's up?" I try to sound as happy to see him as he is to see me. *Why is he so excited to see me? He doesn't even know me. Hell, I don't know myself. I should be more gracious, it's better to have a friend in this high school-shaped Purgatory than not.*

He adjusts his leather Patagonia backpack. "Not much. I'm so sore from lacrosse practice. My neck and shoulders are crazy stiff." He stretches, causing his button-down shirt to lift, exposing his abdomen. "Dude, is the Mercedes your car? That's a sick ride." He flashes a flirtatious grin. "Black leather interior, dual exhaust, very sexy!"

I can't tell if he's flirting with me or my car.

I smile, but it falters when a thought pops into my head. *Is the car a witchcraft bribe? Do they think they can buy me into training?*

"You know, I have a match tonight at St. Andrews. You should come. Then there's going to be a huge party at Poppy's house to celebrate our victory."

I nod, not exactly in the mood to party. "Yeah… maybe, thanks."

Nick takes it with a wide grin. "Come on, I'll walk you to your first class." He gives me a little nudge. His little "nudge" practically topples me over.

I can't help but chuckle at his early morning exuberance. *Who acts like this at eight in the morning?* We breeze through the stained-glass double doors. Nick instantly becomes like a big brother as he trolls the hall loyally at my side—a big, muscular, Hulk-like brother—all the while giving me sideways glances.

"What?" I ask self-consciously. I adjust my oversize blazer and unwrap my scarf around my neck as we stop by my locker. It's the first time I've been able to get the lock open on the first try.

Nick frowns, studying me. "There's something… different about you. I just can't figure it out." He gazes at my face, goes down my neck, slinking down to my legs, sheathed in white tights today. Too cold for knee highs.

I could help him out and say I ditched my contacts at home, but his puzzled expression is far too entertaining. *Maybe I actually made a friend.*

"Oh, duh, you got a haircut, right?" He pretends to smack his forehead. I chuckle. "Nope."
He nods. "Alright, I'll guess it though."
We stop outside Mr. Edwards' classroom, standing huddled in the doorway. Students eye us walking past.

Nick grips his backpack strap. "So, I've got trig this hour, but I'll pick you up after class to walk you to history." He sounds like a working parent dropping off their child at day care. Suddenly paranoid that he's stalking me, I remember he's in my history class as well. I agree and duck into the classroom.

Mr. Edwards gives me a quick smile as I tread into the classroom, my head bent low. I take my seat in front of Jack without any commentary this time.

Books are circulating the classroom as Mr. Edwards writes the title "Macbeth" on the board. *Of course, he picks a play with witches.*

"Hey, O'Reilly," Jack whispers softly, leaning forward in his desk, "I would like to apologize about yesterday."

I keep my eyes forward, watching Mr. Edwards write character names on the whiteboard. "What happened yesterday?" I ask, pretending to forget. He saw me in the hall and, like a flip of the switch, avoided me.

"I can't…I know this sounds lame. I shouldn't have been rude. I can't explain it, but I am sorry," he says sincerely, and repentant. "I'm not sure what came over me."

Mr. Edwards places a copy of the play on my desk, then turns back to the whiteboard. I stare down at the worn cover; the tip of the right top corner has been ripped off. "It's fine Jack." *I have worse things to worry about.*

"O'Reilly, I—"

Mr. Edwards coughs, then clears his throat, calling attention to himself. "Would someone like to start us out by reading Act One? I'm not dividing everyone up by characters, I certainly learned my lesson from the Romeo and Juliet escapade of '09." He flips his book open, then lifts his head, his eyes darting to the back of the room. "Ah yes, Molly, you can begin. Thank you," he says.

I flip open my book. A note written in beautiful script falls out. It's from Mr. Edwards. The parchment smells like butter scotch and chestnuts. Did he really spray his note with cologne? I glance up at Mr. Edwards. He gives me an encouraging smile.

> *My Dearest Eleanor,*
> *I apologize for my atrocious behavior last night. I was possessed with self-righteous indignation which entirely overcame me. To lash out as I did was truly shameful. What a horrific introduction to your illustrious history and true identity. My dear Eleanor, I hope in time you can forgive me, you must discover, and uncover, your true nature in a time set by yourself, not your mother, not your loving aunts, and least of all by me, but by your own hand. At present, I hope you feel you can speak to me on these or any other matters in which you find yourself in need of assistance.*
> *~ Winston Balthazar Leopold Edwards*

I glower at the note. *I don't want help! I don't want to become a witch! Do I have no control over my own life?*

A glowing self-hatred envelopes me. *I'm normal, I'm my father's daughter. I'm not losing him even more than I already have.* I glare at the printed words in the book as I crumple up Mr. Edwards note and toss it into the trash can a foot away.

I continue to stare at my book. *I won't do it. They can't make me. I'm not a witch. I'm not. I'm just Eleanor O'Reilly, Floridian by birth, beach worshiper by nature. I control my destiny. I'm not one of them. I'm like my dad. I'm normal.* A low, quiet hissing sound comes whispering out from the center binding of my book.

I frown. *What the heck?* There's a low pop, a spark, and a little wisp of smoke. *Okay, seriously, what the hell?* My book quivers, shudders, then is engulfed in flames! Giant amber flames consume the book and lick at my hands before I let go. The yellow pages curl into themselves, turning black and smoldering.

A few girls scream. A few boys cheer and yell. "Yeah! You stick it to ol' Billy Shakespeare!" Nearly everyone takes out their phone to record.

I knock the book off my desk to the floor and stomp on it repeatedly. The grey swirling smoke activates the sprinkler system, soaking the entire room and its occupants. Girls cry about their sopping wet hair. Mr. Edwards stares in utter shock. Jack looks as horrified as I feel.

Winston snaps to attention and waves his hands about trying to call everyone's attention. "Okay, okay! Don't worry, the sprinklers will shut off!" Mr. Edwards assures. He blinks as water dribbles down his face.

The sprinklers immediately stop. Given how abruptly the water stopped spraying, Winston must be the culprit somehow.

Winston takes off his tweed coat and slings it onto the back of his desk chair. "Okay ladies, why don't you go to the bathroom and dry off. Gentlemen, grab some paper towels and we'll try to soak up some of the water from the carpet. Shall we?" His boisterous tone sounds like he means to rouse a cavalry.

Jack's damp hair curls around his ears. I watch him leave with the herd of boys to fetch paper towels.

There's a knock on the door. The salt and pepper haired gentleman who was berating the custodian outside yesterday pops his head in, clearly flustered. The Windsor knot of his tie looks too tight around his throat. "What is going on, Mr. Edwards?" His steely eyes gaze around the room as students exit. His hawk nose is sharp, and his blade-like cheekbones are even sharper. His slim lips are pressed in a firm thin line, his dark beady eyes snap to Mr. Edwards.

Mr. Edwards raises his hands and fastens a friendly smile to his formerly perplexed face. "Ah, Headmaster Archibald, t'was a harmless lark that set off the sprinkler system," he assures. "No harm, no foul."

"Harmless!?" shrieks a red-headed girl standing in the back of the classroom still holding her bag over her head. "I just had a keratin treatment; my effing hair is wrecked!"

The Headmaster glares back at Mr. Edwards.

I escape with the throng of girls towards the bathroom, but I practically walk into the wooden bathroom door. Someone has slammed it shut and locked it behind them.

"Absolutely not, Pyro-Psycho!" one of them shouts.

I lean against the locked bathroom door and wilt. Headmaster Archibald stalks back down the hall towards his office, his cheap loafers smacking against the tiling. I fish around my bag for Kleenex and use a few fresh ones to ring out my hair. I can feel my damp hair begin to frizz and wave, and with a binder I found at the bottom of my bag, I toss my hair up in a bun. *How did that happen? Was there something incendiary in the book bindings? Mr. Edwards claimed it was a prank... was it him?*

The rest of the class is spent trying to mop up the standing water on the floor. Mr. Edwards didn't once glance in my direction. I get on my hands and knees with the rest of the class pressing our paper towels into the rough blue-ish green carpet. The Headmaster ensured that the janitorial staff will bring in fans for the carpet, but Mr. Edwards' classes will need to be held in the library for the rest of the day. There's a hum of energy in the classroom as nearly everyone's phones are buzzing.

"Phones off please, you know the rules," Mr. Edwards scolds, pointing to a wooden sign hanging at the back of the classroom between framed accolades.

Jack glances over at me. "Hey, are you okay?" he asks, pressing his paper towel to the floor. I notice his knuckles seem slightly bruised and swollen.

I drag my teeth over my bottom lip, still deliberating on that front. "Yeah," I mumble, still confused by the whole event. *Had I done that? No, of course not! I can't do magic! It doesn't make sense. None of it does.*

Two girls huddled by the closet share something on one of their phones. They both grin at me, then duck their heads, giggling.

I bend my head, feeling my cheeks burn.

"You didn't get hurt?" he questions, crouched on one knee. Jack reaches for my hands, turning them over, palms up. He delicately massages my palms, my fingers curl closed, nearly holding his thumb in my hand from his touch. Like flowers lift their heads towards the sun, my cells open and follow his movements. *How many nerve endings does the palm have? How can something so simple feel so…amazing?* I roll my lips in between my teeth, holding back hiccups as my skin tingles.

My eyes rise from our hands, meeting his steady gaze. His thumbs stop massaging as his eyes peer into mine.

The bell rings.

Jack releases my hands.

"Eleanor, I would like to see you after class, if you don't mind," Winston calls from his desk. A loud "oohing" fills the room as students spill out of the classroom. A few boys yell out it was their fault, to go easy on me, and if I get a detention, they want one too.

Mr. Edwards pulls a wet chair out next to his desk and motions for me to come and sit.

When I sit down on the cushion, the chair is dry as a bone. *What the—?*

His hazel eyes drift over to the open wooden door of the classroom. It slowly shuts with a quiet click. Students are so caught up in their own world that no one even noticed. He leans back in his plumb velvet wingback chair, lacing his fingers over his middle. "Now, tell me what happened," he says, his voice hard with authority but blunted with sympathy.

I peer down at my hands, completely free of injury despite having held the book while it was ablaze. I run my fingers over my palms, not receiving the same sensation as when Jack had touched them. "I don't know what happened. I was just reading, and the book—I don't know, it just caught on fire," I say, cringing at my pathetic explanation.

He rocks back in his chair. "Hmm," he muses, concentrating on my face. He straightens up, something behind me calling his attention. "Yes, Mr. Townsend?"

A freckled face boy peeks his head in. Nick cranes around him, trying to peer in at me. "Uh, Mr. Edwards, can we come in?" He nods his head back towards the crowd gathering in the hall.

Mr. Edwards sighs. "Inform your fellow students that class will be held in the library today, Mr. Townsend. We'll begin our reading of Macbeth; I shall join you all momentarily. First, I need to speak to Miss O'Reilly here as another student played a reckless prank on her and I must get to the bottom of it."

"What happened?" Nick shouts, trying to get past the inquiring student.

Mr. Edwards waves them off and signals them to close the door. He turns back to me, settling back down in his seat, resting his hands on his rotund abdomen. "I have a responsibility to inform your aunts about this, Eleanor. Now are you okay? You didn't get burned at all, did you?" He questions, frowning.

I shake my head, looking away. Thick droplets of rain pitter patter down the lancet window. The outside a somber gray.

"Why don't you illuminate me on the event that led up to you transforming my third favorite Shakespeare play into kindling?"

I wrap my soggy blazer tightly around myself, shivering. "Do we have to do this now?" I peer over my shoulder at the door; Nick is practically pressing his nose against the fogged glass. "I've got class, a friend waiting for me, and by now we are definitely late for second hour."

Mr. Edwards appraises me, then turns to his desk, tugging out his top drawer and pulls out a small tin and a tobacco pipe. "I'll provide you with a note." He sternly gestures for Nick to vacate the door with a flinty glare.

I'm about to voice my objection, but something stops me. Heat snakes down the inside of my blazer, slowly warming until the polyester fibers are completely dry. My starchy button up and skirt get the same toasty treatment. Even my tights and Chelsea boots become pleasantly balmy. Like magic.

I settle in my seat, cautiously watching him scoop tobacco from the square tin and dump it into the bowl of his pipe. "I don't know what happened. I was really... angry, and without warning, it burst into flames. Maybe someone threw something, or..." I grapple to find another excuse.

He unlatches the window and pushes it open, letting the rain drill into the windowsill. "No," he says simply, before placing the pipe between his lips. Without lighting a match, the pipe begins to smoke. "That display of pyrotechnics was caused by you and you alone." He blows out a cloud of smoke. The smoke automatically flows out the window in a steely swirl.

"Overcome with rage, you accidentally set your book ablaze…you are powerful indeed."

I fold my arms across my chest, unable to look at him. I feel sick to my stomach. My head swims feverishly. I tug at my collar. The top button isn't even near my throat, but it still feels like I'm choking.

Winston blows a smoke ring out the opened window. He watches with satisfaction as it obliterates in the heavy, sleeting rain. "Miss O'Reilly, why *are* you so resistant to witchcraft?" he gently prods. Silence stretches out uncomfortably as he releases more smoke. He has it snake between his pudgy fingers before slithering out the window. "Eleanor?"

I nibble on my bottom lip, trying to search for the words. "I—my dad—" I stop. My voice quivers and my eyes turn glassy. "How well do you know my mom's family?"

He ponders this, looking up from the corner of his eye. "Since I was a young chap. Through the various covens the Edwards became acquainted with the Byrnes when we would sojourn across the pond. Marie was about eight, if I recall correctly. I don't believe your mother was even born yet. Why do you ask?"

I swallow. "But my dad?"

He releases an ordinary puff of gray smoke. "Of him, I never had the privilege; however, I've known of him and about him since your parents' union."

The welled-up tears that have been gathering throughout our conversation settle back behind my eyes. "Well, he wasn't a witch, and now he's gone. We were close." I stop, imagining him here, sitting in this brick room with soggy carpet, wondering what joke he would use to defuse the situation.

Memories glitter behind my vision in quick flashes, like falling confetti. Cheering for Margaret when my dad gave her little bike that final push after he had taken off her training wheels. My dad rushing home from work the day Shannyn had her braces removed with peanut brittle, caramel corn, and other former contraband.

"We used to tease that we were going to start a folk band, me on the violin and he was going to learn the banjo," I say with a chuckle, then sniff back more tears that I know will never fall. "He even went out and purchased one." I wrap my arms around myself as if to keep myself from collapsing inward. "We loved horror movies and Humphrey Bogart. Black olive pizza and crispy croquettes after a day at the beach. My father was my hero. I don't want to be so different from him." There's an uncomfortable tightness in my chest. It's as if my heart is being crushed.

I peer down at my knotted hands in my lap. "And then when I think about witchcraft, it's like there's this fury inside me. It feels almost *foreign*, and not my own. I don't know where it's coming from…"

Winston takes another drag of his pipe, pensively.

I gaze at my fingertips devoid of swirl or curving lines. I often wondered if they were all connected, and now I'm certain of it. "My entire life has been a lie."

Another large puff out the window, only to dissipate in the rain.

Mr. Edwards swivels towards me. "You no longer need to be a stranger to yourself, Miss O'Reilly. With those unique eyes of yours, and, of course, your aunts have informed me of the rest. Like it or not, you are becoming a powerful witch indeed. Your mother can't stop the transformation that is happening to you. Until you are ready to accept it, you must mind your temper and your emotions. I was there to prevent further incident this time, but intervening won't always be possible. When you feel that energy build, redirect it, and defuse it." His stern warning comes with an admonishing brow.

I blanch. "I don't know what that means," I admit in distress. "Are you saying I could accidentally start another fire?" My heart hammers in my chest. I feel the phantom heat in my hands.

"Or worse." Winston pulls out a brass pocket watch from his vest, flicks it open and clucks his tongue. "If I expect to have any pupils in the library, I better attend to them. But Miss O'Reilly, from what I have ascertained of your beloved father, he wouldn't want you to declare war against yourself. Don't be afraid. You might even find that through your training, you'll feel that communion you seek," he says cryptically. He waves his hand over his pipe bowl, as if creating a vacuum. The embers extinguish, and the smoke vanishes. He places his pipe back in his desk drawer. He suddenly materializes a yellow pass from his pants pocket and hands it to me.

"You can go now, Miss O'Reilly," Winston says, dipping his head low to meet my nervous gaze. "Just remember what I've said and be careful."

I nod. "Yeah okay, I'll try." I pick up my book bag; the leather is warm and dry to the touch. Winston escorts me to the door and turns in the opposite direction from the one I take.

I steal a glance back at him, watching him trot to the library.

My entire world is slipping away, transforming into something I do not recognize. There's something deep inside that's clutching to the life I knew with my dad even as I'm dragged toward this unknown life of magic and witchcraft. Even my mom is clinging to the life before, but she must feel it slipping too. Knowing this is out of my control is one thing, but knowing it's even out of my mother's too is something else entirely. My grip on the book bag tightens. Whether I like it or not, I belong to magic now.

# Chapter Nine
## Viral

I apologize to Mr. Andersen, handing him my note before rushing to my seat. He dismisses me and continues with his lecture on the civil war up at the lectern.

"Brother, fighting against brother," Mr. Andersen stressed enthusiastically, wearing a union hat. "The blood-soaked fields, you could see the steam rise from the bodies in the early dusky dawn…"

Nick keeps glancing over at me anxiously from across the room where he's confined. His stare doesn't break even when the end of the class bell rings. Instead, he scrambles to my side, pushing students out of the way.

"I seriously need your phone number. I kept wanting to text you. It was driving me nuts," Nick complains, walking out after class with me. "I had to hear from Blaire Putnam about the fire. The Headmaster is losing it and I couldn't get ahold of you," he muttered tersely.

We stop at my locker so I can retrieve my violin. *What did Mr. Edwards mean that witchcraft could bring me closer to my dad? Can witches talk to the dead?* My heart flutters at a different prospect. *More importantly, can I bring him back?* My hand pauses on the plastic handle of my case. *Maybe I can skip the rest of the day? I can go home, tell the aunts I'm ready to train and be talking to my dad before dinner is even served.* My heart leaps a little in my chest. *I miss you so much, Dad.*

"Eleanor? Hello?" Nick waves his hand in front of my face.

I snap my locker close. "Sorry, what were you saying?"

He groans. "Your number?" He takes out his phone from his back pocket. "Okay, I'm ready." His thumbs hover above the screen, impatiently.

I shake my head, flustered. "Oh, uh yeah." I spit out my phone number.

Nick slides his phone into his back pocket with a sigh of relief. "Did you get in trouble for the fire?" he questions. "Mr. Edwards can be such a bastard. No sense of humor. I have him for intro to philosophy seventh hour. He's the worst. I mean, who cares about some shitty play? I hope he went easy on you." He places his enormous paw on my shoulder, unintentionally weighing it down.

My face deepens in color. "Um, no. He knows I didn't do it. Someone just pulled a prank on me," I lie. "New girl hazing."

Nick's eyes turn cold. He shakes his head slowly, his jaw set firmly. "Who did it? I swear I'll get 'em back. I heard Jack was talking to you yesterday. Was it him?" Nick's knuckles crack when he tightens his fist.

I feel oddly protective. "No, of course not. We don't know who did it. But it wasn't him."

Nick steps in front of me, blocking me from going through the auditorium doors.

People step around us.

"Nick, let me pass," I say, annoyed. *Why is he acting this way? He literally met me yesterday.*

Nick laces his fingers behind his head, releasing a jagged breath. He drops his arms. "I'm sorry, I just, I feel bad I wasn't there to prevent it from happening."

I resist the urge to tap my foot, waiting to walk past. "It's fine, I just want to get to orchestra." *Not really, but I do want to end this bizarre conversation.*

Nick holds the back of his neck. "Look, I won't be at lunch today. I've got a lacrosse meeting with the team. But Noah doesn't play, so he'll be there. He'll keep an eye on you."

I frown. "Wait, do you mean keep an *eye out for me?*"

Nick nods. "Yeah, yeah."

"Alright, well, I'll see you later." I sidestep around him and slip through the doors. *Okay, that was seriously weird. And possessive. Is this normal? Am I the problem? Maybe this is what it's like being friends with guys? They come off a little 'roid ragey?*

As I pass the Massachusetts wall murals, I notice the image of the white rabbits hanging upside down from a line, their red eyes staring lifelessly into nothing.

"Try not to start any fires in here. It's old as dirt, and we'll all burn," a cellist murmurs, strolling past me. She tosses her long amber hair over her shoulder, glancing at me, if only to punctuate her snide remark.

"I'd say good luck with your scales, but I doubt you'll find them," I utter under my breath.

She stops, her jaw falling in dramatic fashion. "Excuse me, did you just body shame me?"

"A real musician would have gotten the joke," I mumble, ambling my way past her.

Ms. Sewall stops me on the stairs. "No, not today. Have a seat. You'll join us when you're ready," she dismissed, pointing out to the empty audience.

I don't argue. Instead, I ignore the self-congratulatory smiles amongst the orchestra and spend the rest of the hour receiving an icy silent treatment. I pluck at a loose thread on my plaid skirt, listening to the squeaking strings. *I wish I had my headphones.*

My phone trills in my bag. Then goes silent. And goes off again. And again. And again.

I dig through my bag, hoping to find my phone before Ms. Sewall can hear the beeping. I nearly drop my cell to the floor. I have fifteen new text messages, a few from numbers I don't recognize. There are a few links to a video clip of me throwing down my burning book and stomping it out. My eyes furiously fly to the number of views. My heart slows; it hasn't gone viral. Yet.

Shannyn: Ell what is going on?
Margaret: OMG Eleanor is this u!!??

Sweat bleeds out across my brow. *I look like a freak.* My eyes slide from side to side, meeting the judgmental eyes of the black clad puritans painted on the walls, the farmer's daughters, their barking hounds, the red-eyed rabbits, all staring at me. *I need to get out of here.* The air feels like it's getting thin, and my throat is closing. Risking the demerit, I grab my violin, sprint up the carpeted walkway, and throw open the doors.

Hunched over, hinged at my waist, I gulp for air like a fish beached on dry land. *The video doesn't start until after the fire. It's okay.*

"Hey, you alright?" a warm hand circles on my back.

I leap back, only to see Trixie's stricken face. My heart pounds.

Her frozen face melts into a puckish grin, and she scrunches her button nose. "Sorry, I didn't mean to scare you. Are you feeling sick? I have something for that," she says brightly, swinging around her taupe crochet bag.

I shake my head. "No, I'm fine, thanks. But I might need a pass if you have any extra of those with you."

Her sapphire eyes twinkle mischievously. "Of course. What are we ditching today?"

I close my eyes and breathe out my nose, still feeling nauseated from the video. I didn't even reply to my sisters' texts. *What am I going to say? Hell, what am I going to do?*

Trixie takes hold of my shoulders, "why don't we sit down, you look like you might faint," she says while steering me over to the wooden bench beneath the stained-glass window. "Is this about the video?"

"You saw it?" I say through clenched teeth. Resting my elbows on my knees, I hold my face in my hands.

She nods, then pulls her waist length golden locks to one side. "It'll be okay. We don't go viral. Vivienne Mather once uploaded a video of me talking to some flowers on a fourth-grade field trip to the botanical gardens."

Still holding my head, I turn to face her, steeling myself for her answer. "Did the plants talk back?" *Is that part of magic? Inanimate objects can converse with us.* I think back on this little clown marionette Margaret won at the Florida state fair. *If that thing starts talking to me, I'm out.*

Trixie releases her tinkling giggle. "Of course not, silly. It's just healthy for the plants if we whisper to them. But you don't have to worry, The Committee makes sure those videos don't go wild."

I slump back against the brick wall. "Yeah, The Committee that my aunt and your parents are on?"

She gives my shoulder an encouraging slug. "See, you're getting the hang of it. Besides, it doesn't take magic for teenagers to lose interest in something faster than you can call a broom. You'll be old news by Monday." Her entire face breaks out into a dazzling white smile, I nearly need to shield my eyes. "I've got an idea. Let's get some take out for lunch! Dotty and Ray's have the *best* fried chicken, you'd think it was magic! And don't worry, we'll be back in time for the pep rally," she says, holding out a hand to hoist me up.

"Do we have to?" I say reluctantly, allowing her to help me up. "I'm not one for pep rallies."

"But they're so much fun! We sing the school's song, the show choir performs and they're state ranked. Trust me, you don't want to miss it." Trixie links arms with me and leads us to the student parking lot.

The tide inside me shifts to relief. The rain from earlier now comes down in tiny pinprick snowflakes. I peek over my shoulder at the school's pointed archways and lancet windows. I grip my blazer close.

Trixie and I climb into a pink-finned Cadillac parked in the last row, farthest from the school. She quickly adjusts the temperature dials on the dashboard. A tepid whisper of heat eeks out of the vents. A tiger's eye stone dangles in a knit holder from the rearview mirror.

"Do you like the Carpenters? What am I saying, of course you do. They're amazing," she says, pushing a tape into the console. She sways along to "Please, Mr. Postman".

I nod, eager to put some distance between me and the school. I watch as the small, wet flakes drift to the ground and disappear. The stony sky darkens as more clouds gather.

Trixie's windshield wipers squeak while feebly batting away the snow. She keeps glancing at me, then back at the road. "I see you've given up on the contacts, huh?"

I blush, turning my face to the window. "Yeah, I didn't see a point."

Trixie nods in affirmation. "Absolutely. I think we need to be more accepting of your kind." She turns the dial on the radio up.

I'm about to agree with her, but I stop, confused by her words. "What do you mean by that?"

Trixie slows down, approaching a red light. "Has anyone talked to you about your eyes?"

I sigh, sounding more like a growl. "No," I say between gritted teeth.

She shakes her head. "Our history is fairly complex. I'm still trying to understand it myself. So, I'll give you the abridged version. Your eyes indicate you're a different kind of witch than the rest of us. And let's just say most covens don't really accept your kind."

I find myself bracing for further explanation. I try to rest my hands on her cracked white leather seats. "And what kind is that?" I shiver, either from the damp cold that easily seeps through my school uniform or in anticipation of horrible news.

Trixie's eyes dart to me, then back to the congested street. "You're called 'Nefari'."

I swallow. "Why do I have a feeling that isn't good?"

"Because it's not." She suddenly wrenches her wheel to the right. "Oh my gosh, parking! There are never spots open this close!" she cheers, easing into a parallel space. She grins widely at me. "you'll love it here, but first you need a coat. Your blazer won't cut it." She climbs over her seat into the back seat and scrounges around on the floor that resembles the bottom of my closet. She pulls up a crocheted poncho, then shakes her head and tosses it. Next, a 1950's letterman's sweater, then a fringed jean jacket, and she continues digging until she pulls out a yellow, hooded wool coat with wooden toggles, that flare out at the waist. "This will be perfect."

"Do you live in your car?" I ask, glancing back at the loose jewelry, patchwork pants, and throngs of gladiator sandals littering her floor. Sleet blurs the windows. *If only this were sandal weather.*

"Of course not, but you never know when you'll meet someone who needs a little something. Here, keep it," she says, handing me the coat while buttoning up her own turquoise fur-lined parka. The color makes her eyes glow incandescently.

Once inside, Trixie takes my hand and pulls me to the back corner booth, away from the large bay windows and close to the bar and bubbling coffee pot.

A waitress wordlessly drops two menus off and continues her rotation around the sleepy little café.

Trixie stares at her, her eyes intensely following the older waitress until she disappears into the kitchen. She shakes her head, settling back down in her seat.

"Everything okay?" I ask.

She nods, opening her plastic menu. "Yeah, sorry. I thought she was a witch I knew, Doris Calloway. She's friends with my parents. We haven't seen Doris in a while."

I cock a brow, thinking back to where I've heard that name before. "Yeah, I think my aunts mentioned her."

Trixie shrugs her shoulders, literally shrugging off her worry. "Anyway, I'm starving."

We both flip through the plastic menus. Trixie prattles on about their life-changing chicken.

I chew on my thumb nail chipping off the dark maroon nail polish, not really reading the menu. My suspicions were correct. There's something wrong with my eyes, and if the old adage is true about them being gateways to the soul, what do mine say about me?

"Do I want the chicken? I mean, I did have it just yesterday. So does that mean it's the BLT?" Trixie ponders, pointing a pink polished finger to her narrow chin.

I lower my menu to the table, then softly pull hers down as well. I want her to see my eyes, to tell me the truth. "What does it mean to be a Nefari?"

Trixie drops her head lower, leaning over the table. "It's not something I should tell you."

*You've got to be kidding me.* "Trixie, you already have. Please, why does my mom want me to wear contacts and why does it freak out Mr. Edwards?"

I seize her hand, giving it a tender squeeze in a manipulative attempt at forced sisterhood.

All the sparkle leaves Trixie's eyes, replaced by pity. "There's not much I can tell you. We don't talk about Nefari witches." She retracts her hand and nonchalantly flips to the back of the menu. "And maybe I'm wrong," her eyes scanning the beverages, "your mom isn't a Nefari, you've only just turned seventeen, so you couldn't have possibly made that choice on your own. Know what, I'm for sure getting the buttermilk chicken. That's why we came here." She turns around, raising her hand. "Ma'am, we're ready."

We eat our lunches in silence. Well, at least I do. Trixie giggles about her boyfriend, Sebastian Moon, about finishing up her witches training that she began exactly on her birthday in February, something about a gathering of witches, and of course, the exciting pep rally she eagerly wanted to get back in time for.

On the drive back, she sings along to The Carpenters and occasionally nudges my shoulder to join in. I reticently stay still, sheathing the chaotic stream of questions that plagued my mind.

*Maybe Trixie's right. There's nothing to worry about with my eyes. Maybe I truly have an albinism unrelated to witchcraft.* Trixie refused to elucidate further into the "Nefari history". But the small, fragmented pieces she did divulge makes it seem unlikely that I could be one.

I replay her words over again in my head, turning them about, trying to find any hidden meaning or subtext there. A "Nefari" is a type of witch, a bad type. Either you inherit that state from your mother or you have chosen it by misusing your magic. My eyes didn't suddenly turn violet when I burned the book; they've always been this way. My mom's eyes aren't purple. They're a light, average shade of blue, *beautiful* but perfectly normal.

Anxiety melts away from me while I settle a little easier in my seat, satisfied that I can't possibly be a Nefari. Instead, I have a normal genetic anomaly that has nothing to do with witchcraft. My mother never seemed scared of my eyes until recently, but even then she seemed fearful for them, not of them. *Mom is probably just worried witches may greet me with apprehension because of my eyes.*

I lean my head against the window, drained but resolute. I didn't think the fire would be the least of my worries today.

"Come on, we've got to hurry! It's already started!" Trixie pulls me through the front gate. We slosh through slushy puddles gathering on the cobble stone as we dash across the courtyard to the very back of the school where sits an old stone church, the windows glowing.

The students are on their feet cheering, allowing us to creak the old wooden doors open and easily slip into the last open pew. My muscles melt in the unexpectedly warm stone chapel. I unbutton my coat and slide the hood off my head, appraising the church's agonizingly tall arches, stained glass windows (this school never met one they didn't like) and lack of any kind of religious denomination. However, high on the wall above the pulpit and organ is a ghostly imprint of where a cross used to hang.

Twelve girls, all in varying forms of perfection, stand poised to the right of the Headmaster. They lift their chins, chests out, elbows out, hands clasped below the bust. Vivienne Mather steps forward, flaxen hair lying flat behind her shoulders like a silken veil. She smirks, smiling at someone sitting in the front row. The choir hums in perfect harmony, taking Vivienne's lead as she angelically sings out a Taylor Swift number in benevolent reverence, delivering the hot single in a gospel rendition.

"Oh my goodness, this is so good! I've never heard this before. I love it!" Trixie whispers in my ear, bobbing her head to this new supernal hymn. "I knew you were trouble when you walked in…" she sings along.

I peer over at my new friend before glancing around. A few heads curiously stray to me, but they gloss over Trixie completely. She continues to sway next to me, oblivious to her alienation. *Would this be my fate as well? The fire will cause universal disdain?*

The choir bows and tepid finger snapping breaks out amongst the student body. Trixie, not getting the memo, claps wildly and hoots for an encore. Not one head turns back at her. The shunning continues.

Headmaster Archibald adjusts his striped tie, tucking it back into his tailored buttoned-up suit coat. "Wasn't that lovely? How about another hand for our *Knighting Gales?*" he suggests, snapping his boney fingers too close to the mic. "I would like the co-captains of the track team, Blaire Putnam and Elijah Courtenay," he pauses as a lanky boy and a spindly girl step up to the raised platform and stand left of the podium amongst polite applause, "our varsity crew team captain, Jack Woods," he pauses as Jack rises from the front row, no blazer, crooked tie, lopsided grin as he joins the other two students to thunderous applause and a smattering of standing ovations. The Headmaster claps him on the back proudly.

Jack lifts his hand to the student body, giving an uncomfortable nod. I notice now that his cheeks are a rosy hue. His eyes flitter to the student body, going from face to face, pew to pew until he stops at the very last pew. A small smile blooms across his face once more.

Students continue to hoot and holler, shouting Jack's name and clapping enthusiastically. Trixie keeps nudging me in the side with her elbow.

"Last, but certainly not least, our varsity la crosse captain, Nickolas Andersen! Let's give him a hearty round as they have their opening season scrimmage tonight!" the Headmaster states, a little too loudly into the microphone.

Nick steps forward, bowing jovially to the applause that's less ferocious than it was a moment ago. He makes his way to the podium, leaning forward towards the mic. "If I could just say a few words."

Headmaster Archibald's smile is a tight line on his angular face, but he graciously steps aside.

"I want to thank our coach," he turns his attention to the far-left side of the church where the faculty are standing against the walls beneath the ornamental windows. Our American history teacher steps forward to more applause and cheering. "And my amazing team," he pauses, rousing a little more admiration, "I want to dedicate our win to someone special. Tonight's game may not count to get us to state or nationals, but it's still important that we give it our all and I will be doing just that, not just for the team or just for Griggs Academy, but for my new girlfriend. Baby, I'm winning this game tonight for you!" He points, almost aimlessly, out to the congregated students.

My brows lift in surprise. He hadn't mentioned a girlfriend until now. When Nick's eyes land on me, he grins.

Like falling dominos, the entire student body turns their heads back to me one by one.

# Chapter Ten
## Ouija

As if fearing the early day dismissal might be retracted, the students stampede for the parking lot the moment Headmaster Archibald dismisses us. Only a few linger, Jack being one of them.

The teachers talk amongst themselves, some nursing coffee mugs held close to their faces. Winston looks like he might fall asleep listening to Ms. Sewall. I can't imagine what they have to talk about.

Trixie turns to me. "I'm working on earth tonight."

I slide my arms back into the coat sleeves. "As opposed to working in space?" I quip back, still sitting on the wooden pew.

She giggles. "Eleanor O'Reilly, you are seriously my favorite. But no, silly. Earth is a branch of magic. Potions, healings, it's my favorite branch and the one I'm best at." She pretends to dust off her shoulder. "Want to come? It'll be so much fun!" she says, nearly bouncing in her seat.

Mr. Edwards is leaning against the stone wall, arms crossed, his head tilted slightly downward while Ms. Sewall is still prattling on. It's possible he actually fell asleep. I think back on what he said to me. *Through your training, you'll feel that communion you seek.* If there's a chance I can talk to my dad, I'm not waiting another day. I'm so anxious, it's like there's a hummingbird fluttering around my ribcage. *What will I say to him?*

I look back at Trixie. "I can't, I have to get back. But maybe some other time?" I reject, gently.

Trixie shrugs. "Okay, see you Monday, then." She pulls up the hood of her parka and strolls away, whistling the choir's tune.

When I look again, Mr. Edwards is gone. My eyes frantically sweep the church. There are only a few faculty left. Ms. Sewall is berating some male student. Nick and his team are talking to their coach and the Headmaster, while Jack, hands in the pockets of his chinos, lingers on the very fringe of a group of students snapping selfies and laughing loudly. His eyes find me.

Nick steps in front of him and rushes down the aisle towards me. "Hey, you're still here. Did you get my text to wait for me? You never replied." He whips out his phone to check. Realizing there's no text from me, he drops it back into his jacket pocket.

My mouth gapes as I struggle for words. *Did you call me your girlfriend in front of the entire student body without ever having asked me out? I've never had a boyfriend before. Is this how that works?* My mind reels nervously. No one would call Nick unattractive. He looked like a walking Instagram filter, or if Jason Momoa was seventeen and German. But I'm not ready to date, no matter how attractive the guy is. My dad's gone. I just learned I'm a witch. This is *actually* a situation where it's "not you, it's me," but I can't say that.

*I gotta play this cool.* I brighten my posture, trying to fix a playful smile on my face. "I didn't know you had a girlfriend. You need to introduce me so we can all be friends," I say, feigning ignorance.

Nick's eyes bulge slightly, his cheeks bloom a few shades of red. He adjusts his man-bun. "Um, Eleanor, I—" he stops as a group of kids tread over to us, Jack trailing behind.

Vivienne stops by in her cape coat and red beret with a diamond pin. She parts her ruby red lips in a feline smile. "That was a beautiful tribute, Nick. I didn't know you two were together," she says, batting her eyes. "Boy, you sure do move fast."

"He wasn't talking about me. We're just friends," I say casually. Nick mutters something under his breath and shakes his head.

"I hope your injury from English today isn't so severe that you can't attend Poppy's party tonight," Vivienne says. A redhead with an asymmetrical bob and bowler hat steps forward as if on cue. Vivienne's sloe eyes dress me down. She clucks her tongue, appraising my old, scuffed up boots. I scrunch my toes uncomfortably, in a wash of inadequacy. A slight disapproving sneer appears on her painted lips. Her hourglass figure could still be admired in her short, flouncy coat. I can't stop staring at her pore-less face. Her faithful disciples hover around her, each with a handsome boy in tow. The cloud of confidence that follows them is tangible, and it smells like Hugo Boss and Clinique.

"I'm sorry to disappoint, but I can't." As I pivot to face Nick, my eyes pass Jack; his features are etched in disappointment. "I have to get home. My aunts are waiting for me. Good luck with your game tonight, or meet, or whatever you call it," I say, giving him a genial clap on his biceps. *Dang, that thing is huge.*

My boots click on the stone walkways as I hurry out the door, pretending I can't hear them snicker behind me.

The sky is a marble slab of swirling grays. A storm is passing. The drive from school to my aunts feels eternal, hitting every possible red light. I nibble on my bottom lip. *What will I say to my dad?* The first thought that springs to mind is crying out how much I miss him. My mind can't seem to move past that.

As I pull up the driveway, I see Blue-Eyes peering down from the tower window. The ravens that have taken residence in the dead tree take flight when I park.

"Sally, Marie?" I call as I amble into the house. I hang my coat on a hook and toss my school bag below.

"Well, if it isn't the little pyro," Sally says, sauntering down the spiral staircase.

I cringe, shrugging off my blazer. "How did you find out?"

She cocks a thin brow. "Margaret showed me the twelve second clip. Though I must say, my favorite version is the one with that Usher song playing while you put out the flames. Tres bien!" she says, in perfect annunciation.

I brace myself. "Am I in trouble?"

Sally cackles, tossing back her pixie head. She then descends the rest of the stairs, cocktail in hand. "Oh babe, not a bit," she says, slinging an arm around my waist.

Marie comes bounding into the living room behind us, a herd of cats in tow. "Oh, Ella dear, we were so worried. Are you alright? Winnie called. He assured us this whole thing is going to blow over." She then buries me in a hug.

"Eleanor," I politely correct as they pull me down onto the couch with them. "Are you going to tell Mom, assuming my sisters haven't already?"

Sally grunts and Marie shakes her head.

I settle more into the sofa and lace my fingers in my lap, choosing my next words carefully. I have to let the aunts think they've won, that I'll be trained reluctantly, but I want something in return. "I spoke with Mr. Edwards about training, and after the fire, I've come to the conclusion that I must be trained."

Aunt Marie sniffles back a tear. "Oh, Ellie sweetie, we're so proud of you. You're making the right decision." She wraps me up in another hug.

"Well, I believe this calls for a toast," Sally decrees, her eyes rolling to the side. Cabinets in the kitchen open and close, glasses ting, then a cork pops. A cat shrieks.

Marie snags one of the three bubbling champagne flutes that comes floating in. "I suppose just this once, Eleanor," she says, handing me the second. I sniff the alcohol and scrunch my face. I've never had a taste for it.

"More for me, then!" Sally snatches my glass. "Well ladies, it looks like I'm double fisting it." She downs them both. "Five more of those and I can get a pleasant buzz going." She turns to me. "So, Ell, should we get started?"

Marie finishes her glass and sends it levitating back into the kitchen. "Sally, have you forgotten, Maggie-pie has soccer tryouts tonight. We actually need to leave here soon." She holds up one of her long necklaces that has a working clock charm.

Sally sighs, peering down at her outfit. Black leather pants and a black bell sleeve sweater with a lightning bolt cutout striking between her breasts and ending just above her navel.

Marie grimaces at her sister. "I laid something out for you on your bed." She tugs on the hem of her chunky knit turtleneck. "I will be changing as well." Picking up her purring cat, she trudges up the stairs.

Sally stands and stretches, her shirt lifts, exposing her razor-sharp hipbones. "Well, I better go change into "soccer mom". Hopefully, there will be hot divorced dads there tonight," she says, perking up a little at the prospect. Sal throws me a playful wink, stepping around me.

I jump up after her. "Um, Aunt Sally, since I'm going to be trained, I can start using magic, right?" I fidget with a loose thread on my skirt.

Sally cocks her pencil thin brow, her foot hovering above the first step. "Technically, that's true, but you don't know what you're doing, so practicing magic while untrained can be dangerous."

"Has that ever stopped us before?" I jest, softly punching her in the arm.

She chuckles like she's onto me. "Us? I may look like I was born yesterday, because of the skin treatments, but I wasn't. What's your angle, kid? Fake ID? Cheat on your finals? Bitch at school needs to be taught a lesson? Cause that's not allowed. Other than the finals and fake ID, those I can help you with," she answers deadpan.

I shake my head. "No, it's nothing like that. Do we have a way to communicate with the dead?"

Blue-Eyes slowly slinks down the stairs.

Sally lets go of the railing and pivots towards me. "Have you been speaking to the dead?"

"No, but I would like to. Can we?" I pray she can't hear the desperation creeping into my voice.

Sally frowns. "Not easily, if we don't have the gift." She pauses, regarding me closely. "Are you hearing voices, babe?"

I shake my head, then stop. The birthday dinner comes out of my gauzy memory and into the forefront. "Yeah, actually, I've been hearing a voice. Not clearly, though. And it seems to belong to no one." My brows knit. *How did I forget about that? Maybe the shock of the floating food blocked it out.*

Sally takes hold of my shoulders and closes her eyes, drawing deep breaths through her thin pointy nose. "I don't know. I can't be certain. Though the essence I'm sensing, I don't think you have a veil connection." She opens her eyes and drops her hands. "I'm guessing you were just communicating with your familiar."

"Familiar?" I question.

Sally shrugs one shoulder. "Or guardian more accurately, every witch has one." She grips her hips.

I stare at her dubiously. "I don't think I have one."

Sally tosses her head back, laughing. "Oh, Ellie babe, I think we both know who your guardian is. Now you want to reach out to the beyond…" Sally puts a long, scarlet-painted finger to her chin, pondering. "I believe we still have that Ouija board."

My eyebrows rise in surprise. "Just an ordinary old Ouija board? Like in the movies?"

Sally nods. She walks around me down the hall, stopping at the towering bookshelf. "Ah ha!" She finds a brown box at the bottom. "We normally use this as a cheese tray when we have a wine tasting." She brushes dust off the box and squints at it. "I guess we've been skipping the cheese part." She discards the box into my hands and sweeps her hands off on each other.

I pull off the cover and glance inside. The rules are stapled to the inside cover, and the planchette idles at the side. I gaze incredulously. "So…I just follow the rules and as a witch, ghosts will supposedly communicate?"

Sally shrugs. "There aren't rules for witches, just put the planchette on the board and don't bother holding on."

I frown, slightly let down by the fact that witches speak to the dead using a Parker Brothers game. I was expecting spell books, candles, chanting, maybe a crystal ball of some sort. *Although, now that I think about it, that all sounds as puerile and lame as the board.*

Marie comes stomping down the stairs wearing a pastel track suit and visor that reads "Go Soccer Players" in homemade stitching. With a furrowed brow, she rounds on Sally. "You aren't dressed. Did I not say we had to leave? Maggie-Pie is almost ready to go."

Sally throws her hands up in surrender. "Sorry, I'll go change right now."

Marie growls. "There's no time for that now. Here, just put on the shirt I made you." She tosses an oatmeal-colored top to Sally.

Sal holds it out and scowls. "Did I not say black? What in the beige hell is this?" She turns her shirt around and lays it flat against herself. A smiling picture from Margaret's social media three years ago is screen printed across the front.

Marie impatiently rolls her eyes. "I wanted to match." She unzips her windbreaker, revealing a beige top with Margaret's soccer team photo from last year. "Oh and," she stops and digs around in her paisley quilted purse, "baseball cap instead of visor like you asked." Out pops a purple ball cap, it floats over to Sally, slapping itself down on Sally's head. The hat reads: Margaret O'Reilly's #1 Fan.

I roll my lips inward, strangling back a smile. *There's no way Maggie has a clue about any of this.*

Sally cranes her head over the stairwell. "Margaret, we should go!"

"Coming!" she answers back. Maggie comes galloping down the stairs, pulling her hair up into a ponytail. She stops at the foot of the stairs, dropping her arms to her side as her face flushes. "What...are you guys...wearing?"

Marie springs to life. "Oh, do you like them? When we heard we were taking you to tryouts tonight, I made them."

Margaret blanches. "You guys didn't have to do that. Really, you guys can just go wear normal clothes...that don't have my face on them," she says, mortified.

After shrugging into her leather jacket, Sally pulls a silver flask out of the inside breast pocket. "Don't worry, it's all on theme," she says, taking a swig. A rhinestone studded soccer ball sticker glitters on the flask.

Maggie hangs her head, accepting defeat. "Okay, let's just go."

Marie scrunches her face up in a smile. "Kitties, let's go!" four cats come out strapped with matching soccer visors. "We're taking the minivan," she states proudly. "We bought it after Helen called."

Sally groaned. "It's a total mood killer. Let's take anything else."

I amble over to Margaret as the aunts bicker about safety ratings and appearances.

I gently nudge her hip with mine, tucking the box under my arm. "Maybe it won't be so bad," I tease.

Maggie sneers. "Easy for you to say. You drive a Mercedes to school and neither of them takes you." Then she perks up, a light returning to her eyes. "Hey, I heard you were going to be trained, that's awesome. So jealous."

I shrug. "Yeah, I guess." *I better be able to bring Dad back.* "Wait, how did you know? I only just told the aunts a bit ago."

"Sally texted me."

"Fine!" Sally yells. "But we keep the shag carpeting inside!"

"Deal," Marie agrees.

Sally shouts over to us, "Margaret, grab your things. We are going to take you to dinner after to celebrate. Eleanor, we left money on the counter for your dinner and take-out menus are in the drawer next to the landline. Cats, come along."

Margaret heaves her sports bag up onto her shoulder and follows our aunts out to the van. Sally stops and slowly pivots on her spiked heel.

"Eleanor," she calls.

I move the box, holding it to my chest, lifting my head to her.

She cocks her head to the side. "Remember this: if you speak out into the void, the void will *always* answer back."

I roll back on the balls of my feet and nod. "Okay." I tighten my hold on the cardboard box housing the board, resolute on my plan.

Her dark eyes scour mine as if searching for something below the surface. "If I were you, I wouldn't do what you're planning on doing. Be careful." She finishes and slips into the garage.

I tiptoe over to the front windows and watch as their wood panel van peels out of the garage, kicking pebbles into the air before disappearing behind the gulf of trees. The ashen sky with concrete clouds blots out the sun, giving the afternoon an evening pallor.

I sigh, peering about the mustard-colored living room and listening to the house breathe around me like a death rattle. The pipes clang, the walls wheeze with the slightest breeze, and the wood groans from the expanding and contracting wood.

I move over to the couch and place the box down on the coffee table. Blue-Eyes tip toes down the stairs and two other cats creep around the corner.

My mouth feels like Death Valley. *Maybe I'll finish my homework first.* Blue-Eyes leaps onto the Barcalounger. Trepidation pumps through my veins with every pound behind my ears. I blow a gust of air through my mouth and push myself up off the couch. My former resolve wavers like a mirage in a desert.

I head upstairs, eager to escape the cats and put some distance between me and the board. I purposely advert my eyes from the table, not wanting to see that stupid box with the creepy writing again. My nerves ease when I practically hurl myself into the tower bedroom. My senses are immediately calmed by the scent of rosemary and lavender.

Pulling out a waffle knit sweater and olive-green joggers, I drop my uniform to the floor before falling back onto my bed and scrolling through my phone, killing time. I answer Shannyn's texts, my mom's inquiries to how I'm settling in, and wish Nick a good game, though I'm dubious I phrased it correctly. My thumb flicks through video after video, influencers dancing to the current song of the moment, musicians I follow, internet personalities performing hilarious impressions. Not once do I run into the video of me stomping out the blazing book. For just a few minutes, everything feels normal. I'm just seventeen and the world is still spinning like it did two weeks ago.

I roll over onto my back, discarding my phone on my pillow. My stomach pitches with a hollow grumble. I haul myself off the bed, remembering the aunts left money for some delivery. Pulling on some thick fuzzy socks, I trek back down the two sets of stairs. I stop once I pass the living room to the kitchen. *What did I just see?*

I tiptoe in reverse and peek my head into the mouth of the living room. Every candle on the many shelves is lit and the Ouija board is out of the box and poised in the center of the table. Blue-Eyes is perched on the table, his ragged tail sweeping back and forth. My mouth hinges open in disbelief. "Did you do this?" I ask rhetorically. My pulse quickens and my hands quiver at my sides. *This is a magic house. Witches live here. Unexplainable things happen.*

Blue-Eyes dips his head, almost like he's nodding at me. My stomach flips as he continues surveying me.

The grandfather clock on the second story chimes the hour. "I don't care. I'm going to order some dinner," I say, fighting the tremor in my voice.

I stroll to the kitchen as if attempting to convince the house that I'm not so easily unsettled. I hum my favorite Muse song while I fish around the drawer for takeout menus. I pull out the top three: Village Tavern, Red's Sandwich shop, and The Flying Saucer Pizza. On each menu, the aunts have circled dishes, but whether they're to either warn others off or recommend, I can't be entirely sure. I drop two flyers back in the drawer and keep out The Flying Saucer Pizza one. The description of the circled Space Invader's pizza nearly makes me salivate.

I reach for their landline, a white phone attached to the wall with a long curly cord. *Who even has these anymore?* Then I stop, holding the phone just a few inches from my face. My chest tightens. The entire house is still and hauntingly quiet. Not a creak, not a purr or meow. I can't breathe. It's as if an icy hand reached down my throat, strangling me from the inside. There's an electric feel in the air, a static, like standing in a vacuum.

There is but one sound that slices through the stagnant air. Quick erratic scrapes from down the hall.

Someone is moving the planchette across the board.

# Chapter Eleven
## The Rescue

My heart thumps heavily in my chest, like it's trying to break through its boney cage. I hang up the phone, my ears still perked, listening to the quick swishing of plastic on wood. Each footstep I make walking down the dark hallway feels heavy. Every creak of the wood deafening. I release quick shallow breaths approaching the glowing living room. The scraping is a quick *swish, swish, swish*, almost in fury. *Please be the cat, please be the cat, please be the damn freaking cat…*

Hiccups bubble up my throat, making my entire body quake. My eyes gloss. The sight of Blue-Eyes, deathly still, watching the planchette flicking across the letters on the board with an almost terrified expression sends a sinking chill from my flesh down to my bones.

The narrow, heart-shaped planchette halts mid-stride. The point of the planchette steadily rotates until it aims at me.

Blue-Eyes dives off the table and scurries over to me. He rubs his boney body against my legs. My eyes zero in on the board. The beige planchette pivots away from me, sliding over to the H, E, L, L, O.

*This is what I wanted, right? Who else would be interested in talking to me other than my dad?*

I cautiously tiptoe around the coffee table and sink into the sofa. The room feels smaller, like the house itself and all its occupants are creeping in closer to get a better look.

I drag my teeth over my bottom lip. *This is so dumb. Why would I interact with a board that set itself up on the table? This is a bad idea. Remember, if you speak out into the void, the void will always answer back. I have no idea if this is my dad. This could be anyone.*

The planchette glides over to the E, then to the L, E, A, N, O, R.

I lean over the board and swallow hard. "Hello," I squeak. *This isn't my dad. He never called me "Eleanor".*

The planchette moves so the round glass on the middle encircles new letters so quickly my eyes whip back and forth, trying to keep up.

YOU'RE RIGHT, it spells and continues, ELLA. YOUR NAME IS ELEANOR ELIZABETH O'REILLY, BUT TO ME YOU WILL ALWAYS BE MY ELLA.

"Dad?" I cry. "How do I know it's you?" *Wait, did he read my mind? Do I have the gift? Or maybe my dad just has a connection with me?*

Blue-Eyes appraises the board with an expression I can only describe as skeptical. What the hell does a cat have to be skeptical about? It's my ghost. I rack my brain, trying to think of something only he would know.

"What did you want to call our made-up folk band?" The planchette started moving before I finished speaking, having heard my thought.

THE FOLKING AWESOME O'REILLYS.

That's right. I hear a scoff in my head. My eyes flick to Blue-Eyes watching the board.

I anxiously pluck at a hangnail, still unsure. I frown, and think, *okay, what is my favorite an—*

SEA TURTLE, AQUAMARINE, MASHED POTATOES, ROOTBEER, VERTIGO, and ONCOLOGY.

It took nearly five minutes to spell everything. "Oh, I'm actually not sure if I still want to specialize in oncology—" I stop, he listed my favorite things and greatest ambition. My heart squeezes. There's a dry burn in the back of my throat, desperate for a tearful release. "Dad?" I croak. "It's really you, isn't it?" I feel my shoulders crumble despite feeling uncomfortably exposed and vulnerable.

The Ouija piece delicately moves. YES.

I fall forward, my hands gripping the table as I shudder. The air no longer holds the aroma of patchouli and candle wax. Now it's replaced with the smell of linen, the scent of the ocean, and Calvin Klein cologne. Like invisible arms encompassing me, I'm filled with a comforting warmth. "Oh, Dad. Everything's a mess. We miss you so much. Mom is just… she is so broken. What are we supposed to do?" I sob.

The planchette slowly glides across the board until it's resting against my hand on the table. I sniffle and chuckle. "I love you too," I murmur back. "Dad, I need to know. Is there a way to bring you back? Would you know that?" I ask that question more to myself.

The planchette slides over YES.

I gasp. "Is there a way we can bring you back?"

YES.

I sit up straighter. "How? Just tell me how and I'll do it. Oh, Dad, we miss you so much."

The planchette flies across the board, too hastily for me to read anything.

"Dad, Dad, slow down," I say, unable to keep up with the jerky movements.

IN YOUR ROOM, THERE'S A KNIFE…

Blue-Eyes leaps upon the board, causing the planchette to clatter to the floor.

"What the hell?" I shout. I jump up, ready to shove him off. "Get off!"

With an arched back, he slowly shakes his head at me, his eye contact steady and unwavering.

"Um…you don't tell me no." The temperature rises in my cheeks. "That's my dad, you ass—"

All the candles immediately extinguish, cloaking us in a cloud of smoke and darkness. "No, Dad! Don't go! Please! Please don't go!" I collapse to my knees, sandwiched between the coffee table and the couch. Sitting in the gaping dark, I'm enveloped in despair. No matter how many cats are near, I feel haplessly alone. I wrap my arms around myself, dry sobbing. My heart had still been stitching itself back together after the accident, now it's been ripped open again and left bleeding out on the living room floor.

He was here, so close that if I close my eyes, I can pretend we were just texting each other. *How did it come to this?* My mind reels, shuffling through the events since my father's passing. The funeral, the move, my mom leaving, learning I'm a witch. Nothing feels right, nothing feels real. I'm fractured. And unlike the song, I'm uncomfortably numb.

There's movement on the table, and I push up off the floor. My legs shake as I grope the walls searching for the light switch, feeling the raised threads of the Damask wallpaper underneath my palms. I find the brass switch and flip it. Relief swiftly fills my veins, and I let out a held in breath.

I lean back on the doorway, taking in the electric glow of the room. It somehow feels looser, like it's exhaled a sigh of respite. Even the air flows with a sense of normality. The supernatural presence has completely vanquished.

I rock forward on the balls of my feet. With crossed arms, I glower over at Blue-Eyes. "I'm going to contact my father again and I will bring him back," I state threateningly.

Blue-Eyes dips his head. His eyes, unflinching, never leave mine. With an arched back and a straight tail, he releases a loud, terrifying hiss.

I jump back, then shake off my nerves, refusing to be rattled. "Whatever," I say back in spite. I spin on my heel and head upstairs. I slam the door shut, causing the door frame to shudder. I flop onto the bed, awash with exhaustion that permeates and weighs down every molecule.

My eyes flutter closed. I try to replay the words from the board in my mind. My father answered "yes", that there's a way to bring him back. *How would he know that if he didn't know about witchcraft? Perhaps after he passed away, he somehow came into all knowledge? I don't know, but I know that was him.* There was an unmistakable familiarity.

Before Blue-Eyes rudely interrupted, it appeared my father was informing me about a knife in my bedroom. *Did he mean my room back home? No, he couldn't have. He must mean the tower bedroom. But how will a knife bring him back?*

Tink, tink, tink, thunk, tink.

I peek one eye open, hearing a strange muted clicking.

Tink, tonk, tink, tink.

I frown, sit up, and listen.

Tink, tink, tink.

I slide off my bed and creep forward towards the large pentagon window. Thunk!

Before I reach the window, a large rock flew up to the glass, leaving a little spidery crack. *What the hell?* I jump back a foot. *Who is throwing rocks at the window? One of my aunts' scorned lovers?* I really wouldn't be surprised.

"Eleanor!" someone yells. "Eleanor O'Reilly!"

I shuffle back to my window in a huff. With great effort, I slide the window up. Below on the gravel drive are Nick, Tripp, Pete and Alden. They each drop the remaining stones from their hands. Nick dusts his hands off by rubbing them together, the rest brush their pants' legs.

I stick my head out the window.

"What are you guys doing here?" I shout without thinking.

Nick steps forward, cloaked in his shearling jacket. "We kicked their asses! I sent one of their midfielders out on a stretcher!" Nick calls, then fist bumps Pete.

"That's…great," I answer back. The gravity of the night still held me. I had reached into the beyond spoken with the departed spirit of my father. Discussing a lacrosse game now seems so facile.

"Come down! We're here to rescue you!" Nick yells, his voice dripping with unbridled excitement. The boys shake his shoulders, playfully pushing him aside as they fall to their knees in playful begging.

"Please, dear sweet Eleanor, will you come with us?" Pete calls up before giving a low bow, nearly tripping over when Nick pushes him.

"We've come all the way from Wakefield, practically to the middle of nowhere to save you. Hell, are we still in Salem?" Alden shouts, ending with what sounds like a genuine question.

I roll my eyes and chuckle, leaning my elbows on the windowsill. Despite myself, I have to admit I'm flattered, but also confused. Since moving to Salem, there's been no shortage of boys eagerly offering to carry my books, supply me with answers to any and every test, not to mention the pharmaceuticals. Nick and his crew just happen to be the most persistent and attentive.

They break out into a drunken, out of tune, out of sync barbershop quartet. This sort of thing only ever happened to Shannyn. My fickle heart aches, refusing to let me ignore the disappointment I feel that Jack isn't out there serenading me, maybe even riding up on a white steed. He is a Grigg's knight after all.

"Don't make us drag you out here!" Tripp finishes, laughing.

*Okay, all the sweetness is gone. He wrecked it.*

"I'll go up and get her," Nick assures his friends.

A cool spike shoots down my spine. *They can't come in here!* There are potions, magic herbs, burning incense, spell books, and cats…

Nick is on his way to the unlocked front door. "Wait by the truck, we might be a bit," he orders his friends.

I panic.

"Fine! I'll be just a moment. STAY OUT THERE!" I yell down. Nick stops and hops off the porch, walking back to his mates. I shut my bedroom window and turn to get ready.

I shake my hair out of its ponytail and fluff it, allowing the hair to wave down past my shoulders. Sitting down at my vanity, I dot around my eye with some concealer, hoping to rid myself of the ugly redness. Next, a sweep of eyeliner and a few brushes of mascara; there isn't time for anything else. I pull off my ratty waffle knit sweater, tossing it on the bed. *Do I have anything that would help me fit in here?* In my bra and leggings, I march over to my wardrobe just as someone pushes open my bedroom door.

# Chapter Twelve
## Hell of a Party

My heart skips a beat, nervously expecting Nick to come waltzing in. A wave of relief washes over me when instead it's just Blue-Eyes. I roll my eyes at him and sort through my wardrobe while Blue springs onto the bed. I tug out a square neck cotton dress with a China pattern. *Too formal?* I shove it back in, frustrated with my lack of fashion, and of course, with being forced to go in the first place.

I groan, digging through drawers only to be interrupted by an impatient honking horn outside. I yank on some straight-legged, high-waisted black jeans, a tattered Yacht Club men's sweater I thrifted, and a bejeweled Peter Pan collar I clip around my neck. I slip into my high-tops and grab the black leather jacket Shannyn gifted me after she broke up with the one who gifted it to her.

I sprint down the stairs, skipping every other step. *Wait, do I have a curfew?* The thought almost makes me chuckle. *Sally enforcing a curfew? She'd probably ask me to bring back some booze.* Another blast from Nick's truck's horn intrudes on my thoughts. *I have to go.*

Blue-Eyes appears at the front door, his tail casually swishing back and forth on the Persian rug. I stride past him and close the door behind me. My breath hangs in the cold air in puffy clouds.

The boys hoot and catcall, hanging out the windows of the enormous silver truck.

"Get in, girl! Noah is already at the party and has probably already drunk all the good stuff," Pete hollers, his fist playfully pounds the door.

Gravel crunches behind me. *What the hell?* I glance about. Blue-Eyes saunters to my side. "You're absolutely not coming."

He just stares.

I quicken my pace, and so does he.

I stop and face him. "Okay, assuming you can understand me, you follow me into that truck, and I put you in a woodchipper."

His mouth curls in a challenging smirk.

I sprint the last few yards and rush into the open doors of the truck. The boys help me up and into the cab, guiding me by holding my back, elbows, and one bold hand on my bottom. I climb into the second row, squeezing between Pete and Alden.

I wiggle my nose against the assaulting scent of body spray and sweat. "So, where does Poppy live?" I question, trying to adjust myself between the two boys.

Nick leans his head back while he pulls out of the driveway. "On Foster Street in Marblehead. Not too far."

"About fifteen minutes. But we drive fast." Alden winks at me.

I tuck my hair behind my ears and nod nervously, my stomach forming tight knots. This will be my first high school party. I always yearned to attend the iconic teen bash of a classic high school party. Back in Florida, my invites were perennially absent. I lace my fingers in my lap. My chance is finally here, and yet it feels…wanting. Although, I loathe to admit it, I'm glad for the distraction. I have a daunting task ahead of me with literally no idea how to accomplish it. My mind whirls, picturing my father walking up the aunts' porch, gathering my mom in a passionate embrace before excitedly turning to me and my sisters. *What would we tell his family? Surprise! We made a mistake, Dad is actually alive. Could we return to Florida and live our lives? Would he want to stay here?*

I place a hand over my heart, feeling a strange and unique sliver of pain. I take a breath against this unfamiliar sensation. There's an unusual tug in my chest at the thought of leaving Salem.

"You look nervous," Nick says, glancing at my perplexed face in the rearview mirror.

I shrug, dropping my hand from my heart.

Tripp, having flipped around in the front seat, cocks his brow and pulls up his mouth in an impish grin. "Something wrong with your chest?" His eyes dart quickly downward, then back to my face.

I swallow and push through a smile. "Uh no, I'm fine."

"Want me to check?" Tripp asks.

Nick slugs him in the arm. "Dude, don't be gross."

Tripp chuckles. "What, bro? I was being nice. I've been told my hands work magic." He wiggles his fingers at his friend.

"Just on yourself," Pete quips next to me.

Nick's eyes continuously peer back at me through the mirror.

Alden snakes his arm around my shoulders. "Hey, selfie time," he pulls out his phone from his green bomber jacket pocket. "Smile," he says, pointing his phone at us.

Before I know it, he's snapping the picture and Pete's hand is suddenly claiming my knee. The flash nearly blinds me.

Alden whines, examining the shot. "Eleanor, you look like a hostage. We'll take another one once we get inside," he grumbles, shoving his phone away.

"I think we'll be a little busy," Nick assures, smiling over at me.

Pete tightens his grip on my knee.

I keep my face serene, staring straight ahead despite my pounding heart and erratic nerves. I feel like a piece of meat tossed into a lion's den.

We speed up a street framed by trees with hopeful little spring buds dotting the branches. The gas streetlamps gives it a quaint New England air. Nick slows down coming to a towering iron gate and lowers his window. "Shit, do you guys remember the passcode?"

Tripp runs his hand through his chin length amber hair. "Yeah, damn, what is it? When I was dating Bethany, I used this all the time."

"Bethany Ambrose lives on Foster? I thought she lived on Ocean Avenue in the capital," Pete pipes up, annoyed.

"Capital?" I question, wondering if my fifth-grade civics was failing me.

Pete smiles at me condescendingly, finally removing his hand and pulling out his phone. "The mansion they're talking about looks like the actual Whitehouse, and not just in size," sounding rather unimpressed. "Pretentious and ridiculous."

Alden shakes his head and answers before Tripp. "No, you idiot. That's her cousin's place. Only the Woods live there. 38-something Ocean Avenue. You know, near Castlerock park in Marblehead. My dad sold the Woods that house."

My stupid heart flutters.

Tripp smacks the dashboard, like something just occurred to him. "Oh, oh, yeah, yeah, yeah I remember now, 881536," he informs, pointing to the silver box. "There's a story to how I remember that—"

"And no one wants to hear it," Nick says, punching in the numbers. The gate creaks open and Nick peels through.

I crane my neck trying to see out the windows. We pass clapboard Victorian mansions that only the chicest of individuals would call "cottages". There was something perverse about calling a nine-bedroom, five-car garage with an Olympic lap pool in the backyard a "cottage".

Nick slows his truck, approaching a private drive framed by high concrete pillars. He coasts down a cobblestone driveway encased by towering trees, then the vegetation clears, opening to a glass and chrome residence with jutting angles and an onyx waterfall in the front. There are ten to fifteen cars scattered about the long drive. Through the transparent walls, you can see about thirty to forty teens carousing through the illuminated house.

Nick helps me out of the car and guides me past the water feature to the doorstep that is covered in vomit. The viscous trail leads to an unconscious freshman with a marker mustache and male anatomy scribbled across his cheek.

Nick doesn't bother knocking, just pushes open the steel door. Club music with heavy beats blasts in our faces.

The acrid smell permeating the house makes my stomach queasy. The aroma is a pungent mixture of perspiration, liquor, and excessive perfume.

Nick nods his head and shouts close to my ear, "The party is upstairs!" He motions towards the platinum staircase to our right.

In the corner of the upstairs main living area is a DJ spinning at a turntable. A topless adult male works as an actual bartender behind an ebony bar surrounded by crystal decanters lit up with track lighting. In the open kitchen, people orbit a keg like small moons thirsting for a substance less "silver spooned"; however, there's still an attendant squirting the frothy liquid into cups so we wouldn't have to sink as low as to serving ourselves.

Canapes and charcuterie are offered on silver tiered trays on a narrow marble table. When I imagined the iconic high school party that Hollywood immortalized, I pictured lettermen jackets, beer funnels, someone's Spotify playlist streaming from the home speakers, and maybe a bag of chips if anyone thought to bring something. But here in Salem, at least in the Grigg circles, there's never an expense spared.

Girls squeal as boys cajole them onto the furniture, intertwined. Most of the attendees are upper classmen with a few freshmen setting up phones on ledges to shoot videos of themselves dancing. My heart pounds in time with the pulsing music. A few girls rush past us as boys chase them down with squirt guns. With Nick's entourage in tow, we squeeze through the crowd of partiers. Most are sheathed in designer duds paying a heavy premium for that authentic secondhand look.

The boys at my side quickly disperse, hoping to find a lucky cup with a party favor inside. Pete plops down on a leather sofa and begins making out with an inebriated teen I recognize from the choir performance today. Nick, however, stays hovering at my side as we amble through the crowd to the small sitting room near the back of the house that overlooks their private dock on the bay.

Nick places a heavy paw on my hip and pulls me close to yell in my ear again. "Maybe I can find us a room." Nick wears a large, cocky smile.

"What?" I start to panic. *Is he kidding, or does he actually think we are going to hook up?* I take a small step back from him.

"Hey, look! O'Reilly is here!" a boy over by the fridge calls. A few others clap in response.

"I need a drink; do you want one?" Nick asks. He doesn't wait for a response as he stalks off to the keg in the kitchen. He is quickly engulfed by teammates holding each other, shouting drunkenly, thrusting red Solo cups into the air.

***

I sit on the sofa, bored out of my mind, watching the clock on the wall. It says Nick left me just forty minutes ago, but it feels like several hours. Noah and a few others had pulled him into one of the back rooms. I'm not sure if I'm grateful or not that he's busy. I nibble my lower lip. Maybe I'm being silly. Perhaps this is just how guys act. In Florida, boys never paid me much attention.

Sure, I've gone on a date once when I was fifteen, but he spent most of the time on his phone and then asked me if Shannyn was moving back to Florida after her freshmen year was done. I don't understand what suddenly changed. My looks sure haven't. My eyes are just as purple as before. I inconspicuously glance at my chest. I'm just as boob-less, which was a nickname I received in freshmen gym; and nothing has changed. *Gosh puberty can be cruel.* Even Margaret is more endowed than I am. My stomach is flat but far from defined and I have literally no hips.

I wince, peering down; I have the body of a fifth-grade boy. My looks and actions remained the same; the only thing that changed was location. *Could that be it? In Florida I was the albino ugly duckling, but in Salem a porcelain swan? How can that be?* In Coral Gables I was that girl with no breasts and a constant peeling sunburn (seriously, in eighth grade I was nicknamed "the lizard") but in Salem my pallid features seemed *desirable?* I shake my head at myself. *Nah. No way. I'm a new toy at best. By the month of May, they'll be bored. And knowing me, it'll probably be even sooner than that.*

I grimace to my left, noticing that the couple next to me has produced a thick blanket from somewhere and is now making obscene noises underneath. I squeeze the bridge of my nose. *I want to get out of here. I don't even want Nick to return. Who knows what he'll want to do when he does.*

Four girls prance into the room, claiming this space for stripping and watching purposes only. One girl stakes the glass coffee table in the middle of the room for her platform as the other three girls drunkenly take their clothes off, dancing seductively to a club remix of "Pony".

I flee from the couch and trudge into the next room where a makeshift game of beer pong is being played on a glossy grand piano. A group of onlookers' cheer watching a scantily clad lot playing strip poker.

Noah, wearing only boxer shorts and socks, tosses down his hand onto the green felt table. "Two pair! Take it off!" a boy sitting next to Noah stands up, shrugging off his jeans while three other girls disrobe with faux reluctance.

"Pete, what the hell, dude?! You just spilt your freaking beer all over me, you idiot little transfer tool!" An angry boy roughly shoves Pete back as a minor scuffle breaks out between the observers and the kid who was formerly playing pong. The girls squeal in excitement as they jump out of the way of the sudden brawl.

*Maybe I'll call a ride service?* I frown, *do I have any money in my account? Ugh, would Nick be willing to take me home? I don't think his friends would notice our absence.* My eyes scan the room to see if Nick is here.

I amble down the hall, stopping at each door. The first is a bathroom where four kids are holed up in the jetted bathtub. The rest are locked bedroom doors and an office where a group of kids are huddling around several monitors.

There is no sign of Nick, but I can feel someone's gaze on me, following me as I meander about the party. By the bar, there's a trough of ice and beverages. I dig past the White Claw and other hard seltzers and grab a Snapple most kids were using as chasers. I pull out my phone to check my bank account.

"With the finest drinks at the tip of your fingers, you settle for juice," Jack says, sauntering up to the bar. He leans on his elbow, peering over at me from the corner of his eye, a smirk playing at the edge of his lips.

The topless bartender turns his attention to us, lingering at the end of the lit-up glass bar. "What will it be? Cosmo? A rum and Coke?"

Jack shakes his head and answers confidently. "Macallan, neat."

The bartender pulls up a large glass bottle with a blue label, pours it into a disposable cup, and slides it over to Jack.

The bartender swivels to me. "And for the beautiful lady?"

I shake my bottle in my hand, showing him. "I'm covered, thanks." I glare at my phone, irritated as my bank login keeps failing.

Jack takes a few steps closer to me, holding his cup. "Of all the gin joints," he quotes with a playful grin.

I fight against a smile, giving up on my phone sliding it into my pocket. "Here to celebrate for the team?" I pop the lid off my drink.

He leans back against the bar with the languor of a man with nothing but time. "I'm nothing if not an ardent supporter." He tips his cup to me.

I chuckle. "Sure. So, when is *your* first game?" I question before taking a sip, hoping the liquid will keep any interfering hiccups at bay.

He grins. "For crew, they're called meets, and we have a home meet in two weeks. You're welcome to come and watch."

Despite the chaos around us, I feel electricity go through me from his gaze. I try to look away casually, but out of the corner of my eye, I can see him draw closer. And closer. Closer. Until...

"Would you like to get some air?" he asks, his body keeping a friendly distance, but his lips close to my ear.

I nod, peering across the room. I'm unable to meet his stare, my dia-phragm quivering with potential hiccups. That's when I notice Vivienne prowling through the party. Her eyes hone in on Jack, and she stomps her way over to the bar in black suede boots, cut-off shorts accessorized with a Gucci belt, a sage eyelet lace bustier, with a pastel kimono and a velvet choker. She irritably sucks on a silver vape pen approaching her target. Her sycophants hover nervously in her periphery, exchanging glances with each other, clearly deliberating on how best to support or assist her. Poppy adjusts her babydoll dress, her eyes apprehensively sweeping up and down her leader.

I straighten up like I've been caught red-handed. Jack slumps back and I slide a few feet away from him.

"Cosmo," she barks. "And I'll take a glass, not a plastic cup like some creatin."

Her friends mumble for a few rum and Cokes while two of them exca-vate some White Claws out of the ice.

Vivienne's lips resemble freshly picked berries. She stabs the silver pen in between her lips and sucks deeply. "Jack," she says in a saccharine voice.

"Vivienne," he replies coolly.

She plays with Jack's button-up shirt, undoing a button exposing his sculpted chest. He brushes her hands away. She continues unperturbed, pressing against him. "We're expected at brunch tomorrow. My parents are already in Boston for the weekend, so I thought I'd catch a ride with your family. You know how I hate parking downtown. I don't understand Allen's aversion to valets."

Jack polishes off the rest of his drink and places his cup on the bar top. He shakes his head at the bartender, rejecting a refill.

I bite down on my lip, staring at my stupid shoes with unsightly scuffs. I'm an interloper, a fraud, a fake. I shouldn't be here. Vivienne and Jack clearly have a history probably going back generations. Their union is likely sealed in blood with iron clad prenups and generous bequeathments. Summers in the vineyard in matching seersucker suits, toasting with other ivy league legacies, to industry!

Vivienne takes her cocktail, sips, then sighs, cocking her head at me as if just noticing me. "Look at you. You came," she says, mockingly sweet. "Aw, and you robbed a homeless man's clothes. So cute." She screws up her face as she speaks.

"Ready?" Jack asks, dipping his head close to mine.

My heart quickens, and a shiver works its way down my spine. My chest flutters as I smell him over the musky reek of the room. His scent is san-dalwood, leather, and bergamot. I become hyperaware of every stitch of clothing on my body and how stiff they feel against my skin. I think of my slouchy sweater with only a thin lace bralette beneath. I shift, meeting his gaze. I feel completely naked despite my layers.

He takes my hand and escorts me through the throngs of drinking teens, his hand protectively holding mine. My heart thumps wildly as my hand feels so small and delicate in his square, manly hand that wraps so perfectly around mine. He continues to hold me tenderly until we reach the porch that's nearly free of teens and offers somewhat fresh, body odor-free air. Only a few couples smoke at the various sun tables we pass as we make our way down to the dock, allowing us space and privacy. The weathered planks stretch out surprisingly far into the dark, churning water.

We claim a white painted bench haloed by the glowing doc light. We say nothing as we sit down, relaxing against the rigid back. Jack runs his hands down his exhausted face. I peer away, suffocating the bizarrely brazen desire to reach out and stroke his cheek.

I let out an unsteady breath, feeling like a shaken soda ready to explode. My pulse is ricocheting throughout my body. Stealthy, I peek over at him and his cool exterior.

The icy bay breeze tousles my hair. I try to tame it by tucking it behind my ears.

"Are you okay?" Jack asks, scooting a little closer.

I keep my mouth clamped shut, shuddering against my hiccups. I nod, gazing at the shoreline with the lights dotting the neighboring docks in the dark.

Jack chuckles. "Been having fun?" he questions incredulously. It's quite obvious that *he* hasn't been enjoying himself. Despite being invited to these events, Jack rarely, if ever, attends. At least, that was the impression he gave and the whispers I had heard at school. *I wonder why he decided to come tonight.*

Drawing deep breaths in through my nose, I finally feel my hiccups calm, allowing me to answer freely. "No," I answer flatly. I pull my legs up on the bench, wrapping my arms around them and resting my head on my knees, shivering. I peer at Jack's rolled-up sleeves despite the frigid temperature.

Jack's nose and cheeks turn rosy. "Why'd you come?" he asks, sounding more out of curiosity than accusation.

I throw him a glum smile. "Would you believe me if I said I was kidnapped?"

Jack emits a rough chuckle as if caught off guard. "By your boyfriend, I'm guessing?" he says teasingly.

I drop my legs from the bench. "He is *not* my boyfriend. I don't know why he said that. Gosh, I mean, I met him what—two days ago!"

Jack's eyebrows rise. "Has it really only been that long?" he asks, so quietly it sounds like he's questioning himself.

*My thoughts exactly.* I internally cringe at myself. *What is wrong with me?*

His mouth blooms into a smile. "Eleanor?"

I frown and hang my head. "Looks like you know my name now." *Well, that game was short-lived.*

His grin widens. "It wasn't hard. It's the name that's been buzzing about the school for the last forty-eight hours." He places his arm on the back of the bench, his fingers just brushing my shoulders. "So why did you finally come to Salem?"

*What does he mean "finally" come to Salem?* My mouth turns arid. "There was an accident. My dad passed away." The admission feels like a rock sagging low in my stomach. *Should I have admitted that? What if I can bring my dad back? He said there was a way. My natural skepticism keeps me from fully committing.*

Jack's smile crumbles into sympathy. "I'm really sorry. I can't imagine how hard that must have been." His hand hovers above my back, hanging in midair, grappling with indecision. Slowly, he lowers it to my shoulder blade, a safe, friendly spot. He massages it gently in a friendly, comforting circle.

I'm being ripped in two. Part of me wants to tell him to keep his pity to himself, that my father is merely gone for the moment but will be back soon. The other half, the more rational, grounded, still-unsure-about-magic part, wants to disintegrate into a million quivering broken pieces. I settle on being silent.

"Do you miss where you're from?" he softly prods.

My spirits lighten ever so slightly at the thought of home. Florida. Florida in all its tropical wonderfulness. "A lot, actually. I'm from Coral Gables. It was perfect. Not too far from the beach, a quick drive downtown." My eyes mist, imagining South Beach with my friends, my parents running marathons together in the Keys. Live music. The shops. My school. My dad. All of it gone.

"Are you going to go back there once you graduate?" he asks.

I shrug, then shiver despite my coat. "I still have another year, but yeah, maybe. My parents met at the University of Miami. I thought maybe I'd go there for med school or something." It dawns on me that I haven't given it much thought. My older sister Shannyn followed her boyfriend out east, but I had always planned on staying local. But now my home is gone, so where do I go from here?

"Med school," he notes, impressed. His eyes survey my face, lingering on different features, every freckle, every eyelash, every strand of color in my iris.

I turn away, facing the dark rippling water reflecting long shafts of light from the house. "So, you and Vivienne seem…close," I murmur. I think back on their family's brunch plans tomorrow. A stupid spark of jealously ignited inside me, overhearing their plans.

He momentarily turns stiff. I've clearly breeched a topic he wishes to stay untouched. "It's complicated with Viv. We *used* to date, used to being the operative term. But our families run in the same circles. Remaining cordial is more or less a familial obligation."

I nod along. "Do you have many of those?"

He chuckles darkly. "You have no idea. Being a Woods comes with more strings attached than Pinocchio. And I do have to admit there are a lot of privileges to it. I'd be foolish to deny it, but more often than not, the burden outweighs the good."

Using the toe of my shoe, I grind some bracken on the wooden plank under my feet. "So are you two getting back together or…"

"No, no, no, no, no," he quickly cuts in. "She struggles to acknowledge the breakup, and I'm sure the Mather's still have a date blotted out in June two years from now at The Plaza, but it's over. It's been over *officially* for eight months now, but it's been done for me a lot longer."

A secret smile unfurls, hidden behind a curtain of my hair.

"Eleanor?"

Turning towards him, I allow myself to fall into his gaze. I inhale a shaky breath, taking in the gilded glow of his hair in the dock light. How the yellow bulb illuminates all the varying golden glints of his blonde perfection. My stomach wobbles. He's too beautiful, too untouchable, an Adonis you only actually see in cologne ads or Hollywood. He's a living, breathing, airbrushed portrait. His only blemish on an otherwise paragon face is a scar just above his right eyebrow. But if anything, it just adds to his roguish charm.

Jack surprises me by reaching over, taking my hands in his, warming my icy fingers in his palms. "You're freezing," he says, looking half froze himself. "I've got an extra sweatshirt in my car; let me go get it for you." He heads down the dock at a brisk pace, glancing over his shoulder at me before he disappears out of sight and into the shadow of the lawn.

I can't help it. I expel a girly sigh before rubbing my hands together, then blow on them, trying to warm them.

*"Cold?"*

I smile, turning toward the voice. "No way, that was sure quick," I say, to empty air. I glance about, startled. My heavy breathing comes out in wispy white clouds. I struggle to my feet, taking a few steps back. "Hello?" I call weakly. A scream rips up my throat as something black leaps out of the darkness.

Blue-Eyes lands lithely on the bench.

# Chapter Thirteen
## It's Just a Broken Nose

I blanch at the sight of the stupid cat. "What the hell are you doing here? How did you even get here?" I ask in futility. I'm literally speaking to a cat.

*"I stole passage in the troglodyte's truck bed,"* Blue says, staring up at me, having answered me telepathically.

My flesh breaks out in goosebumps. I grind my teeth, glaring. *So, it is you I've been hearing in my head!?*

*"Yes."*

*And you can hear my thoughts?*

*"Obviously."*

"Great, that makes you what, my familiar, or my guardian or something?" I say aloud.

*"Apparently."*

I cock a skeptical brow. "And you're British?"

*"I hail from Essex."*

*And you're dead?*

*"Not by choice."*

I groan and collapse onto the bench. "You've got to be kidding me. I get the dead cat?"

*"And you're no picnic, either."*

I glare at him, then notice something in his rigid form is missing. I crane my neck, peering around him. "Where's your tail?"

He turns his head indignantly towards the black water lapping against the pylons. *"Clearly, it has fallen off."*

I grimace. "In your grave, though, right? It's not like back at the party somewhere?"

*"It fell off in the back of the truck. That prig drives like an imbecile."*

My eyes close irritably. "Are you saying I need to go get your tail?"

*"Do you always struggle to follow a conversation? Naturally, I require you to fetch it for me."*

"That doesn't make sense," I quibble. "I thought whatever happens to your body happens to," I motion to his form, "your spirit or whatever you are. So, I'm grabbing your spirit tail?" I ask, muddled. *I still can't believe I'm talking to a stupid cat. A stupid dead cat.*

*"And I can't believe I'm talking to an insipid adolescent girl, yet here we are. I'm stuck between the living and the dead for reasons far too complex for you to comprehend. My current state is more than just spirit but less than full-bodied. What happens to my current form can affect my body and vice versa."*

*So, in other words, you're high maintenance...*

*"No more so than you, I gather."*

Jack's hollow footsteps clomp down the dock as he jogs towards us at a gingerly pace.

*"Just shut up, okay?"* I insist.

*"He can't hear me. Only you have that pleasure."*

*I know, hence the order.*

Blue scoffs.

Jack reaches me. His ears, nose, and cheeks are turning scarlet in the cold. He's now clothed in a double-breasted wool coat. He hands me a grey hooded sweatshirt. "Not exactly stylish, I know, but it's clean and thick, so it'll keep you warm."

I tug off my leather jacket and slip the cotton sweatshirt over my head, deeply inhaling his scent left on the clothing. I feel dazed. *If I could bottle his aroma, I would. I'd wear it every day. I'd douse all my belongings in it. I sound so creepy right now.*

*"Yes, you do. Unequivocally so."*

I glower over at Blue-Eyes. *I really dislike you.*

*"Well, look at that. It turns out we have something in common after all."*

I adjust the large sweatshirt and examine the insignia on the front. "Elite Boxing," I read aloud. "Do you box?" I pull my hair to one side and pull the hood up, hoping to revive my ears from the burning cold.

He shrugs one shoulder. "Remember when I spoke of familial obligations," he says, to which I nod. "Boxing is one of them." He glances at Blue-Eyes before doing a double take. "Whoa, hey little guy, where did you come from?" Jack raises his hand to stroke Blue's head. Blue lets out a shrieking hiss, and Jack quickly retracts his hand. "Okay." He glances back at the house, glowing in stark contrast to the engulfing darkness. "I don't think it's Poppy's." He bobs his head about, examining the cat. "Does he look a bit mangey to you?"

"To say the least," I mumble.

"Oh no." Jack bends down at his knees, crouching to examine Blue. "He seems to be missing his tail."

*"Incredible, Sherlock Holmes can't outwit Mr. Woods. His observational prowess is unmatched."*

*You are such an ass.* I move closer, feigning concern. "Should we take him to a shelter? Maybe they could help him? Although, euthanizing him might be the only recourse."

Blue-Eyes bares just a hint of fang at me.

I roll my eyes.

Loud thunks echo up the dock. "There you are!" Nick shouts. He stumbles drunkenly, trying to run down the dock. "What the hell, I've been looking everywhere for you." He continues to run, his lumbering footsteps land heavy on the wooden planks of the dock. Thunk, thunk, thunk.

I whip around and squint into the darkness. "Nick?"

Jack rises from his crouched position. "Hey man, don't run, you're going to fall in," Jack shouts wearily, not wanting to dive into the frigid water after him. He stands tense, arms slightly waved out, watching him make his way to us.

I scrunch my nose, from the cheap booze wafting off of him.

He wipes his mouth with the back of his hand. His shirt is missing and the only article of clothing he's wearing are his jeans and someone else's jacket. He's even barefoot. "Hey! Why are you out here with *him*!?" He clenches his fists.

I peer nervously at Jack. "We were only talking," I timidly assure. "We just came out here to get some fresh air." It was the truth, and yet I still feel like I'm lying to him, that there is a debt between us yet to be paid. My stomach twitches nervously.

Nick throws his red cup over our heads, just missing Jack's head by an inch as he chucks it into the water. "You came here with me! You're supposed to be with *me*!" Nick wobbles as he yells. "*I* brought you here!"

Blue-Eyes adjusts, so he's on all fours, staring up at Nick. He and Jack take a step forward. "There's no betrayal to be had, Andersen. You don't own her," he states firmly and calmly. Jack had to be 6'1" or 6'2" at the very least, but Nick *still* towers over both of us like a brawny, massive troll.

"There's no betrayal, meh, meh, meh," Nick mocks. "You know you sound like a pretentious tool, right?"

Jack fights back an amused smile and forces his mouth into a smooth line. "Fair enough, but you won't order her about."

"Just shut up, bro." Nick sways, looking a little queasy.

Jack adjusts his stance, holding out his arms, preparing to catch him if he starts to fall. "We should help him back inside," Jack suggests, glancing over at me.

Nick sways a bit more. His face is a disturbing pallor with a slick, slimy sheen. His eyes roll to the back of his head, and he takes a stumbling step forward.

"Whoa, big guy." Jack quickly steps closer to steady him. "Let's get you inside, man."

Nick struggles against him. "What the hell, get off me. Eleanor, let's go," he says, giving Jack a sluggish shove.

Jack, completely unperturbed, takes Nick's arm and pulls him around his broad shoulders, hoisting him up a bit as Nick's knees buckled. "Want to hold his other side, O'Reilly? I think it'll take both of us."

I slip under his right side, wrapping my arm around Nick's waist. I cringe, feeling Nick kiss the top of my head. "I've got him," I say, feeling Jack carrying most, if not all, the weight.

The trek down the dock is a slow daunting task as Nick would sometimes thrash against us, insisting he didn't need help only to nearly collapse to his knees.

He turns to me with breath that could wilt flowers. "You're so freaking hot, Eleanor. I'm going to rip your clothes off. We're going to do it all the time," he mumbles half-consciously, his head lulling to the side. "I've got your picture in my room. I take your picture all the time."

Jack tightens his grip on him, his jaw clenched. "Take my advice, *bro*," he says, darkly sarcastic. "Stop. Talking."

I hold his thick wrist, keeping his arm in place around my neck. *He's been taking pictures of me?* I roll my lips, deliberating if I should speak up at this. I feel silly. I've always wanted to be desired and now I'm drowning in buyer's remorse.

We carefully maneuver Nick up the stairs and into the house. Jack struggles to adjust Nick's weight as he slides open the glass door.

"Poppy!" Jack calls as we haul him through the kitchen. His friends Hale and Poppy are lip-locked straddling the glossy black piano bench. Hale detangles his fingers from Poppy's tight red curls.

Poppy warily whips around. "What?" she cocks her brow at us. "What the hell is wrong with him?"

"He needs a place to rest," I shout, straining underneath him.

Nick's head lulls and rolls to the side.

"What room is available?" Jack questions impatiently.

Hale licks his lips. "Try Poppy's, we're done in there," Hale says, gripping his girlfriend's waist.

Poppy balks at Hale. "Ew, no! I don't want him barfing in my bed!"

"White door at the very end of the hall." Hale points. "Pop, let's get the champagne and hit the hot tub. Who's with me?" A cheering crowd hollers its approval.

Jack and I tow Nick down the hall and dispose of him onto a frilly four post bed. I roll my head, stretching out my neck muscles feeling a kink from Nick's arm. I spy Blue wandering about the room, mumbling about the extravagant eyesore of a room.

Jack reaches down, leaning over Nick's prone, unconscious form. He pats Nick's coat, digging through the pockets before rummaging through his pants pockets wincing.

I frown, perplexed. "What are you doing?"

Jack's eyes light up. "Got it!" he straightens up, retrieving Nick's phone from his back pocket. He lifts Nick's hand, holding out his forefinger to unlock it.

I tread over to Jack's side and quietly watch him flip through the photo gallery. Chills rip from the crown of my head to the end of my toes; there are hundreds of pictures of me. Photos of me walking to my car after school. Before school. The lunch room. Class. Orchestra. Disembodied pictures of my legs. My body. Face. Hair. Me driving home and pulling up to the house. I didn't even realize he had followed me home. *What the hell? How did he take so many in such a short amount of time, too?*

Jack flexes his jaw, breathing out his flared nostrils. He selects the entire folder labeled Eleanor, then the backup files, and finishes by emptying his trashcan of discarded photos into the ether. "Alright, I emptied his cloud, gallery, and trashcan. You're safe now." He smiles at me and tosses Nick's phone onto the bed. He snatches Poppy's tortoise shell waste basket and places it next to Nick on the bed.

He turns to me and asks, "Would you like a ride home?"

My shoulders settle with relief. "Yes, please."

*"Oh goody,"* Blue says drolly in my head.

Jack nods his head to the door. "Come on, I'll show you to my car."

As we quietly slip through the house, mostly unnoticed as the party was hitting a fever pitch with the arrival of students from a rival school. Vivienne sits perched on top of the bar, smiling devilishly at the tension sweeping the party.

"Hey," Jack calls over to Pete, sulking on the stairs surrounded by empty cups.

Pete pushes himself to his feet and ambles over. "The king of William Griggs is talking to me? I shall vlog this moment for posterity," Pete murmurs sarcastically, then flings out an arm before bending over in a low bow. "What do I owe this great honor?"

Jack, completely composed, continues, "Nick is in Poppy's room, the last room down the upstairs hallway. He's passed out. You might want to check on him in a bit to make sure he's okay, maybe even get him home. Poppy usually provides a car service when she's hosting. Use it," he orders firmly.

Jack pulls the front door open for me. As I walk through, I notice in my periphery Jack mouthing something to someone upstairs.

The number of cars in the driveway has tripled since my arrival. Vehicles are sprawled out across the lawn, blocking others in. One has a dented fender as they parked up on the granite fountain.

I peek over at Jack as we walk down the drive, squeezing between cars. "So, king, huh?" I say teasingly.

Jack rolls his eyes, turning sideways to slide between closely parked beamers. "Pete's just a bitter guy."

"Yeah?" I say, following suit. Blue-Eyes easily follows behind me.

"He's a scholarship student. He was actually pretty cool when he first came. Last year, we had trigonometry and fencing together. We weren't friends, but weren't enemies either. I don't know if he didn't get into the school he wanted, but something's changed. And I believe he had a thing for Vivienne, but being the snob she is, she wasn't interested."

I nod along, recalling my conversation at lunch with Nick's crew on my first day here. "I think everyone has a crush on Vivienne."

Jack chuckles as we reach the end of the cobblestone driveway. "Not everyone," he quips.

"Wait, did you say fencing?" I question.

Jack grins. We stop at the end of the driveway. I shiver, gripping Jack's sweatshirt around me. "So...did you borrow the invisible jet?" I joke, glancing around the barren road, huddling beneath the streetlight.

Jack points his chin to the right of us. "My grandparents are in New Haven this weekend, so I parked at their place." Jack takes a step, then pauses, glancing around me. "Did I just see that cat?"

I peer down at my feet, then swivel about. I squint into the darkness, trying to peer through the thicket of trees. "Um...I don't see anything." *Blue, where are you?*

*"Keeping myself scarce. I'll meet you at his motorcar."*

Our pace is slow, deliberately so. I draw out each footstep, keeping our stride meandering. Thin whispers of grey clouds drift over the waxing moon. Stars twinkle like diamonds pressed on black velvet. We both crack into shy smiles and coy chuckles as we catch each other stealing glances.

I cross my arms, tucking my chilly hands under my arms for warmth. "Are all your parties so extravagant?" I ask.

Jack shrugs, sticking his hands in his coat pockets. "More or less, I assume. To be honest, these aren't really my scene. I like club music as much as a jackhammer in the ear. The monotony alone makes my ears bleed."

I laugh at that, my smile nearly reaching my ears. That was a comment my dad would have made. I peek over my shoulder, spotting just the tips of the sheet roof of the house. "I hope Nick won't be too pissed that I ditched him," I say, my grin fading from my face completely. My brain flashes images from his phone.

"I doubt he'll remember his own name in the morning. But you shouldn't be worried about his feelings. You should be wondering how to obtain a restraining order," he says, peering over at me apologetically.

I turn my face forward, feeling uncomfortably ashamed for reasons I can't define. Trees and shrubbery to my right jostle like something is running by. A branch snaps, leaves crunch from a few yards off. I stop walking, turning my attention to the tangled grove.

"Eleanor?" Jack asks, pleasantly, like he was savoring my name in his mouth. He steps closer to me. "Everything okay?"

There's further rustling. Then it stops.

*Blue, is that you?*

*"What is taking you and that boy so long? I'm sitting by his front right tire. Hasten your pace."*

I tentatively search through the trees, unable to see far as the thicket is cloaked in darkness beyond the streetlight's reach. "Did you hear something? Like someone walking out there," I ask, using my head to point to the dense grove.

Jack cranes his neck, struggling to see anything beyond the opaque trees. He continues to search, standing up on his toes, stepping forward.

I turn as a small grey rabbit hops out onto the blacktop. It wiggles its little nose, staring directly at me before scampering off into the woods.

"I don't see anything, but maybe it was that cat we saw, or someone from the party." He shrugs. We continue walking, but Jack subtly inserts himself between the encroaching foliage and me.

The trees thin out until parting completely. We approach yet another spiked black iron gate. "A gated home within a gated community? A little extreme," I tease.

"Ah, the Godspeed's do enjoy their security," Jack says, flipping open a silver box and punching in a code. The towering gate creaks open.

"Godspeed?" I ask, walking through with him.

"Mom's parents," he answers as we stroll. The driveway is a slick black pavement. Small solar lights adorn either side of the drive. A white sports car gleams in the darkness but is dwarfed by the gabbled roof, shingle-sided estate that mimicked the quaint aesthetic of a summer escape but with acreage and comfort of a palace. Flower boxes dangle below each window, the pristine white shutters glow against the sand-colored home.

Jack, fishing his keys from his pocket, gazes at me staring up at the house. "Want to go in?" he asks, a crooked grin on his ridiculously handsome face.

I blush, having been caught gawking. "It's beautiful. Quite different from the modern architecture of their neighbors," I say, nodding towards Poppy's.

Jack rolls his eyes. "Don't remind me. My grandparents rant and rave about neighborhood standards and the nouveau riche." Jack turns, brightening up, "but this is my car."

The sleek, white, antique ride glistens, a phantom against the blacktop. The two-door vehicle sits low to the ground. The mustang emblem practically glows.

Jack smiles proudly. "It's a 1967 Shelby GT500. It was originally my dad's. He said if I could fix it up, it was mine. It was my project last spring." He glances over to gauge my reaction.

I give a weak nod. "It's nice," I say, smiling.

He chuckles. "But?" he prods softly.

I shrug. "I know my car says otherwise, but I don't know anything about cars," I admit. I knew guys wanted girls that knew their way around a vehicle just enough to set them apart from the bimbos, but not enough to impugn their egos. I figure I should just come clean now.

Jack executes a casual shrug of his shoulders. "Yeah, truthfully, cars aren't exactly my forte either, but my father presented a worthy challenge," he says playfully. "No matter, I can still appreciate a classic."

I smile, impressed. I bend forward, appraising the tight squeeze of the sports car. *It looks like Blue-Eyes will need to walk home.*

*"Thank for your concern, but I'm already inside. Locks do not confound me."*

I reach for the passenger side door and tug, eager to get in and hide the stupid cat. It doesn't budge. I pull a few more times. Nothing. Frustrated, I pull one more time. A spark flares within my chest.

"Here, let me get that for you," Jack says. He quickly strides over to the passenger side door to let me in.

I try again, wanting time to hide Blue. "Oh, I've got it, really."

Jack takes a few steps, hands up in surrender. "Okay, I'll let you get it," he relents with just the tiniest hint of smugness.

I pull at the handle, but the door still refuses to open. I yank a little harder and shake it. Again, I feel a spark, an electrical surge from my chest down to the pit of my stomach. It subsides as I let go of the handle. I glance behind my shoulder to see Jack watching me, somewhat entertained.

*Blue, you better be hiding under the seat.* "I give up," I say, retreating from the car.

*"Don't worry about me. Do you have my tail?"*

*Crap! I forgot it.* I cringe. *There's a ratty dead cat's tail in Nick's truck. I'm not getting it.*

*"Yes, you are!"*

Jack chuckles. "The door gets stuck. I need to replace the latch. You must have a feel for the door to get it open," he replies kindly to my frustration. Jack steps around me, moving towards the door.

With my growing aggravation, the voltaic feeling rings out throughout my entire body now, percolating at my fingertips.

The car door flies open, smacking Jack square in the face. He tumbles backward, landing flat on his back. His eyes fall shut as blood splatters across his face.

# Chapter Fourteen
## Unconventional Cures

"Jack!" hastily I fall to my knees at his side. "Are you okay?"

His eyes flutter in a daze at the sudden attack from the car door.

The electric sense rushing through my veins disappears. "Oh my gosh, your nose!" I cry, as blood gushes from his nose in thick, crimson dribbles down his mouth and chin.

*Blue, did you do that to him?*

*"Not that I didn't enjoy that, but no, I don't have the capability. We familiars don't have the same power as those we serve."*

Jack swipes beneath his nose but the blood keeps gushing. He scrambles to his feet and spits out a mouth full of blood. "I have no idea how that happened." He cups under his dripping nose. "It just doesn't make sense," he mutters to himself.

I lift Jack's sweatshirt up, but he waves me off. "No, no, keep it. You're cold." The flow slows into a trickle. He wipes his nose on the black of his hand, wincing.

I reach for his keys. "Your eyes are watering up. Why don't I drive?"

I think of the time my older sister, Shannyn, broke her nose during a softball game in middle school. My mother wouldn't let the coach (a physician) set it. Instead, Mom raced her home where she had the "cure" in her bedroom medicine cabinet.

My father hadn't been thrilled by her methods. "Are you sure about this, love? That looks like dried sage," he had said. He hovered behind my mom as she eased in a small bundle of herbs into both nostrils. Shannyn screamed in pain for just a moment, causing Dad to scramble around Mom to yank the herbal pads out of Shannyn's nose but she held up her hand stopping our dad, insisting they were suddenly soothing. The following morning, she removed the shriveled leaves from her nose, black eyes gone, with sharper smelling senses than before. Shannyn even insisted that her nose miraculously appeared more symmetrical than before. I regret rolling my eyes at her now.

Looking at Jack, I'm sure the aunts have something like that at home. "I'll take us to my aunts' house; I actually have something for broken noses."

Jack drops the keys into my open hand. "It just needs to be set. We have a family physician on call."

I shake my head at him while walking around to the driver's side. He climbs into the passenger's seat, carefully closing the door with an almost fearful hesitation. "I promise you won't regret it. My mother's a nurse. I have supplies that will help."

Jack eases his chair back. His nose no longer dripping. The dark blood crusts around his mouth and chin, making a scabbing goat-tee.

I slowly back out of the driveway and pull through the gate.

*"Forgetting something?"*

*Ugh! How badly do you need your tail?*

*"I will claw apart the immaculate interior of this vehicle until it's returned to me."*

I growl.

"Everything okay?" Jack asks thoughtfully.

I tightly grip his thin steering wheel. "Yeah, I have to make a quick stop. I left something in Nick's truck." I stop just outside Poppy's driveway. "I'll be fast." I leave his car running and dash off into the dark where Nick's truck is parked. I climb and tumble into the truck bed, falling on something soft and padded. I feel fur under my palm. I squint in the dark. The fur is thick, white, and rounded like a wreath. I frown, perplexed. I grapple for my cell out of my back pocket and flick the flashlight on. The white fur is attached to a puffy turquoise coat. Trixie's coat. *Why the hell is this here?*

I gaze back up at the illuminated house, crudely displaying the partiers behind the glass like a specimen in a zoo. The bartender is no longer at his post, the DJ nodding his head idly to a slower beat. *Could Trixie be up there? But why would her coat be here?* There could be a chance this isn't even her coat; this is hardly a one-of-a-kind parka.

I dig through the pockets, hoping to find some kind of identification. I pull out loose daisy petals, cinnamon bark, and a teaspoon. I smile despite myself. This has to be hers. But how did it end up in Nick's truck? I peer back up at the house, thinking of my new schoolmates there. They all universally avoid Trixie. She said she planned on training tonight. *They must have taken her coat in a prank. Jerks.*

I tuck her parka under my arm and search for Blue's tail. I flash my light around and fumble over lacrosse sticks until I find a long, skinny black tail curled in a U. I snatch it and take off running.

"Forgot your coat?" Jack questions, his nose completely congested, giving him a muted nasal sound.

I wedge Trixie's coat and the tail between our seats. "Yeah. How's your nose?" I ask. I type my aunts' address into my phone.

"In 500 feet, use the far-right lane..." The GPS voice orders.

Jack closes his eyes. "It's numb, so it's my head that hurts now."

I think back on that spark, the flame that was fanned inside me. *Did my frustration cause it?*

*"You need to mind your emotions until you are in full control of your powers, or his nose won't be the only thing of his you break."*

"Jack, I'm really sorry about the door," I whisper repentantly, cutting off Blue-Eyes's voice in my head.

"It wasn't your fault. It was mine. The interior sticks and I've been needing to replace the latch for a while," he says.

I coast to a stop at the light. "How did you break your nose those other times?" I question.

"Once in boxing and once doing BJJ. Hazards of the trade," he jokes.

I flick the blinker. "BJJ?"

"Brazilian Ju Jitsu. I actually prefer it to boxing, but Allen boxed in high school and college, so did my brother Marshall. They're both college champions. Allen is very proud of that. My preferences are secondary to the family legacy," Jack murmurs dryly. "Besides," he says, mimicking him, "it's the poor man's fighting. There's no dignity in it."

I roll my lips in between my teeth, picturing him in those little shorts, red boxing gloves and tightened, sweat gleaming muscles. Blue hisses in my head, causing me to swerve a little on the road which wakes me from my daydream.

"Allen? I take it that's your dad?" I question. I pull up to the last intersection before I veer towards the woods where my aunts live.

"Yep, that's Dad."

"You call your dad *Allen*?" I ask mildly, wondering if I should even pull at that thread.

"Yeah, I think he prefers it that way," Jack explains. "Some see 'dad' as a title of honor, and some, like Allen, see it as a sinking anchor to one's pride."

I give Jack a glum smile. He seemed to turn dark at the thought of his father. It turns out that everyone's got "daddy issues". Mine comes with a coffin and Jack's came with boxing gloves.

"Box, crew, busy guy, do you do anything for fun?" I ask, peeking over at his bloodied face.

He weakly opens his eyes; they're beginning to swell. He glances over at me before shutting his lids once again. "I like to paint."

"Paint, like houses?" I crack.

He pulls the corner of his mouth in a crooked half smile. "Abstract, mostly. I've done some mixed media. I was mentioned in *Art Forum* last spring. They featured an oil abstract I created back that Christmas. Being a successful artist is a long shot, but I can't live with a "what if". I've got to at least try." He sounds like he's rehearsed that line a thousand times, probably only repeating it to himself.

My eyebrows leap up my face. I glance over at him, reclined as far back as he can be in his classic Mustang. His wool coat gapes open, blood stains the lapels. His chiseled jaw slacks, drawing breath from his parted lips. I grin, turning back to the road. His gorgeous features camouflage the hidden depths, calling out my prejudice against a dazzling smile and paragon eyes. "Jack, that's amazing. Seriously, that's a big deal."

Jack frowns to himself. "I haven't told anyone that yet. It happened almost a year ago," he says in an almost confused whisper.

The quiet hum of the engine is a white noise against the serene silence. It's a comfortable silence that neither of us feels the need to break. The effortlessness of his company feels foreign, yet right. I nearly reach over to grip his hand, but I resist just as the judgmental sounds of the GPS lady punch through the quiet.

"In a thousand feet, you'll arrive at your destination."

*"Thank Brighid, I need to get out of here."*

The tires kick up pebbles on the driveway that ding against the wheel well. I unintentionally stop a few yards from the dead oak. "Sorry," I apologize for the abrupt stop. I pull his keys from the ignition, placing them on his thigh. "Well, this is my aunts' house. Um, come on in, you can wash up and I've got stuff for your nose."

I peer up at the house. The second story is dark, including the tower. I must have beaten them home. *Do I need to leave the door open for you?*

*"Just get him out of the car. I can take care of it myself."*

The lawn appears silver in the light of the moon. I climb up the porch steps sheathed in shadow, then hesitate under the awning. *Is there a ghost inside? I couldn't have imagined talking to my dad. Is he still here?*

*"No, he is not inside."*

*How about you wait till I address you before butting into my thoughts?*

I wince, praying the front door isn't locked. The antique brass knob turns when I twist it. I'm flooded with relief when I push it open. I spin around, noticing Jack is rooted in his place, gazing up at my aunts' estate.

"Are you coming?" I ask.

He raises a skeptical brow. "You... live *here*?" Dried blood flakes off when he speaks.

I fold my arms across my chest. "Temporarily, until my mom finds us a new place."

His face holds a look of disbelief as his eyes survey the Victorian haunted house I currently call home. There is something on his mind. *Does he know my aunts? Does he know about my family's secret? I wish I knew what he was thinking.*

He scrunches his face as he delicately touches his nose. "Okay, what do you have for me, O'Reilly," he teases as he strides up the porch steps towards me.

I flick on the lights. "Everyone's out. I'm not sure when they're getting back," I say, feeling like I'm giving him a warning.

Jack's eyes drift about, taking in the house. "So, we're alone…?"

My heart flutters.

He meanders into the living room, and his smile grows when he sees the dangling chandelier and the rubber spider tied there. He studies the mismatched furniture, the bizarre photographs framed on the wall, and then the cats that come creeping out of the crevices. *Why couldn't the aunts have taken all the cats?*

I wave over to the velvet chaise in the corner. "Why don't you take a seat? I'll go grab the stuff."

"Mind if I wash up?" he asks, pointing to his blood-stained face.

I blush. "Of course, bathroom is the second door on the right," I say, pointing next to the bookshelves in the hall. Then I remember, I've never used that bathroom. My stomach lurches. *What could my aunts have in there?* "Here I'll show you." I rush down the hall and swing the door open. Relief spills over my senses. It's a completely *normal* bathroom.

Jack sidesteps around me. "I'm sure I could have found it." He gives me an amused smile before closing the door.

I throw open all the glass cupboards looking for some kind of first aid kit. I find a black plastic box with a white cross encased in a red circle. *Bingo.* I pull it down to the counter and pop it open. Inside is a half empty bottle of whiskey marked with a post it note reading: break glass in case of emergencies. I shove it back where I found it. I find mason jars of uncut oats, dried leaves, twigs, and other indecipherable items.

Blue-Eyes springs onto the wooden island in the middle of the kitchen. *"Cupboard above the sink, fetch the dried parsley. Your aunts have the ingredients, but you'll need to assemble."*

For Jack's sake, I do as the cat bids and search for the jar of parsley. Luckily, Marie has labeled the jars in this cupboard. I pull out the cylinder labeled Parsley. There's only a small amount left at the bottom, dried and curled. I frown, examining it. "Is this enough?"

Blue nods his head once. "*Now coconut oil, arnica, comfrey…*"

*Slow down!* I pull down a vial filled with oil, but I don't see anything labeled as arnica or comfrey.

"*That jar to your left, with the yellow petals. That's arnica. The purple flowers on the third shelf are comfrey. The bottom shelf has jarred rue.*" Blue-Eyes watches me carefully. "*In the drawer where they keep the silverware, they have twine and eucalyptus leaves.*

I follow each of Blue-Eyes's instructions. Taking the arnica, comfrey, rue, and parsley, I wrap the eucalyptus leaves around the petals and herbs, tie it with twine and oil the leaves with the coconut oil. The leafy pads are about the size of exceptionally large pills.

I feel silly for what I'm about to do, but I know it will work and I must admit it, Jack has a nose worth saving. He can tease me all he wants if it means fixing his nose…that I broke.

*And this will work?*

"*Marie blesses everything before she jars them. It'll work. Ease one into each nostril, then push up. They shouldn't be visible once inside the nasal cavity.*"

The bathroom door creaks open. I can hear him head back down to the living room.

I place the remedy in my palm, take in a nervous breath, and meet him in the living room. He's perched on the chaise I had originally recommended.

He rises to his feet when I enter the room. His face is blood free, but his nose is swollen and bent slightly to the right.

Our knees bump into each other as we take our seats. I stare at my feet, unable to meet his gaze so close. Breathing suddenly feels uneasy, as if I can feel the house reacting to this unfamiliar presence, this stranger that looks so foreign, shiny, and new in this old relic. I can feel the room stretch and yawn around us, settling in for a new show. One quite different from the one they witnessed earlier in the evening.

I can feel him turn, like a lighthouse beam rotating away, glancing about the room. "My mother would be impressed with the crown molding," he says politely. "And is that an actual gramophone?"

I roll the leaves about on my palm. "Yeah, would you like to listen to something?"

Jack shrugs, still examining his surroundings. "Do your cats have names?" he asks, motioning towards the lurking felines.

I roll my eyes, disarmed. "They're not mine." I glance down at the herbs. *Do I surprise him? I feel like if I tell him he'll fight me on it.*

The cats find spots on the opposing loveseat, armchair, and windowsill to lounge and stare, putting my teeth on edge.

Crescent shadows are blooming under each eye. I adjust, ready to pounce, when Jack turns to me. "So, you have an older brother Marshall, then sister Honor…anyone else?" I prod, buying myself some time.

"Just me. Marshall just finished his last year at Yale Law and my sister Honor is a junior at Harvard."

I sit up a little taller. "Yeah, Shannyn is attending Harvard. Art history," I say. My heart sinks. "You guys will probably have a lot to talk about." The moment Jack looks into her doe eyes, I'll be a distant memory. *Thank goodness she's loyal to Lennox.*

"Probably more to discuss with Honor than me. Are you the youngest in your family, then?" he asks, moving a few inches closer to me.

Blue peeks his head around the corner.

"No, I have a younger sister, Margaret. She's at St. Prudence, or whatever it's called. She's in middle school, but she'll be at Griggs next year." My heart pounds in my chest, the remedy turning clammy in my moist hand. "Lay back," I say, placing my hands on his chest, easing him back.

He hesitates, then slowly reclines. His body is still, and his lids fall closed, like we're about to practice a scene from Romeo and Juliet.

I can't help but stop and admire him. With his eyes closed, I notice how long his eyelashes are and how full his lips…

"*Stop!*"

Blue-Eyes' mental intrusion makes me jump a little.

"Are you going to suggest icing it now, doctor?" he teases, eyes still closed and in a prone position. Even with his swollen nose, he is still impossibly handsome, painfully so.

Hic. "I'm going to touch your nose, delicately, I promise." After a brief hesitation, I glide the herbs into his nasal passages, trying my hardest to be gentle. The tips of my thumbs slide up into his nostrils until I feel resistance.

Jack calls out in pain as his sinuses water. "What in the world are you doing?" Jack springs to his feet, furiously plucking at the herbs. He winces and wiggles his nose about trying to dislodge them.

I struggle with his hands, trying to pull them away from his nose. "I know it sounds weird," I strain to keep his arms down, "but I promise it'll work!" I insist.

He exhales loudly through his mouth.

I hold his strong jaw in my hands. "Leave them in overnight. I know it seems really strange, but I promise by morning you'll feel better. Trust me," I say, internally cringing at myself.

His face relaxes at my touch.

I withdraw my hands and retreat a few steps back.

He releases another uneasy breath. "Eleanor," he says, in a congested voice.

I bite against a budding smile. I stare down at my toes, scrunching them against the carpet. I feel him draw closer. He reaches for my hands dangling at my sides. I can't look up. My stomach wobbles like a bent bicycle wheel, and I can feel a hiccup forming in my chest.

Gravel crunches against tires on the driveway. The house rumbles and groans as the garage door moans open. I pull out my phone and glance at the time: half-past twelve.

"Your mom?" Jack asks, hearing my family arrive. He drops his hands and takes a respectful step back. He has an air of confidence and ease at the prospect of meeting my parent.

I shake my head. "Nope, that would be my aunts and my sister. My mom is back in Florida for a few days." I'm dreading my aunts' boisterous entrance. "And I'm sorry."

Jack frowns at my apology.

*"You should have shoved him out the back door of the kitchen."*

Marie is yelling for the cats to pile out the van, Sally and Maggie are chattering away.

I sigh, too enervated to race him out of the room.

Margaret pushes open the garage door and a clowder of cats, now free of visors and vests, dart around her into the house. "Hey…" She says, strolling into the living room. An amused smile forms on her impish face.

"Oh, Eleanor!" Sally sings, stumbling into the house, still dressed like a soccer mom from the 80's. Her Persian cat, Pyre, dashes into the room and hides under the sofa.

I peer over at Jack, who appears intrigued.

Sally trips into Margaret, leaning on her for support. "Well, who do we have here?" She straightens up and adjusts her boobs under her screen-printed shirt.

Maggie chuckles, watching her. "Sally took us to a karaoke bar up in Boston after try outs. They have a drink there named after her. She may have had a few."

Sally advances towards Jack.

I shoot Margaret a look. "Please tell me Marie drove, sober.".

Maggie nods. "Part of the way. Once we got into town, they let me drive."

"Great, you don't even have a permit," I argue under my breath.

Maggie rolls her eyes at me.

Jack extends his hand out to my inebriated aunt. "I'm Jack Woods. I attend William Griggs with your niece." His G's are pronounced heavy from the broken nose.

"Enchante," Sally slurs in a terrible accent. She places her ring clad hand on his to be kissed.

Jack hesitates, glancing over at me, apprehensive if he should oblige her.

Marie thankfully comes barreling into the room, interrupting Sally's advances and giving Jack an out. "Eleanor Elizabeth O'Reilly! Were you contacting the dead while we were out?" Her hands grip her curvy hips. She stops and her face falls when she notices Jack extricating himself from Sally shimming into his side. "Oh, you have company."

I squeeze my eyes shut and cringe. *I'm going to die. I'm going to die. I'm going to die.*

*"I would stop repeating that if I were you."*

I feel my temperature rising. *I need to get him out of here.* Jack is greatly entertained, soaking everything in.

Sally places her head on his shoulder. "This is Jack, Eleanor's *friend…*" She bats her eyes at him.

Marie smiles sweetly at him. "I'm her Aunt Marie," she says, crossing the living room toward us. She swings out her hand, shaking his. My aunt stops giggling at the handsome stranger and scrunches her face in a befuddled frown. "Is there something wrong with your face, dearie?"

Sally scoffs at her sister. "Are you kidding? This mug is perfection." She snatches his chin and turns his head a hundred and eighty degrees towards her.

"No Sal, look. Something is off." Marie motions to his face. Her confused expression falls into horror. "Oh goodness, is that blood? Yes, that's blood. That's a lot of blood!" Marie grips the lapels of his wool coat, her head whips over to me. "Eleanor, is this your doing? Did you make him bleed?"

Sally hangs off him, her spikey hair brushing against his cheek. "Was someone getting fresh? Eleanor can be such a prude."

Jack blanches. "No, it was nothing like that. It was an unfortunate accident with a car door," he insists politely.

Marie looks at me, stricken. *You?* She mouths.

"And now he needs to go," I announce, snatching Jack's hand and forcefully pulling him to the door.

Jack hops over several cats, waving back to my family. "It was nice to meet you all!"

I slam the door behind us and lean against it, as if barring anyone from following. "I'm really sorry about them. They don't get out much," I repentantly joke. I fold my arms across my chest at the noticeable nip in the air.

Jack shoves his hands into his coat pockets, laughing. "They seemed... nice. Friendly," he says, his eyes drifting from my face over to the living room window and waves to somebody behind me.

I swivel to see the aunts and the cats staring from the window.

"Do you often communicate with the dead?" he says, wiggling his fingers at me. "You live in Salem now. They have plenty of ghost tours if you're into that sort of thing."

I exhale, wincing against the door. "No, it was a stupid inside joke. Dead dad sort of thing," I lie, gazing over at the withered tree.

Jack grimaces. "That's awful. I'm really sorry. There are "too soon" jokes and then there's that."

I wave it away, wondering if I've gone too far. I push off the door. "No, it's fine. They mean well. Tragedy, comedy, they run a fine line here."

The porch light flashes on, drenching us in white light.

Jack dabs the side of his nose and smiles. "I better get going, um, thanks for your help."

My stupid heart skips a beat. "My pleasure."

He grins. "I bet it was."

I narrow my eyes, a smile of my own forming. "And don't take any of that stuff out of your nose. Sleep with it in. And I'll know if you took it out," I caution cryptically.

He chuckles, striding down the porch steps. "I promise," he calls. "Good night, Eleanor." He slides into the driver's seat.

I sigh, watching him pull out of the driveway and down the road, leaving a dust cloud behind him. I close my eyes and rest against the front door. Jack Woods. I smile quietly to myself before drifting back into the house.

# Chapter Fifteen
## La Caeli

My aunts stand guard at the door when I walk back into the house.

"He's yummy," Sally says, smacking me in the arm.

Marie links arms with me. "Pumpkin, we need to know. Is that Jack Woodland kid hurt because of you?"

The three of us fall back onto the couch, causing cats to hiss and squirrel out from under us. Margaret is lounging in an armchair with Phoenix purring contently in her lap.

Marie pats my knee affectionately. "Sweetie, I thought you were irresponsibly communing with the spirit world," she says, as if that's the most normal thing to ask in the world.

Maggie turns her head, waiting for an answer.

I shake my head, unsure if I'm ready to answer them honestly. I look to my sister who is listening curiously. I can't tell them, especially with Margaret in the room. "Ah yeah, it didn't quite work out."

Marie nods. "Good. What Sally advised you to do was not only foolish, but reckless."

Sally groans. "Ugh, enough. Tell me about the boy!"

I lay my head back on the sofa, looking up at the shimmering chandelier. "We were just hanging out," I say sheepishly.

Marie adjusts in her seat to get a better look at me. "And he got into a fight with a door?"

My stomach twists. "I don't know. I couldn't get it open, but I wanted it to open and it kind of flung open and smacked him in the face. But I think I fixed it." I close my eyes, exhausted. If I was being honest with myself, I had hoped my night would have ended in erupting fireworks with a cinematic kiss. But no, it ended in a fashion more akin to my current lifestyle: blood, embarrassment, and felines.

Sally and Marie exchange indecipherable glances.

I heave myself up from the couch. "Well. I'm going to call it a night. Oh um, do you have a needle and thread?"

Marie scoops up her chubby white cat, holding it under her chin while she tickles its small ears. "What color, sweets?"

I peer over at Blue sitting on top of the stairs. "I need black."

Marie rummages through a drawer in her sewing room, which was just an annex off the kitchen with half-finished quilts piled in the corner, needle point hoops hanging off the walls, and boxes upon boxes of various button collections.

Blue knowingly follows me up to the tower.

I place a record down and lift the needle. Stevie Nicks cries out, *wait a minute baby, stay with me awhile...*

"Do you have your tail?" I ask aloud, holding the needle and thread, feeling Blue-Eyes silently slink in behind me. I sit down cross-legged on the bed. Blue hops up, circles, and finds the right spot to sit in front of me.

"*I think we should seek your aunts' assistance; I hear you musing about using glue...*"

I roll my eyes. *If you don't like what you hear, stop listening. I know how to sew.*

I thread the needle and adjust the cat. His fur is rough and matted, but the skin beneath is thin, malleable to my needle.

"*You did well tonight, fixing his nose,*" Blue says. "*Perhaps training you won't be a completely unachievable feat.*"

I sigh. He just couldn't help but tack on some snide remark. I tug the thread, pulling it taut. "Please tell me you're not the one training me."

"*Of course not. I was merely observing on behalf of your aunts. When you aren't whining, you follow directions well.*"

I hold the needle aloft. "You do realize I'm sewing your tail on, right?"

"*Yes, against my better judgement. Please make sure it isn't crooked.*"

I release a growl and continue dipping the needle into the fur, piercing the skin and pulling.

Blue-Eyes's ears twitch, his head turns. "*Don't be honest. For her sake.*"

*What are you talking about?*

There's a knock at the door and Margaret pops her head in. "Hey, got a minute?"

I wave her in. "Of course."

Her coppery locks drip down the shoulders of her terry-cloth robe. She cocks her brow as she comes in and claims the corner of my bed. "Really?" She motions to Blue-Eyes.

I roll my eyes with a shrug. "Apparently, he's my cat. Turns out we don't get to pick our familiars, they pick us."

"*Hardly! We're celestially assigned.*"

Margaret reaches forward, tickling his forehead. "He's cute, in a broken sort of way."

I give his tail a little pull, feeling where any loose stitching might be. There's none to be found. It's an impressively tight seal. "So, what's up? How were try outs?"

She looks down, playing with the belt of her robe. "Fine, I've been recruited to three different private schools. The rep from William Griggs wanted to make sure I was coming next year for her team. But that's actually not why I came in here," she says, her tone turning serious.

I flick my eyes to her, then back to the task at hand. I finish on the last stich, tug, and tie off the thread. "What's going on?"

"Did you try to reach Dad?" she questions, bending her head to force my eyeline.

My heart picks up the tempo. "Yeah."

"Did he answer back?" she leans against the canopy post, bracing herself. "*Lie.*"

I stare down at the comforter and pick at a loose thread. "No."

"You're lying," Margaret quips.

I shake my head, daring to look at her. Her green eyes are welled up with thick, globby tears that spill over her freckled cheeks. She swipes her nose on her thick cuff.

"*Lie better.*"

My heart skips a beat and sinks, tumbling into the pit of my stomach and drowning in guilt. "He said there was a way to bring him back."

Margaret scoots closer, sniffs, and brushes away the flowing tears. "What do you mean? Like he can be with us again? How, how?"

"*You went in the other direction with that one. Why do I bother?*" Blue hisses at me and leaps down from the bed.

I ignore him. "We were interrupted. I want to contact him again with the aunts' help this time."

Margaret shook her head, staring at me pleadingly. "No, Eleanor, Marie was fricken pissed with Sally that she encouraged you to seek spirits out. They can't know. They won't help." She grips my hands, and I notice her fingernails have been nibbled down to nubs from anxiety. "I heard them on the way home tonight. They plan on starting your training tomorrow—err, today. What if afterward we got the aunts out of the house and we tried again?"

"*No, out of the question.*"

*Butt out, this is between my sister and me.*

"*No, you're my charge now. Forget it.*"

"Tomorrow night," I agree.

Margaret gives me a teary, optimistic smile and pulls me into a hug. "Thank you. We're gonna get Dad back. Oh my gosh. Our family will be complete again." Her body trembles in my arms.

*"I will take no pleasure in your failure. You have done your sister a disservice. I'm disappointed in you, Eleanor."* With his newly attached tail, Blue stalks off from the bedroom.

Margaret releases me, her face all puffy and red from crying. She runs her fingers under her eyes. "Okay, now that's done. Tell me about Jack. Did you seriously break his nose?"

We fall into a pile of giggles, just like we used to. Curled up on my bed, we gossip about school, magic, boys, and Salem. Throughout the discussion, Blue-Eyes's words haunt me, making me doubt the possibility of bringing my dad back. I drown him out, focusing on the present with Maggie, laughing so hard she snorts.

By 3:00 a.m., we are drifting to sleep buried under layers of protective blankets. It felt so natural, so right, talking and whispering like we used to before the accident.

***

"Okay Eleanor, let's get a move on it!" Sally shouts while she swats my backside. Margaret moans and rolls out of my bed, declaring she's getting more sleep in her room.

I lift my head off my pillow and glance at my phone on the nightstand.

I want to cry. "Are you crazy? It's six in the morning!" I whine and shove my head under my pillow, which Sally rips out of my grasp. "Maggie and I only went to bed a few hours ago."

In response, Sally levitates the pillow and sends it sailing to the other side of the room. She points her left first finger at the window, making the curtains pull back and the window slide open.

"There's tea simmering in the kitchen for you." She then strips away my bedding, leaving me in a clenched ball, shivering in the middle of my bed. "Be downstairs in ten minutes or trust me, you don't want to see what will happen if I have to come back up here." She wears a wicked smile across her face. "And wear black," she adds. She wiggles her brows and giggles to herself before heading back down the stairs.

I groan, dragging myself out of bed. Fighting against a yawn, I throw my hair up in a loose bun, toss on a holey Led Zeppelin tee that used to belong to my dad and some leggings before trudging downstairs. I pat my cheeks, trying to wake myself up.

Just as they had instructed me, the aunts are both clad in black. Sally is dressed to kill in a sleek black leather skirt and thin black sleeveless sweater while Marie is bundled up in a thick ebony cable knit turtleneck with velvet trousers in the deepest shade of onyx. They're both huddled around the dining room table, fenced in by old leather books and candles. They whisper to each other over their steaming tea in delicate floral porcelain. When I enter the room, they both straighten up in their seats, appearing alert.

Marie smiles sweetly at me. Her typically untamable, frizzy reddish grey hair is pulled back with an antique butterfly clip. Her hazel eyes follow a chinoiserie teacup and saucer floating towards me from the kitchen.

I pluck it from the air, feeling the strange transformation from weightless to weight in my hands. A small silver teaspoon zips over with some honey, dunking it into my cup without a hint of a splash.

The chair in front of me at the table pulls itself out for me. I swallow. "Thanks," I say, hesitantly taking my seat. As I sit down, the chair lunges forward, halting at the table's edge.

"Drink up, dearie. We need you awake and ready. Plus, it'll take care of those dark circles under your eyes." Marie then dumps a spoonful of sugar into her cup.

I peek into the cup. *What could be in here?* The amber tea with sinking leaves looks perfectly average. "Well, bottoms up," I say, lifting the delicate cup to my lips. The liquid is only a few degrees warmer than room temperature. It first tastes like peppermint and lemon, and then strongly of Red Vine Licorice. "Interesting tea," I murmur, smacking my lips with mango aftertaste.

My head feels airy, like it might float away. I take a stabilizing breath. A muted popping sensation begins in the center of my being before waving out to my limbs, as if I've got bubble wrap under my skin, jolting every pore and molecule in my body awake with a subtle pop. Unlike the jittery feeling of coffee, I feel roused from a perfectly restful slumber with summer sunshine beaming from the inside out. My eyes flutter. "Whoa ..."

Sally chuckles. "I made mine a double with an Irish splash." Her floating teacup tips at me in a friendly fashion before drifting into her open hands.

Marie glances around. "Where is Blue-Eyes? He should be here for this."

Sally rolls her eyes and recrosses her legs, bumping the table. "That little scamp ran off. He refused to cooperate," she replies curtly before slurping her last sip.

I gaze down at the swirling wood grains of the table, ruminating about his judgmental look last night and his disappointment in my decision to be honest with Margaret. *Ugh, a cat is dissatisfied with me. How did I get here?*

Sally drums her long crimson nails on the table. "Eleanor," she begins, her cherry painted lips pulled back in a devilish grin, "we'll be instructing you on your first branch of magic today. You'll use it every day and it's the easiest to master—well, for the most part," she amends with a little giggle. Every object in the room—candles, books, a glass bottle of bourbon—floats in the air before rotating around us like a carousel. Candles bob, books twirl, and the bourbon pours itself into my aunts' empty cups before settling back down to their original spots.

Marie stabs her sister with a sharp glare. "Sally, we're trying to teach her, not show off!" Her face folds into soft crinkles as she turns to me. "Sweetie, before we harness the air, we must first learn where this power comes from."

Sally pretends to snore. But Marie plows on. "Being a witch isn't a choice. It's a heritage, a destiny passed down from generation to generation. Although you can find covens all over the world, ours hail from the Celts and Druids. But we all come from the same source."

I polish off my tea, no longer experiencing the previous sensation to the same degree. "So, did our ancestors worship Satan, Gaia? What?" I prod, not quite sure if I want to know the answer. My father was raised Catholic, and we were far from devout — we typically only attended mass on the important holidays.

Marie opens a dusty leather tome, thumbing through the yellowed and crinkled pages. She stops somewhere near the middle and slides the book over. In the center of the page is a painting of a maiden with long kinky curls sitting under a fig tree. She's wearing a delicate Grecian dress in a pale ivory with a lamb on her lap and a cat curled next to the roots of the tree. "We call her Brighid. But she is known by various names by different covens from all corners of the world. She is our creator, forming us from celestial dust. She was tasked with creating guardians of the Sons and Daughters."

I raise a brow. "Okay, so we aren't...*human?* And who are the Sons and Daughters? They sound like a cult." *I wish my mom was here.*

Sally exhales, bored. "No, we aren't human. We're witches. Our celestial purpose is to bring enlightenment to non-witches and fight against dark forces that seek to destroy the sons and daughters of the creator of the world," Sally says mockingly dramatic, with wiggling fingers.

My stomach churns and my mind reels. I battle the urge to argue with my aunts. Despite wanting to shout how wrong they are. "Okay, so there is a God. Everyone who isn't a witch is a son or daughter of God, and witches are a different breed entirely. So are witches, like...angels then?"

Marie shrugs her shoulder. "We've been known by that, angels, guardians.

But that's why we wear black when we train. We honor the dark cosmic material whence we came."

"Plus we look bitch'n," Sally interjects, pulling her sweater down slightly.

Marie clears her throat, calling back my attention. "There are five branches of magic," Marie says, opening a new book, pointing to the pentagram. "They all have a single incantation which allows us harness it to our will. Today we will work on just one." Marie's thick finger points to the west point of the star, "air."

"You see, we never move the object," Sally says. "It's the surrounding air we control. The current, the flow, it allows us to levitate." She pauses, forcing a book to fly up from the table in a figure eight. "If we wanted to, we could create a tornado, shape mountains, wear down valleys. When harnessed, we can create a wind that could change the world."

Marie practically stutters trying to butt in. "B-B-but we try not to affect the weather, we try to keep a balance in nature," she informs sharply. "Besides," she looks at her sister drolly, "the average witch couldn't do that. You would need to have a gift with air or an entire coven of witches assisting. But again, Eleanor, we don't do anything destructive like that. It goes against our code."

With my elbows on the table, I hold the sides of my head. "Code?" I question, struggling to keep up.

Marie opens her mouth, but Sally quickly interrupts. "For heaven's sakes, we can go over all the boring stuff later. Eleanor, don't do anything that could cause the sons or daughters harm. Done. Moving on." Sally then smiles deliciously. "Now, to control the surrounding air, you must call to it. For that to happen, you say this," Sally slides a different book in front of me. Beneath the chapter titled "Wind" is the handwritten word "Caeli". "It's pronounced see-lee. It means "air" in Latin. I don't know who in our line switched the incantation from Gaelic to Latin, but they did, and this was what was handed down."

Marie gives a dismissive wave of her hand, causing the books to all hop to attention and leap back onto their shelves. Candles dance and twirl back to their original positions. Sally's eyes slide to the swinging kitchen door. A simple glass of water comes floating in, landing gracefully in front of me.

Marie settles into her chair. "Okay, Eleanor sweetie, try to lift that glass of water." Marie motions to the small glass cup in the middle of the table.

I move my hand towards the cup.

"Stop!" an annoyed Sally blurts. "Use your powers, babe, seriously." She returns to drumming her nails against the tabletop, waiting.

"I don't know how," I counter in frustration. I cross my arms, wanting to quit.

"Eleanor, just focus on the glass." Marie's eyes narrow in on her target.

I shake off my agitation and blink several times before leveling my stare at the glass with as much concentration as I can muster. Once again, I feel that same sparkling electricity surge through my body from the pit of my stomach, just like it had last night with Jack's car door. It courses through me, sparking at the very tips of my fingers. I ignore the feeling and continue to stare at the cup. *Move, jump, dance, lift off the table, just do something, you stupid cup.* A spidery crack jolts down the side of the glass before it bursts, sending small shards jetting across the table and spraying the water everywhere. Hic. I leap out of my seat, backpedaling from the table.

Hic. "I'm s-s-sorry—" hic "—I'm so sorry! I'm done. I can't do this!" Hic. Panic grips me and my hands quake. Hic.

Marie shooed me back down to my seat. "Oh no, no, no, don't worry, sweetie. We were expecting much worse. We had to set you up to fail so you could identify the sensation without having any control over the element." Her eyes never leave my face while she mends the cup using her magic. Every shard comes back together. The water on the table evaporates. "Fire. I used heat to mend the cup and evaporate the water," Marie explains with a child-like grin.

"Fire is my domain, sister. You should stick to water," Sally says irritably while water slowly fills up the glass. "Now, did you feel that power surge within you?"

I hold my hands up to them. "Wait, pause. Why do you guys keep saying things like that? Am I only to use one branch of magic once I learn?"

Marie shakes her head. "Oh no, dearie. Once you are fully trained, you'll discover you have a certain proclivity towards a certain branch. I'm known as a water witch. I can accomplish things with water that typically would take nearly an entire coven. Sally excels with fire. But like you just saw me using the fire spell, you can use all five elements, but you'll find you have a particular strength. All witches do."

I pick at my thumbnail, mulling all this over. "What about my mom?"

Marie reaches across the table for me but can't quite get there. Trying to be amiable, I extend my hand, allowing her to give it a gentle squeeze. "Earth. Your mother's potions are more potent and powerful than any witch I've ever met."

Sally places her hand on top of ours, her rings sparkling in the light. "Our baby sis is the most powerful witch in the family, and I say that with no reluctance," she pauses, "well anymore."

Feeling a little silly, I retract my hand and my aunts follow suit.

"Now, did you feel that little spark, almost like something is electric deep inside you?" Sally asks.

I nod.

Sally smiles. "That little power surge was your magic trying to figure out what you wanted. There is a way to control that, to either push it down or harness it." Sally pushes the cup a little closer to me.

"Now say "La Caeli", in your mind, not aloud. But before you say it, visualize the cup coming towards you," Marie instructs intensely. "Show your magic what you want."

I nod once more, too nervous to actually speak.

I let out a slow breath of air, my eyes focusing on the glass. That electric sparking begins. I imagine the glass slowly lifting off the table and delicately levitating over to me. *La Caeli,* I whisper in my head. The glass wobbles, almost tipping over. I narrow my eyes, determined not to fail. The cup lifts a smidge before going back down. It lifts again and moves only a few inches towards me. The glass shutters, nearly tipping over as it rests back down on the tabletop. I grin to myself. *I've got this.* I picture the glass sliding over to me on the table, deciding not to risk spilling by having it float. *La Caeli.* I hold my hands out on the table, and just as if someone had slid a milkshake down a diner's counter, the glass comes sliding to me with ease.

The electric feel ceases. The task is complete.

My grin breaks ever wider across my face, and I lift the glass triumphantly. "Did you see that!? I did it! I made that glass move!" I take a gulp from the glass. I scrunch my nose as the water tastes like how the house smells, stale with a thousand different incense flavors.

My aunts smile at each other and back at me.

The cup refills to the very lip of the glass. Most likely from Marie.

I put my elbows on the table, ready to continue. "So now do we work on fire? Water? What else?" I ask, feeling strangely powerful, like I can conquer the world.

Sally snorts as Marie gazes at me sympathetically.

"Oh no, dearie. We aren't done with air yet, and that's all we'll do for the day. Anyway, my darling, when you feel that electric pulse inside you, that surge of magic flowing freely in your veins, you can turn it off and not use your magic. This is very important to learn right now while you are still developing your power."

Sally leans forward, interrupting her sister. "That happens to even experienced witches. When there are so many massholes on the road, we want to make their car explode for cutting us off. We need to turn off our magic before that happens," she says, cracking her knobby knuckles. "When I was first training, I imagined my magic as a light switch, when I'd feel my magic wanting to control the situation before I was ready, I would just picture myself flipping the switch," Sally explains with an encouraging smile.

Marie looks at her sister in surprise. "That is the best advice you've ever given to anybody," she states, impressed at her sister's suggestion.

Sally scoffs, crossing her arms. "Hardly. Who do you think gave Stevie Nicks her first shawl?"

Marie ignores her sister. "Okay, Eleanor, just do that. Imagine that magic light switch inside you." She pushes the glass of water closer to me. "Eleanor darling, now think about going for the glass. Tell yourself in your mind that you want to lift that glass and when you feel your magic wanting to serve you, imagine a pulsating magic switch and flip it, okay?" Marie instructs.

Sally frowns. "Ugh, why is it pulsating?"

"You can do it," Marie concludes, elbowing her sister in the ribs.

I take a deep breath, feeling pathetically foolish for having to focus on my simply picking up a water glass. *I'm going to pick up the glass. I want to lift the glass of water.* Apprehensively, I reach for the cup. I can feel the pressure inside me, the tiniest little spark firing. The glass begins to shake and shiver. I withdraw my hand. I was so close to lifting it, but my magic was about to do that for me. *Okay, I can do this. I've done this kind of task every day. Seriously, I should be able to do this.* I move for the glass again and, of course, the pressure and electric sparks begin as well. I picture myself flicking off a light switch. The surging inside me continues to flow. I take another deep breath, my hand so close to the shaking glass. *Stop. You're my power. I control you.* The water cup stands still. I quickly seize the moment and grasped the glass in my eager fingers. Water trickles over the side onto my hand. My eyes fly to my aunts in victory.

"Okay, good job Ellie-pie, that's it for the day," Marie states. With a snap of her fingers, she clears the table and takes the cup from my hand.

I shake my head. "Wait, what are you talking about? I just got started!" I complain. I glance at the cup, my eyes gazing into the transparent glass, *La Caeli.* My power seizes the cup and smacks it back down on the table. I wince as it lands roughly and spilling the water. "Sorry," I mumble.

Marie admonishes me with a look that wouldn't scare a kitten. The water lifts in crystal clear droplets and falls into the hydrangea in the corner. The glass zips off to the kitchen. "Eleanor dearie, you are exhausted. You don't even know it yet. Your first day always takes a lot out of you, physically and mentally," Marie says pityingly while softly patting my shoulder.

I don't argue, instead I tacitly agree and quietly shuffle out of the room. I can hear the aunts snickering to each other as I run up the stairs, taking two by two. A cat shrieks as an unfortunate tail meets the bottom of my heel.

"Sorry!" I call over my shoulder as I slam the door before the horrifying cat could seek any kind of revenge. I plop down in the middle of my bed, my eyes scanning my room, looking for anything light that I can levitate. My head snaps to the left as my cell phone rings on my dresser across the room. *Perfect.* It's small and light. I carefully concentrate on my phone and say, *La Caeli* in my head. My eyes home in on my target. The cell phone quivers, then lifts off and floats towards me, dipping a few times. It suddenly feels as though I'm experiencing a brain freeze before spreading. My body aches, my muscles pulsate like I'd just run several miles. My cell phone drops to the floor.

I drag myself across my bed and hang over the side, straining for my phone. By the time my fingers grasp it, the ringing has ceased. My phone's screen flashes, showing I have a missed call from my mom.

With herculean effort, I roll over onto my back and rotate so my head can be on my pillows. I give up halfway, unable to keep adjusting. My sore limbs melt into the bed like quicksand. I wonder if Jack's nose is healed as my brain drifts away to unconsciousness.

# Chapter Sixteen
## Sacrifice

My eyes weakly open from a deep sleep. A gloomy shroud rests over the room given I slept the afternoon away until—I snatch my phone—'til 8:00 p.m. I yawn and stretch out across the bed, my clothes clinging to the slick sweat down my chest and back.

Maggie pops her head into the room. "Wet the bed or sweaty sleeper?" She's wearing washed-out high-waisted jeans and a Lululemon knock-off tank crop top, with her white sports bra barely visible underneath. She has the same gift Shannyn has, the ability to take any last season clearance item and turn it into runway-ready haute couture.

I tug at the shirt stuck to my skin. "I think it's exhaustion from training this morning." I slide out of bed and wiggle my toes until I feel ready to push onto the balls of my feet. My legs aren't as wobbly as I had expected them to be. I bend and straighten my knees, waking up my body. "So, what's up?"

Maggie gives me an incredulous stare. "Seriously? Hello? Remember, we kind of had big plans for tonight." She glances over her shoulder and decides to shut my bedroom door. "I think it's fate. I mean, I thought we were gonna have to orchestrate something, but Sally has a date tonight and Marie has a Committee meeting," she says in a hushed tone. She peers down at her hands, her fingers splayed out, and shakes her hands full of nerves. "We're supposed to contact Dad tonight. I can feel it. Everything is magically working out." Her sage green eyes glisten with hope.

I roll my lips in between my teeth, remembering the promise I made to her last night—err, this morning. I have no response. *Do I have what it takes to bring him back? What if we reach out and he doesn't answer?* There's still a part of me that feels this is too good to be true, that we can't just bring our dad back from the dead. I peer down at the crescent moon scar on my right kneecap. *If witches can bring him back, why hasn't our Mom tried? She may have given up witchcraft, for the most part, but she would still do everything in her power to bring him back, so why hasn't she?* I feel a terrible pang of guilt at realizing Blue-Eyes was right. I shouldn't have told her. My heart sinks.

Maggie places her hands on her defined hips, determined not to crumble with emotion. "Do you know everything we need?"

I shake my head, still staring down, avoiding her.

"Well, Marie hid the board, but luckily for us, she's terrible at hiding things. I found it under the sink. I already swiped it and placed it under the couch." Margaret moves towards the door, then stops when she notices I'm not following. "Come on, let's say goodbye and get started." She fiddles with the doorknob. She licks her lips, her bottom lip trembles.

Everything inside me breaks. I follow Margaret down the stairs and into the living room, and we both plop down on the sofa. Maggie unfolds her legs onto the coffee table, causing two cats to scatter. She casually flips through a trashy magazine advertising the latest pregnancy scandal of a cheating celebrity.

I nudge her foot with mine. "Are you pretending to read?"

Maggie rolls her eyes at me. "No, I'm actually reading. You might want to do something too, so you don't look so suspicious," she mumbles. Her eyes go to the size of saucers and her mouth falls open. "Oh my gosh, he's the father? But he's so old! Ew!"

"That 'ew' better not have been directed to me," Sally says sternly, carefully clomping down the stairs in platform heels, tight black jeans with shredded knees, and a strapless red lace corset.

Mag drops the magazine on her lap. "Aunt Sally, you look hot!"

Sally twirls for us when she reaches the entry. "Thank you. These are my lucky jeans, after all." She pats her thighs.

"Why do you even bother getting dressed at all?" Marie gripes, strolling in from the kitchen. As per usual, Marie is dressed more conservatively, still in her thick turtleneck from earlier, her erratic hair pulled up with a scarf. She crosses her arms and scowls at her sister.

Sally shrugs, pulling out a black fringed shawl with large embroidered red roses off the hook. "Because I see no point in getting arrested twice in one month."

"Do we know this victim?" Marie asks.

Sally gives her sister a quizzical look. "It's Hamlin Smith, from the post office."

Marie shakes her head, throwing her arms up in the air. "Great, there goes the mail arriving on time. Can't you date someone out of state?"

Sal wraps the fringed shawl around her thin shoulders. "You know I don't limit myself to state lines. But what is wrong with you? Why are you being such a witch bitch?"

Maggie snorts, a giggle next to me.

Marie stomps to the coat rack and snatches a wool poncho. She glances wearily in our direction, then steps closer to Sally and whispers, "Ennis Goode is missing." Her voice is so low I can just barely hear it.

Sally frowns, then speaks behind a bejeweled hand. "He's that tasty senior at Salem State, right?"

Marie glares at her. "Fanny, Doris, and now Ennis. I have to go." She turns to us. "I'm so sorry, my sweets. There's a drawer of takeout menus in the kitchen." Marie then digs through her quilted purse and floats a few bills over to the table. "If you want to watch television, we keep it on a cart in the closet. Just wheel it out."

"Don't wait up!" Sally says with a devilish wink before leaving.

Marie continues. "'I won't be out too late." Marie blows us kisses then shleps her voluptuous cat out the door. The lock on the front door flips, the chain lock pulls itself across.

Maggie grins. "I'll never get used to that." She slides onto her knees and reaches deep under the couch. Newton and Persephone sprint out from under it. Maggie tugs out the Ouija board and arranges it on the table. She takes a deep breath, holding onto the table as her eyes search the board. "Okay, so what do we need to do?"

I suck in my cheeks, thinking. Part of me wishes we could just watch TV instead. I don't know why. I'd give anything to get Dad back, but there's something…off about this. There's a current of hesitation inside me, recognizing that this all came too easy. *I mean, reaching out to the spirit world one time and my dad was ready to answer back?* And *there's a magical way to bring him back that Mom didn't bother trying?*

"Eleanor?" Maggie impatiently interrupts. "What did you do last time?"

I think back on the room last night. All the lights were out, the room was washed in an ethereal glow of candlelight. "I think we need candles."

Maggie looks about the room. "Okay, can you light them with magic?"

I shake my head, staring at the table. "No, I haven't learned that yet."

Margaret hops to her feet, undeterred. "Well," she says, glancing about, "there's like hundreds in the room." She motions. "I'll go check the kitchen for matches." She hurries off, skidding slightly in her socks.

My stomach trembles with trepidation. *Blue?*

Nothing but silence.

*I'm scared. I don't know what to do. I want to see my father again. More than anything, but…what if I'm wrong about this?* I suddenly realize that I haven't fully accepted his passing. Telling myself he's dead still felt like a pernicious lie of the darkest kind. Hiding in the shadowy crevice of my heart is the hope this is all just a bad dream I'll wake up from. Dead fathers happen in movies and to other people, not to me. Not my family. He's just away on another business trip. If we fail at this tonight, if I fail, I must accept it. He's not coming back.

*"You need to end this. It's not too late."*

I can hear cupboard doors open and close, drawers pull out.

*But there's a chance.* I hold my head in my hands, elbows resting on my knees. *I'm scared if I do this, I could fail, but I'm petrified that if I don't do this, I'll truly never see him again.* The indecision eats away at me like little fire ants crawling beneath my skin. *I miss him so much. You don't understand.*

*"I don't have to. You can't do this, Eleanor."*

"Awesome! We can do this. I've got the matches," Margaret announces, bounding back into the room. She tosses me a box and holds one herself. "You're practically a foot taller, you get the higher candles," she orders, going about lighting the wicks of the long stem candles on the bottom shelves.

I scratch the long stem matches and ignite the candles out of my sister's reach. She shoves the small match box into her back pocket and flicks off the lights, allowing the flames to paint the room in a yellow glow. I expected the task to take longer, but instead I find myself being pulled to the couch by Maggie, eager to get started.

Maggie pulls her phone out and flicks her thumb across the screen. "Okay, so I looked up the rules online and—"

I shake my head. "Those apparently don't apply to us. We simply put the planchette on the board and wait." My voice is monotone, emotionally dead.

Blue appears at my side.

Margaret places her hands on the planchette; I shake my head and move her hands. Maggie leans forward, resting on her forearms on her thighs, gazing at the board. "Come on, Dad. We're here. We're ready to help you," she whimpers. I watch as she adjusts the board, making it perfectly parallel to the table's edge. "We're here, Dad."

The seconds tick on.

The cats in the room shift positions.

The house emits a moan when the heat kicks on.

And the seconds turn into minutes.

"Maggie, I don't think this is working. Maybe we should try to convince the aunts to help us. They'd understand, I'm sure," I say, sounding unconvincing even to myself. I turn towards the board pleadingly. *Dad, are you there?*

Margaret shakes her head, refusing to take her eyes off the board.

"No Eleanor, they won't. We are Dad's *only* shot. We can't just give up on him." Her face becomes blotchy, bubbling tears gathering in her eyes.

We both gaze at the board, silently praying the piece will move.

The tension in the room tightens as we keep staring.

"*Eleanor—*" Blue begins.

"Do we need to touch it at least?" Maggie questions, moving her hands slowly towards the board.

I quickly shake my head. "No, we don't touch it." I ring my hands in my lap, watching the table.

"*Eleanor,*" Blue tries again.

The planchette begins quivering then slides across the painted letters. H-E-L-L-O.

Maggie practically hurls herself onto the board. "Dad! Oh my gosh, it's you! Dad!" she cries, her hands shake as she's unsure what she can do.

I reach for her shoulder. "Maggie, we don't know it's him yet."

The planchette keeps moving, swiping slowly over letters so we are able to keep up.

I lean forward, hovering above the board. "Hello...my little red rose," I read aloud.

"Eleanor, it's him! It's him!" Tears pour down her cheeks as her voice cracks. "Dad, I love you. I miss you so much."

The glass slides over the E. I keep reading. "Ella, I need your help."

My sister leans against my leg, gripping my knee. "Our family knicknames. He's the only one that ever called us that. Oh, Dad!" She sniffs and wipes her nose on the back of her hand.

Blue-Eyes sits stiff next to me, his eyes fixed on the board.

"What do you need us to do, Dad?" I whisper. My heart clenches, waiting for him to answer.

S-A-C-R-I-F-I-C-E.

Margaret cocks her head, watching studiously. "Did I read that right?"

I frown. "What do you mean, sacrifice? Like a human sacrifice?" This isn't right. My dad would never suggest something like that.

The planchette continues to glide across the letters: BURN PYEWACKET.

I squint, unsure if I caught the spelling correctly. "What's a pyewacket?" My heart settles a little. *Maybe it's a plant? Or a spell of some sort?*

BURN THE BODY. EVISERATE THE SPIRIT.

*Burn what body? I don't understand.*

"My body."

*What?* I adjust in my seat, peering down at Blue.

*"Blue Eyes is only a moniker given to me by your aunts. My real name is Pyewacket."*

"Dad, we don't know what that means," Margaret shouts, desperately trying to cling to our father's message.

*How could my dad know Blue Eyes' real name before we did?*

MY DEAREST ELLA, YOU NEED TO SPILL YOUR BLOOD OVER PYEWACKET.

My stomach lurches. *This isn't right. This isn't Dad.* My eyes glisten.

*"No. it's not."*

"Margaret," I say, pulling her back from the board as the piece goes flying over letter after letter furiously. "I'm so sorry. That's *not* Dad."

HELP ME. HELP ME. HELP ME. NOW. NOW. NOW.

Suddenly, there's a strange rattling coming from the kitchen, like a drawer struggling to open.

Margaret's eyes go as wide as saucers. Her head slowly turns toward the darkened hallway, out of the candlelight's reach. "Was that a drawer?"

DO IT. DO IT. DO IT. DO IT. DO IT. The planchette continues to move vigorously.

Persephone leaps from her perch from the back of an armchair and lithely lands on the board, nipping at the planchette until she can finally stop it, knocking it and herself to the ground. Startled, my sister and I both jump to our feet. Blue joins in, wrestling the planchette with Persephone. Blue-Eyes and Persephone become tangled as the planchette escapes their claws. The tabby cat nips and bites at the board piece, but it zips away too quickly. Blue leaps off Persephone's back in a black blur as he pounces, forcing it back down.

The rustling in the kitchen continues.

Maggie reaches over and clasps my hand in hers, shaking. "What do you think that is?"

We flick the light on in the hallway and slowly approach the kitchen. We flip on every light we pass. The kitchen light easily illuminates the entirely white painted room. The far-left corner drawer next to the sink keeps thumping as something is desperately trying to pry it open.

Margaret pants, unable to catch her breath. The air in my lungs constricts as I watch the unattended drawer violently shake and rattle until finally the drawer rams open, disturbing everything inside.

A long silver kitchen knife levitates out of the drawer; the terrifyingly sharp point poises itself in our direction.

I swallow. "Run."

# Chapter Seventeen
## The Only Way is Through

Margaret's hand in mine is slick with perspiration as we sprint to the nearest room. From the dining room, we fling ourselves into Marie's sewing room and lock the door behind us. I throw myself against the door, acting as another barrier. There's a tap, tap, tap against the wooden door.

Margaret peering up at me from the floor, her eyes still wide as her mouth makes a horrified oh. "It's out there! It's still out there! Get away from the door, Eleanor. What if it stabs through?"

Like a specter, Blue-Eyes walks right through the door. *"Thank goodness. I thought I might get stuck."*

The tapping gets stronger, stabbing the door with such ferocity I swear I can feel the point right between my shoulder blades.

*"Eleanor, go to the window. You two need to get out of this room before—"*

The knife clatters to the floor.

The closet next to us pulls itself open, exposing an antique sewing machine. It's in the room with us.

"Margaret, climb out the window, right now!" I order through clenched teeth.

Gratefully, Margaret doesn't argue. She slides the window up and sticks one leg out, straddling the windowsill. "Ell, come on! You have to come! Or I'm not leaving!"

*"Go!"* Blue echoes.

I dash to the window. Maggie hops down onto the lawn, and I shove one leg out the window just as the sewing scissors rise out of the drawer. I can hear it whistle through the air as I duck my head under the raised windowpane. I whip my head around, expecting the sound of shattering glass. Instead, I hear a quiet thump. The scissors have pierced Blue completely through the ribs to the other side, and now they've pulled free and turn to face me just as I leap from the room.

My sister and I are crouched down in the bushes below the window. I wrap my arms around Maggie as we both shiver, but not from the cold. *Blue, are you okay? Oh my gosh, Blue-Eyes?*

*"You need to hide! Now!"*

Too scared to speak, I snatch Margaret's hand and tug her to the back-yard. We race to the darkened tree line out of reach from the shafts of light thrown by the house. We sink to our knees in the dark. *Now what? What are we supposed to do? Hide till the aunts get back? Oh my gosh! My aunts! Will this hurt them!?*

*"We need to destroy the board, cut off communication."*

The sound of glass ricochets. The sewing scissors glide through the air, going around the perimeter of the house; disappearing in and out of the light and shadow.

*I think it's outside with us.*

*"Open the back kitchen door."*

I turn to Margaret, clutching her hands in mine as she whimpers. "Maggie, I need you to stay here."

"No, please, don't leave!"

*"Eleanor! Stay hidden. Use your magic. Open and slam the kitchen door. Now!"*

I close my eyes, envisioning the back door opening and slamming shut. *La Caeli.* I can't hear the door creak open — we're too far away — but I hear it slam. Hard. I open my eyes just as the long sewing scissors zip around the corner and crashes through the glass window of the back door.

Cats hiss and cry out. There's a crashing sound.

*Blue, is it killing the cats?*

*"No, they are creating a distraction. The scissors are trapped in the bathroom. It's looking for a new weapon. Bring the board out to you. Quick!"*

As I did with the kitchen door, I imagine the board sliding off the table, skidding across the floor, opening the front door just enough for the board to slip through and come to us in the woods. *La Caeli.* I release a cry as my brain feels like it's being squeezed inside my skull.

"Eleanor!? What's happened? What should I do!?" Maggie cries, seizing my shoulders. "Eleanor?"

My shoulders curl inward, my bones feel like they're splintering. There's a high pitch ringing in my ears and my mouth goes dry. I fight to keep the image in my mind, but it's like holding a blanket with a pinky against a line-backer ripping it away.

"Oh my gosh, Eleanor! Something is coming towards us! We need to run!"

I force my eyes open against the intense pain. The wooden board wob-bles and dips while floating to us, hidden behind foliage. It drops to the ground in front of us.

My lungs burn like I've been holding my breath for far too long. I collapse till I'm on all fours, feeling like my body had been stretched on a medieval torture rack. "W-w-we need to…" I can barely speak. My jaw feels loose and untethered like it's dislocated. "Burn it. I don't think I c-can…" I gasp for air, feeling like I might hurl. *Blue, what can I do? I don't know the fire spell, and I'm too weak to bring anything else out. Blue?*

Margaret springs into action, furiously digging through her pockets. "Here! I've got the matches." She strikes a match and drops it onto the board. A blue flame ripples out across the wood before it's completely engulfed in orange flames.

The house behind us goes silent.

*Blue, please answer me. I think I'm dying.*

*"It may feel that way, but you're in one piece. You just overextended yourself."*

Flames dance in Maggie's glistening eyes.

I stretch out my fingers on the soft earth, feeling the cold blades of grass against my skin. I slowly feel like I'm being pieced back together. My popped joints feel eased back into place. My muscles mend themselves like they are reattaching to the bone.

Margaret and I watch as the board blackens and cracks down the middle, destroying it beyond recognition.

Maggie peers over at me. "I think it's over. I don't—I don't know, it's like I can't feel it anymore," she says.

I shut my eyes, closing off visual distractions to feel a presence. There's nothing. Just my sister and I trying to catch our breath.

*"It's over."*

Relief fills me as I nod. "It's gone. It's safe to go back." *Blue-Eyes, are you okay?*

*"I'll be fine."*

"Do you need any help to get inside?" Margaret kindly asks, her voice small and quiet.

I shake my head, pushing myself up off the ground. We say nothing as we trudge back through the yard. We both stop, gazing down at the shattered glass on the back steps. We carefully step over it as we're only wearing thin socks.

"I'll get the broom." Margaret says, opening the closet next to the pantry. Inside the small closet hangs about fifteen old fashion brooms you'd see in period films, the kind you could imagine a witch soaring through the air on. Leaning in the corner is a modern yellow broom with a dustpan resting beside it.

"Are you sure?" I ask. "You can go check on the cats?" *They're all still alive, right Blue?*

"*Yes.*"

I sigh a breath of relief, grateful Maggie and I don't have to clean up something so visceral and nightmare-inducing as brutally murdered cats.

Maggie sweeps up the glass. "It's fine. I think Blue-Eyes got hurt. You might want to check on him." Phoenix hurries into the room and rubs against Maggie's legs, desperate to console her.

I amble into the dining room just as Blue is limping in. His ribcage is dented inward on one side. "*You did well . . .*"

*Thank you.*

"*I'm not done. You shouldn't have had to do any of that if you had listened to me. You weren't speaking to your father. You knew the entire time you weren't. You were just hoping in vain.*"

I can't look at him. I ball my hands into fists, frustrated. With either him or me, I'm not sure.

"*Bringing someone back from the dead has never been done. To my knowledge, there are only theories. But even with those theories, all of them claim there is a price to be paid. A price that no one with any morsel of morality would pay. Do not attempt this again. Now, I have some bones that are begging for attention. Follow me. I'll show you what to do.*"

The door gently swings open. Margaret hobbles in from the kitchen, favoring one foot. Phoenix keeps close to her.

"What's wrong?" I ask, rushing over to her.

She stops me, holding up one hand. "I'm fine. I stepped on some glass. I've already taken it out. It was small, but I still bled a little. I'm just going to go wash my foot off," she says flatly. Her face is drained of color and emotion.

I silently follow her to the stairs and listen to her close the bathroom door behind her. I run my hand down my face, feeling the shame of the destruction I have wrought tonight. I sense Blue watching me. *Please don't. Don't say anything.*

Blue nods his head towards the kitchen. "*Come on, everything we need is in there.*"

Following Blue-Eyes's instruction, I gather nearly identical herbs that I used to fix Jack's nose. Jack. It feels like it's been a month since I've seen him. Even tonight it feels like an entire week has spanned the few hours my aunts have been gone.

I snap Blue's rib bones cautiously back into their place and use a cloth bandage to wrap the healing herbs around him. "Will this work?"

"*Sometimes it does. Sometimes it doesn't, due to the strange state I'm in. If the bones don't mend, there's always glue. Wood glue seems to work best."*

Blue-Eyes rests on the island in the middle of the kitchen while I tend to the living room. When I enter the room, the cats are pushing pillows into place, hiding a torn knit throw under the sofa. Some of the candles have melted into puddles on the shelves. While I blow out the remaining wicks, the front door creaks open. My heart stops and my stomach clenches. I turn on my heel. Marie shuffles in, her head is bowed and her shoulders sag.

"Marie?" I question.

She squints at me, a sad smile on her face. "Hi, sweetie." She places Miss Priss down on the floor, who exchanges a look with the other cats.

I exhale, and my shoulders relax. "How was your meeting?"

She sighs, her nose rosy and her eyes glassy. "Not very well, I'm afraid. But I'm not currently at liberty to discuss it." She dabs under her nose with a cream-colored hanky. "So, what did you girls end up doing for dinner?" she questions, sliding her poncho over her head. She hangs it and her purse on a hook. "I'm a little pecked myself."

I open my mouth, trying to think of a reassuring lie about a quiet night in but my mind is too exhausted. "We didn't end up ordering anything."

Marie looks at me with a furrowed brow. "Is everything okay?" Her eyes tick about the room, searching for anything out of place. "Would you girls like me to whip something up?" she offers generously.

I turn facing her. "You wouldn't know how to make my mom's meatloaf, would you?" I ask, thinking of Maggie's go-to comfort food.

She smiles at me, her apple cheeks making her eyes small slits. "Of course, honey. It's our mother's recipe." She turns for the kitchen. "I'll call you when it's ready."

I thought ascending the spiral staircase would be an insurmountable task, but the more I move, the easier it gets. Light peeks out from under Margaret's door.

Maggie is curled up on her bed, Phoenix is cuddling into her. She doesn't lift her head or acknowledge my presence. Her eyes are puffy, the skin around them blotchy and red.

I sit down opposite her. I want to reach for her, but I hesitate, unsure of how receptive she'll be. "Maggie, I'm so sorry."

She sits up, disturbing Phoenix who adjusts on her pillow. Still not looking at me, she asks, "Do you think that was the same thing you spoke to last night?"

I gaze down at her small, freckled hands. "Yeah. I do. I thought it was him because it knew things."

"Yeah. Me too," she replies, her voice flat.

The back of my throat burns, pleading for tears. "I'm really, really sorry. I was wrong. I should have known better." I dare to peer over at Margaret. She's staring off into space; I'm not even sure she's listening.

Her lower lip trembles. "He's really gone. He's not coming back, is he," she asks rhetorically.

My heart further breaks into a million pieces, never having put itself back together after the news. Accepting the truth takes those tiny hurting pieces and grinds them further. I gently shake my head. "No. Dad—" my voice croaks, my jaw quivers. But I know I need to say it aloud. I need to say it for both of us. "He's dead." Lost in my own grief as I had been, I'd thought I was the only one who hadn't believed it, but it turns out Margaret hadn't either. Even before we knew magic existed, we both held onto a silent hope, a prayer that Dad was simply away. We could survive his absence if it was only temporary. It wasn't temporary, and we couldn't ignore it any longer.

Maggie and I collapse into each other. Holding each other so tightly it feels we might disintegrate into one another. We cry—she with tears, I without—realizing there is nothing else we can do. Our father is dead, and we have no choice but to live with it.

# Chapter Eighteen
## Mud Fights and Healing

I don't remember if I got dressed for bed or not. All I can recall after reaching my room is how my bed felt. My body felt like a small stone on mounds of goose feathers.

I tried to persuade Margaret to stay and spend another night in my room, but after we had a good cry, she insisted she just wanted some time alone.

"Besides," she said, while she walked me to her bedroom door, "Mom's called like ten times. I should probably call her back." She sounded like she was dreading the call, like Mom had known what we were up to. Perhaps she had.

"Aunt Marie is making Mom's meatloaf, which I guess is actually Grandma Colleen's meatloaf if you're interested," I said, trying to cheer her up.

Thankfully, she gave me a half smile and agreed to meet us down for dinner. Marie gratefully, wasn't angry about the kitchen window but acted suspicious of us while we ate in the living room and watched "Bewitched" on their small rollout TV. Margaret didn't tell me how the conversation with our mother went, but I watched her in between bites, waiting for her to break.

"Goodnight!" I called as they dug into a sheet of brownies. I couldn't hold vigil with them as my body ached, desperate to sleep.

I stir as I feel a tempered heat rise in my cheeks. Despite the rapidly rising temperature, the scorching heat doesn't fully wake me up. Internally, I'm aware, but my body doesn't rouse from the deep sleep, almost like I'm under a spell. *No, this is just sleeping paralysis, this has happened before. I just need to relax and soon my body will respond.*

"Thou shall not suffer a witch to live," a low, commanding voice bellows.

My skin burns. I can't get my mouth to move or my eyes to open. *Who's there?* I call out nervously in my head. *Is this the entity from tonight? Maybe it's back to finish the job? It wanted to spill my blood over—gah, what was the name? Blue-Eyes! Blue, I need your help!*

"You had been warned prior to your crimes…"

There's suddenly an unbearable pressure on my eyes, like someone is pressing down on them with all their strength. My sinuses are scorched, the orbital socket about to crack. *Blue-Eyes, you damn cat, why aren't you answering me!?*

"…you have been judged and found wanting…"

I want to scream. My flesh is on fire. Has someone shoved me into an oven? My skin feels crispy, the moisture once there charred. I suck in a breath, ready to shriek in pain, but I can't release it. *Am I dying? Someone please help me! Help me! I'm burning! Anyone! Please!* I curl my fingers into a fist, feeling my skin crack as I bend them.

I feel someone's mouth against my ears, their icy breath tickles my sizzling skin. "Your time is coming…Eleanor O'Reilly…just like I had mine."

A suffocating veil is lifted, and I can finally breathe again. A surge of cooling air fills my oxygen-deprived lungs. The heat dissipates within seconds. My skin all over feels cool to the touch. My eyes lightly open, fluttering as sweat clings to my lashes. I sit up the moment I'm able. I put my hand to my sternum where the burning started. I gaze over at the bedroom window overlooking the front lawn and drive. The white gauzy curtain floats in the air like a ghost in the breeze.

My body is slippery as I peel my blankets back, wet with perspiration, and tiptoe to the open window. My skin breaks out in goosebumps in the frigid air. A small brown bat gazes at me from under the roof eaves. It takes all my might to slam the window down and swipe the lock.

Blue is fast asleep on the tuft recliner near the door. I reach into a dresser drawer and pull out a long sleeve tee and boxer shorts, putting them on before crawling back into bed. Curling up under the duvet, I keep feeling the blow to my chest I would swear was real. My body trembles, recalling the pain. It was just a bad dream. I've experienced this sleep paralysis before in my bedroom back home, but never anything like this. The fire felt so real. I squeeze my eyes closed, afraid of what will happen if I fall back asleep.

"Eleanor?" someone calls from far away. "Eleanor! Come on! Eleanor! Eleanor!"

My eyes weakly open. Margaret stands over me, snatching a decorative pillow that had fallen to the floor and whacks me with it. "I can't believe you're still in bed! I've been calling your name for like ten minutes," she complains with a forgiving smile.

Yawning, I sit up, glancing over to the empty chair where Blue-Eyes had been sleeping. "It's Sunday, the day of rest," I complain, flopping back down on my pillow.

Margaret chuckles. "Well, it's one in the afternoon, sleeping beauty," she chides with a roll of her green eyes. "Aunt Marie and I just got back from the farmer's market," she stops and gives a catlike grin, "and Sally and Hamlin are in Atlantic City till tomorrow. Marie is pissed!" Margaret sits on the edge of the bed, hungry to share some gossip. "She said that if Sally attempts to elope again, she's kicking her out for good." She wiggles her eyebrows at me for good measure.

I nod weakly, trying to find amusement in the story but coming up short.

"What's wrong?" Maggie questions, tilting her head at me. Her concern falls into realization. "Suffering from last night?" Maggie doesn't wait for an answer. She inches closer to me, placing her hand on top of my knee. "I talked to Marie last night about Dad and missing him," she shoots her hands up in defense, "I didn't tell her about the Ouija board stuff I swear, just talked about Dad and that kind of stuff. We did a spell together; well, *she* did the spell, but Marie did it on me, for my grief. I feel a little better. Like, I don't know, like I'm filled with Dad's love for me or something. I can't explain it, but it feels like the spell heightened our love and memories, which dulls the pain. You should try it. We used like moon bathed water," she says, shaking her head in disbelief.

I pull my mouth into a half smile. "I'm glad Maggie. I just had a bad dream," I say, running my hands down my face.

"Yeah, I'll say," Margaret mutters, appraising me while she tucks her red hair behind her ears. "I was a little scared last night too, so I had Phoenix sleep next to the door and I kept my lights on all night," she admits sheepishly.

I nod, staring down at myself. I'm covered in visible gross sweat from head to toe. My shirt has long damp sweat stains.

"Well, Marie wants to do some retail therapy, because she's so mad at Aunt Sally. We are going into Boston to meet up with Shannyn to do some shopping. Wanna come?" she offers hopefully. "It's actually gorgeous outside. I'm not even bringing a coat."

I run my hands down my face, not feeling up for a sojourn into the city. "Nah, I've got a ton of homework to do, and I haven't practiced my violin all weekend, plus I need to do some laundry."

Maggie still stares at me, concerned. "Okay, well, just text if you need anything, okay?"

I agree, and she gazes at me once more before closing the bedroom door.

I wait a few minutes until I can hear whatever car they're driving today pull out of the garage. It nearly takes all the strength I have just to get out of the perfectly doughy bed. Despite my grogginess at the start, my day is fairly productive. First, I throw on some clothing that doesn't smell like I had just worn it to run a marathon. I pull on an oversized white t-shirt with a small breast pocket and light-colored blue jeans. After conquering some homework, I practice my violin, then search the house for the laundry room only to find the washer and dryer behind a sliding closet door off the kitchen. The washing machine looks like it hasn't been used in years.

Most of the cats mosey about the house, ignoring me. Never in a million years did I think I'd feel even remotely comfortable in a house full of cats by myself. I drop to the couch and flip through channels without any streaming services, like it's the 90's. Nothing's on. I switch off the television, toss the remote onto the table, and roll onto my side, propping my head up with my arm. I stare at the remote, imagining the remote floating up and doing a figure eight in the air. *La Caeli.* A quiet spark flutters in the center of my being, light as butterfly wings. The remote lifts gracefully off the table and glides into a sleek figure eight. It hangs in the air, knowing I didn't want it to rest on the table just yet. Using my finger to guide it, the remote levitates about the room, drifting by the window, weaving between shelves until I order it to rest on top of the television set. I exhale, waiting for my body to spasm and quake in pain, but nothing comes. Nothing but the tiniest hint of soreness after a mild work out or stretch.

I extend my fingers, gazing down at my hands. *I'm getting better.*

Blue-Eyes strolls into the room and leaps onto the fainting couch next to the window, basking in a pillar of sunlight shining through.

"Where have you been?" I question, sitting up.

*"Around. I had some business needing attending. Why the inquiry?"* he sends back, sounding a little annoyed.

I roll my eyes. "I was just curious, Blue."

His eyes slide to me. *"Perhaps you should call me 'Pyewacket'. That is my actual name."*

*That's a really weird name. But sure, Pyewacket.*

*"Oh yes, and "Eleanor" is so felicitous to the ear..."*

A thought occurs to me. *How did that entity know your real name last night?*

*"I'm not sure. But I wouldn't dwell on it. We don't know to whom or even what you were speaking. If it was a demon, they are known to be manipulative, and sly."* Pyewacket leaps down from the couch and stretches out on the rug. *"Hmmm, bishop to F8. I believe that puts you in check, my friend."*

*What?* I frown at him, confused.

*"I'm playing chess against Mortimer, the familiar of Winston Edwards. This is why I chose the Sicilian defense, you old cat. You just can't help yourself."* He chuckles. *"No, no, you'd played the King's Gambit last time."*

*Seriously, even the dead cat has plans today.* "I don't see a board anywhere," I point out the obvious.

He sighs, irritably. *"The board is at his home. I'm just communicating the moves, no different from playing over the telephone."*

*Oh yes, we've all been there,* I huff internally.

*"What do your fellow youths say today? 'Touch grass'?"*

I try not to growl, getting up off the couch. "Enjoy taking the piss out of each other," I say in a terrible cockney accent, heading to the garage door. I notice Blu—err, Pyewacket wince at me.

The garage door lags and rumbles when I push the remote. The sweet purr of the engine seduces a smile out of me. I cruise down the gravel drive peering up at the tree canopies, noticing new buds sprouting on the barren branches. A soft pitter patter of rain sprinkles down lightly tapping the roof of the car. I flip on the car's Bluetooth and raise the volume to BØRNS's "Past Lives". His hypnotic vocals fill the car, followed by the heavy synthetic beats.

I pass a brown wooden sign indicating Highland Park up ahead. I wonder if the city knows my aunts have a home in the middle of Salem woods. Jack seemed confused, then surprised by my current residence. But the way he hesitated in his car, it belied something other than mere confusion. I drive past a golf course until the road serpentines from pavement to dirt and veers off into the trees.

I apply a little pressure to the gas pedal as I peer up out my window. The blue sky appears to be done ringing out the moisture from the pale clouds skirting across the sky. A red cardinal perches on a branch, its scarlet plumage striking amongst all the green and brown. The gravel on the road becomes sparse, as the narrow road is more mud than rock. Approaching a fork in the road, I aimlessly take a left around the bend. I squint, seeing a dazzling white mustang pulled to the side of the road several yards ahead. Someone is sitting on the hood of the car, back facing me. *Could it be?* I coast to a stop.

Climbing out of the car, I nearly stumble. "Hey, excuse me, everything okay?"

The gorgeous blonde head hangs back. "Of course, you would find me…right now," the man replies in a complaint.

I grin. *It is him.* "Jack?" I confidently venture.

He straightens up, turning around as his mouth pulls up in a crooked smile. His blonde hair gently rustles in the light breeze. "Here to save me?" he questions playfully.

Stepping around his car, my sneakers keep sliding in the mud. "Do you need saving?" I ask with arms folded, feeling a little chilled, having yet to acclimate to New England weather. I examine his face, searching for the telltale signs of a break. His nose has a perfectly straight, symmetrical slope, with the tip perfectly level.

He squints at me staring, but his face relaxes as he realizes something. "It worked."

The confirmation of his obedience to my insane suggestion propels a pleasure-filled smile across my face. "You really did what I said?"

He nods, then scratches the side of his nose. "I had every intention of telling you that you were wrong tomorrow at school, but to my surprise, it worked." He shakes his head incredulously. "I've never been to a witch doctor before, so what are your rates?" he teases.

I roll my eyes at him. "More than you can afford." I glance about, taking in our surroundings. "What are you doing out here, by the way?"

A delicate pink creeps into the apples of his cheeks. Holding the back of his neck, he peers over at his car. "Getting lost, but I got a flat tire and no jack. I stupidly lent it to Stephin and never got it back."

I tilt my chin in the direction of my car parked just a few yards behind his. "You can check my trunk. I'm sure I've got something you want."

Jack chuckled, his shoulders bouncing as he laughs. "Oh, yeah?"

I roll my eyes once more with a sigh. "Haha. You know what I mean. I think there's a kit in the back you can use."

Jack walks towards me. His sea-green eyes peer down at me, gazing at my lips before stepping around me to my car.

I release a pent-up breath, my hands trembling at my sides. I grip my hips, my eyes lifting to the recently sprouted leaves. Rain from the abrupt shower clings to the canopy, occasionally trickling down. My feet sink ever so slightly in the mushy ground.

"Got it," Jack calls, taking a black case out of the trunk. "The lug nuts appear to be the same size, but there's only one way to find out." He strides past me and kneels down at the front right tire. His denim clad knee squelches in the mud.

I keep peeking over my shoulder at him while he works, watching his muscles flex while he turns the wrench. His face is tense while he concentrates. Jack was strangely harmonious in contradictions. His jaw severe and sharp, his eyes soft and supple, his grin is sly and sexy, his clef chin noble and gallant.

His eyes flick over to me. "What? Do you think I'm doing it wrong or something?" he questions, with just the slightest hint of nervousness.

*How should I know? I've never done this before.* "No, that looks right," I reply.

Blushingly, my eyeline slides back to him. He frowns, tightening the last nut. He's so overtly gorgeous, masculine, and perfect. Jack Woods, the captain of the crew team, the boy who dresses like he just walked out of a high-end modeling shoot, the boy that's such an obvious choice to fall in love with. The "Harvard-legacy Adonis" is hardly my type.

"Damnit." His knee slides and he loses his grip.

However, is there *something* behind those emerald eyes that isn't so genuine? Shiny surfaces and all that, Jack, appearing to be the golden boy, has an indescribable, hidden edge to himself lingering just beyond the periphery. It's like he's always hiding something. But maybe I'm just being paranoid, uncomfortable that someone like him is interested in someone like me.

Jack rises to his feet, a clump of mud stuck to his jeans. "I'm glad you found me," he says, handing me back the vinyl tire kit.

I can feel his eyes on me as I stride back to my trunk, tossing the kit back in. My keys feel heavy in my hands while I stand idly by my driver's side door, not feeling ready to leave. "So…" I rack my brain for something cool or clever to say. "Um, where were you headed?"

Abashed, Jack's eyes are fixed on the hood of his car. "Ah, nowhere in particular…just killing some time until I meet up with my coach."

I flick a glob of mud off the toe of my shoe, hiding a smile. "Okay, well, I'm glad I could help. Anymore car problems or broken bones, just let me know," I say, trying to sound flirtatious. Carefully, I measure my steps, one foot directly in front of the other, alternating the shake of my hips attractively, or at least attempting to be.

I press on the gas, but my tires just spin and squeal. I thump the pedal revving the engine, but to no avail. *Oh, come on!* I even try rocking back and forth in my seat, growling out curses, trying to get this stupid car to move, but the tires just spin hopelessly. Jack doesn't even try to conceal his amusement.

"Would you like some help?" Jack inquires, playfully smug, traipsing through the muck to the back of my car.

*No.* I don't want help. I want to look independent, sexy, and cool. I slam my foot on the gas again, determined to get out of the mud by myself. Jack is shouting to me, but I'm distracted by something deep within me. It's quiet at first, a mere flicker of power. My magic knows exactly what I want, and before I can concentrate on turning it off, the power surges through me. There's a loud thud against my trunk as my car lunges, nearly flies forward. I wrench my wheel to the right, narrowly missing Jack's Mustang, and then stomp on the brakes with both feet. My car slides to a stop on the gravel road. In the rearview mirror, Jack is nowhere to be seen. I throw the car in park and immediately hop out.

"Jack? Jack!" I yell, racing back to him.

Jack pushes up off his stomach until he is on all fours, then ambles to his feet. Thick, viscous mud covers him from head to toe. He uses the inside of his sweatshirt to wipe his mouth clean. He still spits out the mud that made its way into his mouth.

"Jack I'm so sorry! Are you okay?" I peer over his entire form, looking for injury, but he seems to be okay, other than the thick coating of muck that covers him. I roll my lips in between my teeth to keep myself from giggling. I snatch a green cardigan from the passenger seat. "Here, you can use this to get cleaned up."

He nods, accepting my offering, then spits out more mud as he wipes multiple clumps off his nose, cheeks and eye.

I whip my hand up to my mouth to cover a laugh, my lips trembling against a torrent of giggles snorting out.

He raises a muddy eyebrow and smiles. *Damnit.* Even covered in mud, he's still handsome, adorably so, and his teeth freaking sparkle against the dark muck.

He fumbles with a heavy wad of mud in his hand. "So, you think this is funny?"

Narrowing my eyes at his stupidly beautiful face, I swallow my laughter and drop my hand. "You wouldn't," I warn, taking a cautious step backward. *Jack wouldn't dare. Especially since I'm wearing a thin white shirt. He's far too much of a gentleman... right?*

I barely have time to register his movement as a mud-filled hand moves across my face and into my hair, caking my bun in muck. His right arm wraps around my waist, pulling me close as he shakes his head, whipping mud about and dragging his face over my shoulders and collarbone. His hair paints me in streaks of sludge.

The more I squirm, the tighter he grips me. "Jack! Stop—please—I can't—breathe!" I choke out through my laughter. My chest crushes against his solid pectorals. Jack snags my flailing arms, keeping me ensnared. My feet stagger in the mud, sending us tumbling to the ground and rolling into the shallow ditch.

Jack landing squarely on top of me. He studies my startled face and chuckles. "Are you okay?" he questions with a playful grin after. A thick clump of mud glops from his forehead onto mine.

We both pant, out of breath. Our legs are tangled, and our hips are aligned. His square hand cradles my head while the other lingers on my hip. I shiver beneath him. My body tingles, aware of every movement, of every breath he draws. My gaze slides from his full lips to his eyes, a dangerous act that has me falling into that beguiling sea green.

There's a hunger in his stare, powerful and yearning. He adjusts his weight so he's balancing on his knee and elbow. "I apologize. I just couldn't help myself. Missed opportunities and all that." Reluctantly, he pushes up and off of me. Or maybe I just hope he's reluctant. He graciously extends a hand to me, then effortlessly hoists me to my feet. Together, we climb out of the trench.

I place my hands on my hips. "I don't know what I'm going to do," I say, peering over to the car. "I don't think the Mercedes was meant for a mud wrestler." I suddenly frown as I imagine the beautiful, smooth leather interior covered in sticky, leather-ruining gunk.

Jack steps forward, pausing before placing one hand on my elbow and brushes his fingers over my lips removing a lump of mud. Despite the muck, his fingers going over my lips cause a shiver to go up my spine. *Did he move it so he can kiss me? Am I about to get my first kiss!? Truthfully, I didn't imagine all the mud when I dreamt of this moment.*

The air in my lungs constricts. I can't breathe. I lean slightly forward only for Jack to drop his hand from my elbow.

He nods his head to his car. "I've got my gym bag; you can use the clothes I was going to change into." I watch as he trudges to his car, pulling out a shirt and towel.

I shoot him a playful frown as he returns. "So, if you had this all along, why did you use my cardigan earlier?"

Jack grins but chooses not to answer. "The towel and shirt are clean," he says. "You can sit on the towel to protect your seat and I'll turn around if you want to put this on," he says. He steps around to the driver's seat and lays out the towel.

With my back to him, I peel my slimy top up over my head. I steal a peek over my shoulder; Jack is respectfully facing my car. I pull my arms and head through, trying my hardest to avoid caking his black tee.

"All clear. Thanks, Jack." I motion to his shirt. "What are you going to do?" My heart flutters in my chest just saying his name. *Is he a witch too? Is that why it feels so right, so good to be near him?*

Jack shrugs. He tugs the hem of his shirt, pulling it over his head and tosses it onto his closed trunk. My mouth goes dry at his cut form. He pops the top button of his jeans.

"Oh." I hastily pivot away from him. "Sorry."

He chuckles. "It's okay."

I can hear his jeans thunk on top of his trunk.

My face feels feverish, my skin too tight. My heart pounds in my chest, squeezing up into my throat. Flashes play before my eyes, my top removed, his body crushing against mine. Our mouths melting into each other. Our hands furiously exploring. Another spark of power ignites within me. *Oh, gosh. Don't do anything!* "Um, ah, I've got to go. Uh, I'll see you at school, Jack. Thanks for lending me the shirt." I shield my eyes, rushing to my car.

Jack calls after me. "Eleanor? Wait, I wanted to ask—"

I shake my head, creeping one eye open to find my door handle. "I'm sorry, I really need to go! See you tomorrow at school, okay?"

I race back to the aunts' house, never daring to peer back. *What the hell was my magic trying to do? Gosh, what is wrong with me? Are my hormones somehow connected to my magic? Ugh, sometimes being a witch is the worst.*

I leave the car in the driveway and trudge up the veranda steps. The mud is now dry and has formed a craggy shell on my pants and skin. Bits of dried mud falls to the floor as I walk. Thankfully, everyone is still in Boston.

I spin the nozzles and bang the copper pipes before steaming hot water bursts from the showerhead. I inhale his scent on the shirt before taking it off, leaving it puddled on the floor next to the rest of my clothes. The sludge slithers and slides off my body, darkening the water whirling down the drain. At first, I feel disgusting with my slimy hair tumbling free when I let it down, yet inside I'm warm—fuzzy, pleasurably tingly. *Jack Woods.*

*"Stop. Please. Just. Stop. No more."* Pyewacket snaps abruptly in my head.

*Go back to your chess. Or block me or whatever.*

*"I've got an errand. Get all of this out before I get back."*

I roll my eyes and use a homemade Himalayan salt scrub with jojoba oils and jasmine. When the water runs clear, I lather in a moss-colored shampoo that smells like spring and mountain air. *Oh, Jack. Jack Woods. Mr. Jack Woods. Jack something Woods.*

My eyes pop open when I hear something clatter.

My hands quiver and my stomach drops.

The clawed planchette sits in the center of the tub. It's cracked glass eye staring up at me. Something red drips off the tip and swirls down the drain.

# Chapter Nineteen
## Sketches and Dubious Dates

I adjust the towel wrapped around my head while sitting at my desk in the bedroom. The planchette looms under the desk light. I finger the broken glass, tracing the crack.

Pyewacket saunters in through the door and I hold the planchette out to him. "Did you drop this in my shower?"

The thin black cat stretches, raising his butt up in the air. The tip of his tail is missing fur, revealing the smallest hint of bone.

*"What like as a prank?"* he questions telepathically, eyeing the game piece.

I irritably shrug, tossing it back onto the desk. "I was taking a shower, and it dropped in."

Pyewacket leaps up onto the trunk at the foot of the bed and lounges there, one paw dangling off. *"That sounds like something Gunther would do. He's Lennox's familiar, and he is rather perturbed; he missed the scuffle. Prig. I told Pyre taking him in would be a mistake."*

I gaze back at the planchette, my stomach still unsettled. *Wait, Lennox Burroughs, Shannyn's boyfriend is a witch?*

*"Yes, he comes from a powerful line. Rather two very strong lines that intertwined. It'll be very interesting to see what comes from Shannyn and Lennox's offspring. Whoever has the strongest bloodline magic determines the line. Rarely is the blood so perfectly matched you have both lines pass. The matriarchal bloodline in your family is unparalleled. That's why you come from a long line of daughters upon daughters."*

I nod, not feeling a genealogy lesson as I hold the cursed planchette.

Pyewacket regards me pensively. *"I rather doubt you're being haunted. The board was destroyed. Ponder upon it no longer. Sally plans on training you after school, a possible 'double header' depending on how you do. This means a copious amount of rest. The sooner you are trained, the safer you'll be."*

I smile at that. *It's cute that you worry about me.*

He lifts his head up, staring at me quizzically. *"You misunderstand me. I meant the safer it will be for those around you. To put it delicately, you are a walking time bomb; it would be best if you were treated like a leper until you gain better control.*"

I roll my eyes. *You're seriously the worst.* I march past him and pull pajamas from the closet.

*"They call that projection, my dear."*

"Eleanor!" someone shouts from the first floor. The staircase thunders as the aunts pour into the house and Margaret charges up the staircase. "Eleanor! Oh my gosh," she gushes, bursting into the room just as I slide on some sweatpants and an old, tissue paper-thin *The Who* tee. Maggie shuts the door behind her and rushes to the bed.

"Okay, so first we went into Boston and saw one of my favorite influencers filming in the exact restaurant we were at! Then Sally calls us and needs to be bailed out of *jail!* Marie was furious, but Shannyn came with and Sally has a tattoo on her shoulder blade of a chainsaw on fire. She has no memory of getting that!" Margaret bursts out laughing.

"You're kidding," I say grinning, my eyes over drift to my desk. I carefully hold my smile in place. *Pyewacket, hide the planchette. I don't want Margaret to worry.*

Thankfully, he doesn't argue. Instead, he inconspicuously slinks over and knocks it into the trashcan.

Margaret meticulously details Marie's epic tantrum in the police station before moving onto the rumor that Lennox is ring shopping for Shannyn, a rumor that's not surprising in the slightest.

Maggie skips to the door. "Come on, Marie is doing breakfast for dinner and I'm sure she's still giving it to Sally."

After an icy dinner with the aunts, I'm relieved to see the planchette is still in the wastebasket when I return to the room. I crawl into bed and collapse onto my pillow. When my eyes flutter open, the bedroom is completely different. The walls are rugged grey flagstone, there's a bubbling black cauldron in the hearth, and taxidermy birds of various species and size dangle from the ceiling.

I'm no longer in bed; in fact, the bed is completely gone. Instead, I stand next to a torture rack. I rub the slimy, bitter coating on my tongue against the roof of my mouth. My teeth feel long, fuzzy, and almost pointy.

There's a loud clomping outside, like clanging coconuts. Through the window, I see I'm several stories high in a stone tower. Below I spot Jack riding a majestic white mustang to rescue me.

Just as I'm about to call out to him, I hear a sniffling cry to my right. Next to me is a beautiful maiden with a golden crown on top of her cascading canary-colored curls. Her features seem familiar: the pinched nose, the regal, sharp cheekbones. *Vivienne?* She is bound by heavy iron chains jutting from the walls, crying out for help. Her eyes well up with tears at the sight of me, causing her to wail even louder for Jack's rescue. Her pale pink dress shimmers in the torchlight, making her alabaster skin glow.

On the wall is a full-body mirror framed in bones. One glance in the mirror and I recoil; I'm *hideous*! My eyes are blood red, with a hint of black woven into my dirty-colored irises. There's a large grotesque wart on the tip of my long, boney chin. The over-crowded teeth crammed about my green-ish brown gums are pointy, yellowy-grey with some kind of gelatinous muck smeared across them. Instead of the radiant complexion like the princess, my skin has a tint of green, like fungus. On top of my rat nest hair, I've got a comically large witch's hat. My dress is black, filthy, with dried blood and other unidentifiable substances. The smell emitting from me makes me nearly wretch.

"I'm coming, my love!" Jack yells gallantly from the ground. I peer back down from the window to see the glorious prince climb up the wall stones to bravely save his captive princess. Not me, the captor.

"Stay back, you beast!" Jack leaps through the window with his sword drawn. The steel blade glints in the filtering sunlight.

"No, Jack! Please!" I cry, but my voice comes out raspy, inhuman.

Jack ignores my plea and runs for the beautiful damsel. I don't move. He breaks her chains with his sword, then holds her tenderly while she cries into his shoulder. I watch as he passionately kisses her, deeply, their mouths opening to each other's.

Jack helps his precious princess climb out the window and then glares back at me with pure disgust. My body aches with the hate that radiates from him. His leg hangs inside the tower room as he straddled the ledge.

"Jack, please don't do this!" I run to him.

I stop as his sword presses painfully against my chest. Tears stream down my face.

"I could *never* love such a *vile* monster as *you*!" His eyes hold my stare before he runs the sword through my chest.

Suddenly I'm back in my bed, panting. I swear I can feel the sting of the blade penetrating my breastbone.

I roll over in bed, and a cool breeze washes over me. My bedroom window is open again, my lace curtains floating in the chill night air. I tiptoe to my window and slide the window shut. It's pitch-black outside, not a single star visible. The branches of the dead oak tree out front bend like curling fingers against the wind. Three of my aunts' cats tiptoe about the yard on the prowl.

I quickly crawl back into bed, my heart still pounding from the dream.

I place my hands on my chest where the blade had gone through. That tiny spot below my bust line throbs. *How could a dream cause physical pain? But it was only a dream. A terrible nightmare.* I close my eyes, hoping I won't dream of him again tonight.

\*\*\*

"Ouch! Marie, when I asked if you could give me a halo braid, this wasn't exactly what I had in mind." I wince as a lock of my hair gets painfully tugged by my aunt's magic while she gulps some tea from across the room.

Her brows knit as she gives me a sympathetic smile. "Sorry sweets. It's nearly done." She twirls her finger in the air.

I yelp as my head is yanked to the left. Pins nearly scalp me as they hold the braid in place. "Thanks," I say, picking up my messenger back off the floor. "I'll see you after school."

Sally breezes through the kitchen doors, her face slathered in a goopy-looking green mask. "Take it easy today, because when you're done with those pointless studies, things will get lit," she says with a smirk. A fiery snake is slithering between her fingers, carefully never touching her skin. She snaps her fingers, extinguishing it.

I chuckle awkwardly. "Yeah, no one says that anymore."

"Told you," Marie mumbles into her teacup.

Sally grips her hips irritably. "Okay, if you don't get that broom out of your backside, Marie, I swear I'm burning the house down."

"I'll see you guys later," I say under my breath and head for school.

The sky is a cornflower blue with cotton candy clouds that drift lackadaisically. I keep fingering my braid that wraps around my head. I wanted to do something special, so I took over an hour getting ready this morning. *And for what? He could have kissed me, but he didn't. He didn't even ask for my number. But I didn't exactly give him a chance. I ran out of there before my magic could strip him or whatever. Gosh, I'm such an idiot.* I peer down at my chest at that tiny spot on my sternum that still slightly throbs. *Is this just in my head? Is my magic causing it to hurt? Stupid dream.*

I lift my eyes to the school steps. Trixie is stepping inside. A daisy crown sits on top of her head. Her blonde wavy hair sways as she walks.

"Trixie!" I call, holding her turquois parka tucked under my arm and Jack's belongings draped over the other.

Several heads swivel looking back at me, surprised, frowning in confusion, with a few disgusted expressions.

Trixie spins around, spotting me, and her eyes crinkle above a broad smile. "Hello, friend!" her eyes drop to the coat I'm holding. "*You* took my jacket!" she takes it from my arms. She leans close to me while kids walk around us into the school. "I had to walk home without it. I was so cold and too tired to warm myself up."

Trixie links arms with me. "I'm sorry. Wait, you were at the party? Where?"

Trixie dismisses me with a jingling little giggle. "Of course not. I'd finished the Earth spell last night. With flying colors, I might add. *So* easy. *Too* easy. So, I moved onto the mind spell. You should know you looked right at me," she whispers to me, mumbling from the side of her mouth.

I frown. "What are you talking about? I didn't see you."

We stop at my locker. She leans her shoulder against my neighbor's locker. "You and Jack were walking. Remember seeing a cute little bunny?"

I nod slowly at her, sliding my things into the tight rectangular space. "Yeah. Wait—are you saying you were the…"

"Bunny? Of course," she replies, like it's the most obvious thing in the world.

I think about the music box at my aunts' place with the witch crumpling up like paper into the rabbit. The photograph of the fluffle of rabbits in the bathroom. I crane my head forward so only she can hear. "Yeah, what's up with all the rabbit stuff? We can, like," I glance about quickly, "turn into them?"

She tucks her wavy flaxen hair behind her ears. "Not really. We can't perform *actual* transfiguration. It's just an illusion, part of the mind spell. In 17th century Salem, it was safer for witches to meet in disguise, and rabbits were the agreed upon animal. They blend in easily. After a few tries, I totally nailed it. I was desperate to try it out, and I knew you'd be at the party, so I biked over, left my coat in Nick Andersen's truck and worked the spell." Trixie continues peering at my befuddled face. "I took my coat off because it helped me get into the right mindset for the spell. Cool night air on my skin, not so encumbered."

I slap my locker closed as every muscle and tendon in my body feels weighed down, completely overwhelmed down to my sinew.

"Well, I need to get to Latin. I'll see you later," Trixie says, air kissing both cheeks before prancing away. "Love the hair, by the way! I'm sure Jack will too!" she shouts cheekily before ducking into her classroom.

I lower my head and shrink into Mr. Edwards' classroom. I take my seat just as the bell rings. Jack's desk remains empty.

I place his folded towel and shirt down on his desk.

"Good morning pupils," Winston greets everyone and slides a new copy of Macbeth across my desk.

I nod my thanks. I open the play, glancing over at the door, wondering if Jack is coming. *I did my stupid hair for nothing. I really am an idiot.* I slump in my desk, annoyed that I tried to pathetically impress him, annoyed that I even care, annoyed that I'm so disappointed he's not here.

"Poppy, could you pick up at the beginning of act II, please?" Mr. Edwards asks, perched on a grey stool in the front of the classroom.

Poppy, never lifting her eyes from her phone, gives him one finger indicating she'll be ready momentarily. "Sorry. Emergency," she says, sliding her phone into her purse. "I could recite it in French, German—" she flexes.

Mr. Edwards interrupts her, almost amused. "The original English will be just fine. Accent optional," he jokes.

Everyone turns in their seats as the classroom door opens. A slightly flustered Jack hurries into the room. His striped tie is crooked, his blazer is folded over one arm and of course his hair appears perfectly windblown tousled. He's so attractively disheveled I force myself to look away before he can catch me staring.

"Sorry, I don't have a note," he apologizes.

Mr. Edwards waves him to his desk and motions for Poppy to continue.

I purse my lips, hiding a smirking smile as he makes his way over. I tuck my nose into the book and continue to scan the line Poppy reads aloud despite my attention is devotedly elsewhere.

Jack leans forward in his desk. I can feel his cool, minty breath caress my exposed neck. I suddenly became hyperaware of the distance from his lips to my skin. A feverish tingle swells inside me.

"I'm late because of you. Thought you should know," he whispers.

I frown, only slightly turning my head. "How so?" I question quietly.

His breath tickles my neck. "I can smell everything."

I immediately want to do a sniff test on myself. "Excuse me?" I ask, slightly mortified.

"Ever since you fixed my nose, I can smell everything. I didn't know fresh eggs have a smell, they do. I can smell every chemical used in the laundry detergent and it makes me ill. I'm wearing the same clothes as Friday because they aren't freshly laundered."

"I apologize, your towel and shirt are also freshly laundered," I say teasingly. I can hear him inhale his laundry behind me.

"Mmm…" He says smelling his shirt I gave back.

"I promise your heightened smell will fade," I whisper to him.

"Before the smell of the entire school makes me gag?" he mutters under his breath.

"Am I part of that group?" I want to shovel my question back into my mouth the moment it leaves my tongue. *What if I do smell bad to him? Why do I have to sit in front of him?*

"Are you asking me to smell you?" he playfully replies.

"Okay Poppy, stop there please," Mr. Edwards instructs. His knees creek as he rises from his stool. He plucks his round reading glasses off his nose, pocketing them into his tweed jacket. *Did the man ever wear anything else?* He paces stoically in front of the room. "Now, can anyone explain what Macbeth meant when he said, "Methought I heard a voice cry 'sleep no more! Macbeth does murder sleep,'—the innocent sleep, sleep that knits up the ravell'd sleave of care"?" Mr. Edwards questions the entire class, his eyes slide from student-to-student waiting. "As I have studied this play since I was merely a lad, I've ascertained that…"

"You smell nice, Eleanor," he says, stretching out my name like he was savoring it on his tongue. "Your hair looks nice too, whatever that's called," he compliments in the most boyish way possible.

The temperature in my cheeks could melt candle wax. He likes the way I smell. I want to giggle. I want to dance. I want to twirl. I want to die. *Idiot.*

Winston's head snaps in our direction. "Mr. Woods, do you have a question? Or some interesting observations you would like to share? Maybe you could explain Shakespeare's motif. I do believe it was you who objected at the beginning of term to reading this play as you had already made a study of it last year." Mr. Edwards turns the entire class's attention to us, popping the little bubble Jack and I had created for ourselves.

Jack settles back in his chair. I stay forward facing, my eyes never lifting from my book. "Yes," he says as easily as if he was always planning on addressing the entire class, "Correct me if my interpretation is completely unsupported," he begins with an air of sincerity, "But I believe William Shakespeare wrote this as perhaps a warning that corrupting power due to unrestrained ambition can only lead to one's destruction. I feel that Macbeth's principal theme is contingent on the belief that if our ambition is not in check with absolute severe moral or social confines, we will create a path of devastation," he states with precision and ease. "The characters' goals propel them to commit atrocity after atrocity, with the help of the revelations given by the inimical witches. Macbeth even goes mad with guilt, but still doesn't halt his horrific actions because of his lust to achieve his lofty ambition. Once one is hell-bent down a malign path, it is difficult to stop. This leads me to believe, despite it's never fully confirmed, that Lady Macbeth commits suicide, the futility—"

Mr. Edwards waves his hands and an excited expression playing at the edge of his lips. "Thank you, Mr. Woods, that'll be all. We have yet to reach Lady Macbeth's conclusion."

"Yeah, spoiler alert," I teasingly chastise.

"But Mr. Woods has brought to our attention with Macbeth—," Mr. Edwards begins again, turning his eyes back to the rest of the class with pure delight.

I notice to my left every boy in class is peering over at us. *Why are they staring like Stepford husbands? Do I have something on my face?* I sink lower in my seat and pretend to be absorbed in the play. I nibble on my bottom lip as heads slowly swivel back to the whiteboard.

I can feel Jack's eyes on me. I slowly swivel in my seat, catching a quick glance at him, hoping he won't notice. He's holding his book up, but he lets his eyes linger on me before dropping to the opened play.

I drop my gaze to his notebook laying exposed on his desk. They're clearly notes for another class. My eyes sweep over his meticulous handwriting to the corner of the blue-lined paper where there's a small, incredibly well-done sketch of—*me*, my knees are pulled into my chest hiding my body while something is sprouting from my back, like wings. I'm laughing in the drawing, my hair long and in waves spilling over my shoulders. My legs tucked into me, covering my exposed body. There was a curved shadow at my kneecap, like a crescent moon. It's a scar I had on my right knee from attempting to go longboarding with my dad. I had scraped up against some coral and received a C shaped scar from it. *How does Jack know about that scar?* Below the sketch is a date. I squint, trying to get a better view. Jack snaps his notebook shut and shifts in his seat, his eyes now following Mr. Edwards, tucking his notebook away.

I whip back, facing the front now trying to catch up with the discussion. Another student has been reading, but I haven't been following along whatsoever. A discussion breaks out about whether the witches were real or just a hallucination.

Winston wraps up his lecture as the hour is nearing its end. I try to peek over my shoulder inconspicuously, but Jack didn't take his notebook out again. The scribbled date below the drawing doesn't make sense. It's got to be some mistake. The date was March first of this year. My birthday, and two weeks *before* I moved here to Salem.

When the bell rings, Winston is still giddy from Jack's input that propelled his lecture about symbolism and modern representation.

In the time I take to scoop my belongings off my desk, Jack is already gone.

# Chapter Twenty
## Ghost in a Glass

I crane my neck, trying to see over everyone as I search for Jack, but he's slipped away in the gulf of students.

"Hey, looking for me?" Nick asks, strolling up to me. He grins, peering down at me, but there's something about his smile that makes me believe he's nervous. His lips twitch.

"Hi," I reply dryly, not even slightly in the mood for him.

Nick adjusts the strap of his backpack on his shoulder. He glances about the hall, shifting his feet, and his smile slowly reclines in an apologetic position. "Actually, I was hoping to run into you. I think I drank—no, I *know* I drank way too much. I barely remember the party at all." He stops taking a breath, "and if any of my ex's are to be believed, I was probably a jerk. I'm really sorry. I hope I didn't scare you off because I can be such an ass."

I feel the ice inside me melt somewhat. *Maybe the pictures are normal? Maybe I've been flirty and leading him on?* My shoulders roll forward and I uncross my arms. "Okay, I accept your apology. We're friends," I say, nudging him in the arm jovially.

"Walk you to class?" He nods his head toward the hall.

We walk in step together, Nick pounding kids' fists as we go. He hovers by my table as I take a seat. "I've got something for you." He produces my leather jacket from his backpack.

I stare at it, shocked and confused. "Oh my gosh, I didn't realize I left it! Thank you," I say, taking it from him. I scrunch my nose; it smells like beer and beef jerky. *There's got to be a way to clean the leather.*

"Of course." Nick's face holds a broad grin, his chest is slightly puffed as he stands up straighter. He gives me a quick wink before he takes his seat.

More students flood in voicing sporadic groans and complaints. I put my jacket on my lap and glance up at the board. The word "Quiz" is written on the whiteboard in big block letters. Mr. Andersen, standing in front of the class, hands out the three-page stapled quiz.

Mr. Andersen scratches at his freshly shaven face. I hadn't noticed how broad his face was until now. "I don't want to hear any complaining," he states with an easy-going smile. "There are eight multiple-choice questions, six true or false and three essay questions," he explains as kids are already flipping through the pages hoping to find the quiz to be as easy as Mr. Andersen's demeanor. From whispers I've overheard, at least half the girls have crushes on him, but he's unanimously adored by everyone. It helps that he can keep up with pop culture references and the current binge-worthy show.

"Okay, you have forty-five minutes." Mr. Andersen hit some buttons on his phone, "Begin... now."

Seated in the back of the classroom, I'm the last to receive the quiz and have no chance to flip through the questions before Mr. Andersen's timer began.

1)    The skirmishes between British troops and the colonial militiamen occurring in Lexington and Concord kicked off the armed conflict. This occurred when?

      A)    April 1775
      B)    February 1775

*"Eleanor..."*

I circle A.

*"Eleanor..."*

Moving onto the next question, I pause, realizing it's a trick question. *Pyewacket?* I mentally call out. *Stop bugging me. I'm taking a quiz, unless you want to help me with it. You were around during the Revolution, right? Pyewacket?*

*"Eleanor..."*

A hissing, maleficent whisper drifts nearby, outside my head this time. The whisper is soft and subtle, like slowly letting air out of a bike tire. My eyes dart about anxiously. The girl I share the table with is absent, leaving me to sit by myself. The rest of the class is busy burrowing their heads in their test papers.

*"Over here..."* The voice calls softly in my mind, highlighting the femininity in the voice. It's definitely not Pyewacket. This seething voice wafts around in my head like a poisonous fog.

My pulse quickens. *The Ouija board, the planchette. Whoever we reached is talking to me now.* My head throbs painfully at my temples as the whisper chuckles almost like a low purr from a pussy-cat lounging on a stuffed pillow.

*"Get ready, Eleanor."* There's a strange, almost sultry quality to the voice. Despite the seductive edge, it's like an audible black stain on snowy white silk.

I glance at the window to my left, only to jerk my head back, doing a double take. My hands tremble on the tabletop as my heart stops. My reflection is completely absent from the immense glass window beside me. Staring back at me is a beautiful woman with thick auburn hair, curls stacked upon her head like a Greek goddess. Her oval face is sculpted and severe, her cheekbones defined as if crafted by a chisel. Her doe eyes are coal black, a vicious abyss of churning darkness framed by wickedly high arched eyebrows like a 1930's film villain. Her stare doesn't waver as it remains steadfast and volatile, as if I were staring down the barrel of a gun. Her full ruby red lips pull back in a terrifying yet alluring smile.

There's a painful stabbing in my chest as I feel an unexplainable surge of dislike eclipse into the blackest loathing. Air traps inside my constricted lungs. My eyes hold her icy stare as fiery hate blares inside me, vibrating in every cell. *Who is she?* I don't even know why I hate this woman, this transparent woman whom I don't even recognize. But I do. More than anything. There's second's warning crackle, the window explodes in a terrifying cacophony. The shattered glass ricochets in every direction, causing everyone to leap up from their seats and rush to the opposing wall.

A few kids shriek in disbelief and fright, but most are stunned into silence. Shards of jagged glass have embedded themselves in the walls and on tabletops. I stay in my seat, staring at the window in shock.

"I've been cut. I swear I can feel a cut somewhere!" A girl cries. She runs to Nick for inspection. "Can you see it?!" She shimmies up and down, shaking her chest, trying to dislodge any glass.

Everyone hastily begins checking themselves, making sure they hadn't been scratched and weren't carrying any glass on them. Miraculously, everyone seems unharmed, myself included.

"I know I'm bleeding! I can feel when my body is bleeding! So I have a cut somewhere!"

"I don't see any cut, Beth," Nick assures, looking her over. He raises his thick black eyebrow as he watches her maul her clothing and hair.

Mr. Andersen, standing slacked jawed, snaps to attention. "Is-is everyone okay?"

I can feel this pleasure trickle inside me, completely foreign and separate, like a sliver sliding under my skin. The window frame doesn't have even a single splinter of glass left in it. *Had I shattered the window? Or was it the woman somehow?*

"Eleanor?" Mr. Andersen shouts. I suddenly realize he's been repeating my name over and over to get my attention. He crouches next to me, glass crunching beneath his loafers. His eyes sweep over me. "Are you alright?"

"I'm so, I'm—I'm so sorry," I stammer. "I don't know what happened, I—," I stop before I accidentally out myself. "I was just sitting there and then someone—err, something…just…I'm not sure how…but…"

Mr. Andersen tilts his head side to side, still examining me. "Eleanor, Eleanor, it's not your fault," he assures. "Someone must have thrown a rock at the window, or the changing temperatures caused it to fracture and burst. This is a very old building." He gazes at me with large, baffled eyes. "How are you not hurt?"

Despite my objections, Mr. Andersen dusts my hair, feeling for glass. Finding no cause for alarm, he still insists that I go to the nurse's office to get checked out. A few boys, Nick included, offer to walk me down to the office. The girls can't help but look annoyed. Instead, Mr. Andersen instructs Nick to go get the janitor and everyone else to continue checking themselves over.

I pick up my bag off the table. There's a square outline around where my bag sat, but no glass landed near my belongings. I nervously swallow some hiccups before ducking out of the classroom, avoiding the group of seething or curious gazes.

I keep expecting glass to sprinkle off me as I walk down the hall, but nothing comes. *Who the hell was that woman?* She said my name and stared at me like she had known me. But not just known me like a friend, but really *knew* me. *How is that possible? Seriously, who is she?* It feels like more than that stupid Ouija board. It's like there is a locked box at the back of my mind that contains answers about her. I know her from somewhere. I just don't know how…

*** 

I'm promised the nurse will see me shortly, so I scroll through my phone, peering at pictures posted by friends back in Florida. It feels like a different lifetime now. I'm not sure how long I can flip through pictures pretending everything is normal, that I didn't just make a window explode while a ghost was staring at me. My blood runs cold thinking of her stare. I don't know who she is, but one thing's for sure: we hate each other. *But why? Why am I feeling like this?* It feels as if something dark, heavy, and slimy crawled into my body and has begun to rot.

I scratch my scalp. My braid has loosened and a few pieces have escaped.

*Okay, think. I've never seen that woman before in my life. She was probably the person communicating through the Ouija board. But if she is, then how did she know all those personal details about me? If she's been haunting my aunts' house, she wouldn't have known those answers. Unless she followed us from Florida. But why? This doesn't make any sense.*

To the left of the nurse's office, the boy's locker room door opens. Hair still wet from the shower, Jack steps out. The collar of his white shirt is damp against his neck. His tie is draped around his neck untie. Pink spills into his cheeks when he spots me.

I quickly busy myself in my phone, pretending I don't notice him. I zero in on a picture of my old friend's dog as I can feel him come closer until he sits next to me. *Please don't address the drawing I saw when I was spying. I'm sure you have a reasonable explanation.*

"Hey," he says, his voice is uneven, unsure.

I lower my phone. "What's up," I say casually. My head suddenly fills with the scent of expensive manly soap.

He tilts his head, gazing at me, concerned. "I heard about the window incident. Are you okay?"

"What? How? It like… *just* happened?" I balk.

Jack leans on his elbows, resting on his knees. "My cousin Bethany, she's in the class. She took a picture of it. Does Mr. Andersen know what happened? Beth is saying a flaw in the glass. Callum's stepbrother is in your junior class and claims a freshman threw a rock at the window." He flashes me his phone, showing me the picture circulating around the school of the empty window frame.

*Perfect.*

Jack straightens up. "Are you okay? You didn't get hurt?" His eyes sweep over me, concerned.

I nod, then let my head fall back. "Yeah, I'm fine. Window's not."

Jack coughs, clearing his throat nervously. "I don't want to pry, but is…anyone giving you…" He stops like he's searching for the right word, "harassing you? Or bothering you? Maybe someone with an overactive camera?" he says, curtly ending the last part.

I shake my head. "Nick has that class with me. He didn't do it. He's fine," I say, not quite sure why I'm jumping to his defense. *Well, doesn't matter. He didn't do it, anyway. I did.*

Jack nods thoughtfully. "Well, would you tell me if you notice anything?"

Exasperated, I shrug. "Sure. I doubt I'll find anything."

Jack, however, doesn't look so convinced. "So, I'm sure you're aware, we don't have school on Wednesday. I was wondering, would you like to come sailing with me?"

I glance down at his hands; he's nervously playing with a cuticle.

My heart flutters. Butterflies take flight in my stomach, and for a moment, the window, the magic, that woman, none of it matters. "Yeah, I would love to."

He grins at me; his worried fingers relax. "Perfect, it's a date. Could I get your number? You know, to coordinate?"

My lips curl into a smile. I peer down at my shoes. "Of course," I say before reciting my number. He quickly types it into his phone, and I jump a little as my phone buzzes in my lap. "Oh gosh, did you already text me? If you did, that would be so cheesy," I joke, secretly hoping he did.

Heard about the window, I think it is best for you to come home. Just leave, we'll call in an excuse.
This is your Aunt Marie, not Sally. Xoxo

"Nope, that wasn't me," he says, sliding his phone back into his pocket.

I frown at my phone. "Yeah. Honestly, I'm actually not entirely sure who this is." *My aunts are so weird.*

Jack rises to his feet. "I better get going. I'll catch you later?"

I wave goodbye and immediately regret it, knowing how stupid I look. As soon as Jack turns the corner, I speed to the parking lot, unsure whether I'm relieved to cut the rest of my classes.

"Sally, Marie?" I call out, walking into the house. Cats are meandering about, and a swanky, Dixieland jazz record plays from their gramophone.

Marie pops her head out of the greenhouse and Sally descends from the second landing. Marie hurries over to me, nearly mowing down three cats scrambling to get out of the way.

"Oh, my dear, are you alright?" Marie gathers me into her, her hands probe my clothing looking for glass. "What happened? Do we need more practice controlling your magic?"

Sally clears her throat, her high heels clacking against the wood stairs. "Are we ready to begin?" she questions, wearing a red sparkling evening gown with sequence flames.

Marie cocks a brow disapprovingly. "What happened to wearing black?"

Sally grins, her elbow resting on her wrist. She snaps her fingers. The sparkling flames on her dress ripple up the bodice before consuming the sleeves, leaving the dress completely black like it's scorched. "To the kitchen." She points the way before leading the charge.

Marie sighs. "Sal, we need to talk about this window incident with Eleanor," she says, placing her hand on my shoulder. "I don't think learning another branch is appropriate at the moment. She needs to work on control. We don't want anymore broken windows."

Sally drops her head back petulantly. "Why? It was probably ugly anyway. I'm sure Eleanor did them a favor. Besides, accidents happen, it's part of the learning process. She'll learn further control the more she learns her magic."

Marie stares at me with concern, but soon relents, and we follow Sally down the hall.

The white kitchen cupboards glow against the room sheathed in darkness. Blackout curtains drape in each window, white long stem candles balance carefully on the countertops. In the middle of their kitchen island is a metal bowl, a stick, and several leather books.

"More grimoires?" I ask, fingering the edges of the page. "We might need some more light if we plan on reading these."

Sally shrugs, strolling to the other side of the island from me. "I put those out for Marie's benefit."

Marie pulls up a stool, sitting close to me. "Eleanor, sweetie, these books contain entries from witches dating back to the sixteenth century. These women didn't just scribble something down for no reason. We are to study their words, their advice, their accomplishments. As much as Sally pretends not to care, when she trained, she pored over every book out here. Without these, she never would have developed her power the way she has. The same goes for all of us. These women," she places her hand on the thickest book next to us, "they were creative. They figured out just how far their power of fire could go. Learn from our ancestors; they have much to teach you."

Sally frowns skeptically at her sister. "I can't tell if that was a compliment or not. But no matter, the show must go on. Eleanor, just as when you learned the air spell, it's all about measured control. You picture what you want your magic to do. But the more physical action you put into it, the easier it is at first."

I perch on the stool next to Marie. "Physical action?"

A candle levitates over to us, wax tears drip across the floor.

"Yes, yes, I'll clean it up, Marie," Sally snaps before her older sister can say anything. The solitary candle comes to a stop and rests directly between Sally and me. "Not to brag, but this branch of magic is my gift. I've never needed the physicality; fire always obeyed."

Marie coughs and clears her throat, signaling to Sally to get on with it.

"But others need a little more help. Technically, no, you don't have to move any part of your body, but often witches, young and old but especially newbies, need to move their hands, or blow, something to better bind the feeling of control to the spell. Like so," Sally bends her head closer to the candle, the flame extinguished, "I'm going to say the incantation in my head, then I'm going to blow on the wick to light the candle."

Marie leans close to my ear. "I like to snap my fingers."

Sally lightly blows on the wick, igniting a powerful flame. She straightens up. "Easy. Now your turn."

The flame vanishes, and like a sudden vacuum opened in the room, there's no smoke to be found.

"The incantation is *Ne Feerah*. Picture the wick igniting, then blow," Sally instructs, nodding at the candle.

Leaning on my elbows, my mouth hovers above the candle. Sweat prickles my neck. I glance at both my aunts. "And you're prepared with a fire extinguisher if this goes awry?" My stomach bubbles like a cauldron.

Marie tilts her head, gazing at me kindly. "Why do you think I'm here?" Marie asks, more of a statement. "I'm far better than a fire extinguisher."

I turn back to the candle. I picture a perfectly innocent flame. A small, non-threatening, totally extinguishable flame. *Ne Feerah*. I whisper out a breath onto the wick. I hastily pull back, not wanting to burn my eyebrows off. A small spark burst from the wick before a tiny orange flame flickers to life. "Oh my gosh! I did it! You guys saw that, right!?" I practically bounce in my seat. I pull at the collar of my starchy school blouse, feeling a little warm.

Marie claps her hands together. "Brava! Brava, our little Ellie!" she leans over planting a kiss on the side of my head.

Sally bows her head at me. "Well done. Now, moving on." She picks up an ordinary stick, about the length of her forearm.

Marie shakes her head. "No Sal, she's not ready for that," she argues.

Sally turns an icy eye to Marie. "She lit the candle on her first try. Your first time you lit mother's curtains on fire. She can handle this." She hands me the stick like a baton. "I want you to light the entire stick while holding it. If the fire is obeying your command, it should not burn you."

I peer over to Marie uneasily. "Okay." I place the stick back down on the island's counter and shrug off my jacket. My armpits feel like moist caves and beads of sweat trickle down my breasts and spine. My slick fingers grasp the stick, gripping it between my thumb and forefinger. Closing my eyes, I imagine the entire stick engulfed in a flame, leaving a little space for my fingers, bending away from my body. *Ne Feerah*. I open my eyes to see the stick smoking. A flame ignites and crawls down the stick, creeping closer and closer to my fingers. The fire stops, then begins on the other side until it reaches the very end.

"Well done!" Marie exclaims excitedly. "Oh, my dear, perhaps fire is your talent!"

Sally smiles. "Good, we could use another fiery broad in this house."

My hand quivers as the flame licks away at the branch dangerously close to my skin. When my fingers start to burn, I yelp and drop the stick into the empty metal bowl, shaking my hand as if it's on fire. I peer at the tips of my finger and thumb. My skin begins to bubble and blister.

Marie hops off her stool and takes my hand, examining the damage. "I'll get the aloe and goat's milk. Sally, I think we are done for the day."

Surprisingly, Sally agrees. The blackout curtains drop from the windows and all the candles blow out. Grey smoke swirls and dissipates. "Now Eleanor, since we are cutting our training short, you're gonna have to read these." She stacks the books and pushes them over to me, never actually touching them. They make magic look so effortless.

I examine the top book's cover and the gold flame etched at the top. Inside, the pages are yellowed, cottony, and thin in the beginning. I can smell the age as I carefully flip through the pages. Blue lines etched by witches through the ages who added their own suggestions. I frown, peering closer to one entry's author. Sally Cliodhna Byrne. She drew pictures of dancing fire balls and witches clasping hands about the fire. She wrote poems, suggesting that adding the incantation to a poem made it more potent and thus the fire more powerful.

Sweat from my forehead drips onto the page. I wipe my hand across my face. "Okay, it feels like an oven in here. I blame all the candles."

Sally chuckles. "It's your first time working the spell. Your body's temperature is rising. I recommend an ice bath."

"Already set up," Marie informs, looking up to the ceiling.

By the time I'm stripping for the bath, my clothes are soaked through. My entire body trembles as I step into the tub. Steam rises around me. My teeth chatter and I hold myself at my elbows, leaning my head against the lip of the tub. I can feel the floating ice chunks shrink as my body acts like a hot coal.

By the time the ice has completely melted, a metal bucket filled with more comes bounding in through the door, replenishing my tub. It takes three more ice refills before I stop perspiring.

After the bath, I can only bear to wear a bralette and light cotton jersey shorts. I pour over the various spell books. One witch, a great-great-great-grandmother of mine, used the air spell to help cool herself after overworking the fire spell. I consider it for a moment, but I can't help but picture a cyclone whipping around my room, destroying everything I own. I continue reading through the passages, my different ancestors theorizing how all the elements connect, how we set our own limitations.

I instinctively lean closer to a page clearly torn from a school notebook and spliced into this ancient grimoire. The author is my mother when she was seventeen. She expressed her struggle for a steady stream of heat. She broke it down to molecules and organic chemistry, suggesting that if we better understand science, the better control we'll gain over the element. I devour page after page, chuckling at a few of my mother's misspellings but enjoying her amateur thesis.

My neck aches from being hunched over. I stretch my arms above my head, then eye my textbooks and violin case by the desk. My arms drop to my sides and my insides sag. *I have at least an hour each of calculus, physics, and French.* I run my hands down my face. *Why did my mom have to pack my schedule?* A thought occurs to me. *She didn't anticipate I'd be busy with witch training.* I want to snatch my phone and send her an angry text, but knowing how my dad would feel if I lashed out in spite, I send her a kind "miss you" text instead.

I turn back to my mother's writings and trace her scientific sketches. They're actually well done; I didn't know she could draw. I lift my eyes from the page as Pyewacket strides into the room.

"*Have anything you'd like to share?*" he questions before leaping onto my bed, sitting across from me.

I roll my eyes. "If you wanted to know how great my training went, you should have been there," I say sullenly.

Laying on his stomach, he lays one paw over the other, trying to level me with a gaze. "*I was talking about the damage to private property. I've seen you use your magic; you could have prevented such a catastrophe. Do you want to be found out, you silly child?*"

I drop the grimoire onto my bed. "It was an accident. You seriously think I wanted that kind of attention?"

"*Then tell me what happened,*" he demands.

I exhale, internally mumbling expletives.

"*I can hear all of that.*"

I fold my arms across my chest indignantly. "It was an accident. I think I saw the person, creature, I don't know, a ghost maybe? The thing we spoke to on the Ouija board. It was a woman, beautiful, but off somehow." I picture her face, her sharp model-like features. She was stunning but scary, like a bejeweled scabbard over a blood crusted machete. "She had auburn hair, sharp features, black irises."

I stop recalling her eyes so clearly burned into my memory. Her eyes weren't just black, they were threads of purple, like an onyx with veins of amethyst. "There was a hint of purple. She was a reflection in the window, calling to me. I could feel how much she...hated me. And I hated her. But I don't know her, at least I don't think I do. She had full lips, pouty almost. Her skin alabaster." Despite the warmth, I feel a shiver down my arms. "She was taunting me. I don't know if she broke the window, or I did." My chest rises and falls faster and faster. I'm about to break down into a dry sob. "I don't ever want to see her again. What if she comes back?" I ask in a quivering whine.

Pyewacket has a faraway look on his face as he stares off towards the pentagon window. His thoughts are quiet, muddled, and undecipherable.

"Do you know her?" I inquire, feeling a strange pang of betrayal.

"*Yes.*"

"Who is she?" I cross my legs, wanting to fold into myself protectively. "How do you know her?"

Pyewacket remains silent, his eyes fixed on the window, his body is still as he's not breathing. "Her name is Elspeth. I was her familiar, long ago."

I frown, befuddled. "So, she's like coming back to claim you?"

He shakes his head. "*No. She's dead. We were executed together.*"

Questions keep jumping in my head, like popcorn. "How? Why?"

"*It was the sixteenth century. She was on trial for witchcraft to which she was found guilty.*"

"Did they have any proof?" I ask, doubting they had any, thinking back on everything I know about the Salem witch trials.

"*Yes.*" He shut his eyes as if wanting to shut out an unpleasant memory.

"What?" I ask.

"*She stabbed a small child, offering him to Satan.*"

A tinkling, eerie lullaby begins to play.

"What the hell is that?" I ask, glancing about, searching for the source. I close my eyes, trying to locate the source of the music. I crawl to the edge of the bed and peer over.

Under my head is the creepy black music box with the red carved writing. The lid is propped open, the rotating spring is empty, creaking as it turns. On the floor next to the box is the witch, its body shattered.

# Chapter Twenty-One
## Missing

I barely taste my food at dinner. I push my roasted carrots around my plate with my fork.

"*Stop being a child and eat,*" Pyewacket says, sitting at the end of the table to my left.

I roll my eyes at him. *Maybe I'll start listening to you when you start being honest with me and quit keeping secrets. Why is Elspeth reaching out to me? Did she smash the jewelry box? Why would she smash the creepy jewelry box? How is she even able to do that? Is it because she wants you back for some reason? If so, she can have you. I won't put up a fight. I want her to go away. I need to know how to get rid of her.*

Pyewacket turns back to his tuna tartare, disregarding me completely.

"Eleanor, hello?" Margaret says, waving her hand in front of my face.

My head snaps up, looking from my plate to my sister. "I'm sorry, what?"

Maggie looks at me incredulously. "Mom wants you to call her after dinner. She thinks you've been screening her calls."

I rub my temple, all of a sudden feeling incredibly exhausted. "I haven't been, I've just been really… busy." I turn back to my uneaten dinner.

Margaret reaches for a roll and her butter knife. "Well, call her before she suspects anything."

I idly slice a pea in half. "How long am I supposed to keep my training a lie?" I mumble, still sour from Pyewacket's unnecessary evasiveness.

Sally swirls her wine in her goblet, examining the liquid inside. "Just until you're done training, by then it's too late."

"I still think we should just be honest. Helen isn't unreasonable," Marie insists.

Sally glares at her sister. "Are you kidding? Do you think it was reasonable to never tell her kids that they're witches?" She stops and takes a swig. "And you think I'm the ridiculous one in the family."

"A certain flaming chainsaw would back me up," Marie states dryly.

Sally drops her fork on her plate with a loud clatter. "It's practically gone now. Helen's old remedy worked, okay?"

After dinner, the aunts have me use my magic to clear the dining room table, scraping the plates and stacking them neatly in the kitchen sink to soak. Maggie did her best to keep her jealous grumblings to herself and even gave me a word of encouragement when I accidentally dropped the gravy boat on the floor, breaking off the handle.

I pace my bedroom nervously, wondering if I should wait for my mom to call me and get going on neglected homework. I peer at my phone's screen, my thumb hovering over the call icon. I growl to myself and keep striding my room. *I don't have time to sit on the phone. I need to clean up the broken box still under my bed and demand Pyewacket stop playing games with me.* I pause, letting my arm hang at my side. *Maybe I am avoiding my mom. How could she lie to us for so long?*

I fall back on the bed, and without giving myself another second to chicken out, I hit call. My mom answers after three rings.

"Eleanor," she whispers. She sniffs like she has been crying.

"Hey Mom," my heart softens hearing her melancholy. "Are you okay?" I ask lamely. *Of course, she's not okay; Dad is gone.*

She sniffs again and releases a quiet whimper. "I'm sorry, it's just been a hard day today. Dad had some loose ends I needed to tie up."

I want to apologize for my resentment. I want to comfort her, I want to tell her something, anything that would help, but instead I curl up on my bed listening to her speak. She explains she has finished things with the house and has been dealing with attorneys and wills and my father's "lovely" family. She tries to make light of things joking about Mr. McDaniel's putting Lydia in her place, and my uncle Richard roping the family into a crypto scam. Despite trying to enliven the conversation, her voice still trembles with grief.

I think about the spell for grief Margaret did with the aunts. There has to be several spells that could help her through this, yet she chooses not to. *Why?* It has to be more than just wanting her children to grow up like my dad. But he's gone now, so why keep up the charade? Is there something else she's hiding?

My mother was hesitant to hang up the phone, but she forced a brave voice and expressed how much she missed me. I roughly jab my graphing calculator, struggling with my calculus homework. *I'm a witch, there's got to be a spell to do this.* I read through the differential equations as my calculator stalls. The numbers blur on the page. I squint, staring as the X's as they start to vibrate on the page. I feel a quiet simmer inside of me. I place the paper back down on my bed and close my eyes. *Is my magic trying to serve me?* It doesn't feel like the air or fire are reaching out. It's something new with almost crystalized clarity, a small direct light on a singular dark spot. I open my eyes; the equations are solved and complete. I snatch the paper, holding it up close. The answers are written in a perfectly neat script, but close to my hand. The ink, however, is a shiny metallic silver. I can practically see my reflection on the numerals. *How did I do that?*

There's a knock on the bedroom door. "Ellie?" Marie calls.

"Come in." I uncross my legs and gather up the books on my bed.

Marie waddles in; three cats follow. "I just wanted to say goodnight, dearie. I have a Committee meeting tonight at midnight, lots to get done before The Gathering." She watches me stack the spell books and workbooks on the desk. "I'm so glad you're studying magic so diligently."

She turns to the bed and her eyes zero in on my finished homework. "Eleanor," she chides, picking up my homework. "You shouldn't be doing your homework with magic. It's not breaking the witches' code, exactly, but it is heavily frowned upon." My aunt turns on her heel, handing me back my calc worksheet.

My brow knits in confusion, taking it from Marie. "I wasn't even meaning to. I have no idea how I did it. I'm still not even sure what's possible."

Marie holds her hands in front of her. "You exercised the mind spell. You didn't actually fill out your homework, it's an illusion. These answers will most likely fade before you hand it in. You are seeing what you think your instructor wants to see." Marie clucks her tongue at me. "Just this once, and this one time only." She points her forefinger towards the worksheet. A few equations correct themselves and the ink sinks lower into the page, like being struck down by the mechanical levers of a typewriter. "Those answers should stay on that paper for a few weeks, at any rate. Do not tell your Aunt Sally, I'll deny everything," she warns. "Sleep well, my darling." She kisses the top of my head. "I'll send up some willow bark tea for your head. It's going to hurt."

My temples throb, and as I brush my teeth, my brain feels like it's being squeezed. I practically crawl up the stairs and collapse into bed. On the nightstand next to the bed rests a steaming floral teacup. I lose consciousness as I reach for it.

My legs are crossed at the ankles, wind tangles in my hair as I sit side-saddle on my broom. Pyewacket rests inside a leather satchel swung over my shoulder. My stomach drops and my mouth goes dry. I grip the broom, terrified, sending it jerking upward. *Crap! Crap! Crap!* My entire body quakes with fear. *Why, why am I flying? And why would I ride it like this? Pyewacket!? Help me!* I'm going faster and faster up towards the sky. The trees look like small broccoli stalks beneath my dangling feet.

"She's cheating!"

"Send her down!"

"No, send her up. The higher she is, the harder she falls..."

"Eleanor, is that you?"

"Eleanor! Get up or you're going to be late for school soon!" Marie hollers from the landing.

Groaning, I roll off the bed. The tea from last night spills all over my pillow. I pull on my uniform and snag my suede u-heel ankle boots, questioning my decision to wear tights. I don't even have time to eat breakfast as I dash off to school, arriving just after the bell.

Taking my seat in English, I find myself anxiously waiting for Jack to show. I didn't get a chance to put on makeup; I barely had time to brush out my hair. *Do I look good?* I hate that I care. Why should it matter what he thinks? He's *just* a boy. A gorgeous, kind, funny, sweet boy with the greenest eyes I have ever seen. I notice several seats throughout the classroom are vacant.

"He's not here."

I glance to the back of the classroom. For some reason, Vivienne is seated next to Poppy who is tapping away on her phone, grinning devilishly.

"Who?" I mumble, pretending not to know who she's talking about.

Poppy giggles and rolls her eyes as Vivienne cocks a thin brow on her perfect heart-shaped face. "Jack, of course. The crew team is away on a meet. A bunch of us are cutting out early to go show our support." She pauses and smiles, her eyes narrow on me. "Want to come?"

I have an uneasy feeling; this is a trap. I shake my head. "I'm good, thanks." I turn back to face the front as Mr. Edwards strides to the front of the classroom.

Poppy whispers something to Vivienne, causing them both to laugh.

"Good morning. As I'm sure you have all noticed, we have a new pupil. Miss Mather will be joining us for the rest of the year," he says, gathering papers from his desk.

Vivienne pulls her silken hair to one side. "Yes, because Mr. Fowler is sexist," she retorts, examining her fresh manicure.

Mr. Edwards clears his throat, piqued at the chuckling students.

At the end of class, I wait for Vivienne and Poppy to exit, saving me from having to walk past them.

"Eleanor, are you alright?" Mr. Edwards questions, gazing at me quizzically.

Vivienne and Poppy stop at the door, glancing at me.

I nod, tucking my hair behind my ear. "Yeah, I'm fine."

Vivienne and her lemming exchange glances before finally leaving.

Winston peers at the door, closing it behind them. "Eleanor, are you certain you're well? I'm aware of the glass in Andersen's room."

I place one hand on my temple, scrunching my face. "Yeah. It was an accident. I thought I saw something, and I'm not sure what happened."

Winston rocked back in his chair, placing his hands on his tummy. "There were witnesses that a student possibly from St. Michael's threw the stone."

I groan, letting my forehead rest on the desk. "That's a rumor. I don't know how that started."

Winston coughs. "I started it. I may have also planted some…memories. The mind is so very malleable, memories especially so."

The classroom door opens and students tramp in.

I gather my belongings, unsettled and confused by his admission. "Um, thanks, I think," I say before quickly dashing out. I run into Nick in the hall.

Relief floods his face when he sees me. "Finally, I thought that old tool kidnapped you. Hurry, I can't get another demerit." Nick snatches my hand and hauls me down the hall to the classroom. "I was really worried about you. I heard you had to leave early."

Mr. Andersen swoops in the moment I enter, prodding me about my wellbeing. "The police are investigating, and the perpetrator will be apprehended," he assures while I slide into my seat.

Blood drains from my face. "Wait, seriously?" My stomach twists like a coiled snake, making me feel nauseated. *This can't be happening. What are they going to do when they don't find anyone?*

Mr. Andersen delivers an engaging lecture on the real Paul Revere while I finish the quiz I was unable to yesterday.

Trixie catches up with me in the hall after class. "Eleanor, I was really worried about you. I wanted to come to your home but my parents advised against it. Are you okay?" she inquires kindly. Her hand moves so quickly I almost don't notice her hand slipping a red columbine and basil in my coat pocket. Each day, I've been finding leaves, flowers, and herbs in my pockets.

"Yeah, I'm fine. I guess a student threw a rock or something," I reply, stopping at my locker for my violin.

Trixie gives me a sly, conspiratorial smile. "Right, of course," she says with a wink. "I heard he even had a hook for a hand." She wiggles her eyebrows at me. "So, are you excited about Friday? I'm getting a brand-new dress for it. My mom took me to Esmerelda's, and she's seriously a genius," she says excitedly. "She embroidered chrysanthemums all over the bodice and skirt. They're the same color as the dress, but they add some charm and texture. Do you know what you're wearing? Other than a dress, of course."

My violin case keeps bumping me in the leg as we walk. "What are you talking about?"

She scrunches her impish face at me, amused. "Oh, Eleanor, it's only the best night of the year. The Gathering! We wear period costumes, there are contests, music, dancing! It's seriously the best." She stops talking, taking in my befuddled face. "Oh, I'm sure you're going! Marie is on The Committee; Sally always takes part in dancing naked around the fire. You'll be there, I just know it." Trixie rambles on about the delectable food, the famous witches that attend, seances, potion making, and more. Thankfully, most of the students in the hall either had pods in their ears or continued their shunning of Trixie, ignoring us completely.

Orchestra drudged on, dragging out every shrieking minute until finally the end of the hour bell granted me mercy.

"Eleanor," Ms. Seawall called after me. "I counted eighteen mistakes. Perhaps instead of chasing boys, you could start practicing."

I continued to mutter under my breath as I marched off to lunch.

"So, Eleanor? What are you doing Wednesday? You know, our day off?" Nick probes as he takes a swig of my soda and then returns it to my tray. I don't have many pet peeves, but back wash is definitely one of them. I pick the bottle off my tray and place it on his.

"Um, I'm going sailing with Jack," I answer before taking a bite of my pizza.

The table falls silent. All the boys peer over at Nick towering next to me. They cower, waiting for the volcano to erupt, killing us all in its massive, terrifying wake.

Nick surprises everyone as he takes a pensive bite of his roast beef sandwich, not seeming too perturbed. "Seems like you're spending a lot of time with Jack," he says while he chews. "Are you guys what, like a couple or something?"

I shrug. "We're just friends. We're all just friends," I say, trying to get my point across loud and clear.

He balls up his fists, and then… relaxes them. He straightens up. "I just worry about you, that's all. And I've known Jack for a long time. I can't stand him. That whole golden boy act is crap. He's *not* a good guy. He took Vivienne away from me my freshmen year. He became the captain of the rowing team his sophomore year when that spot wasn't his to have. It was my cousin's. Jack likes to take things that don't belong to him. Just trust me on this, you'd be better off cancelling your plans," he states like a command, then chomps off another bite of his sandwich. He swallows and forces a smile. "So, I was thinking we could go up to my family's cabin tonight and spend the night. The bar is stocked, my parents just finished putting in a hot tub—"

"Swimsuits optional?" Noah chimes in.

"You're keeping yours on, bro," Alden retorts.

Nick laughs at his friends. "Bikinis are optional."

I don't wait for him to rearrange my plans any further. "I can't, Nick. I'm sorry, I agreed to plans with Jack. I'm not just blowing them off."

"Bring him along," Tripp suggests, causing Pete and Nick to grimace.

"I'll ask," I lie. Playing referee between Jack and the boys was not how I wanted to spend my evening.

Nick glares at Tripp for the suggestion, to which Tripp mouthed back, *what?*

I finish my lunch and prepare to leave just as Nick's hand lands on my knee with a soft squeeze.

"Are you just going to ignore me?" Nick questions me, his every word encased with ice.

I hold back a growl. "What are you talking about?"

He throws his hands up. "Jack! I told you he's bad and you're still going out with him!?"

I shrink beside him. "I appreciate your warning, but I would like to make up my own mind. Besides, Jack and I are just friends," I say gently, noticing now that several people have turned towards the table.

Nick's fist slowly curls closed.

My stomach drops. *This needs to be over. I need to get away from him.* But I'm too scared to get up. My palms are slick with sweat. I stare at my tray. My magic bubbles deep within me. I nearly cry out when my head pulsates. There's no switch to flip, no way of stopping whatever is coming. The bell rings loudly overhead, surprising and confusing the students in the lunchroom but reluctantly obeying its trill. Kids start dumping their tray and trudging out of the room questioning the time.

"What the hell, it's eight minutes early," Noah complains, glancing at his phone. "I'm not moving."

I take this opportune distraction and make my escape.

"Nice work," Trixie jests when I take my seat next to her in anatomy. "Though of all the hours to shorten, why lunch?"

My head still pounds. "It was an accident."

Trixie snickers. "Those are happening a lot."

That stings, probably more than Trixie meant it to. But it is happening a lot. I feel a total loss of control, like I'm strapped on some kind of psychotic rollercoaster, turning me, flipping me, with no way of ever getting off it. Is this just my life now? Will training fix anything?

"How long have you been training?" I whisper just as Ms. Albert turns off the lights and flips on the television fastened to the wall.

"Well, I turned seventeen in February, and I only just finished last weekend. But I had read all our family's grimoires, and checked out spell books from The Committee's library since I was like eight. Why do you ask?" Trixie doodles flowers and leaves in her book.

"No reason."

How different her training must have gone. She had sixteen years of preparation. I had a tough revelation upon moving to Salem. Part of me wishes I had grown up like Trixie, but then again, would I have been so close to my dad if I knew we were basically two different species? Already, I feel a distance from my memory of him now that I'm training. With each spell, an abyss grows.

The sound of wind chimes jingles. Trixie reaches into her macrame school bag, pulling out her phone. She gasps, staring down at her glowing screen. Before I can even ask if everything's okay, she turns to me, stricken.

"Doris Calloway has been missing and now her son Rivers is too. Our families are super close. Rivers just turned seventeen in November," she whispers, tears gathering in her deep blue eyes.

I lamely pat her shoulder, not sure what to do. "I'm really sorry. Is there something going on? I think I heard my aunts talking about another missing witch from Salem State or something." I squeeze my eyes shut as my headache continues to pound and cause my ears to ring.

Trixie shrugs and pulls out an embroidered hanky from her pocket. "I don't know. My parents don't talk to me about Committee business. But River's younger brother, Casen, messaged me. It's serious. Their older brother, Vic, is coming back from Liverpool to help the search for his family. I'll be right back; I need to call Casen. He's only twelve." Trixie materializes a pass and strides up to the front of the class.

I wish I could be more help, but the pain raging in my head is hitting an unbearable fever pitch. I consider ditching the rest of the day, but I can't miss my calculus test. Trixie never returns to class and the rest of the day is fraught with the worst headache of my life. When I get to my car, I lean my head on the headrest, unable to drive home. I close my eyes and lean my seat back. *I'm pretty sure I failed my calc test.*

Like a ripple moving across a smooth lake, my headache gradually irons out. I lift my head and open my eyes, nearly crying from relief. I'm not in my car anymore. I'm standing in a freezing creek, my feet burn in the cold. I quickly amble to the rocky bank surrounded by dense forest.

*What the heck?* The stars in the sky are blotted out by the glowing full moon illuminating the vegetation below. I'm still in my school uniform, but barefoot. I feel the sharp pine needles and pebbles beneath my feet. I wrap my arms around myself, shivering. *How did I get here? Is this a dream?* There's a rustle of twigs breaking behind the trees and a strange moaning sound. I rush to hide behind a bolder, bracing myself for whatever is coming. A herd of bleating goats trots past, pushing through underbrush and trudging across the river. One goat stops and peers over at me, his eyes scarlet and wide. His stare is so intense I almost expect him to speak. He nods his head across the shallow river. Without thinking, I follow. I curse, stepping on the sharp undergrowth. *Where are my boots? Why couldn't I have been wearing shoes?*

The trees peter out. I scrunch my nose as I suddenly smell smoke. We stop at a clearing and peer down into a valley. The red-eyed goat stops at my side as the rest of his herd trudges on, going down a beaten path into the valley. Nestled between hills are wooden colonial homes, shops, and farms, but every building is engulfed in flames. Men, women, and children come running out screaming. My eyes furiously slide from burning dwelling to burning dwelling. In the center of this little village sits a gallows with six hanging bodies strung deadly still.

"What is this? What am I seeing?" I question either the goat or myself. I glance at my sides expecting to see the goat, but he's gone. I hear a patting of hooves. I slowly turn, spotting the goat behind me several yards, breaking into a run right for me. "Wait!" I put my hands up instinctively, glancing over my shoulder at the steep drop. The homes are ashes now. The ground is littered with bodies.

I whip back around to see the possessed goat lowering its head, about to ram into me. Just as its curled horns collide with my body, my ears are filled with the sound of blaring sirens and someone shouting my name.

My eyes fall open and I tumble back to reality. I'm lying on the parking lot pavement, cradled in Nick's arms. He's shaking me, yelling my name, and begging me to wake up. The sky is pale pink. Blue and red lights flash from a nearby firetruck and an ambulance comes bounding down the road.

# A Spell for Visions

*(For those seeking that which is hidden)*

## Ingredients:

Valerian root      Chamomile tea      Mugwort
Wolfsbane candle      Virgin oil      Celestite
Tiger's eye stone      Moonstone
Lily of the Valley Candle with witch's bone

## Instructions:

Place the blue candle to your left and the white candle to your right. Place the celestite next to the blue candle at the six o'clock position, and the tiger's eye stone next to the white candle at the midnight position. Place the moonstone under your pillow. Hang the valerian root above the bed.

Drink the entire cup of tea, then let the night take you as you speak the incantation into the dark.

## Incantation:

*In whispered words, I conjure dreams,*
*Through blessed chants, my mind's agleam,*
*In shadows, dreams dance, and play,*
*A realm of magic, where visions hold sway*
*Brighid Oculi*
*Blessed be*

# Chapter Twenty-Two
## Dreams and Visions

My limbs are heavy, and my brain is still foggy from the dream. "Nick, what's going on?" I ask, leaning away from him, still wrapped in his arms.

His jaw falls open, his eyes expand to the size of saucers. "Eleanor!" he snatches me back, burrowing his face in my hair. "I thought you were dead. I totally thought you were dead."

I try to wriggle out of his grasp, to no avail. I peer over at my car; my door is open and the window has been smashed out. "Did you do that?"

Nick finally releases his hold. Tears paint his cheeks and dribble down to his stubble. "Eleanor, I banged on your window. I honked my horn. You weren't waking. I seriously thought you died. Bro, you looked so pale," he defends anxiously. His eyes search my face, the shock of me waking is still hitting him.

I grind my teeth. "I'm *always* pale. Nick, you shouldn't have done that," I say, just as the ambulance pulls into the student parking lot. I hastily scramble to my feet, wobbling. I nearly topple over, but Nick springs up, gripping me at my waist. I stumble back until I'm completely leaning up against him. He wraps his arms around my waist intimately, holding me close.

The ambulance grinds to a halt, and paramedics come rushing out. For the next hour, the paramedics poke and prod me. Nick answers the police's questions; I notice he's friendly with one officer who keeps leering over at me and nodding at whatever Nick is saying.

Thankfully, Sally and Marie come to my rescue. The two insist I don't need an ambulance ride to the hospital, that simply some rest at home will be enough. Sally applies more lipstick and thanks Nick for looking out for me before peeling out of the parking lot in the red Mercedes that's currently missing the driver's side window.

Marie swings her arm around me. "Let's get you home, sweets." She kisses my temple. Marie graciously waves to the medical team and police officers. "That Andersen boys seems quite enamored. Are you two…"

I shake my head. "No, absolutely not. He's just a friend," I growl.

Marie nods at me thoughtfully. "It was very kind of him to look after you. There could have been something truly wrong."

I lean back in my seat to rest my head; the tension wheezing out like a deflating balloon. I think back on Nick's pained expression, his eyes ringed with worry. I mean, the kid cried, thinking something happened to me. But he's been such an ass! However, since my first day in Salem, Nick has kept an eye out for me—but also *on* me. *Ugh. I just can't right now.* I shut my eyes, too exhausted to debate Nick's intentions.

Marie scrunches up her face in a painfully polite smile. "Pumpkin, this is the part where you fill me in on what happened," she says, approaching a red light.

I run my hand through my hair. "I don't know. I think I may have caused a bell to ring early today. I don't know if that was my magic, but right after, I had like a level ten migraine. I passed out in the car after school."

Marie switches from park to drive when the light turns green. "And so little Nickolas thought he'd call 911?" she questions, as if not quite buying my story.

I shrug. "Yeah, I guess. Apparently, I was really out of it and he couldn't wake me up. I was having a super weird dream." My many nightmares flash before my eyes: Jack climbing the tower, flying across a full moon, a freaking goat ramming me off a cliff. I mean seriously, what the hell!? "Marie, are dreams a form of magic, or whatever?"

Marie slows down to snail speed, approaching our turn. "They can be. Tell me about them."

"Ever since I started training, I've been having nightmares. They're kind of odd, but really intense. Like I was stabbed in one and I woke up with horrible chest pain." I place my hand on my sternum, recalling that sharp blade penetrating my skin, cracking through bone.

I frown, peering down at my hands, realizing the dreaming started before. The night I turned seventeen, I went to bed early, feeling ill. I grip my seat in Marie's car as my stomach drops. My skin breaks out in goosebumps. I wore a private school uniform, just like the one I'm wearing now. In the nightmare, I was lying in a large bed with deep blue blankets. First, I saw a spider crawling on my Converse, then I saw one crawling out of my white anklet sock, and suddenly hundreds were crawling up my shins, up my skirt, down my blouse, tangling in my hair, biting my scalp, heading into my nostrils, crawling across my clamped lips. I woke up screaming, batting them away, only to realize I was perfectly fine in my normal bed. I squeeze my eyes shut recalling a furry one creeping across a school patch, an emblem of a knight.

How is that possible? How could our magic even account for that? Just thinking about the spiders makes my skin itch.

Marie stares out the windshield. "Well, hmm… dreams can just be that, ordinary dreams, but they could also be visions of things to come or things that have already come to pass."

I scratch at my head, suddenly feeling uneasy. "How would I know the difference, and how does that work with our branches of magic?"

My aunt purses her lips as she pulls into the garage. She says nothing, but nods for me to follow her. We pass the cats, eager to greet us, and head up the stairs.

"Marie, hurry up. We're going to be late for Margaret's game. And we are in charge of drinks, so I was thinking we could just get—"

"No," Marie shouts back from the top of the stairs. "Follow me," she says sweetly, taking me by the hand. We walk around the table and into the room left of the bathroom door.

Inside the room, the slender tabby cat Persephone lounges on pale yellow bedding neatly made over a queen size bed. The feline immediately sits up and appraises us intruders. The bedroom has short, stiff beige carpeting that matches the walls. A gilded oval mirror hangs at the head of the bed between two long column windows sheathed in gossamer curtains. To the left of the closet are shelves and shelves of books, vials, candles, beakers, and dried flowers hanging upside down.

Marie marches over to the shelves, examining a wooden box. I find myself drifting over to the simple rustic wooden dresser. There's a glass jewelry box with pressed violets, pansies, and baby's breath. My mother's favorite bouquet. She has framed pictures of her holding trophies amongst a cheering team, prom photos, movie ticket stubs and photo booth pictures shoved into the frame of the fastened mirror. This was her childhood home. In a clay catch-all-dish are tubes of homemade lipstick, home brewed roll-on perfume, a string of pearls, and bejeweled bobby pins. I find my eyes welling with tears that will soon sink back into oblivion. *My mother never let us in. Why couldn't she just have been honest? Did she think my father wouldn't accept her?* I brush my fingertips beneath my eyes just in case this time they would fall.

"Ah ha! Got it!" Marie says, retrieving a long blue candle and a long skinny white one. "Your mother made these; she is so gifted with things of the earth. I wanted that to be my gift, but alas, it wasn't meant to be." She steps around the bed. "Blue is for dreams, white is for visions. Now visions can come in the form of dreams, but they are far more specific. Tonight, you will light both of them. If you have the gift of visions, which is in the branch of the mind, it won't matter that you lit the dream candle. Visions will overpower it." She hands me the slick, oily candles.

I finger the white candle as it feels lumpy and slightly curved. In fact, it has a precise sort of lumpiness to it. A thinner lump at the top, then the second and third lump feel thicker, a little more substantial. "I still don't understand what you're saying." My thumb strokes the white candle. "It's like there are bones in this."

Marie smiles sweetly. "Oh, there are, sweetie. The bones of a witch's middle finger, she too would need the gift of foresight to bewitch the candle. Helen paid a hefty price for this."

"What?" I drop the candle on the bed. *Maybe that's why my mom wouldn't tell us about herself, because she was a graverobber. This is still making no sense.* I despondently plop down on the corner of the bed. "Okay, Marie, explain this to me like I'm an idiot."

Marie pulls out my mother's rolling desk chair and plops down. Her face holds a patient smile, or maybe a condescending one, I'm not sure. "Okay, pumpkin. There are witches, very few, that have visions of the past, present, and future. Some only of the past, some only the future, some get all three. Visions fall under the mind spell. You see, as celestial creatures, we are all connected. The material used to create the Sons and Daughters was partly used to make us as well, and thus we are connected to the actions of others, their ripple effects. If you knew all things, why, you could practically predict everyone's actions with a mathematical equation. Our magic can do that for us, then it reveals a portion of it to us. Like I said, very few witches receive the gift. And we can burn a candle that was blessed and made with herbs that are used to help expand the mind. But rarely are they clear to witches not gifted in that area. Now blue is burned if you are suffering with disturbing nightmares and dreams. Lighting this candle will relax your mind. It will iron out those anxious worries that plague your sleep. But if you light both, one cancels the other out. If you don't have the gift, your dreams will turn pleasant and normal, the kind of dreams you experienced before your turning. But if you are given the gift of sight, your vision will sharpen. The vision will become less hazy, metaphorical and clear."

"Metaphorical?"

She nods. "Yes, you see, your magic is still working itself out. Even your gift has to stretch and feel its way through you. I've read accounts from witches with the gift and their visions were typically more dream-like than real, but over time, they lost that fantastical mirage. This would also explain your headaches; you're using the mind spell without the proper training."

I pick up both candles, feeling the weight of them in my hands. "So, when I go to bed tonight, I light both of them?"

Marie hands me a crinkled, stained sheet of paper. "The directions are right here. Helen wrote them down, so you can trust this will work."

My brows knit, peering down. "It's weird to think my mom once embraced being a witch."

Marie giggles. "Oh, yes. My baby sister was very talented. She was so good at everything that it took forever to really discover her gift. When she turned seventeen, there was never a struggle. She knew the incantations from watching our parents, and of course Sally and me. What a natural. Fully trained in a week," Marie shared proudly. "Discovered her predilection towards the earth that summer when her cures needed just her blessing instead of multiple witches for better potency."

"Then why?" I rise to my feet, startling Persephone, sending her running under the bed. "Why would she keep this a secret? Why would she turn her back on all of this, on you guys, her entire family? Her coven?" I shout in accusation. "Maybe I wouldn't be so scared right now! Maybe I wouldn't be haunted like I am! But no! Instead, I'm lost and more terrified than I have ever been!" I'm finding my chest heaving up and down, my mouth becoming arid. "Maybe my fingers, my eyes, all of that wouldn't be so confusing, my magic not so confusing. How could she do this to us? To Dad!? He *loved* her! He loved her so much! He loved her no matter what! He would have accepted her! I know he would have!" I exclaim, my throat going hoarse. Emotional tremors rock my body. I want to scream further, hit something, cry, curse, kick, curl up in a ball on the floor and never get back up.

Marie doesn't look taken aback by any of this, not disturbed in the slightest by my hysterical outburst. Instead, I'm shocked when she pushes off the chair to her feet and pulls me into a hug. I'm rigid at first, standing ramrod straight in my righteous indignation. Her hand rubs little circles on my back.

My muscles slowly buckle, one by one until I've melted into her hug. "I just—want to understand."

"Perhaps I've given you poor advice. Next time you speak to your mom, you need to ask her," Marie whispers.

I imagine how that conversation will go in my head. I can't decide between icy silence or defensive screaming.

Marie tentatively releases me from her embrace.

The bedroom door swings open. Sally stands there with her hand on her cocked hip. "Uh, hello? We are late for our niece's game. I want to be there if that little weasel elbows our Maggie."

Marie rolls her eyes at her sister. "Just because Margaret said that girl has that reputation doesn't mean it'll happen to our girl. Besides, you would never break one of our most sacred codes and hurt someone," she says like a stern warning.

Sally rolls her eyes. "I wasn't going to hurt her. But if her duffle bag were to burst into flames—"

Marie throws her hands up in the air. "Enough. We are not doing that." She turns back to me. "Sweetie, follow those exact instructions and you'll be just fine. If you need any crystals, check the dining room cabinet."

To my dismay, the aunts decide to leave all the cats here. I get on my hands and knees, digging through the bottom cabinet, looking for a moonstone. They had a celestite and tiger's eye on the top shelf, but no moonstone. I actively fight against my inner cynic at the thought of healing crystals and magical tea. The Eleanor I was a few weeks ago would be laughing her head off, pulling up studies about the ineffectiveness of all this "hippie garbage". *Maybe Marie Curie just needed crystals, and she'd have survived radiation poisoning,* I would have mocked.

I reach as far back as I can, my ear pressed to the wooden drawer, practically dislocating my shoulder to stretch to the far back. *How deep is this thing?* My fingers stumble into a box; inside I feel a slender stone in the shape of a small egg. *This must be it.* I pull my arm back. A moonstone rests in the center of my palm.

*"If you are searching for a moonstone, there are three in the kitchen."* Pyewacket shares, walking through the door.

I roll my eyes irritably. "Thanks, now you tell me. You're really proving how useless you are." I shut the cupboard door and rise to my feet.

*"You could have asked me…"*

I cock a brow. "Oh yeah, cause you've been around. You've been a big help." I stroll past him and head to the bedroom to place the stones next to the candles for later.

Pyewacket keeps his distance as I catch up on homework in the tower. My heart is strangely…at peace. I'm able to concentrate on the task at hand. I outline my essay due Friday for Winston, study for the French midterm next week, and even practice the new concerto we are attempting in orchestra. *Is it just because I'm finally confronting my mother about witchcraft? Maybe Marie used some kind of spell on me while she hugged me. Or possibly it's even simpler than that: I needed to scream, to release all that pent-up frustration.*

By the time I finish using the half-life concept to describe the rate of decay of an isotope, I can hear the jubilation in Margaret's voice coming through the floor.

"Undefeated!" Maggie cheers, seeing me coming down the stairs.

I laugh. "Isn't this your third game?"

"Does it change the fact we haven't lost yet!?" she hollers. She pulls me in for a sweaty hug the roars far too close to my ear.

Sally giggles, standing in the corner watching. Marie glowers with her arms crossed.

Margaret reaches her arms up over her head, stretching. "I'm gonna take a shower."

"Dinner will be ready soon, sweets," Marie grumbles.

I frown, following my aunts down the hall. "Am I missing something?"

Sally snorts into her hand, laughing.

Marie glares. "It's not funny. She could have gotten hurt! We don't know what her reaction will be to such a concoction."

I stare at them both incredulously. "Um, what did you give my sister?"

Sally dismisses us with a wave of her hands. "Oh, it's nothing. She asked for a drink and I gave her the wrong bottle," she says nonchalantly.

"What!? You got my fourteen-year-old sister drunk!?" My mom is going to kill Sally.

Sally straightens up, gazing at me as if wounded. "Of course not. It's an herbal juice I got from Molly and Polly's. It's all natural, a witch's brew to help loosen things up. She drank it and *loved* it, by the way." She leans across the kitchen island to better lecture her sister hovering by the refrigerator.

"Just stop," Marie chastises. "You aren't as innocent as you're pretending. Now, help me with dinner. Margaret requested Cuban sandwiches and I don't have the foggiest idea how to make it," she admits apprehensively.

I look up the ingredients on my phone and pass it to my worried aunt. Together, the three of us use magic to pull items from the fridge, slice the bread baked yesterday, and ordered the ingredients we didn't have from a witch food delivery service.

"And we couldn't just use a normal delivery service?" I question, opening the front door to retrieve the deli meat wrapped in paper and tied with twine.

"We like to support witch-owned businesses. Besides, that pork had to appear invisible and fly from the shop all the way through the woods to our humble abode. Now, you're telling me you'd rather have someone manhandle our food?" Sally questions, lifting a thin brow.

I hand over the meat. "Okay, yeah, that's pretty cool."

Margaret devours her sandwich like it's the first thing she's eaten in weeks. The shower apparently helped sober her up. "That might be the best Cuban I've ever had."

Sally opens her mouth and lifts her finger, about to cut in.

Marie elbows her in the ribs. "Don't."

I giggle, taking another bite of my sandwich. Mustard drips onto the plate.

Marie rubs her hands together. "Now, Eleanor, Winston informed me that you don't have school tomorrow. How about we train you in water magic?" she asks, practically bouncing in her seat.

I nibble on my lip. "Um, I can't."

Everyone turns to me.

"Why not? I'm sure you'll be fabulous," Sally says, sipping her cocktail.

"I kind of, I don't know—I might be going on a date tomorrow. Or a hang out. I'm not sure what it is. But Jack asked me to go sailing tomorrow." I stare at my plate.

Sally scoots her chair closer. "And you've accepted, haven't you? That boy is fiiiine. If he was just five years older..."

"Just five?" Marie says disapprovingly.

I tuck my hair behind my ears. "Yeah, um, I said I'd go sailing. Is that okay? Maybe we could train after?"

Marie nods sweetly. "Let's train before, just to be safe, then you go have fun. Just mind your thoughts. We don't want more accidents on our hands, especially if you're going to be out at sea..."

I roll my lips in, holding them between my teeth. My diaphragm quivers. *What if I do something? I broke his nose already. What else could I do? Drown him?* I imagine a dreamy sailboat, Jack shirtless, wearing linen pants flailing in the water as something keeps pushing his head below the salty waves while I stare murderously helpless. *I don't want to risk hurting him again. Maybe I need to cancel.* My body vibrates as hiccups stream from my chest popping up in my mouth.

I reach for my water. There's a small waterspout swirling inside the goblet. Before I can bring the glass to my lips, Pyewacket leaps onto the table, knocking it from my hand and sending it crashing onto the floor.

"What the heck are you doing?" I shout, leaping from my seat.

"It's no worry. Easy clean up," the aunts insist, not even rising from the chairs. The glass is swept up and the water immediately dried. A new goblet comes dancing in, landing lightly in front of me.

I close my eyes and imagine ice from the freezer and a root beer from the pantry, carefully levitating into the room, then utter the air spell mentally. I can hear the bottle bang against the counter, knocking into the door, but eventually the ice and beverage make their way over to my cup.

"Very good, Ellie-belly!" Marie smiles, clapping her hands.

After dinner, I collect what I need for my tea and the other plants needed for the spell before saying goodnight to everyone.

Pyewacket sits patiently on my trunk, his head poised towards the door.

"I would suggest they euthanize you, but I doubt that'll really help me in this situation," I mutter sarcastically. "Can you turn around or close your eyes?" I order, getting dressed for bed.

I toss my uniform into the hamper and make a mental note to do laundry. I ignore Pyewacket's watchful eyes as I place the candles in brass holders on either side of my bed. I squint, deciphering the difficult scrawl.

Blue candle to my left side, white candle to my right. Saying the incantation in my head, I blow on the wicks to light them. I grin; I don't think the novelty of magic will ever wear off. The instructions say to place the moonstone under my pillow, the celestite stone next to the blue candle at the six o'clock position, and the tiger's eye to my right at the midnight position. I hang the Valerian root above my bed and sip my simmering tea seeped with mug wort and chamomile.

*"This is a fool's errand,"* Pyewacket sends, leaping onto the bed.

*Please go away. You tried to wreck dinner, you've been blowing me off, just go.* I pull back the duvet and climb in. I picture the light switch flicking off. *La Caeli.* The overhead lights immediately switch off, leaving the room in an amber glow from the candles.

Pyewacket tiptoes up the bed until he is level with my head.

I groan, rolling over, only to whip back to face him. I sit up on my elbows. *La Caeli.* The lights turn back on. I lean closer to the dead black cat. He has fresh blood on his last few remaining whiskers, the rest of his face is matted in dried blood. There's a slice going down his shining blue eye. "Oh my gosh, Pyewacket, what happened? Did you kill something? Is this from the glass? Did you cut yourself?"

There's a giggle, a low quiet giggle that if I breathed just a hair quieter, I wouldn't be able to hear it at all. Despite the low volume, I feel a further tear in the universe, a fissure striking across its very foundation. I hear distant petrified screams, smell smoke, hear goats bleating, a child's cry, and that low, satanically sweet giggle causing my insides to recoil.

"Elspeth. It's her, isn't it? Is she doing something to you?" I question anxiously.

*"I don't believe it's me she's after. But I've stymied her attempts."*

I sit up more. "She wants to hurt me. Why? What am I to her?"

Pyewacket shakes his head. *"I know not. I haven't worked out how she's able to reach through the veiled gate. It hasn't been possible till now. But I don't believe she's terribly powerful. Most of her attempts have failed without my intervention."*

"Why does she want me dead? Tell me the truth," I demand.

*"Truly, I know not. I've been counseling with Mortimer. There must be a spell to quell her. But such magic is unknown to us."*

I don't accept his answer and continue to rack my brain for answers. "What could it be? Envy? She's upset that you're my familiar now?"

Pyewacket stares thoughtfully. *"She always was a jealous mistress, but her true intentions are veiled from me."*

I settle back into my pillows and pull my blanket up to my chin. "Pye, how scared should I be?"

Pyewacket circles to find a comfortable spot. *"Be cautious, not fearful. Her power can never reach its full potential from purgatory. But I won't let harm befall you."*

My lips pull up in a half smile. *La Caeli.* The lights turn off. "Thanks."

*"You're still a major pain in my arse and make me wish I was comfortably dead."*

*Well, on that note.* I roll over; my eyelids heavy, like sandbags, slide shut. Each muscle in my body melds with the bed, ironing out every ripple and tension until my body is loose and malleable.

My eyes flutter open, the lids feeling as light as butterfly wings. I'm standing in the middle of a long and quiet road. The soft glowing stars are speckled across the night sky. Houses dot the sidewalk with lush trees planted by the road and in between the darkened houses. It appears to be a silent suburban night.

Like a string is anchored to my chest, I feel a pull to the large stone house to my right, just three houses down. I tiptoe across the street, making my way to the house.

I frown, peering up. The home is the biggest on the block, with an ornate deep-blue door that perfectly matches the blue flowers planted under each window. Outside the perimeter of the white-picket fence and between the sidewalk is the paragon of climbing trees. The house, with its large bay windows, wide front porch, imposing stone archway, is, in all frankness, boring. It's nice, beautiful even, but perfectly ordinary. *Why am I seeing this?*

I gaze up and down the vacant street dotted with posh looking streetlamps. Not a single stray cat or dog or even a randomly parked vehicle can be seen. Even the lawns seem to be cut at uniform level. The street is finely paved, the sky a normal black. Nothing could be described as fantastical or even interesting. Even my outfit looks normal and from my closet. I'm wearing jeans, sneakers, and a long sleeve shirt advertising the orchestra camp summer after the eighth grade. If it wasn't for the nip in the air and the lack of Spanish architecture, I'd swear I was back in Coral Gables. Picket fences, average cars not too nice but not shabby either, a perfectly ordinary night in the most average neighborhood in America. No whimsy, no strange characters on parade. *Maybe this isn't a dream, but a vision…*

Suddenly, the third story window's light flickers on. A bright yellow light shines across the freshly manicured lawn. I step back onto the road, trying my best to peer into the window. *Who's up there?* Headlights cut through the darkened street coming right at me. I quickly leap onto the sidewalk, stumbling in the process. The car comes to an abrupt yet silent halt at the curb, cutting the engine almost immediately.

I glare over at the maniac who almost ran me over. The windows are tinted black, making it impossible to see into. The driver kills the headlights. A person dressed completely in black steps out and around the car. A black ski mask obscures his face.

*Oh crap! Crap, crap, crap, crap! That guy is going to burglarize that house!*

He strides right past me as if I'm invisible and scales the tree. He doesn't stop climbing until he reaches the top, parallel to the lit window.

I rush to the tree and mount the branches, deciding to join him, figuring he can't see me anyway. It feels oddly invigorating to stretch my arms climbing higher and higher. I peer down through the branches, not realizing until now just how high up I really am. A light breeze rustles the branches and my confidence. I'm fairly certain you can't die in your dreams, but the pain is very real. I glance over at the man clad in black rubber necking then back to the glowing window.

A beautiful blonde girl takes out her ponytail and shakes out her wild and wavy hair. She saunters about her room before sliding her shirt up above her head and tossing it into a bamboo hamper.

I lean forward, squinting. *Trixie!*

She flips on some music and sways to some old school *Carpenters* wearing a yellow lacy bra with neon blue cotton underwear. *We've Only Just Begun* can be heard outside. That song always creeped me out. How did anyone ever find that song romantic? It sounds like the soundtrack to a serial killer.

The man doesn't move from his spot, observing her prance about.

"Ugh," I groan aloud. He's a pervert. A peeping tom. "What is wrong with you?" I hiss at him, despite he can't hear me. I turn back to Trixie. *Is there a way I can warn you? Does my magic work in visions?*

With one arm, he grips the thick tree branch he's straddling, and with his other hand reaches into his pocket.

*Ew! Ew! Please don't be doing anything gross!*

He takes out a tape recorder and places it close to his lips, whispering. *I didn't think peeping toms took notes.* His eyes stay fixed on her window.

Carefully, I crawl farther up my branch to get a better look at him. His eyes are calm and direct, not wild with lust. My heart pounds; a feeling of dread fills every pore, washing me in unadulterated fear. This guy isn't here because of an unrequited love or some undeniable attraction he has to the seventeen-year-old. He's dangerous.

"What am I supposed to do?" I cry. "Go away! You creep! Stay away from her!" I shout, uselessly.

My eyes scan from the gazer back to Trixie. She keeps disappearing into an adjoining bathroom, then reappearing with a toothbrush in her mouth, checking her laptop before going to spit out her toothpaste into the air. Her spittle slithers in the air like a floating snake slinking into the bathroom.

*Wow, she's good. Oh, wait! Crap!* This perv just witnessed her doing magic. I glance over at the intruder and watch as his eyes scan her room, now earnest in search of something. His eyes fold into slits, his cheeks lift, smiling under the mask.

I frown and lean forward, baffled at what he could be staring at. In view was the end of her white four post bed. There's a desk with an open laptop, a large wooden bookshelf filled with books, a vase of flowers, blue ribbons, a teddy bear, and an elegantly dressed porcelain doll.

Trixie strides back in the room and slides in her retainer. Meanwhile, the lights and the music all turn themselves off. Trixie then slides into bed.

The waiting continued for what seemed like hours before he ventures out onto a long, thick branch inching closer and closer to the first story roof. He springs like a lithe cat onto the dark gray surface. He quietly, yet quickly, scrambles up to Trixie's window from the ivy-covered trellis.

*Oh, no! He's going to go in! I have to stop this!* Trying to follow in his footsteps, I climb out onto the branch, trembling nervously as I have no idea how I'm supposed to get him out of her room. A soft breeze whispers through the trees. The branch shakes slightly underneath me and I hesitate. After taking a deep breath, I leap through the air. A grunt escapes my throat as I smack against the gutter and tumble to the ground. I've for sure broken something. I try to sit up to no avail. I can't feel my legs. Panic sweeps over me.

There's a loud thump next to my head. The man has jumped the rest of the way down. I squint in the dark, trying my best to see what he has tucked close to his body. It's a floral book spackled with hipster Lisa Frank stickers. In swirly cursive, it reads: Diary; and in small hand-written letters: Property of Miss Trixie Faye Caldwell, Witch Queen of the Universe.

I let out a weak chuckle and wince in pain, realizing a rib or two is likely broken. *All this for a freaking diary? I hope it's a good read, perv!* Then a thought dawns on me. What secrets has Trixie shared with her diary?

# Chapter Twenty-Three
## Drowning in the Backyard

I move my tongue around, rolling short, wiry hair in my mouth. I numbly peek open my eyes and reach in my mouth, pulling out a strand of black cat hair. *Gross! I'm breathing in rotted cat hair!*

"Pye!" I groggily call out, shutting my eyes again. "New rule, my bed is forever off limits until you shave all your hair." When I adjust my pillow, my fingers knock into something smooth and cold. The moonstone. It must have wriggled out while I was sleeping.

I spring up to a seated position. The blue candle is nothing but a hardened, melted puddle. The white candle is still aglow. Without a moment's thought, I say the air spell in my head and extinguish the candle. I squeeze my eyes closed, recalling the dream from last night. It's fuzzy at first, like looking at something above the surface while you're underwater. Slowly, the images become clearer and clearer until—Trixie. I was outside Trixie's house. Some creep took her diary. *But why? Is that just the guy's kink? That pervert is just into girl's diaries?*

Pyewacket arches his back, stretching out. *"Find something black. Your training resumes soon."*

*Pye, did you see my dream err vision last night?*

He turns to me, his eyes fixed on my face. *"No. But I heard you recalling it. Sounds like the Caldwell's need to up their security."*

I dig through the drawers, searching for black clothes. "It's weird though, right? I see a man steal Trixie's diary. Why would someone do that? But maybe it's not a diary at all. Maybe it's actually a spell book, a grimoire?" I pull out black gym shorts and a black ribbed tank top. I pull my hair up into a bun, waiting for a response from Pyewacket.

He tilted his head to either side, musing so quietly to himself I can't hear. *He needs to teach me how to do that.*

*"I doubt I could instruct you. You have as much control over your thoughts as an*

*inebriated toddler."*
  *Jerk.*
  *"Tosser."*
  My door creaks open. "Eleanor? Are you ready?" Marie calls.
  I lean my head out. "Coming!" I look back at Pye. "Please think about what I should do. As a dead cat, I'm sure you have advice that would really help," I mutter sarcastically. This is how ridiculous my life has become.
  I rush down the stairs, surprised to be greeted by Mr. Edwards and Marie standing at the bottom. I slow my pace. Heat creeps into my cheeks as I feel indecently exposed in my shorter shorts and tank top.
  "Um…hey, Mr. Edwards," I say lamely, with a nod.
  "Miss O'Reilly." He tips an imaginary hat in my direction. He's dressed in his usual attire, button down, sweater vest, perfectly straight bowtie and pleated trousers. He places a gentle hand on Marie's shoulder. "I'll leave you to your training. Please think about what I said."
  Marie gives him a reluctant smile. "Okay, Winnie." She slowly turns, watching him trot down the veranda and into his sand-colored Cadillac. She scrounges around in the pockets of her black, floor-length cardi and pulls out a crumpled tissue to dab at her eyes and blow her nose.
  "Everything okay?" I ask, descending the last few steps.
  My aunt nods quickly, shoving her damp tissue back into her pocket. "Come, we're training out back today," she says, pointing down the hall to the back door in the kitchen.
  The lace curtains are drawn and tied back, revealing the aunts have replaced the broken glass. I think of the possessed scissors crashing through, and chills ripple down my spine.
  The sun is bright and beaming, basking us in its warmth, not quite to the degree of Florida but a welcome change from the usual slurry of snow and rain. We walk out onto the uneven cobblestone courtyard where Sally, shaded by a floppy black sunhat, is seated at a metal table, her legs crossed at the ankle resting on the table. A pitcher of herbal tea swimming in ice is pouring itself into a teacup in front of her, then without spilling a single drop, it fills the other two cups.
  Sally slides her circular black sunglasses down her pinched nose to give us an incredulous look. "What crawled up Winnie's butt and died?"
  Two chairs slide out for Marie and me.
  Marie sighs, peering up at the clear sky. "Not everything is your business, Sal."
  Instead of the typical stack of books and candles, there is only one book. A light blue leather-bound tome buckled closed with a leather strap. On the

cover in silvery swirly letters is the word "Uisce".

Sally removes her feet off the table. "You know! What's going on? He totally rebuffed me when I initiated our usual sexual repartee."

I pick up my overflowing cup and sip, trying not to slurp. *It tastes like home.* Honeysuckle and lemon. My mom would always brew her own herbal tea during the summer.

"Not now, Sally. It's time to train Eleanor. She has a date to get to," Marie says, surprisingly encouraging as she reaches beneath the table and pats my knee. "Let's not keep her from her beau."

My stomach knots, still unsure if I should cancel. *Maybe training today will be enough to help keep me in check.*

Sally narrows her eyes on her sister. "This isn't finished." She wiggles her eyebrows at me. "But yes, let's not keep Eleanor from her—are the kids still using 'bae'?" she frowns.

I chuckle while taking one last sip of my tea, then shake my head.

Marie points her stubby finger at the title of the spell book. "It's pronounced ish-ka. It's what our family and all Celtic witches use to call upon water. We can control bodies of water, pull the moisture from the air, even pull it out of the ground. Magic is so malleable, dearie, you set your own limitations. Now, just like calling upon the air and fire, imagine what you are asking your magic to do, say in the incantation internally, and let your magic serve you."

"Why do we say it in our heads and not out loud?" I ask, then whip around as the back door opens and an empty glass pitcher glides over to the table.

Sally cuts in, answering before Marie can. "It's easier to communicate with our inner selves. We process thought automatically, so you can focus all your energy on that one precise thought as opposed to having to open your mouth, send the signal from your brain down."

Marie looks taken aback.

Sally rolls her eyes. "I know things. Stop being surprised."

Marie flips the book open to a specific page and slides it over to me. There are molecular models, sketches of evaporation cycles, ground water, nimbostratus clouds, cumulus, and cyclones. "Just remember, there is a balance in nature. If you make it rain, you could cause drought elsewhere. So, if you find yourself needed to tip the scale, make sure it's truly worthy of the risk." She pushes the tome over to me. "Add this to your personal study."

"Now, Ellie babe, fill the pitcher," Sally orders, sitting up a little taller in her seat.

I frown, still muddled on the mechanics. "How? I just gather moisture from the air?"

Both the aunts nod. Sally leans forward, eagerly watching, while Marie's head rests in her hands waiting.

*Sure, this will be easy.* I shut my eyes concentrating, imaging the water vapor in the air, the slow-moving molecules, picturing them gather making droplets into the pitcher. *Uisce.* In my mind's eye, I see the pitcher fill up with crystal clear water. My magic flares within me like turning on a gas stove.

Something cold and wet rolls down my cheek. And then another and another. I peek an eye open. A single grey cloud unfurls over the backyard, rain trickles down slowly in a soft pitter patter before picking up speed.

Sally's mouth downturns, her eyes fold into pitying slits. "I was afraid of this."

Water pours down like a faucet. The rain streams into little rivers bending away from my aunts like dribbling over an invisible umbrella. Water flows down my face, slicking my hair to my face and soaking me to the bone.

The pitcher is now filled and overflowing from the heavy shower, the storm cloud ringing itself out like a dishrag. Then it slows, the thick heavy droplets that before had hit the ground like bullets now peter out into a softly blowing mist until stopping altogether, like someone put a kink in a hose.

"Did I do that?" I question.

A fluffy pink towel comes zipping out of the house and flops onto my head.

Sally whips her head at Marie. "I could have dried her off, or Eleanor could have."

Marie brushes her off with a wave of her hand. "I want her to, but I don't want to exhaust her out." She gazes at me from across the table. "Well, not quite what we had in mind, but you did fill the pitcher." She cranes her neck, peering over me. "See that water barrel over there? Now, don't use the air spell. Call upon the water and lift it out of the barrel in a cyclone."

I turn my chair to face the barrel that sits a few yards away near the house. My skin feels loose and my body weighed down like a trash bag full of liquid. I roll my shoulders, trying to move as this bloated feeling is expanding, drooping. I touch my face, checking to see if I have jowls as my cheeks feel floppy. My skin is overly moist but not jiggly to the touch despite my insides feeling wobbly like jello. I close my eyes. There's a trickling sensation of water dripping out of my ears. I struggle to ignore it and focus on the spell. I picture a gigantic stirring stick circling the barrel, causing a natural cyclone, then I imagine reaching in and pulling it out, the water swirling and spinning.

The aunts clap, prompting me to open my eyes. There's a waterspout lifting five feet into the air, then it halts, splashing right back into the barrel.

My aching body slumps over in my seat; I feel like my pores are about to stretch out and burst like a sprinkler system. The towel draped over my shoulders is now soaking wet from the water seeping from my skin. My mouth lulls and water dribbles out. "S-s-s-somethings-s-s-s wrong," I gurgle. My arms hang over the armrests and my legs are splayed out.

"Oh, dear," Marie says, eyeing me sympathetically.

Sally chuckles at my expense. "Well, that is an extreme reaction. I think it's safe to rule out water as her gift. I knew she would be wet for a while, but…"

My heart pounds anxiously, my eyes dart to them, frightened. "Is-s-s-s this really bab?" I utter, the water burbling in my mouth.

Marie jumps back, watching me bloat. She furiously flips through her spell book. Sally marches up to me with a determined look on her face.

"I'll dry her out," Sally says. She holds out her hand at me like a crossing guard.

My flesh itches and my heart races. "S-s-s-stop!" I cry out. Blisters bubble across my tight skin. My body feels like it's been set ablaze. *She's boiling me alive!* I release a strangled scream as more water chokes me.

Sally immediately stops, horrified when her eyes appraise me. "Marie! Did you find anything?" she rushes over to Marie, hovering over her.

Marie and Sally exchange panicked looks. I can see their mouths moving, but they're too far away to hear. Sally uncrosses her arms and Marie points to me. My fingers swell to a point that it's agony to bend them, soon becoming impossible. My nails feel like they're about to pop off. The tops of my feet jiggle with water.

"Helb!" I gurgle, struggling to push water through my nostrils as water flows from my mouth. My eyes roll to the back of my head and my lungs scream for air. My body suddenly feels weightless, my head falls back, and water drips off me. *Am I seriously going to drown on my aunts' patio? Is this really how I die?*

*"Eleanor, you are allowing this to consume you. You need to fight this."*

My thoughts become scattered. I see my dad smiling, pushing me on a swing. Birthday candles. My parents asleep in the hammock in the backyard. Broken dishes. Frayed rope.

I'm landing somewhere. My head knocks into something. My eyes burst open, I cough up water rolling over to my side. Water still leaks from my pores and gathers in the basin. I gasp, catching my breath. *How did I get in the bathtub?*

The aunts tower over me, their eyes intensely fixed on me, almost as if they're seeing through me. My chest heaves up and down and my body feels like it's being rung out like an old dishrag. I bend and stretch my fingers and toes. My cheeks no longer sag and warble. I shiver, feeling my skin breath in and out, pushing out water like a pump.

"Mom?" I mumble out, disoriented.

"This doesn't make sense. Most witches without the gift secrete a little water, but I've never seen anything like this," Sally hisses to her sister. Her hands continue making concentric circles above my body.

Marie shakes her head, sending her cheeks a flutter. "I don't understand it. It appears as if her magic is rebelling. But that can't be. Did she try to do this to herself, maybe tried a different spell after the waterspout?"

Sally shakes her head. "No. Even if she did, her own magic can't hurt her. Not like this, anyway."

I weakly lift my head, but it immediately clunks right back down against the porcelain tub. "What's w-w-wrong with me?" I stutter, trembling.

My aunts lower their arms, once again gazing over at each other with knit brows. A Duran Duran song starts playing and Sally whips out her phone.

"Polly, hello. Yes, yes, we do. Thank you. Can you send over the stewed cactus flower? Alright, thank you. When can Zoey bring it over? Oh good, thank you." Sally hangs up the phone and slides it back into the pocket of her sundress. "I'll be back. I need to go to the greenhouse. Zoey is bringing something from Molly and Polly's that should help." Sally glances at me shivering in the water trickling out of me.

Marie sits down on the toilet lid, nervously playing with the raw amethyst pendant on her long brass necklace. "How are you doing in there, pumpkin?"

I try to lift my arm to flick a halfhearted thumbs up, but my arm is far too feeble to move. "I need to text Jack…" I pause, needing to breathe, "we need to cancel our date." My heart sinks only slightly, a little too overwhelmed by this aquatic episode to give it the full mourning it deserves.

I can feel Pyewacket's presence in the bathroom.

"Eleanor, is there anything…you want to tell me? Perhaps there's something you've been keeping to yourself."

My eyes flutter close. *Yes.*

Sally strides into the room holding a turkey baster. "Okay, Ell babe. I added honey to make it taste sweeter."

Marie hops to her feet. "What is in that, Sal?"

Sally kneels next to the bathtub and tilts my head back. "A recipe tried and true. Dried clovers, four leaves of course, onion root, pumpkin seeds, and a stewed cactus flower. We had everything but that."

My mouth falls open weakly. Sally puts the baster at the back of my throat then squirts it in. I struggle to gulp it fast enough. The taste of the bizarre concoction tastes the way freshly cut grass smells. I can feel every lump as the tea cascades down my throat. Water instantly stops dripping from my ears.

Marie reaches over and grips her sister's hand. "That was excellent, Sal."

I squeeze my fists with a surprising amount of pressure, pushing out water like balled up sponges. With an unattractive grunt, I find the strength to sit up and lean against the tub's wall. My chin rests on the lip bathtub. "I think I'm going to stay away from the spell."

"Oh no dearie," Marie says, shaking her head at me. "You need to practice. If you struggle with this, it's vital you master it."

Sally brushes water from my cheeks. "How are you feeling, squirt?"

I exhale, feeling the weariness slowly drain from me, along with more water. "I feel like I just chugged an espresso. It's like an energetic force is possessing my body." I run my hand, which is not back to its normal size, down my slick arm. "Do you know when I'll...dry out?"

The aunts rise to their feet. "Soon. Once you start moving, it should come to a close."

Pyewacket watches Sally and Marie help me to my feet while sitting in the sink. *"Don't tell your aunts about Elspeth. Not yet, anyway."*

*Why not?*

*"We don't need them meddling. Not when we know so little. When the time is right, you can tell them. Your mother, too."*

There's a knock on the bathroom door. Marie helps steady me as Sally opens the door.

Margaret stands there wearing gym shorts and a K-Pop Tee. She smiles mischievously. "Um, that super-hot guy is at the door. I let him in."

Sally glances back at us and zooms out of the bathroom.

"No! Sally, don't do anything!" I nearly stumble trying to catch up with her. Marie follows, nipping at our heels.

The four of us stop on the staircase and peek out over the banister at him.

Jack is standing with his back to us, his hands in his dark khaki shorts as he surveys the wall with all the framed photographs. He tilts his head appraising the photo of women encircled standing hand in hand wearing white cotton dresses.

"I need to meet that kid's father. Maybe he's a chip off the ol' block," Sally whispers, practically salivating.

"Shh!" I whisper.

Jack's head whips, jumping slightly. His cheeks color spotting me. "Eleanor," he says, a crooked smile unfurling.

I step past Sally and Margaret. My hair still drips water down my back. I look as if I just fell into a pool with my clothes. My feet leave little wet footprints down the stairs as I walk. My skin prickles with goosebumps from the chill.

Jack's sea-green eyes take in my appearance, the way my damp clothes cling to my body. He breaks his stare as I come closer. "Did you just go swimming?"

My knees quiver, almost unsure if they can hold me up. "Something like that."

He grins at me, his eyes peering into mine like transparent windows leaving me completely bare. "Would you like me to come back later?"

I shake my head, water still prickling on my scalp and arms. "Sorry, I hadn't heard from you. I wasn't sure when we were going," I say anxiously.

Jack's face becomes flushed. He waves a few fingers, peering past me.

I peek over my shoulder and cringe. Sally, Marie, and Margaret are all still standing on the stairs, observing us like animals in a zoo.

Jack frowns and reaches into his pocket. "You responded to my text message." He flashes me his glowing screen. He texted me good morning and asked if I was still up to sailing. I responded with a yes and agreed to eleven thirty. "Was this not you?" he asks, sounding amused at the prospect that other occupants in the house set this up.

I glare over at my confused family members. "No. I didn't see these. But the time still works." I turn back to him. "Let me go get ready. Um, do you want anything? Tea? Soda? Water?" I offer, internally wincing at the thought of water. My entire body is still soggy.

He smiles. "I'm fine, but I'm also okay if you go in that," he says flirtatiously, his eyes sweep me up and down.

I giggle nervously and clamp my mouth down on a hiccup I can feel swimming up my throat. I scowl at each family member in turn as I rush past them.

Everyone follows me up into the tower.

"What am I going to do about the water? I'm still… leaking," I groan, plopping down on the trunk at the foot of the bed. My underwear and shorts squish beneath me. I hang my head back, ready to cry. "I thought trying to figure out what to wear would be the hardest part."

*"Not too late to cancel. I don't trust him."* Pyewacket waltzes into the room.

Maggie cocks her head, studying me, her lips pursed, eyes narrow. "I've got something you can wear. Leave it to me." She dashes away before I can respond.

Sally runs her hands through my hair like a heated comb. "I can already feel the water is slowing down. Marie, are you doing your part?"

I glance over to my curvy aunt sitting at my desk, holding the bloodied planchette close to her face.

"Is this," she sniffs, "cat blood?" her eyes flash to me. "Eleanor?"

*Do I lie? Should I be honest? Pye?*

*"Be vague. For now."*

I straighten my shoulders and arch my back as my hair is hot to the touch. "You're not burning my hair, are you, Sal?" I ask, catching a whiff of burnt hair.

"Of course not, babe."

"Eleanor?" Marie tries again.

I peer back at Marie. "Remember, we used the Ouija board? The cats weren't too happy about it and attacked the planchette. Py-Blue-Eyes put it back in my room, maybe to punish me or something."

*"Not bad. Though I don't appreciate being cannon fodder."*

Marie nods skeptically and places it in the trashcan.

"Got it!" Maggie exclaims, rushing back in. She tosses me a pair of faded jean shorts and a beige crochet top with a boat neck and cap sleeves.

"This will barely reach my waist," I complain, holding it up to myself.

Sally cranes her neck, looking over my shoulder. "Yeah Maggie, do you have anything shorter? Oh, I have this leather bustier that would be adorable!"

Marie leaps to her feet. "Nope. Nope. Absolutely not!"

I place the top on my lap as Sally continues to dry out my hair, nearly sizzling my scalp in the process. "Thanks Maggie, this will work," I say before Sally can recommend anything else.

Margaret kneels in front of me with a tackle box filled with makeup. "I'll use only my waterproof stuff." She dabs a little concealer on me. "I take it you're not super sweaty. This is just the fun part of training?"

I exhale roughly through my lips, making a raspberry. "Yeah…"

"Eleanor, don't move. You're going to make me mess up." She sweeps blue eyeliner above and below my eye.

Sally stops fingering my hair and steps back, scowling. "Marie, are you making it humid in here? You're making her hair all frizzy."

Marie's hair is nearly at afro status as she concentrates on me. "Yes, where do you think all the water from Eleanor is going? The teacup is already filled with water, but she still had a long way to go."

"Okay, you're going with beach waves. I'll get my salt spray. You can thank Marie. I was going for dominatrix straight while I dry, but we'll have to make do." Sally stomps out to the bathroom. "Jack, you sure I can't offer you a drink?" she shouts from the landing.

"Are you almost done?" I impatiently inquire, knowing Jack will need to be rescued soon.

"Mascara is done, now a little lip stain and you're all set." Margaret rolls a tube across my lips, then tosses it into her box. "I'm an artist," she compliments with a wink.

Everyone filters out so I can get dressed. The shorts are a little snug, more so than I typically wear. When I raise my arms, the top lifts just about my bellybutton. *This is so not me.* I appreciate long, protective layers, preferring loose tops to form fitting. Modest opposed to exposure. I think of something my dad said when Shannyn was debating the merits of spaghetti straps. *"You're lovely. Everything else you show is extra. Not everyone who sees you is worthy of you."* My heart winces. *I wish you were here to lecture me, Dad. Would you say Jack is worthy?*

I slide into some brown leather sandals that originally belonged to my mom and tread down the tower stairs.

Maggie rushes to me when I reach the landing. "Here," she says, handing me a vintage lunchbox with the old school "Strawberry Shortcake" gang on the front. "Inside you've got breath mints, sunblock, lipstick, and band aids because you never know." She gives me a devilish look. "Then there's stuff in there from mom's secret medical closet that Marie suggested. They're all labeled, but be careful, some of it totally looks like weed. Don't want Salem Vice to crash your date.".

I give my sister a hug, toss my cellphone into the box.

Two cats are rubbing their bodies against Jack's legs. He holds a teacup near his lips, nodding to whatever story Sally is telling him. When he spots me coming down the stairs, his mouth breaks out into a smile. He eagerly sets his teacup and saucer down and makes his way over to me.

"You look beautiful," he boldly compliments.

I'm now sweating out of nerves rather than magic. I inconspicuously wipe off my hands in my jean pockets while I avoid his eyes. "Thanks," I mumble uncomfortably. *Why am I acting like an idiot? The hottest guy on the eastern seaboard, maybe the country, perhaps the world, just called me beautiful.*

Marie scurries to her feet from the sofa, clattering her teacup and saucer onto the coffee table. "Jack, you two are going sailing?"

"Yes," he nods. "I've rented a boat for the day out of Pickering Wharf. I packed a picnic, and depending on the current, we might stop in town for dinner. I believe Sally has my phone number."

Sally lifts her glass in confirmation.

*Ugh, I'm sure she's the one who texted Jack from my phone.*

Marie fidgets with her necklace, her eyes sliding from Jack to me. "Just be careful, don't try anything foolish, and for heaven's sake, please be careful."

Jack regards my aunt thoughtfully. "I promise nothing will happen."

Her eyes zero in on me. She wasn't warning him. She was warning me.

*I will,* I mouth.

*"Would you like me to accompany you?"*

*Absolutely not.*

Jack opens my car door for me. When he starts the engine, an acoustic bass and snare drum fill his car. He turns the song off. "Sorry about that," he says, pulling out of the driveway.

"No, no, I liked that. It sounds familiar," I say, recalling the lyrics that held a current of British pop-punk.

Jack chuckles. "It's an older band," he says, verging on bashful. Jack glances back at the house before cruising down the road.

"That didn't sound like an "oldies" tune. What kind of music do you like?" I ask.

His cheeks darken in color. "If I tell you—"

"Please don't say you'll have to kill me," I tease with a roll of my eyes.

"I was going to say, don't make fun of me."

I laugh, giving him the scout salute.

"I'm doubting your scout status, but I really like late nineties, early thousands music. Blink-182, what you just heard. The Killers. The Foo Fighters are probably my favorite band of all time. Some Linkin Park. Radiohead. Brand New. Then further back you have Zeppelin, ACDC, and occasionally The Eagles," he lists.

I can't help but smile listening to him.

"What about you?" he asks.

I shake my head to refocus my thoughts. "I have a very eclectic taste," I answer. "I love Eliza Rickman, Florence + The Machine, Zeppelin, and a lot of others."

"Any guilty pleasures?" he asks with a grin.

"Are we still talking music?"

He chuckles and gives me an approving look. "Yes, unless you have something else in mind?"

My hands shake in my lap, worried he's going to find out just how uncool or unfunny I actually am. "I can rap all of Shoop by Salt-N-Pepa."

Jack laughs, nearly barking. "No way. I have to hear this!"

I blush. "Maybe one day." My phone buzzes, rattling inside the metal purse. I unlock the box and retrieve my phone.

"So, what about books and movies?" Jack continues.

I'm about to answer him when I click on the text message from an unknown number.

RIVERS AND DORIS'S BODIES HAVE BEEN FOUND.
DON'T BELIEVE THE LIES.
THEY'RE SAYING IT'S MURDER SUICIDE.
IT WASN'T. IT WAS AN EXECUTION.

# Chapter Twenty-Four
## Sloop John B.

As this is the first warm day of the entire spring season, the New England harbor is teaming with life. We stroll past a packed oyster bar, patrons sipping cocktails under umbrella-clad tables. The Wharf is filled with red brick and clapboard establishments, many with witchy themes. *Oh, if they only knew.*

Our hands brush each other as we walk down the sidewalk. He protectively places his hand on the small of my back when we pass a crowd taking up most of the sidewalk. When a car takes a fast corner, Jack inconspicuously slips to the other side of me, guarding me from the road full of what my aunt calls, Masshole drivers. I tuck my smile away, secretly enjoying his gallantry.

Jack offers me his hand when we step down onto the dock; the old wooden planks rattle beneath our feet with each step. We pass yachts of various sizes and age. The largest is a two-story vessel dripping in affluence and luxury. In bold golden letters on the stern reads *The Commodore*, and it's docked only three boats away from where we're headed.

"It's this last one down here," he points to a modest sailboat with a small galley.

We stop at the very end where there's a man sitting in a folding chair wearing a sun-bleached sweatshirt and holey gym shorts. He rises to his feet when we approach, and a grimy smile curls on his unshaven face as he peers down my legs.

"You Mr. Smith?" he asks.

Jack steps forward, fetching his wallet from his shorts. "Yes, I reserved for the entire day." He flips through several large bills.

The man cranes his neck, peering over him at me. "Yeah, the reservation's good till eight. You need me to show you how to work it?" his eyes never leave me while addressing Jack.

Jack dips his head, blocking his view. "No, your services aren't needed."

He forcefully hands the folded bills over.

The man nods. "Life jackets are in the galley. Want me to get them?" he asks me, ignoring Jack completely.

Jack takes my hand, leading me onto the stern of the boat. "I can take it from here, thank you," he says curtly.

"I'll be here at eight to help tie up." He winks at me before walking back down the dock.

I sit down on a padded seat, gazing at Jack as he rigs the boat.

"Callum! Slow down! My Manolos weren't designed for docks that are cheap AF!"

Recognizing that voice, I rise from my seat and lean over the rail. Down the way a group of teens are trickling down the dock, stopping at The Commodore.

I notice Callum Philips from my physics class; I don't know the other boys' names, but I've seen them hanging around Jack. Vivienne is tucked under a floppy straw hat wearing high-waisted striped-linen pants with a matching bandeau top. Her friends are similarly dressed in floral print rompers and stylishly oversized sunglasses. I watch as they arrange and rearrange themselves for selfies.

One of Jack's friends, I think his name is Hale, shakes up a bottle of champagne and pops the cork, splashing foam all over the girls who squeal in delight, feigning annoyance.

"Everything okay?" Jack questions, walking up from the small galley. He follows my eyeline over to his frolicking friends climbing aboard the luxury yacht. A captain steps out and greets them, instructing them aboard.

Jack curses under his breath. "Let's give them a wide berth. We'll venture out in just a moment." Jack places two life preservers on the seat across from the seat at the helm. He adjusts the mainsail and heads to the bow to deal with the jib.

I chew on my bottom lip, glancing from Jack to his friends, trying to understand his irritation. *Is he embarrassed to be seen with me?* I tuck my hair behind my ears and peer down at my glowing legs neglected by the sun. I look from my legs to my chest to my wimpy arms. *Boobless-O'Reilly* they taunted at my previous school. I think of the spare room I have in my A-cups. *No hips. Practically flat chest. No muscle definition. Complexion of a ghost. Purple eyes.* As the massive yacht detaches from the dock and motors out to sea, the girls are already stripping into their bikinis despite the chill ocean breeze. I stare with envy at their golden bodies, ample assets, and Pilates-defined limbs. I tear my eyes away. *Yeah...I'd be ashamed to be caught with me, too.*

Jack continues to wait until there's plenty of distance between us, then pushes us off. "You ready?"

I limply nod, wishing the date was already over. I cross my arms over my chest, wishing I had more clothes on, or better yet, wishing I was someone else. Shannyn owns every room she enters, and now Margaret is starting to capture men's attention, even though she's completely clueless about it. I wish I had on a parka, or an invisibility cloak. I feel so stupid for even trying.

"Careful," Jack shouts to me, hoisting the sails.

I turn around as the wind pulls us from the dock. I study the marina, taking in the church steeple poking out from behind the colonial shops, the warped and sea-stained wooden planks of the marina, boats tied to their posts, and an antique sailing battleship that looks straight out of a history book on the revolutionary war. Tourists gather about taking pictures.

Jack sits casually at the helm with an insouciant air that could only come from a well-versed sailor. With one arm resting on the metal rail and the other on the helm, he turns to me. "Eleanor, everything okay?"

I find myself shrugging and nodding at the same time.

He regards me dubiously. "What's up?"

I sigh, pulling my feet up onto the seat so I'm sitting crisscrossed. "I don't know. You seemed—desperate to hide from your friends." I throw my hands in the air, when he hangs his head, "I get it. Your friends don't like me."

"That's not true," he insists. "Callum and Stephin have threatened fist-icuffs about asking you out. Callum was planning on making his move at the party and Stephin may have been texting the wrong number," he admits sheepishly, possibly guilty like he's the one who sabotaged.

I play with my thumbnail, chipping away at the dark nail polish. "Then why did you not want to be seen with me? Breaking guy code or something?" I feel only slight relief that not all his friends despised me.

Jack checks the halyard, then turns in his seat to face me. "I'm sorry. My family's social circle is stringent and Grigg's is small. We aren't friends out of mutual admiration or common interests. I didn't want them to see us and insist we come aboard. I could say no, and I would have said no, but it would have gotten back to Allen that I blew them off. There are certain families you can't refuse."

I nod along, listening. "From what I hear at school, you're *the* family you don't mess with."

Jack ran his hands down his face, this conversation souring his mood. "My parents collect people based on beneficial connection. You appease others even if you are perceived to be on top, that way your menagerie stays perpetually pristine and devout. I used a stupid alias like Mr. Smith because I don't even want my parents to know my plans. As far as they're concerned, my future has been carefully mapped out and there is no deviation." Jack turns back to the helm, easing us out of the mouth of the harbor.

I think about our conversation on the way home from the party, his parents carefully laid plans, his old school "betrothal" to Vivienne, and the endless slew of expectations. I feel a sudden wave of gratitude for my family.

The frigid breeze coming off the Atlantic whitecaps gives me a shiver.

"I brought an extra sweatshirt and there are blankets in the galley." Jack peers over his shoulder, "um…just in case you're cold."

"Okay, yeah, thanks," I say, unsure how he knew I had a shiver. My arm brushes against his as I walk past him and down into the small galley. My head barely escapes, brushing against the low ceiling.

On the navy blue and white-striped couch to my left is a picnic basket, folded fleece blankets, and two sweatshirts, a gray one with a gym logo and a dark blue with a crew team symbol. I grab the gray one and press the soft cotton to my nose. It smells like him. I slip it over my head and slide my arms through. *Jack will need his other sweatshirt.* I snag his Crew Team sweatshirt and head back up.

"Here," I say, tossing it to him.

He pulls it on without hesitation. The moment he settles back in his seat, hand on the helm, he glances back at me. "How did you know I wanted it?"

I pull my knees up into my chest as I sit in the corner opposite him. "Probably the same way you knew I wanted one too," I state. It comes out more like an accusation than I meant it to. Something hangs in the air between us, an obvious secret neither of us knows how to address.

Jack gives a quick nod. "Yeah, well, despite the sun, it's still only March," he says nonchalantly. He swivels in his chair. "So, how many offers did you get today?"

"Offers?" I question.

He chuckles. "Mason Platt was going to ask you out to his parents' vine-yard property, and I already told you about Callum and Stephin."

I shrug. "Mason from orchestra? He never approached me. The only invite I received was from Nick and his friends."

Jack nods. "Did I just ask first?"

My stomach knots nervously. *Yes, but that didn't matter. I'd rather be here with you than any of the others.* I hiccup, my shoulders lift with the interruption. "Do you have," hic, "water?" The boat takes a rough wave and rocks.

Jack straightens up, pointing his finger down the stairs. "Oh yeah, there's some Pellegrino, lemonade, and root beer in the mini fridge beside the bathroom.

*How did he know to get root beer?* Hic! I nearly trip down the stairs trying to escape. My chest seizes with a barrage of hiccups. Hic! I whip open the fridge and pull out a bottle of water. Water dribbles down my chin and shirt. The boat rocks and I brace myself against the bolted table.

"Are you hungry?" Jack shouts from the deck.

Hic! I hold water in my mouth, then roughly swallow. "Sure," I answer. My shoulders stop trembling, and my chest stops heaving.

"Then I'll drop anchor," he calls back.

I hear the crank reel releasing the anchor and the whoosh of the sails being dropped.

I feel discombobulated. My head swims with feverish confusion. There's an undeniable magnetic pull between us that shouldn't exist for a boy I barely know. *How does he know my drink of choice? How did he know I was cold? I mean, of course it is March in New England, not Miami Beach in the summer, but still. And why do we always seem to find each other? Like in school, or a crowded party, or even the middle of the forest? Could he be a witch too? Maybe that's why I feel a spark, a mutual connection through magic.* My heart flutters at the thought.

Jack clomps down the ladder steps into the galley, nearly bumping into me in the cramped space. He inclines his head forward towards me to keep from hitting it against the ceiling. He smiles at me. "Do you want to have lunch down here or up on the deck?"

The boat rocks again, tilting him closer to me. He plants his hands on either side of me, steadying himself, his right foot firmly between mine. His cheek brushes the side of my head. I place my hands on his chest, leaning against the countertop. I feel his steady heartbeat beneath my palm. Jack's nose brushes mine; his lips part, his breath tickles my skin. My skin tingles, feeling him so close. Our hips press together. He slips one hand under my chin, lifting it towards his face, while my left hand slides up the back of his neck, gripping his hair. My heart pounds wildly in my ear. Our breath becomes heavy as we keep meeting each other's gazes, asking—begging for permission to go further. I lean forward, my chest compelled against his. Our need to kiss becomes dire.

*Oh, no.* I tense in his arms, tilting my head away ever so slightly as my diaphragm shutters. My nerves are catching up with me. My diaphragm convulses and I release a loud hiccup. Then another. And another... and another.

Jack moves his hands to my hips, pulling his head back. "Are you okay?" he questions. A small, concerned smile plays at the corner of his lips.

Hic! I recede into myself, but he continues to hold me in place. "Yeah," hic, "when I get," hic, "nervous," hic! Hic!

Jack's eyes sparkle as he fights back a grin. "Do you need water? How can I help?" He's sincere, but still slightly amused. His lips twitch, battling against a smile.

I gently push him back onto the couch, forcing space between us. I whip around and throw back my water, holding it in my mouth and counting down.

He rises from the couch, but I hold up a finger, asking for another minute. He holds his hands up, palms forward.

I forcefully swallow the water, then squeeze my eyes shut. I take deep breaths, compelling my nerves to relax.

"Eleanor," Jack says sweetly.

I keep my eyes shut.

"Eleanor."

I peek my eyes open, holding the bottle close to my lips just in case they start again.

His lips are in a gentle smile, but his eyes pierce with intensity. "You're safe with me, I swear."

I gulp back more water. *I wasn't worried about that, even if I should be.*

Jack turns, picking up the brown wicker basket. "Why don't I bring this up top and set things up? Want to get us some drinks?"

I watch him climb back up. *Ugh, why am I such a freak?* Even before I became a witch, I was a mess. I snag a glass bottle of lemonade and my water but wait to head up until I know my nerves have completely settled.

"Jack?" I spin on my heel. He's laid out a plaid blanket on the bow of the ship. I carefully maneuver over to him, squeezing past boom and mast. Jack's lying on his side, propped up on his elbow, and in front of him are eggshell-colored plates filled with fresh fruit, bread, dried meat, and cheeses.

I toss him his lemonade. He deftly catches it and chuckles. "I promise not to spill any on you."

I roll my eyes with a smile. "I appreciate that." I pick up a chocolate-covered strawberry and take a bite, then hold out the plate, offering him one.

He waves his hand at it. "I'm allergic, but thank you," he declines politely.

I lick my lips as the juice drips from the berry. "Then why did you bring it?"

He shrugs, unscrewing the cap of his drink. "I had a feeling you'd like them."

I adjust in my seat, deciding to curl my legs to my side. "I do. Thank you. I'll keep the plate over here then." *How would he know? Ugh, stop. I'm just being dumb. Chocolate-covered strawberries are one of the most cliché date desserts.* I reach for a slice of smoked cheese, brushing my fingers against his as he reached for it too.

He pulls his hand back. "Ladies first."

"So…" I begin, "you graduate soon, where are you going to college? I'm sure you've heard back." I'm grateful he doesn't bring up my hiccups, nor the fact I was ready to jump his bones down in the galley. But of course, my hiccups stopped us. I quietly sigh. If the opportunity rises again, I'm plowing through them. I'm sure you can't hiccup and kiss at the same time, and if I do one before the other, perhaps kissing will win out.

Jack stares down at the veritable buffet he provided. "I got into Harvard."

My eyes bulge, despite not being all that surprised. "Jack, that's amazing. I mean Harvard is the dream school." It hits me, Jack told me already he doesn't want to attend that University.

I dip some bread into the peppered olive oil, grateful I have something for my hands to do. Plus, eating is helping keep my irritating hiccups at bay. "So, where are you actually going?"

Jack looks up at me, almost surprised. "I'm going to RISD, Rhode Island School of Design. I've already sent in my acceptance and memorized their course catalog. I just haven't told my parents yet. The deadline to accept Harvard's offer isn't due yet." His eyes are stormy, his face undecipherable as he bites down on a slice of dry sausage.

"Why haven't you declined Harvard's offer?" I question.

Jack rolls onto his back, placing one hand behind his head. "I'm putting off having that conversation with Allen."

I follow his example and lay back, basking in the sun. I close my eyes against the glare. "So, how far is that from Salem?" I question, hoping he can't hear the disappointment in my voice that in a few short months he'll be leaving.

"About an hour and a half," he answers, sounding almost as mournful as I feel. "And you want to move back to Miami? Next year, after you graduate?" he peeks over at me.

I exhale pensively. "I did, but now I'm not so sure." I imagine my childhood home, realizing I no longer belong there, but don't feel like I belong anywhere else either.

"Think you might want to stick around here? Or maybe in Providence, Rhode Island…" he asks, trailing off.

I giggle, unable to look at him. "So, were you invited on the Bezos yacht?" I joke.

Jack smiles, rolling back onto his side to pick at more food. "They may have brought it up, but I let them know I was otherwise engaged." He lifts his eyebrows, peering at me.

I take a swig of my water. It feels like we are dancing around each other, but carefully, so guarded and afraid. *Is he hiding the same thing as me? I have to know without giving myself away.* "Do you know everyone at Grigg's?" I question.

He shrugs one shoulder. "Uh yeah, more or less. Why?"

I tug a cherry off its stem with my teeth. "How well do you know Trixie Caldwell?" My eyes search for some kind of reaction. Is he protective of a fellow witch, or repulsed like the rest of the population?

He nods before taking a sip of his drink. "Pretty well. In fact, her older sister Quinn... or was it Miranda? One of her older sisters dated my brother Marshall for a month before she broke it off. And Trixie and I have gone to the same school since kindergarten."

I frown at him. Nothing in his body language, tone, and words gave me anything to go off. "If you know her so well, why don't you talk to her? I usually see her by herself."

Another shrug, but he frowns thoughtfully, as if he never thought about it before. "She's always been... a little odd. But really nice. I don't know, we were friendly, everyone was relatively friendly then suddenly, kind of recently she was sitting alone every day at lunch and kept to herself."

*Great, I'm actually more confused than I was before we started.*

"Can I ask you—a weird question," Jack says, playfully serious.

"Sure," I say, skeptically.

"Were you wearing colored contacts your first day?"

I sigh. "Nope, these eyes are all natural." I wave to my eyes.

He shakes his head. "No, they were brown."

My shoulders drop. "Yeah, I did. I thought I'd try having normal looking eyes at my new school." I watch his face relax, accepting the answer. *I'm not getting anywhere. I should ask my aunts if there's a way to test someone if they're a witch.* I smile, just to myself thinking about the archaic tests performed on the early puritan people, *yeah that's not what I was thinking for Jack.*

I lean back on my palms and stretch out my legs crossing at the ankles, enjoying the toasty feel of the sun on my skin. "Why do you ask about my eyes?"

Jack chews on a pastry, then dusts his hands off when he finishes. "I was curious."

A thought occurs to me, and my head slowly turns in his direction. "How did you know that my brown eyes were the fake ones? Why didn't you assume I started wearing purple-colored contacts?"

He freezes. His calm, easy-going façade slips, revealing an exposed nerve. After a moment, his rigid form melts back into the careless, lazed look of someone on vacation. "The brown looked fake. Those actually look real." He nods to my face. "Now to ask you a question, do you know how Macbeth started on fire?"

My body tenses in the same fashion. Our tiptoeing dance is slowly turning into a tightly squeezed tango. I finish off my water hoping to prophylactic my hiccups. "I really don't. Or at least, I didn't at the time," I say, close-ish to the truth. Jack sits up, listening keenly. "Mr. Edwards didn't give me a lot of information, but I guess it was a trick; the prank was supposed to be played on someone else, but I got the book instead."

Jack nods thoughtfully.

"Okay, my turn." My eyes narrow on him. "Why did you hesitate when you came into my house when you broke your nose?" I didn't understand his hesitation that night. He didn't appear fearful; it was something else entirely.

He blushes, ducking his head slightly. "Okay, this is going to sound completely ridiculous…"

I'm about ninety-nine-point-nine percent sure that he can't say anything that would appear strange or ridiculous to me at this point. I've been talking to a dead cat and recently discovered I come from a very long line of witches.

He continues somewhat bashful and rushed. "That home isn't supposed to exist. Since I was a child, my friends and I have trolled the woods looking for the "most haunted house in Salem". No one has ever been able to find it. I swear the dirt road that leads to your aunts' place wasn't there until recently, but clearly the house is old and has been there for a long time. I was just shocked to find that you live in one of the oldest living legends in town," he explains with a chuckle and a careless shake of his head.

*Is even my aunts' house magical? At this point, who knows?* I snag a cube of smoked gouda, embracing the sound of waves against the hull. I turn my head towards the horizon, spotting a familiar sparkling white vessel. "What do you think Vivienne's crew is up to?"

Jack glances over to where my eyes are fixed. "Right now, Vivienne is probably complaining about her bikini top, the girls shivering the entire time because this is Massachusetts and not the Maldives. Soon they'll be branching out to different areas of the boat to hook up," he says, sounding mind-numbingly bored.

I chuckle uneasily. "I take it you're speaking from experience. Would you and Vivienne call dibs on an estate room or did you both prefer the sundeck?" I tease. It's true, I have no claim on Jack, none whatsoever, yet my jealousy is anxiously plucking away inside me. *Is Jack even a virgin anymore?* And if he isn't, was it Vivienne?

Jack shifts uncomfortably. "Would you like some more prosciutto? I think we've got more in the fridge," he offers, conveniently avoiding the question.

"I don't know how you could date someone like Vivienne and then go out on a date with someone like me," I mumble, staring out at the calm bay.

"Seriously?" he asks. "Vivienne and I were just shoved together. Being with her was never my choice. Being with you is," he says boldly, confidently.

My heart skips a beat. My eyes fall to my lap, too nervous to face him. *I can't tell him I want him too. That's too brash, too transparent. He'll see my weakness, see how fallible I am and how easily he could hurt me.*

"But your parents want you to be with Vivienne…" I say, suddenly feeling like I walked out of Hocus Pocus and into a Jane Austen novel. *Was Jack spoken for? Were we just biding our time until Jack's number would be called?* I shake my head. *Every high school relationship has an egg timer that ends at graduation. Why should we be any different?* My pathetic heart sinks.

Jack gives me a glum smile. "Well, Vivienne's cousin Keaton is currently in a relationship with Marshall. Going strong for about a year now. Selfishly, I hope Marshall marries Keaton; it'll probably let Vivienne and I off the hook because our families will want to diversify our genetic portfolio. But it doesn't matter what my brother does. It's my life, who I date is my choice. I'm prepared to be cut off after graduation if it comes to that."

I'm struck by the devotion in his eyes. "Okay," I say, unsure what I'm agreeing to. *Are we declaring ourselves?*

His blazing look softens. "Do you want some of my lemonade or I can go get you something more to drink?" he asks, chivalrously.

"Sure, I'll take a sip," I say, not wanting him to leave even for just a moment.

He reaches his arm over towards me. I lean over, my fingers enclosing over his, taking the beverage. As soon as he releases, I drop the glass bottle, not sure if it was from the condensation or the lustful spark between us.

"Crap! I'm so sorry." I scramble to clean up. Thankfully, none of it landed on the food. Instead, it just soaked my side of the blanket and splashed on my shorts. "I'll go get you another one."

He waves me off. "No, don't worry about it, really. It was more than halfway gone, anyway. But man, we are really unlucky when it comes to lemonade," he jests, giving me a dazzling smile. He pats a spot next to him. "You can come over here, if you want. It's dry," he offers.

My legs feel shaky as I step around our picnic and lounge next to him. Our legs press together in the narrow space. He picks up his hand and nervously, hesitantly places it on mine.

I don't know who started moving first, but I find myself in a reclined position laying side by side, our hands intertwined.

*Don't hiccup. Don't hiccup. Don't hiccup. In through your nose, out through your mouth. In through your nose, hold it, release through the mouth.*

Jack rolls onto his side, facing me. "Are you okay?" he asks gently. He peers into my eyes, looking for permission before every move.

I nod, too nervous to speak.

Jack places his left hand on my hip. He leans closer.

*This is it! I'm going to get my first kiss. On a sailboat. With the sweetest, hottest guy I've ever met.* I shut my eyes, ready to feel his lips on mine. Suddenly, my magic flares inside me, like lighting a paraffin torch. My magic is alive and ready to strike. *No, no, no! Don't do anything!* It surges down each limb.

"Wait, Jack." My eyes flash open. Before I can place my hands on his chest, stopping him, he is suddenly flung away from me. For a brief moment, I see the confusion and terror in his eyes. His body flies clear over the railing and splashes hard into the choppy water.

"Oh my gosh! Jack!" I scurry to my feet and frantically search the dark water for him. There's no sign of him. "Jack!" My heart pounds in my chest and my hands quake while gripping the railing. *Where could he be? Where is he? He has to know how to swim, right?* My eyes swell with fearful tears. "Jack!" I scream, nearly delirious with fear.

I can feel an undulating surge of adrenaline. Despite being engulfed in sheer panic, I sense a strange smile deep within. My magic is… happy? My magic relaxes inside me, like the task at hand is complete.

I squint, spotting his golden hair through the waves. He's still submerged a few feet below the surface. No bubbles, no flailing. He's perfectly, deadly still.

# Chapter Twenty-Five
## Memories

Without a moment to think, I leap over the railing and dive into the water. *Oh my gosh, please be alive, Jack! Please be alive!* I'm stunned by the frigid ocean temperature seizing my limbs. The icy water burns against my skin. I fight through cramping joints and breaststroke underwater towards him. He's slowly sinking, his limbs floating limp at his sides. Somehow, the water is even colder below the surface. I reach Jack, wrap my arms around his chest, and furiously paddle upward.

Our heads finally breakthrough the surface. I gasp for air, then take a face full of water from a small wave. It's everything I can do just to keep his head out of the water; there's no way I can get back to the boat in time. Without checking for onlookers, I squeeze my eyes shut and picture both of us springing from the water and landing gently on the deck of the boat. My magic awakens, slithering out of a cavern within. *La Caeli.*

Instead of shooting out of the waves like I had imagined, we gracefully lift like a balloon. We drift through the air and land on the deck. Jack splays out, his head lulled to the side. I kneel at his side, tapping his face. "Jack! Jack!?" *Chest compressions. You can do this.*

*"You did this..."* a slithering whisper slinks out from the corners of my mind.

My jaw quivers and I whimper. Instead of CPR, I imagine the water in his lungs flowing up his throat and his breathing returning to normal. *La Caeli.*

A stream of saltwater trickles from his mouth into the air until it sprinkles back into the ocean. I watch his chest compress up and down until...

Jack's eyes burst open. He gasps, his head bobbing as he coughs.

"Jack!" I cradle him against my chest. "You're okay. You're okay." *I'm an idiot. I should have cancelled today. How could I have done this to him?* "I'm so sorry. I'm so sorry!"

Jack's coughing settles down and his breathing slows to a steady rhythm. His eyes flutter closed, his body limp with exhaustion.

*Margaret's lunch box, maybe she packed something that'll help.*

I pull off Jack's sweatshirt, heavy with seawater, and toss it to the side, then rush to the stern where I left the purse. When I crack open the tin lid, small glass vials of mixed herbs, flower petals, and other liquids spill into my lap. My hands shake as I read each label written in my mother's elegant handwriting. Broken bones. Burns. Headaches. Numbness. Blindness. Memory loss. I stop and examine the strange blue liquid with the memory label. I strain to read the tiny written direction and purpose. To suppress recent memories, ingredients include milk of the poppy, ashwagandha, bog fungi, ginger, blue algae, and sacrificed calla lily. *Whatever that means.* I put that one to the side. Lacerations. Sore sinuses. I snag the sore sinus vial and the memory vial, then rush back to Jack.

I ease his head onto my lap again. According to the directions on the memory vial, he should only take a few sips; anything more and he could lose hours. I uncork the top and methodically pour a few precise drops past his parched lips. Now for the sinuses. This vial came with a dropper. I put one drop of the clear liquid in each nostril.

I watch his chest rise and fall and place my hands on his soaking wet chest. I imagine his clothes and body drying, his clothes feeling dryer fresh. *Ne feerah.* My palms percolate with heat. *You will not hurt him.* I can feel his soggy sweatshirt become fuzzy with warmth. I peek my eyes open and withdraw my hands. His hair curls more than usual from the sea salt, but at least it's dry.

I tenderly move his arm so one is pulled from his body and the other placed behind his head. I curl up next to him, not quite in his arms but close enough, like we had just fallen asleep together.

Jack's body reacts to my proximity and rolls over towards me, draping one arm over me. "Eleanor," he whispers, muffled with sleep.

I'm too emotionally drained to smile and release a sigh of relief instead, just grateful he's okay. He's sweetly dreaming of me, but in reality I'm a nightmare. As he slumbers, I trace his nose and cheeks, then dust the salt out of his eyebrows. "You need to stay away from me," I whisper. "I could have killed you." *This should be easy. I barely know you, you barely know me. We can easily sever whatever this is. I don't love you. Of course not.*

My heart sinks at the prospect, then picks up pace, realizing just how out of control I was. *Why would my magic want to hurt someone I care about? Could it have been Elspeth? But why would she want to hurt Jack, and how could she have any reach over* my *magic?* I snuggle closer to Jack, feeling a prickling chill, like watchful eyes on us. *How can I keep you safe?* A dark cloud reaches out over the sky, draping us in grey shadow. I gulp back against a lump forming in my throat. *How do I even keep myself safe?* One thing is for sure, I can't wait for Pyewacket to do something. I need to speak to the aunts about Elspeth.

My hands are trembling. I grip his sweatshirt, hoping it will calm them down, but my whole body is quivering. I want to cry. I feel so overwhelmed as my predicament keeps twisting and coiling into something obsidian and sinister.

Jack smiles in his sleep and his eyes sleepily drift open. His smile widens and he pulls me closer. "Hey," he says, as if he was awaking from a casual nap. He closes his eyes while he tucks me into his chest. He releases a peaceful breath. His hands run through my hair, cradling my head. A finger gets caught in the cold, wet tendrils. I feel his loose body tense, his eyes creek open as he frowns. "You're wet, how did you get so wet?" he questions sleepily yet concerned as he feels my damp back.

I shrug and sit up, leaving the warm comfort of his embrace. "Oh, I think we knocked over some drinks. I'm not that wet." I say, wondering if I risk performing the fire spell to dry off more.

Jack nods, accepting my answer. He yawns, stretching his arms up above his head before sitting up. "I'm really sorry. I can't believe I fell asleep." His brow knits and he pulls at his clothing. "I feel—grimy. Maybe we took a wave. Though…how did we sleep through it?"

I shake my head. "I don't know. We were cuddling together, then we were waking up."

Jack smiles, taking my hand in his, intertwining our fingers. "I remember the cuddling." He smiles crookedly. He tilts his head, studying my face and tepid smile. "Eleanor? What's wrong?"

My mouth goes dry. *Do I do it now? Or should I wait? I mean, we still have to sail back to shore. Do I have to do this? Yes, I can't date him. I've broken his nose and nearly drowned him already. What else could go wrong?* I immediately end that train of thought before my magic can react to it.

I shake my head and try to force a better smile. "Sorry, I think I'm still out of it. Deep sleep and all."

He gives my hand a gentle squeeze. "If you're sure," he says, with slight skepticism.

I nod, then my attempt at giving him a playful wink gets him to laugh.

Jack hoists himself up onto his feet and dusts off the dried salt. "I think I left my cell down in the galley. I'll go check the time."

As he makes his way down the ladder, I quickly scramble to my feet and pick up all the fallen potions and other date aids strewn about next to my purse. I quickly snap it shut and fall into a lounge position on the couch just as he's coming back.

He slides his phone into his back pocket. "Wow, we slept for about an hour." He rubs his sternum painfully, then rolls his shoulders and cracks his neck.

"You okay?" I question.

He frowns. "My chest is really sore. Maybe I slept on the deck wrong," he says, slightly teasing. "If I had known we'd need a nap, I'd have suggested the bed down in the galley. Though I can't speak for the cleanliness of the sheets," he says warily.

I chuckle, feeling a blush bloom in my cheeks, most likely turning them splotchy. Despite the near disaster from moments ago, I still have to fight back images of us frolicking in the narrow galley bed.

"Sorry," he smiles awkwardly. "So," he claps his hands together, "do you want to continue to tour up the coast? I can teach you how to sail," he says, alluringly.

The word "no" rests at the tip of my tongue, but instead I hear myself say, "sure, that sounds great."

While we clean up the picnic, Jack eyes where we slept almost mournfully, like he wasn't quite ready to let go of me. His square hands knot the rope, crank the anchor, and hoist the sail.

When we're underway, he takes a seat in the captain's chair. I follow his arm as he points out different landmarks on shore: a lighthouse, historical homes, and colonial looking restaurants with signs boasting they have the best clam chowder in the state. The sun is shining brightly, reminding us summer is right around the corner.

As soon as I claim the seat across from him, Jack picks up my legs and places them on his lap. With one hand on the wheel, he uses the other to rub the arch of my left foot. I snort behind my hand, trying my best to swallow my giggles.

"What?" he questions, self-consciously. "Am I that bad?"

I shake my head. "No, I'm sorry, I'm so ticklish," I say, holding back a peal of laughter.

He raises a brow. "Really?" he tightens his hold.

"No! Don't!" I squeal as he pulls on my feet, keeping them in place as he tickles from my toes down to my heels.

I squirm in my seat laughing, trying to wiggle away. "Stop!" I cry between fits. As my writhing body worms out of the seat, I feel Jack's hands on my legs, then my waist, pulling me onto his lap so I'm more or less straddling him. I snatch his wrists, holding his arms down. "No more, or I'll start tickling you," I threaten, catching my breath.

Jack grins, his green eyes dazzling. His gaze falls to my lips. His firm hands move from my waist to my back. Every nerve ending in my body tingles at his touch. For a moment, I wonder if my skin glows just beneath his hands. Before my heart can explode in my ears, or my hiccups can trumpet their humiliating interruption, his mouth is on mine. My body melts into a puddle in his lap, and I fall deeper into him and his kiss. His mouth opens to mine, preventing me from anxiously analyzing my performance. Around us is nothing and everything, all at once. His mouth is urgent, hungry on mine, like he's been waiting all his life for this. My lips move with his, matching his intensity. My hands run through his hair as his arms wrap around my body, pressing me against him.

We break apart to catch our breath. He clutches me in a vice-like hold, like I might just disappear if he gives me an inch to do so. I rest my head on top of his as he lays his on my collarbone.

I can feel his pounding heart nestled behind marble-like muscle. My heart bangs in tandem. *How did this happen? I'm supposed to be saying goodbye, not 'kiss me now and forever'.* Everything inside me wants to weep as I feel a crack ripple through me. I just made it ten times harder on myself to say goodbye. *Can I even do it?* There's a scratching, gnawing sensation at the back of my mind, screaming to get out, something I've tenderly known since we ran into each other in the hallway. I love him. *And I'm an idiot.*

Jack smoothly maneuvers me so that I'm sitting across his lap, allowing him to drive the boat. My arms wrap around his neck as his right arm snakes around my waist. We sit in comfortable silence, neither of us feeling the need to break this perfectly incandescent spell we are under...at least for now. We can always break up tomorrow.

"When is your birthday?" Jack questions, out of the blue.

I chuckle, caught off guard. "March first. You?" *Is he asking because he knows that this last birthday was special, that I'd ascend to witchcraft?*

"September third," he replies. "Favorite flower?"

"Daisies, and you?"

"I think I like daisies now." He gently smiles. "Favorite food?"

"Cuban. What's with the twenty questions?"

He shrugs. "I want to know everything about you."

I scrunch my nose in an awkward smile. "There's not much to know. I'm rather boring." *At least with what I'm allowed to tell you.*

His gorgeous blonde hair is tousled softly in the ocean breeze, making him even sexier than what's fair for a hormonal witch having to mind her thoughts. "Oh," he stands up with me, carefully placing me on my feet as he adjusts the sail. "Careful," he calls as the boom swings around and he pulls me out of the way. Jack eyes the horizon and the grey clouds gathering despite the beaming sun overhead. "We should probably turn around now; I don't like how those clouds look."

I take a comfortable seat on the back couch, once more enjoying watching him work. He glances back at me with a grin before continuing. Jack pulls the wheel to the left, heaving the boat to the side, and the sails fluff up with captured air. "What did you do for your birthday?" he asks as he sits back down at the helm.

My stomach clenches and my jaw clamps. I would have jumped ship to avoid this question. I swallow. "Um, nothing really. What about you?" I question, hoping to change the subject back to him.

"Oh, come on, you must have done something. It was only two," he squints, thinking, "three weeks ago."

I peered down at my feet, feeling ashamed.

"Did you do something bad? Did you get drunk? Tattoos? Bad piercings?" Jack teases gently.

I shake my head at him. "No, my dad passed away the next day."

Jack straightens up. His smile vanishes, replaced with sympathy. "Eleanor, I'm so sorry. I didn't know it happened around your birthday. I—" He grapples for more apologetic words. His eyes search my face repentantly. "I'm truly sorry, Eleanor."

I shake my head, not wanting to get into it. "He had a seminar in Jacksonville that weekend. One driver rushing and another driver sleeping." He was hit head on by a semi. The driver had fallen asleep at the wheel. Dad was killed instantly. Six cars altogether in the pileup. My dad was the only one that died. "So, tell me about your family. You have an older brother and sister, what are their plans after they finish school?"

Jack places one protective hand on my knee while keeping the other on the helm. "Marshall just graduated from Yale law. He interned for a Supreme Court Justice and he's being courted by several large firms, but I believe he wants to move to Boston. He couldn't stand New Haven, and he's not a big fan of D.C. However, Allen wants him to set roots there in Washington, keep connections strong, remind certain politicians who lines their wallets. And Honor, I think, is studying foreign affairs. She wants to be a correspondent. So, when she finishes up at Harvard, I doubt she'll come back here."

The water is becoming choppy, causing us to bob and splash. I tuck my hands into the pocket of his sweatshirt I'm wearing. "Are you guys close?"

He gives my knee a little loving squeeze before retracting his hand and standing up, fixing something with the sail. "Only that we share

DNA. You'll see," he assures.

"Oh, I will?" I ask, folding my arms at him, jokingly smug.

He flashes me a grin. "Yeah, I want you to come to dinner next week. It's better to rip the band aid off right away."

I swallow, all teasing drains from me. "Your family sounds terrifying. Besides, I thought you try to keep your life a secret, *Mr. Smith*," I point out, hopefully not too harshly. I picture his sister adorned in pearls and Dior's latest confection while the men are swathed in Armani. I try to steady my heartbeat, reassuring myself that meeting will never take place. At the end of this date, I have no choice but to say goodbye.

He nods, then readjusts his hands on the helm almost nervously. I watch him struggle with something internally until he rights his shoulders, confident in whatever conclusion he has come to. "I didn't want today to be spoiled, and I'm hoping that perhaps I can now introduce you as more than a friend. I'm sorry if I'm being a little too presumptuous in that."

I turn away, unsure of what to say. *I don't want this to be the end, but what can I do?* I nibble on my lip, knowing he's painstakingly waiting for an answer.

"You don't have to give me an answer. I know this is all sudden. But would you be willing to think about it?" Jack asks, a tepid whisper of hope in the timber of his voice.

*I need to continue my training. Maybe if I complete all five branches, my magic will finally be under control and Jack will be safe. Safe and with me.* I rise to my feet and walk over to Jack. A hiccup is building, but I place my hands on his shoulders and press my lips against his. My pulse quickens and my body comes alive when he pulls me into him at my waist. His mouth devouring me as before. A hiccup pops out of my mouth when our face's part for air.

Jack smiles, resting his forehead against mine. "I've got you," he assures me, attempting to assuage my nerves. "But does this mean we're together?"

I shut my eyes and nod my head against his.

Jack practically cheers, wrapping his arms around me and lifting me so even my toes can't touch the ground. He stops himself from saying something and instead buries himself into our embrace.

As we settle back into our seats, we look for any excuse to skim our hands against one another or brush our feet together. He tucks my hair behind my ear while we make our way back to the harbor.

Anxious about the prospect of meeting his incredibly intimidating family, I ask rapid-fire questions, hiccupping as I interrogate.

"My father, 'Allen Marshall Jackson Woods IV, of the Boston and Salem Woods', runs White Stone, the investment firm. He occasionally golfs, but honestly, his hobbies revolve around his work."

"What about your mom?" I probe.

Jack sighs. "My mother Evelyn Godspeed-Woods, chairs a variety of charities. She's always traveling. She prefers Paris this time of year."

The fickle wind slows down our sojourn into the harbor, though neither I nor Jack seem all that eager to end the date.

Jack continues. "My brother, Marshall Wallis Anthony Woods," he says, with a mockingly puffed out chest, "because of course we all need multiple names to really show a sense of self-importance, will probably be your best bet. He's fairly easy going. He enjoys polo, harassing country club waitressing staff, and trips to the vineyard," he describes.

Our families couldn't be more diametrically different if they tried. Sure, my grandmother Lydia on my father's side came from old money and would be able to snob it up with the best of them, but her children took the old money and made it new, flaunting wealth and means while also draining it. I roll my eyes, thinking of my mother's side, a staggeringly long line of Celtic witches.

"Would your sister Honor like me?" I ask meekly.

Jack smiles gently at me, describing her interests of frequenting different fashion weeks around the world to working as editor and chief of The Harvard Crimson, to spending her twenty-first birthday in Morocco courting some prince.

"So, short answer is *no*, your sister will also not like me," I say, hanging my head back, peering up at the blue sky overly diluted by grey clouds, knowing rain is imminent.

It was hard to keep my jaw from dropping hearing about Jack's golden legacy from a family that the phrase "Keeping up with the Joneses" was probably coined after. I used to think my parents were intimidating.

Jack gives me a little encouraging tug. "I don't care what they think, Eleanor. I just don't want to hide you. They aren't going to change my mind and honestly, you being so different from them is a bonus in my book. I really like that you're so different."

*You have no idea.*

# Chapter Twenty-Six
## Saint Tropez

As we approach the wharf, the bustle from earlier has largely died down. The weather has shifted from perfectly balmy to ominously gloomy, causing tourists to tuck away into shops and indoor dining and leaving the seagulls to peck to at the leftovers on the docks.

Jack and I exchange glances as we both peer over at the far end of the dock where The Commodore is stationed. If he's at all nervous or bothered, he disguises it skillfully, shooting me a smile and a wink.

My stomach twitches. *We were going to have to face his friends eventually.* I stare over at Jack, still unsure how he'll act.

Jack turns his focus on directing the boat. He expertly eases us into place with such precision you'd think some other force was guiding us. The man we rented the sailboat from pushes up off his lawn chair and wanders over to us. Jack throws him the rope to tie the boat in.

"You two get wet?" he smirks.

Jack ignores him and instead instructs him on the rigging. Jack lends me his hand helping me out of the boat. With one hand he clutches the picnic basket and the other he affectionately holds my hand, occasionally bringing it up to his mouth bestowing a kiss.

"Dude! Jack!" Stephin calls from the top deck of the Commodore. He ironically wears a fedora and a white windbreaker without a shirt on.

I try to shrink away, but Jack proudly wraps his arm around my waist, pressing me against his body.

"Get up here!" Stephin yells, thrusting a brown bottle in the air while a rolled white paper bounces between his lips. "Come on!" He motions for Jack to join him. "Dude! Let's go!"

Hearing the commotion, the rest of Jack's friends come trickling out of the main cabin onto the deck. The string of party lights strung about the yacht flicker on just as the dock lights illuminate. Poppy rides on Hale's back, giggling. Callum leans against the railing, his arm slung around another girl's neck. They all call out to Jack, trying to cajole him aboard. Vivienne, however, hovers in the peripheral, holding a cocktail glass leaning against the doorway. My eyes flick over to her, meeting her murderous gaze.

Callum stares at us with a jovial grin. "Bro, you missed it. Stephin tried to do a backflip from the top deck, ripped his pants—"

"Pissed his pants more like it," pipes up the tallest of the group. I think Bennet is his name.

"Aye!" Stephin shouts from up top. "Come on, Jack," he shouts, nodding his head toward the ship.

"You can bring Eleanor," Poppy assures, quickly spying a peek over at Vivienne as if asking permission.

Jack turns to me. "We do not have to go over there. Truly."

I can feel everyone's eyes piercing my back as I deliberate. "If we get this over with now, maybe it'll be easier at school Monday," I suggest, deflated.

Jack brings his mouth close to my ear. "The moment you want to leave, we'll go." He kisses my cheek, making the skin feel aglow. *How does he do that?*

Jack is yanked by his friends over to the professionally staffed bar as I'm flocked away by Vivienne's friends. He glances over his shoulder at me, his brows knit in concern. *"You okay?"* he mouths, trying to gauge me.

I smile and shrug, hoping to appear congenial. They lead me over to a dark leather sofa decorated with nautical throw pillows. When Poppy plops down next to me, all the other girls follow suit, all except Vivienne who is still at the mini bar with the boys.

"I don't think we've all been properly introduced," Poppy says, struggling to command her words from slurring. "Now that we are all friends, this is Caroline Chen," Poppy nods to the girl immediately to my left who I recognize from anatomy class; she glares flatly at me. "Hazel Bartlett, Margot Ruiz, Sienna Hastings and, of course, you know Viv," Poppy says, glassy-eyed and tipping her crystal flute towards her friend leaning on a barstool.

"She's pretty famous," Margot pipes up. "she was featured in Teen Vogue as 'One to Watch'." Her brown eyes turn hard, gazing at her friend more enviously than supportive, I realize.

I nod along, peering back over at Jack, surrounded by his friends. He listens to Hale while he unscrews the lid to a bottle of water. The boys all start laughing about something, and Callum claps Jack on the back.

"What is it? You look mystified," Hazel says smugly.

I pull my gaze from Jack and glance about the grand room with its dangling crystal chandelier, a busy staff ready to serve. "Yeah, I guess. Wasn't exactly expecting this in the harbor."

Sienna scoffs, not looking up from her phone.

"Salem is the new Manhattan, thanks to Allen Woods. He forced Wall Street to take notice," Caroline states matter-of-factly.

Margot retrieves a small silver Gucci case from her beaded clutch and flicks out a long cigarette. "So, are you and Jack like together now?" She lights the paper with a bedazzled lighter and blows grey smoke into the air.

Hazel leans across her friend to get closer to me. "You landed the whale, you know," she chimes. "I mean, his godfather is the Secretary of State."

Sienna crosses her long legs at the knee, leaning back into the pillows. "That's one of his least impressive anecdotes. His family was invited to the royal coronation, all those tacky weddings, the Woods know everyone and are involved in everything," she says, sounding bored out of her mind. She runs her hand through her blonde pixie, pushing her bangs back from her forehead. "Movies, politics, fashion, global networks, there's the Woods. Okay, seriously, does anyone have a Xanax?"

Poppy digs through her purse.

Caroline rolls her eyes at her friends, downing the rest of her drink. "Not that any of that matters to you, of course," she murmurs, eyeing me. All her friends give her an indecipherable look. She balks, falling back on the couch. "What? Like Vivienne hasn't had dibs since birth? Her parents want that match as much as she does," she concludes.

Hazel giggles. "I bet while they were dating, they switched out her birth control with tic-tacs," she says dropping her voice just in case Vivienne is eaves dropping from across the room.

The girls giggle with exaggerated eye rolls.

Sienna sighs, her lanky arms resting on the back of the sofa. "They've never stopped dating; this is just their twisted foreplay. Jack plays with something and Vivienne hooks up with Bennet to make Jack jealous. Round and round we go," Sienna says, twirling her bejeweled finger in the air.

"No offense," Hazel says to me with faux consideration. "If it makes you feel better, the Woods boys give *the* best parting gifts. My stepsister hooked up with Marshall for a while and when he ended it—"

"Over text," Sienna interrupts.

Hazel continues, "she got a Harry Winston. It's like her favorite thing in the world now."

Poppy laughs drunkenly. "*That's* how she got it?"

Hazel glares at Poppy. "At least she didn't give it up for crappy mother-of-pearl earrings."

The girls argue Cartier vs Bulgari and Tiffany's vs Winston. Watches are out, tennis bracelets are back, and there's never an excuse for rose gold.

Every time Jack tries to escape the bar, his friends guide him back. My pulse races at the mere prospect of meeting the Woods family. No matter how futile this dinner seems, given the fact that Jack and Vivienne are written in the stars, my body is still wracked with nerves. I bite down on my lip, concealing bubbling hiccups.

The catty chatter continues, dissecting the graduating class, rating the teacher's looks, and congratulating each other with their ivy acceptances.

"Where's the bathroom?" I ask, glancing around the group.

Caroline points down the hall and I quickly push up to my feet and hurry from the room. I feel their scrutinizing stares with every step I take.

I close the door behind me and face the mirror, mortified. My nose and cheeks are rosy from the sun, my hair is frizzy and erratic. My mascara is smudged beneath each eye. I snatch some toilet paper, wetting it and dabbing under my eyes. *What was I thinking? How could I suggest we do this!? I look so scruffy!*

Frantically, I comb through my hair with my fingers and toss the hair over one shoulder as if this look was by choice. I grimace. *It doesn't matter. Are Vivienne and Jack actually together? Would Jack disobey his parents and ditch their plans? He said he's going to RISD, but he hasn't even told his parents yet nor declined his Harvard acceptance. What if he chickens out?* I twist the ends of my hair, feeling everything is stacked against us; if it isn't my magic, it's Jack's illustrious family.

The bathroom door swings open. Vivienne slips in and locks the door behind her. She leans against the door; her eyes slide from my hairline to my shoes. Her plump lips curl into a sneer. She lifts one perfectly quaffed brow, her eyes still leveling me. "You're not as clever as you think you are."

I fold my arms across my chest, withering beneath her scrutiny. My eyes fall to the golden straps of her shoes. "I wasn't aware I thought I was all that clever," I mumble.

Vivienne tilts her head condescendingly, appraising me once more. She plucks at the grey boxing sweatshirt hanging off my frame. "Not really your shade. But it's so comfy, right? I used to pick that one too. Until my skin started reacting to common fabric."

I scrunch my toes inside my sandals. "Can you please move?" I wave to the door, still staring down like a coward.

Vivienne takes a step forward, causing me to take three steps back until my back is pressed against the beveled shower door. "Many have tried, all have failed. You're just a plaything, something new, a muse." She grins wickedly, her face inches from mine, "so have your fun, get a shiny trinket or two, but don't for one second think you've suddenly landed yourself a Woods. You haven't. And you won't."

"And you have?" I challenge her, somewhat under my breath.

Vivienne laughs, practically barking in my face. "Oh, you really are *adorable*," she coos condescendingly. "You have no clue what you're trying to mess with. You think Allen or Evelyn would let this little dalliance continue?"

I straighten up more, forcing Vivienne back a few inches. "We're in high school. I think you can suspend your engagement panic," I say, beckoning some boldness. The room feels like a funhouse closet, the walls closing in.

Vivienne purses her lips, amused. "I'm not worried you'll mess up our engagement. Those papers were drawn up years ago. It's common in our circle for the men to momentarily slum it. You know, get it out of their systems before they buy the rock."

I shrug, trying to sidestep her, desperate to escape this cage. "Well, it looks like you have nothing to worry about then." I slip past her, but she spins on her heel, snatching my arm tightly. Her manicured nails painfully dig into my flesh.

"For your own sake, back off. You don't mean anything to him, you're simply delaying the inevitable." She tightens her hold on my arm. "Ask him about Saint-Tropez, do it. His answer might surprise you," she says, summoning an insouciant air in her voice while gripping me like a vice.

She releases her grasp around my arm and instead loops hers with mine. A maniacal smile clicks into place. "Sit next to me at dinner, mmkay?" she squeaks with a bounce of her shoulders. Despite being two inches shorter than me, she successfully tows me out of the restroom. Her lemmings immediately gather at our side. Jack frowns, spotting Vivienne's arm firmly intertwined with mine.

Jack and his group of friends drift over to us. Jack peels off from them and steps between Vivienne and me. He eyes me with concern.

"Robbie, seat two more places at the table," Vivienne orders a swarthy-looking waiter. He grins at her, despite having at least five years on her. Vivienne steps around me, claiming Jack's other side as if I'm invisible. "Do you remember that chef, Pierre something, from that fishing trip?" she says, finishing with a giggle. "Allen was so mad at Marshall," she continues to laugh despite Jack's obvious indifference. "Well, he's here, and unlike last time, I made no promise to provide the main course."

I lean towards Jack's ears; his entire body turns to me, reacting to my movement and brushing Vivienne aside. "Can we go?" I whisper.

Vivienne rushes to my side. "Oh no, Eleanor, this is a Michelin-rated chef. Allen Woods flew Pierre over from—goodness, where is he from? Jack, was it Saint Tropez?" She peers up at the ceiling, tapping her chin.

Jack's eyes slide to her sharply, but he hesitates, then drifts back to me.

"We must be getting back," he says brusquely. He places his hand on the small of my back with a tenderness that catches me off guard.

We walk silently down the sidewalk. Venders are closing their pop-up shops for the day, and there's a new flow of people coming out for dinner and the pleasant seaside ambience. Jack pulls me close as a large group stampedes down the sidewalk towards us.

There's been a storm in his eyes ever since Vivienne opened her mouth. His thoughts cloud his face; he keeps opening his mouth to speak, only to clip it shut again.

"I'm sorry," I say as we meander closer to the parking lot. I nervously wring my fingers. "It was my idea to join them. I'm sorry.".

He frowns, stepping closer. "Do you think I'm mad at you?"

I say nothing.

His shoulders fall at my silent response. Then he drapes a comforting arm around my shoulder and presses his lips to the crown of my head. "No. I'm the one who should be apologizing. I know they can be—nasty. Especially Viv. Today was supposed to be ours. I shouldn't have put that on you. I'm sorry, Eleanor." He gives me a gentle squeeze, elevating the mood.

I smile, letting myself fall into him. My eyes wander across the street just as Jack asks me about dinner. Across the way, Trixie is in a pair of bell bottom overalls and a rain slicker while she tapes a red flyer to the light polls.

Jack unlocks his car and props open the trunk, placing the wicker basket inside. "I don't know how you feel about lobster, but there's this great little place not far from here."

I glance at him, then back at Trixie. "Um, could you excuse for me just a second?" I dash across the street, narrowly dogging a biker. "Hey," I say, greeting her softly.

Her blue eyes are fierce, almost wild. She pulls me in for a squeezing hug. "You got my message," she breathed.

I think back on the cryptic text at the beginning of the date. It was from Trixie. "Yeah, I'm so sorry. My aunts haven't said anything," I say.

Trixie shakes her head bitterly, curling her lips in an angry pout. "It's because the Committee is keeping it under wraps. But I knew them, Ell. Doris would never do this, neither would Rivers. It makes no sense."

I pull her back into a hug, unsure of what else to say or do. "I'm really sorry." I gaze down at her hand hanging at her side. "What are these?"

Trixie hoists up the scarlet sheet. "I'm looking for the real perpetrators." Bold black letters declare that Doris and Rivers Calloway were murdered in cold blood. Cash reward for any information.

Indiscreetly, I sniff the paper; it smells heavy of incense.

Trixie's looks about the street, almost paranoid. "I dripped compelling oil on the papers. Hopefully, if anyone knows anything, they'll feel compelled to reach out." Trixie points to one of the many personal cell number tear aways she provided.

I try to hand her the flyer back, but she shakes her head, insisting I keep it. "I'll try to talk to my aunts, see if they know anything, but I can't promise they will even if they do smell your flyer," I say, folding it up. "Trixie, I know your family goes way back with them, but why do you think it wasn't just a horrific tragedy?" I try to grapple with the dream I had of Trixie and her journal. *It couldn't be a coincidence, could it? Friends of hers are murdered and someone steals something so personal to her?*

Thunder booms above our heads, like a heavy marble ball rolling across hard flooring. A whisper of rain begins to drizzle. I pull the hood up over my head of Jack's sweatshirt.

Trixie takes a few conspiratorial steps closer to me. "I think this has been going on for a long time. Witches going missing, only to be found dead in the most random of circumstances. But the covens are refusing to even discuss it." Trixie looks about again, anxious before continuing. "We are being hunted. The signs are everywhere."

Despite the rain turning into a full downpour, soaking me to the bone, the hair on the nape of my neck stands on end. Her words echo in my skull; *we are being hunted.* The natural cynic in me wants to laugh and jab about tinfoil hats, but since moving to Salem, I've had to completely reevaluate my understanding of the world. *Maybe Trixie is right?*

Jack trots across the street to us, a black opened umbrella in his hand. "Hey, Trixie," he greets, holding his shelter over us. He takes in my distressed expression, then Trixie's. "Everything okay?"

Trixie's ocean eyes swell with emotion. She sniffs back tears. "Lost some family friends…pretty brutally."

Jack winces. "Was it that mother and son that passed in Greenwich?"

My head immediately snaps in his direction, which he picks up on.

"It's all over the news," he says in explanation, almost defensively. He swivels back to Trixie, spying the flyers she's clutching. "I could help hang those if you want." He eyes the block lettering shouting from the flyer. "Tips? I'm sorry, I thought the police had closed the case?"

Trixie tilts her chin up in defiance. "*They* have. *I* have not."

He nods pensively, taking in everything Trixie is saying. "Is the family doubtful of the findings?"

My eyes dart from Jack to Trixie. She purses her lips, possibly determining how much she should explain.

"Trixie Faye Caldwell!" a woman shouts.

Trixie's eyes leap to me in alarm. "Go!" she hisses, giving me a little shove. "Hide in the store or something till we leave! Go!" She spins me around and shoves me into the stoop of a candle shop.

Jack's face crumbles in confusion. "What is going on?" he asks us both.

Trixie whirls him around so he's no longer facing me, hiding in the stoop, but instead faces the newcomers who shouted Trixie's name a block away.

I turn my back to them and face the glass door advertising in-house made candles. I step into the corner next to the door as a couple brushes past me, hurrying in out of the rain.

"Trixie, what is this all about?"

"I can't explain, but they can't see Eleanor," she whispers back. I can barely hear them above the rain pounding on the pavement.

"Why?" he whispers back.

"Trixie," an older female voice says scoldingly.

"Mom, Dad, you didn't have to come down here," she says indignantly.

"Jack Woods, it's been a long time. I hope your family is doing well," the woman says cordially.

"They are, thank you. My condolences for your loss," Jack says, ever the gentlemen.

There's a quiet pause.

"Thank you, son," a male voice replies politely.

More awkward silence.

Jack coughs. "Well, I better be going. This belongs to the store; I'll leave it right here." He shakes something out, then steps into the stoop.

I peek behind me, seeing his umbrella resting in the corner for me.

"Trixie, I'll see you tomorrow at school. Mr. and Mrs. Caldwell," he says.

The Caldwell's are silent, probably watching him leave.

"Trixie Faye Caldwell, you're being reckless and irresponsible!" her mother chastises.

"We already combed around town taking down the flyers," her father firmly informs.

"What were you thinking?" her mom shrieks.

"My dear, let's not make a scene," he says in a hushed tone.

A loud exhale. "Trixie, let's go home. I'm brewing some tea, you'll feel better. I promise," her mother assures in a strained voice.

"The Nefari have nothing to do with this," Trixie declares loudly, boldly.

"Trixie!" her mother hisses.

"This was human-on-witch murder," Trixie continues to counter.

"This was a horrible, terrible tragedy. But right now, we need to be there for Cloud. He lost his wife and son. No matter what you think. And poor Casen and Victor, they will need our support as well. Don't be selfish, Trix," her father says sternly.

"Fine," Trixie relents.

I wait a few minutes before I dare peek around the corner. The Caldwells have left. I slide open Jack's umbrella and dash through murky puddles racing to his parked car idling in the lot.

I close and shake out the umbrella before sliding into his warm car. I cup my hands around his small heater.

"Here," he says, taking my hand in his and blowing his warm breath, trying to warm me and sending tingles up my arms.

I smile, wondering if I could grab him and kiss him again. But the thought of Trixie shoving me away from her family sours my smile and kills the butterflies fluttering about my stomach.

"Why did Trixie hide you from her parents?" Jack questions, pulling out from the parking space. He glances at me, then back at the street.

I shake my head. "I don't know. Maybe her family has some kind of beef with mine. My Aunt Marie works with her parents," I say, thinking of the witches committee they're all on.

Jack nods, accepting my answer. "It's still really weird, though."

The streets have nearly become rivers from the storm as we drive through town. "Would you like to stop for dinner?" he asks.

"I think I need to get back, but rain check?" I tease, pathetically.

Jack, ever the team player, chuckles at my lame joke. "Sure," he agrees, then bestows a tender kiss on my hand. "Now, if you would take out your phone, we're going to see what Eleanor O'Reilly was last listening to." He adjusts his Bluetooth to my phone.

An old Evanescence song plays, and we both laugh. Jack surprisingly knows the words. He skips around, stopping at a song by The Who, next Led Zeppelin, then Placebo.

Jack bobs his head along to the music. "I have a feeling you're a very complicated girl," he concludes.

"HA! You could say that. But then again, I could say the same thing about you," I say, reflecting on the conversation with Vivienne's flock and stupid Saint Tropez. *Was Vivienne just screwing with my head? Whatever happened between them, is it even any of my business? It was before I even knew him.* I open my mouth to ask him only to chicken out.

Jack gets lost trying to find my house, to his great frustration. I redirect him once, then twice, then a third time.

"Normally, I pride myself that I can get myself anywhere. Maybe you should write down the directions for me," he says, playfully defeated. He coasts into the driveway and kills the engine, holding the steering wheel, staring down. "I'm sorry," he apologizes for the umpteenth time today.

"For what?" I ask. It wasn't Jack who shoved me into a stoop to hide.

"I know Viv's friends have teeth, and I can only imagine what Vivienne must have said to you. I tried to keep her occupied, but I lost track of her," he says, as if she was a rabid animal.

I unbuckle my seatbelt, turning myself in his direction. "They were fine. Mostly bragged about you. And Vivienne brought up a trip or something to Saint Tropez. She wanted me to ask you about it," I say.

He freezes, his jaw set in a hardline. "Going on the boat was a mistake."

I play with the strap of Margaret's purse. "Did something happen?"

Jack cranes his neck, peering low out of the windshield. "That cat, isn't that the one from the party? Did you bring it home?"

I bend forward, trying to look out of the fogged-up glass. Pyewacket sits on the top step of the covered veranda.

*"It would be best if you came inside. Now."*

"He's...a long story. But yeah, that's sort of my cat. I better go inside," I say despondently. I place my hand on his car handle.

"Eleanor," Jack says. He places his hand on my knee, stopping me from exiting, then gives me a small, hopeful smile. "Despite the bizarre run-in with Trixie and the unfortunate time on the yacht, I had a great time today."

"Yeah?" I say, as my dumb heart picks up speed.

He nods, his grin becoming more confident. "Yes. Best date I've ever been on." Jack leans forward, his hand cupping my cheek.

Just as my eyes flutter closed, there's a loud watery smack. Our heads whip forward, facing the windshield. Pyewacket sits on the hood. His right ear starts slumping under the hard rain.

"I better go. I'll see you tomorrow, Jack," I say, feeling the pleasure of his name on my tongue. Before he can change my mind, I rush into the rain, snatching the stupid cat and racing up the steps. I wave goodbye before heading inside.

"Ugh, you smell even worse when you're wet," I say, dropping him on the floor stepping inside the warm house.

*"Someone is in trouble,"* he sends, cryptic and amused.

With a roll of my eyes, I head into the living room, prepared for the post-date interrogation.

Perched on the couch is my mother. She's holding Persephone in one hand and the bloodied planchette in the other. "Eleanor..." She says coolly.

My stomach drops.

# Chapter Twenty-Seven
## Welcome Home

My emotions are in constant conflict. On the one hand, I'm relieved my mother has returned, but I can't help but worry about what she found.

"Mom, you're back," I say lamely, lifting my brows and pushing on a smile.

Sally and Marie are sitting on the floral love seat. Their eyes silently follow me as I enter the room. I give my mom a nervous hug and a peck on the cheek.

My mom motions for me to take a seat next to her. "Were you trying to contact your father?" she asks, holding up the planchette.

I open my mouth to voice some defense, but I stop, staring at her face. Her eyes are encased in scarlet rings, which are unfortunately on-brand for Mom these days, and her brow furrowed in sympathy. "I don't know what the aunts told you, but—"

"Excuse me? I'm no narc!" Sally exclaims, causing her teacup to rattle on its saucer.

Marie's eyes roll to the ceiling. "Narc? Seriously, Sal?"

"It wasn't your aunts," Mom chastises. "Persephone informed me."

My eyes move from the regal looking tabby cat curled next to my mother to my aunts. "How? Can cats text? Email? Should I start expecting Pyewacket to call me on my cell?" I feel like my brain is melting asking such asinine questions.

My mother sighs. "I know you know about everything, Eleanor. Marie and Sal filled me in on your training, the accidents at school."

I fold my arms across my chest, falling back into the couch in a slump. "Something you should have told me a long time ago," I grumble crossly.

My mom's gaze remains even, unaffected. "I had my reasons. Still do."

My brow falls into a glare. "Are you serious!?" I leap up from the couch, needing to pace. "Mom, I was freaking out! All these things were happening to me and I didn't know why! *You* should have told me! But you lied to me! For my entire life, you've lied to me, all of us! Did you lie to Dad?"

My mom tilts her head to the side, watching my tirade with a quiet annoyance. "Eleanor, can we please take down the dramatics? Of course, your father knew, *and* he supported my decision."

"Then please tell me why. Why did you keep it a secret?" I ask, sitting back down and scootching closer to her.

As if calculating something, Mom glances quickly at the aunts, Marie peers down at her feet and Sally gives a 'blink-and-you-miss-it' shake of her head. She turns her gaze back to me. "It's…"

I ball my fists in my lap. *She's going to say it's complicated.*

"Complicated, Eleanor. One day you'll understand," she assures, pulling up her defenses, closing ranks with her sisters.

I heave myself up off the couch. "Yep. And it looks like today isn't that day. Welcome back," I mumble petulantly, spinning on my heel to leave.

"Excuse me," Mom pipes up, "we aren't done here. You went against the aunts' wishes and tried to contact your father—twice! You were even advised not to by your familiar," my mother says firmly, and yet also casually, as if this isn't the first time we have spoken about ghosts and familiars.

My lower lip trembles, my body slumps with emotional exhaustion, this conversation taking its toll on an already whirlwind of a day. "I'm sorry—I just," I stop, my eyes burn wanting to cry, my throat tightens and stings, "I miss him."

Mom leaves the couch, crossing over the room to me quickly. She pulls me into a hug, her arms are tight around me, shaking. "I'm not mad," she breathes, "you just scared me, Ella. You were messing with such powerful forces. I'm sorry too." She strokes my hair.

My stomach lurches at the nickname "Ella". Only my dad ever called me that. But the stabbing pain isn't as potent as it was before. I sniff, releasing my mom from the embrace. My mom hesitates before letting go.

"So, what does this mean? Can I keep training?" I ask, fearing the answer.

My mom nods, brushing my ratty hair off my shoulders. "I'm going to help. My sisters told me about the window and the fire. It's common for accidents to happen in the beginning."

Marie rushes to her feet, clasping her hands together. "Oh see, Helly, everything worked out." She skips over to us, placing a hand on our shoulders. "I've been waiting for this moment." Thick tears roll over the apples of her cheeks.

Sally lifts to her feet with a roll of her eyes. "I can't believe either of you ever doubted me. I told you all would be fine. Now, that nonsense is dealt with." She pauses, giving my mom a look before turning to me. "Ell babe, I want to hear about that yummy date!"

My mom frowns. "Date?"

Sally gently pushes us both back onto the sofa, then perches eagerly on the ottoman.

"I thought Marie said she was just out with friends?" Mom asks.

"Did I?" Marie feigns ignorance, fluttering back down to her seat. A tea kettle comes whizzing into the room, followed by two teacups and saucers. "Tea?"

I watch as mint, honey and a lemon come levitating into the room. This magical sight, commonplace in this house, still leaves me mystified. The sprig of mint drops into the cup my mother plucks from the air. Honey drizzles itself and the lemon peel falls away like a woman dropping a nightgown from her body. A lemon wedge wrings it out over my mother's delicate cup.

"Oh Helly, over here," Marie says, holding up her hand.

My head snaps to my mother. Her eyes slide to me and back to her sister.

Antique teaspoons come dancing into the room, plunking themselves into everyone's cup. My mom is doing this. Not only is she making things float, but she does so with such elegance and precision. The items glide through the air like swimming dolphins, gracefully getting to their targets.

A decanter zips into the room going straight for Sally. It deftly stops, pours into Sally's cup, then hurries back into the kitchen. *Now, that was not my mother.*

"Oh, I made some honeysuckle cookies," Marie says, wanting to add to the frenzy. Cookies come bobbing in, dropping two on everyone's saucer. As everyone's items float back to the kitchen, it strikes me that each witch's magic has its own unique accent. Marie's spell flutters and drifts like dandelion seeds in a breeze. Sally's zips like a knife cutting through the air. And Mom, her magic is like a polished, choreographed dance.

I can't help but gawk while her spoon, unencumbered by hands, stirs the tea floating at her side. There's a small part of me that screams "stranger danger", but despite the foreign feel of her magic, I can still see *my* mom shine through. It was like for the last seventeen years I've seen my mother through cataract-ridden eyes, but now the veil has been lifted; this is the real Helen O'Reilly. A mother. A sister. A witch.

"So, go on Ella. You've been here essentially for two weeks, and you've got yourself a boyfriend now?" Mom says, a little smile playing at the corner of her lips.

I shake my head. "No, it wasn't like that. At first. I guess we're dating. Maybe. I don't know." I take a large gulp of my tea. The steaming liquid trickles down my throat, warming my entire body. I feel my nerves calm, my senses relax. Every tense muscle softens. I settle into the back of the couch, taking another sip. "I think Jack asked me out to figure out our relationship. By the end of it, we decided to be a couple. He even wants me to meet his family." *Wait, why am I sharing so much?*

My mom nods along, listening thoughtfully. Marie dips her cookie into her tea and Sally looks at me, annoyed.

"Any nudity?" Sally questions deviously, wiggling her skinny eyebrows at me. "Or handcuffs?"

"Sally!" Marie snaps at her wild sister.

Sally rolls her eyes dramatically. "What? Remember that date I went on with Nathaniel Marcus and we got arrested, Marie? We went skinny dipping in Mr. Finnel's pond?" she shivers. "Probably not the best idea in November."

"Wild youth?" I ask.

Sally chuckles. "No, that was last year."

Marie exhales irritably while my mother appears mortified at her sister.

Sally waves her ring clad hand for her teacup to go rest on the coffee table after hovering so close to her. "Are you telling me, Eleanor, there was no action? A boy that fine and you both just came to the resolution you should be a couple?" she prods skeptically, cocking a brow.

I take another sip. "No," I answer simply. "We made out. Twice. First time he initiated, second time I did." I stop, my frowning deepening. *Why did I just say that?*

Sally grins wickedly as my mother winces.

"And that's all that happened?" Mom asks anxiously.

I shake my head. "No," I answer matter-of-factly.

Sally laughs and claps her hands together.

My mother blanches. "What?" she squeaks. She places her hands to her temples. "Eleanor..."

"I tried to kill him." *Why am I saying all of this? What is wrong with me?* My heart keeps pumping in a steady rhythm, rejecting my attempts at panic.

My mother's eyes flash open, both my aunts stare.

"What?" they all ask in unison.

My eyes casually bounce from stricken face to stricken face. "He tried to kiss me, or at least I think he was going to. But just as he was going to, my magic started waking up and I was about to stop him because I was unsure what it was going to do, but I flung him from the boat and held him under water till he passed out," I state flatly before finishing off my tea. *Is that what happened? Did I really hold him under? What the hell is wrong with me?*

Mom flinches but recovers. "Eleanor, why would you do that?"

My head is swimming, I feel a strange swishing inside me like a shaken bottle of water and oil. I fight to react, to shovel everything I just said back in, but instead a cold blanket of calm honesty envelopes me. "I didn't mean to. I tried to stop it. But all I could do was watch in horror. I did jump in and save him." I go onto explain how I demanded my magic obey me. I thanked them for advising Margaret what to pack in the purse and that I used the memory suppressant on him.

Marie holds her hands up. "Now Helen, before you get furious..."

My mother wheels on her sisters, pursing her lips. Little angry lines appear on her face. "It's illegal to brew memory spells. It's been outlawed for at least twenty years."

Sally rises to her feet, stepping between Marie and Mom. "Helen, it was from your cupboard."

"It was legal back then. You should have gotten rid of it," she quips.

"It sounds like it came in handy with your daughter today, so..." Sally trails off, weighing her hands up and down.

"Is that all that happened on the boat?" Mom asks as everyone settles back down.

The buried part of me cheers for that simple little modifier *on the boat*. I don't feel compelled to tell her Trixie hiding me from her parents. "Yes," I reply truthfully. I peer down in my empty teacup, spotting a strange milky residue. "Did you...slip me something?" My heart once again tries to pound, but instead remains calm and even.

My mom peers at my aunts, but Marie shakes her head. They both face Sally.

Sally shrugs, polishing off the rest of her drink. "Just a little something. Eleanor is so taciturn, it's hard to get a straight answer. I didn't think she was going to tell us she nearly killed her date," she says with an incredulous chuckle. "I give it a few more minutes."

My mom appears to be deliberating something. "Eleanor, has your magic been acting on its own accord? Almost like it has a mind of its own?"

I nod, not trusting myself to speak.

They all exchange confused, worried glances.

"What does it mean?" I ask nervously, my heart slowly picking up pace.

Mom looks to her sister, then back to me. "I honestly don't know. But we can't delay your training. Tomorrow after school, do not make any plans with friends. Come straight home." My mother peers over at Marie in earnest. "Marie, you're on The Committee. Do you think you could get me into their library?"

Marie gulps uncomfortably. "I'd need to get permission. You've been gone a long time; you'll probably need to meet with the head of the coven and then the head committee chair."

"Who is it now?"

"Head witch is Agatha Caldwell. Head Chair of The Committee is Mercy Wicklow."

Sally makes a disgusted grunt. Mom's brows knit in confusion.

Marie dismisses Sally's grumble. "Oh, Mercy is just a stickler for the rules. And she's the reason why we've been so safe."

Sally chuckles darkly.

"Tomorrow. Please, Marie," Mom says.

I didn't realize Trixie's mom was the leader of our coven. *What did that even mean, anyway?* "Mom," I say anxiously. "Um, don't mention me to Mrs. Caldwell, please."

My mother looks taken aback at my request. Her eyes narrow on me. "Why don't *you* want me to mention you?" She prods, almost knowingly. It's clear she too wants me hidden and now wants to gauge just how much I know.

I shrug. "Trixie suggested to keep my distance."

"Their youngest is Trixie. She's Eleanor's age," Marie says just as my mom opened her mouth, about to ask.

"Mom!?" Margaret rushes into the house, dashing through the living room, stampeding over the cats. She throws her arms around our mother in an all-encompassing bearhug. It takes me a moment to realize Margaret is trembling. "I missed you so much," she whispers.

Mom kisses the top of her head. When the hug ends, they stay entangled, Margaret with her arms around our mom's petite waist and mom's arms protectively cupping Maggie's shoulders.

"Ell, oh my gosh, how was your date?" Maggie asks, leaning against Mom.

Sally snickers.

"It was interesting," I answer.

"Did you guys kiss?" Maggie probs wickedly.

"They made out twice," Sally replies under her breath.

As Margaret squeals, Marie giggles.

"Okay, okay, I don't like this kind of talk," Mom says, waving everyone down.

"You're such a prude," Maggie teases before pecking Mom on the cheek.

"Let's get dinner going, please. It's getting late and you girls have school tomorrow. Maggie, how did that history test go?" Mom asks, ushering us all towards the kitchen.

"Argh, I hate having to memorize dates. I suck at it. There's no way I got anything higher than a B, and that would be a freaking miracle," she complains.

"Language," Mom chides, breezing through the kitchen door.

"Mom, I said 'freaking'," she retorts.

Our mother rummages through cupboards, noticing empty shelves. "Marie, Sal, when was the last time you went grocery shopping?"

The aunts exchange a look with each other.

Marie smiles guiltily. "Well, sister, we aren't exactly experts in the kitchen, unlike yourself—"

Maggie quickly interrupts, "Aunt Marie, what are you talking about? You guys are amazing cooks! I've had some of the best food of my life since moving here. No offense, Mom," she quickly amends.

"Wait, have you guys been getting the meals catered?" I question. I had just chalked up our sensational meals to magic.

Mom leans against the counter, staring deadpan at Marie. "What did you do?"

"Everything they ate was edible," Sally defends.

Blood drains from mine and Margaret's faces. Our ears tune in, dreading the punchline.

"Well, Margaret did eat a napkin accidentally, but that was completely Sally's fault. I told her to clear the table of all inedible objects!" Marie accuses.

Maggie's jaw falls open.

"What?" Mom snaps.

"Oh, it was plant based, I mean look at her," Sally motions to Maggie who's lost all color in her face, "she's fine."

I wave my hands, calling for attention. "I'm sorry, but what happened?"

Mom turns, answering for them. "They took some food, probably odds and ends, and performed the mind spell, making you believe you were eating a feast."

"We wanted to make a good first impression. I did make that meatloaf Maggie wanted," Marie insists. "Out of the real ingredients," she clarifies.

"That stops now. No enchantments, just actual food. Now, let's see what we can make," Mom says. They all gather around the refrigerator, craning their necks, peering in. "Okay, lamb stew it is. Maggie, come with me into the greenhouse. Marie, chop the onions and carrots. Sally, get the cauldron to a boil." Mom stops at the doorway. "Ella, peel the potatoes, but do *not* use your hands," she orders with a small smile. Maggie follows her down the hall.

Potatoes come floating from the pantry to the sink.

"Thanks, Sal." I search the drawers for the potato peeler. After reciting the air spell in my mind, the potato lifts and the peeler hacks away at the potato in short staccato slices. My eyes stare intently at the rotating potato. *La Caeli.* The faucet flicks on and the naked potato slips under the stream, rinsing off before dancing over to Marie to be cut.

As another potato lifts in the air, my eyes catch something dart across the lawn. I squint, leaning closer to the window. The potato and peeler tumble into the sink. A fuzzy brown bunny sits in the shaft of light cast by the kitchen lights. It's beady, little eyes stare at me.

"Hey, I'll be right back," I call. I flick on the back patio light, my sandals slapping against the cobblestone out back. "Hello? Trixie?" I whisper into the moist night air. The rabbit dashes out of the pillar of light and to the edges of the yard. I stop, squinting. Within a blink, I see Trixie in her normal form, hiding behind a tree. She peeks out, waving me over urgently.

"I'm coming," I call out in a hushed tone.

Trixie grips me in a hug. "I'm sorry I had to do that. It was so unkind to you. You must know it was for your own protection," she insists, holding onto my shoulders.

"Does this have anything to do with my eyes?" I question, peeking over my shoulder back at the house. Thankfully, no one is staring out at us from the window. Pyewacket, however, slinks out of the shadows, joining us.

"Is this your familiar?" she asks, softening her face and bending down towards him. She reaches out to ruffle his ears, then immediately pulls her hand back, looking at him sympathetically. "I think something just crunched with his ear." She straightens up. "I'd give him some mug wort."

"Trixie, I still don't understand why you had to hide me. You say my eyes might make me a Nefari or something, but you still talk to me," I say, confused.

Trixie nods, taking my hand. "You're my best friend. I don't care what you are. But my parents are bound by committee rules. I overheard them talking in the study tonight. My mom thinks some Nefari are behind Doris and Rivers' deaths. My dad is still in denial about the whole thing."

I shake my head as if trying to clear it. "Okay, so they might suspect I'm one of them, but would they really think I would hurt strangers I've never met?"

She nibbles on her bottom lip nervously. "You're new to town. There's been an uptick in witch disappearances and murders since about the time you arrived."

"That still doesn't make sense. I could easily prove I had nothing to do with them," I insist.

Trixie gives my hand a gentle squeeze. "You don't understand. That doesn't matter. If they believe you're Nefari, they'll have no choice but to kill you."

A chill electrifies my spine, causing the hair on my arms to stand on end. Hic. "And," hic, "this is because of my eyes?" Hic. "I can just wear contacts." Hic. "Right?" I question nervously, gripping her tighter. My hand becomes slick with anxiety.

"I think so. I mean, there are other ways of telling, but they'd need to suspect you to perform the tests. No one suspects anything yet," she assures.

Hic. My pounding heart rattles my ribcage. "Okay, I'll hide my eyes." Hic. "That shouldn't be an issue." I take a few deep breaths to abate the onslaught of hiccups. "Is this why you came? To apologize?" I ask. My chest settles. *I have a plan. I'll wear those brown contacts. Most people at school think the purple is fake, anyway. Everything will be okay.*

Trixie steps even closer. Her blonde hair begins to twist and curl in the mist. "You asked about my diary today."

I nod, focusing on my breathing.

"I can't find it. It's gone missing…"

In the dark woods, a tree branch snaps.

# Chapter Twenty-Eight
## A Decent Proposal

Trixie refused my invitation to stay for dinner, saying she needed to get back as she had snuck out. Within a blink, she was back in her rabbit form. She dashed away, cutting across the yard to a clearing where she parked her car.

*"I must speak to Amethyst. She needs to be kept abreast on Trixie."* Pyewacket peers up at me. *"She's being quite irresponsible. That was wise to instruct her on the use of locks. Protection spells are wildly unreliable."*

My eyes scan the woods as I hear more twigs breaking. "I think something is coming," I say, taking several steps back.

*"I believe it's time to return to the house. Come,"* Pye orders telepathically.

I don't argue. I quickly back peddle until I'm encased in the light thrown from the house. I'm too scared to turn my back to the woods. My pulse quickens, pounding in my ears. There's a heavy dread in the air so palpable I half expect it to form a visible fog.

"Pyewacket, what's happening?" I whisper. I feel something, a force extending towards me like outstretched fingers in the darkness.

*"Elspeth."*

"Eleanor?" my mom calls from the backdoor. "What are you doing out there? The potatoes should be cooking."

"Sorry," I shout back over my shoulder. *I'm going to make a run for it.*

*"Go."*

*Are you coming?*

*"Soon. Go now."*

I whip around and race back into the house, nearly toppling my mom. I smack the back door closed and flick the brass lock. With my back against the white door, I take a deep breath. "Sorry," I say, meeting everyone's curious gaze. "I thought I saw something in the yard."

"Then you got spooked?" Sally questions.

I nod. "I'm just being stupid."

Margaret chuckles. "Well, I wasn't going to say it," she teases. She returns to stirring the cauldron with a long wooden paddle. "Ready for the rosemary, Mom."

My mom hesitates, her gaze fixed on me. She exhales and turns back to the hearth. "Okay, are the potatoes *that I had to finish* soft?" she says with a scolding tone.

Marie glances over at me, still holding vigil at the door as if I can keep Elspeth out. "Everything okay, pumpkin?" Marie questions, floating over the button mushrooms and chopped veggies.

I nod. *Pye, is everything okay? Pye?*

Pyewacket strolls through the back door, leaving a few clumps of hair behind. *"Yes."*

"Sally, enough red wine!" Mom chastises.

"Oh Helen, it helps bring out the flavor in the meat," she counters.

"Yes, as an accent. This is going to taste only of wine."

"I really don't see a problem here." Sally lifts her hands in the air, confused.

"Girls, please set the table," Mom says exasperated.

We gather around the table to eat. The ladle circulates around the table, carefully scooping and pouring into everyone's bowl. Either due to the excess wine in the meal or just the bare relief of my mother's return there's a jovial air while we eat. Marie teases Sally about her recent ill-fated tattoo. Margaret excitedly shares about her soccer team and a soccer camp this summer in North Carolina she's desperate to attend. Mom informs us about her plan not to return to work, at least for a while. I find myself, however, unable to join in their buoyant conversations. Elspeth is still haunting me. Destroyed Ouija board or not.

*Pyewacket?*

He leaps up into the empty chair seated next to me.

*I think we need to speak to Elspeth. I can't believe I'm going to say this, but we need to reach her by any means necessary. Even if it means using another Ouija board.*

*"Oh, my giddy aunt."* He thinks this with a near audible growl or whatever the cat equivalent is. *"I was told adolescents are daft but... You're just taking the piss out of me, right?"*

I roll my eyes at him while scooping up a potato with my spoon. *You're right, of course.* I reply sarcastically. *I think it's better to keep being haunted by her. I don't have other things to deal with on top of this.*

*"I told you I'm handling this. You need to focus on training before you're well in it. Your obligation to Trixie is finished. You told her to be careful and she will be. Your objective needs to be on controlling your magic. That's it. Not snogging boys, not*

*hunting down clues, and not trying to reach that bloody Elspeth."*

I drop my spoon into my nearly empty bowl with a loud clank. "May I be excused?"

Mom nods. "You don't want anymore rosemary bread? It's your favorite."

I shake my head, sending my bowl into the kitchen sink. "I'm pretty tired. Long day. I'm glad you're back, Mom." I give her a kiss and head upstairs.

I roughly brush my teeth after my shower.

Pyewacket saunters in. *"Still being petulant, are we?"*

I finish in the bathroom, ignoring him, then slam my door behind me, wishing he can't just walk through. Thankfully, he doesn't follow me. I quickly work on some homework before crawling into bed. The bedroom door opens just as my brain drifts to sleep.

The ground is soft and spongy under the soles of my feet. In typical dream fashion, each footstep feels heavy as I pad my way across the moors. The sun is just breaking over the horizon, sending great streaks of orange and red chasing away the dark. My hair rustles in the breeze. My ribs feel crushed inside an early century corset. I stop and peer down at my plain 17th century dress. My waist is tightly cinched and accented by a tied apron. Suddenly, strong square hands encircle my waist. A firm chest is pressed against my back. A hand guides my head back as his fingers trail up my neck. Lips press against the hollow beneath my jaw.

*Jack. So, it's one of those dreams.*

My head lulls as his lips explore my neck. His fingers flick at the laces up my back. With each tug, I feel my dress loosen until I can feel my back completely exposed. My eyes flutter open as he lightly drags one finger up my spine. Something small and black moves in the distance, scampering closer. *Pyewacket? What the hell are you doing here!? Get out!* Despite my shoulders keeping my dress up, saving me from indecent exposure, I still clutch my dress.

Jack whips me around to face him. He's in a billowing laced-up white shirt and tight black pants. His mouth meets mine with ferocious passion, moving against mine like he too understands we must move quickly as I can wake up any second.

*Pyewacket, leave!* I untuck his shirt from his pants, but before I can lift it over his head, he clasps my hands trapping them in his, and firmly keeps them at my side. Jack slowly, almost condescendingly, shakes his head no at me.

*Don't you want to be with me?*

Jack twirls me around, forcing me to face forward. We are no longer standing in a misty English moor. I'm on a rough wooden platform. Sharp splinters stab my feet. I squint, trying to peer out as we've gone from dawn to dusk in a blink. We're in a clearing in a forest. There's a large crowd below dressed as puritans. I see Vivienne and her posse and the rest of the kids from school making up the mob. I gaze terrified at the horde, some with hungry faces, some with apathetic eyes. Several film us on their cell phones, two girls are touching up their makeup, others are pointing and laughing.

Jack gives me a hard shove forward until I'm standing over a trapdoor. A noose dangles down from a beam over head.

Suddenly, I have searing pain between my shoulder blades. I scream, falling to my knees and writhing in pain, begging for it to stop.

Two arms reach out, yanking me to my feet.

*Pyewacket, help!*

Pyewacket slinks his way through the crowd. "*It's a dream, Eleanor. Wake up.*"

"No! It's real! It's real!" I cry out. The burning pain is beyond intense. Spittle bubbles in my mouth; tears fill my eyes. I can't think of anything beyond the scorching sensation between my shoulder blades.

Pyewacket leaps onto the gallows. He hisses at the tall puritan men standing guard. "*Then we need to run until you can wake yourself from this. Now! Go!*" Pyewacket hisses at the men, his back arched and his tail straight, his black wiry hair standing on end. The men jump back, giving me enough berth to run, nearly stumbling down the steps. I race as fast as I can down the dirt path leading deep into the densely opaque forest. Pyewacket somehow catches up with me.

My lungs burn and my muscles ache as I try to force a sprint. *Why would Jack do this to me?*

"*Keep going, Eleanor. Faster! Faster until you wake!*"

My entire body is a pulsating throb as I feel invisible chains latch onto each limb. My heel hits something solid, practically bruising the bone. I plant my other foot down, still trying to run. I cry out as that heel feels fractured and bruised too. My elbows thump back against an impenetrable force.

My eyes fall open. I'm tangled in my blankets on the floor next to my bed. I gasp for air; my feet throb from pounding the floor in my sleep. I sit up, groaning, and run my hands down my face. "Pyewacket!" I grumble out, heaving myself up off the floor.

Pyewacket lifts his head. His entire body lounges on my pillow at the top of the bed.

"Were you actually in my dream?" My entire body is sore. I stretch hoping to ease the pain in my back and neck.

Pyewacket frowns. "*I possibly dreamt the same dream as you. Whether we occupied the same dream space, I'm not sure.*"

I stifle an irritable moan. *I can't even have privacy in a dream. Great. But I do appreciate your help this time.*

Pyewacket releases a disgusted grunt. *"If this is going to be a common occurrence, perhaps you can stop altogether with the — ahem — romantic dreaming."*

I growl and chuck a pillow at him. I snatch my uniform from the wardrobe and race to get ready as I know Winston is a stickler for punctuality. I borrow some of Margaret's matte lipstick and slowly trace my lips hovering close to the bathroom mirror. Those kisses, the pain, it all felt so twistedly real. I purse my lips, stupidly wondering if lips can look too plump. I dig through her tackle-box-turned-make-up-kit, searching for some mascara. This is the second dream where Jack has hurt me. *There's no way my dreams are telling me something. It's just my subconscious manifesting my fear of intimacy. Yeah, that sounds right.* I snag Maggie's antique hair pins we picked up at a thrift shop near South Beach.

"Mom? Maggie?" I call, reaching the dining room. There's a basket of bagels next to some whipped cream cheese and a note pinned to the basket.

*Ella,*
*Took Maggie to school. I packed you a lunch. It's in the fridge.*
*Remember, home right after school. Have a great day! Love you! Xoxoxo*
*Mom*

I shove the brown paper sack into my satchel.

There's a banging coming from the greenhouse.

I tiptoe down the hall.

"Are you serious, Marie!? What were you thinking? Those weren't carrot seeds you bought from that kid! Look at those leaves!" Sally screeches. "We can't bring these to The Gathering!"

"He said they were organic!" Marie argues.

"Did he also tell you they're best dried and rolled!?"

The drive to school is riddled with puddles as dark water floods the ditches and drainpipes. Salem is struggling to dry out after the storm, but the picture perfect blue screen sky, without so much as a puffy cloud, promises a good return. I smile to myself, having lucked out finding a parking spot next to a gleaming white Mustang.

My stomach twists into large knots at the prospect of seeing him. *But did Jack change his mind? Are we not actually a couple?*

I follow the stream of students through the front gates.

"Yeah, that's her."

"I've tried to look her up. She literally doesn't exist."

My eyes dart about, noticing students tilting their heads together, whispering conspicuously.

"She's not… *un*fortunate looking."

"Her eyes aren't doe, they're bugged eyed."

Nick paces in front of the doors and straightens with a wide smile when he sees me. I feel like a jerk because nearly every one of his smiles I give a grimace in return, even if it is internal. *How do I break up with someone I'm not even dating?* I suck at tactfully maneuvering through social cues, especially with boys. *Do I have to confess my feelings for Jack?*

He swings the door open, only missing my face by an inch. "Whoa, careful! How was your day off?" he asks, surprisingly without any hint of malice.

I duck inside, letting my hair cover my blushing face. "Um…it was ah, good. I mean, it was fine. What about you? How was your day off?" My words come out hurried and nervous. As we tread down the hall, Alden, Tripp, and Pete fall into step behind us as if instructed to form an awkward barricade.

Nick adjusts his long sleeve, pulling it down slightly past his wrists. A small, mischievous smile cracks across his face. His eyes crinkle in glinting squints, as if he was enjoying some secret joke. "It was…interesting." Then he mumbles something to himself under his breath.

I nod along as if I'm in on his wicked grin. "Really? What did you do?" I pull my satchel up on my shoulder to keep it from slipping. "Did you still go out to your cabin?"

He coughs, hiding a chuckle. "Oh, no. Um, we did something else. Just… guy stuff."

"She gets around," a girl hisses to her friend.

"First Nick, then Jack, then what? The entire junior class?"

My hands quiver at my sides, I bend my head low and rush to my locker. My pace slows as I turn down the hall.

Jack is leaning against my locker, waiting for me. He looks up from his cell phone, a grin spread across his handsome face. He places his phone back into his pocket and reaches for me.

"I'll see you after class, Eleanor," Nick murmurs and stalks off, his friends glancing from Nick to me and back before they hurry after him. Nick glowers at Jack while passing by.

Jack, completely unperturbed, takes my hand. My eyes dart about, noting the onslaught of stares from nearby students. I swear one even took a picture.

"Hey," I say timidly. I crack open my locker, placing my violin and bookbag inside.

"So," he begins in a tone that hints he's gearing up for something, "my parents will be home at the same time for the first time in months. On Friday," he says, marveled. "I would like you to join us for dinner."

I shut my locker door. "This seems really… quick."

Jack peers at me with knitted brows. "I know. I apologize if this feels like an ambush. But this unfortunately is a necessary evil when dating in my family. I don't want to hide you. The sooner my parents know about us, the better it will be."

The warning bell trills.

"I don't know, Jack. I've never done the whole meet-the-parents thing. I'm not sure I'm ready."

He nods, compassionately. "Don't worry about it then. I'll cancel," he promises softly. Jack places his hand on my lower back as we shuffle to class. Girls' faces light up, spotting us like creatures on safari. Guys nod to me and pound Jack's fist.

Vivienne cuts us off at the door. She shoots us a tight smile before opening the classroom door. "After the cute couple."

Jack rolls his eyes at her as we step aside and into the room.

Mr. Edwards stands in front of the whiteboard writing character names, themes, and quotes from Macbeth. "Good morning students, I hope everyone took advantage of yesterday's holiday and worked on their reading of Macbeth. If not, I dare say you've come unprepared and unarmed for today's trial," he teases menacingly. "Everyone, take out your computers. On the board you'll see the site where you'll be writing your essay. I'll enable the internet, so no cheating."

He glances in my direction for a fraction of a second. I shrink back, wondering if my aunts told him about some of my homework I *unintentionally* cheated on. "Your essay should be two thousand words. Choose an interesting argument on behalf of one of the characters I've chosen on the board or expand upon a quote. You have until the final bell. Begin."

I select the witches and start formulating their defense. Try as I might, my mind keeps circling back to the Woods and the cancelled dinner. *I'll have to meet them eventually. Should we wait and see what happens with us?* I think back on my dream; such a tantalizing start, only to transform into a nightmare. Jack's lips on my skin, that desire burning in the back of my throat for more. The burning. Something burning on my back. *Jack would never do something like that.*

I peek over my shoulder at him. His hands are typing furiously, but his eyes flick up, meeting mine. His lips pull up in a small, quiet smile and winks.

Heat fills my cheeks and I turn back to my computer. Every time we're together, some catastrophe befalls him. If we aren't meant to be, then why is it when I see him, I feel something come alive inside me? There's a bizarre combination of peace and excitement. A perfect feeling of completion and a certainty that I'd follow him to the ends of the earth. *Is there something wrong with me?*

I fight against using my magic to complete the essay and type as fast as I can to catch up. My mind still swirls with apprehension. *Argh. On my hierarchy of problems, meeting Jack's parents shouldn't even be in the top five. I have Trixie and Elspeth to worry about. Not to mention training. Terror at the prospect of meeting the boyfriend's parents is something reserved for normal girls.*

The bell rings right before I reach the last paragraph. *If only I knew the mind spell. My grades are seriously taking a hit right now.*

Everyone closes their computers, shoving them back in their bags. Several girls audibly review their essays together, determined not to tank their 4.0 GPA. Vivienne dismisses Poppy and lingers silently in the back of the classroom, watching Jack like a predator.

"Hey," Jack says, rising from his desk, "I have a presentation at the Commons, so I won't see you until after school," he informs regrettably.

I shove the laptop into my bag and pull myself up to my feet, trying to shake off my annoyance at an unfinished essay. "I'll miss you," I reply quietly.

Jack smiles, wrapping an arm around my waist, causing me to jump. He quickly withdraws his arm. "Whoa, I'm sorry. I didn't mean to startle you."

I shake my head. "You're fine. I'm just…jumpy this morning."

Students trickle into the classroom. Jack gives a little wave before walking back. Vivienne follows him out, throwing me an icy glare first.

"Miss O'Reilly, can you wait in the hallway for me? I would like to speak to you," Winston says, pointing a pudgy finger to the hall.

Nick looks relieved to see me. "I thought maybe you ditched me."

I adjust the strap of my bag weighing down my shoulder. "No, sorry. Mr. Edwards wants to speak to me. You should probably go without me."

The last few students coming to Mr. Edwards's second hour class trot in and shut the door behind him.

"It's cause you're hot," Nick states brazenly, "Mr. Edwards always has an excuse to talk to the hot girl in class," he accuses.

I flinch, disgusted by his salacious accusation.

The classroom door creaks open and Winston steps out. He gives Nick a disapproving glance. "Mr. Andersen, I believe you have class this hour, no?"

"Yeah, I was just waiting for Eleanor. We were going to go to class together…"

Mr. Edwards twirls his finger around, motioning for him to turn around and leave.

Nick's knuckles turn white, gripping the straps of his backpack. "See you," he growls before marching off.

I sigh, knowing I'll have to deal with that later. "Is this about my essay? I was so close to finishing it. I was having a hard time concentrating, which I get is no excuse. But if you knew what was going on, I think you'd give me a freebee with this one."

Winston tugs at his bow tie and flaps his tweed coat to cool off. "No, this isn't about your work. Eleanor, has Marie said anything to you?" Sweat dribbles down his rosy face.

I appraise him skeptically. "No, I have no idea what you're talking about. Are you alright?"

He exhales despondently. "Well, I believe I have my answer."

I frown. "Answer to what?"

He leans against the row of lockers, his hands shoved into the pocket of his trousers, his eyes downcast to the floor. He reaches into his coat pocket, retrieving a small wooden box.

I gasp. "Did you propose?"

He tosses me the box. I fumble, drop it, and quickly snatch it back up off the ground. Inside, nestled in crushed velvet, is a cushion cut emerald encased in a wreath of glittering diamonds on a yellow gold band.

"Wow." I snap it shut and hastily hand it back, too fearful something, anything, could happen to it in my possession.

"It was my mother's." He places it back into his coat pocket and glances inside his classroom.

I frown and run the toe of my shoe along a crack in the terrazzo tile. "I kind of thought you were dating Sally, not Marie," I admit, thinking about the house party and the way Sally hung on Winston, whispering who knows what in his ear, causing him to blush. But then again, Marie was also all over him, too. *Ew, I'm not pulling that thread.*

He coughs, straightening up, righting his shoulders. "Um, yes, well, it's a very complex entanglement, but never you mind that." He shakes his head sadly. "Well, there we have it. My apologies for keeping you from your studies. This was selfish and inappropriate."

I surprise myself when I stand in front of his classroom door, cutting him off.

He peers at me, muddled. "Yes?"

"You have Trixie next hour, correct?"

He nods slowly. "Yes. What is this concerning?"

I step back from the door, feeling silly for being so brash. "She's kind of…going through something right now. Um, some close friends passed away. And…" I lose my words, unsure how to continue.

He exhales, his shoulder sag. "Indeed. Doris and Rivers. I spoke to Cloud just yesterday. Truly a shame."

I step closer, glancing down both hallways before continuing. "She doesn't think this was a murder/suicide. And I had—I don't know, like a vision or something of someone breaking into Trixie's bedroom."

"Good gracious," he says, astounded.

"He didn't, like, hurt her or anything, he just stole her diary. I just—I have a bad feeling. We need to look out for her, okay?" I ask worriedly, gnawing my bottom lip.

Winston stares at me pensively. "Trixie Caldwell won't be in school today, nor tomorrow. Her mother, Agatha, informed the school she'll be out. Most likely, she's assisting her family with preparations for The Gathering. Perhaps I should speak to her father, Harrison," he muses to himself.

I nearly leap in alarm. "No! We can't get her parents involved. At least, not yet. Or if you do, please don't mention me in all this."

He peers deeply into my eyes, causing me to stare at the ground uncomfortably. "Alright you have my word. I'll leave you absent from our conversation. But I will speak to them. Here," he pulls a yellow slip from his pocket. He slides it into my hands. My name and excuse magically appear in the margins. "Now hurry on. Pip, pip," he nods towards Mr. Andersen's classroom down the hall.

Mr. Andersen stands before the class, addressing everyone. I hand him my note, and without looking at it, he waves me off to my seat. "In the upcoming weeks, with the partners I will assign, you will be presenting a dissertation on an appointed topic. It'll be important for you all to remember why I structured this course the way I did. I explained in the first quarter, does anyone remember?" he searches the room.

Bethany shoots her hand up. "We started from the present and worked back through time because you explained to understand the expansive picture of history. We first needed to work back to see causation."

"Excellent," Mr. Andersen replies excitedly. He turns to the board.

I glance over at Nick sitting sullen at the corner table, refusing to look over at me. I roll my eyes facing forward, annoyed, realizing there's nothing I can do that'll make him happy.

My hand cramps trying to keep up with the notes from Mr. Andersen's lecture. I'm still jotting last minute dates when the bell rings.

Nick darts from his desk and I do nothing to stop him. *Maybe he just needs to cool off from whatever set him off.*

At lunch, Nick's crew called me over to sit with everyone at lunch. I hesitated with my tray, gazing over at Jack's table. Vivienne, Jack, Margot, and Hale were missing from their usual seats. Reluctantly, I plop my tray down between Nick and Alden.

The boys are eager to share their exploits from their day off that Nick was curiously absent from. Noah shares his adventure at B.C.'s Alpha Kappa Alpha spring fling. Pete interjects, claiming he wasn't the only one who hooked up with a sister before displaying his recognizable brown "battle wounds" on his neck from an aggressive college freshman. Tripp gives Nick a hard time about punking out and canceling on them.

"I had other things to do," he answered simply, barely touching his lunch.

In Calculus, Sienna kept shooting me knowing looks, grinning like a canary killing cat. Another girl, one I didn't even know her name, referred to me as Mrs. Woods. By the last bell, I'm practically sprinting to my locker.

My heart slowly accelerates as I take the books needed from my locker, placing them in my messenger bag. I pause, my finger hovering over the spine of my physics book. *Something's wrong.* I feel a strange pull. I peer down the hallway. Everywhere, students are popping open lockers, retrieving belongings. Nick comes speed walking down the hall bulldozing kids in his haste. He doesn't slow his pace or even glance back at me.

I look down the hallway he had just rushed from. A strange pulse throbs inside me. I snap my locker close and walk against the flow of exiting traffic. The farther down the hall I get, the sparser it becomes. At the end of the hall, someone is leaning against the towering stained-glass window.

"Jack?" I call down the dim hall.

Jack turns his head away from me.

My stomach twitches anxiously. *Did I do something?* "Are you okay?" Alarms go off in my head, seeing red droplets on his collar shirt. My eyes fly to his face where his lip is swollen and split. "Oh my gosh, Jack. What happened?" I practically fall onto him, reaching for his face, but he takes my hands and places them on his chest instead.

"Nothing. It's not a big deal."

Nick was taking off down the hall like there was a fire. "Did Nick do this?"

He rolls his eyes. "Andersen has no idea how to punch. If he had better footing, his right hook could have far more power," he critiques dryly.

I sigh. "Let's be grateful he doesn't," I say, gazing at his blemished, beautiful face. "I'm shocked Nick isn't missing a tooth or two," I say, unsure if I'm disappointed or not.

Jack shrugs, pulling me close so our hips rest against each other. "I don't like unfair fights. Besides, I can't blame him."

"For what?"

His top lip is swelling even more, turning purple and flopping as he talks. "I'd want to punch him too if he won you over. Though I wouldn't *actually* do it."

I groan, resting my forehead against his chest. "This is about me?"

His hands slide down my back, his fingers trailing down my spine.

The nightmare. The laces. The burning. A shiver goes up my spine in tandem.

"It's okay. Andersen doesn't scare me. Now," he pauses, running his finger over his lip, feeling the lump forming there. "You wouldn't happen to have any of your magical cures on you?"

"Sshhh!" I hush, "don't call them that," I say, peeking about. Thankfully we're completely alone. A light comes on in my head. Every year for school, my mom made us a small "emergency kit", homemade band-aids that miraculously kept us from ever scarring, hand sanitizer, tissues that seemed to cure any allergies, and a lip balm that treated cold sores, dry skin, and cuts. "Actually, I do!"

He laughs. "Of course, you do."

I dig into my bag. *The kit should still be in the side pocket . . . voila!* Inside the plastic case I pull out the little clear disk and unscrew the lid. The balm smells like plumbs, mint, and chamomile. I delicately massage the clear goo into his swollen lip. His breath tickles my fingertips. Like an out-of-body experience, I see flashes of him kissing me in a field, his lips caressing my skin. Then the scaffolding, the burning, the hanging. A hiccup escapes my mouth, then another.

His lips quiver as he fights back a smile. "Am I making you nervous?" His hands grasp my hipbones through my bulky skirt.

My magic is waking up and begins to whisper into my veins. It's warm yet sharp, like it plans on defending itself. Possibly against Jack. My magic flares. Hic. "I've got," Hic, "to go." I throw my belongings back into my bag and practically run to the student parking lot, still feeling his phantom kisses and the burning flesh on my back. My magic settles as the distance between us grows.

# Chapter Twenty-Nine
## Blessed Be

I swear I can still feel that searing sensation on my back as I drive home. *How can a dream affect me so?*

I kick off my shoes and toss my things up on the hook in the entryway. Pyre, Gunther, and Cat meander down the stairs while Miss Priss and Newton bat and claw at a furry ball rolling about on the floor. The grandfather clock on the second landing chimes and a bedroom door closes. There's never a stillness in the aunts' house. If it isn't a kettle screaming in the kitchen, it's the cats hissing at each other, or the vacuum running itself around the house.

"Hello?" I call. A feather duster swirls between candles and photographs.

"Ella? Come in, I'm in the greenhouse," Mom answers.

The floorboards creak beneath me as I walk past the dining room.

The greenhouse is a picture window glass room attached to the back side of the house. White wooden beams run down and across the room while towering plants brush against the ceiling. The floor is littered with hundreds of clay pots filled with assorted succulents and herbs, and running the length of this especially spacious room are flower boxes many bursting with spectacular blossoms of the most exotic colors.

Mom stands towards the back of the room near a tall countertop. She's wearing a black turtleneck and black trousers resembling a less curvy Marilyn Monroe, more like Kim Novak in *Bell, Book, and Candle*. I think of what my dad used to say that when she would walk into a room, even wearing her scrubs, he would forget to breathe.

Mom pinches a clear glass dropper over a boiling beaker. "Go change into something black. We've got some training to do." She glances over at me, then back to the Bunsen burner.

I chuckle with a roll of my eyes. "My wardrobe needs more black."

Opting not to dig through my dirty laundry, I nearly empty my drawers until I find my black jeans and a black top with skinny horizontal white stripes. *Close enough.* I jump as something silently crawls out from under the bed, but it's just Pyewacket. "Any chance you could be less creepy? It's like *Night of the Living Dead* in here." To avoid a lecture from my mom about my hair in my face, I pull it up in a tight ponytail. "Coming for my training?"

*"Ah yes, let's see if you burn down the greenhouse..."* Pyewacket quips as he climbs down the stairs with me.

"If you remember correctly, I aced fire training," I retort.

Pyewacket chuckles. *"Cleats..."*

*Cleats?*

On the last step, I stumble over Margaret's stupid soccer cleats, collapsing to all fours and ripping the knee out of my pants. *Dang it.*

Pyewacket chuckles darkly, his tail slowly swishing side to side as he strolls down to the greenhouse.

"Mom, can we dump our familiars? Maybe I can get an upgrade?" I grumble, limping and dusting myself off. "And can you tell Maggie to pick up her crap?" I plop down on a wooden stool irritably.

Mom is bent over the table, peering deeply into a beaker changing colors from a neon yellow to a dark, emerald green. "We are assigned to whom we are assigned. Familiars are spiritual guardians: that bond is extremely sacred." She motions to her tabby cat wandering about the greenhouse. "But what happened to your knee?" she questions with a glance.

"Tripped. Now I've got a hole and my knee is scraped," I whine.

Pyewacket leaps up onto one of the tables. *"We've established that observation is not one of your gifts."*

*Jerk.*

*"Cockwomble."*

I pause for a moment. *Okay, I'm stealing that. Cockwomble.*

*"Plonker."*

My mom's face holds a small smile. "Perhaps it was fortuitous you tripped. You can use what we brew today." Mom straightens up, placing her hands on her trim waist. She walks over to a rough-hewn white desk, pulls out a cracked leather book, and levitates it to me. "You can keep this one. It has all your basic plants for healing."

Each page is titled for whatever ailment you're hoping to attend to; swelling, sleeplessness, headaches, upset stomachs, bruising, rashes, abrasions, and more. Under the elegantly scripted title of the ailment are pressed herbs taped to the page with written inscriptions detailing how to cultivate the desired properties and how to administer.

"Every young witch should have these memorized. Now, anyone can collect flora and create natural remedies. But only witches can bless the natural materials, making them more potent. It allows us to pull forth properties that no one else can." My mother takes me by the hand, leading me deeper into the glass enclosure.

At the very end of the room is a white wooden table adorned with what appears to be a 19th century chemistry set.

"Today, my little Ella-bean, we're going to work with wild lettuce, nature's morphine and sleep aid. Wild lettuce has over fifty species in the wildlife genus. For today, we're just going to be working with prickly wild lettuce or Lactuca Serriola. Here, come closer so you can see the barbarous leaves."

I glance around the worktable. "Did you bring gloves?" I question.

She smiles at me, knowingly. "No, sweetheart, we don't need them. Now, when working with plants, speak the incantation aloud." She demonstrates this by leaning her head close to the plant. "La Narine'," she whispers close to the leaves. She examines the plant, satisfied. "Here, feel." She takes my hand and runs it down the prickly leaf. The sharp edges brush my skin like lamb's wool. "Works on all defensive plants. Any thorns or prickles, just whisper the incantation "La Narine" and you awaken the plant's softer nature. Now, of course, if it didn't have any barbs to worry about, we could just get started."

My mother points out the milky white substance emitting from the stem when cut, explains how to dry the leaves, how to use the fire spell to speed up the bubble and boil.

"Eleanor, are you writing all of this down?" she probes, turning up the heat on the leaves.

I flip my composition notebook around, showing her my diligent note-taking. "If you're using the fire spell to dry, why are we using Bunsen burners and hotplates?"

My mother places the wooden spoon in my hand and tells me to stir the bubbling liquid. "Something you'll come to realize is that using man-made tools to assist is very convenient. Especially when this extract is so easily burned. Eleanor, I didn't say stop stirring," she says, waving her hand at me.

I quickly go back to stirring, after which Mom, attempting to keep this more interesting, uses the air spell to strain the mixture. Directing the liquid with her hands, it streams out of the small black cauldron and hovers a foot or two above it, like a mossy green rain cloud. Droplets trickle down from the floating mass back into the pot, leaving coarse stems and seeds floating. She waves the wet debris into an empty clay pot, parting the soil with in and sprinkling them down into the dirt before delicately combing it over.

I've seen my mom garden hundreds, even thousands of times, but never like this. It's hard for me not to mourn for this side of her she's kept hidden for so long. At seventeen, I shouldn't be just getting to know my real mom.

She continues with her instructions. "Two tablespoons of pure alcohol, and a tablespoon of water. Do you see how viscous it is? This should loosen it." She pulls my spoon out of the mixture, slightly exasperated. "Just use the air spell. You're not stirring fast enough. Go on."

I imagine a little cyclone spinning faster and faster inside the pot and say the air spell in my head. *La Caeli.*

"Perfect. Now I add just a pinch of sugar to make it more palatable. Keep the spell going to help mix it in," she says, placing a hand on my shoulder.

Mom takes the brownish green liquid and pours it into a glass vial with a rubber dropper attached to the lid. She unfurls a white, blank sticker across the glass. "Now write pain relief then in small letters the species, and no more than four droplets for extreme discomfort."

I quickly scrawl the directions as instructed.

"Now, before we seal it, we whisper the incantation into the bottle. This is very important, Eleanor. To avoid corruption, we have to finish the spell with 'blessed be'." She passes me the open vial. "First whisper 'La Narine'."

I bring the vial up close to my lips, not too close to my nose as it smells absolutely vile. "Do I need to close my eyes?"

"Up to you."

Just in case, I close my eyes. "La Narine, blessed be." The mixture brightens from a murky shade to an earthy, mossy green. My eyes bulge. The new aroma is like a fresh spring morning, earth after rain, a completely untouched meadow. "Mom, that's amazing."

She grins, handing me the lid. "You did very well, Eleanor. We'll continue making cures and other potions, but you need to get the herbology books off your aunts' shelf. You need to be able to identify the flora in an instant. If you have the gift, this will take no time at all," she assures. "Now take this," she slides me a shot glass filled to the brim with blood red liquid. "This will help with the effects of training."

"Great, is a tree going to grow out of my ass now?" I mutter sarcastically.

"Language," she chides, then fights back a smile. "No, but often young witches complain of dizziness, vertigo, and exhaustion. It should give you some energy without making you jittery."

I take up the glass, examining the strange crimson liquid. "What is in this?" I take a whiff. It smells like American Beauty roses. "It smells good, but I don't exactly want to drink a rose…"

My mom stares at me impatiently. "Just drink it, Eleanor."

I squeeze my eyes shut and shoot it back. "Hmm, tastes like a liquified gummy bear."

Mom shakes her head with a smile while clearing up the table. The cauldron floats over to the farm sink and rinses itself out, followed by the spoons. "Do you have an inkling of what your gift might be?"

I sit down on the stool across from her. "Definitely not water, I'm terrible. But maybe mind?"

Mom cocks her head at me. "Interesting, you haven't trained in the mind yet, so what makes you think that will be the one?"

I lean my elbows on the table. "I keep having dreams or visions, whatever. I performed a spell to have clearer visions, and it actually worked, but does that mean I have the gift, or was it just the spell? And the dreams haven't stopped. They're still super confusing, but they're consistent," I say, reflecting on the most recent dream.

My mom leans her head on her palm, listening to me. "It could be your gift. Oftentimes when you're young, your magic is working out little kinks. Especially if your gift is in the mind branch of magic. What dream came true?"

I roll my lips inward between my teeth while I cautiously consider whether I should tell my mother about Trixie's break in. I have no reason to lie to her. "I had a dream about Trixie Caldwell, someone breaking into her bedroom and stealing her diary. I just found out it's gone. But that's the only dream that's come true so far. I mean, last night I dreamt about Jack standing in a field with me, then suddenly I was on scaffolding about to be hanged. I mean what the heck does that mean?"

"Well, for one, it means I want to meet this boy," she states firmly.

I roll my eyes. "You don't have to. It's still super new. As in yesterday, new. But it's weird, too. Today, I felt this weird pull and then I find out Jack had his lip busted by this mouth-breather that is *supposedly* my friend," I growl, slumping lower on the table. "It's gotten so confusing, Mom. People thought I was quiet and weird back home, but now I have more admirers than I know what to do with. Especially my "friend" who punched my boyfriend in the face," I disclose practically out of breath.

Helen sighs with an almost expectant air. "You never know how strong it will be — it varies from witch to witch — but all are affected."

I sit up. "What are you talking about?"

My mother reaches across the table, taking my hands. "It means you need to be careful. There's something called the Power Lust. It affects non witches, especially men. The darker the heart, the more powerful it becomes for them. There are anomalies, of course, but that tends to be the rule. It always manifests in romantic displays, but when taken too far, it can become aggressive, dangerous, even deadly."

I frown, feeling something recede inside me. "Why? Why would they be affected by us?"

"There's no definite answer, but it's commonly accepted that they subconsciously detect our power, and they want it for themselves."

My heart sinks and my throat dries. *Is Jack affected? Is his heart dark and he only wants to contain me? No. That can't be him. I can feel his heart, his intentions.*

Mom watches me concerned. "This friend of yours that laid his hands on Jack, he might be too far gone, lost to the guiles of the power lust. If that's the case, you need to withdraw slowly so he doesn't become dangerous. Cutting him off at once could cause him to lash out. But if he's still reasonable, then you set *firm*, friendly boundaries. And you're bringing Jack to dinner on Sunday. No argument," she states, trying to level me with a look that Dad would have called adorable.

"Mom, how did you know Dad was the one and not just a victim of the power lust?" I question in earnest. "I mean, was it when you told him you were a witch? Was it like the show "Bewitched"?"

Persephone pounces onto the table and curls up, purring next to my mom. She laughs. "No, I didn't wait until my wedding night to tell him about witchcraft. Once I knew he was the one for me, I displayed a few spells, and showed him some potions. A few weeks and a CAT scan later, he realized he wasn't crazy. He was honestly excited, and fascinated." Her smile turns sad and her eyes glassy. She quickly busies herself picking up dry leaves off the table and looking about for an empty mason jar.

I chew on my bottom lip. "Not to press, but *how* did you know he was the one?"

Mom turns away, doing a quick sweep under her eyes with her fingertips and causing a stabbing feeling in my chest, making me bleed with guilt.

She clears her throat, forcing on a smile. "We are created in pairs. Most often, that pairing is with another witch, but for whatever reason, we are twinned with a human. Our spirits complete one another. When our soulmate is awakened, they will have dreams of us for three consecutive years. Your father's last dream of me was the day before we met at school. These dreams can happen at any time in one's life. More often, it's when they're pubescent. But there are some late bloomers out there."

My heart stops. *The sketch that had to be me. Right? I mean, it even had my scar. Could he have been dreaming of me? How would I even ask that? Hey Jack, have I haunted your dreams lately? And when I say lately, I mean for three years without fail?*

*"Please allow me to accompany you when you ask him, in those* exact *words."*

My heart pulses so powerfully, I can feel it throughout my limbs. "Mom, I think Jack—as lame as it sounds, I think he might be the one. Like, *the* one. I mean, did you have a pull with Dad?" I ask, imagining the invisible thread between Jack and me, leading me towards him when he was in pain. There had to be something to that.

Mom smiles softly. "Yeah, we did. You always do with your mate. But like I said, you're bringing him to dinner on Sunday. Period. Now let's go get cleaned up for dinner. Marie should be arriving home with Margaret any minute." She slings her around my shoulders as we head for the kitchen.

While I help Mom prep a salad, I feel lighter, like a weight has been lifted off my chest. I finally have direction with Nick, the rest of the male population at school, and where I most likely stand with Jack. Seeing how Nick is resorting to using his fists, I need to lay firm boundaries now before they go too far. And Jack, wonderful perfect Jack, I'm going to marry him and give him witch babies. The feminist in me wants to kick myself, but the other half rejoices knowing that *all* of me is his.

*"And what of the dream? I believe it was he who shoved you toward the noose…"* Pyewacket slinks into the room, intruding on my thoughts at the least convenient time.

Marie and Maggie come bounding into the kitchen, laughing. Maggie is dressed in a seventeenth century coat and britches, including a powdered wig and hat.

"What is this?" Mom exclaims, greeting Maggie with a kiss on the cheek.

Marie wipes away tears from laughing before going for the fridge. "She's a funny kid, sis."

Maggie grins. "For our midterm project, we are reenacting the Boston Tea Party set to the lyrics of "Rich Girl", by Hall and Oats. At an all-girls school, I think it works on so many levels," she says.

Mom frowns. "That has cussing. Can't you pick another song?"

Maggie rolls her eyes. "I'm going to go get changed. I'm starving."

At dinner, Maggie recreates her part in the production, explaining they were the only group to do a performance.

"Where is Sally tonight?" I ask, spearing a juicy tomato.

Marie places her glass back down, the ice tinkling in her cup. "She was asked to help bewitch the cemetery for The Gathering. It's going to take several covens to help protect us."

"What do you mean?" Maggie asks.

"Well," she pauses, chewing on a mouthful of salad. "Because The Gathering is held at a public place, even at night, we need to be invisible. Any witch can perform the mind spell to trick the human eye for a moment or two, and there are witches that can go for hours maybe even a day if that's their gift, but to achieve several hours of a large gathering we will need many witches praying and whispering the incantation in place. I'll be heading over tomorrow morning with your mother to help."

Maggie's slacked jaw slowly retracts until her mouth performs a sly feline smile on her impish face. "I seriously can't wait to be a witch." She probes Mom and Aunt Marie for more information on The Gathering. They discuss the music, the food, dancing around an open fire for all ages.

"Is it true they dance naked under a full moon?" I question, recalling a comment Trixie had made.

Mom nearly chokes on her water. "They haven't done that for many years. And even when it was allowed, it was segregated. No male gazes. The men had their fire and we had ours. But they haven't done that for a very long time now," she assures us uneasy.

Maggie's eyes bulge and she smacks the table with her open palm. "OH my gosh! The photo in the bathroom, of the woman dancing around the fire, that was you!"

Mom's face is stricken scarlet. "Marie please tell me you don't have a picture of that!"

Margaret and I fall onto the table in a heap of giggles and disbelief.

"I was nineteen and that was the last year they were allowing it," mom grumbles. "Everyone just eat," she orders indignantly.

"Helly, it's a small picture, not pornographic whatsoever. Now, Ellie, did you see Winnie today?" Marie questions, before sipping on her glass of wine, peering away from me.

I nearly drop my fork. "Um…yeah. I think you should call him."

Mom glances from Marie to me. "What's going on?"

Marie and I stare at each other.

"Mr. Edwards proposed."

"He proposed!?" Mom asks excitedly. She waves for Marie to show her the ring.

Marie exhales, slumping in her seat, holding her head with one hand. "It's just—it's so complicated at my age."

Mom's eyes slide over to Maggie and I. "Girls, why don't you head upstairs," Mom suggests, her brows pushed up high on her forehead as she motions for us to go.

We quickly clear our plates as Marie pours more wine into her glass, starting to blubber.

"Hey," Mom says, taking my hand as I turn away to go upstairs. "When you go to bed tonight, after studying up on your botany and schoolwork, close your eyes when you lay your head down and demand answers," she says hushed.

I spend the evening practicing my violin for an hour and finishing up some calculus homework, then I turn to the added work of studying the yellowed, stained book my mother gave me. I take notes on the varying locations of where the plants can be found, and that if you sacrifice a Calla Lily (cut mid stem under a full moon with a silver blade), the blood of the plant will be far more intense.

My jaw practically unhinges when I yawn while pulling on my sweatpants and t-shirt. My eyelids feel laden with cement. My body settles into the folds of my bed; even my bones seem to sink in. *Magic, listen to me, give me answers.*

I can't pry my eyes open. Lifting my head off my pillow isn't even an option. My body is falling, falling, falling…through the mattress and past the floor into an abyss. I'm completely untethered, feeling nothing, no whooshing air around me. I'm just slowly withdrawing downward.

There's a strange unfurling sensation encompassing me, like being unrolled from a bolt of satin. Then there's pressure, an immense crushing pressure that fills every pore and steals my breath.

As quickly as those new sensations come, they vanish, replaced by sound and smell. Birds chirp, a brook burbles, and the smell of fresh earth overpowers the senses. I try to inhale, but something is keeping my chest closed. The surrounding smell is pure, fresh, and foreign. When my eyes are finally allowed to open, they do so without effort.

Dapples of sunlight break through flourishing tree top canopies in angelic shafts. I'm lying down outside. There's a creek a few yards away and a grove of trees above. I'm wearing petticoats, a suffocating corset, a shift, and a white cottony blouse under a front lace up vest. *Oh great, not another one.* I clutch my head at my temples as my brain still feels like it's tumbling. The meridians of my body feel swollen, the liquid beneath them swirling. I blink several times, trying to get my bearings. I push to my feet, my toes curl inward. I lift the voluminous folds of my skirt to peer down at my white stocking clad feet shoved into buckle shoes far too small for my size ten feet.

I roll my neck and stretch out my limbs, glancing about. *Who should I expect to ambush me this time? Maybe Nick will kill me this time, or Vivienne.* Either would be a welcome change. I continue to squint about, waiting. Nothing. *Maybe I should start walking?*

I wade through the tall grass, stumbling in these stupid shoes, until I find a makeshift road. I peer down to my left, then my right, without the foggiest idea of where to go. The ground slants ever so slightly towards my left. I step out and meander down the slope, stepping around an unsightly pile of old horse dung. *Wow, my dream is really going for authenticity.*

I pass the clearing of trees into a colonial town of stone houses and wooden shops. A blacksmith smashes his hammer down onto his anvil. A woman beats a rug hanging from a line. A farmer herding sheep shuffles down the lane. One black goat trailing in the back halts, separating from the herd and staring in my direction. Flies buzz about, one landing directing on the goat's unflinching eye.

"They're getting' the witch! Ya ken!"

I'm nearly knocked to the ground as a group of children come running from behind me. I duck and shrink away, squeezing my eyes shut and waiting for shackles to encircle my wrists. I crouch down ready to start swinging.

"Out of the road, miss!" a surly man shouts. He gives me a rough shove, sending me tumbling to the ground and knocking into a barrel at the side of the path. "What the devil are you doing?" a British Redcoat with a musket barks at me. He continues marching with three other soldiers.

My chest squeezes; I struggle to catch my breath. Men, women, and children straggle behind, the crowd growing with each dwelling they pass.

"Come, they're gettin' the witch." A dirty-faced woman with visible fleas extends her hand to me, offering to hoist me to my feet.

On impulse, I place my hand in hers, letting her assist me to my feet. We hurry along with the crowd that smells worse than any locker room I've ever been in. Their rank body odors wafting in the air makes me gag. The cheering crowd slows to a stop outside a stone hovel. Someone throws a bottle that shatters against the stone. The crowd murmurs. Kids run back from the doorway, huddling into their parents. I strain to see over heads. *Is it Trixie?*

I glance about, scrambling for some indication of what's happening. *Maybe I can start a fire? Or hell, it's just a dream, maybe I summon an east wind to blow those Redcoats away?*

An earsplitting shriek explodes from the house. A cat screeches.

"Excuse me! Excuse me! Move! Please!" I push my way through the rubber necking crowd. I get strong armed by a guy that reeks of urine. "Let go!" I try to wriggle from his grasp.

The mob frowns and grimaces at me before turning back to the house just as the soldiers haul out their prisoner. I instantly freeze, my eyes glued to the shackled woman. Her burnt brass hair ruffles in the breeze. Her flinty glare scans the crowd. I immediately recognize that thin oval face with cheekbones sharp as daggers. Her thin lips, bloodied and curled back in a sneer.

Elspeth.

The hoard of onlookers spit and curse as she walks past. I fight my way to the front of the hungry parade of peasants eager to watch her receive her comeuppance. Elspeth screams and threatens all that witness this.

We pass a pillory and the lone black goat watching the scene with an almost human expression. We go farther past town, past settlements, and past farmland, the crowd diminishing the more we walk. By the time we reach a stone castle, there are only four of us left.

The castle's wooden doors have shut, locking us out. Two Redcoat guards stand poised at the entrance. I inch closer to the tower, trying to remain inconspicuous while I try to find a way in, but the guards boorishly shoo me away.

*Great, now what?* I peer up at the stone fortress, looking for some fissure, a foothold, anything that would aid me in getting inside.

"Be gone!" the soldier orders again, this time stepping forward, ready to grab hold of me.

I shoot my hands up in surrender and back peddle away. I sit down several dozen yards away under a tree and survey the castle from a distance. *Think, think, think. You're here for a reason. You asked for answers; well, here they are.* I squeeze my eyes shut, my elbows resting on my knees.

My eyes flash open. I glance about, hearing a woman's voice.

"Worry not, Pyewacket. Death be not the end."

*"My queen, we must capitulate."*

She chuckles condescendingly. "No. Me master will not yet receive me, ye groveling tripe. Tis rumored there is a spell for rebirth. Death shall not be me end. Let them burn me physical form, for the spirit shall live on."

*"There's never been a record of any such spell,"* Pyewacket argues. *"I fear what you seek is impossible."*

"Your knowledge is shallow, me friend. I know the dark magic our lord possesses. I shall be burned on the morrow's dawn, but I fear not. Ye will serve me, for this night I call upon a sacrifice most wicked…"

My heart stops, my mind reeling with this new revelation. Elspeth wants to return. That's why she's haunting me. *She must think she can possess me or something. Maybe because her familiar was incorrectly assigned to me? She's been planning her return for centuries. She must think I can help or…I'm in her way? Wait, what is the sacrifice she's planning?*

My eyes are suddenly open. I'm back in my bedroom filled with morning light. My body is restless, like I haven't slept for even a minute. I sit up, grateful I stayed in my bed this time.

"Eleanor…"

My eyes flash to the wardrobe. There in the dark, obscured by shadow, lurks Elspeth. She steps forward into the shaft of morning light, her eyes furious and her mouth menacing. She extends a hand towards me.

I press my back against the headboard as an involuntary scream erupts from deep within me.

"Pyewacket!"

# Chapter Thirty
## Creepy Crawlies

Before my scream can sting my throat, Elspeth vanishes. Pyewacket vaults onto the bed; his blue eyes dart about alarmed.

My hand calms my chest as it heaves up and down, struggling to catch my breath. "Elspeth was here." I flop back onto the pillows, fighting to slow my hammering heart. "I saw Elspeth get arrested. I think I know why she keeps trying to communicate." I prop myself back up on my elbows.

Pyewacket settles at my feet, his tail slowly swishing back and forth. *"Go on."*

"She wants to come back. And she's targeting me because you are now my familiar, which still doesn't make sense, but there it is. I think she keeps trying and failing. Has she tried to possess me? Is that why my magic goes haywire?" My eyes search the cat's face looking for some tell. But he's a cat.

His eyes remain steady. *"Yes, she has tried, but always failed. I've managed to thwart her every time. Unless she finds a way to increase her power, she'll stay where she is."*

My phone's alarm sounds. I quickly switch it off and swing my legs out of bed. "Can we banish her?"

Pyewacket sits up. *"No! No, not yet. I need to speak to her."*

I throw open the door and head to the bathroom with Pyewacket close behind. *You need to speak to your queen…?*

Pyewacket freezes outside the bathroom.

I splash water on my face and snatch my toothbrush. *I don't understand why you would need to speak to her. She is literally haunting me.* I stop scrubbing my teeth and slowly pivot, facing him. *Are you still loyal to her?* My skin tingles. *What if he's been helping her this entire time? Maybe you're not my familiar; you're still hers?* I look at him sideways, considering if I have a spy in my midst.

*"The audacity. I…"* Pyewacket descends the stairs two at a time.

*That wasn't an answer.*

There's a faint high pitch ringing in my ears, then a muted silence, the kind of dead air when someone hangs up the phone.

*Fine. He referred to Elspeth as his queen, and he does nothing but disparage me.* I finish in the bathroom and dress for school. After checking the weather, I leave my blazer on my bed, grab the button-down sweater vest, and hurry downstairs, keeping my eyes peeled for a pouting Pyewacket.

"Breakfast?" Mom asks, placing a plate of eggs and sausage on the dining room table.

I glance at my phone. "I have like a minute." I take a seat and scarf down the food. The eggs are heavenly. Then I stop, rolling the eggs over into my cheek. "These are real eggs, right?"

Mom chuckles with a roll of her eyes. "Yes," she promises.

Margaret comes bounding out of the kitchen, still in her pajamas. "Like the eggs? I helped."

I frown. "Aren't you going to be late for school?" I question with a cocked brow.

Maggie grins. "I get to skip. Mom says I can do errands with her for The Gathering. Lots of prep before the big day tomorrow."

My mouth falls open, ready to spout an objection of unfairness. *Jack.* I click my jaw shut and continue to shovel the rest of the eggs away.

Maggie laughs. "I told you she wouldn't want to stay. Not with Jack at school waiting for her, ready to make out between periods."

The full water glass on the table lifts and floats over to Margaret, high above her head.

"Mom!" she shrieks.

"Eleanor," Mom chides dryly.

The cup returns to the table, still full.

"Speaking of Jack," Mom says, arms folded. "Don't forget to invite him for Sunday dinner at seven."

I finish breakfast and push the plate away. If I invite him here, he'll insist I meet his family. "There's a chance I'm going to the Woods for dinner tonight." *Hopefully not.*

The kitchen doors fly open and a drenched Sally bursts through. "Um, Helen, we might need you in the garden."

Margaret brightens, "Can I help?"

Sally nods her head in haste. "Grab some buckets, Red, and follow me."

While my Mom is busy addressing the commotion, I slip from the dining room. Pyewacket lounges in the dead oak tree as I pull out of the garage.

*I still want an answer.* I send, but for the first time since arriving in Salem, I feel like my mind is my own. I grind my teeth, switching gears. *Could he do this the entire time!?*

By the time I get to school, I'm surprised I still have any teeth left. I survey the parking lot searching for a specific car. In the last spot, farthest from the crowd, is the white mustang. I step on the gas and steal the spot next to him. The butterflies that have taken permanent residence in my stomach take flight. *I left so abruptly yesterday he probably thinks I'm an idiot.*

Students loiter in the courtyard, relishing the rare chance for vitamin D. Boys roll up their sleeves and loosen their ties. Girls roll down their knee-high socks into anklets and hike up their skirts; several unbutton their blouses to daring levels. I scan the crowd but don't see Jack, so I quickly head into the school just as the Headmaster comes marching out.

"I've got demerits for anyone whose attire has been altered!" he threatens, holding up slips of paper. I brush past and stride down the hall, eager to see if Jack is waiting beside my locker.

My face falls. I skip my locker and trudge straight to class. Several students have already taken their seats, but not Jack. Curiously, there's a bottle of water on my desk. I sit down, picking up the bottle, confused. I glance about, but no one indicates ownership. I place it on the corner of the desk.

"Just in case you get nervous," Jack says, sliding into his seat behind me.

I purse my lips in a smirk, turning around in my seat. "I should be okay. I think I'm getting used to you," I tease.

Jack's grin shines broadly across his beguiling face. "In that case, what are you doing tonight?"

My stomach twitches anxiously. "I believe I'm going to dinner tonight at your house."

His brows lift, taken aback. "Really? What changed your mind?"

I exhale. "Because my Mom is insisting you come to dinner on Sunday."

His head falls back as he releases a guttural laugh. "Well, look at that. I assume I've been invited to discuss doweries."

My cheeks flush and I swivel around in my seat.

I can feel his lips close to my ear as he leans forward. "Tell your mom I accept."

"Miss Grear, can you start us off at the top of act V please," Mr. Edwards instructs.

"I have two nights watched with you…"

The moment the bell rings signaling the end of class, Vivienne stops at Jack's desk, scrolling through her phone. "Did you invite Eleanor tonight?"

Jack immediately straightens up. He notices my face surely draining of color. He shakes his head at me. "After dinner, my parents are taking the jet into New York for drinks, meeting some friends and stuff." *We won't go,* he mouths.

Vivienne's eyes slide from her phone to me, then to Jack apprehensively. "I know your dad prefers Mathis for drinks," she turns to me, giving me a mockingly sympathetic smile. "It's an exclusive club. Tacky movie stars aren't even allowed in." She turns back to Jack, opening her mouth to continue, but Jack interrupts.

"Ah yes, just captains of industry. They're never tacky," he says to me sarcastically. Jack guides me out of the classroom with a protective hand on my back. Vivienne nips at our heels.

"All I was saying was you should convince him to do something more fun. The plaza is classic," Vivienne wheedles, stepping in front of us into the hall. "Ooh, the Rainbow Room has that one signature cocktail you love, though you'll have to tell Marshall to behave himself this time."

Jack refuses to meet her eye.

Vivienne, unperturbed, turns to me. "I'm sure you'll enjoy Marshall's antics, Eleanor; all the new ones do. See you both tonight." She shoots me a wink before joining her friends by the lockers.

My bag weighs me down more than it did before class. "You're sure Vivienne isn't coming to dinner tonight?" I bemoan.

Jack leans against the neighboring locker. "I promise. My mother insists if they're home together, guests are prohibited. And that's been stringently enforced for the last two years."

My hand grasps the spine of the book and pauses. "Then how am I allowed to come?"

He smiles, sliding closer, his arms encircling my waist. "The bylaws of the Woods Estate contain a loophole for significant others."

I nibble on my bottom lip. "And I fit that classification?"

He chuckles lightly. "You're the *most* significant." He plants a small kiss just below my jaw.

I lean into his touch, my eyes falling shut. How can he make every nerve in my body shiver in pleasure by the simple action of his mouth meeting my skin? *Is everyone's skin as sensitive? Are my senses just heightened being a witch?* My head nearly lulls when he pulls his lips back. He pulls my body close until our hips are pressed and our legs are tangled.

"Boundaries, Mr. Woods," Headmaster Archibald says, striding past us.

Jack doesn't move, his unflinching gaze dipping to my lips. "I'll see you in orchestra." He gives me a quick peck on my cheek before strolling away, glancing back at me before stepping into his class.

My silly heart skips a beat. My head still feels cloudy and caught in the hall when I walk into history. Elspeth, Pyewacket, my magic, it all keeps drowning me in abject hopelessness, but Jack is like a beacon of light, or a raft pulling me safely to shore. When I'm with him, I feel weak and invincible all at once. My eyes drift to the repaired window to my left. My reflection is obscured by the glass.

"Eleanor O'Reilly," Mr. Andersen calls.

I snap to attention.

Mr. Andersen smiles, possibly from having called my name more than once. "Your research partner is Nickolas." He points to Nick staring up at the front of the class.

*Great.*

I roll my lips in between my teeth, peering at him. *Is he just a victim of the power lust?* His body is tense, hunched over his book, refusing to acknowledge me.

As I stare at him, hoping he'll eventually turn, I think about my mother's warning: withdraw slowly to avoid him lashing out, or remain friends with strictly set boundaries. *Do I even want to stay friends?*

"I'll give your research topics in the upcoming weeks. But it wouldn't hurt to meet with your partner and do some preliminary research on the various topics written on the board." He motions to subjects listed scrawled at the edge of the whiteboard. The bell trills. "There's the bell. Have a good weekend, everyone."

I scramble to get my violin up off the floor and my bookbag, but Nick has already hustled out of the room. One thing is for sure, regardless of whether we stay friends, I need to smooth things over before they escalate.

Peering out into the dark auditorium, I wonder where Jack is seated during orchestra.

"Emily, that was a beautiful solo, but you still need to work on holding out on those whole notes," Ms. Seawall instructs.

A strange pulse suddenly begins in the back of my head. A tug on a line. A bizarre blip like on a heart monitor. I jump in my seat; my violin nearly topples from my lap to the floor.

"Quiet!" Mr. Seawall shouts. "Now Charlotte, as first cello, I expect..."

Something — or someone — is trying to reach me. *Pyewacket? Elspeth?* Whoever it is, reaching out to them might be a disastrous move. I rub my thumb over the repeating shocks in my fingertips. My magic is a quiet, rhythmic stream veining throughout my body. *Wait, what is this? What are you going to do? You're my magic. Be still.* I close my eyes, reining my magic in. The flow of magic settles back down as if crawling back to sleep. *It listened. I barely had to do anything, and it listened.* There's a twinkling smile in my heart.

"Eleanor!"

My eyes flash open. Ms. Seawall towers over me, clapping her hand two inches from my face.

Ms. Seawall's stale coffee breath hits me like a brick as she cranes her neck closer to me. "You owe the entire orchestra an apology for your lack of respect. People not paying attention go splat!" she claps her hands together again, practically catching my nose in the process.

My body goes stiff, an icy chill drips from the crown of my head downward. "Excuse me?"

Her thin pursed lips curl menacingly, the moment she realized she struck a nerve. "Did you not hear me? Were you not paying attention, or did you fall asleep?" she straightens up, squaring her shoulders victoriously as my jaw hangs. "Accidents happen when careless people aren't paying attention, you should know that better than anyone."

The tide of my magic rises like ditches flooding in a storm. My face feels fiery, my cheeks scorched in scarlet. The sparking shoots up and down my arms, no longer limited to my fingertips. My breathing quickens as my temper escalates.

The orchestra attends to their instruments, lifting their bows to their strings as Ms. Seawall raises her arms.

I squeeze my eyes shut, vying for control of my magic. My mind is assaulted by images of the accident, my father's eyes going wide with terror, his car getting crushed like a tin can. *Stop.* Screeching brakes, his body mangled collapsing metal. *Stop it!*

"Hurry up, Eleanor, or I will call that mother of yours."

A loud pop of glass. Then another. And another.

My eyes leap open; the antique stage lights are bursting one by one. Jagged glass fragments litter the stage and grey smoke swirls from the broken bulbs.

Ms. Seawall whips her head in my direction.

*Oh, crap. That was me, wasn't it? And she knows...*

The orchestra is aghast, but Ms. Seawall wobbles at her podium, clambering for composure. She waves her hands. "It's alright, everyone. Isabella, go get Headmaster Archibald and the janitor," she orders, her hands still fluttering in the air. Isabella Campbell hurries off stage. "Alright, the rest of you..."

She stops, examining her left hand, she turns it palms up. Ms. Seawall shrieks, smacking her palms together. "What? No! NO!" she stares in horror at the tops of her hands, furiously brushing them down her sides. "NO!"

"What the hell?" Brenden Michaels utters. The orchestra students gasp and anxiously whisper to their stand partner.

"Spiders! Get them off of me! Spiders! Help me! Help!" she claws at her neck, leaving long, wrathful scratches in her skin. She grabs at her throat, choking and coughing. She stamps her feet, grinding the heel in her splat-tered saliva. She scratches at her scalp, ripping clumps of greasy black hair out of her tightly wound bun.

Everyone leaps up out of their seats, searching for these unseen spiders.

"What is she talking about?"

"What is happening?"

"Do you see anything?"

"She's lost her mind!"

Ms. Seawall releases a blood-curdling scream, plucking unseen assailants from her eyes.

*Stop! Stop this right now! I don't want this! Stop.* My magic is like an inde-pendent being inside me, using me for its own desires. *This isn't me. I'm not doing this. Elspeth? Elspeth, stop! Right now! No more! Please!*

"*Eleanor,*" Pyewacket squeezes his way into my already overcrowded mind. "*Divert it. You may be unable to shut it off by finding a new target to direct your energy.*"

Ms. Seawall grips the collar of her beige blouse and tears open the buttons. She wrestles her top off and throws it to the floor, revealing her old-fashioned torpedo-shaped bra and sallow skin. She digs her nails deep into her flesh, leaving trails of blood as she claws away at invisible spiders.

"Someone stop her!" someone shouts from the audience.

Most have their phones out filming.

"*Focus, Eleanor. Sweep the glass back from the stage. You can do this.*"

*I can't. What if the glass goes flying and I make everything worse!?*

"*You won't let that happen. Do it now.*"

Ms. Seawall has kicked her skirt off and is now stomping on it, still howl-ing hysterically. Jack leaps up onto the stage, nearly slipping in the broken glass. He doesn't slow down, sprinting to Ms. Seawall and locking his arms around her stopping her from causing more damage to her body.

"Someone call 911!" he shouts. "Now."

She wriggles and writhes against him, screaming about the spiders biting her.

I shut my eyes, trying to drown out her wails. I imagine the shards of glass inconspicuously sweeping back until each piece sits below the shattered bulb. *La Caeli.* My unbridled magic slows and softens within me, going from a full-bodied entity to a phantom. I peek my eyes open. Everyone is moving around on stage, distracted by Ms. Seawall and Jack. I intently watch each animated piece of glass inch away like crawling glass insects. Shards of glass glide soundlessly across the stage until they are a safe distance away.

Headmaster Archibald and a jumpsuit clad janitor rush up the stage steps.

My magic quiets down, still percolating at the surface.

"*Well done,*" Pyewacket sends, sounding uneasy.

"Ms. Seawall, Tammy!" The Headmaster pushes Jack aside, gripping her by her bony shoulders wrecked with scratches. "Children, you're dismissed. Go. Now. Leave. Nelson, help me." The janitor rushes to his side, picking up Ms. Seawall's top and using it as a makeshift blanket, covering her. The three of them shuffle away backstage towards her office.

*This couldn't be me. My magic reacted without me. Pyewacket, was Elspeth using my magic to hurt Ms. Seawall?*

"*Possibly, with your permission…*"

It takes a moment for everyone to move. But once everyone does, the whispers and nervous giggles begin.

*My permission? I didn't want this. I was upset and I wanted her to stop but… I was upset, I could feel my magic awaken and I didn't care. I was just so angry. Pye, did I do this on my own?*

"*I believe Elspeth influenced you.*"

Jack crosses the stage for me. "Are you okay?"

I'm still seated, feeling like a patient coming out of surgery, disoriented. I place my hand in his, letting him help me to my feet. My fingers feel numb and fumble with the silver latches on the violin case.

"I can't believe that happened. Was it something with the bulbs bursting that set her off?" Jack questions as we walk to lunch.

"I don't know," I mumble.

Jack pulls open the cafeteria doors, leading me in. Instead of joining the line for food, he digs through his bag and retrieves a large brown paper sack advertising The Lobster Shanty. "Had it delivered last hour. Two lobster rolls, fries, and just in case you aren't a fan, I got you a salad. It was the most neutral option," he says with a nervous smile.

His teeth, gleaming and white, dazzle me into momentarily forgetting what I've just done. I smile, falling into his easy demeanor. "You take the salad, I'll take the rolls," I tease.

The joy in his smile makes his eyes twinkle. "Where would you like to sit?"

I scan the lunchroom looking for an empty table, knowing I can't bear to sit with his friends. Various tables gaze over at us, including his usual post. Standing so close to Jack, I find myself encased in his glow and how the entire school reveres him. They stare like a god walked among them. I spot Nick's table, his back to me, but Noah and Alden watch us intently. "Would you sit over here with me?" I nod my head towards the table.

His eyes follow where I'm motioning, and he looks at me incredulously.

"Um, I guess. You do realize he punched me in the face yesterday, right?"

I nod lamely, glancing at his perfect lips, blemish and bruise free. Of course. "I know, I think, maybe if we can all work out our issues, it might be for the best." *I hope. At least, it might not get any worse.*

All the boys look up as we approach, all but Nick.

"Could we sit here?" I ask, balancing an awkward smile on my face.

Everyone scoots over, making room. All but Nick.

"Thanks," Jack says, pulling out a chair for me before sitting down himself.

The boys exchange looks. Jack seems completely oblivious to their admiration and deference. Nick takes a bite from his sandwich, munching on it like he's trying to penalize it.

Jack attempts to break the awkward silence of the boys gawking and chewing. "You boys are playing Deerfield tonight, right?"

"Deerfield was yesterday, tonight's Milton. We leave after next period," Tripp answers.

Noah smiles, his cheek full of burger. "Is it true that you stole Milton's mustang from their headmaster's office?"

Jack's face holds a coy smile before taking a sip of lemonade. "I plead the fifth."

The boys all laugh, pushing each other.

"Told you," Tripp says, lightly punching Pete in the shoulder.

"Then you filled his desk full of thongs and bras," Noah says, grinning wickedly.

Jack chuckles with a shake of his head. "Nah, I believe that would be my older brother when he was at Grigg's. I merely took their mascot." He peeks over at me.

I do everything in my power not to lean into him, wanting to rest my head on his shoulder. I take a bite of my sandwich instead.

"So, what did you do with it?" Pete asks.

Jack blushes, peering down at his half-eaten roll. "Um, I left it on display in one of the dormitories at Windsor."

The boys laugh uproariously, hooting and cheering him.

"The girls of Windsor are so hot, damn," Tripp says enviously.

Jack gives me an uneasy eye with the new direction the conversation has taken.

"Whoa guys, guys!" Noah holds up his phone close to his face, calling for everyone's attention. "Bruh! Mrs. Seawater or whatever had a nervous breakdown and striped on stage!" he flashes everyone his phone of a video playing on screen, the sound muted.

My food turns sour on my tongue.

Everyone grapples for their phones.

Even Nick finally breaks and reaches into his pocket. He scrolls through a text chain. "Ms. Seawall has been taken to the hospital. She's been put on leave indefinitely."

*Pyewacket, did I just break the most sacred of witch's codes?*

*"Almost. You didn't take her life."*

*What are we going to do?*

*"I don't know."*

# Chapter Thirty-One
## The Woods

School couldn't end soon enough. All anyone could talk about was Ms. Seawall's freak out, especially after the videos had gone viral. By the last hour of the day, Headmaster Archibald was shooing news crews away from the premises.

Jack and I linger next to our cars, watching the scene unfold. Before we part, he texts me his address, informing me dinner will be at six sharp.

"Mom?" I call, walking into the house.

I stride past the table on the second story landing and knock on my mother's bedroom door. "Mom?"

The door creaks open. Her bed is besieged by stacks of tomes, but no Mom. *I'll just try her cell again.*

Several of the books have blank covers. Some seem waterlogged and dried out, their pages stale and stiff. But the book that drew me back in was a threadbare covered book with frayed edges and a large two-dimensional eye drawn in reflective silver where a title should be.

I flip through the first few pages. The script in the book frequently changes from messy chicken scratch to elegantly written script to shorthand and code.

One question in particular in regard to the Nefari is the matter of rehabilitation...

*Once the eye color has changed, there is no restoration of...*

The extermination order of the Nefari remains ever prudent...

*The lack of humanity is just the beginning...they know no kindness, just malice...*

I snap the book close and tuck it under my arm and scurry from my mom's room. Ms. Seawall's screaming is at the forefront of my mind. *Is that what happened with me, my magic knew only malice, just like the book said. Or was Pyewacket right and it was Elspeth with my permission?*

I place the book on my nightstand, determined to refute any perceived connection I have to the Nefari. Just because Trixie is convinced doesn't make it so. I glance back at the book. *I don't want to be one of them. I never made a choice. This can't be right.*

Pyewacket crawls out from under the bed. *"Before you convince yourself of anything, perhaps more study is required."*

My heart falters, reaching for the book and flipping open to a page with sketching. Sketches of eyes with unnatural irises fill the page. "I doubt it. My eyes are lavender Pye. There's no point trying to convince myself otherwise," I grumble, fishing for a debate, hoping he can dispel my worry. I turn another page, titled Binding.

"Eleanor?" There's a soft knock at the door. Shannyn peeks her head into the room.

I close the book and place it back on the small dresser. I frown, confused. "Hey, what are you doing here?"

She steps into the room. Her long blonde hair is pulled up into a messy ponytail, and her face is splotchy and red with a glistening sheen. She's dressed in a hot pink sports bra and white biker shorts, her defined abs brazenly on display. "I just got back from my run," she explains, still catching her breath, "but I'm in town for The Gathering. Lennox will arrive tomorrow morning." She rolls her head from side to side.

"Yeah, Mom and the aunts have been preparing nonstop. I didn't realize this was such a big deal." I peel off my sweater vest, tossing it onto my bed.

My sister's eyes widen as she nods. "Oh yeah. Coven leaders all over the world fly in for this. Last year was my first time; it was incredible. Well, you'll see. I think Margaret and Mom are out picking up everyone's clothes for tomorrow. I can't remember what store they went to, but it was a mistake not to go Esmerelda's. She's the absolute best." She sits down on my desk chair. "I commissioned her to make my dress for the dance competition this year. Just wait 'til you see it, it's incredible. Depending on which element we're dancing with, the dress will change colors and textures. Plus, it's covered in these little glass beads that look like iridescent raindrops. Simply amazing," she says, grinning with self-satisfaction.

When she looks over at me, her face slumps. "What's wrong?"

I shrug. "Nothing. Just a lot on my mind. I'm meeting my—" I stop, unsure if I'm willing to call Jack my boyfriend and be berated by inquiries.

"Your boyfriend's parents? Oh, yeah, Mom told me about Sunday dinner," she says.

I run my hands down my face. The whole thing is overwhelming, and yet, somehow meeting a family as intimidating as the Woods isn't even my biggest problem at the moment. *How did I get here?*

Shannyn heaves herself up. "Boyfriend's parents are easy. I've never had a bad experience."

I roll my eyes, falling onto my bed. "Yeah, that's because you're you."

Her eyebrows lift. "Meaning?"

"Everyone loves you. To meet you is to love you."

Shannyn rolls her eyes at me and crosses the room. "Yeah, it's super easy being me. I'm going to take a shower." She closes the door in a huff.

I groan, knowing I'll probably have to apologize later. For what, I don't even know.

I scrounge around in my wardrobe and drawers, completely lost. Dress pants? Or a dress? Sleeves or straps? Minimalist or maximalist? I throw myself on my bed and google *what to wear when meeting your boyfriend's parents*. One article suggests dressing akin to Nancy Reagan, and another recommends not shaving due to gender stereotypes.

I can hear Margaret and my mom enter the house. Tim McGraw blares from what is most likely my mom's cellphone speaker.

I hang my head off my bed, deciding if I want to tell my mom about Ms. Seawall, thereby getting grounded and taking this completely out of my hands. But I don't want to disappoint Jack.

*"If you spent even half as much time worrying about training as you do your…"*

*Beau?* I offer, hoping to land on the point sooner.

He shakes his head, slinking around the room. *"Let's leave the French out of this, shall we? That young man shouldn't be your priority."*

Whether I want to admit it, he is a priority. I feel him when he's not around and when he is, I can barely breathe.

I resume my search, pulling out a simple blue dress with peasant sleeves. I hold it up to myself. *What am I supposed to do? I have one branch left to train in and they're the ones dragging their feet, not me. Besides, you won't help me with Elspeth. I want to banish her, but you two need to speak first, so where does that leave me? Unable to do squat.* I squeeze my eyes shut, trying to close out the image of Ms. Seawall clawing away at spiders.

I hang the dress back up, feeling just as lifeless as it looks. *Pye, I didn't mean to do that. I never ordered my magic to torture her. I was mad, but that was a vast overreaction.* A terrifying thought occurs to me. *Will the witches' Committee hear about this? What would happen to me?*

Pyewacket pounces onto my desk chair. *"Typically, for a young witch in the dawning of her magic, they would be lenient. You would be observed for the rest of your training. Restrictions would be placed on you regarding when you could practice magic unsupervised. However, you are an atypical case. Your eyes separate you from the common witch. You have eyes of the Nefari without the prerequisite. Why is that? But they won't ask that question. You'll just be treated as one of them."*

The prerequisite of either practicing the forbidden magic or having one of my parents pass it down to me. But does that really matter? My eyes are still lavender, Pye. I lay across my bed on my stomach, I peer over at my cat. *Pyewacket, you said Elspeth was most likely influencing me. Is that true, is she trying to take me over?*

*Elspeth can't possess you. I believe her spell of rebirth only partially worked. She didn't descend entirely into the afterlife; she's caught in purgatory. Those in purgatory are stuck between life and death. They barely have possession of their own spirit. In a way, it's a fate far worse than death. Without the line of communication with you, she's less than a ghost."*

"And I opened that line of inquiry up more when I communicated with her through the spirit board, didn't I?" I question aloud.

He gives a simple nod.

I sit up. "Pyewacket, I have to do something. I can't allow her to influence me to hurt others or cause harm like she did that night."

*"The board is burned, I don't believe she can have that level of authority again without it."*

*Are you willing to take that chance?*

"Hey! You would not believe what I just did." Margaret glides into the room and hops on the bed. "I flew on a broom! With mom's help, of course. It was freaking awesome!" Her eyes bounce from a pile of rejected clothes to a second pile of rejected clothes. "What do we have going on here?" she asks with a smile.

I shake off the dower conversation with Pyewacket and roll over to face my sister. "I'm meeting Jack's parents tonight. Nothing to wear." I feel empty, like all my nerves have been scooped out.

Maggie claps her hands "I love fashion emergencies. Okay, let's see what we're working with?" She slides to the floor and rummages through piles.

"Eleanor! Some of these things are mine. You suck at returning stuff," she complains, plucking items out of the pile.

"Sorry."

Another knock at the door and Shannyn slips in smelling of vanilla and amber. Her hair lays down her shoulders perfectly straight, like spun gold. She holds up a white, eyelet lace, spaghetti-strap dress with hook-and-eye closures keeping the bodice tight. The lower half is a pleated skirt with a simple black ribbon tied loosely around the waist. "This is Chanel. It's my best dress, so if anything happens to this, I'll burn you at the stake," she teasingly threatens.

My sisters ignore me when I ask them to turn around while I change. I barely have the dress up before they begin tugging and fastening.

Maggie examines me thoroughly, fighting against a smile. "We'll have to stuff the chest."

"Way ahead of you." Shannyn stuffs the dress with what looks like chicken cutlets.

My sisters argue about my hair and the virtues of chignons or a classic braid. "I bet you anything his mother will have a chignon," Shannyn says.

"A braid will make her look like a Pollyanna," Maggie counters.

We settle on my hair pulled half up with a silver barrette. Margaret strings a silver wishbone necklace around my neck. Shannyn finishes my makeup, barking at me to look in all directions and not to pucker too much.

Once they declare their work complete, I assess my appearance in the mirror; my dewy-looking skin shimmers under the overhead light. My lips are the color of peonies, and my collarbone is striking under the thin straps of the dress. My waist is cinched, bringing attention to my suddenly ample chest. *I wonder if they'd be mad if I grabbed a chunky cardigan to hide under.*

"Don't you dare," Shannyn says sharply, interrupting my thoughts.

"What?"

"I know what you're thinking. You act like I don't know you, but I do. You're not covering up like some old bag-lady."

I roll my lips inward, holding them between my teeth.

"Eleanor Elizabeth O'Reilly!" my mother yells, storming up the stairs.

*Oh, crap.*

My sisters glance at each other, confused.

The bedroom door flings open. Mom marches over to me holding out her cellphone. The infamous video plays on a loop on her screen. "Did you do this!?"

My body goes cold. I have no defense, so I look away.

"Eleanor! How could you?" She turns the phone back to her and grimaces.

I want to quibble that she deserved it, that she has been hounding me since I got here, that what she said about Dad was unforgivable, not to mention what she called my own mother. I feel that spark of anger extinguish within me. *I sent a woman to the hospital because she said mean words to me? Only a monster would do that. Maybe I am…*

"It was an accident," I mumble.

"Well, you aren't going tonight. You're grounded. This was too big, Eleanor." She pinches her the bridge of her nose. "You could have exposed yourself; I mean, what if this gets back to The Committee?"

"Mom, I saw that video," Shannyn interjected. "No one knows it was Eleanor. Besides, from what I hear, she had it coming. And you'd be lying if you said you never wanted to do that to Tammy Seawall at some point. I've heard the stories."

Mom roughly exhales through her nose. "That doesn't matter. I never acted on it."

Shannyn chuckles at our mom's response. "The aunts already approached me about training her with the last branch. Once she conquers that, Mom, the accidents will stop," she assures, to my surprise.

Mom folds her arms, deliberating. "Fine. Curfew is at ten, young lady."

I tuck away my grateful smile, knowing her curfew will exclude me from the clandestine cocktail hour filled with people who already hate me. "Okay…I guess, if you insist," I say, pretending to be disappointed.

Margaret hands me a beaded clutch. "The aunts didn't supply this one. It'll only fit a cell phone, so good luck," my *younger* sister advises.

Mom stares at me nervously, gripping her hips. "Ten o'clock, Eleanor. And please, for goodness sake, be careful."

My bedroom door creaks open and silver heels with crystal cluster embellishments come prancing in. "They're Louboutin knock offs, but they'll do," Mom utters slightly begrudgingly. "They're my favorite."

I wedge my feet into the narrow heels with a pointy toe. My mom gives me a peck on the cheek as I wobble on my way out to the car.

*"There's willow bark in the glove box; it might stave off a heart attack…"*

I nearly swerve into oncoming traffic as Pyewacket crawls out of the footwell onto the leather passenger seat. "What the hell!? What are you doing here!?" My GPS loudly instructs me to take the next exit. "Jump out! Now! I can't be late."

Pyewacket stretches insouciantly, his skin stretches, outlining each bone in his spine. *"I was sure Helen would forbid you to go. She's far too soft. After today, I'll be escorting you more often."*

*You. Are. Not. Coming. Inside.*

*"I need to be around to intervene in case you go off your trolley again. I saved your arse today."*

*Yeah, and you weren't at school.*

Pyewacket lips curl. *"Just drive on."*

I inhale until my lungs fully inflate, then release through my nose. *I will not hiccup tonight.*

*"What's the expression? If there's a will…"*

*Shut up.*

I slow as I approach a gate that can't be less than thirty feet tall, then crane my neck, peering up. A brawny man with a clipboard steps out of a brick booth disguised as a pillar. A gun is strapped to his bulging chest. Pyewacket creeps under the seat again.

*If anyone sees you, I'll deny knowing you and join in on the hunt.*

The man bows his head, peering into my car, looking about. "Name?"

"Eleanor O'Reilly?" I whisper, as if I'm unsure.

He takes a step back. "Park in the circle and leave the keys on your seat."

The narrow road to the house is like driving through a dark green tunnel. My nerves kick up about ten notches as I pass under the shadow of tightly packed trees and shrubbery. The leafy tunnel opens revealing the majesty of Jack's home.

Now my stomach is doing backflips. A long, perfectly rectangular pond with five sprinkling geysers sprays up the middle. Nick's friends had referred to the home as "The Capital", but even that was being modest. This white, federal-colonial mansion is the epitome of American royalty, like Buckingham Palace with a splash of George Washington.

Standing at the front doors, my hand hovers in the air, not sure if I should knock with my hand or use the antique door knocker. *It looks centuries old. Is it just for decoration? Do they have a doorbell? If I knock, will anyone hear me? Oh gosh, is this what dinner is going to be like? Maybe I should just call Jack to let me in.*

I glance at the time on my cell phone before scrolling for his number, but I nearly drop it when the black French doors open.

A bald man who looks like if Mr. Clean was also a retired MMA fighter steps forward wearing a baby blue polo, a conspicuous earpiece, and khaki pants. "Miss O'Reilly, come in," he says with an indecipherable accent.

"Thank you," I whisper nervously. My hands quiver at my sides while I step into the marble and gold encrusted foyer. There's a round table with fresh, aromatic hydrangeas poised in a crystal vase.

"This way, ma'am." Mr. Clean escorts me down the left hall until we stop in what I assume is their private art gallery. The elongated windows are adorned with drawn red velvet curtains that ruffle out on the floor like scarlet waterfalls. I feel like a mouse tiptoeing into a museum after hours. Each baroque painting is accompanied by a light and a plaque. Chaise lounges and divans are scattered about the room, methodically angled to best appreciate the priceless pieces on the wall and the towering sculptures in the center.

"Please take a seat, ma'am. I'll fetch Mr. Woods." With a bow, he staunchly strides away and disappears down the hall.

I gulp. *Which chair am I supposed to sit on?* I eventually select a large armchair in the corner of the room wedged between two oil paintings, a Picasso and a Dahli, according to their placards. Shannyn would be in heaven. *Maybe she can text me some talking points?* My eyes scan the room, wishing I had taken an art appreciation class so I could sound somewhat intelligent over dinner.

I cross and uncross my legs, then adjust in my seat. This armchair has no give. It's like being perched on a boulder; a very expensive, chic boulder. My eyes fall to a small gold plaque at the base of the wall that reads Dolly's Roses. I squint, reading more. *Oh my gosh, this chair belonged to James Madison.* I leap up, realizing this chair is a piece of American history, not furniture. I remain standing and fold my arms, careful not to bump into anything. It's like being in the Met, just with fewer crowds and more rules.

A booming laugh echoes from down the hall. It isn't Jack's. This laugh has more gusto, more stature. I can't help but think it's the kind of laugh you'd hear from a king watching the court jester right before a beheading.

I step closer to the doorway while still safely ensconced in the room.

"You're kidding? A real screamer, huh? That's why I've given up on the sport. I'll never be satisfied. They recruit the same type and it leaves nothing but disappointment. Team sports are all the same." The booming male voice sounds too young to be Jack's father. "I'm telling you only one technique actually works, full proof. No Hail Mary. Ha. I don't keep trophies, big difference. Yeah, yeah, he's a CrossFit champion, I think. Of course, I still play. I just prefer to go solo. Hey, look at the top tier, they aren't playing doubles. Oh, you know Allen."

I return to perusing the paintings on display, trying my hardest not to eavesdrop on this stranger's conversation that's perfectly lost on me. I stop at a modern sculpture encased in glass. It looks like twisted and fraying steel balancing perfectly on platinum rings.

"Iyad informed me you had arrived. There was a part of me that didn't quite believe it."

My heart settles in my chest. With my back to him, I hear him draw closer until his arms are around me. "What do you think?" he questions as we both stare at the immense sculpture.

I shrug, the back of my head resting against his chest. "I've never been one for modern art."

He chuckles softly. "Yeah, neither are my parents, but Allen got into a pissing match with Zuckerburg, and well, here it is." Jack turns me around, taking my hands. His eyes tumble from my lips downward. His brows lift and his mouth parts. "You look beautiful." He gazes at me like *he's* unworthy, as if even in a room as spectacular as this, *I'm* the thing to admire.

I shrink back under the scrutiny. "It's my sister's dress. I feel overdressed, or maybe underdressed? I don't know." I try to cover myself up by folding my arms. I only now notice Jack's attire: light grey slacks, matching coat, pristine white button up, no tie. His outfit, most likely in the six-figure range, cuts his slender form into something bold and regal. I peer down at myself, feeling like a flea market bargain next to the Hugo Boss cologne commercial. I stare up at his face, seeing an exhausted, hounded look. Dark circles cup under his eyes, his handsome features almost haggard. Only hours prior, he seemed perfectly fine.

"Hey are you okay?"

He shakes his head, waving my question away. "You look perfect, Eleanor." His smile is peaceful when my name leaves his mouth. He tips my chin upward, pressing his body against me. His lips caress mine, moving tenderly, with one hand on my lower back and the other cradling the back of my head. I stretch on my tiptoes; the heels of my feet lift out of my shoes as our kisses quicken in passion. His arms tighten around me and I struggle to reach until suddenly I'm more level to his mouth and… I'm *literally* levitating. *Crap!*

I break our mouths apart and push myself back down into my shoes.

Jack frowns, opening his mouth to speak.

"Mr. Woods, Honor has just arrived. Your family is waiting," the brawny butler announces from the doorway.

Jack sighs, straightening up and adjusting his lapels. "I promise this won't be too painful."

Jack guides me hand in hand down the hallway until we stop at a brass caged elevator. I stay silent as we take it up to the third-floor formal dining room, too nervous to speak.

The elevator doors open to an immaculate dining room. I take a gulp of air, forcing my hiccups to stay put. The elegant room is sophisticated in simplicity, but with the architecture of a cathedral with tall ceilings encased floor to ceiling in dark grain wood with a marble fireplace that ten grown adults could party inside. No artwork, no knickknacks, no personal artifacts of any kind. Instead, adorned on either end of the room are two enormous gold frame mirrors giving the illusion of eternity in either direction.

His family is huddled near the fireplace, conversing. Two men in tailored suits are standing with their backs to us, one of whom is regaling the group with a story. An elegant woman, svelte and chic wearing linen pants and a cream-colored cashmere sweater, sits in a high back wooden chair. A much younger woman in her twenties leans against the chair in a black tiered skirt, and an embroidered tulle long sleeve top. The women, whether intentional or not, both have their hair pulled up in a tight chignon.

The woman in the chair tilts her head, peering around the men.

My throat constricts nervously. I didn't realize I'd be meeting his *entire* family tonight. He said his older siblings don't even live in town anymore; his older brother lives in D.C. and his sister attends Harvard in Boston.

Jack strolls up to the group with a confident rolling gait and gives my hand a gentle squeeze. "Allen, Marshall, Mom, Honor," he calls to attention, "this is my girlfriend, Eleanor O'Reilly."

A scorching heat rises in my cheeks as I shyly wave.

The broader of the two men is the first to turn around. He has a broad jaw, flinty eyes, and a clef chin with salt and pepper hair that is more salt than pepper. Allen Woods, the family patriarch, regards me skeptically in a navy suit, a light blue button up with a matching pocket square. With his defined cheekbones and strong features, he resembles what Mattel would design if they were making a sexy Gordon Gekko Ken doll. He forces a polite diplomatic smile with a slight bow of his head.

Evelyn rises to her feet, tugging gently at the hem of her cashmere sweater. "Welcome, Eleanor," she says, coldly. Her white pants are immaculate, not a single loose thread, not even a wrinkle, like they were sown directly onto her elegant frame. Even her shoes were white and spotless, shining against the light. She holds out her hand, smooth as silk, for a delicate handshake. Her wedding ring catches the light from the chandelier, nearly blinding me.

"This is my mother, Evelyn," Jack says, motioning to the picturesque statue before me.

Her smile is small and measured, not causing a single wrinkle. Her face gives only the slightest indication of her age. Evelyn delicately retracts her hand from mine. She rubs her fingers together as if there was some kind of residue left behind by our shake. "My daughter Honor, and my son Marshall," she says, nudging her daughter lightly.

Honor's tightly bound, sandy blonde locks shine as brightly as her mother's ring. Her mouth forms a charming, gracious smile that belies her sharp, curt eyes that pierce her target.

My heart pounds in my ears. *Please, just let this night to be over with already.*

Marshall looks more modern in his sharkskin wool blend tan suit. He salutes me with his half-filled scotch glass before giving me a wink.

Jack's siblings favor their father's razor-sharp features, accentuating either their brawny handsomeness or lissome beauty, while Jack's looks are more inclined toward his mother's elvish allure, even down to the clear sea-green eyes.

My eyes slide from face to face anxiously, not sure what to do or say. I jump slightly as the twelve-foot door swings open. An older woman with a pageboy haircut and matching polo and khakis leads a crew of identically dressed attendants who silently place small square plates on the dining room table.

"Oh, good. I'm starving," Marshall complains, eyeing the servants.

Allen extends a hand towards the table. "Shall we?" He strolls to the head of the table, his wife to his right and Marshall to his left. Honor takes a seat next to her mother and Jack pulls out a chair for me two down from his brother, and claims the middle for himself.

I squint down at my plate, unsure of what I'm seeing. On the plate rests an oversized glass spoon. In the bowl of the spoon is some kind of raw pink fish curled and arranged like a flower, dripped with some kind of sauce on a juicy, clear nest. "What is this?" I whisper to Jack.

"Arctic char gravlax with white grapefruit. There's a set menu. This is served on the third Friday of every month. Allen insists on predictability and consistency," Jack explains, annoyed by the monotony of it all. He shakes out his cloth napkin and places it on his lap.

A woman hurries in with a bottle of white wine and fills everyone's goblet, except for mine and Jack's. Instead, somehow servants materialize beside us and place bottles of sparkling water next to our empty glasses.

I make a quiet study of how everyone eats their first course before I begin, reaching for the same size fork as everyone else. Jack gives me an encouraging smile.

Allen appraises me with stony eyes, slowly chewing his fish. My eyes fall instantly to my plate. My fork rattles against the glass when I try to spear my fish. Before I can even take a bite of the first course, the plates are being cleared. Everyone remains silent, sipping their drinks as bowls of creamy soup are placed in front of us. "Black walnut soup," Jack informs. The soup's buttery aroma causes my mouth to immediately salivate.

After ten minutes, another course is presented: a bite-size serving of smoked white fish served on a comically large plate trimmed in gold. No one speaks. Obviously, "family time" was more about familial proximity than actual bonding and discussion.

Throughout every course, each family member superciliously peers at me in turn. All except Marshall. The few times he glances at me, it's like he's staring at a call girl, something cheap and made to serve.

Under the table, Jack reaches over, stroking my knee.

"More wine, miss?" the pageboy-haircut woman asks Honor.

Honor's eyes turn to ice. She turns her head toward her with a disgusted scowl. "No. Not if you plan on serving the same swill as before. No. Get me the '96 Cabernet Sauvignon. Now," She dismisses.

Evelyn shudders at the sudden break from the quiet. She glares at her daughter sideways. "It's unbecoming to yell at the staff, dear."

Honor shrugs, pushing her glass away. "I didn't yell, mother. I forcefully stated what I wanted. Besides, did she get that chardonnay from the cellar, or did she scoop it from a puddle?"

Allen rolls his eyes at his daughter before taking a tentative sip from his own glass. "Perhaps your education is being wasted. Maybe your future is as our sommelier."

Jack's sister rubs her left temple. "Well, fire whoever is currently filling the position. I'm embarrassed for them." Honor pushes away another uneaten plate. "I'm not eating this." By the look of her sunken cheeks and thin frame, it seems she hasn't eaten in months.

"Sweetheart, that bottle was over three grand. The notes are perfectly balanced," Evelyn chastises.

Allen shakes his head, scrunching up his face like he tastes something truly foul. "Evelyn, dear, talk like this is vulgar in front of guests." He pushes his empty plate forward.

Evelyn apologetically smiles at him with a solemn nod.

"I pay my dog walker more than what that bottle is worth, mother," Honor snaps.

"Unsightly," Allen mutters, just before dabbing his mouth with his cloth napkin. After that, the main course is served, roast pheasant with quince, blackberries, and honey. Everyone is silent while the old plates are taken, and the new ones placed on the table.

"Quite right," Evelyn says, picking up seamlessly where the conversation left off. Her eyes flutter in my direction, as if only now remembering I'm still here. "Eleanor, where are you from? I understand you are new to Grigg's?" Her question sounded polite and earnest, then she immediately turns to a servant waiting silently against the wall. "I want a Sazerac," she orders, her smile vanishing. Her eyes shoot daggers at the servant before turning back to me, her amiable charm slipping back into place.

"Yeah—I mean, yes, I am new to Grigg's. I'm from Coral Gables, Florida," I answer. My hands shake in my lap.

"How lovely," she says just as a short glass filled with a reddish-brown liquid and a curly lemon peel balancing on the edge is placed before her. I'm unsure whether she was speaking to me or the servant retrieving her drink.

I watch as Allen takes a precise bite of his pheasant. He seems to shift the supple meat in his mouth before swallowing. "Evelyn, how was your meeting?" he questions, staring forward at nothing in particular.

She gently places her glass down with an exaggerated sigh. "Oh, Dorthea Hastings has broken the rule about black tie engagements. You should see the flowers she's chosen. Apparently, galas for the global climate initiative should look like a first communion in Sicily. Thankfully, Violet Cummings is calling Leo's people and we'll get it straightened out."

I can't help but stare at Jack's father while he finishes his plate, gazing at nothing while his wife drones about table linens and catering. Given his commanding presence, stature, and sense of power, he's probably accustomed to lingering eyes. Allen, by all rights, could be considered handsome in a polished Prime Minister sort of way. But there's something off about him. He has a look about him, cold as stone, like some part of him has died inside, leaving behind a stately, animated corpse in a power suit.

After pushing her plate away and keeping her glass close, Evelyn continues, "Speaking of Violet, she and Henry just had their rose garden completely re-landscaped. It's really something. I think we could use a new grounds artist. Those lilies in the back are looking quite ill."

Allen nods his head. "Whatever needs to be done."

Evelyn finishes her drink, seeming more relaxed. "Good, I have several ideas. Perhaps even a Japanese water garden. They're all the rage."

"For tacky hotels," Honor mutters under her breath.

My fork hovers over my plate, too nervous that spearing my food might accidentally cause a noise someone at the table might find disagreeable. I carefully push my food around, my stomach churning with nerves.

"Marshall, how's that new assistant working out?" Allen prods, holding a confident smile on his lips.

Marshal flashes a bright grin, leaning back in his chair. He clucks his tongue, glancing over at me quickly. "She's working out well. She's not scared to go that extra mile."

Allen shakes his head before dabbing at his mouth with his plumb-colored cloth napkin. "I don't trust her. Anyone who went to Cornell can't be trusted." He and Marshall chuckle conspiratorially.

Jack rolls his eyes.

Marshal devours every last morsel, accidentally scraping his knife against his plate, much to his mother's dismay. "Jack, you need to come and check out my new place. We just finished renovating the rooftop gardens, added a hot tub, sauna." He nudges his brother with his elbow.

Jack nods limply.

Allen finishes sipping his wine and motions for it to be refilled. "And how are things progressing with Keaton?"

Evelyn perks up at this question directed at Marshall. "Oh yes, are we still thinking the Mandarin in December? Or was it Endicott in October?" she questions, mostly to herself.

Marshall coughs and stretches his neck like he's struggling to swallow. "We've decided to take a break. I've been spending time with Blaire Hornsby, actually. She's going to be flying in with us tonight since Keaton is in Tokyo, anyway."

Jack stiffens, his eyes anxiously dart to his brother, his fork hovering in the air by his mouth.

Allen mulls this new information over, slowly cutting his meat. "The Secretary of Defense's daughter?"

Marshall scrapes his teeth against his fork, plucking the meat off and chewing with a smile.

Allen nods his approval while Evelyn roughly chews her food with discontent.

"Is it wise for her to come? The Mather's will be in attendance," Evelyn despairs, her drink clutched tightly in her hand.

Marshall rolls his eyes at his mother. "It's fine. It was a mutual decision to take a step back. She hates D.C. as much as Honor does," he comments.

Honor shoots him a tart, shriveled smile with narrow eyes.

Everyone falls back into silence as we move onto decadent sorbet, through the salad course, and finally the fromage course of soft cheeses, nuts, and fruit. Honor nibbles the edges of an almond like a squirrel.

"Jack," Allen begins sternly, "I spoke to the freshmen dean today. Apparently, they have yet to receive your acceptance. I expressed that they must be misinformed because my son will be attending in the fall. But don't worry, it's been taken care of. You're even staying in the same dormitory as I did."

Jack clenches and unclenches his fist. His eyes stay fixed on the table.

Allen chews his food smugly. "You're eighteen. You shouldn't need your daddy to take action. I expect a certain level of maturity."

Jack grips his fork, trying to simmer down before taking his first bite. "It wasn't a mistake," Jack states, his emotions about to boil over.

Allen shakes his head, brushing him off like he's just some fly buzzing too close. "We'll talk about this later, when you aren't trying to impress your girlfriend, Ellen."

"Eleanor," Jack corrects pointedly.

Allen is no longer listening. He motions to the staff to begin clearing while Evelyn scrunches her face at me with an apologetic, yet patronizing smile.

My heart pounds behind my ears. It's like the entire room has been turned into a vacuum, sucking out all the oxygen. I'm not sure if I can do another course.

"So, Eleanor, what do you like to do...for fun?" Evelyn asks with a tight, closed smile.

I swallow the sour brie, glancing over at Jack whose knuckles strain white, his lips in a severe line.

"Um...I like to play the violin. I'm actually in the orchestra at school," I offer, hoping my oblation will be accepted.

Evelyn places a hand to her chest in alarm. "I was informed of your conductor's episode today. I'm on the board. It's a shame you had to witness such a violent break," she says with a disbelieving shake of her head. "I'm aware that she was ambulanced to the hospital, but I'm unsure of her status."

Honor releases an amused snort, her glass pressed to her lips.

Allen shifts in his seat, causing all of us to turn to him. "Were you one of the "helpful" students who filmed the entire ordeal?" Allen addresses me for the first time tonight, his voice brimming with contempt.

I peer over at him, almost pleadingly. "No, I wasn't sure what to do," I say, almost desperate, like a cross examined witness. I can't help but flinch when I meet his eye. It's as if my pale skin is completely translucent and every flaw, every mistake, is lit on display. And whatever Allen sees in me, he doesn't like it. Not even a little.

"Does Ms. Fischer still work there? If she started stripping during class, I'd demand she get a raise," Marshall utters to Jack quietly.

Allen calls over to the head of the wait staff. "We'll be skipping the coffee. Tell Charles to bring the car around." He tosses his napkin onto his plate and pushes from the table. Everyone stands from their seats, perfectly choreographed and nearly in unison. I scramble to rise in kind.

Allen shoots Jack a cantankerous glare before gazing over at me, shrinking beside him. "Pleasure to meet you..." He appears to struggle to find my name, but immediately disregards it and moves on. "Evelyn, Honor, your things have already been sent to the St. Regis. Marshall, Jack, your things should be on the chopper."

"I won't be attending tonight. I sent word to your secretary, your assistant, and your assistant's assistant. I have arranged plans this evening," Jack states calmly.

Allen does a double take at his son. "Excuse me?" He takes a bullying step forward, causing me to take an unconscious step back. Jack, however, stands his ground, his shoulders square and his gaze matched.

"Darling," Evelyn says, placing a delicate hand on Allen's forearm. "Jack staying behind simplifies the evening. If Blaire is taking the chopper with

us too, we have no room for him anyhow. I think we can let him miss…"
she pauses, her eyes flicking over to her son from across the table, "just this
once," she says like a warning.

Jack's shoulders fall slightly.

Allen brushes away his wife's hand. "Fine. We don't have time to argue.
The Farnsworths and Vikanders are already there." He tilts his head towards
Jack. "We'll continue this discussion when I return from Munich on Tuesday.
I expect your course load and major declared upon my arrival." He turns on
his heel, swiftly exiting the room.

Evelyn gives me a morose smile. "It's regretful we didn't get to speak
more. Perhaps I'll see you again," she says, as if there is little to no chance of
that happening. She turns her dour gaze to Jack and shakes her head before
following her husband out.

My heart falls like a lead balloon. His family didn't hate me; it's even
worse than hate. I'm completely and utterly inconsequential. They have no
reason to loathe me because I won't be around long enough for it to matter.
How did Vivienne put it? A passing amusement?

*"Perhaps this is for the best. Maybe this way, Jack won't become collateral damage
in your training…"* Pyewacket sends.

*I know, but…* I stop myself from even thinking the words.

*"I'm painfully aware of your feelings, miss…"*

*Then you know how badly this hurts.*

*"It will for a time, until you find your matching spirit. Then you'll forget all about
these cantankerous arses."*

"I'd say you're being ridiculous, but you already know that." Honor delicately reaches for her long step glass. "There are worse fates than ending
up at the most prestigious university in the country." Honor finishes her
glass and nearly slams it down on the table. Her eyes sweep over me before
settling back on her brother. "You can always keep your pet on the side with
her imposter shoes," she murmurs, raising a brow.

"Don't," Jack warns sharply, holding up his first finger towards her.

"No." She places her hands on her impeccably small waist. "When you
step out of line, the rest of us pay as well." She stomps away, towering in her
spiked high heels. "Time to join us in the real-world, Jack," she calls over her
shoulder.

Marshall slings his arm around his brother's shoulders, giving him a
friendly squeeze and jostle. "Bruh, you don't know what you're missing. Phi
Beta Kappa girls are *insane*. They look like they've been grown in a lab for *one*
purpose," he says with a dark chuckle. "Blaire was a Phi Beta Kappa." His
affable expression knits into an apologetic frown. "I'm sorry about Keaton,

and that I couldn't spare you. We just don't work. We make less sense than Allen and Evelyn."

On the contrary, I find his parents perfectly matched. Both have glares that can wilt entire gardens in a flash.

Jack stares at his brother. "It caught me off guard, that's all. Your engagement status doesn't affect me," he states, his mouth in a resolute line. His eyes hold a stormy, faraway look.

Marshall continues as if Jack hadn't spoken. "But hey, isn't Vivienne going to Yale? That gives you a little break. *And* I bet Evelyn and Allen will let you wait until *after* law school before any announcement is made. That gives you seven years of freedom. Go enjoy it, little brother." He attempts to ruffle Jack's hair, but Jack dodges his hand.

Marshall laughs, stepping around him. "And *Eleanor*," he says, emphasizing my name, proving he remembered it, "pleasure meeting you." He takes my hand, kissing one each, staring into my eyes. "But as I'm now looking at you," he says, conspicuously eyeing my entire form now, gliding from legs to bust to waist to my bust again, "it was clearly not enough of you. You wouldn't be willing to turn around for me, would you?"

"Marshall," Jack snaps.

His older brother takes a step back, hands in the air. "Take it as a compliment. I have exquisite taste, and apparently, so does my little brother." He winks with a guilt-free grin, then gives me a once over with pursed lips, shaking his head to himself before leaving.

Jack runs his hands down his face, releasing a pent-up groan. "Unbelievable. I'm truly sorry. How they behaved is unforgivable."

His fingers are spread as he leans his palms flatly on the table.

"It's okay," I assure. Placing a gentle hand on his shoulder, I feel unbelievably grateful for my family. I think of my sisters helping me get ready for tonight, my mom lending me her shoes we all considered fancy. Even my zany aunts are so intertwined in my life, I can't think of life without them now.

He shakes his head. "No. You deserve better," he says, bitterly. "And I should have known better. I don't know what I was thinking. This was a mistake. I don't need their approval," he says, more arguing with himself. "I can't believe I fell for their crap. They'll never change." Jack's hands tremble on the tabletop as his head hangs forward.

"I think I should go," I mumble. I can't bear to see him struggle in turmoil because of me.

Jack's face crumbles. "I'm sorry, Eleanor. Would you stay? I've got something I want to show you." He straightens his back and pulls me into an embrace.

As soon as my heart skips a beat, I know he's won.

Jack takes my hand and leads me down the hall. He opens a white door and sweeps me into his bedroom. Now I'm nervous for a whole new reason. He's brought me to his inner sanctum, the room in the house that is his and his alone. His tidy room could fit four or five of the attic room in the aunts' house. Black double doors lead to a spacious terrace overlooking the enormous backyard with an Olympic-size pool and a magnificent view of the ocean. I swallow, spotting his king-size bed placed proudly in the middle of the wall.

Jack strolls to his spacious closet, removing his jacket and placing it on a hanger.

My pulse quickens. My head swims with contradictory emotions. *Why did he bring me to his bedroom? We don't have to worry about privacy. His entire family left.*

Jack glances over at me with a crooked grin as he unbuttons his shirt.

# Chapter Thirty-Two
## A Picture is Worth a Thousand Words

My face goes flush. My mouth goes dry. I can't take my eyes off his bed. *Was this it? No way! We literally* just *started dating. Am I even ready?* I nearly stumble in my heels.

Jack slips on a charcoal t-shirt.

Air rushes from lungs. I feel a pathetic smile on my face, unsure if I'm relieved or not. "This is a nice room," I say awkwardly, motioning about.

Jack nods, slipping his hands into his pockets. "Thanks, but this wasn't what I was talking about." He holds his hand out for me, standing idling at the edges of his closet.

I raise my brow, skeptically. "Okay…"

We step farther into his brightly lit closet that's roughly the size of my aunts' living room, but better furnished. We stop at his shoe island in the middle. He fingers under the ledge until there's a loud click. The entire shoe block clacks and shifts a few inches. Jack shoulders the marble shoe island, forcing the heavy thing to slide. A hidden cement staircase is revealed beneath it.

*This is either the coolest closet ever, or the creepiest.* "Is this where you stash all your girlfriends?" I joke nervously.

He gazes at me through gentle eyes. "Actually, I've never shown this to anyone before. You're the first," he says in an almost reverent whisper.

Jack helps me down the three flights of stairs, each flight becoming increasingly brighter until we are bathed in a luminous yellow light.

"You should think about installing railings," I lightly tease.

"I'll call a contractor tomorrow," he replies with a wink.

I half expect either a cellar for a serial killer, your typical unfinished basement, or even a luxurious man cave. Instead, I've entered another art gallery. The raw cement walls are speckled in canvases of varying sizes and subject matter. The room is surprisingly cozy and warm; there's even an

electric fireplace against the wall. Enormous throw pillows litter the unfinished floors that are partly sheathed in ornate Persian rugs.

"Take a look around," he suggests, taking a few steps back towards an
old wooden bar. The marble top looks like it's been ripped right out of a
1920's speakeasy. "Can I get you anything? Soda, mineral water, mocktail? Or
after dealing with my family, hard liquor?"

I chuckle. "I'm okay, thanks." I kick off the high heels and stroll towards
the closest wall of canvases. The series is filled with agonizing lines across
a myriad of splashing colors. There were paintings slathered in vibrant oils
bursting their images to life.

Music plays from speakers placed about the room. Jack sings along, a
little off key.

"On that Midnight Train to Georgia," he sings, making me giggle. "Okay,
I can't sing. But I love this song."

I grin, wishing we could stay down here forever. I turn back to the paintings, taking a step closer, craning my neck, examining them from different
angles. On every finished canvas, scribbled in the corner, are the letters JTW.
"What's JTW?"

"Jack Tennyson Woods," he answers.

*Even his name is sexy.*

"Jack...these...these are amazing. Did you do all of them?" I ask,
awestruck.

"Yes, some aren't finished yet, so don't judge me too harshly."

The sequence of canvases continues around the room, some rectangular, some square, but all arranged closely together. Stretched across the
largest wall is a vertical canvas displaying a thick tree trunk, its bark scarred,
the branches reaching out across the other canvases. The earthy branches
then morph into something completely different. One branch becomes a set
of hands clasping a ball that looked like the moon. Other branches turn into
a twisted bar of music, a murder of crows, rays of light bursting through
darkness, and disembodied legs of a family in bed together. The paint is
thickly applied, giving the entire "tree" a moving shadow.

My eyes drink in his artistry. The paintings speak to me in ways no other
painting ever really has. I feel like I finally understand Shannyn's passion
for art. "Your work is incredible. I can't believe you did these," I confess. I
continue to stroll about his basement-turned-studio, my eyes sweeping over
the unexpected beauty. This is a skill far beyond a simple high school art
class. This was a life of dedication. I was now in Jack's world.

Jack appears next to me, taking my hand, sending sweet shivers up my
arm. *How has my skin not adjusted to his touch? How is it that every time our skin*

*caresses, every nerve awakens?*

"Here, I want to show you something else." He nods his head toward a hanging sheet dividing a small corner of the room away from the rest of the gallery, like a sacred secret tucked away from the multitude of paintings on display. "These are for you," he says as he opens the curtain for me.

I duck under the white hanging sheet. My heart squeezes its way into my throat as I gaze at another wall covered floor to ceiling with his work. The painting directly in the center is a still life of a transparent vase of flowers, but the buds on the end of the stem are colorful butterflies bursting to life, taking flight off their long, graceful stems in fantastical surrealism. I wanted to follow their delicate flight off the canvas, watch them gracefully flutter in the air. Taking a step closer, I realize their wings are broken pieces of stained glass. Or was it just painted to look that way? I want to stroke my fingers over the painting, but I resist. "I think this is my favorite," I say, smiling.

Jack nods, his hands tucked behind his back, observing me. "Yes, I remember," he whispers.

I frown, not understanding his meaning. Next to the magical butterflies is a round canvas of a pale-yellow house, quaint with flowering bushes and flower boxes beneath each window. The modest home is dwarfed by the surrounding Mediterranean designed mansions. My eyes bulge. The mailbox at the gate is dented with a chipped flag. The second-story window far to the right is painted a bright yellow, indicating a light is turned on in the room. My room. In my old house. "Jack, how—how is this…?"

My eyes fly to the next painting of a girl laughing in a white silk gown. Her black hair has an almost blue tint, like a raven's wing. Her mane is wild, blending into the trees behind her while skipping away from the artist. Below it is a square, porcelain tile where Jack painted himself holding the girl, the beautiful siren in a blue ball gown nestled into him. He looks—so peaceful, yet torn with worry as he clutches her, tucking her close.

On a round, possibly leather canvas, the same girl is lying on her back in a field of wildflowers—daisies. Her blackish hair laid delicately about her amongst the flowers. Her cotton white sundress is ruffled around her thighs like she had fallen down, settling to the side of her legs. Her eyes are closed, her face serene, her heavily painted lips hold a small, tranquil smile. I peer down at my dress. *Is it the same one?* She does look like…but no, she's way too beautiful. But that was for sure my old house.

"Jack, you painted…" I stop, my eyes fall to the biggest canvas of all, resting on the floor against the wall, stowed away in the corner of his secret gallery. A haunting violin, resting at an angle to the upright bow, but the bow is…*unique.* It's much longer, disproportionate to the instrument itself, and it casts a strangely shaped shadow. Behind the instrument are dark vertical shapes. I examine closer, noting it's actually a city skyline. *Wait, I recognize that building, and that one there is a hotel. It's the hotel my parents always stayed at for their anniversary.* The view is if you were standing on Brickle Avenue. My eyes slide back to the violin, only now realizing it's the silhouette of a woman and the curve of the violin was her small naked hip.

I turn to him. "You painted me." My spine is the strings splicing down the body. On my shoulder blade is a crescent moon and star with a little date indicating the time the ink was put there. I turn to Jack, pointing out the astronomy on my shoulder. "That was a henna tattoo I got at a music festival in Miami. It lasted for like a month. Jack, I got that tattoo when I was sixteen. How…" I spin back, facing the artwork again. There is another small, obscure marking in the middle of my back, one that I can't make out very well. It almost looks like an upside-down smiley face, maybe? Or perhaps a horseshoe? It's too dark to tell. Maybe it's nothing. But every scar, every freckle on my shoulders are accounted for. "How can that be possible?" *Maybe Jack has been experiencing what I've been dealing with, visions, out of context, nonsense visions. In fact, perhaps Jack's family weren't assholes, they were just witches. Could it be? No, there's no way I'm that lucky.*

Jack throws his hands up as if surrendering. "Eleanor, I'm sure this looks terrible. Like I'm a stalker or something. But I promise, it's not like that," he says, then amends with an in spite-of-himself smile, "which I'm sure is what a psycho stalker would say. But it's the truth."

*Here it comes. You're a witch and we're going to live a magical life together. I don't care if I'm meant for someone else. I choose you. I'm going to be a doctor. You'll be an artist with your own gallery. We'll have magic babies together and live happily ever after.* My heart beats wildly, about to burst with pure joy. I'll be his witch and he will be mine. I suddenly get a mental image of Jack in his little boxing shorts, making things fly and myself doing something or other, probably watching and drooling. *This has to be it, right? He's a witch.*

Jack struggles for words.

I stepped forward with a soft smile that causes Jack's face to furrow in confusion. "Jack," I say softly, "it's okay, you can tell me. Jack, you can tell me anything," I urge gently. *Maybe I could go first? If I tell him I'm also a witch, that might make it easier for him.* "Jack, I know what you're trying to say, and it's okay."

I reach up to cup his face, but instead he takes my hands, holding them in his. "It started when I was fifteen. That's when the dreams began."

My heart stops. *Wait, fifteen…?*

He releases his hold on me and paces towards his work. "This is going to sound impossible. Because it *is* impossible. I don't understand it. But almost every night, I dreamt of this incredible, beautiful girl." He waves his hand to the painting of the violin, the girl running, then several canvases I hadn't even noticed, with lavender eyes gazing from the wall. "She would always be so close, but I could never reach her. I didn't know her name, where she was from." He stops gazing up at an abstract of lavender eyes over a stormy sea. "You were my muse and my tormentor." His eyes drift down to a small square canvas of me with gray wings and a dress made of rain and mist. "You were the best dream and the worst dream I've ever had."

I feel feverish and lightheaded. Feebly, I reach for the wooden stool he has placed in front of an unfinished piece; my knees buckle beneath me just as I sit down. *This is real, this is really happening.* My insides feel wobbly, like something is changing inside me. My heart skips a beat. Jack Woods is my fate. In a way, it feels harder to believe than witchcraft. Yet something feels…right. A lock sliding into place, a piece pressed perfectly into the hole of a puzzle. Something in my heart recognizes him. I felt it that first day of school. And I resented it. I didn't want to depend on anyone, didn't want to feel that pull, that tether. But here I am, knowing nothing will ever be the same again. I'm seventeen and my soul has found its mate.

His eyes implore mine for forgiveness. "I know you must be freaking out right now. It doesn't make sense. I've tried to analyze it, that maybe I somehow came across your social media and you imprinted on my subconscious. But I *never* go on social media. The closest I've been to Miami is the Bahamas. So, unless you were vacationing there during my freshmen spring break… I don't know how it's possible, but it's true. I've been dreaming of you. For years. I've listened to you play your violin a million times. I've memorized your laugh, the way you concentrate when you're working on something. I promise I'm not crazy—or maybe I am, but I couldn't keep this from you any longer." His eyes downcast to the floor as if waiting for an impending death sentence.

I feel my heart settle in my chest, at peace with this revelation. "I believe you. I don't think you're crazy—I…"

Pyewacket interjects before I can finish. *"One revelation at a time, if you please. Let's adjust to the idea that we are now stuck with him. He's still a teenage boy. Your secret puts not only you at risk, but your family, too."*

"I wanted to tell you the truth the moment I first saw you in the hall. I almost did." He kneels down in front of me. "This is why I wanted to introduce you to my parents. I wanted to make this…more real in a way. No more keeping it in shadow or shut away in my studio. You matter most to me." He unexpectedly graces my knee with his lips, caressing that C shaped scar. And suddenly I realize there are pleasurable nerves in the knee.

"May I have one?" I ask meekly, nodding to his work.

He smiles. "Any of them, all of them, what's mine is yours." He offers me his hand, helping me off the stool.

I stride over to the canvas the size is a little bigger than a teacup saucer. The painting is voyeuristic, peering at an out-of-focus couple through tall blades of grass. They're only visible from the shoulders up, their arms tangled around one another. I hold it up to him, showing him my prize. Jack grins, delightfully surprised by my choice.

As we stroll quietly content towards the staircase, I peer back at the gallery, knowing one day those pieces will hang in our house.

Back in his closet, he slides the shoe island back into place. Then he chuckles to himself, shaking his head, mystified as he closes the closet door.

"What is it?" I question, smiling. I place the small painting next to my purse and skip back towards him.

He intertwines our fingers. "I can't believe I told you that I've dreamt of you for years and you just believed me. You saw the paintings, but you didn't question it. You didn't press me on it, didn't accuse me of being a psycho. Don't get me wrong, I'm very grateful, but still. You acted better than even my best-case scenario."

I shrug. "Yeah, well, I've heard crazier things. Besides those paintings, there wasn't a freckle out of place. You even got this birthmark." I roll my right shoulder forward, pointing out the little bow shaped mark.

Jack brushes his thumb across that little bow. His eyes fall shut when he presses his lips against it. When he pulls his head back, he delicately slides the thin white strap of my dress down off my shoulder, letting it lie limply on my arm.

I let out a pleasure-filled breath as his lips trail up my shoulder and over my neck until his mouth longingly lands on mine. He ardently opens his mouth to mine, igniting a fire within me. My arms wrap around his neck as he grips my waist. We peddle back, my feet stumbling over themselves, forcing me to allow him to support me, practically carrying me. We fall back onto his bed, our kisses hungrily devouring each other. He supports his weight, laying on top of me without crushing me. My hands passionately explore the hard contours of his chest and arms. Running my hands over his body feels strangely natural, like my hands already know him and feel at home there.

I can feel Jack's hands tremble with a desperate desire to traverse my body. His hand moves from my waist to my hipbone down to my thigh. His lips graze my collarbone and pull down my other strap. My hands run wildly through his hair.

Jack pulls back, panting. His eyes searching my face fervently, devotedly. "I love you, Eleanor. With all my heart. I only ever want to be with you."

My lips feel nearly bruised and swollen from the feverish kisses exchanged between us. My heart contains an unfamiliar mixture of rapture, euphoria, and yet utter contentment. I've never belonged to anyone—other than my parents, of course—and certainly no one has ever belonged to me.

"I love you too," I whisper. I wait for fear of rejection to wash over me, the illogical worry of abandonment, but it doesn't come. Instead, declaring my feelings leaves me stronger and somehow made whole.

The uneasy feeling of not being ready begins to ebb away slightly. *Am I ready? What am I even asking myself?* Whatever happens, it's with the boy who loves me, and I him. And unlike typical high school romances doomed to end at the changing of the graduation tassel, our bond was celestial, forged in the stars before we even had consciousness. Whether we liked it or not, our souls perfectly align. Thankfully, I like it *very* much.

He asks with his eyes if he can go further. His hand glides up higher on the outside of my thigh, causing my skirt to fall higher, dangerously so. Our frenzied pace slows. His forehead rests against mine, peering into my eyes, our hips pressed together. Our eyes close as he dips his head towards mine. Our lips move so gracefully together it feels like a waltz. *I love you.*

"I love you," he whispers, as if in reply. "We don't have to do anything tonight. We'll take it slow," he assures as if sensing my nerves.

Just as my heart feels ready to burst into blissful confetti, a stabbing pain ripples out from the center of my body. I feel gutted. I bite down on my lip, stifling an excruciating scream. Every pore, every cell in my body feels as if they are being stretched. My joints burn, my lungs ache, even my bones seem to splinter under my twisting flesh. *I'm going to die. Oh gosh, I'm going to die! Pyewacket, what is happening to me?*

*"I don't know. This is vexing. I've never seen this before."* Pyewacket grunts, then curses suddenly feeling the same pain I am.

Jack's hand slides up my ribs just inches away from a zone he eagerly wants to cross. "Are you okay?" he asks, pulling his head back. His face is suddenly etched with concern.

I take a deep breath, fully expanding my chest. Jack lifts himself off, giving me space while staying affectionately close. The heavenly high we shared evaporated, but the pain seemed to weaken once panic took over and my joy deflated. Just as I thought I was about to succumb to my agonizing demise, it was over. My body relaxed.

"Eleanor?" he repeats anxiously. "Are you alright? Did I hurt you?"

I shake my head. "No. I'm okay."

Jack studies my face, unsure if he should be worried or not.

I reach up and cup his handsome face, feeling a little stubble under my palm. "I'm okay, really. I had this weird chest pain for a moment, but it's gone. It only lasted for like five seconds."

Jack's eyes involuntarily fall to my chest, then he immediately looks away, blushing.

"Jack?" a female voice calls, his door creaks open.

Jack releases a low growl close to my ear.

We both look over at the sudden intrusion. Vivienne shuts the door behind her, folding her arms across her chest.

Instinctually, I tighten my hold on his biceps as if bracing for a Real Housewives-level freakout.

Instead, Vivienne laughs with a careless roll of her eyes. "Sometimes, Jack, your predictability is astounding to me." Her eyes snap over to me. "He looks for any excuse to get out of cocktail hour. You're just the latest one."

I hastily adjust my straps and pull the hem of my skirt down. Jack adjusts until he's in a seated position on the bed. "Get out, Vivienne."

She drops her black Greca Goddess Versace bag onto his dresser, and casually flips her flaxen locks over her shoulder. "Do you have anything good to drink in here? You used to."

Jack strains to keep his anger in check. "There are plenty of drinks at the St. Regis. I'm sure if you leave quickly, you might just make it."

Vivienne strolls over to a refrigerator hidden amongst the mahogany paneling along the wall. "That's all right. I think I left a bottle of Belvedere. Or, ooh, do you have any of that Beluga left over?" She digs through the freezer, retrieving a tall glass bottle studded in crystals. "Oh, this stuff is great. Eleanor, you must try some. You'll never be able to drink anything else."

I shake my head, slowly sliding off the bed. "No, thank you. I don't drink."

Vivienne shrugs nonchalantly. "Have you asked about St. Tropez yet?"

Jack glares at her, and through clenched teeth, says, "Get. Out."

Vivienne chuckles, unscrewing the lid. "Jack, if you two are going to "date"," she says using air quotes, "she should know the truth." Her eyes flick over to me, the sharpness in her gaze is paralleled to Evelyns.

I steel myself, trying to prepare for the barrage of salacious details of their steamy vacation that I'm sure rivals any twisted, dark fantasies you might find in the back of a bookstore. My heart aches. *I have to forgive whatever he did with Vivienne in his past. He didn't even know me then, at least not in the flesh. And if any teen soap opera is to be believed, sex is normal in a relationship, right?* My heart hurts. *Is it wrong that I wish he had waited?*

"We made promises to each other that no matter who he dates or spends his time with, we'll end up together. We even exchanged the rings his father gave to us."

*Wait, does that mean that they hadn't?*

"Okay," I say, not quite seeing the dilemma. "Teens do stupid things all the time. I'm sure you've told Poppy you'll be BFFs always. Everyone makes dumb promises they don't keep."

Vivienne quickly pulls the bottle from her lip, laughing. Vodka dribbles down her chin as she nearly spits. She wipes it away and shakes her hand. "You still don't understand, do you? You aren't one of us. We're so far above you, you're nothing."

My stomach drops.

Jack reaches into the top drawer of his nightstand.

Vivienne continues, "Jack and I will move forward as planned, and there's nothing you can do about it. Get pregnant, we'll get rid of it. Scream and cry, we'll commit you. Hang around sulking, we'll call the lawyers. Jack not only assured me of our future, but our parents as well. You don't turn your back on a vow made to Allen Woods. Why do you think he was so gracious to you tonight? He knows a plaything when he sees it."

I reflect back on dinner. Allen couldn't have been ruder if he had spit in my eye. I almost smile, relieved. *Perhaps I'm a threat after all.* "If I'm temporary, Vivienne, why are you here? Why do you care?" I mumble, wishing I could sound braver, bolder.

Her skin blazes in scarlet, her glare reaches a new level of loathing. "You stupid girl. You don't know what you've just done."

"Do not threaten her, Vivienne. St. Tropez doesn't matter. I told you we were done. And I meant it."

Jack's bedroom door swings open, two bulging polo wearing men march in, turning to Jack.

"Martin, Gregorio, Vivienne would like an escort out. See that she makes it to her car safely," Jack says calmly.

Vivienne scoffs. "Nice, Jack. Fine. I'm gone. But remember what I said. Allen is the most powerful man in the world, and he chose *me*." She spins on her heel and pushes her way through the muscle men. "Get out of my way."

The men nod their head to Jack and follow her out, closing the door behind them.

"I'm really sorry about that," he says, scooting across his bed to me.

"Jack, did you and Vivienne…ever…you know…" I ask, dreading the answer. She's an Aphrodite, the most intimidating girl I've ever seen. Her looks are perfect, to say nothing of her confidence.

Jack releases a sigh. "No. But I'd be lying if I said I never wanted to. I very much did, but when the opportunity arose, I began dreaming of this other girl, and ever since there's been no one else I wanted to be with, Vivienne included. I'm sorry I didn't tell you about France. I've been avoiding it because, honestly, when I break that promise I made to Allen, I know how he'll react, and it won't be good."

I turn to face him. "Do we even have a chance, then?" I ask, my heart shattering into a thousand soul-crushing pieces. *How did we go from ecstasy to despair so quickly?*

*"Hormones, most likely. But Eleanor, as much as it pains me to admit it, if you two are soulmates, you'll be together. Twinned souls are a supernal business that must be taken seriously."*

*But how? Vivienne's right, Jack's dad is crazy powerful. And know how I know that? He's so powerful he doesn't come up on a Google search. His lackeys take credit in the media while he pulls all the strings.*

Jack places a reassuring hand on my back. "I've got a plan. Next week is spring break, we'll be in Ibiza. I'm sitting down and telling him about RISD. They'll certainly cut me off. I'll be banned from his home, accounts, trust fund, all of it."

I sigh, and my shoulders sag. "Jack, you don't realize what you're saying. A life of privilege starts to seem normal and almost quaint; it makes it hard to live without. My cousins have no idea how to survive without money, because until recently, they never had to."

"On my eighteenth birthday, I came into a portion of my trust fund. I started buying and selling stocks that my father's political friends do. I've already repaid the trust and placed ample funds in a Swiss bank account that he can't touch. But you're right, I've lived a life of privilege. I have much to be grateful for, but I'll give it all up if I have to. There's just no going back to life without you. I've long passed the Rubicon," he declares. "With those new savings, I have enough to pay for school and start a new life with you and even pay for whatever school you choose. I don't even have to go to RISD. I'll go wherever you want to. I love you." He tenderly kisses my lips, gently pulling me back down onto his bed.

I cuddle into his side, placing my head on his chest knowing despite what Jack was proposing, we are embarking on a treacherous path.

*"You have no idea…"* Elspeth whispers.

# Chapter Thirty-Three
## Buried

I wake to the raucous of slamming doors, breaking glass, and arguing aunts.

I'm not even sure how I got home last night. Everything's such a blur. After Vivienne was escorted off the Woods's estate, and we cuddled, we discussed our future. Since arriving in Salem, Jack had planned to blow off spring break with his family and friends in Ibiza, but now he was going to use that time to drop the news about Harvard and Vivienne. After I voiced my concern and asked to be left out of that conversation — to which he agreed — he gave me a tour of the estate and grounds. Jack even jokingly floated the idea of skinny dipping in the heated pool, but by that time it was nearing my curfew, so we made out in my car instead. It was *awesome*. My head felt disconnected, dizzy from passion, love, and the emotional whiplash of the evening. But thankfully, I didn't experience another bizarre episode of pain.

"No, Helen! She had no right! I can't do this anymore! I need to move out!" Marie thunders emotionally.

"Fine! I know a place you can go!" Sally counters.

I groan, rolling over in bed. "It's too early…" I grumble. I squeeze my eyes shut against the shouting.

"Sisters, please. Sal, what you did was wrong, and you know it," my mom reasons. "And Marie, hair grows back."

I peek one eye open. *Wait, what?*

Footsteps thump up the tower stairs. "Eleanor?" Mom calls sternly.

I whip the covers over my head as my door swings open. "You're still in bed?" she huffs.

"Yes," I mumble sleepily. "You guys kept me up 'til two giving me the third degree." My blankets magically roll away from me, causing me to retract into a shivering ball. "Mom!"

She flicks one finger at my bedding and with the other makes my dirty clothes fly to the hamper. "*I* didn't keep you awake. I was in bed by twelve."

"Sally and *my* sisters wouldn't leave me alone. They kept looking up Jack online and asking questions. Can't I get one more hour?" I question, exhausted. I reach for my blankets but can't unroll the blanket log my mother created.

"Another hour? Eleanor, it's already nine, on the morning of The Gathering," she quibbles before flicking the curtains open, drowning the room in sunlight.

I sit up, propping myself up on my palms. "I don't even want to go." I stop, hearing how petulant I sound and readjust my tone to be a little sweeter, a little more groveling. "I was thinking maybe I could spend the day with Jack…"

"No," she answers simply.

I groan. "Why do you suddenly care about The Gathering? We've never gone in the past," I say with a roll of my eyes.

Mom grips her hips, staring at me with only a quarter of Evelyn's potency. "Eleanor, if we want to embrace our witchcraft, we either go all the way or not at all. The Gathering is more than a festival. It's a celebration of mother Brighid coming into the full power of her maidenhood. We celebrate every spring solstice."

"Two weeks late…"

"Well, we work with the venue availability. Now get a move on it or I'll have Sally brew her pheromone potion in here and let me tell you, it doesn't smell good," she threatens. "So, get downstairs. We could use your help."

I pull on some leggings and an old school t-shirt with our tiger mascot that looked nearly identical to Kellogg's Tony the Tiger, then hurry downstairs, only now realizing that Pyewacket wasn't in my room when I woke up.

I come to an abrupt halt in the hallway. *What in the creepy hell?*

Plopped in the middle of the hallway is a naked Miss Priss. Not a single white hair could be found on her pudgy body (which wasn't actually as chubby as I was expecting). Her jowls hang in a glaring, unnerving scowl. I delicately inch around her, careful to not make eye contact as she follows my movement.

Bubbling liquid can be heard even from the dining room.

"Oh my gosh, Sal, that reeks. Are you sure that's the recipe?" Margaret questions gaging.

I open the door, spotting Margaret sitting on the counter, her legs dangling while she pinches her nose.

I gasp, clapping my hand over my nose and mouth. The smell of sulfur, old urine, and overcooked Brussels sprouts permeates the kitchen.

Sally, standing on a stepping stool, is bent over a black cauldron on the hearth, rapidly stirring with a wooden spoon. Her furrowed brow drips in sweat. "I think it needs more heat." The fire beneath it grows.

"No! You added too much hair! You didn't need that much!" Marie shouts, pouting on a wooden stool at the center island. "Miss Priss is delicate. She needs her full-bodied coat."

Margaret hops down. "I've got to get out of here or I'm going to puke. Hey Ell, would Christian come and hold my hair back if I did?" she teases.

I fold my arms indignantly across my chest. "Ugh, I shouldn't have told you that story. Only Trixie ever called him that."

"Ell babe, we've got eyes. That hottie is smoldering," Sally says, stirring faster. "Alright, my little girlies, I'd leave so you don't accidentally get splashed. Marie, I'll need your help bottling this."

Margaret and I happily exit, running straight into our mother in the dining room filling up wooden crates with glass bottles filled with different colored liquids. The lids are wrapped with twine and sealed with wax.

"Where's Shannyn?" I question, noting her absence.

"She went with Lennox to meet his parents for brunch," Mom explains without pausing or taking her eyes off her work." "I was supposed to go as well, but I'm just so far behind. Maggie, hon, can you hand me that bottle with the light green fluid?"

I nonchalantly pick up a bottle full of blood red liquid and read the label: *Bat's Blood*. I put it down, disgusted. "His parents are coming to The Gathering?"

"Of course, Lennox's parents are being honored tonight," Mom says. "Their family hails from two of Salem's most powerful witches, George Burroughs and Tituba."

"Is this for every witch in the world? How can Salem host something of that size?" Margaret questions.

Mom carefully writes out the ingredients on a label. "In the United States, there are three locations for The Gathering: West, Central, East. And not everyone comes. Many witches celebrate at home these days, but this year it's Salem's turn to host, so Committee leaders from around the world will be in attendance here," she explains, ending her writing in a little flourish.

Maggie and I get to work fetching ingredients for Mom while she explains these will be used to barter at the Gathering.

"That's right," Sally says, entering the room. "There's no money allowed at The Gathering. You bring your goods and trade them. Your mom's cures are legendary. People will pretty much trade anything for these babies."

*Pye? Where are you? You're starting to worry me.*

Mom's cellphone vibrates in her pocket. "Oh, no. Shannyn is bringing Lennox back to the house. I can't have company like this," she says, looking herself over.

"What are you talking about, Mom? You look great. It's just Lennox," Maggie says.

Mom doesn't say anything and instead gently closes her eyes, softening out the worried lines on her face. Her pale lashes become long and dark, like she has run them with designer mascara. Her platinum blonde bob that before was slightly frizzed now straightens and glosses itself like a professional blowout. Her baggy Mother's Day t-shirt hanging off her petite frames ripples and fades away like mist, revealing a metallic gold day dress, sleeveless with a tea-length skirt. Her faded blue jeans have vanished completely. Even her white 'mom shoes' have been replaced by bejeweled, pointy-toe flats.

Mine and Margaret's jaws drop with no hope of ever coming back up.

"Mom, that was like some serious Cinderella action," Maggie marvels.

Our mother smiles with a little wink.

"But why so formal?" Margaret inquires.

Mom tucks away a knowing smile. "I think Shannyn will be coming home with some exciting news." She turns to me, holding out a bottle filled with purple liquid. "Give this to your familiar, it should help him stay more or less in one piece tonight."

I take the small vial eagerly and slip it into my pocket. "Thanks, Mom."

*Pyewacket, I've got a surprise for you. Hello? What is going on? Are you mad at me or something? Please just answer me.*

"*Pyewacket isn't available...*"

"Elspeth?" I whisper. The dining room feels still, eerily so. "What did you do with Pyewacket?"

I feel a sudden sharp pain in the center of my forehead as an intrusion of my thoughts takes over. Polaroid-like images shuffle through my head; Pyewacket being dragged out of my bedroom by a shadow, his head banging against the stairs, his ears being wacked off by the trauma. Fresh mounds of earth piled next to his tiny grave. A lead block placed on his chest.

"Eleanor, where are you going?" Mom calls after me, but I can't stop to explain. I sprint to the backdoor and step out into the garden, grabbing a spade sticking out of a newly pruned plant.

*How does she still have this much power!? I thought it wasn't possible!* I fall to my knees in front of the freshly packed grave and begin digging. I keep digging until my spade clanks against something hard, then I drop the spade and claw away at the dirt. I unearth the small ebony box and pry open the lid.

Inside is Pyewacket's lifeless body. The dark chunk of lead has caved in his ribs. I hastily reach in and toss the block into the pile of dirt next to me. "Pye?"

After a moment, Pyewacket lifts his head, looking like it's ripping into two separate heads. I cringe, a little squeamish at the sight. His spirit rolls over and springs out of his grave, leaving the body behind. He curls his hind legs in, stretching out his front legs and back, then shivers and cracks trying to straighten out.

I let out a pent-up breath of relief.

*"I must employ your mother's help. It appears I have broken."* He sends, peering down at his small, dented chest. His head looks oddly spherical without his ears. *"I believe I left those on the stairs. Might I prevail upon you to fetch them for me?"*

"It was Elspeth. She's the one who did this to you, right?"

He nods, not without difficulty. *"Yes. I reached out to her. I believe our connection was too strong and she was able to...well...retaliate. But not before I ascertained some information. Eleanor she's connected to the missing witches..."*

The back door falls open.

"Eleanor! What are you doing? Get inside!" Mom calls.

Pyewacket watches my mom stick her head back inside. *"I'm not quite sure what she said. Feel like sewing?"* He peers up, going side to side where his ears should be.

I shake my head trying to keep up. "What about Elspeth and the witches? Is she killing them somehow? Pye, Trixie is convinced that Doris didn't kill her son, or herself," I say, thinking of Trixie's pained face. "I don't understand Elspeth's power here. I thought she was in Purgatory, but I've seen her. I saw her reflection in the glass at school, she reached out for me from behind my wardrobe. And now this, not to mention the havoc she wrecked the night of the Ouija board."

Mom bangs on the door, waving for us to come inside.

*"We'll continue this later, you have my word."*

"Eleanor! Come into the living room!" Margaret yells excitedly as we enter through the back door.

"The size of that thing! Wow!" Sally cheers.

"What's going on?" I ask, my hands still caked with dirt as I amble in.

Everyone is gathered in the center of the living room, Lennox included. His arms are wrapped around Shannyn's waist, head on her shoulder. Everyone is smiling, giggling, and holding glass flutes filled with bubbly liquid. Mom wipes away tears despite her broad smile.

"Ellie, dear," Marie spins around, handing me a glass. "Have some sparkling cider with the rest of us." She frowns at my dirty hands and mud slick pants.

"What are we celebrating?" As soon as the question leaves my mouth, I spot a large emerald-cut diamond on a diamond-studded yellow band on Shannyn's finger.

My jaw drops. "You're engaged?"

Lennox grins ear to ear. "Yep! I had to beg, but she finally said yes." He kisses her cheek.

"Oh, shut up no you didn't," Shannyn says, giggling. She lightly slaps his forearm slung around her abdomen.

Sally elbows my mom gently in her side. "I can't believe you knew this entire time and didn't say anything!"

Mom smiles over at my sister. "They asked me not to, they wanted to be the ones to tell everyone. Besides, unlike some people in the room that should remain nameless I can keep a secret." She eyes Sally.

Shannyn gazes at her huge engagement rings as she speaks. "We're thinking of keeping the ceremony in town, maybe The Hawthorne in October or the Ipswich Country Club. Lennox's dad has a connection, though I think I want something a little more glitzy, more glamorous," Shannyn explains, mostly talking to herself as she isn't looking for suggestions. "The Crane Estate in Ipswich would be perfectly dramatic, or do we want to rule out a destination wedding?"

Mom nods along, smiling until she gives me a double take. "Eleanor, what happened? Why are you so dirty?"

All eyes fall to me.

"Pyewacket needed some help." I peer down at my muddy knees and hands. "I won't give you guys a hug, but congratulations. I'd say welcome to the family Lennox, but you've been an honorary member for years," I say, tilting my glass at him.

"Thanks, Ell," he replies with a playful wink.

Pyewacket clears his throat. "*As lovely as this is, there's the problem of my ears.*"

"Eleanor, why don't you get cleaned up? We need to start getting ready," Mom says, eyeing a clump of mud loosening on my knee. She levitates the drink from my hand, whizzing it to the kitchen to be scrubbed.

"*Ears...*"

I make my way to the sewing room and snag a thin needle and black thread. Everyone throws me strange looks as I methodically comb the stairs for the missing cat ears. The small furry triangles are practically invisible against the dark wooden steps. Eventually, I find them on the fourth and sixth steps.

"Hold still," I tell him, perched on the trunk at the foot of my bed. I cringe as the needle cuts through something crunchy.

"*Make sure they aren't lopsided.*"

*Will it make a difference?*

"*Shall we detach your ears and find out?*"

I roughly tug on the thread, accidently making his head jerk. "We're alone now, so tell me, what has Elspeth done?"

"*Gentle,*" he begs as I pull the thread taut. "*She's connected to the missing witches.*"

"She's got that kind of power? I thought a ghost — or whatever she is — she doesn't have that kind of reach…"

"*She doesn't. The connection occurred when she was alive.*"

Now I'm completely confused. "But Elspeth was alive in the sixteen hundreds. This doesn't make any sense." I struggle to wrap my mind around it while I sew the other ear.

"*Unfortunately, that's all I have for the moment. Tonight, at The Gathering, I'll keep my ear to the ground, so to speak. See if any of the familiars have heard anything. Regrettably, when a witch dies, so does their familiar, but maybe they shared something before it happened.*"

"You're going to The Gathering?" I question, finishing the last stitch.

His eyes slide over to me. "*Of course. All familiars are expected to attend. Worry not, for you shall see little of me.*"

I tie off the knot and cut the string. "Done." I examine my handiwork and frown, noticing his right ear is a little crooked.

The grandfather clock on the landing chimes the hour. I need to get ready. But Elspeth can't be allowed to do this anymore. She may not be able to kill, but she can cut. She tried to force me to spill my blood that night over Pye. Then I remember, yesterday when I took that grimoire from my mother's room about Nefari witches, dark magic, and vengeful spirits. It had a chapter titled Binding. Pyewacket didn't want me to banish her, but perhaps I could bind her powers back to Purgatory.

I snatch the grimoire off my nightstand and search for a binding spell. Not only do I find one, but all the materials are already in my room. I squint as the chapter is handwritten.

*Nefarious Witches have displayed the ghastly ability to haunt. If a banishing incantation hasn't worked, as a banishing is often impossible against the spirit's consent, one must use a combination of earth magic and the mind spell to bind their powers to the plane from which the spirits are extending themselves…*

*Pyewacket, do you think this will work? I don't know the mind spell yet, but this doesn't require the mind spell's incantation, just the earth spell's.*

Pye bends his head over the chapter, reading the directions and ingredients. *"It does seem promising. The annotations from other witches claim the spell's prowess."* His eyes bulge, dipping closer to the page. *"Eleanor, am I seeing this ingredient correctly?"*

I peer over to where he's pointing.

*Place a bone from their familiar into the virgin candle's flame.*

I exhale, then glance over at him back away. "Pye, before you say no, she buried you, with a lead brick. Which you'll have to explain to me why the brick, but there's no telling what she'll do next. Please," I plead.

He glares. *"So, I should just pick my least favorite bone then?"*

I shrug. "I don't—wait, Pye, your teeth. They're bone. Can I have a tooth?"

Pyewacket hisses at me and trudges back to where I'm sitting on the floor. He opens his mouth. *"The back molar, if you please. No reason to look like a familiar from Appalachia."*

I reach into his open mouth, cringing, and tug on a slimy undersized tooth in the back of his mouth. I struggle to get a good grip on it. *La Caeli.* The tooth breaks off his grimy, slippery gum. Pye curses.

Holding the tooth in my hand, I carefully read the instructions. I light a wolfsbane candle, then the lily of the valley candle next to it. I dust off the grave dirt from my pants onto a little saucer placing a clover on top. I drop the tooth into the flame. *Ne Feerah.* "Blessed be." Purple smokes drifts from the candles, intermingling and swirling upward.

*"Come, you must let it sit."* Pyewacket nods to the door.

I say a prayer in my heart that it'll work and slip from the room.

The house is a flurry of energy and chaos as five witches prepare for the evening with only one bathroom with proper lighting. The second I start my shower, Margaret bangs on the door demanding I hurry up. Then Marie. Then Sally, who irritably shouts that we need more bathrooms.

On my bed is a black garment bag. My stomach coils and uncoils at the prospect of going tonight. Still wrapped in a towel, I unzip the bag. Inside is a dark crimson dress with a full skirt, tight bodice, long sleeves, and a scoop neck. I run my fingers down the fabric. It's eerily like the one I wore in my dream. My pulse escalates, I can hear my own screaming, can feel the flames licking my skin. I withdraw my hand as if I've been burned. *Maybe I shouldn't go...*

*"You won't be allowed to stay home. You might as well get moving."*
I suck in my waist, buckling the bodice with a little magical assistance. I dig through my closet looking for appropriate shoes, gasping for air. *Stupid dress.* Barely able to bend, I settle on the closest pair, my black high-tops, then tie the white apron around my waist and join the huddle in the bathroom.

Margaret sits on a stool while our mother has her long red locks gathered, pinning them up. "Are you sure you want to do a bonnet, Maggie? You have so much hair," Mom says through clamped teeth as she holds a bobby-pin.

Maggie looks at her freshly painted manicure matching her dark emerald dress with an ivory apron. "Yeah, I told Marie I'd join her."

Mom smiles, continuing to pin her hair. Shannyn sits on the lip of the tub, puckering her lips while peering into an antique gold compact. She wears a terry cloth bathrobe over her navy-blue dress with a square neck.

Mom glances at me leaning against the door frame. "Oh, good. The dress fits. I had to guess on your measurements," she says, sliding the ivory bonnet onto Maggie's pinned updo.

Maggie leaps up from her stool, turning her head about in the mirror. "Wicked," she says with a wiggling brow.

"Eleanor, do you want me to do anything with your hair?" she offers.

Margaret skips past me into the hall, giving me enough room to enter. I see now that my mom is wearing a beige dress with long sleeves that end in a point. The textured fabric has ivy embroidered on the cloth in the exact same shade of beige.

"You look beautiful, Mom."

Mom, always uncomfortable with flattery, colors at the compliment. "I've got an idea." She pushes me down onto the stool and wraps my tendrils around the curling iron, giving my hair more gloss and direction. Next, she takes black eyeliner and draws a little star on my cheek.

"Perfect," she says, admiring her handiwork. She grips my chin, looking deep into my eyes, holding my stare. Her eyes bear into mine with severe concentration.

"Um, mom?" I frown, trying to wretch my face away, which only causes her grip to tighten. "Mom, you're pinching."

She blinks several times, as if breaking from the forced staring contest. She nods her head, satisfied, and smiles. "You look great, Eleanor."

I glance in the mirror to see if she smudged my make up or left a mark. "What was that about?" My face is perfectly made up without any red marks.

"Nothing, love," Mom answers with a shrug. She glances over at my sister working her lip liner. "Shannyn, let's not gild the lily, shall we?" She gives her knee a little nudge.

We meet Marie and Sally downstairs. Marie is wearing a dark tan dress with a full white apron and bonnet, holding back Miss Priss, who's hissing at Sally.

Sally is, of course, in a black puritan dress that she would probably have been hanged for. Her scoop neck is so low with her breasts squished so high that one little jostle or hiccup and she'd suffer a major wardrobe malfunction. Her scarlet lips part in a mischievous smile. "Little pre-gaming?" she says, glasses come floating in.

Mom shakes her head. "No, no, no, we're back on the wagon, aren't we?" she says, looking at Sally pointedly, holding her hips.

Sal rolls her eyes. "Of course, I'm just bringing in that pitcher you made. If there's liquor in there, you only have yourself to blame," she says, bringing in a cloudy glass carafe. The pitcher carefully pours everyone a full cup.

Mom smiles. "Chilled lavender and honeysuckle tea. Enjoy."

"Bloody hell, Helen," Sally mumbles before taking a sip.

"To the Byrne-O'Reilly sisterhood." Mom raises her glass high in the air, then drops her hand, leaving her long stem glass floating there. She assists Margaret's glass as we all do the same, our arms hanging down at our sides. "Blessed be." We chorus.

"Well, let's make the best of this boring beverage. Drink up, witches!" Sally cheers, snatching her glass from the air.

# Chapter Thirty-Four
## The Gathering

We all pile into Marie's wood-paneled van. The cats meow their complaints at having to sit on crowded seats, or laps, or the floor.

Pyewacket hisses up at me, sitting next to my feet. *"This is insulting."*

*Tough, I don't want to be covered in your hair. Besides, your broken side kind of freaks me out.*

*"Marie was kind enough to break them back into place. Hence the black cast."*

I take out my cell phone, seeing I have two unanswered texts. One from Jack, and one from Trixie. *That's a cast? I just thought you just lost a ton of hair.*

*"You really are as observant as a doornail."*

*Freak.*

*"Blighter."*

*Why couldn't they just heal you with magic?* I send confused.

*"Decaying bones are a little more difficult to treat."*

I text Jack back congratulating him on his crew team's win and tell Trixie we'll be arriving shortly. "Do you know where you're meeting up with Lennox?" Mom questions Shannyn while sitting in the back with Margaret.

"Yes, after opening ceremonies, over by Helga's Rune stand," she answers before turning back to Margaret, discussing possible bridesmaid dresses.

"That color is going to clash with my hair," Margaret chides. "I like that silk dress," she says, scrolling through Shannyn's phone.

We drive through historic Salem, then park outside a general store. The setting sun streaks the sky in beautiful pink and orange strands on the horizon. Marie explains we will need to walk the rest of the way to Old Burying Point Cemetery. The cats part from us, insisting they have their own entrance for The Gathering.

Mom links arms with me as Shannyn and Margaret do the same. Strangely, no one passing by gives us any strange looks in our historical costumes. They barely glance in our direction beyond checking out Shannyn's backside as we pass.

"Mom," I begin, as we turn a corner, Marie promising us it's only a little farther, "aren't you a little concerned about me being here?" The worry I've been actively suppressing can no longer be contained. "Won't they mistake me for a... Nefari, or whatever?" I whisper. The sky has already lapsed from brilliant red to muted dark blue.

Mom cuddles into my arm. "There's no fear of that tonight. Just enjoy yourself. This will be a magical evening."

"Hurry ladies, we are running late," Marie mutters.

Sally and Marie quicken their pace when we approach an iron gate. A man casually dressed sits on a rocking chair at the entrance, smoking a tobacco pipe. The quiet, barren cemetery stretches out behind him.

He tips his baseball cap at us. "Evening ladies. Nice night for a walk," he says cryptically, gazing at Marie.

I grip the iron bars, peering into the historic graveyard. Grey headstones dot the ground. Most are sinking or off kilter with faded engravings. The headstones are so thin they look more like Styrofoam props left out from Halloween. Dirt paths serpentine through the hauntingly quiet burial ground.

Marie steps forward. "Yes, but I'd rather skip across the stars."

"Enjoy the milky way." He nods to Marie. "A dress makes it hard to run," he says to Sally in a similar fashion as before.

Sally opens her mouth only to look up from the corner of her eyes, thinking. "Oh, damn."

"Every year." Marie grinds her teeth.

"Mom, are we the first ones here?" Maggie asks muddled, staring at the vacant cemetery.

"Oh! Oh! But tis far more fashionable!" Sally says, self-congratulatory.

The man sighs, peering at Sally with an annoyed familiarity. "Then give it a go," he replies dryly, in code.

Shannyn steps forward, her skirt trails on the sidewalk.

He studies her face before speaking. "It looks like rain," he says.

Mom puts her arms around mine and Maggie's shoulders. "Don't worry about a secret pass code. You girls are with me. It's just for adult witches."

Shannyn winks at us before stepping through the gate and vanishing. Maggie and I rush the fence, our eyes peeled, searching for her.

"Have you seen the seven wonders?" he questions Mom.

"Yes, and I'm the eighth." She bows her head to him. "Girls, let's go!" Mom shouts over to us.

The aunts excitedly take our mother's hand and step through the gateway, disappearing into the ether. Margaret giggles, clasping my hand as we take an exaggerated step over the threshold, waiting for a zap or a spark, something possibly unpleasant.

As if our ears have emerged from underwater, we're bombarded with sound. Heavy Celtic drums pound in a cheerful beat as fiddles dance and bagpipes bellow. Spoons join in clicking and clacking. Hundreds of witches clap to the beat, some dance with friends around grave markers, but most wander about, weaving in and out of the historic headstones. Fireworks explode overhead in vibrant colors and shapes.

There are more wooden stands and tented booths than there are headstones. The male witches are dressed as early puritan farmers or judges, most with either black sixteenth century hats or modern witch hats. The female witches are far more diverse in their varying shades of dresses. Some wear simple white bonnets like Margaret and Marie. Many wear real flower crowns like my mother and Shannyn, and many wear knit witch's hats like Sally.

Marie heads to some spitting fountains while Sally skips off to the levitating rings of fire. Shannyn has already left us to meet up with her newly minted fiancée.

My mouth waters at the smell of smoked meats and freshly baked bread.

Flags from countries all over the world hang over different stalls, but the most prominently displayed flag is the green, white, and orange flag of Ireland. In fact, most booths serve food like bangers and mash, fried cabbage, colcannon, potato soup with cabbage, Irish soda bread, ham soup with cabbage, corned beef, and cabbage. Cabbage, cabbage, cabbage. Ireland has really graced our shores. Growing up, whenever Mom got homesick for Ireland, she'd make a feast primarily of cabbage and potato.

Margaret seems to notice too as she's glancing about, pointing to a stall with different colored four-leaf clovers that appear to be waving at us. "Okay, are those clovers dancing? And is this a witches' gathering or Irish Fest?"

More fireworks explode. Children holding magical sparklers shooting out fireballs run past us. The music speeds up in a ruckus Irish tune.

Mom nods to a group of witches we pass. Several gasp and speak behind cupped hands to their companion. "Well, our coven descends from the Celts and this was our year to host. Next year will be the South American chapter. Oh gosh, I miss those fried plantains," Mom muses as we meander about. She returns a curtsey to another group of witches.

"Mom," I say, glancing about seeing witches that were lounging against headstones leap to their feet, acknowledging my mother with dropped jawed awe. "What is happening? Are you like…famous?"

My mother rolls her eyes, her cheeks blooming. "Our family's line is… well known. It was a bit scandalous when I left the coven. Anyways, come on, let's get something to eat." Mom treats us to some fish and chips and a drink called an Irish Fairy, which takes like Sprite mixed with fresh juices.

As we wander from booth to booth, I keep my eye out for Trixie, but I've yet to see any sign of her. Or Pyewacket, for that matter.

"Oh girls, look over there. I loved this when I was younger. Let's go!" Mom tows us over to a red tent where a great number of younger children have congregated. Margaret shoots me an incredulous look.

The banner reads: My Very First Broom. Mom shoves us forward until we are practically stumbling into the stools that sit too low to the ground with our knees uncomfortably jutting into our chins. On the table set for third graders are staffs of either ashwood, hazel, or chestnut. The bristles you have to assemble yourself are made of twigs, corn husks, or straw. A colorful witch walks around the short tables offering to help the youngsters.

"Girls, come on, the brooms come in all sizes," Mom chides.

Maggie and I share a glance. *For Mom.*

"Add cinnamon bark," Mom suggests as we assemble our brooms. "Maggie, Ella, that's blessed vanilla over there. Make sure you oil the tip with it." Our mother gets impatient with us as she wedges herself in helping. "Now take three strands of hair from your head," she instructs, then releases an irritated sigh when we give her dubious looks. "Just do it, girls." Mom plucks six hairs from her own head and hands us each three. "Now, take mine and your own and weave it in with the twine. A mother is aways connected to her children. There, now keep those brooms in your room and if anyone means you harm, the broom will fall." Mom makes her way over to the vender, offering packets of seeds she produces from her apron pocket in exchange for the brooms we made. He excitedly accepts and kisses both my mom's hands.

The three of us go back to exploring the cemetery. Clutching our newly made brooms, we pass more stands boasting of exotic drinks and food from around the world. Many are selling Gathering souvenirs like eternal burning candles, enchanted feathers, jewelry, and large black cauldrons.

Beyond the makeshift shops and food stands are booths advertising various contests. One was even a spit fire contest that I'm certain I saw Sally rushing over with a feathery quill to sign up. Then there's a kissing booth with a sign reading: Kiss me, I'm a witch! And: Free Tarot Reading with Every Kiss. A boy with black and neon green hair eyes Margaret up and down.

"Let's keep walking," I mutter around my mother to my sister.

"Cats! We've got kittens, cats of every size and color! Get your cats here!" Male witches arm wrestle atop a wooden barrel. The men use fire, rain, wind, and mind trickery to manipulate a win. The larger of the two men is practically drowning in his own personal rain cloud, while the other man had what I think is a badger clawing at his leg. Amongst the gawkers exchanging paper bets is Mr. Edwards holding an overflowing glass stein. The man with the gnawing badger slams the other man's arm down. Winston cheers, breaking out in a jig, his kilt flapping. The badger dissipates in a cloud of smoke.

"Eleanor! Ell!" Trixie shouts over the throngs of witches. She stands tallest among her crowd. Her face beams, waving over to me from across the way. It's strange to see her enveloped in such a crowd given her pariah status at school. Her dress is mustard yellow with baby's breath and dark marigolds woven into her golden locks. Her beauty is ethereal, like a magical fairy from a storybook.

"Mom, can I catch up with you guys?" I shove my broom under my arm and pick up the folds of my skirt.

"We'll meet you at the stage for Shannyn's event," Mom calls out. I dash over to Trixie who is nearly bouncing with excitement.

"Eleanor, I'm so glad you're here!" she says, squeezing me into a vice-like hug.

I feel my back crack. "Yeah, me too!" I wheeze out.

She releases me, only to cup my face, peering into my eyes with relief. "Oh, good." Trixie slides an arm around my waist. "Guys, this is my friend Eleanor O'Reilly, her family are the Byrnes!"

There are three girls and four boys. The boys seem in protest of the dress code as they're dressed in white from head to toe under gray trench coats. Two of them have facial piercings. They appear as if they are trying with great effort to look menacing, but instead look like dejected members of a late-nineties boy band.

One of the boys closest to me, the one with the eyebrow piercing and hazard orange hair, takes a step closer to me as if to get a better look. "You're seriously a Byrne?" he questions with a bemused smile.

I shrug. "I guess, but that's my mom's maiden name. I'm Eleanor O'Reilly," I answer simply.

The girl with the streaks of bubble-gum pink in her hair laughs, throwing her whole head back. "You're kidding!" She turns to her female friend. "Told ya. Hand over the money. And no Yen! I want straight up American dollars!" she teases.

Her petite friend glares at her. "You know, that's racist!" she accuses with a tight smile. The debtor tosses a ten-dollar bill in the air, causing it to fold into a crane and fly over to her friend.

The friend who won the bet turns to me, happily snatching her prize. "Your last name might be O'Reilly, but here, you're a Byrne."

"I'm sure you're going to compete, then. Broom flying?" a girl questions, her eyes flick to the broom under my arm.

Before I can speak, my mind flashes to the dream I had several nights ago of flying across the moon on a broom with witches threatening to end me and sending me falling to the ground. *Was that some random dream or a warning?*

*"Why take a chance? Don't show off, Eleanor. Keep your feet on the ground. Your ego isn't worth a broken neck."* Pyewacket slinks to my side and sits next to my foot, peering up at the crowd.

"Is this your familiar?" the girl who made the crane coos, bending down to pet him. "He's so…" she trails off, examining his slightly matted fur, his crooked ears.

*"Dash it all. I knew you made them crooked."*

She wearily eyes Pyewacket's crinkled whiskers and cast wrapped around his middle. "Cute," she says, her face scrunched slightly repulsed, withdrawing her hand.

*"Well, her familiar looks like an arse face."*

Trixie skips over to the only boy without fake piercings. His thick, black hair hangs like a curtain mid neck, his russet skin highlights his defined cheekbones and chin. There is no denying it, the boy is hot. He's no Jack, though.

Trixie holds onto his hand while gazing up at him with dreamy schoolgirl eyes. "Eleanor, this is Sebastian Luna," she says in a nearly reverent whisper, with a flutter of her long lashes. "His family hails from the Chilean coven. His parents are actually one of the honorees tonight," she beams.

I shake his free hand. "Hey, nice to meet you."

He nods. His eyes scan my face as if trying to discern whether I'm friend or foe. Feeling awkwardly scrutinized, I glance behind me seeing someone make dark gray smoke from a fire the shape of dancing skeletons.

"Okay, can we eat? I'm starving and would kill for a kabab," a girl in her group complains, peering at Trixie, clearly establishing her as their leader.

"But we need to stop at Molly and Polly's stand first. I heard they brought their dragon water again this year. Plus, Zooey is stuck helping at the booth, so we should say hi," another boy interjects.

Trixie glances at me, then back to her friends. "You guys go ahead; I'll meet you at Molly and Polly's. Here," she retrieves small white flowers with bowed heads from her purse, "These are my snowdrops. Polly's been pestering me for a sample for years. This should get everyone a round of drinks and then some."

Sebastian gives his girlfriend a kiss on the cheek before leading the herd away, but not before shooting me a warning glance.

*What the heck?*

"*He doesn't trust you.*"

*Obviously.*

"*Trixie informed him of your vision of her diary.*"

*How did that make him angry?*

"*He's worried for her. He's not sure if you're to blame or not.*"

*Am I?*

"Oh, my giddy aunt," he sends exasperated. "*Are all modern teenagers so self-centered? Or are you a special case?*"

*I'm sorry I'm worried I put my friend in danger,* I think sarcastically.

"*We haven't even ruled out if it's simply a case of tom foolery. Your vision didn't give us much to go on.*"

The moment her friends are out of earshot, Trixie's smile vanishes. She snags my hand and hauls me past several booths until we are huddled on the outskirts of the festival by the fence.

"Trixie? Trixie, what is going on?" I struggle to catch my breath in this stupid corset that makes it nearly impossible to breathe. Pyewacket can barely keep up in his cast.

Trixie bends her head close to mine. "I found something in the archives."

I frown, not following. "What do you mean?"

"There's a library of witchcraft where The Committee meets. I was going through the archives and found something I wasn't supposed to." She stops and glances about again, paranoid. "Darn it. I think one of the wardens is listening." She nods to a male witch walking several yards away.

I peek over my shoulder at him. "I think we'll be okay. Trixie, what did you find?"

"What's happening with all the missing and murdered witches, it's happened before."

My stomach drops. An icy, fearful chill streaks from the crown of my head down my spine. "Tell me." *Does she know about Elspeth? Was Elspeth responsible for the "before"? Pyewacket said she doesn't have the power to kill.*

"*Nor does she.*"

"All dancers to the east stage, all dancers to the east stage," someone announces.

"It's all connected to the trials in the sixteen hundreds, I'm sure of it," Trixie says, her eyes blazing. A white and orange cat tiptoes out of the dark, making me jump. The cat scratches Trixie's buckle shoe, and Trixie drops down to her cat with a smile.

"So, I don't get it. Whoever is doing it now was around during the trials?" I question.

Trixie continues to stare at her cat. "You're right." She lifts her eyes to me, clasping my hands once more. "Eleanor," she says desperately, "we can't talk right now. Find me at midnight when all are gathered to dance under the full moon. We'll meet back here." She scoops up her cat and hurries away.

I release an anxious breath. *It should be over though, right? If Elspeth was somehow…influencing Nefari to harm witches, she can't anymore. Her power has been bound. Did I do this? When I reached out for my father and communicated with Elspeth instead, did I bring her forth?*

My stomach continues to lurch, threatening to purge everything that I've consumed this evening. I join the flow of people assembling in front of the largest of all the stages set up for the evening. *This isn't my fault. This isn't my fault. Oh gosh, what if a bunch of witches are dead because of me? I think I'm going to be sick.*

*"Don't get yourself worked up. Elspeth has very little power in this realm."*

"Eleanor? Whoa are you okay?" Lennox questions concerned strolling up to me. "Going to hurl?" he pats my back as I stand hunched over, my hands on my knees. People peek over their shoulder at us and stamp forward, giving me a wide berth.

"I've got some ginger root," he offers. "With some peppermint my dad blessed, so it's *very* potent." He pulls out a cling wrapped brown strip. "You chew it like gum, Buroughs family specialty."

I unwrap the gum and pop it into my mouth. "Thanks, Len," I say, gratefully chewing the most powerful tasting peppermint gum I've ever had. My mouth tingles.

"No problem, sister-in-law," he jests with a nudge of his elbow. He glances up, then waves his arm up over his head. "Helen, Mom, over here," he calls out to our mothers chatting at the very edge of the crowd. They squeeze their way over to us with Margaret and Lennox's brother trailing behind.

"Eleanor, don't you look lovely," Sariah compliments, air kissing my cheeks.

"Thank you, I love your feathers," I say, enjoying the calming effects of the gum. I wave to the feathers in her hair and the necklace around her neck.

"I'm honoring my ancestor, Tituba," she says with a respectful bow of her head.

"Guys, guys, here she comes!" Lennox says, nodding to the stage.

Twelve dancers now donned in skimpy, sparkling leotards with itty-bitty skirts. They look similar to professional figure skaters, if those figure skaters had more skin-revealing peek-a-boos in their costumes with embellishments plastered to their skin. As promised, Shannyn's dress stands out in a bare-ly-there pink Lycra with a lightning bolt striking down her chest, swathing across her navel, ending on her hipbone. Crystals dangle from her costume like she just emerged from a shimmering pool. Though my sister could wear a garbage bag and still dazzle.

A male witch in a kilt takes center stage holding a microphone. "Good evening, witches!" The crowd cheers, and he does a little jig in response. The dancers politely clap behind him, eager to begin. "Back by popular demand, the dance of the angels! The rules are simple, the last dancer standing is our winner. Now, no hexing or charming. If another dancer is caught cheating, they are immediately disqualified..." He eyes a few dancers before continu-ing the rules.

"Mom, can we go up front? I can barely see," my 5'3" sister complains.

Mom nods to her, still speaking to Sariah. Margaret and Lennox's younger brothers snake their way through the audience for a better view.

"Let's go, Shannyn!" Lennox shouts over the music and boisterous crowd.

The presenter takes a bow and steps aside, allowing the dancers to take their positions and the band readies their instruments. Someone behind the stage blows a train whistle, practically blowing out my eardrums, and the band takes off in a traditional Irish number. The dancers immediately begin to river dance with such ferocity I thought they may *actually* fly off the stage. Shannyn's pink dress shimmers, transforming into a beguiling blue. I join the audience clapping away to the music until suddenly a dancer disappears, as if she has fallen right through the stage.

"Lennox! What the heck happened to the girl on the far left? She's gone!" I say, tugging at Lennox's shirt sleeve.

At first, he doesn't take his gaze off my sister, but after a moment, his dark brown eyes dart to where the girl vanished. "Oh yeah, that girl on the end sunk. Haven't you seen river dancing?" Four more dancers fall through and disappear, leaving only seven left on stage.

"I've seen river dancing, but I don't remember dancers falling through the stage."

"Here, I'll show you." He snaps his fingers and I float up about four feet into the air, enough to get a good view of the platform. I nearly lose my breath seeing they aren't dancing on a stage at all. Under their feet is a pool of swirling water; they are literally river dancing. My brain struggles to process what my eyes are seeing. Another dancer sinks. But from this angle, I can see them swim to the side and climb out. Several of the fallen dancers are wrapped in towels, too exhausted to dry themselves off magically. A few of them are crying, complaining that it wasn't fair.

The music stops and the remaining six dancers strike a pose. Shannyn hasn't even broken a sweat. A firm wooden floor appears under their feet. "We have our finalists!" the same witch as before announces.

The whistle blows.

The fiddlers draw back their bows and begin playing at a dizzying speed. *Maybe next year, I can join them.* The dancers leap about on stage, twirling, kicking their legs up while dancing on literal fire. I've never seen legs move so fast! Flames lick up their feet and legs, turning any remaining water into steam. As Shannyn twirls, the blue of her dress scorches away into a bright, blinding yellow.

A dancer cries out in pain. She stumbles but quickly ambles to her feet. Nearly every dancer is in excruciating pain. One of them jumps off stage, rushing over to put her feet in a metal bucket of ice. I can see her blisters from several yards away. Two witches clad in silken red and white sprint to her aid, rubbing some ointment I recognize from our own medicine cabinet.

"How are their legs not on fire?" I shout to Lennox. The competition is completely lost on me. Why would anyone want to do this? Even if they can be healed after, who would want to endure the pain?

Lennox bobs his head to the music and clapping along in time. "You have to work different spells while dancing. You'll be disqualified if you put the fire out, but a lot of dancers do the mind spell to make themselves numb and then get treated for third-degree burns later. But while you are concentrating on doing spells, you still have to do the dance while looking as graceful as my angel up there," Lennox explains, gazing up at Shannyn.

I feel a tug on my heart. *I miss Jack.*

*"Of course, you do…"* Pyewacket bemoans.

The crowd erupts in thunderous applause as Shannyn is the last one standing. The flames are extinguished.

"Whoa! They didn't even get to round three!" Lennox hollers over the cheers.

"What was round three, dodging bullets?" I tease sarcastically.

The MC comes running out, thrusting Shannyn's hand into the air. "We have a winner! The lass with the magic feet, Sssssshhhhhaaaaaannyn O'Reilly!" he screams. He hands over what appears to be a Venus Fly Trap in a terra cotta planter.

"Oh wow," my mom gasps, clapping vigorously.

Lennox cranes his head close to my ear. "That's a Rafflesia crossbred with a Butterfly Orchid. Only a few witches have successfully bred them.

Their seeds and juices produce a truth serum, can extend human life, cure leprosy; it's even been known to restart a heart that was thought past hope."

I glance at my mother again as she eyes the award enviously.

Shannyn, of course, receives more thunderous applause. After she executes a perfectly elegant curtsy, she accepts the award, then like a gazelle leaps off the stage and over the gasping audience into Lennox's open arms. Like moths to a flame, their mouths become practically fused together.

I abashedly turn away at their publicly displayed intimacy. As the crowd disperses, I see Winston a few yards away next to a rotating pig on a spit, holding my Aunt Marie tenderly. I bite my lip, wondering if she's broken his heart.

Pyewacket coughs as if clearing his throat. *"Think again, I do believe I see an emerald on her finger…"*

My heart swells with a quiet, relieved joy, and I can't help but grin. *Elspeth is bound, Shannyn's getting married, and now Marie. I'm with Jack. Maybe things can actually be okay.*

*"Eleanor, it's time. We need to meet Trixie,"* Pyewacket sends, peering up at me.

My shoulders slump. I selfishly want to walk away from investigating. Since arriving in Salem, there has been nothing but obstacles, but now my life finally feels like it's settling. I've got an amazing boyfriend, though that term seems trite now that I know we're soulmates. My family is finding happiness after the tragedy of my dad. Even my mom's smiles seem to be real.

*"Eleanor, witches are dead."*

*I know, but I'm not Nancy Drew. What can I do?*

*"We need to hear her out. Elspeth didn't take that diary, and we don't have evidence to prove it was a prank. Until then, we need to entertain any alternatives."*

*True.* I sigh. *Let's go.*

I accidentally trip into a headstone, nearly cracking my knee on it. When I reach the agreed upon spot by the fence, I rub my knee, cursing under my breath. I sit down on the thin short grass, massaging my knee.

*"Enough, your knee is fine. Do you see her anywhere?"*

I roll my eyes at him. I peek around, squinting in the darkness. The floating lamps and candles from earlier have all been extinguished, drawing people closer to the fire at the center of the Gathering.

"Do you think she forgot?" I ask, still glancing about.

Pyewacket leaps up onto a thin headstone, carefully balancing on the top. *"No. Amethyst doesn't know where she is either."*

I wait until half past midnight, but Trixie never shows…

# Chapter Thirty-Five
## Truth Comes Light

I slide my phone out of my pocket on the drive home from the Gathering and type out another text to Trixie.

Hey everything ok? I was at our spot. Please call me.

In red letters, I receive: Message Failed. Just like the last four. I shove my phone back into my pocket and start nibbling on my thumbnail nervously.

*Pye, do you know what's going on?*

Mom glances over at me approaching a red light. "You doing alright over there?"

I shrug. "I was looking for Trixie tonight but couldn't find her, and now none of my texts are going through." The odds of anything bad happening are low. We were at a witches' gathering with heavy security. Still, something feels wrong.

*"It's far more likely she got in trouble with her parents for taking whatever she did from the archive."*

"I'm sure it's fine. She probably just forgot." Mom peers down the road to her left, then her right. Traffic is clear, yet the light remains red. "Come on," she complains under her breath. With a flick of her hand, the light becomes green, and she floors it through the intersection.

"Mom, did you just turn the light green?"

She spies me from the corner of her eyes. "Yes, and it's advanced magic because you need to picture the other light going to yellow and red, all the while imagining yours going green, so don't even try it."

I roll my eyes and chuckle. A flake of mascara breaks off from my lashes and falls into my eye. I pull down the visor mirror and am taken aback by the color of my eyes. They're dull, plain blue. Not a speck of lavender to be had. *But how...* then it hits me. My mother did this when she was helping with my make-up. That's why she stared deep into my eyes. I find the small trace of mascara and finger it out of my eye before closing the visor.

"So, is it permanent?" I ask flatly, leaning against my seat. I know it's childish, but it feels like a betrayal. I wouldn't have been able to go if my eyes were left purple. *It's still unfair.*

Mom slows as we drive through the heavy wood. "No, it's not permanent. It'll most likely wear off by morning. But whenever you're around other witches, you need to have that glamour on you."

"Glamour?"

"Glamours are just part of the mind spell. Your eyes aren't *actually* blue now, it's just an illusion to others. I'm fairly surprised you see it."

I slump in my seat. "Can't we just prove I'm not Nefari?"

Mom squeezes my knee sympathetically. "I love you, and we'll figure this out, but in the meantime…"

"Yes, yes, a glamour it is." I glance back at Margaret, head lulled to the side, mouth hanging open. "Someone partied her way into an early coma."

Mom chuckles. "Yes, we stopped by Molly and Polly's. She mixed beverages, gave her a nice energy high, then came the crash. Your dad experienced the same thing. His first time attending, he mixed Molly and Polly's dragon water with their agave mint elixir, and well, he couldn't stop laughing for a good twenty minutes and spoke in puns for over an hour. Thought I'd kill him," Mom says, shaking her head with a sad smile.

I frown. Wait. "Dad came out for The Gathering?"

She nods. "Three times actually. Once when we were engaged, then after our elopement, but after that I got pregnant with Shannyn and couldn't travel. We came back when she was around three, and that was it."

My heart practically skips a beat at this new information. I have to repeat my mother's words as I struggle to process them and understand. "You were still part of this world when Shannyn was born?" *What changed? Why would they suddenly stop? My mother gave up her entire world, and for what?* Like a blindfold lifting from my mind, I suddenly understand. *I* was the reason. Shannyn is four years older than me. They suddenly stopped attending The Gathering and pushed all witchcraft from their life, including mom's family and friends. I think of my first birthday photo, Shannyn desperately trying to blow out the solo candle, Mom crouched down between us, Dad behind the camera, my infant eyes a bright, undeniable lavender.

"Oh…" My heart breaks and my eyes swim with tears that'll never fall.

Mom pulls into the garage and shuts off the car. Margaret, Phoenix, and Persephone are all still asleep in the back. "Eleanor?"

"You gave up your life for me, didn't you? I'm the reason you stopped doing magic, why you shunned everyone. You weren't ashamed. You were trying to protect me."

Mom says nothing, just stares out the windshield, her expression unreadable. "Maggie," she calls. Margaret doesn't move. "Maggie," she calls a little louder, causing my sister to stir.

Margaret yawns, stretching her arms out above her head. "Yeah?"

"We're home, time for bed," Mom says. The cats all lazily stretch, looking displeased at having been woken. Pyewacket rolls his eyes at them, watching from the middle seat.

"Okay," Maggie says sleepily, sliding the van door open. The cats lethargically follow her into the house.

Mom turns to leave.

I place a hand on her thigh. "Mom," I say, my vision blurry with tears that will never actually fall. "I'm sorry."

My mother stares at me straight faced, her eyes hard, like she's insulted. "I regret nothing, Ella. I would do it all again in a heartbeat."

"But what changed?" I implore, wracked with guilt. "My eyes are still lavender. Why couldn't you just do a glamour on me? That way you wouldn't have to give up your family."

Mom sighs. "Glamours are short-term solutions, and they aren't reliable. I would never have risked it. And what changed is…" she pauses, her eyes becoming glassy, and she struggles, swallowing, "your dad was human, his presence protected you. With him gone now, I need more help. That's why we live with my sisters. I can't protect you on my own."

I nod, my throat burns, begging for quenching tears. "We uprooted Margaret. You quit your job because of me. You sold our home."

"Your father was my home. The place I sold was just a house. My sisters, you girls, our little coven, this is now home. Like I said, Ell, I would have done it all again. Now it's late, you've got training in a few hours." Mom gives my arm a little loving pat before going inside.

*I can't believe she did that for me.*

"*Of course, you can't. You're not a mother. Speaking of which, inquire if she would fix my ears. My right ear is sewn on so far back I'm shocked it's not attached to my arse.*"

Pyewacket follows my mom into the sewing room, and I escape to the bathroom to shower. By the time I've finished, my eyes are back to their typical purple.

The night has left my legs sore, and I have a bruise forming on my knee. My calves cry when I haul myself up the tower stairs into the attic room. I reflect on my mother's words as I dress for bed. I've treated this home as something temporary. This was just my aunts' home. But my mother moved into this home when she was fourteen. Her formative years were spent here. My sister is that same age now. This place *is* my home. This room has been given to me. As long as my family, my little coven, lives within these walls, it's home.

I crawl into my bed, snuggling my head deep into my pillow. I can both smell and feel Pyewacket come into my room and curl up on my bed.

*Ears fixed?*

"Yes. You could learn a thing or two..."

*Yeah, yeah, good night.*

"*Slumber well and deep, for Mr. Woods arrives for dinner in sixteen hours...*"

I immediately picture Sally flirting, Marie measuring him to knit a sweater, my mother interrogating him, and me, slowly dying from humiliation. *Thanks for that.*

I pull the blankets up over my face, snuggling deep into my bed, curling into a ball. I feel my face relax, my shoulders slack, my breathing slow and I can hear a seagull's lonely call from somewhere far...

The sand is warm and toasty between my toes. Waves drag across the sand and recede back into the ocean. My cheeks and nose feel sun kissed, the salty tropical breeze tousles my hair, and I can finally open my eyes. The light bouncing off the turquoise water nearly blinds me. I hold my hand over my eyes on my forehead as I peer down the white sand beach. It's utterly vacant in either direction. I know this beach. I know that resort off in the distance. I know those sloping palm trees that make for a perfect hammock spot. I'm at Smathers Beach in Key West. This is my favorite beach in the world.

*Now, this is a dream I can get on board with. Pye, are you here too?* I glance about, but he's nowhere to be found. I'm completely alone. I peer down at myself, seeing my linen blend overalls with my white one-piece swimsuit underneath. I half expect to see my family come bounding down the beach or out of the ocean with snorkels. But no one is coming. I sit down in the sand, doing another once over up and down the shore. This beach is never empty; even in a hurricane, kamikaze surfers would be seen trying to catch a wave. But this is a dream. Those rules don't apply here. In dreams, anything goes.

*But why am I here? Am I coming back to Florida for a trip? Mom surprising us for spring break? If this is Shannyn's destination wedding, am I extremely under dressed?*

I lean back on my palms, watching the gentle waves lap up the sand. I wiggle my toes deeper in the sand until my feet are buried up to my ankles. I pat the mound of sand covering my feet and listlessly poke holes into it. I let my knees fall open; the sand collapses, freeing my feet. I glimpse down the empty beach again. I puff out my cheeks and blow through pursed lips, waiting for something to…

Inky black clouds roll on the horizon. A crackle of thunder spiders across the sky, lightning illuminates the entire beach in a flash. The sun sinks back behind a stormy blanket, unfurling with an ominous roar. The air is electric, and dangerously still.

I clamber to my feet and squint, trying to see through the storm. I peer up, waiting for the heavy downpour. My eyes drift down the shore, then I do a double take. A dark figure is strolling along the beach, their black dress whipping in the wind that's steadily picking up. I continue staring, trying to figure out who the thin woman is. Red hair tumbles about her face. Her features become sharper as she comes more into focus, her narrow oval face, slender eyes, and pinched nose.

Elspeth.

She's no longer obscured by a crowd of vengeful villagers, no longer a reflection or a shadow. Her cheeks are ruddy, and her skin alabaster. This is the most solid, most full-bodied I've ever seen her. She has a scrappiness about her boney structure. There's an obvious roughness, a grit down to her marrow.

Her Iris's are vicious and obsidian in color. Elspeth's thin lips curl in a malicious smile, devilish and delicious.

I shrink, glancing about wondering if I should make a break for it. *Could I outrun her? I'm not fully trained. There's no way I can defend myself. But this is my dream. Can I control the outcome?*

A lump forms in my throat; my knees shake, melting with fear.

Elspeth comes to a stop, tilting her head. "Hello, Eleanor."

I put my hands out as if I can create a force field. "What do you want? Go away. Leave me alone!" I shout.

She clucks her tongue at me. "Now, that's no way to speak to me."

I take a few steps back from her. "Actually, I think that's the perfect way to speak to you. Stay away from me. Stay away from my family. And stay away from—Blue Eyes." I order.

She arches a thin brow. "Blue-Eyes?" she says, scrunching her face like something vulgar spilled across her tongue.

I jut my chin out in the air, indignantly. "Yes. Pyewacket was a stupid name. He serves me now, a new name for a better witch."

She laughs, rolling her head back. "Oh me. I thought you would have figured it out by now. Or *Pyewacket* would have."

I glare. "We did. You're connected to the witches dying. But as a Nefari I'm sure you've killed plenty of witches."

She shrugs. "Witches, sons, daughters…none of them mattered. But that's not what I was referencing."

"I don't care what you have to say," I snap.

She strides closer until we are mere inches apart. "Do you not wonder why your eyes are violet?"

I say nothing, too frightened to speak.

"But you know why," she sneers.

I shake my head, begging myself to wake up from this horrible nightmare. "No! No, I don't. It's just a coincidence."

"You lie. You know why your eyes are violet. Why you can't cry. You knew when you saw me in that window, when you sent the glass shattering. I know what you felt." She reaches out to touch me, but I fall onto my backside trying to dodge her, then I hasten to my feet.

"No! Stop! Please!" I plead. Rain falls in heavy torrents, landing on my skin like bullets.

"I'm in your very bones, Eleanor. I created you."

I cover my ears, pleading to be saved. I cry out for Pyewacket to wake me up. For my mom to rush into my room and rescue me. My heart pulses wildly behind my ears.

"You exist because of me. I own you. Your spirit, your body, their mine. Not yours."

I fall to the ground shaking. Tears flood my eyes as rain attacks my skin. I tuck my knees into my chest and cover my head with my hands as the rain is so hard it feels like hail. *It can't be true. She's lying. It doesn't make sense. That kind of power doesn't exist in the five branches of magic! Unless, unless I'm just an illusion from the mind spell. No, no, that can't be possible. None of this is possible.*

"Look at you sniveling on the ground, crying, hiding. Pathetic little girl. You don't deserve to live."

I'm crushed under an impenetrable weight. The thundering tempest swirls around me, hammering me into the sand.

*"Eleanor, wake up. Leave this place,"* Pyewacket whispers in the corner of my mind.

*I can't. It won't let me. I'm stuck here. I'm never getting out.* My body is pummeled by the storm, breaking me down into nothing. *I am nothing. I was never anything.*

*"Don't give in, Eleanor. This is Purgatory. You don't belong here. You're alive. I want you to wake up."*

My body is going limp, numb to the point that I can't feel the rain anymore. Lightning strikes close by and thunder crashes above our heads. My surroundings grow smaller and I'm drifting.

*"No, Eleanor. You need to hold on. Hold on to Helen, to Will, to Jack."*

My mind feels like unspooling thread, slipping, and tumbling until I can no longer grasp it. I try to conjure up a picture of those names, but I can't. The names are sliding away from me until they're unrecognizable, merely pebbles in the sand.

*"Hold on, I'm getting help,"* a strange voice calls out.

"I don't belong here. You do." The woman says to me.

I tuck my knees even tighter into my chest. The tide rises, bringing the ocean's fury even closer. The angry, brutal waves smash against the sand only a mere foot from me. I wonder if I'll be submerged soon. I register grainy bits of sand sticking to my skin and crusting around my eyes.

*"Eleanor, when I count down from three, you will open your eyes."*

"Who is that?"

"No one," the woman answers.

"And who am I?"

"You are no one."

"That's right," I answer plainly. I'm free falling while somehow also motionless. I know water is crashing over me, but I can't feel it. I'm completely paralyzed. There is no fear, no relief, no joy, no anxiety, no love. Just nothingness. The woman looks disgusted and walks away from me. I'm falling, swallowed by the ocean, and alone.

*"Three, Two, One!"*

My eyes spring open. I'm in my bed, and I shoot up to a seated position gasping. My hands quiver, gripping my blankets. My eyes frantically sweep my bedroom. The midday sun pours in from my windows, painting my room in warm light. My homework is open on my desk, my violin rests next to the window seat, and grimoires are stacked neatly by my wardrobe. Everything is where it should be. Pyewacket — Blue-Eyes — stares at me tensely, sitting next to my knees. I notice three long scratches down my thigh, ripe with blood.

My chest heaves in and out as I try to catch my breath, but I can't. My hyperventilating crumbles into dry sobs. "Oh gosh. Oh my gosh. I-I-I…" I wrap my arms around myself, weeping without tears. I feel snatched from the brink of death, from the very gates of hell.

*"That wasn't Hell. That was Purgatory, where Elspeth is trapped. Hell is far worse; you can feel your guilt and sorrows in Hell, and that's all there is."*

I shake my head still overcome. My body trembles. "No, that was worse. I couldn't feel guilt if I wanted to. I felt nothing. I was nothing." My heart speeds up again; I'm about to lose all control.

*"That's because you were still alive here. You first need to lose all sense of things*

*before you become lost in Purgatory. Eventually, you would remember some things. Both good and bad, but you wouldn't be able to touch them. You'd be an empty vessel. But calm yourself, you're back now. And there are ways to keep your spirit from being dragged there."*

*Elspeth took me there?*

*"She called to you; you willingly went."*

I burst out crying again. "I can't go back there, I can't!"

*"Breathe, Eleanor. Breathe. You won't go back there."*

It looked so inviting at first. It's one of my favorite places. So many family vacations, family photos, birthdays, so many holidays were spent there. But it was a poor imitation. The sand was too coarse, the resort was dingy and empty, like it had been abandoned for years. The palm trees too sparse and the water too cold.

I lay down on my side, trying to calm my breathing while still quietly whimpering. "Could you hear what she said?"

*"Yes."*

"Is it true? She created me?"

*"Yes."*

"How is that possible?" My identity is unveiling more layers than I can comprehend. I thought discovering my heritage of a witch was a hard pill to swallow. I'm not even sure how to conceive of this. I feel myself unraveling, leaving me naked, raw, and devastated.

*"I wasn't entirely there with you, part of the luxury of being dead and stuck in this plane. I tried to make myself small so that she couldn't sense me. But her mind was open. I saw everything, including your creation."*

*It doesn't make sense.*

*"After she was found guilty of witchcraft, the night before her execution, she conferred with a demon who granted her access to the sixth branch of magic."*

"There's a sixth branch?"

He nods. *"This magic doesn't only apply to witches, but to humans as well. It is the gift of creation, of bringing forth new life. Like all Nefari, she was promised to rule in Hell after her death. She was warmly received in Hell, but without a body she saw no point in it. She wanted life."*

As I listen to Blue Eyes's explanation, I instinctually grab a pillow and hold it to my chest.

Blue Eyes continues, *"However, she had been deceived. She believed she would be able to recreate her own life, entering a brand new body but with her own spirit, not unlike reincarnation. She tried for centuries but failed every time."*

*What changed?*

*"She spoke to Lilith, the highest-ranking mistress of the Evil One, and far and*

*away the most intelligent. Elspeth worked her way up to Purgatory to be closer to the living. Lilith told her she'd need living DNA, so she scouted different lines of witches for years. That is how she decided on your mother. With Elspeth's DNA mingled with your mother and father's, you were created. That is why you have no fingerprints, why your eyes are lavender. You were created with Nefari magic."*

I let this new revelation sink in. I want to deny it, but can't. I think back on that day when I saw her face reflecting back at me from the window. I hated her, loathed her from the depths of my soul, because deep, *deep* down, I recognized her. I saw my creator.

*"You're a new spirit, a completely original new being. She may have created you, but she does not own you. You don't belong to her. Helen and William formed you; Jack is a part of you. Don't let her manipulate you into thinking otherwise."*

"Am I a Nefari then?" I question, still trying to connect all the pieces, still reeling from the discovery.

He looks down sadly. *"I honestly can't tell you. Nothing like this has ever happened before. You're completely new. You can only be a Nefari if passed down through your parent, the sins of the father and all that, or you yourself have broken the laws that govern witches."*

I sit up. "Well, right there. If Elspeth created me or whatever, then sins of the mother…"

He shakes his head once more, furrowing his brow. *"Except you have two other parents, the ones that provided you with a body. You're unique, Eleanor. The normal rules don't apply. Or perhaps they do, but again, we don't know."*

*Maybe this is why my magic doesn't obey. Why it yearns to do bad things and doesn't want to listen. Maybe my magic has two masters.*

*"Possibly."*

I peer down at my fingertips, running my thumbs over them. "Elspeth couldn't reach me until my seventeenth birthday, her connection to me is through my magic," I say, mostly to myself.

My phone on my nightstand buzzes. I see blood has dripped down onto my bed.

*"None of this changes the fact you need to be trained. You need to show your magic who its true master is. You are more powerful than her, if for no other reason than you're alive."*

My phone continues to vibrate. "Why am I bleeding?" I murmur.

*"I had to cause your physical body pain to bring you back. But I believe in you, Eleanor, and I don't say that lightly."*

Buzz… buzz…

*"For the love of—will you please answer that bloody thing?"*

I snap out of my daze and grab my phone. Unknown number. I answer anyway. "Hello?"

"Hello, is this Eleanor O'Reilly?"

"Yes," I say.

"This is Mrs. Caldwell, Trixie's mother. Is she with you?" Her mother's voice is strained, desperately trying to come across contained and emotionless.

"No. I tried texting her last night, but they kept failing. I haven't seen her since before the dance competition." My nerves kick up a notch.

She draws in a shaky breath. She sounds as if she might be crying. She clears her throat. "She didn't come home last night. We had a row. She was quite upset and insisted she'd find a ride home. Sebastian told us she planned on meeting up with you."

I shake my head, even though she can't see it. "No, she was going to meet up with me at midnight, but she didn't show. I went home with my mom and sister," I say, worried I may sound defensive. "Sebastian hasn't seen her either?"

"No," she croaks. "I must be going." She sniffs and swiftly hangs up.

My stomach drops. *Trixie is missing.*

# Chapter Thirty-Six
## Oculi Tempe

My hands are again shaking when I put my phone down. I hold my head on either side, feeling like my skull might just explode. *This is too much. Too much is happening.* Anxiety wracks my body; I need to move. I pace about my room, trying to gather my thoughts that are blowing in my head like leaves in a windstorm.

I run my hands through my hair while my stomach does backflips. *I need to think. I need to force this to make sense. Okay, witches are going missing. Elspeth has a connection dating back to when she was alive. Some unknown figure stole Trixie's diary. Trixie was researching the truth behind the murdered witches, and now she is missing.*

"What are the chances she's just…hiding out or something?" I ask, circling my bedroom.

*"I'm not sufficiently acquainted with Trixie to say whether she has a capricious nature. Based on that ill-fated phone call, Trixie's absence is unusual for her. Regrettably, I don't believe she has sequestered herself somewhere."*

I crumble onto my bed. "Oh my gosh, what am I going to do? I should have done more."

He trots across the bed to me. *"Let's not start discussing funeral arrangements just yet. You need to keep your wits about you. Training commences soon."*

"I don't care about training right now. How am I supposed to focus on magic when I've got a friend missing?" *Oh, and apparently a third parent or something!?* I begin to hyperventilate again.

A bleary-eyed Margaret pops her head into my bedroom. Spittle gathers in the corners of her mouth as she yawns. "Mr. Edwards and Shannyn are here for your training. I'm going back to bed." She shuts the door behind her.

*"Well, it appears you have no choice, Eleanor."* He levels me with a gaze. *"You'll be a better asset to Trixie and yourself if you are trained. I'll try to reach Amethyst. As long as I can get in touch with her, Trixie has a good chance. Familiars*

*don't live past their masters. Go."* He nods his head towards the door.

I hurry to find something black because of the stupid tradition that I'm sure Mr. Edwards will reinforce. I throw on a black tank and shorts, then hurry downstairs. When I reach the second landing, I see an old motel "do not disturb" sign taped to Sally's door. I chuckle with a roll of my eyes before continuing down the second set of stairs.

Mr. Edwards, with one hand on his waist, is checking his pocket watch. Shannyn sits in the armchair nearest the window, sipping tea from a dainty cup. Neither is wearing black. Instead, Mr. Edwards wears a three-piece suit while Shannyn is in tailored jeans and a sleeveless white turtleneck.

"Is there something about being a witch that makes you go crazy for tea?" I ask, strolling in.

With a flick of her finger, she dismisses her cup and saucer into the kitchen. "I'm a witch. I drink tea and cast spells," she answers sarcastically.

Winston smiles jovially, his mustache playfully waxed and curled. He snaps his pocket watch closed and slips it into his waistcoat. "Good afternoon. It appears everyone is still resting from the wicked delights of last night. I do hope you slept well, as we have the most important, and infinitely the most difficult branch to conquer today." He claps his hands together and rubs them eagerly. "Take a seat, take a seat." He motions to the floral sofa.

I plop down unable to muster any genuine enthusiasm for the training ahead of me.

Winston holds his hands behind his back, chin in the air as he takes a turn about the room. "The mind spell is the most elusive, complex, and misunderstood element of magic. One does not transform the body, not any other object, into the desired form, but merely manipulates—"

"It's an illusion," I interrupt. "Almost like what a magician does."

"Oh, great..." Shannyn bemoans, running a hand down the side of her face.

"Poppycock! Did you say magician!? Sleight of hand!? Parlor tricks? Chicanery?!" Winston storms, stopping mid-stride. The lights in the living room flicker; the glass in the sconces rattle. "Do those charlatans control neuronal cell bodies, neuropil, glial cells!? Can they make someone's mind malleable to their will?" A blue vein pulsates in Winston's forehead that is drenched in sweat and flushed with scarlet.

I open my mouth to apologize, but Winston continues to rant. I look to my sister pleadingly.

Shannyn's eyes sweep about the room, noting the quivering pictures hanging. "Mr. Edwards, clearly, Eleanor is less educated in this branch. Perhaps we can explain it better?" she says in a soothing tone. "All of this is new to her, remember? She meant no offense by it."

The lights quit flickering and the room calms. Some of the pictures are left hanging askew. Winston retrieves a hanky from his back pocket. "Yes, yes, quite, quite right. Apologies for my outburst." He dabs his forehead and the back of his neck before returning it back into his pocket.

He continues his professor's march about the room. "Today will function more as an introduction to the mind spell. To fully grasp all it encompasses is a lifelong study, one which even I myself continue to this day. However, for the average witch, nearly all your spells will affect the occipital lobe, the area of the brain that interprets sight. I'm sure you've heard of witches using glamours or transforming into rabbits, a tradition kept from the seventeenth-century colonial witches. However, you're first generation, so if you feel more comfortable disguising yourself as an owl, feel free," he informs, keeping up his pacing.

"Maybe we should start by sharing the incantation," Shannyn suggests.

Winston politely smiles. "When I assisted in training your mother—"

"You helped train my mom?" I questioned surprised.

He nods his head, his lips pursed, slightly miffed that I interrupted... again. "Your mother is twenty-two years my junior. At least in witch years, I was plenty learned by then."

I frown. "Witch years?"

He sighs, taking a seat in the chair adjacent to Shannyn. "Yes. As you should know, your next birthday will indicate that you have orbited the sun for the eighteenth cycle, but it will be three years till your body reaches that age." He removes his pipe and tin of tobacco from his inside coat pocket.

My jaw falls as my eyes pop. "Ah...I feel like that should have been shared during Magic 101. So let me get this straight. Next year, when I turn eighteen, I'll still look seventeen until I turn twenty, and on that birthday I'll look eighteen?"

His pipe immediately ignites, and he puffs out little clouds of grey smoke. "I see your study of arithmetic's has not failed you. However, I have a sneaking suspicion we will not get to your necessary training," he says disappointedly, his pipe dangling from his lips.

I feel torn in a whirlwind of battling emotions. *Should I be excited that I'll now be aging slowly? Will anyone take me seriously looking so young as a doctor? At least I'll still look good at fifty. Wait, does this mean I'm going to outlive Jack, by a lot? And my friend is still missing...*

Shannyn rights her shoulders. "No, I promised our mother she'd be trained today. Eleanor, focus. The incantation is 'Oculi Tempe'. Just as with the other branches, you must picture what you want your magic to do. As

Winston illustrated, this branch is very complicated. It'll take more concentration. What you imagine will need to be more encompassing." Shannyn rises from her seat and cranes her neck, peering down the hall. An apple gracefully zips in from the kitchen and deftly lands on the coffee table. "Change the Red Delicious, to Granny Smith. Don't close your eyes, you need to stare and watch it change."

I glance at Winston, who nods. I'm not sure why, but there's a part of me that was hoping he would wave it away and dismiss me from training. There's an itch under my skin to get out of here and escape. *I need to find Trixie. I need to tell Mom about Elspeth. But apparently, I also need to change the color of this stupid apple.*

I scoot to the edge of the sofa with my elbows on my knees and stare at the apple. I imagine the ruby shade fading away into a shiny leafy green. *Oculi Tempe.* Nothing happens. I narrow my gaze, focusing on the apple and imagining the red slipping away like a sheet being pulled to reveal the green prize beneath.

Like pixels on a computer screen, bits of red dissolve to green until the entire apple is transformed. I grin, relieved that it worked. "Done," I chime.

Shannyn's smile curls mischievously. "Pick it up."

Raising a brow skeptically, I lift it off the table. The apple immediately fades back to red.

"What the heck?" I say, glowering at the treacherous fruit.

My sister chuckles arrogantly. "All encompassing, remember? Did you imagine it being picked up, eaten, falling, smashing, flying, rotting? You only imagined it on the table. Mr. Edwards told you; this is far more complicated."

Frustrated, I place the apple back down. I steady my gaze, determined, and imagine the different possibilities the apple could encounter. Someone taking a bite out of it, cutting it into slices, falling, bruising, levitating, baked, roasted, peeled. The spongy consistency of a red delicious turning firm, crisp and tart. *Oculi Tempe.* Like a wave, green flutters out from the stem, rolling out all the way to the bottom.

Shannyn waits until the transformation is complete before snatching it off the table. She gives it a gentle squeeze, her eyebrows lifting as she appraises it. She peers at Winston before taking a tentative bite. A look of surprise leaps to her face as she crunches into the apple. She grins, chewing on the bite of her apple. "I admit, I'm impressed."

I settle back into the couch; a mild throb begins at the back of my head. Hopefully, a minor headache is all I'll receive today, given that I technically already worked the mind spell by invoking visions.

Winston's smile straightens into a thin line. His eyes follow something moving about the room. I glance about, not seeing whatever he's staring at.

"Mr. Edwards?" Shannyn calls his attention. "Should we move on with the lesson?"

His stare continues to the hallway before snapping to my sister and I. "Yes, we shall. Eleanor, please stand." He motions with his free hand.

I push off the couch to my feet.

"Turn into a rabbit," he orders before taking a puff.

Shannyn rolls her eyes to the ceiling. "Isn't that a little advanced?"

He stares at me studiously, puffing on his pipe. "She succeeded with the apple. Experiencing any pain, Eleanor?"

I shrug, eager to finish. "Nothing I can't handle." Not waiting for further discussion, I close my eyes and focus inward. I imagine the cottony fur, whiskers, long ears, and fluffy tail. I visualize what it would look like for a rabbit to be hopping around the living room, sitting in the corner, standing on its hind legs, laying down, rushing out the door, exploring the yard, the woods, rocky creek edges, burrows, and bushes. I release a slow breath, pretending that as I release the air, I'm shrinking. *Oculi Tempe.* I continue imagining that my skin is covered in fur.

I open my eyes to see Shannyn and Winston both craning over the coffee table, staring at my feet.

"Brava!" Winston cheers excitedly. "A New England Cottontail, excellent choice. Now Eleanor, to return to your normal form, you need to turn off the flow of magic. You should feel it coursing through you like a current."

*How are they seeing a rabbit?* I look down, expecting to see my legs and feet, but they have vanished. I feel my arms move so that I may look at them, but I see nothing. Peering back down, I see a small tan and white speckled rabbit. "Guys, I don't like this. I want to come back."

Winston turns back to his seat. "Cease the flow of magic, like I instructed."

I close my eyes, focusing on that steady stream I feel winding throughout my entire body. I think of a light switch like my aunts had recommended. *And off.* It continues to flow without interruption. Panic rises. I peek one eye open. Still just a rabbit. *Oh my gosh. Oh my gosh. Oh my gosh.* The bunny starts making stressed, squeaky noises like it's in pain.

"Eleanor, don't panic," Shannyn orders. "You can do this. Your magic belongs to you. It'll listen. Calm yourself, deep breaths and," she draws her hands out, touching her middle fingers to her thumbs in a meditative stance, "stop."

Winston's eyes follow some unseen thing again. "No," he says to no one in particular.

I squeeze my eyes shut. *Stop. Just stop. Stop. Stop.*

"Eleanor, your magic is only half yours. But it resides in *you.* You have the upper hand. Take courage, take charge," Winston commands.

Shannyn's face crumples in bewilderment. "What are you talking about? Of course, her magic is hers. Eleanor, you have to regain your peace of mind. You're getting worked up."

The rabbit is squealing, twitching its nose, and quivering.

"It feels your fear and looks for its other master. You need to reinforce that you are in command of your powers. You have a body, you're alive, it is one with you," Winston states, almost angrily as it continues to watch something.

*Elspeth.*

"Winston, are you having a stroke?" Shannyn questions.

My body is rigid as the magical current courses through me. I want to succumb, to give into its wishes. I think of Purgatory, fading into nothingness, feeling that vast emptiness. *No. Never again.* I straighten my invisible shoulders, lifting my chin in the air, looking inward. *I am Eleanor Elizabeth O'Reilly, you reside within me; I command you. Stop. Now.* Like a crank being turned on a water hose, my magic recedes, slow to a trickle, then ceases.

I open my eyes. The rabbit is gone, and my body is clearly present. I collapse back onto the couch, overcome with relief and drained of energy. *I don't want to do that again.*

Shannyn apprehensively looks from Winston to me and back. "Does someone want to fill me in here?"

My headache, thankfully, doesn't increase, but it does stay on a steady, pulsating beat. I meet Winston's piercing gaze.

"Eleanor has a peculiar relationship with her magic. I believe I need further examination before I can explain it," Winston answers. He cleans out his pipe before placing it back into his suit pocket.

The wheels on Shannyn's face turn at full speed. She's skeptical for sure, but she keeps her cards close to the vest. "Fine," she responds, her eyes sweeping over me. "I need to get back to school. I'm involved in a restoration project." She helps me to my feet and pulls me into a hug. "Be careful," she whispers fiercely. She releases me and walks to the door, picking up her purse. "I'm sorry I can't stay for dinner. Tell Mom I'll call her when I get back to my apartment. Winston." She nods at him before leaving.

Mr. Edwards leans back in his armchair, peering out the window, watching Shannyn leave before addressing me. "Tell me about Elspeth…"

My stomach falls. "How do you know about her? Have you seen her?"

His eyes flick away to the staircase. "She's here now."

I look over to where he's staring, yet I see nothing. "She told you, then? Wait, how are you seeing her?"

"My gift, I can commune with the dead. There's not much she can do from Purgatory." He then shifts in his seat. "You're not as clever as you might think. Sure, you've lived longer, but that doesn't make you more learned. Destroying your familiar won't give you more power in this realm. Your failure lies not in these futile attempts, but in your ignorance of your circumstance. I dare say, if Eleanor was to perish, your connection here would also cease."

The night we used the spirit board, she wanted me to sacrifice our familiar. *Was she trying to kill me too that night?*

Winston coughs roughly and pounds his chest. His face screws into a shrewd scowl. "You can't, you're bound, I feel the binding ties, you have even less power than before," he argues. His lips twitch as his anger rises. Winston's face flames in red. "You don't know Helen O'Reilly. She'll find a cure, and I'll help her if it's the last thing I do," he threatens.

Mom descends the staircase but stops, noticing Winston's glare. "Winston?" Mom inquires, placing a hand on her chest.

Mr. Edwards rips his glare from the staircase, his hands clenched into fists. "I think I must be going," he says. He picks his hat up off the arm of the chair and roughly smacks it down on his head.

*No! Wait! What just happened!? A cure for what!?*

Mom hurries down the rest of the stairs. "You're finished already? Where's Shannyn?"

I shrug, trying to catch up with everything. "She left. Had to get back for school tomorrow. Said she'll call you," I answer, my eyes fixed on Mr. Edwards.

"Eleanor transformed a red apple to green and conjured the image of a rabbit. That should be sufficient for the day," he answers tersely. "And Helen, we must speak when…" he looks flustered and furious, "when I'm in better spirits, but it will be soon. I promise."

Mom's face softens. She places a gentle hand on his forearm. "Please stay. Did you explain the history behind the incantation itself? That helped me. Winston, I know she struggles to control her powers. She needs all the…assistance she can get," Mom says, wincing.

Winston sighs, glancing over at me, then back to my soft spoken, gentle mother. "If you wish me to guide her lesson any further today, I will. But Helen, it's imperative that we speak. Perhaps tonight." He pulls out his pocket watch, examining the time. "It's 3:00 p.m, perchance we can abscond from here to speak at 8:00?"

My mother frowns. "We are having Jack Woods over for family dinner. Maybe after you finish training?" she probes.

My stomach does anxious somersaults as I watch them discuss. *Does he plan on telling her about Elspeth? How is that going to go over? I'm still reeling from it myself. I even forgot Jack is coming to dinner.*

"Ah, good lad. That is acceptable." He nods to my mother. "Tonight after dinner then."

She smiles kindly, but her eyes are nervous as they slide to me. "I need to run into town to pick up a few things. I'll be back within an hour." She tries to make her voice sound light and casual, but I know her too well for that.

Once my mother leaves, Winston settles back down in his seat. His posture is curled and frail. He sighs, straightening up as if trying to boost his own morale. "Oculi, the plural form of oculus, is Latin for—"

I shake my head at him. "I'm sorry for interrupting again, but you spoke to Elspeth. The witch who helped…" The words feel like toxic sludge on my tongue, "the witch who created—who helped make—whatever. We're connected. She explained this to you?"

He exhales, his eyes downcast. "She did, as well as further burdens you may face."

I throw my hands up in the air. "Like what? At this point, what else can she possibly throw at me?" My breathing comes rapid and shallow. I want to cry. Want to scream. Want to hit something.

"I'm aware you moved to Salem because of your father's passing, so undoubtedly you've been melancholy, but have you experienced any happiness recently, no matter how fleeting?" he questions.

I think back on my time here. *Sure, I've been happy with Jack. With Trixie. I enjoyed myself at The Gathering.* A flash of memory recalls the pain when Jack and I said we love each other. The pain was agony, the worst physical pain I've ever been in.

"Yes," I answer. "I was blissfully happy, then suddenly it was like my body was in a trash compactor." I shudder, thinking of that twisting, bone shattering pain.

Winston shakes his head sadly. "Because your magic has a connection to someone in Purgatory, where happiness can't exist, it makes your happiness here untenable. Whenever you feel pure joy, it will attack you. Weaken you. Possibly leave you comatose."

*Oh good, because my life was getting boring there for a bit.*

"But Eleanor," he scoots to the edge of his seat, "we will fight this. We'll find a cure," he assures. "Elspeth doesn't know what she's up against."

I nod, falling back into the sofa. *What does this mean for my future with*

*Jack? How can we be together if he makes me so happy I'll be in a coma?*

Winston rubs his hands on his knees. "Well, we should get back to it. Given your family's Celtic origin, we would normally use Gaelic incantations; however, I've found the Latin terminology to be more affective…"

Winston delves deeper into the incantation's origin.

*"Eleanor, I've located Amethyst. She's alive, but she's lost connection to Trixie."*

*Okay, so… what does that mean?*

*"I don't think she's in Salem anymore. If you're too far from your familiar, your connection becomes weak, almost severed."*

*Do you think Trixie just ran away?*

*"It's certainly a possibility, but I can't be sure."*

I say a silent prayer for my friend, hoping she's alright. And wherever she is, I'll find her.

# Chapter Thirty-Seven
## Lies, Revelations, and Dinner

Winston is still describing the origins of "Oculi Tempe" when Mom returns with four bags of groceries following in the air behind her. She peeks her head around the corner, grim-faced and hesitant.

Winston's back is to me, his arms in the air. "It is said the Vale of Tempe was forged by Poseidon's trident."

Mom fights a humorous smile, noting my desperate face, pleading for us to stop. I clasp my hands, begging.

She chuckles silently, then audibly clears her throat. "Would you like to stay for dinner, Winston?"

Winston blushes, perhaps realizing he's been in his own world lecturing for over an hour. "Well, I wouldn't want to impose."

Mom waves away his objection. "No imposition. We have plenty of food," she insists. "Besides, you wanted to speak to me, anyway."

I can't help but look at her in askance. *How will it look with our English teacher having dinner with us? Isn't there enough pressure tonight as it is?*

Winston smiles, the apples of his cheeks pushing his eyes into squinty slits. "Well, alright then, I accept your invitation. Eleanor, you did marvelous today. Will you excuse me? I must change before supper." He waves to his three-piece suit.

Mom and I watch him climb into his Cadillac Deville. It's almost identical to the one Cruella drove. He honks twice and waves before pulling away.

"What is he going to change into, white gloves and tailcoats?" I tease.

Mom laughs. "I don't know. He's always been...eccentric. I'm happy for him and Marie." She slings her arm around my shoulders, steering us towards the kitchen. "How did training go?"

The grocery bags have all emptied themselves and rested in a neat stack on the island. Veggies and some kind of meat wrapped in paper and tied with twine sits on the counter near the stove. While Mom pulls out her instant pot, which looks oddly out of place in a witch's kitchen, a peeler hops out of a drawer and peels a carrot while floating over the sink.

"It went okay. I kind of got stuck as a rabbit for a bit. Freaked me out," I answer, pulling out a stool from the center island.

She looks at me sympathetically. "It can be scary sometimes, but you'll get the hang of it. Wait, where is everybody? They can't still be sleeping?" she says, glancing at the time on her cell phone.

I point my thumb at the back door behind me. "Margaret has sold Sally on building an underground pool, so they're measuring a space out back, and I believe Marie is in the greenhouse. This all occurred while Winston held me hostage. Do you know all our incantations should be in Latin, regardless of ancestry?" I say, quoting him.

Mom sighs. "Oh yes, I remember." She unties the parcel wrapped meat by hand, which now seems unusual. It's strange how quickly I've acclimated.

"What are we making?" I question, watching more and more carrots rinse themselves and wait in line to be peeled and chopped.

Mom lifts a slab of meat and drops it into the pot. "Pot roast," she answers simply, dripping red wine onto the raw beef.

I flush. "Mom, I was served a seven coarse meal when I met his parents. By a staff. We can't give him pot roast. What will he think?"

Mom's brows furrow, squinting at me. "Well, if he thinks poorly of us, then he's a snob and you can do better. Besides, there's nothing wrong with pot roast. It was your father's favorite."

My heart clenches. "I know," I mumble.

"It'll be lovely, Eleanor. Sally made yeast rolls. Marie is making her lavender honey cheesecake for dessert. And Margaret even volunteered to make a spring salad." She sends the bottle of wine to empty the excess down the drain as Sally is supposedly back on the dry wagon. "Jack is still coming at seven, correct?"

I nod, thinking of his confirmation text during Winston's long-winded lesson. "Yes. Do you need my help with anything?" I restlessly adjust the potatoes next to me.

Mom shakes her head, calling over the onions. "Nope. This is your night, so if you want to start getting ready now, you can," she says. I don't deserve so kind a mother.

I kiss her cheek and dash upstairs.

I toss on some old 'Tegan and Sara' hoping that singing along to the lyrics will drown out my anxiety. Focusing on the task at hand, I decide to straighten my hair and use my natural toned makeup. I can't stop gazing at Jack's painting resting against the wall on my desk. It makes my heart flutter every time I look. I giggle girlishly to myself. *He's really all mine.* I still can't believe it. *I mean seriously, how did I get this lucky?* I pucker in the mirror just as Pyewacket—or is it Blue-Eyes now—strolls through the bedroom door, literally.

*"So, what will it be, Pyewacket or Blue-Eyes?"* he questions dryly.

I roll my lips together, swiveling in my chair to him. "Elspeth called you Pyewacket, so I don't want to call you that. The aunts named you Blue-Eyes, which makes you theirs more than mine. But I like that they referenced your eyes," I say, staring at his strange azure irises. "They're unusual, like mine. What if I just called you Blue?"

He pounces onto my bed. *"A black cat named Blue? Sounds like a terrible song title. Fine. I care not. I thought you would like to hear what Amethyst had to say."*

My heart stops. "What? What did she say?"

*"Amethyst did not go home with her; she was busy doing other things when she left, but she was aware of Trixie walking home. On her way, she ran into Jack."*

*Jack? Jack Woods? My Jack?*

He rolls his eyes. *"Is there any of other?"* He sends sardonically.

I lean against my desk, muddled. "So…then what happened?"

*"Amethyst lost contact."* Blue sounds weary.

*Maybe he knows where she is then. She told me she was fond of Jack, knew him forever. What if she asked him for help? I know he would assist her.*

Blue assesses me dubiously.

"Don't," I warn.

*"With all due respect, you may be blind where that boy is concerned."*

I stomp over to my wardrobe, pulling things off hangers and scrutinizing them before tossing them on the bed. "I'm not blind; I'm a realist. I know Jack, he wouldn't hurt her. Besides, what would his motive be? None. This is stupid. I'm not discussing this," I huff. "Moreover, I thought you were on his side."

*"I never indicated as such. I merely pointing out the bizarre turn her disappearance has taken."*

*Maybe the fight she had with her parents was bigger than Mrs. Caldwell is letting on. Maybe Jack is letting her cool off in one of the Woods's properties.*

*"It wouldn't hurt to ask…"*

*Fine. I will.*

I stare at my pile of clothes studiously, trying to figure out how Shannyn and Margaret would make sense of all this. *I told Jack it was casual, regardless of what Winston's attire might imply.* I pull my 'Velvet Underground and Nico' tee with the bruised Andy Warhol banana. Another old shirt that my dad had as a teen that I inherited. He had me listen to the whole album before I could be deemed "worthy". I turn about in the mirror. *Maybe a graphic-tee is too casual?*

"Pair it with that cardigan with the broach, then those twill shorts and textured tights," Margaret says, hovering in the doorway. "I like your hair straightened, but you need gloss spray to keep it from frizzing."

I plunk down on the trunk, feeling a little hopeless. "What about my feet?"

She squints, pursing her lips. "Ankle boots, for sure."

I pick up the discarded sweater with the bejeweled broach, a hand-me-down from Shannyn after she didn't like the shape it gave her. "Thank you. I was a bit lost."

She shrugs. "What are sisters for?" she gives me a playful wink before skipping back downstairs.

I assemble the look Maggie recommended and dig under my bed hunting for my boots. My phone trills on my dresser. I have it float over to me. Guessing the text would be from Jack, I'm startled seeing Nick's name flash on my screen.

Ell, please read the entire message before you delete it or block me. I just wanted to say I'm sorry. I know I've been acting like an ass. I think it's no secret, I like you. I think I liked you the moment I saw you on the steps. My pride was hurt when you picked Jack. But that's my problem. I have to get over it. I really want to be friends. Just friends. Promise. I hope we can be. I don't know if you're going to be around this week. My parents are taking a trip, so I'm stuck here. Any chance you would want to get our history project done?

My thumb hovers over the delete button, but I'm reminded of my mother's warning. If I push him away, cut him off, ice him out, things could go badly. He might escalate and really hurt someone. Jack assures me he could take Nick in a fight, despite Nick's size, but no amount of fighting skill will help if Nick runs him over with a car or something. I can't risk it.

I quickly type out a reply.

Hey Nick, I appreciate the apology. And yes, we can be friends. My family hasn't even discussed spring break, so it's safe to say I'll be around. Though do we even have a topic assigned yet?

I hit send.

My phone buzzes almost immediately.

Hey Eleanor! I honestly wasn't sure if I'd hear from you. Yeah, if you go to the school's website and click on classes, you can see what topic we were assigned. He does that for the overachievers who don't want to wait till after the break to get started. I guess we are one of those nerds. LOL. We've got early colonial settlers and the witch trials. When would you want to hang and work on it?

I think for a moment.

Will Friday work?

*Hopefully, Trixie will come back by then.*

Perfect. See you then.

I exhale, holding my phone. *Couldn't hurt.* I type out a message to Trixie asking if she's okay and sent it off.

A warm sensation fills my chest. It feels...*familiar.* Calming. Something tugs me to the window. I cross my room and peer down, seeing Winston parking on the gravel drive and Jack coming down the lane.

Blue chuckles. *"Well, this should be interesting. I was worried I'd miss act one."*

Winston, in a bowler hat and a black suit, tips his hat to Jack and shakes his free hand; Jack holds two bouquets in the other.

The heel of my boots clack, clack, clack as I rush down the stairs, clutching the railing as I run. "I've got it," I say, bee-lining past Sally intercepting the door. I'm slightly out of breath when I swing it open.

Winston's hand hovers in the air, about to knock. Behind him, Jack grins at seeing me.

"Come on in," I say, sweeping aside.

Winston chuckles, his eyes bouncing between Jack and me as he strolls past into the house.

Jack steps inside wearing a white button up under a navy cardigan with tailored jeans, a classic choice. He gives me a kiss and says, "These are for you," presenting the largest bouquet of white Gerber daises I have ever seen. *I've never gotten flowers from a boy before.* There are sprays of baby's breath and white roses mixed in as well, adding to the floral aroma. It's the most stunning bouquet I've ever seen. I press my nose against the silky petals and imagine walking down an aisle in an off the shoulder white dress, long train, walking towards my future, holding an identical bouquet. I wish I could force it into a vision and live it for a while.

"Thank you, Jack. I love them."

Jack wraps an arm around my waist and kisses the top of my head.

"You must be Jack, I'm Helen," Mom says, descending the stairs. She glows in a sage green midi dress. Around her neck is the string of pearls and matching earrings my dad gave her for one of her birthdays. She grasps Jack's hand in a warm handshake. "Welcome."

"Thank you," he says, handing off his second bouquet to her. A gorgeous arrangement of colorful lilies, hydrangeas, and yellow roses.

"Oh, how lovely, you didn't have to go to the trouble," Mom says, embracing her bouquet.

"May I say your house," he looks about, "may be my favorite in Salem. Victorian gothic revival, late eighteenth century?"

Mom smiles, pleasantly surprised. "Yes. I believe when my parents purchased this place, they said it was built in 1898. We've made some improvements since then," she says with a chuckle.

"It's beautiful. I like buildings with personality, homes especially." He banters expertly, but his easy nature rings with a sincerity and charm befitting a man, not some high school boy trying to impress his girlfriend's mom. "Have you ever visited Trinity Church in Boston?"

Mom nods. "Yes, gorgeous."

"Hello, Jack," Sally purrs, sauntering down the staircase one step at a time. Sally, shockingly enough, is dressed more conservatively than normal in a simple sleeveless black jumpsuit with a knotted belt that hangs loosely around her boney hips. She sidesteps my mother and pulls Jack into a hug, the bangles around her wrists jingle. She gives Jack one last squeeze before releasing him. "Come on back, it's practically a party. Do you know Winston Edwards? He teaches at your school." She strolls down the hall to the dining room.

Mom smiles with a roll of her eyes. "Here Ella, I'll take your bouquet and put them both in water."

"Thanks," I say as Mom strolls down the hall, commenting how great the flowers smell.

Jack dips his head low to my ear. "Ella?"

I shrug. "My parents are the only ones that call me that, mostly my dad."

Walking into the dining room gives me pause. The formerly peeling dark Damask wallpaper has been replaced with pale ivory and robin's egg blue chinoiserie paper. No longer is there waist-high dark wood paneling; the room is now framed by crown molding and is brightly lit by a minimalist gold chandelier that looked like a disembodied candelabra. Winston is sitting at one end, speaking lowly to Marie seated next to him.

Margaret is biting her lips, fighting a smile when she spies my startled face while setting the table. "Here, Ell, I set a place for you and Jack over here." She pats the chairs across the table from where we're standing.

"Margaret, right?" Jack asks, walking around the table to his seat.

"What is going on?" I hiss to Marie quietly walking past.

"Sally," she mumbles back.

Jack seamlessly pulls my chair out for me, still engaging with Margaret about school. "Grigg's is a little more flexible. As long as you test into advanced classes, you can take any senior level class. But there is a wide range of electives from fencing to folk dancing." He takes the chair next to me.

Margaret takes a seat across from me. "Yeah, I'm very ready for high school."

Mom and Sally march in carrying a pot roast on a serving tray, freshly baked bread, and a salad in a crystal bowl.

Jack hops to his feet, as does Winston.

Mom waves them both down, smiling her thanks. She places the roast in the center of the table and takes a seat. Sally is the first to dig in, slicing the bread she baked.

"Please, Jack, don't hesitate to dig in," Mom says, handing him the serving spoon outright. "So, are you in Eleanor's junior class?"

"No, ma'am, I'm a senior. I graduate in May," he answers while fixing himself some salad.

"Oh, please, call me Helen. Well, that's very exciting. What are your future plans?" Mom questions.

Jack colors at the complicated question.

"What's with the interrogation, Mom?" I butt in.

Brows leap up her face in surprise, though her eyes peer at me sharply. "I didn't realize I was."

Jack shakes his head, pouring himself the blackberry honeysuckle lemonade from the pitcher. "No, it's fine. I'll be heading to Rhode Island School of Design."

"Are you going straight to school or maybe taking a year off?" Sally interjects, filling her plate of mostly potato from the pot roast. "I took a year and traveled. I lived in Brazil, Argentina, Portugal, but my favorite was Peru. All those ruins, the mystery…"

"Men," Marie mumbles under her breath.

Sally's gaze slides to her sister. "I took a vow of celibacy for a full year, and I didn't break it," she snaps.

"But you made up for it after," Marie snipes.

"Rhode Island School of Design," Mom quickly jumps in. "That's very exciting. I barely sketch, and Eleanor's father couldn't draw a stick figure if all our lives depended on it," she jests, then inconspicuously shoots Marie and Sally a look when Jack peers down at his plate.

I feel flushed, just waiting for someone to slip up and use magic or say something even more untoward than what Sally already has. My eyes keep landing nervously on Margaret, who in return gives me encouraging smiles.

Winston slathers his bread in the butter Marie churned this morning. "Mr. Woods is one of my star pupils. We will greatly miss his wit and insight next year. Very sharp, just like his father." He spears a tender chunk of meat and releases a moan when it reaches his mouth. "Truly, Helen, this might be the best roast I've ever tasted. My mother's was always tough and dry."

Jack looks almost shaken as he stares at Mr. Edwards. "You know Allen?"

Winston finishes chewing and carefully swallows. "Very well, actually. You could say we were friends back in the days of yore," he teases with a sad smile. "I'd be rather surprised if he remembers, though."

Jack seems bothered by this, although I can't figure out why.

"So, Jack, what do you like to do for fun?" Marie asks, her face scrunched in a sweet smile.

Jack shares his interest in painting, that he's on our school's crew team, about Brazilian Ju Jitsu, sailing, and traveling. He indelibly charms everyone at the table, surprising even me with his gregarious nature, so different from the man who is so often stoic and pensive. He has everyone laughing with his quick wit, Mom giggling with a napkin pulled up by her mouth, Sally banging her knee, causing Winston's cheeks to go scarlet. Margaret is snorting and Marie dabs at tears.

I struggle to join in, feeling like I'm on the outside looking in. This already feels like a memory. Faded and distant. Sipping my lemonade, I feel adrift, alone and disconnected. I peer at their faces wishing I didn't know Elspeth. I rub my fingertips together. *If Elspeth hadn't created me, I wouldn't be here. Mom and Dad helped, but my spirit is from Elspeth.* It makes me wonder. *Did I take someone else's place?*

I feel a soft nudge under the table; Jack is caressing my knee with his. He's peering at me from the corner of his eyes, curious and concerned, while Marie is regaling everyone with her days at Trinity in Dublin.

*"Someone's coming."* Blue appears at my side from under the table.

There's a loud bang at the door, then the irritating doorbell screeches. BANG. BANG. BANG.

Mom frowns, dabbing her lips with her napkin. "Who could that be?" She hurries from the dining room. Persephone joins her in the hall and stands guard at the door. She creaks the door open. "Oh, hi, Harry, Aggie. What can I do for you?" Mom says friendly but bewildered.

"Excuse us, Helen, we need to speak to your daughter now." Mrs. Caldwell cranes her neck around my mother, standing on her tippy toes. Her eyes, red and full of fire and outrage, meet mine. "You!" She brusquely brushes past my mother.

"Agatha," Mom calls as Mrs. Caldwell marches down the hall towards us. Her husband utters his apologies to my mother.

Trixie's mother stomps into the dining room and comes to an abrupt halt, noticing Jack seated next to me. Her jaw flaps flustered, her eyes dart about. "Jack," she says through clenched teeth, "would you excuse us for a moment? I would like to speak to Eleanor alone." Her glare falls back on me. She steps back startled; her face is ashen and her hand flutters to her chest.

"Margaret, why don't you give Jack a tour upstairs," Sally suggests, rising to her feet, joining my mother's side.

Maggie peers over at me, made uneasy by the intruders and desperately wanting to stay. "Okay," she finally relents.

Jack looks at the Caldwells with a disquieted apprehension. He gives my hand a gentle squeeze before rising to his feet, following Margaret out. He gives me one last look before disappearing down the hall.

Everyone waits, listening to them climb the stairs out of earshot.

Mrs. Caldwell's head snaps in my direction. She tries to make her way around the table to me but Winston pushes out his chair, blocking the narrow path and Marie rushes to her feet.

Trixie's mother puts her hands on her hips, towering over Winston who is still casually seated, appearing as if unbothered by their disruption. "I understand you, Marie. Despite being on the Committee, which will no longer be the case. She's your niece. But you, Winston, I expected more from you. You who honors tradition, who upholds our way of life with such ferocity. To protect that creature is beneath you."

"Hey, watch it!" my mother warns, holding her finger to Agatha. Despite the fury flaming in my mother's voice, I see her hands tremble, her knees shaking against the edge of the table with fear.

My eyes gloss but refuse to do more, despite my desperation. "Please, you don't understand!" I cry.

Mr. Caldwell, who had at first appeared uncomfortable with such confrontation, now pushes his way farther into the dining room. "You know our laws. There's nowhere she can run," he threatens. "We didn't come here for this. But to know you have been harboring one of *them*, you're all subject to punishment." He lifts his hand palm up to me.

Blue hisses, leaping up onto the table as I skid back in my chair.

Sally nods her pointy chin towards Mr. Caldwell's outstretched arm. His suede coat sleeve ignites in flames. "Put your hand down, Harry. You don't threaten my niece. Not now, not ever. Show him, Helen," Sally says, as if knowing why my mother is furiously scrolling through her phone.

Mr. Caldwell curses, extinguishing the flames.

"How dare you!" Mrs. Caldwell screams at Sally.

Winston smiles at Sally's pyrotechnics.

Mom wheels her phone around, shoving it in their faces. "See!? Eleanor is one years old in that picture. See my eyes, normal, now look at Eleanor, she has a condition."

Mr. Caldwell stares at the phone, aghast, while Mrs. Caldwell shakes her head indignantly. "No, no, you…you're manipulating the photo. She is one of them," she insists.

My mother forces the phone into her hands. "Look through the pictures, go through my phone. I can't use a glamour if I don't know what picture you're going to look at. Harrison, Agatha, you've known me for a long time. You know I'd never break our laws."

"But you left," she challenges, her eyes rising to meet my mother's before going back to the phone, furiously scrolling through every album.

Mom crosses her arms across her chest. "There's no law against leaving the coven. And I still served those around me to the best of my ability. Test me if you don't believe me; I'm not lying. Eleanor has a condition. But I knew we would be subjected to this. *That* is why I left."

The Caldwell's both pore over the phone, exchanging looks with one another. Reluctantly, she hands my mom's phone back.

"Satisfied?" Mom questions.

"Not quite." Mrs. Caldwell reaches into her kiss-lock purse and pulls out what looks like a playing card and slams it down onto the table and slides it across to me.

I squint, staring at the strange card. It's faded, aged with a simple picture of a black sun, almost like a tarot card image. "What is this?"

"She's demanding a trial in front of The Committee," Marie whispers, peering over me at the card.

"*If we need to run, Eleanor, we run. I won't allow you to be destroyed.*" Blue vows, keeping his eyes steady on the Caldwells.

My heart pounds. *What? Run? Where? Oh gosh, this can't be happening!*

Mom growls. "That can't happen. With her eyes, no amount of pictures or truth tonic will exonerate her. The Committee follows one line, kill Nefari, period. No trial. No discussion. Kill first, test later."

I stare at my mother, terrified, watching her grapple for control of the situation. One of her greatest fears is playing out before her eyes. She sacrificed everything to protect my secret, left her family behind, her true identity, her home, and now it's all crashing down around her.

Winston crosses his ankle over his knee, resting back in his chair. "Harry, Aggie, why don't you take a seat, and we'll explain why that trial will never come to be."

"Oh yes, it will!" Agatha cries, tears springing to her eyes. "Our Trixie is missing, and she is involved!"

Mom blanches. "What? What are you talking about?"

Winston hauls himself to his feet and eases Mrs. Caldwell into a chair as she collapses in a fit of tears. "Harry, why don't you take a seat next to your wife?" he suggests, waving to the chair and having it pull itself out for him. Instead, Mr. Harrison holds onto his wife's quivering shoulders and resolutely shakes his head.

Winston settles back down in his seat, intertwining his fingers, resting them on his protruding stomach. "Eleanor will not be called to a Committee tribunal for obvious reasons. And if you fight this, you force my hand into sharing the time Quinn gave three girls facial boils that lasted… what was it, eight weeks? I believe it even left a lasting scar on one of those poor girls. If I recall, Harry, you described it as a mere youthful indiscretion. And you, Aggie, were voted in as coven leader that year. It would be a shame to bring those to light," Winston skillfully eviscerates Caldwell's resolve.

Mrs. Caldwell's lip trembles, "It's our daughter. We can't do nothing." Her weeping eyes turn on me. "Eleanor knows more than she's saying."

I want to crawl into a hole and stay there. I can't escape this. I'm going to be judged in the witch community forever. I'll never be accepted, all because of something completely out of my control.

Mom pulls out her chair and calmly sits back down with a look of determination. "I will allow a private trial. Here at the house," she offers.

I balk. My stomach plummets. My skin is becoming sticky with sweat. "Mom, what are you saying?" I ask, my voice breaking with fear.

Mom reaches over, taking my hand. "You have nothing to fear because you have nothing to hide," she states, as if assuring herself as well as me. "How long has she been missing?" Mom probes, sincerely worried.

Mrs. Caldwell sniffs and runs a lace hanky under her nose. "We last saw her at The Gathering. It was nearly midnight."

"And you've spoken to her friends? Your other daughters? Maybe a boyfriend?" Sally prods anxiously.

Mr. Caldwell's barbarous eyes slide to Sally, still seething from the pyro techniques. "Yes, yes, and yes. Sebastian said she was going to be meeting up with Eleanor and that's the last he heard of her, too. And ever since Eleanor has moved here, Trixie has been...*different*."

"Different how?" Marie asks with a knitted brow.

"Defiant, argumentative, speaking blasphemy against The Committee, and now we know why," Mrs. Caldwell answers, glaring in my direction.

I drop my hands to my lap, keeping my gaze low. *Oh, Trixie. You were a better friend than I deserved.*

"Tomorrow at 9:00 a.m., we will hold the trial. No representative, Eleanor must speak for herself," Mr. Caldwell declares, stabbing his finger into the table like a gavel.

"What about her familiar? Trixie's, that is," Mom asks.

"Amethyst hasn't been able to reach her," cries Mrs. Caldwell.

Sally sits back down, crossing her legs, almost relieved. "Well, that's something. Perhaps Trixie will get in touch or even show up before then."

Mr. Caldwell helps his wife to her feet and wraps her shawl around her trembling shoulders. She leans into him, overcome by the whole ordeal.

"Sorry to disturb your dinner party." He peers at me sharply. "We'll see you tomorrow." He and his wife trudge to the door. No one speaks until they hear the door close behind them.

"Eleanor, you need to tell me everything you know!" Mom demands.

"I assure you, Eleanor is innocent," Winston chimes.

Mom exhales in an almost growl. "I know that, but I also think she knows something."

Blue turns to me as everyone falls into a debate about what I know, how much, and what to expect for tomorrow.

I shrink in my seat. *Blue, am I going to be okay?*

*"They'll give you veritas tonic, you'll be forced to tell the truth,"* he sends, nervous.

*But I have nothing to do with Trixie's disappearance, you know this.*

*"I know."*

*Then why do you sound so unsure?*

*"If they ask you about your eyes or the nature of your magic, you'll be forced to confess about Elspeth, putting you in danger."*

*What are we going to do?*

*"We need to figure out how to control their line of questioning."*

*Or else?*

*"You'll be found guilty, and your soul will be burned..."*

# Chapter Thirty-Eight
## To Bare it All

"I'm sorry dinner was so weird," I say, walking Jack back to his car. After the Caldwells left, we finished dinner, meandered through a quiet, awkward dessert where even Jack couldn't resuscitate the mood.

"It's okay. I don't want to be disingenuous, so I need to admit I overheard a little. Trixie is missing?" he asks, as we linger next to his car door.

My heart sinks like an anchor. In fact, my entire body feels like it's plunging downward somewhere dark, somewhere cold, somewhere alone. Somewhere even my family can't reach me. I intertwine my fingers with Jacks, as if trying to keep myself afloat, keep myself in the light. I close my eyes and roll my lips inward.

"Eleanor?" Jack pulls me closer until I'm leaning on him completely.

*I need to do this.* I release my lips and take a deep breath.

"*Eleanor...*" Blue sends wearily. "*I know what you're thinking. Don't.*"

*I don't know what tomorrow brings. He's my soulmate, my other half. He needs to know.* I glance back at the house. Blue scrambles to the living room window looking out. I turn back to him. "Can we go somewhere?"

"Sure." Jack opens the car door for me.

I gaze back at the house. A light breeze whispers through my hair and against my cheek. I picture the Caldwells all hot and full of rage, stomping up the porch steps. *Would I still want to tell Jack about witchcraft if they hadn't come tonight?* I slip inside his mustang and quickly jot out a text to my mother informing her I'm just going on a drive with Jack.

"I'm sorry about Trixie. Are her parents under the impression you have something to do with it?" he questions skeptically.

My chest aches, hoping this isn't just some stupid teenage impulse I'll regret later. "Yes, they think I know where she is or what happened. But I don't. Not really," I mumble.

He slows coming to a fork in the road. "Is there anywhere particular you would like to go, or is this an aimless drive? I'm up for either," he says encouragingly.

"Do you know where Burying Point Cemetery is?" I ask.

He nods. "I do, but I'm fairly certain they're closed. The gates are probably locked by now," he replies.

I shrug. "It's okay, I still want to go." I can't explain it, but I feel a subtle pull there, like that's the place I'm supposed to confess to him.

Jack enters the cemetery into his GPS. "I don't want to pry, Eleanor. I just—I want to be there for you. I hope you know you can trust me."

I nibble on my bottom lip. The aunts—Marie, Sally, Helen, and Winston laid out the rules plain and simple for me: tell no one who you truly are, keep your witchcraft a secret. But those types of rules don't apply to your matching soul. Mom not only told Dad, but she brought him to The Gathering.

I reach for his hand, taking comfort in the warmth of his skin and spying the little fleck of paint stain on his wrist. "I love you," I whisper.

Jack lifts my hand to his lips, bestowing a gentle kiss. "I love you, too."

That night in his room was my first time saying it to someone that wasn't required to say it back. I didn't need trumpets, didn't need the pomp and circumstance that Hollywood rom-coms make those three words out to be. I just needed Jack and the truth. And the truth, the most certain truth in my life, is that I love him. I'll always love Jack Woods. Simple. Honest. Real.

A pinching sensation nipped below my skin. The pain, the unnerving ache of happiness.

Jack coasts to a stop, reaching the graveyard, stopping just outside the entrance. He kills the engine and the lights, then ducks his head, peering out my passenger side window. "Yeah, that is most definitely closed." He nods to the chain wrapped around the gate bars.

"It's okay," I say, putting my hand on the door handle. The air smells damp, like wet leaves. The branches in the flourishing trees bend like small waving hands in the breeze. I shiver and pull my cardigan closed.

Jack walks around the car to me. "This will definitely be the strangest place I've ever broken into," he admits, gazing up at the locked gate and shoving his hands into his pockets.

My face crinkles in a smirk. "Is breaking into places a pastime of yours?" I tease.

He shrugs. "I may have participated in a few unlawful entries," he says with a sheepish grin.

I chuckle, taking his hand and strolling up to the gate.

Jack picks up the padlock, examining the keyhole. "I have to be honest

I've never successfully picked one of these. However, I did witness Marshall open one with black powder from a revolver. It took more than one try and the sound alone alerted my father's security," Jack says with a shake of his head, dropping the lock. "I guess we could climb the fence. It isn't too high," he surmises, taking a few steps back on the sidewalk assessing.

"That might not be necessary." I pick up the lock and close my eyes, visualizing a key made of air, pushing and turning the proper mechanisms. *La Caeli.* The lock pops open. I release a dramatic breath, relieved and shocked it actually worked. I remove the chains.

"Oh wow, how did you do that?" Jack steps back over to me.

"Magic," I answer, letting the chain dangle as I push the gate open.

Jack chuckles, taking my hand. We stroll through the open gate and down a winding path. Neither of us speaks as we casually saunter through the cemetery, admiring the grey speckled headstones.

"Eleanor," Jack begins as we circle back. "Is there a reason you wanted to come here?"

My stomach lurches. *No more stalling. I chose this. I want to tell him.* "Yes." I veer us off the path and to a soft patch of grass underneath a towering tree's barren canopy. This is where the dancing competition was held the night of The Gathering. *Was that really only last night?*

I sit across from Jack, nervously playing with the cuff of my sweater. "I need to tell you something." I pause, letting a few hiccups pass.

Jack reaches through the cuff of my cardigan and gently takes my restless hands in his. "There's no need to be nervous. You can tell me anything."

Hic! My heart pounds. I hold my breath, fighting for composure and against the assault of incoming hiccups. "Jack," Hic, I stop and hold my breath, forcing my chest to be still. Jack gives my hands a loving squeeze. I release the air through my nose. "I'm a witch," I blurt out.

He raises a brow. "Okay. So, you're what, a wiccan? This is Salem, so about half the girls in the public school system here claim to be. Not a huge deal. Though..." he pretends to examine me, "you're not exactly on brand. I don't see any piercings or neck tattoos. You must be new," he jokes.

I shake my head. "No, it's not like that. I'm not a wannabe witch. I'm an actual *witch.*"

"Okay," he agrees amiably, probably still imagining an incense-burning, hair-dye-abusing girl that loves the "witchy" aesthetic yet has no idea magic is real. "Vivienne believes in horoscopes. It's really okay."

I let go of his hands, considering pointing out the printless fingers... but he wouldn't know the meaning of them. I want—no I *need* him to understand. He doesn't even know who he loves or who he's meant for.

"I'm a witch. I'm magical. I've got powers. I mean, "witch" is pretty much a nickname for what we *actually* are. From my understanding, we're something closer to like angels, or maybe demi-goddesses, I'm not sure. But we aren't satanists or whatever, but that's beside the point," I ramble.

Jack's face remains impassive. "Sure. I'm okay with however you identify. I believe Honor even attended a "finding your inner goddess" seminar in the Maldives last year."

*Nope. He's still not getting it. Time for a demonstration.* My eyes dart about the cemetery until I find—a stick! *La Caeli.* The stick lifts off the ground and zips over, deftly landing in my hand.

Jack's eyes bulge to the size of saucers, and his jaw drops an inch. "Okay…how did you do that?"

"I'm not done," I say. *Ne Feerah.* The end of the stick glows for a moment, forming just a small ember. Hardly any smoke, and no flame. *Oh, come on! I need to concentrate. The aunts said adding an action can help.* I narrow my eyes on the end and lightly blow a soft breath. The stick sparks like a firework before folding out reddish orange flames like an incendiary flower.

Jack's face glows from the new flame, highlighting his flabbergasted features. "This has to be some kind of trick." His eyes move side to side, trying to logically explain what he's seeing.

I extinguish the flame. "I've got something better. Here, stand up," I order, discarding the stick. Jack's eyes rake over the silly twig on the ground, probably looking for some kind of ignition trigger. "Jack," I call, reclaiming his attention. "Grab my waist," I command, stepping closer to him, not allowing a single inch between us.

Jack straightens up, placing his square hands on me, encircling my waist. "Eleanor, I don't get what this is."

I place my hands nervously on his shoulders, gripping his sweater. Closing my eyes, I visualized us flying a few feet off the ground, not high in the air, just high enough to cease his doubt while still keeping him from needing to go to the ER if I screw up. *La Caeli.* Nothing can break my concentration. I tighten my hold on him. Slowly, confidently, our feet lift off the dirt path. I keep my eyes closed, not wanting to risk anything. I can hear Jack gasp, gripping me even tighter. Both of his arms are now wrapped completely around my waist.

Peeking one eye open, I see we've lifted higher than expected. We hover up by the trees' canopies. I let out a slow exhale, asking my magic to allow us to descend back to the ground. Jack doesn't release his vice-like hold until after our feet touch down and we're settled for a minute. I peer up at Jack, waiting for some kind of audible response, but his face is waxen and anxious.

As time ticks by, an owl hoots in the darkness and leaves crinkle in the breeze. The night speaks while Jack stays silent.

I step out of his shocked embrace, becoming nervous I've made a grave error. "I needed you to know the truth. I didn't want any more lies," I say in an unfortunately desperate tone. I play with my fingertips once again, thinking about what is missing there.

He slowly lifts his eyes from the path. "Tell me everything."

\*\*\*

"I told you I'm no good with the water spell," I say, ringing out his shirt. "I didn't learn it that long ago, and it didn't go so well." I toss him back his shirt, having dried most of it with the fire spell.

I made flower petals dance in the air, made a small sparking fireball hover above my palm. I even tried the mind spell to make Jack see a unicorn in the cemetery, but it didn't work. And I was too scared to turn into a rabbit again.

Using his flashlight on his phone, he studies my hands, then my eyes, and then my hands again. He settles back against the trunk of the tree we sit under. "I guess it all kind of makes sense. I mean, my dreams of you, the book starting on fire, the window in Mr. Andersen's classroom," he says in almost disbelief. "And I dreamt about you because we're soulmates?"

Jack repeats most of his questions and prods me with what seems to be a never-ending line of inquiries. I answer most of them to the best of my ability. He seems almost as antsy as I feel, so we stroll about the cemetery while stopping for further demonstrations. We finally linger by the fence where Trixie and I were supposed to meet up.

"Really, you fly on broomsticks? And what about warts? Should I be on the lookout?"

I roll my eyes. "That is actually a very offensive stereotype. Apparently, it makes my aunts cry every Halloween."

Jack pulls me into a warm embrace. He lets out what sounds like a relieved breath. "Thank you for telling me. Having an explanation, no matter how improbable it seems—I mean, my brain is still struggling to keep up, but it makes me feel less crazy. Thank you."

I melt into him. "But remember, you can't tell anyone. A witch's identity must stay hidden," I say into his chest as I rest there.

With his cheek resting on top of my head, he whispers, "I promise. I will do everything to keep you safe. I love you, Eleanor." He suddenly goes stiff.

I pull my head back. "Everything okay?"

He nods. "Yes, I just realized my children will be witches. I've never really given much thought to having a family. I mean, obviously I presumed one day, but I actively pushed it from my mind since my family was constantly foisting Vivienne and I together. But now I can see it. We'll be together." He draws my face to him, kissing my lips. "I want our future to start now. Every special occasion, birthday, holiday, I want to be with you. Speaking of which," he blushes, his mouth forms an adorable, crooked smile, "I know I'm supposed to ask you in an elaborate crazy way, but would you go to prom with me? I'm hoping it's not too late, being six weeks away and all," he says, partly teasing.

I can't help but giggle. "Yes, I would love to." I push up on my toes to kiss him. As our mouths move together, perfectly playing off each other's movements I feel the beginning spark of pain causing me to pull back but not ready to leave his arms. I smile, snuggling into him, refusing to let the moment of pain dampen the mood. Because just for a moment I can forget about everything outside of his arms. Trixie isn't in danger. I won't be put on trial tomorrow. And Jack will never have to let me go.

I rest peacefully in his arms as he holds me tenderly and close. My eyes drift open, aimlessly sweeping towards the fence. I notice something scratched there. D67. *How random?*

My phone chimes bursting the incandescent bubble we've made for ourselves. I stifle a groan as Jack reluctantly releases me and I fetch my phone from my pocket. It's a message from my mom.

Spoke to Winston. Come home now. We need to talk.

# Chapter Thirty-Nine
## The Trial

"I hate that my flight leaves in a few hours," Jack complains, clasping my hands to his sculpted chest. "I could still not go."

My heart sighs. "And then what? Just surprise him in the fall when you're in Rhode Island? You need to do this." I kiss him once more.

After we pull away, I run my fingertips over my lips as I watch him back out of the driveway and disappear into the night. It's strange that we've only just begun doing this. With every kiss, it feels more and more right.

I'm still a little dreamy when I walk into the house. Mom rises from the couch in the shadowed living room and flicks on a light.

I squint against the sudden light. "Mom, why were you sitting in the dark?" I step into the room, shielding my eyes as they adjust.

The skin under mom's eyes is blotchy, red, as is her nose. "I know what that woman has told you."

I shrug off my sweater, draping it over my forearm. "Are you going to tell me she's lying?"

Mom sniffs and wipes her nose with the back of her hand. "No. But it doesn't matter. You are *my* daughter. Mine and your father's. I don't care how you supposedly came about. You are an O'Reilly. Period. Winston told me about your magic attacking you when you feel joy; that will also be rectified. I don't know how, but it will. I've already begun looking into different spell books."

"Okay," I whisper back. I rest my back against the banister, wishing I could simply press pause on all of this.

Mom pulls her robe around her tightly, crossing her arms over her chest. "I expected an argument from you. I thought this would be a longer discussion," Mom says, releasing her indignant expression. "This doesn't change anything, Eleanor. Only that we know why you struggle to control your magic," she states firmly, still steeling herself for a fight of some sort.

"And why my eyes are purple, why I can't cry, or fingerprints," I say, glancing down at my hands.

"None of it matters. You're my daughter, whether you like it or not," she snaps, getting heated again. I realize now, watching her eyes turn hard, gazing away from me, that her fight isn't with me, but with Elspeth. "I like that boy, by the way. He's welcome back anytime," she says, still sour from how the conversation began. "You better get to bed; tomorrow is a complicated day."

"I'm sorry," I apologize. Dealing with grief and now this.

Mom waves me away with her hand. "Just go to bed, Ell. I'll see you in the morning."

I pass Blue on the steps.

*"We don't need to speak till morning,"* he sends petulantly.

*Works for me.*

I know I won't be able to sleep, so I attempt to tackle some of my homework, but I can't concentrate either. I move on to practicing my violin only to keep screwing up the fingering, and I can't for the life of me get the E string to tune correctly. I peruse various grimoires reading up on the inner mechanics of the mind spell. How to close your mind from your familiar. How to summon visions. Full body glamours. And how spiders are a Nefari calling card.

The grandfather clock down on the landing chimes the hour as I pace my room. *What if they ask me about my eyes?* My stomach keeps turning over. *Oh, Trixie, where the hell could you be?*

I trudge back to my desk and open my French notebook, but I keep messing up. I throw my pen at the wall, knowing the only way I'm going to pull an A in this class is to suddenly become fluent. I let my head collapse onto my arms folded on my desk. *School doesn't matter like it should. I don't know where my friend is and there's too much happening that is completely out of my control.* My eyes feel dry and heavy as grey morning light sweeps my room at 5:45 a.m.

Blue paws at my feet. *"Eleanor, wake up. The Caldwells are on their way."*

I whip my head up, disoriented. My neck and back throb from falling asleep at my desk. I rush to get ready, making the mistake of asking Blue how I look.

*"A little puritanical, like you're trying too hard. But never mind all that, they aren't here to judge your wardrobe, just you. Be downstairs looking ready before they get here."*

I fight the urge to argue and rush downstairs only to fidget on the couch waiting for them to arrive. Blue sits dutifully by my side.

There's a light thumping coming down the stairs. My mother is dressed in jeans and a cowl neck sweater, looking just as anxious as I feel.

"Don't hold anything back," Mom warns, taking a place next to me.

By the time the Caldwells arrive, Marie has set the coffee table with a delicate tea set and shortbread cookies while Sally prepped me on how to skirt around the truth.

"Sal, she'll be fine. I will interject if they are asking things they shouldn't," Mom says. She crosses her arms while an irritable frown hangs on her face.

We all jump at the crisp, hardy knock at the door.

Marie waves us all down, dusting off her hands on her peasant skirt and hurries to the door. "Aggie, Harry," Marie swings the door open, ushering them inside. "Has there been any word from Trixie?"

"If there had been, we wouldn't be here," Mrs. Caldwell snaps. After a deep breath, she adds, "I'm sorry, it was a long night." She now has a softer tone, sounding more like Trixie.

"I'm sorry. Eleanor is in the living room," Marie says, motioning towards the couch.

Mr. and Mrs. Caldwell remove their coats. Somehow, they look even thinner than they did last night. Their clothes drape from their frames like withered scarecrows. Neither of them looks like they have slept, given the bloated bags under their eyes. All the fire and furor from last night seems to have been extinguished.

Sally calls two rigid dining room chairs into the room, placing them directly across from me on the other side of the coffee table.

I don't realize my hand is shaking until my mom grips it.

They sit down wearily, exchanging disheartened looks. Mrs. Caldwell opens her mouth to speak, only to be interrupted by a knock at the door.

Winston scurries into the house, not waiting for anyone to answer. He tips his hat to everyone before removing it and taking a place next to Marie. "My apologies for my delay," he says, just before Mrs. Caldwell tries to speak. "I was going over our bylaws. Miss O'Reilly is entitled to a representative of non-relation, even in a private inquiry."

The Caldwells don't have it in them to quibble over rules. Mrs. Caldwell retrieves from her quilted purse a small glass vial with inky black liquid. She holds up for everyone to see, then empties its contents in the teacup closest to me. The moment the ebony substance hits the tea, it turns translucent.

Mom nudges me to pick up my cup.

My insides quiver; I feel like I'm about to hurl. *I don't want to do this, Blue.*

*"There's nothing to fear. Winston will intervene if it goes awry."*

I put the cup to my lips, inhaling the lemon balm tea. I'm unable to detect the added elixir. I shoot the warm tea back like a shot, worried the foreign substance would have a strange taste, but it doesn't. A little dribbles down the corner of my mouth and I wipe it away with the back of my hand.

I lean back on the sofa, feeling oddly relaxed. Even my diaphragm that was trembling moments before seems to calm itself. My joints loosen and my head becomes airy, like a summer breeze gently caressing around my skull. I half expect my eyes to slump down in a lazy haze. But instead, they feel bright, wide and unlocked, like attic windows thrown open, allowing as much light in as possible.

Mrs. Caldwell scoots to the edge of her seat, her hands folded in her lap. "Eleanor, do you know what happened to Trixie?"

"No," I answer, simply, truthfully.

"Has Trixie ever expressed desires to run away?"

"No."

My mother's eyes anxiously slide from Mrs. Caldwell to me.

"What were you two planning on discussing at midnight at the cemetery gate?"

"She found some stuff in the archives about the missing witches," I explain, not holding anything back. "She wanted to share these with me because I'm the only one who believed her that Doris and Rivers didn't kill each other or themselves."

Mrs. Caldwell's eyes fall closed for a moment; she sucks in a shaky breath. Mr. Caldwell looks at his wife with an almost *I-told-you-so* look on his face.

When Mrs. Caldwell opens her eyes, they're even glossier than before. "Eleanor, do you have any information that could help us find our daughter?"

"Possibly," I say, honestly unsure if my visions are connected to her present disappearance.

Mom gives my hand a little nervous squeeze.

Winston adjusts in his seat, hooking his ankle over his other knee.

"Then tell us," she demands impatiently.

"I had a vision of a man coming to Trixie's bedroom window, waiting until it was safe to go inside and steal her diary. I told her about this and she said she couldn't find her diary when she looked for it."

The Caldwells look at each other, confused.

"Eleanor, are you a Nefari witch?" she asks next.

*"Do not answer that,"* Blue orders.

Winston slaps his hand on the arm of his chair. "Out of line," Mr. Edwards halts the proceedings. "We have established Helen isn't a member of the Nefari thus Eleanor couldn't have been born a member, and we've proven the shade of her eyes isn't a recent development as she was photographed having violet eyes early in her life. Next question, and if you continue to ask about the Nefari, we will put an end to this inquisition and I'll bring forth a black vote, Agatha, to have you removed as head of our coven for abuse of power."

My mouth hurts like I have a hot burning coal resting on my tongue. My temples throb and jaw quivers, desperate to speak. *I need to answer them. I have to tell them about Elspeth.* My stomach lurches as if it'll force me to hurl the truth from my body.

"Fine," Mrs. Caldwell capitulates bitterly. "Did Trixie ever speak to you about her diary?"

The new question seems to have swiped the slate clean, putting my body at ease after the Nefari question. "Only that she couldn't find it after I told her about the vision I had," I reply.

Mrs. Caldwell cradles her forehead with her fingertips. "This just doesn't make sense. I don't understand," she whispers to her husband.

Mr. Caldwell straightens up. "Did Trixie ever confide in you about suspicious happenings?" he asks, taking over. "Someone following her? Threats? Worries?"

I shake my head. "No. She was only ever suspicious of the deaths and disappearances of the other witches."

Mr. Caldwell ponders this, scratching at the stubble on his chin. His eyes casually sweep to Blue, then back to me, only to do a double take, darting back to Blue nestled into my leg. He frowns. He squints, startled, his train of thought completely interrupted. "What is wrong with your familiar?"

I glance down at my gaunt, scraggily, undersized cat. His whiskers are bent and mostly gone.

*"And just what is he getting at, exactly?"*

*You're ugly.*

He peers at me from the corner of his eye. *"Words hurt, you know,"* he sarcastically sends.

"Harrison, familiars are not subject to questioning, you know this," Winston warns sharply.

Mr. Caldwell sighs. "That wasn't part of the formal line of questioning, Winston. But there is something clearly off about her cat."

"Any question you pose while she is under the guile of veritas tonic is an official inquiry. Do you have any further questions for her? If not, let's put this order to a close," Winston says sternly, holding onto the lapel of his coat.

"Do you have anything else to tell us *in regards,*" Mrs. Caldwell emphasis's, peering over at Winston, "to Trixie's disappearance?"

The pressure I was feeling from the previous question is immediately relieved. "No, I don't. I really wish I did. Trixie is my friend, probably the only *real* friend I've ever had," I answer openly. My brain can't help but go back to all my friends before Salem teasing me past the point of humor, "forgetting" to invite me to outings, and being perennially unable to ever pay me back for things.

Mr. Caldwell rests his forehead against his wife's head. "We should go. What if Trixie comes back and we're not home?"

His wife's ashen face brightens for just a moment, then falters. Her eyes swim with tears. "Thank you for your help, Eleanor." She looks at my mother. "We won't bring up her *condition* to The Committee. You have our word. But unless she masters a glamour, or you do," she looks over at me, then back to my mother, "I wouldn't bring her around The Committee. Mercy won't hear you out, nor will she wait for a baby picture," she warns. Her voice is flat and deflated.

"Thank you, I appreciate your silence. I pray Trixie will be home soon," Mom says, walking them to the door. Mom leans her back against the door as soon as they leave. Her chest inflates with air then she slowly releases.

"Can I come down now?" Maggie calls irritably from upstairs.

"Yes, it's over," Mom answers, eyes still closed.

Margaret comes stomping down the stairs. "I don't understand why I couldn't be down here while the Caldwell's were here," she murmurs.

Mom pushes off the door, striding back into the living room. "Eleanor, if you have any more premonitions, or visions, or whatever, I want to know about it. *All* of them," she orders tersely. "Now," she straightens up, snatching her purse off the hook in the entryway, "I have to take Margaret into town to pick up new cleats. Then we're going to Reds for brunch. Do you want to come?"

I shake my head, turning away from her. I can feel the shutters of my mind drawing closed.

"Anybody else?" Mom opens the offer, sounding exasperated with me.

Marie and Winston take Mom up on the offer and follow her out. "I've never been to a sporting goods store," he says, sounding like a man out of time instead of just looking like one.

Sally peeks out the window and waves goodbye, then spins on her spiked high heel. "Ell," she begins, uncharacteristically soft and agile. Her bony hands, clad in outrageously oversized rings, take up my hands. "Your mom won't say this to you because, well, everything with your dad," she sighs, peering down at our hands, "you need to prepare for the worst with Trixie. When witches go missing, they tend to not come back. I don't want you to be caught off guard if this goes sideways." She pulls me into a hug, letting my head rest numbly on her lean shoulder.

I don't know how to feel. Call it denial, call it naivety, but I'm not willing to give up on my friend just yet. She wouldn't have just thrown in the towel with me because the odds don't seem in my favor.

Sally's rings clink against each other as she lovingly runs her hand up and down my back. "Am I doing this right?" she asks. "I was never very maternal."

I grimly smile. "It's okay," I say, releasing the hug.

Sally tries to give me a warm, encouraging smile, but it instead curls upward, looking desperate, almost manic. "Why don't we work on some magic? What would you like to learn? I could teach you how to make that dragon made completely out of fire like I did at The Gathering. I did win first place," she says, wiggling her eyebrows at me.

I bite my lip, thinking. Trixie was looking into the missing witches, and then she goes missing herself. It can't be coincidence. *I have to get to the archives. Whatever she found there could help me find her.* My eyes flick up to my aunt's eager face. "Can you give me pointers on how to use a glamour?" I ask.

Sally grins wickedly. She shakes her head back and forth. Long blonde hair tumbles down from the crown of her head until she has long flowing locks a la Cher circa 2000. "Sure, I can."

An antique hand-held mirror comes flying down from her bedroom. She holds it up to me, framing my face. "Close your eyes. Imagine exactly what you want. The closer to your natural look the easier it is to maintain. Next, say the mind spell, then open your eyes."

For the next several hours, I test out different eye colors on myself. But every time Sally flashes a light on them, turns the lights off and on, or makes us leave the room, the color fades back to purple. If I blink too many times, it fades purple. She splashes water on my face. Purple. Blows air in my eye. Purple.

"Can't we just keep trying, please?"

"Um, no. I need food as do you. Besides, the more frustrated you get, the weaker your concentration gets. You need a break." Her black, shimmery palazzo pants drag on the floor as she saunters to the kitchen.

*"She's right, you know."*

I huff, falling back into the floral sofa. *Why am I so bad at this? I was able to disguise myself as a freaking bunny, but I can't maintain a stupid eye color? Maybe I should just find those stupid contacts my mom gave me?*

*"You're messing up because you want this too badly. You need to calm your mind and your nerves. And no, the contacts are no good. She wanted you to wear those if you are just passing another witch, not elbows deep in the archives next to someone on the committee. They'll tell the difference."*

I cock a dubious brow. *But a glamour will fool them?*

*"No, actually. They'll sniff that out, unless you're doing another glamour. Try changing the length of your hair and when you get to the archives change the length again, they'll feel the glamour and assume it's from your hair. Pubescent witches are constantly fiddling with their hair. It'll see perfectly ordinary to them."*

*Argh! So not only my eyes but my hair now,* I think frustratingly.

*"Well, eat up. You'll need your strength."*

Sally puts on some trashy reality TV and we both devour an egg salad sandwich on her freshly made bread overflowing with alpha sprouts and paprika.

A woman on TV screams at another plastically preserved woman, threatening to pull out her synthetic-looking extensions. Sally giggles, cheeks filled with egg. She mumbles at the woman over and over again to hit her. "When it turns physical, that's when it gets really fun. No one knows how to hit worth a damn, so it's a lot of hilarious flailing."

Sally gets her wish. The middle-aged woman gets slapped across the face.

"Woo haaa! Now we're getting started!" Sally cheers.

My phone chimes. I scramble to turn on the screen. Hoping Trixie has answered one out of my hundreds of texts. Though I'm not disappointed to see it's Jack.

> Hey couldn't get through. I've reached Spain. My dad arrives tomorrow. Gives me time to prep what I'll be saying.
> I love you and miss you.

I wish he was here. But I can't dwell on him. The moment our sandwiches are finished and the fight on TV has settled, we resume our lesson.

"Arg! Damnit!" I curse when my blue eyes resort back to lavender. "I can't do this," I shout against my hands, cupping my face.

Sally snags my wrists bringing my hands down. "Ell babe, come on. Quiet your mind, deep breaths. You've got this."

*"Eleanor, find your happy place. Obviously, not too happy, but a peaceful, restful place. Then picture what you want, all the while holding onto that tranquility. Say the incantation, and open your eyes, knowing your magic will serve that desire."*

I take the mirror from my aunt, holding it out in front of me as I close my eyes. I picture Jack walking off his Gulfstream towards me with a spring break tan and dazzling smile. *He picks me up, crushing my body into his as his lips hungrily meet mine, caressing down my neck. His hands sliding from my waist to—*

*"Ugh, stop. Bloody hell. It's like being in Sally's mind. That is not what I mean. Peaceful not randy. Stop with the snogging. Just relax."*

I clear my mind and think of Jack painting in a studio, the sun sweeping the floor as his brush expertly drips and runs across the canvas. *I'm sitting on the couch looking through medical journals and taking notes. Dinner is bubbling in a pot in our kitchen.* My heart suddenly feels at ease. *My eyes are blue. They're blue when I roll them, look left, look right, up, down, open, and closed. They're blue in the light, dark, dusk, dawn, indoor, outdoor, in my room, house, car, archives, whether or not people are looking at me, they're blue. Oculi Tempe.*

I open my eyes, and they're blue. They aren't a vibrant blue or uniquely blue. They're just a plain, dull blue, not a tinge or speck of purple. Sally tests them by startling me, splashing me, lights on and off, running outside and back inside. She aggressively nods confirming they stayed boring old blue.

"Now turn it off," she orders.

I close my eyes, focusing my magic, quiet it down and open my eyes. She grins. "You did it."

Sally promises to work on my hair after dinner. Marie and Winston went back to his place for a quiet dinner. Margaret shows off her new purchases and Mom goes into detail about Shannyn's wedding plans.

"August, if you can believe that. It gives us no time to plan," Mom complains, clearing off the dinner plates.

"I like the colors," Sally says, looking at the palettes Mom brought home. "Cream and blush. Is that wedding talk for white and light pink?"

We wait till Mom is in the bathroom taking her bath before we go back to practicing.

"And why aren't we telling your mom?" Sally questions when we move into Marie's sewing room.

"Because she'll make me nervous and I can't deal with that right now," I say determinedly. We both perch on the guest bed that was left out after Shannyn's visit.

I picture the short style and say the spell in my head, but I fail again. And again. And again.

"Stop trying to do a pixie. Do something more realistic. Not everyone can achieve my level of sexiness," Sally says, running her hand through short spikey hair.

By the time I accomplish a jaw grazing bob, I'm sweaty, fatigued, and the clock is striking midnight.

I crawl into bed with Blue, exhausted from all my complaining, laying across my feet.

Tomorrow, I go into the belly of the beast. Tomorrow, I go to The Committee.

# A Spell to Escape Purgatory

*(For those who belong in the realm of the living)*

## Ingredients:

Wolfsbane Candle        Hyacinth Candle
White Selenite Stone      Black Hematite Stone
Rose Hips Candle with Witch Blood
Scattered Objects of Pain – nails or broken glass

## Instructions:

Scatter the objects of pain in an area the size of your body. Light the three candles around the objects of pain.
Place the selenite at one end and the hematite at the opposite end Lie down on the objects of pain with your head toward the selenite. Have your familiar keep watch, as it repeats the incantation.

## Incantation:

*To flee purgatory's grasp so tight*
*Seek living plane, in the shimmering light,*
*With blood, and pain, your soul shall rise,*
*Escape the purgatorial ties*
*Blessed be*

# Chapter Forty
## Archives

*"Will you stop pacing? You're giving me a headache. We will get to the library. Not that I'm completely for this plan. I'm not even sure it's wise."*

"Yes, but you're not stopping me. I have to help Trixie," I whisper.

*"Hence, me escorting you rather than thwarting you."*

I glance at the time on my cellphone, Mom is still out on her run, and I want to be gone before she gets back and either gives me chores, insists on further practicing my magic, or calling venues for Shannyn's wedding (Mom has forbidden her from "wasting" her money on a wedding planner, not when you have sisters that can help).

There's movement in Marie's room. The floorboards creak and moan. I spin around when her door opens. *I need to get to the archives, and I can only do that with Marie's help.*

"Oh sweetie, you scared me. What are you doing up so early? Aren't you kids on holiday this week?"

I nod, hopefully not too vigorously. "Yeah, but I was wondering if I could come with you to the committee. I want to check out their library." I anxiously wring my fingers.

Marie's face falls into a sympathetic smile. "Oh pumpkin, I don't think that would be a good idea. I've got several meetings today, and I don't think we should play with fate."

My smile slumps. *No, I'm not giving in that easily.*

"Marie," I begin. "I've been practicing. My eyes will stay blue the entire time. But it's important; I need to do some research, and I promise to share with you anything I find."

Marie looks deep into my eyes, examining the blue. She flips the lights on and off. Gently holds my chin, moving my face around. My eyes remain that same dark blue shade. She releases my face and her eyes sweep me over.

"Wait, you changed your hair too?" she asks.

I shrug. "Trying something new."

She runs her hands through my short wispy strands, testing it out. "I'm very impressed. Well, we better get a move on it." she nods to the stairs. "It's in the basement of the Old Town Hall." She glances at Blue, assuming he's coming. "Grab a satchel for him to be in until you get inside the library."

We pile into her wood paneled van and quietly, at a snail's pace, make our way to Derby Square. For just a moment, I feel like a normal tourist as Marie points out the different red brick shops, cafés, museums, and the Derby Square bookshop, her favorite place in Salem. Our footsteps sound hollow across the cobblestone. "We used to hold the Gathering here, but crowd control made it impossible," she whispers.

My stomach knots as we walk up the Old Town Hall. I keep reaching up and fingering my short, angled bob. I adjust the red satchel draped across my chest, then suck in an anxious breath while Marie fishes out her keys and unlocks the green door.

My eyes sweep about, almost waiting for an intruder alert to sound off, but there's nothing. The inside looks like any other building: white plaster walls, wood floors, steel drinking fountains. Perfectly ordinary. A plaque hanging on the walls boasts of the building's historical significance. Blue pops his head out of the bag, glancing about. A woman in a pencil skirt holding a stack of papers strides past Marie, giving her a nod before breezing through a set of wooden doors. Two men come clomping down the hall animatedly talking about yesterday's Red Sox game.

Marie hoists her bag high on her shoulder. "Now sweetie, my meeting is through those doors." Her thumb points behind her. "But if you take those stairs, they'll lead you to the basement library." She dips her head low, whispering to me. "If you get lost, don't ask for help. Just call me. Only witches can see the staircase. A little mind spell illusion. Keeps the library secret." She pats me on the shoulder and nudges me towards the narrow staircase.

I take in the library with great disappointment when reaching the bottom step. I half expected a brick fireplace, rich wooden shelves overflowing with leather-bound books, Persian rugs unfurled across the floor. The smell would be heavenly, like a coffee shop in autumn. Instead, I'm greeted with scratched tiled floors, plain beige walls, rows and rows of metal bookshelves, and squeaky metal carts with piles of rolled up scrolls tied with twine. The only smell is mildew and old paper.

Blue, realizing the coast is clear, leaps down from the bag.

Bookshelves that are spaced too close together tower over me. *I don't know what I was thinking. Blue, I don't even know where to begin. I've never even done research in a library before. Everything I've ever needed to know is online.*

"*Each generation, I think we can't possibly get more hopeless, then your lot comes up…*"

My eyes scan the bookshelves as my fingers run up and down the thick spines. Most of the books aren't titled, so I randomly pull one from the shelf and thumb through it only to end up reading pest control secrets for a blossoming greenhouse. My next attempts aren't any better: headache cures, endless journals on curious cases and illnesses observed by witch midwives, relationship guides that begin with "your familiar and you". I snap the book closed and shove it back onto the shelf.

"Do you see anything, Blue?" I call out.

"*Seeing how I lack the necessary digits to pull out such tomes…no, I don't.*"

I hang my head back, releasing a groan. "Then why did you come?"

"*In case you get into trouble. This is the last place a Nefari witch should be.*"

My eyes despondently survey the shelves. "Is there an even more secret library?" I ask aloud, hoping that if there is one, it'll just reveal itself to us. My line-of-sight glides past the top of the shelf where I see B35 stenciled on the ledge. *Wait, where did I see something like that? The iron fencing where I was supposed to meet Trixie! Crap, what did it say?* I close my eyes, envisioning the black fencing, my eyes focusing on that small, almost invisible etching. *D, D something. D60? D65?*

I run through the stacks, following the sequencing of letters and numbers until I reach the D's. I slow my run, 59, 60, 61… I start pulling out random volumes. There are world maps, books on dead languages, Brighid a History, Athena a History, D67 Death. I pull out the gigantic tome that spans from my waist to my eyebrows, feeling my neglect of the gym as I schlep the book to the nearest study carrel. It lands on the tabletop with a thump. Blue leaps up and peers over the red dusty cover that has two ghostly handprints left behind that aren't mine. *Trixie.* My finger traces the outline of her long forefinger. I shake my head. *I can't get distracted. At least I know I've got the right volume.*

I flip the cover open, causing a dust plume to puff up in a sinus-attacking cloud. Inside the enormous volume are vertical columns listing a witch's name, country, date of death, and cause of death.

*Maria Alejandra Santos. New Spain, 1598. Heart removed.*
*Edda Hope Martin. England, 1599. Burned at the stake.*
*Agnet Albine Joseph Valaitis. Prussia, 1600. Drowned.*

I rapidly scan the columns looking for patterns, but there are hundreds, thousands of names from across the globe spanning centuries. Even the deaths run the gamut smattering of drownings, crushed, burned, quartered, disemboweled, hanged, beheaded, staked, crucified, the rack, iron maiden, something called "broken on the wheel", and even just "volcano".

While scanning the page, I freeze.

*Elspeth McEwen. Scotland, 1698. Tortured, burned at the stake.*

There's an unusual annotation in the margin.

*Familiar's location unknown. Body has been moved.*

*Where was your body?* I ask Blue.

*"Elspeth had arranged for it to be preserved and moved. She thought she'd need me to come back. She arranged for my body to be taken to Salem, as you know."*

I peer back down at the page, thinking of what I read about the connection witches have with their familiars. *Did you feel the torture? Or the burning?* My fingers tremble as I turn the page.

Blue hops down and wanders through the aisle behind me. *"Every second of it. I'm going to see if there's an index somewhere."*

I skip through the centuries. More witches all over the globe, all dying under seemingly random circumstances. There seems to be no connection other than the facts they're witches and their lives ended abruptly. No witnesses, no leads, no connections between them. *Is this all Trixie found? Dead witches throughout the centuries?* When I reach the twentieth century, I start seeing more suicides, car accidents, even deaths listed as simply "broom accident". *Is Trixie trying to tell me none of these are accidents?*

I check the time on my phone; I have three missed calls from my mom and one from Marie. I call my mom back, leaving her a message that I'm with Marie at The Old Town Hall, that my glamour has been holding up, and that I have Blue with me for further protection. Just alone in the library. Marie is looking out for me, too. I quickly listen to Marie's message that her meeting will go past sundown and that I might need to get a ride home.

I snag a power bar from my bag and continue my research. Blue helps me find more tomes recording witches' deaths. None of them seem all that relevant to the current crisis.

Blue leaps back up onto the table. *"You need to let your magic guide you."*

I knit my brown incredulously. "How the heck do I do that?" I growl.

*"No one is here, and all the academic institutions are on holiday, so I don't think we need to worry about secrecy. Lay down."*

Eager to receive some answers, I do as I'm told. I cross my feet at my ankles and rest my hands on my abdomen, then stare at the ceiling, noticing a crack in the corner where there's an unsightly water stain. "Now what?"

"*Close your eyes. Have your mind become a complete blank, then say the mind spell. We don't have any crystals or candles, so hopefully your gift is better developed by now.*"

I deeply inhale, then exhale. *Oculi Tempe.* "Ouch! Blue what the—" something as sharp as a razor sliced at my heel. I immediately lift my head and open my eyes, expecting to see Blue, for some reason, injuring my foot. But I'm alone, standing in the woods. Barefoot. In the middle of the night.

The full moon illuminates the forest below like a spotlight. For some reason, I'm squinting through the tangle of branches and trees, seeing flashlights in the distance cutting through the forest.

Without warning, my legs break into a sprint. My feet are screaming in pain, tortured by the brambles, pine needles, and sharp pebbles. I run aimlessly, sprinting in large zig-zag patterns. Branches scratch and claw at my face and tangle in my hair. My bare legs are covered in mud.

I stumble over a fallen tree limb which sends me sprawling on all fours. My face smacks into the ground, sending dirt and other debris into my nose and mouth. Everything hurts. The pain radiates down through my skeleton to my very marrow. I want to quit. I can't keep running. My tongue runs over the roof of my mouth, feeling a foreign object there.

The pounding of footsteps draws closer. A girl hoots and another boy hollers. Music is playing. It's not quite big band music; more like something from the 1940s. The music is a cheery, jaunty tune, and there's a worn, scratched record sound to it, like you'd expect it to be accompanying an old crackling cartoon. The male singer's voice happily sings, *run, run, run, run…*

Something is clomping through the woods. Something big. *A horse, maybe? What year is this? Was that torchlight I saw? No, torches don't project beams of light.* I peer down at myself, noticing a raggedy t-shirt caked in mud now. I struggle to make out the image. *The Mammas & The Papas.*

"I see her!" someone yells out.

The music swells, *Bang, bang, bang goes the farmer's gun.*

My lungs burn. My entire body is crying out for relief. My hands tremble, fingers splayed out as I scramble to my feet, only to collapse again, unable to make my exhausted legs move. I have to get up. *Get up! Come on! Get up!* The music is getting louder, as is the thundering of feet.

I release a blood-curdling shriek. But it's not my voice, not my scream I hear. It's Trixie's.

I blink and I'm back on the library floor. My chest is heaving up and down. Blue rests against my arms, his head bowed close to mine.

"*I couldn't see it. What happened?*"

I begin to sob tearlessly. "I just saw Trixie get murdered."

# Chapter Forty-One
## Under the Moon

I take a ride service home, spending the entire drive home staring out the window. Blue hisses every time the driver makes a sleazy pass at me. Normally, I'd be confused, maybe even flattered by the obvious flirtation, but not when my heart is broken for my friend. The driver gives me a double take, seeing my hair grow from a chin-length bob to the middle of my back in seconds.

The house is mostly dark, the only light coming from the dining room.

"Sally, that's not a word! You're cheating!" Margaret yells.

I kick off my shoes and head down the hall.

"It's Gaelic. Your mother should have taught you," Sally counters, giggling.

"Ugh, we are only playing in English!" Maggie scolds.

My mother's laughter carries down the hall.

"Hello?" I call. My voice is lifeless, barely more than a croak. The dining room still has the bright chic appearance from when Jack was here on Sunday.

Sally, Margaret, and my mom lounge on the dining room chairs, enjoying a rigorous game of Scrabble. And by the looks of it, Margaret is winning. No surprise there.

"Wanna join? It's way more fun with a fourth," Maggie says before catching a piece of popcorn in her mouth that Sally tossed. "Ha! Got it!"

I shake my head. "Mom, can I talk to you for a second?"

My mom studies my face, and her smile falters. She rises from her chair and steers us to the living room. "What's going on?" she asks once we are safely out of earshot.

My entire body is heavy. I can still hear the music pierced by Trixie's scream. The running. The cuts. The coughing. The choking. It's all too real.

"Eleanor?" Mom questions. She places her hand on mine. "You're shaking. What is going on?" Her fearful voice raises an octave.

I squeeze my eyes shut, trying to purge those images from my mind. "It's Trixie."

Mom begins to gasp but swallows it. "What happened?" She becomes stiff in her seat, steeling herself for the news.

"I had a vision of her running through the woods at night. She was being chased, and there was this weird song playing. She was injured." I try to catch my breath that is just out of reach.

*"Push through your feelings. You're no help to Miss Caldwell in this state. Grief is for later. Think past what you felt in the vision. What did you see? The finer details."*

I release a breath, trying to steady myself.

"I need to call Agatha. She and Harrison need to know," Mom says, reaching for her phone.

I wave my hand, stopping her. "No, not yet. I'm trying to think." I can see Trixie's hands. Clots of dirt clumped under her fingernails. Her scraped bare legs. She wasn't wearing her Gathering dress. "She was in shorts and a t-shirt, like she had gotten home that night." I run my tongue over my teeth, recalling something metal there. A retainer. "She may have even been in bed. Mom, I think she was taken from her house." I rack my brain, trying to recall every detail. "That's all I can remember."

Mom snatches her phone and scrolls to the Caldwells. She paces the living room and lifts the curtain slightly, noticing Marie's van returning. "This is Helen O'Reilly," she says, using her answering machine voice. "We might have some insight with Trixie. Give me a call back as soon as possible."

Mom stares out the window, tapping her phone to her chin.

"Mom," I say, causing her to turn around. "I need to go back to the archives tomorrow to do more research. I had the vision there and Trixie found something, I just haven't made the connection yet."

Mom nods, as if not quite hearing me.

Marie trudges into the house from the garage. Her footsteps are heavy and lumbering. She says nothing to us as she slogs down the hall, her eyes downcast. Margaret and Sally chorus a greeting, but Marie just mumbles a reply on her way to the kitchen. Miss Priss sensing her distress, hops off her tuft cat bed in the corner of the living room and traipses after her.

Mom and I exchange a weary look.

"Marie," I say, entering the kitchen. "Did something happen at your meeting?"

Marie is slumped on a stool at the island, her eyes adrift and her shoulders sagging. "Nothing to worry you about, sweetie."

I walk around the island to her, my mom close behind. "Did they talk about Trixie? What is going on?"

Marie sniffs and her lower lip trembles. "The Committee has forbidden anyone from looking into Trixie's disappearance any further. Same with Doris, and River, and now as recent as this morning, Ryan Christianson in Ipswich."

"What?" Mom says aghast.

"Why would they do that?"

"It has been ruled that Nefari were not involved. We will only investigate disappearances or occurrences if caused by a Nefari witch," Marie murmurs quietly. She heaves herself off the stool, scooping her plump cat off the floor. "I should get to bed. More meetings tomorrow."

"Do Agatha and Harrison know?" Mom asks, putting a hand on Marie's forearm.

"Yes, they're appealing the ruling. Mercy Wicklow is currently in Maine, investigating a Nefari nest. Agatha and Harrison are on their way now." She pats my mom's hand morosely and disappears down the hall.

I pivot to my mom. "We can't stop looking into this. This is ridiculous. I'm going back tomorrow."

Mom holds her forehead, her breathing uneven. "What did I bring you girls into? I didn't realize how unsafe this place was," she murmurs to herself. She glances at me, as if forgetting I was here. "We'll go to The Old Town Hall together," Mom assures before returning to the dining room. "Who's turn is it?" she asks, less cheerful than before.

Righteous indignation steams from me as I flop down on my bed. *What? Because it's not a Nefari problem, it doesn't matter? And who's to say this isn't them doing it?*

Blue sighs. *"It's all very…complicated."*

*But we're still investigating, right?*

*"As your familiar, it is my duty to protect you, and that means understanding any imminent threats. So, for the time being, yes, we must gather more information. But Eleanor,"* he leaps onto my bed. *"You need to keep your wits about you. You can't let your emotions get the best of you. It may cause you to overlook details that could mean the difference between life and death. Detach yourself now; it will only become harder from here."*

I try to settle myself by responding to unanswered text messages from both Nick and Jack. None from Trixie. I type a fast reply to Nick and eagerly get to Jack's. He explained that his father arrived in uncharacteristically high spirits. He still doesn't have high hopes this will go over well, but he's not backing down. He asks if there's any word on Trixie and that it's strange he hasn't heard anything on the news about it.

I roll over onto my stomach, propping myself up on my elbows. "It is weird," I say to Blue.

Blue, in his very catlike way, shrugs. "*Not particularly. You are to avoid police involvement. You put more witches at stake when they get involved. The Calloway's shouldn't have reached out to the police with Doris and River.*"

My brow furrows, thinking. *Maybe the Calloway's didn't contact the police. Maybe it was whoever actually did it.* "The Committee advises against the police because it could expose the coven, right?"

Blue nods.

"What if exposure is part of it? Not *just* the murder. I mean accusing them of witchcraft is pointless nowadays, it's not 1692 anymore. There's a "witch" shop on every corner in Salem." I bite my lip, thinking, my mind reeling as it tries to piece this all together.

Blue gazes at me intently. "*Go on.*"

I sit up, hoping it'll help me think clearly. "They want to expose their connections. I've watched enough true crime with my dad to know that when someone dies, be it an accident, suicide, or homicide, police look into the victim's personal connections, who they associate with and what not. They could track the Calloways to another family, like the Caldwells, or any witch family. Our community is a small one, everyone knows each other. This could send the police down a rabbit hole of strange deaths and disappearances."

Blue peers at me dubiously. "*But wouldn't the culprit be concerned about being caught as well?*"

"Unless you're sure you have this whole thing rigged so that no one can trace it back to you."

"*And this perpetrator has been doing it since Bridget Bishop was accused?*"

"Who?" I question confused.

"*The first person to be accused of witchcraft in Salem. She was actually innocent, not a witch at all. However, she did have a cousin.*"

I raise a brow. "Unless they aren't connected," I counter.

"*Trixie believes they were, and somehow Elspeth is also connected,*" he sends, his eyes dart about as if worried she may be eavesdropping.

I throw myself back against my pillows. "It doesn't make sense." My blood pressure is rising.

"*Try to eat something and calm yourself. We go back to The Old Town Hall tomorrow.*" Blue curls up on a pillow.

After everyone is asleep, I creep downstairs for a snack and some sleeping tonic from the cupboard.

Still awake at 2:00 a.m., I'm snacking on some homemade trail mix and scrolling through social media. I try to resist looking up Vivienne, but my willpower wavers and suddenly I'm scrolling through freshly posted pictures of Vivienne Mather lounging on the beach with…Honor. *Jack didn't mention the Mather's would be joining their vacation.* My thumb flicks past all the jailbait pics. She, Evelyn, and someone I'm guessing is Mrs. Mather are holding up glass flutes that the caption indicates are mimosas. #Mimosaswithmyfavmoms #HaciendaNaXamena

I continue to punish myself by scrolling through. With the number of pictures she's posted, you'd assume Vivienne's been vacationing for at least a month. I pause, spotting Jack in the background of a picture. He's wearing boardshorts and an open button down, somewhat out of focus. He's leaning on his elbows on the bar, his face moody and pensive. I swallow a groan. *He's too beautiful for me. That golden hair. That tan. Look at those abs! Seriously, who looks like this in real life!?*

*"Go to sleep."* Blue growls.

I ignore him and continue to torture myself. This girl has been everywhere. Barcelona. Paris. Milan. Budapest. Amsterdam. Tokyo. And then the less exotic but no less grand stateside locales like Napa, Honolulu, Aspen, Seattle, and Manhattan, just to name a few.

My stomach sinks, and the food in my mouth sours. Saint-Tropez. The last trip where they were an actual couple, according to Jack.

Against my better judgement, I thumb through the countless old videos of them cuddling and making out in hot tubs, Vivienne smiling ruefully at the camera while Jack rubs lotion on her bare back. Dinners together. Yachting together with their families. Breakfasts on private balconies, just the two of them. Swinging in a hammock. Skinny dipping in turquoise water. Riding bikes through town. They look like a perfume ad.

The next photo illuminating my screen causes my eyes to bulge and mouth to run dry. An engagement picture, or at least an imitation of one. The image is of Vivienne's perfectly smooth, manicured hand on top of Jacks. Both wearing matching rings, although hers was decorated with rubies and diamonds in an organized pattern. As Jack's was a plain, dark band with some etching. *We exchanged rings,* she had said to me the night of the Woods dinner.

I move past the pic and stumble onto a video of Jack and Vivienne standing on a candle lit balcony, the exact same one from the previous picture. They're standing, lovingly facing each other, Jack wearing linen shorts and a button up short-sleeve shirt while Vivienne wears a white strapless daydress. Their hands tightly clasped. Allen woods, dressed in his casual vacation best, stands between them, as if officiating. He's speaking but Vivienne has a voiceover in a female robotic voice saying, "Practice makes perfect. This is a vow we'll never forget." Then a cover of Elvis's "Can't Help Falling in Love" plays blocking out any sound coming from the video participants.

I close out of the app and lay back down, kicking myself for opening that Pandora's Box. *I have bigger things to worry about than his past love life.*

I toss and turn the rest of the night, replaying those stupid videos in my head until finally falling asleep right around the time my alarm goes off.

Mom hands me a to-go cup of tea on my way out the door. She also performs the glamour for me, as I'm too exhausted to even attempt it.

"What is our little Maggie-pie up to today?" Marie asks while driving into town.

Mom's been quiet, just nursing her tea, staring out the van's window. "Lennox is giving her and Sally a tour of the campus."

When we reach The Old Town Hall, Mom surprisingly goes with Marie to speak with some Committee members, leaving me to research alone with Blue.

Picking up from where I left off yesterday, I pour over various volumes, scanning countless pages. By the time I reach the mid-1990s, my head is pounding, Breaking for a quick lunch, I dive back into a tome I've already read that recounts the deaths in the Spanish Inquisition. Death. Death. Torture. Torture. More death.

"Those aren't smudges, you know," a deep voice says.

I nearly jump out of my chair and stifle back a scream, seeing Mr. Edwards standing behind me. "What?" I ask, my heart hammering in my chest.

Winston pulls up a chair next to me. Blue scoots over to make room. "Those blue dots, those aren't ink droplets. They're markings. Ruled a human caused death. Red for Nefari."

I whip my head back to the page. After the cause of death is a small dot. "How could I have missed those?"

Winston smiles kindly at me. "Easy to overlook."

I peer over the smattering of dots; some names have neither. *Does that mean it was undetermined? Which dots do I pay attention to?* "I don't see a pattern," I mumble. I run my hands down my face and exhale, frustrated. "Trixie came here. She figured something out, but I can't. I mean, have I been looking in the wrong books? There's nothing to go off of," I complain. I was so convinced the answers would be here, but for the countless volumes littering this library, they offer nothing useful.

Winston leans against the back of his chair and strokes his mustache, pondering this. "She went missing at The Gathering…"

"Afterward, she got home after The Gathering," I interject.

He nods. "And now it's Wednesday."

I shake my head at myself. "I feel like Trixie's life is depending on me and I'm failing her." My lower lip trembles.

He furrows his brow, his eyes falling to the open book. "You might need to start from the present and work your way back. Perhaps you'll see a pattern," he suggests.

His advice reminds me of something Mr. Andersen said when describing his syllabus for the past year, about how starting at the present and working backwards not only explains the destination better but the journey as well.

An elderly couple wobbles into the library, waving and mumbling hellos to Winston.

*Blue, I need more to go on. I think I need to speak with Elspeth. Perhaps she can connect the dots.*

*"You can't offer her anything she wants. It would be a foolhardy endeavor."*

Winston turns back to me. "I must speak with Marie. If you run into trouble, I'll be around. I cancelled my full moon chess match with Mortimer." His knees crack and he groans as he rises to his feet.

My vision. Trixie. The woods. A full moon lighting the forest floor. My head whips around him. "Wait, what did you say?"

"Every full moon, Mortimer and I play a rousing game of speed chess. And we only speak in Latin, just for fun," he answers with a twinkle in his eye.

"There's a full moon tonight?" I ask rhetorically. I slam the book close and gather my belongings. There's still a chance to save Trixie. There's no time to fetch my mother or Marie. "Mr. Edwards, can I borrow your car?"

# Chapter Forty-Two
## Run Rabbit

"Do you think these are the woods, Blue?" I question, coasting to the side of the road.

He claws at the seatbelt strapped around him in the passenger seat. "*You really thought this was necessary? I'm dead remember?*"

"You're *mostly* dead. Besides, we don't need you decomposing all over Mr. Edwards's car," I answer, examining the towering surrounding trees.

"*I've never desired a middle finger more than this very moment…*" Blue grumbles, mostly to himself.

I fish my phone out of my bag as Blue wriggles out from under his seatbelt. "According to Google, this is the densest forest in the area. I remember that for sure in my dream. I thought I was back in Oregon for a minute. But the area is massive. How am I supposed to find one teenage girl amongst all this acreage?" *Why would The Committee close the book on her? If we could just ask for volunteers, we could comb this entire forest in hours. I wonder if the Caldwells got mom's message and are working with the police.*

I flick through the pictures of the forest people post online. I groan and toss my phone onto the dashboard, hopeless. She could be anywhere. I crane my neck, peering up at the sky through the windshield. It's already 4:00 p.m. "Blue, can I do a spell that would lead me to her?"

His tail slowly swishes across the seat. "*Possibly the mind spell, but I'm not certain what you would need to visualize. The mind spell is more complex than you can imagine. It's a—*"

*Lifelong study. Yeah, I got that.* I finish for him, rolling my eyes. *But Trixie doesn't have time.*

"*Work within your capabilities,*" Blue suggests.

*Visions.*

I look around the car hoping Winston might have supplies, but all I find is a tobacco pipe, tobacco tin, and dried mint sprig. No candle. No crystal.

*"You didn't have them yesterday,"* Blue points out.

I sigh. "Yeah, but I'm asking for something *very* specific. She's going to be in these woods tonight."

*"To which I ask again, what is your plan? Take on the mob chasing her?"*

I roll my eyes at him. "No, I told you. We'll hide, I'll call the police, maybe I'll see who's doing this and record them. Exposing them. I'll use my magic and—"

*"No!"* he screams in my head.

*Ow, not so loud! Why can't I use my magic?*

*"Until we know with certainty you are truly Nefari, you can't behave as one. You can't hurt a human, even to save your own life."*

I raise a brow. "How do we know this *isn't a* Nefari's doing?"

Blue shakes his head at me. *"We don't. But until then, no defensive magic. I already lost one ward to the seduction of dark magic. I won't let it happen again."*

*Hello, my eyes!* I point out. *Kind of set in stone, don't you think?*

*"I've told you, you're unique. We can't assume we know anything for certain. Now, put your seat back and relax. Every moment we argue is another moment lost."*

After turning off the engine, I put my seat back, letting him have the last word. Because he's right, I do need to relax and open my mind to a vision, not to winning an argument. I close my eyes, trying to get into the right headspace before saying the incantation. My body goes limp in the seat, my body desperate for sleep. *Maybe…maybe a nap won't hurt. I'm just so tired…*

"Eleanor…"

I can't feel the car seat anymore. I smell…earth. Moss. Pine resin. The air is damp, spring fresh, heady with bloom. "Trixie?" I open my eyes. I'm back in the forest, in the exact place as before. I spot the fallen tree branch and the soggy, rotting log. I whip back around, seeing the branches intersecting and treacherous to run through. I squint up at the sky, holding a hand above my eyes. The sky is moving like a time lapse video. It goes from dusk to dawn in seconds, over and over again. Starry sky, in second blinding noon day sun.

"Eleanor?" Trixie calls melodiously.

"Trixie?" I shout back, unable to spot her in the shifting light. The shadows move all about us with the rotating light, blanketing us in darkness then returning the light. *Damnit.* This makes it impossible to discern our surroundings. The perpetually evolving shadows appear to be rushing all around us.

"Eleanor…" she sings.

I press my palms on either side of my temples. *What does any of this mean? I'm not nearly clever enough to figure this out! Okay, the light keeps changing. Does that mean she's been out here for days? I'll be out here for days? It won't happen for several more days? Why does Trixie sound happy? Is she a spirit and I'm too late? Is she safe? Was she not taken at all?*

I feel like I'm about to collapse.

"Eleanor!" Trixie shrieks, appearing inches from my face. "Help me! Eleanor, you have to help me!" She snatches my forearms, squeezing like little boa constrictors. Her face is dirty with mud, her waist length sandy locks have flowers and clumps of mud dried on the strands. She's wearing a white eyelet lace sundress with cap sleeves and smocking. "Please, help me!" she cries. Her beautiful face crumbles in a tortured sob.

I take hold of her elbows as she still holds onto my arms. "Tell me how! Please! Tell me where you are!"

She pinches her eyes closed as tears squeeze through. "It hurts! Eleanor, it hurts!" she howls.

"I'm sorry! I'm sorry! What should I do?" I cry. My palms are getting sticky and wet at her elbows. I try to take a step back, but she tightens her grip. Blood drips down her forearms from two long, deeply slit trenches on the inside of her arms. Warm, viscous blood pools in my hand. "Oh my gosh! Trixie, you're bleeding. I need to get you help!"

She throws her head back, releasing a heart breaking, ear shattering scream. "It burns! It burns! Help me! They're burning me! They're burning me!" she wails.

I shake my head. "No, Trixie, you're bleeding. How are you burning? Please, help me. I don't know what to do." I join her in a helpless sob. "I'm sorry. I'm sorry. I'm so sorry…"

Her fingers dig deeper into my flesh, the temperature in her hands rising until they are hot pokers fresh from the fire. Her head hangs back, her chin pointed to the sky.

"Ow. Ow. Trixie, you're hurting me. Please!"

Music swells, overpowering both our cries. *So run, rabbit, run, rabbit, run, run, run. Run, rabbit, run, rabbit, run, run, run…*

Trixie slowly creaks her head back up, her eyes wide like a woman possessed.

My heart is pounding in my ears like a bass drum.

*Bang, bang, bang, bang goes the farmer's gun. Run, rabbit, run, rabbit, run, run, run, run…*

"Omega!" she says, her voice inhuman. She shouts again over the music, over the pounding of my heartbeat. "Omega!"

I shoot up to a seated position in Mr. Edwards's car, gasping. We're sheathed in the dark of night. I can barely spot Blue in the car. I continue to gulp, desperately trying to get more air into my lungs. "Her arms," I squabble, "they were...slit. Like she self-harmed." I lean my head back against the headrest, my heart racing in my ribs.

*"Breathe. We've been through this before. Deep breaths. Hold, release."* He keenly watches me from the dashboard.

I shut my eyes and hold my breath for a moment, then release. The ringing in my ear subsides, the pain on my skin quickly fading into memory. My heart slows to a steady rhythm. "I saw Trixie. But she wasn't making any sense. Her arms were cut open, but she screamed about being burned. And when she held me, I could feel it. It was excruciating. More than anything I've ever felt before."

Blue nods along, carefully listening to each word.

"She asked for my help, and she kept saying 'omega'. And there was that creepy music about a rabbit being hunted played. It kept getting louder and louder," I said.

Blue's eyes drift away from me. *"Omega...that sounds...familiar."*

"Do you know it?" I ask Blue. The chilled evening air makes me shiver, so I start the car and turn on the headlights.

Standing in the middle directly in front of the car is a brown hare sitting up on its hind legs, sniffing the air, wiggling its nose.

My heart freezes. Trixie.

It whips its head in the direction of the forest and darts away into the dark.

"Wait!" I turn off the car and I chase after it, stumbling over rocks and tree roots. "Trixie! Slow down!" I hear the snap of a tree branch and whip my phone's flashlight toward the sound. The rabbit is next to a bracken-covered stump. "Trixie!" It sprints away, ducking under and through some underbrush.

I run, not even registering the branches smacking into me, the thorns and brambles scratching me. Blue struggles to keep up as he leaps and ducks with all the agility of a dead cat. "Trixie!" I shout, quickly running out of breath.

My foot wedges under a tree root, pitching me forward. I land on my back with a thud, but I keep moving, somersaulting down a hill. My body is battered by bushes, fallen branches, and stones. I'm airborne for a solid two seconds before landing on the mushy ground of a ravine.

*"Eleanor!"* Blue sends, sounding frantic. *"Where did you go? Where are you?"*

I blink, looking up at the night sky from the flat of my back. I can only see out of one eye. Each breath is agony. *I think I broke a rib. Maybe two.* I try to lift my head to assess the damage, but it hurts too much to move.

*I fell, Blue. I'm in, like, a ravine or something.*

*"Are you hurt?"*

*Yep.*

The moon and stars above my head seem to laugh at me. *What was I thinking? Trixie seems to be okay. But then why was she running away from me? Any sign of Trixie, Blue?*

*"No."*

My eyes drift a yard away where my cellphone is projecting a beam of light against a tree. *I need to get my phone. I need to call my mom. She'll know what to do.*

*"I think I see you. Is that your flashlight down there?"*

*Yeah, that's it.* I get on all fours, crying out in pain, every inch of me feeling fractured. *Oh my gosh, I hurt. Freaking Trixie. Why didn't you stop? I came to save you.* My head throbs and I taste the blood in my mouth. I crawl over broken mushroom caps, dragging my knees, too hurt to put weight on them.

Inches from the phone, my right hand slides on something silky that tangles around my fingers. *Oh my gosh, a dead animal.* I release a yelp and scramble for my phone, shining the light at the unfortunate creature I've crawled upon.

"Blue!" I croak in a broken scream.

Empty sapphire eyes framed by thick blonde lashes stare through me. Her head is lulled in an awkward position, her golden hair splayed out in all directions.

I've found Trixie's body.

# Chapter Forty-Three
## Trixie

The walls are sallow against the fluorescent light. The air has the sterile smell of disinfectant. I cart my coffee cup around with me in the waiting room as I pace, unable to drink it. I'm not even sure why I made it. I hate coffee. I toss it into the trash only to immediately regret it, feeling desperate to hold something. I didn't think I'd ever miss Blue, but I do. He's waiting, probably impatiently, in the car.

"Ell," Mom says, coming back into the waiting room.

I freeze, and my stomach drops. "Yeah?" Blood drains from my face.

Mom holds her hands up, trying to fan down my fears. "Harry and Agatha are speaking to the doctor." Mom holds her hand out, taking mine and easing us both into chairs. Heavy bags sag under my mother's eyes. She yawns, crosses her leg over her knee, and places her arm over my shoulders. I don't even realize I'm trembling until I feel her arm bounce against me.

"What time is it?" I ask, not really caring but needing to fill the silence. Needing to fill my brain with more than just "what if Trixie is dead?"

Mom turns her petite wrist and squints down at her screen. "Let's see, it is now Thursday at 1:30 a.m."

I rest my head on my mom's shoulder, still quivering. Adrenalin still courses through my veins, leaving me fairly numb to my physical pain, but it does nothing to quell the mental anguish. Her blood was dry on her arms. Her eyes were devoid of light. Everyone living has a glow to their skin. Everyone. We take it for granted, but it's there. And Trixie sparkled even more than most. But in the woods tonight, there wasn't so much as a spark.

I fidget in my seat, constantly adjusting. Mom keeps glancing at me. "Is your eye doing better?"

Mom and the ambulance met me out in the woods. I told her on the phone about my fall and, of course, as a mom, a nurse, and a witch, she came prepared. We followed the ambulance to the nearest hospital while my mom forced different herbal remedies down my throat.

"Marie is weaving a dried patch I want you to wear on your eye when we get home," Mom says sternly.

I chew on my ragged thumbnail; my eyes drift about the room, looking for any sort of distraction. A muted television fastened on the wall plays the news with subtitles moving so fast it's a sport trying to read every word before it disappears. "Mom you're an amazing healer, why did we have to bring Trixie here?" I mumble, feeling like I'm being watched by the nursing staff every time they flit in and out of the room.

Mom sighs. "She's not my child. I did all I could for her but I'm just one witch and time is of the essence. This place will help her," she assures sounding less than convinced.

Two police officers pass through the automatic doors, looking like graveyard-shift junkies immune to the late hour. Their boots thump heavy on the title as they hold their utility belts crossing the room towards us. The shorter of the two officers elbows his partner, blushing as he gazes at my mother. They stop, towering over us.

Short cop coughs, clearing this throat. "You're the one who made the call?" he asks, more in a statement than a question.

I shrink in my seat and stutter, trying to answer. *I called my mom first. She told me to call 911. I promise I didn't break the rules. She told me to call you guys!*

"Yes," Mom answers for me, placing an encouraging hand on my back.

"We have a few questions for her," the taller of the two officers says, hands on his waist.

"Could she call, or you could stop by the house tomorrow? Or we could swing by the station. My daughter is really shaken up right now. That's her friend in surgery right now," Mom says, firmly but with her soft friendly smile that has won over more than her fair share.

The police officers nod. "Could we have a word with you over here?" short cop asks, nodding his head towards the coffee bar.

Mom gives my knee a little pat before following them over to the corner of the room, talking in hushed tones, occasionally glancing over at me.

I position myself away from them and tap my foot against the leg of the chair, anxiously waiting for my mom to return. I can't get that stupid song out of my head. *Run, run, run, run…*

The blushing policeman hands my mother a card. Both stay to watch her reclaim her seat next to me before ambling toward the exit.

Mom drops her affable pretense the moment the automatic doors slide shut. "You won't have to go to the station tomorrow. I took care of it," she declares. "Are you ready to tell me what happened?"

I take a deep breath, instantly regretting it. Somehow, the pain is fighting through copious amounts of adrenaline and magical supplements. "Mom, I told you. I thought Trixie was in that rabbit form, so I followed her, tripped and—"

Mom shakes her head. "No, I know that. Before, you said you went out there because you had a vision. Then you fell asleep in Winston's car and had another one. What happened in those visions?"

I lean back in my seat, feeling a new throb in my tailbone. "I saw Trixie and I in the woods. The sky kept changing from day to night, and she told me she was in pain. Then said she was burning, and she burned me with her hands. She screamed "omega", and that run rabbit song was playing and I woke up." I end abruptly, noticing my mother's unnatural stillness when I said "omega". "Mom, do you know what that means?"

She shifts in her seat as the color drains from her cheeks.

I sit up, moving closer to her. "Mom, tell me. I need to know. Trixie said it to me before my vision ended. It has to be important."

Mom shakes her head at me. "I don't know what it is, exactly. I was twelve. I heard Ma whisper that word behind closed doors to my father. But I didn't know what she was talking about. Then my best friend, Erin, her older sister was affected by whatever omega was and they moved. I never saw them again."

I freeze, listening to her. My mother never speaks of her parents. Neither do Sally or Marie. I always assumed her parents died and they were all still grieving. "What happened?"

Mom shrugs with a nervous shake of her head. "I honestly don't know. I haven't heard that term again until now. Ma sounded scared, petrified." Mom's stare is unfixed and distant, her eyes mist with the ghosts of her past.

"I need to find out, whatever it is." *Maybe Trixie will know. But what if she doesn't remember? I still can't believe they were able to detect her heartbeat. It was weak, but still there, the EMT assured me. Maybe Trixie and I can solve this together. Put an end to whoever is doing this.*

Mom and I leap out of our seats when Mr. and Mrs. Caldwell trudge into the room. Mr. Caldwell's arm is securely wrapped around his wife. Their faces look as grave as when they arrived. Mrs. Caldwell sniffs and wipes her face with a handkerchief.

Mr. Caldwell kisses her head before turning to us. "Trixie has passed."

Mrs. Caldwell collapses into her husband, sobbing. He struggles to keep her upright, then gives up. They both slowly crumble to the floor. Nursing staff rushes over to assist.

*Blue... Trixie is dead.*

# Chapter Forty-Four
## Drastic Action

I pass the aunts' sympathetic faces on the stairs. They exchange goading looks with each other, neither knowing what to say. Mom motions for them to follow her into the dining room. No one ever knows what to say in these situations. Even Blue closed his mind and stayed silent. It makes me think of my friends after my dad passed. Lots of sympathetic stares with awkwardly grim smiles and the occasional sprinkling of uncomfortable apologies.

I rinse off the dirt and dried blood in the bathroom; I even discover a small twig in my hair. The unbearable pain of each movement keeps me tethered to reality. My brain keeps trying to patch itself up with a nice band aid of denial. Trixie is okay. This isn't real. Everything will be alright. My ribs cry out when I bend. *No. Nothing will be alright. It is real. Trixie is dead.*

I crawl into bed, unable to find a position that isn't excruciating. Using my magic, I draw the shades and pull my covers up over my head. I'm only asleep for an hour before Marie comes in with a healing patch for my eye. My mom wraps my ribs and forces me to finish a cold tea that tastes the way a damp towel smells after being left on the floor too long.

"Do you need anything else, sweetie?" Marie asks, rubbing the top of my head like a puppy.

"No. I'm fine. Thanks."

Everyone shuffles out, flicking off the lights before shutting the door. Blue settles into bed next to me and quickly falls asleep. His tiny cat snores rattle and wheeze.

*I'm so sorry, Trixie. I'm sorry I couldn't save you...*

I don't leave my bed for the rest of the next day and night. I don't even realize it's Friday until Nick texts me, asking what time we're getting together. We rescheduled it for Saturday.

*"Eleanor, you need to eat something,"* Blue sends gently.

I roll over, facing the other direction. *I'm not hungry.* I don't know what I am, but I know I'm not hungry. But my feelings are…strange. Opaque, even to me. I feel partly responsible, and I don't know if it is due to already having lost my dad this year, but I'm entirely numb. It's like I hit a grief overload and my emotions can't compute anymore.

The aunts, Margaret, and Mom all occasionally pop in to check on me, offering me cookies, liquor, a hug, making sure I didn't accept the liquor from Sally, and just general comfort.

Mom pokes her head into my room and sighs, probably because I'm still hidden beneath mounds of blankets. "Eleanor, your blood needs to circulate for the elixirs to work, so you need to move around the house." Before my door closes, my blankets slide down until they are draped over my knees.

I pull my blankets back up and shut my eyes only to wince when I try to curl into a ball.

Blue claws at my hair, tangling the strands, swishing his tail over my face, nipping at my skin with his fangs until I finally drag myself out of bed. Using my magic, I pick up a few items off the floor, placing them back on the shelf. I take a seat at my desk and go through my school bag, not knowing what else to do. I frown, feeling something papery and delicate at the bottom. It's a miniscule bundle of violets, rosemary, fennel, and jasmine. Probably enchanted by Trixie. I cry tearless sobs and haul myself back into bed, curling in a ball and reveling in the painful punishment I deserve for failing my friend.

***

My door creaks open. "Ell?" Mom tiptoes into the room and perches at the edge of my bed. Her tabby familiar quietly follows her in.

*"Thank you for telling Helen, Persephone. She needs this."*

*What are you guys talking about?*

Mom peels back my covers. She's holding a cup and saucer with a crystal balancing on the edge of the saucer. A candle, new to my room, ignites. "I brought you some tea. I want you to drink every last drop," she instructs.

*"Do it. You can't be shutting down, Eleanor. You need to be focused. Find out what happened to Trixie. We are still no closer to uncovering this malicious, murderous group. I asked Persephone to speak to Helen to help rectify your grief."*

*You can't rectify grief, Blue.*

*"No, but you can put it in perspective. Margaret was able to deal with her grief with a blessing spell from the aunts. You have to do this. No more pity party, as they say. We need to get to work. It's already Saturday."*

*Pity party? You really are a cockswobble.*

*"It's 'cockwomble'. And I'm aware of the pain this inflicts. Pulling yourself up by your broom is never easy."*

*I quit, Blue. Just let my mom and the aunts handle it. I'm done. I failed.*

*"Failure is when you give up. Your mother and aunts don't have the advantages you have. You're connected to this through Elspeth, and possibly more. It needs to be you."*

"Ell?" Mom prods, gently brushing my hair back from my face.

*"Please drink, Eleanor. If not for me, do it for Trixie."*

I moan and adjust so I'm sitting up against my headboard. I take the teacup from my mother and down the bitter liquid in four large gulps. I run my tongue against the roof of my mouth as the tea forms a sweet aftertaste.

My mother tucks her platinum bob behind her ears. "Margaret has a tournament in Mystic. I would like you to come. We're going to get a hotel, make a weekend of it. We haven't done anything for you girls' spring break."

I hand the cup and saucer back to my mom, shaking my head. "I can't…I just want to stay here."

Mom sighs, revealing this wasn't really an invitation. "You can't stay here. Sally's coming, it's going to be fun. I don't want you left alone."

"I'm barely keeping it together, Mom. I don't want to be stuck at a tournament. Please. I'm just trying to get through this," I tell her honestly.

Mom's face softens as does her resolve. "Fine, you can stay because Marie is also staying. But you aren't to go to The Committee library while I'm gone. Your concentration is compromised."

I nod, knowing I haven't found anything worthwhile, anyway.

"The tea should help soon. Let the candle burn itself out," she advises, pushing herself off the bed. "There's more wild lettuce extract in the cupboard if your ribs start hurting again."

I lay in bed listening to Sally, Mom, and my sister talking, trying to muster up excitement for Margaret. They even take one of the aunts' more fashionable cars. Sally honks twice, saying goodbye.

I roll my neck, then each shoulder, stretching out the muscles. My muscles suddenly feel ironed out and my joints greased. The lacerations on my fingers and face have healed into nearly unnoticeable red lines. Even my left eye looks better; it's no longer an angry, demonic-looking red. I couldn't see anything from that eye all day Thursday and thought it might have completely lost its sight.

My phone buzzes on my nightstand, inching towards the burning candle.

"Hello?" I answer before even glancing at the caller ID.

There's a sigh of relief. "Eleanor," Jack says, "I got your message. I'm so sorry about Trixie. I've checked. I can take a flight out in an hour to get to you."

My eyes gloss over, but my heart settles, either from Jack or the grief spell. I'm not sure which. "No Jack, it's okay. There's nothing you can do."

He breathes into the phone. "I wish I could help."

I shrug despite he can't see. "Yeah, but there's no way around it, just through. How's Spain? Have you spoken to your father yet?" I ask, desperate for a distraction.

"We have dinner plans just the two of us in a couple of hours. He'd been putting off meeting with me but finally relented this morning," he says, ending gruffly.

Typically, my stomach would seize with nerves, but I find myself too drained to give into my anxiety. "Good luck," I say, hoping it sounds more loving than how I'm hearing it. "I'm here for you if it goes poorly, and if it goes well. I'm here either way," I say, fumbling over my words like an idiot.

"I love you. I'm going to take us here one day. It's beautiful, but it'd be better if you were here."

"What would we do there?" I ask, leaning against a pillow.

He chuckles sheepishly. "Given the recent unfortunate events, maybe we'll talk about what we'd do later."

I smile, grateful for the brief moment of levity. A dark jealous thought creeps into my head begging me to ask about Vivienne, but instead we exchange "I love you" and say our goodbyes.

*"Good. No reason to pull at that thread."*

I notice it's 10:00 a.m. before tossing my phone back onto the nightstand. I try to get my body moving by doing a load of laundry, fixing some lunch and further studying earth magic, finding the different herbal combinations fascinating, even despite how I'm feeling. There's a dark pall that follows me as I make my way through the house, but as the time ticks by it's getting easier to ignore.

Sitting at the dining room with my physics textbook out and my computer open to the current homework assignment, I type Trixie's name and "Salem, MA" into my phone curious to see if the local news station is covering the situation. There's nothing. I place my cell face down on the table.

"That's a good thing, right? That no one is talking about Trixie?" I ask, still mystified that her story isn't spreading like wildfire online. A beautiful dead teen in the woods, trenches in each arm; the more macabre the details, the greater the chance it goes viral. Yet there's nothing. Not so much as a blip.

*"Tis better this way. Believe me. Finish your studies. I think we should invoke another vision tonight."* Blue stretches across the dining room table.

I blanch and quickly bury my nose in my book, trying to cover my cowardice. I can't bear another vision right now, having to witness endless clues that provide no answers, just actual physical pain. "Maybe. Nick is coming over to work on our history presentation together," I mumble. I take out my calculator, tapping in the numbers and letters of the equation.

Blue stares at me studiously.

Marie comes waddling inside with a bag of takeout floating behind her. The corners of the brown paper bag are wet with grease as it lands stiffly on the table. Marie brushes her hands off, smiling at me kindly. "Oh sweets, I'm so glad you're up and about." She reaches over and gives my hand a little squeeze. "Death isn't the end, just a brief delay in correspondence. Trixie has earned her wings and is in the bosom of our mother Brighid." Plates come flying in from the kitchen, setting themselves on the table.

If only it were that simple. I would love to convince my heart that Trixie has simply reached her hero's end, that she's basking somewhere pearly and glorious. But instead, I mourn the time stolen from us. Our friendship may have been new, but it was real and growing fast. Who's to say we wouldn't have become even closer? Maybe roomed together in college. Gone on double dates with Sebastian and Jack. Been bridesmaids at each other's weddings. Our kids going to school together. Joint family vacations. The possibilities shone bright, like stars across the night sky. But that future has been blotted out. *You're right, Blue. I need to know why.*

I push homework out of the way to make room for dinner. "Where's Winston tonight?" I ask, scooping a generous portion of Pad Thai onto my plate.

Marie's round cheeks turn rosy. "I'll be seeing him a little later. Much to do before our elopement on Wednesday."

I nearly choke on a peanut. "You're eloping this upcoming Wednesday?"

Marie nods before taking a bite of her dumpling. "Yes. We don't want a bunch of fanfare. I've already married once with the whole white dress and flowers. This time, we are doing it sensibly. Mercy Wicklow, head of the Committee, will officiate at The Old Town Hall. There's a little corner office. We'll perform it inside."

I peer at my aunt awkwardly. "Can…we come?"

Marie giggles with a little twitch of her nose. "Of course, pumpkin, you girls will be there, as will Helen, and Sal."

I can feel the grease congeal on my insides after single-handedly finishing the Pad Thai and spring rolls. Marie pulls her chair next to mine as we share some mochi and she shows me on her phone the powdered blue blazer and knee-length skirt she'll wear to her elopement. The practical dress suit is very old-fashioned, very circa WWII. *It's true what they say, couples really start to dress alike.*

"Winnie picked it out," Marie says, taking her phone back and closing out of the picture.

*You don't say,* I think, sarcastically. "It's going to be weird having you
move out of the house, or is Winston moving in?"

"We'll split our time between houses. We're both set in our ways
and enjoy our space. No sense in rocking the boat at our age."

I give my aunt an incredulous look. *Married but living separately?
What's the point?* I think about my future apartment. Paintings adorning
the walls. A ring on my finger. And Jack lying next to me. Pure bliss. But
my aunts aren't conventional, not even by coven standards.

Marie's phone emits a high-pitched chime. "Oh goodness," she
says alarmed, but her face settles in a disappointed frown. "Agatha has
resigned as Head Witch. That's to be expected, given the circumstances.
I just wasn't expecting it to happen so soon. I'm sorry, sweets. I need
to get over to Winnie's." she kisses the top of my head and dashes
towards the door. "I won't be out late."

Using my magic, I send the half-filled containers to the fridge and
the rest into the trashcan. *Do you think I could just straight up ask who did this
to Trixie? Have my magic pull back that veil, so to speak?*

*"Technically, yes. You can send that out into the void. Whether that'll be answered
is dubious."* Blue springs onto the island, sniffs a plastic wrapped fortune
cookie and bats at it with his paw.

"Why does my magic show me what it does?" I question, opening
a cookie. I fold my arms across my chest, leaning against the sink.

Blue moves the cookie around with his nose before sticking out
his tongue and giving the little tan cookie a lick. *"We don't know why a
witch receives the revelations she does."* He takes a bite of the cookie, chewing
slowly. *"Dry. Tasteless. I rather like it."* He finishes the cookie and hisses
when Miss Priss comes too close, trying to steal a nibble. *"She looks like
a hideous mole-rat with her white prickly hair coming in."*

Miss Priss hisses in response, having heard Blue's barbarous remark.
Blue ignores her, enjoying his treat.

The doorbell rings its annoying sound.

*Please make yourself scarce. Spread the word. I would like a relatively cat free
evening. I don't need the headache tonight.* I trudge down the hall to answer
the door. Through the frosted glass, I can see Nick's bulgingly muscular
silhouette in the halo of the veranda light.

*"I'll allow it, but I'll be listening..."* The cats scatter about the room,
hiding in the corners and lurking in the fringes.

"Hey," I swing the door open, getting a face full of mist not realizing it's been rainy all evening. "Come on in," I say, stepping out of the way.

Nick cartoonishly produces a bouquet of roses from behind his back. "These are for you," he says, arm outstretched.

*"How romantic."*

*Oh gosh. Seriously?* I force a smile on my face, accepting the flowering bouquet. "Thanks, Nick. These are…beautiful."

"They're apology roses for being a jerk lately. And there doesn't seem to be any non-romantic apologies for female friends," he says with an awkward smile.

I giggle. "Well, what would you have given Noah or Pete?"

Nick shrugs. "Nothing. I would have just told them not to be a tool and accept my apology, bro."

I laugh an actual, genuine laugh, surprising myself with how easy it came and how good it felt. I can feel the tingling, strengthening power of the tea and candle still burning in my bedroom. "Let me just put these in water."

*"No, no, dry them. They can be used for more than just decoration."*

I tread into the kitchen and decide to put the roses in the refrigerator. *For someone who was just going to listen, you sure have a lot to say…*

Nick looks strange in my aunts' cluttered living room, like a gorilla in an antique shop. His legs stretch out from the couch, making their sofa look child size. "Wanna work in here or…?" He trails off, his backpack is open on the floor next to his foot.

I shrug. "No, this works." I sit in the armchair across from him. "I can put on some music to work to, or I can have something playing."

Nick looks at the old dial TV in the corner of the room on a mobile cart. "That thing works? Wow. It's okay, I doubt we could get "Family Guy" on that thing." He pulls out his MacBook. "Okay, so I've got the thesis outlined…" He makes no mention of me sitting in a separate chair from him as he turns his computer to face me. In fact, he acts perfectly friendly. Perhaps a friendship with him is actually possible.

I chuckle several times as we prepare our project. "Is it just me, or are you actually defending the puritans and their witch trials?" I tease.

Nick laughs with a roll of his dark brown eyes. "I'm not asserting any opinion; that's for our conclusion portion. I haven't even thought that far ahead. But if you ask me, they probably had it coming."

A chill ripples down my spine. "What?"

Nick busts out laughing, falling back against the couch. "I was kidding, O'Reilly. You should have seen your face though. I thought you were about to scream and pummel me with a pillow. Everyone back then was ridiculous and hysterical." His laughter recedes, and he sighs. "So primitive and stupid.

It does make you wonder, though, what will historians think of us one day?"

I exhale, settling back into my seat, turning to my own computer balancing on my lap. "Okay, I sent you the critical dates within the assigned timeline," I say, highlighting online textbook portions and cobbling them together into an email.

"Whoa," Nick says. His face holds a shocked expression, the glow from his computer highlighting and shadowing his features.

"What is it?" I ask.

Nick blinks several times. "Um...I don't know how to tell you this. Ah...Trixie Cadswell—err Caldwell...well, she died."

"How do you know that?" I question.

He turns his computer around. A local news anchor is stationed on the side of the road, engulfed by the forest.

My heart squeezes. "Yeah...I know." I look down at the blinking cursor on my screen. I can't even remember what I was writing. *The news has finally broken. Soon everyone will know.*

*"I doubt the investigation will yield any results. Don't lose focus, Eleanor. We still need to do our own investigating."*

I ball my fists, suppressing the anger percolating inside. I want to make whoever did this pay. Make them hurt the way they hurt my friend.

*"No! Absolutely not. We are not on a revenge mission. This is for protection only. The more we know, the safer you'll be. Cease harboring thoughts of revenge. We will not have this conversation again."*

"Eleanor? You okay?" Nick asks.

I clear my throat. "Yeah, I just need to get something from my room real quick." I rush up the two sets of stairs and into my bedroom.

The flame on the candle is still steady. I grab my amethyst and consider doing a blessing of my own.

My bedroom door moans, slowly opening. Nick stands slack jawed in the doorway. "Okay, this is seriously the coolest bedroom. Ever." He circles about, putting me on edge. Grimoires are littered about the room, but he seems focused on my canopy bed. "I mean, you seriously live in an actual tower. That's huge, by the way. You're like a princess," he says with a playful wink.

*Or like a witch.*

He sits next to me on the edge of my bed. His face loses all excitement, instead holding a pained expression. "I know you were friendly with Trixie. I'm sorry for your loss," he says, a little too formal and clearly uncomfortable. Which I'm fairly used to at this point.

"Thanks," I reply. He snakes an arm around my back and waist, fumbling us into a strange hug.

He strokes my hair and pats my back. "I'm here for you."

I'm rigid in his embrace and return the pat on his back. "Thanks, Nick."

He releases me just as my phone buzzes. There's a text from my mom asking how things are going and a text from Jack informing me he'll call me in the morning. He ends it with "I love you."

Nick's eyes narrow on my text.

I respond to my mom and hold off on replying to Jack. "Well, should we go back downstairs?" I say with a shrug of my shoulders.

Nick stares down at his feet. "Can I ask you something?" he asks rhetorically. "What do you see in him? I know he's super rich and stuff..."

I roll my eyes at his petulant tone. "You think that's why I like him? We just have things in common. Similar interests." I say, watching Nick fidget with his hands. I notice a small black smudge on his wrist. Maybe a birthmark or something?

"I hate to admit it. I've always been a little jealous of him. And now I'm doubly jealous. I think you're amazing, Eleanor. And I know I blew it," he says, dismally.

I shake my head pityingly. "No, Nick, that's not it. You didn't do anything wrong."

His hand swiftly moves to cup my face, his wrist coming into full view. I squint at it as he pulls me in. His lips press against mine, too aggressive, too wet, and extremely unwanted. His other arm grips my waist, tucking me into his as he tries to ease us down, but I resist.

"Nick, stop," I say, tearing my face away from his. With my hands on his chest, I try to shove him away.

My homemade broom resting against my desk clacks to the floor.

His lips land roughly on my jaw. He drops his arms, leaping up from my bed to his feet in aggravation. "Damnit, Eleanor!" he thunders. "What is wrong with you!?" He picks up a grimoire and chucks it against the wall.

I instinctively duck, despite it didn't fly anywhere near me.

In a fury-filled rampage, he picks up my bottle of perfume and smashes it against my mirror, causing the glass to shatter. He picks up another book, hurling it at the wall and breaking the binding.

Blue leaps through the closed door, screeching. He pounces on Nick's neck, biting and scratching.

"What the hell!?" He rips Blue free from his neck and throws him at my window, cracking the glass.

"Blue!" I scream, rushing to his little broken body. His tail has detached from him.

*"I'm fine. Get out of here."*

"JTW, wow, I wonder who that is!" Nick picks up the small painting from Jack, throws it on the floor, and stomps on it. His eyes are crazed as he looks for the next thing to break.

"Nick! Stop! Get out! Leave right now!" I shout.

Nick's barrel chest heaves up and down; his hands are shaking at his sides. He seems lost and disoriented, completely out of control.

*Is this the power lust?*

*"Yes, he is entirely possessed by it. You need to get out of here. Fly if you have to."*

Nick digs into his pocket, retrieving a knife. "I love you, Eleanor. I loved you since I first saw you. But no, you only want Jack!" he screams, flicking out its long steel blade.

I put my hands up, shrinking and back peddling from him. "Nick, you don't want to hurt me. Please. Please don't do this!"

He takes a dangerous step closer. "I'm not doing this, you are! You did this to me! You don't belong with him! He doesn't want you like I want you!" he shouts, extending the knife outward.

My door swings open, slamming against the wall, startling both Nick and me. Winston stands in the doorway, his eyes jump from me to Nick, assessing us. His line of sight falls to the knife, held out towards me.

Nick makes a sweeping motion towards Winston's middle, but his arm stops mid-swing and his wrist snaps backward. The knife clatters to the floor.

Nick cries out, clutching his injured wrist to his body. He eyes Winston terrified and shoves past him and sprints down the stairs.

"Don't come back!" Marie calls after him.

My hands are still quivering. "Winston, you…you hurt a human."

His eyes are troubled, his split-second actions catching up with him. He straightens up. "Are you alright, my dear?"

I nod. "Yeah, but," I look to my window, seeing Blue struggle to his feet. "Nick saw you perform magic…" I scoop up Blue, stroking his fractured body in my arms.

Winston's face drains of color as his eyes drift.

Blue crawls off my lap and lays next to me when I slump onto my bed, the marking on his wrist flashes in my mind. It wasn't a birthmark; it was a tattoo of a pyramid. The base was a silhouette of a rabbit mid run, its ears made up half the structure's wall on one side. At the top of the pyramid, just below the tip, was an eye, like the marking on the dollar bill.

*A rabbit. It can't be a coincidence. I think he wasn't surprised by Trixie at all. And now, he knows Winston is a witch too…*

# Chapter Forty-Five
## Branding

All day Sunday, I jump at every sound, convinced that Nick and a hoard of Salemites are storming the house, but instead of torches and pitchforks they've come with rifles and Molotov cocktails. *What would have happened if Winston hadn't come? Would I have used my magic against him? Would I have been too scared to concentrate? I'm probably only alive because of Winston Edwards.*

Marie helped me fix the window, sweep up the glass, and bind the grimoires back together. Unfortunately, she could do nothing for Jack's painting.

"I can use the mind spell, make you think it's mended and looks the same," she offers.

I shake my head. "But I'll still know it's destroyed."

Blue drinks tonic from a bowl for his cracked bones and fractured spine while complaining all evening about not being compensated for all the work he does.

I keep hoping Winston will stop by or even check in, but he never does.

"Are you going to turn him into the Committee?" I ask Marie, standing at the sink shucking corn for dinner.

Marie pauses, then sprinkles salt into the pot of water. "No. I doubt he did much harm. Winston is a truly powerful witch. I'm sure he just startled that nasty little brute."

"And if he did...?" I mumble.

Marie brushes her hands off on the tea towel. "I don't know. Winnie might insist. Anyway, did you speak to your mother? Did she say how close they were?" she smiles sweetly at me, maneuvering us to a new subject.

"They're an hour out," I say, floating the cobs of corn over to the pot. "Aunt Marie, what are we going to tell my mom about Nick?"

Her face drains, like air slowly being released from a balloon, her color disappearing in her cheeks. "I really don't know, pumpkin. Your mom is dealing with so much right now..." she hesitates, pursing her lips. "Okay. We

Burned

have to tell her. But let me do it," she suggests.

She gets no argument from me.

Maggie, Mom, and Aunt Sally arrive just as we are setting the table. Their high spirits quickly dampen when they spot me in the dining room, a rather somber start to dinner.

"How did your project go?" Mom inquires, dishing up a helping of green beans onto her plate.

My eyes slide to Marie, who giggles uncomfortably.

"Long story, sis. We'll talk later. But I have an announcement. Winston and I will be eloping on Wednesday. You're all welcome to come. The ceremony will be held at The Old Town Hall," she announces, holding her water cup up high in celebration.

We all clinked our glasses, cheering her news.

***

"Can't we just glue it on this time?" I complain, trying to get ready for school. I struggle to get ready as I feel lethargic and irritable. Jack called me explaining he won't be back now till Wednesday due to the weather. Apparently, they took the jet to Gstaad to finish up the break skiing. I'm hoping that's a good sign.

*"Glue? I'm going to pretend that was a snide remark and not an actual suggestion."* Blue snatches his tail with his mouth and sauntering through the door, leaving a tuff of hair behind.

I slip on my light grey sweater vest, leaving it unbuttoned, temperatures permitting. I struggle to push Nick from my mind. *What am I supposed to say to him when I see him? And why do I feel embarrassed? Like I am the one who should be ashamed? He kissed me and took out a knife!* After Marie told Mom, my mother sat me down with a stern, fear-filled lecture.

"Eleanor, you avoid him at all costs. I'm going to call and see about switching classes so you don't see him," she promised.

*Good luck,* I thought sarcastically. The student body is small and making it highly unlikely that I could possibly avoid him.

The student parking lot is slow to fill, the drudge of returning to school after a weeklong vacation. Almost the entire student body, all one-hundred and fifty of them, have returned with fresh sun streaks in their hair and raccoon eyes from oversized sunglasses.

I spot Poppy and her crew traipsing arm and arm through the gates, basking in Vivienne's absence. They giggle and snap pictures of themselves as they move in a herd, their skirts hiked dangerously high, showing off their tawny legs.

Hazel glances over at me from behind her shoulder as I schlep my things to my locker. "Oh my gosh, Eleanor, I didn't see you there. How was your spring break? Did you take an early flight in? I thought everyone was still stuck in France?" she questions confused, holding up her friends who roll their eyes in unison.

"Your knowledge of geography is frightening. Gstaad is in Switzerland," Margot Ruiz hisses.

"She didn't go. It was a Woods-Mather affair," Caroline Chen corrects.

"Mistresses aren't allowed to go. Why do you think Marshall and Allen get so antsy," Sienna Hastings says, gazing at her manicure.

"Where did you go for break? Somewhere…" Poppy questions, eyeing my pale arms and legs, "cold perhaps?"

I sigh, desperate to get to my locker. "I stayed in town."

They squint at me, imparting condescending smiles.

"I'm sure Jack missed you," Poppy says with a wink. Hale comes up behind her, wrapping his arms around her waist.

"Come on, we've got assembly in the chapel," he whispers in her ear before swiping his tongue up her ear.

Her shoulders shoot up as she squirms. "Ugh! Hale, I hate that!" She squeals scoldingly.

"Why do we have an assembly?" Margot questions annoyed, looking up from her phone.

"Probably to talk about finals coming up and you know, the dead student," Hale says, pretending to strangle Poppy. She gives him a shove.

I turn away, my stomach churning. I push past them and shove my belongings into my locker. Students flow behind me talking about breaks and their gratitude for the get-out-of-jail-card assembly.

Before heading to the chapel, I peek into Winston's classroom. The lights are off and the room is empty. *Maybe he's already at the assembly.*

I slip in after all the straggling seniors and find a place in the last pew. Winston is standing alone at the side of the room below the stained-glass window of a tree.

Dean Sather approaches the podium and taps the microphone. "Welcome back, students. I hope everyone had a safe, fun break. As you all know, finals are approaching. Outside the office has your adjusted schedule that begins next week."

I glance about the congregated students, all of them whispering, sharing photos, gossiping. None of them caring about Trixie. I thought there would at least be pretenders, that suddenly with her death there would be a flood of faux mourners who claimed to have loved her, looking to soak up the sympathy of a dead "friend". But instead, it's like she never existed at all. I'm not sure which is worse.

"Here at Griggs, we expect the best. Our top students are accepted into the most illustrious universities in the world, and of course, the underachievers go to Cornell," he says with a self-satisfying smile and a smattering of chuckles. He exhales, forcing his lips to turn down as he grips the lectern. "It is with a heavy heart that we mourn the passing of a student here at Griggs Academy. Trixie Caldwell was a junior here and a fine student. Her parents are upstanding members of the community, and we will not tolerate any gossip nor comments to the press. We have been informed that the investigation into her death is ongoing. Mrs. Henry, our guidance counselor, has cleared her schedule for any students in need of support."

A woman in a pink turtleneck and Griggs blazer steps forward, giving a little wave, as if forgetting she's being mentioned as a resource to help with the loss of a student.

Mr. Edwards stands with his arms crossed and his face impassive.

"Now we have a few words from our drama club before you are all dismissed for second hour," Mr. Sather says, gathering his papers.

The moment the assembly is adjourned, I race out of the chapel, hoping to catch Mr. Edwards. But as I rise from the pew my eyes do a natural sweep over the students, spotting Nick, cavorting with his friends with a bright blue cast around his wrist...

*There's no way. He has to be faking it. It can't be.*

"Mr. Edwards," I call after him in the crowded hallway.

"Miss O'Reilly," he greets. "Is there something you need?"

I open my mouth but stop just as Nick saunters past us, walking into history class, sporting his injury for all to see.

Winston's gaze follows Nick to class before peering back at me. "Yes?"

I glance about, watching students trickling off into classrooms. I wait until we are alone in the hall. The bell rings out loudly above our heads, but I disregard it. "He's wearing a cast," I point out.

He gives a quick nod. "As I observed."

I take a step closer. "Do you think there will be consequences? Like, with The Committee?" I whisper.

"Not with The Committee, no."

My stomach knots. "But you will from someone else?"

His jowls droop and his mustache is brushed, laying bushy against his top lip. "You need to get to class, Eleanor." He produces a pass from his coat pocket. "Give this to Mr. Andersen." He motions towards the classroom and steps into his own.

My skin prickles with sweat and anxiety when I trudge into Mr. Andersen's classroom. He says nothing, accepting my note and waving me to my seat.

I refuse to even look in Nick's direction. Not only does he not deserve an ounce of my attention, but I worry that I might do something magically defensive.

At lunch, I sit at Trixie's empty table. Not a single student looks in my direction, as if I have inherited her cloak of invisibility. Even Nick's table seems preoccupied and doesn't bother with a glance.

Throughout the day, kids whisper about Trixie, looking up articles on their phones about how she was found, and of course, the gruesome, juicy details of her demise.

"The P.I. my mom regularly hires is friends with the lead detective. It looks like it was a relationship gone wrong," Hazel whispers to a friend behind me in French class.

"I thought it was suicide," the girl corrects.

"Yeah, it was, but she did it because of who she was sleeping with…"

I accidentally snap my pen, spilling black ink on my desk and hand. I draw a shaky breath, forcing my magic back down.

I've never been so grateful for the end-of-the-day bell. I call my mom to let her know I'm heading to The Old Town Hall to do further research.

Growling in my front seat, I stare at the mirror, my eyes flickering from blue to violet. "Come on, focus," I groan to myself. *Deep breath. Tranquil place.* I feel my heartbeat steady, and my body relaxes. *I've got this.* I imagine my eyes changing to blue and remaining that shade in all circumstances. *Oculi Tempe.* I open my eyes and smile, grateful for the simple shade of blue.

Taking Winston's advice, I take down the most recent volumes of death records. The timeline, however, is a year behind. I take pictures of pages listing names, locations, and deaths. Nowhere am I seeing any reference to omega.

Book after book, dead end after dead end.

"You're the girl who keeps coming here," a woman says behind me.

I turn around, spotting a slender woman with jet black hair is streaked with grey, wearing a pristine pants suit. Her heart-shaped face and deep-set dimples give her a beautiful irresistibility, but her dark eyes, wreathed in thick long lashes lend her an air of mystery. She looks like a young woman in her thirties, trying to appear in her sixties. Her skin is luminous and creamy, her lips full and scarlet.

I blush and tuck my hair behind my ears. "Um, yeah…"

She tilts her head at me and smiles. "I like that. This younger generation,

I fear, doesn't care enough about our history, not appreciating that it's *their* history. Is there something specific you're looking for?"

I close the book. "Yeah, I'm looking up some of my ancestors that have been lost over the centuries. But it's kind of daunting," I say, motioning to the rows and rows of books behind her.

She peeks over her shoulder. "Some of our more modern scribes have begun digitizing the records. If you type in a name or location, it should come up," she says.

I fight a chuckle at having a search engine explained to me. "Um, that would be great," I say, rising from my seat.

"It's back in our computer lap. You need the key code," she steps close to me. "It's Salem," she says with a clever wink, "but don't pass it around."

I smile. "Thank you. I really appreciate your help."

She holds out her hand for me to shake. "I'm Mercy Wicklow. I'm your Committee leader," she states with a humble smile.

My smile fractures. This is the leader of the Witches' Committee for *all* of North America. My hand trembles in her grasp. This is our fearless leader. The champion of Nefari destruction.

I scramble to pick up my book bag and hurry through the towering shelves to the small inconsequential looking door in the far corner. I quickly type in the code, repeatedly glancing over my shoulder.

Locks slide behind the door and I'm in. I lean against the door as soon as it shuts, my heart racing in my chest. There are eight computers in the windowless room to choose from, and I pick the one farthest from the door. As the computer powers on, a sickening paranoia fills my brain. *There's only one escape from this room. What if she sent me in here to corner me? No, she was nice. But she didn't even ask for my name, as if she knew... No. no. no. I'll be fine.*

The computer's homepage asks me if I want to access the archive. I click yes and type in my inquiry. Omega.

Within seconds, thousands of names, dates and pictures pop up. Trixie's name is the latest on the list. There's even a picture of her skin just below the collarbone, a burn. More of a branding, actually, a little smaller than the size of my palm. It's the horseshoe shape of the omega symbol. I scroll through the names, recognizing them from my aunts whispering about the missing witches. Doris and Rivers Calloway are listed, both with burns on their bodies. The locations of branded witches show up everywhere in the country and the world. Seattle, Napa, Chicago, Austin, then Barcelona, Tokyo, Budapest, Paris. And those are just the last few years. But what isn't given is who's doing this, or why.

I click on a footnote that reads: *for further information, see "Malleus*

*Maleficarum" also known as "The Hammer of Witches".*

I print out the twenty odd pages and nearly jump out of my skin when there's a knock at the door.

"Miss, Miss? We're closing now. Come on out," a crotchety, old voice calls out.

"Okay," I answer, gathering my belongings and rush out to my car.

After some cajoling, my mom relents and allows me to eat dinner in my bedroom so I can finish up some "homework".

*"My tail is attached again, no thanks to you . . ."*

"I'm very happy for you both," I say, cross-referencing the printed pages with the notes and pictures I've taken. I stab my baked potato and take a bite. "By the way, the omega is a brand witches have been receiving since," I look at the earliest date, "the late fifteenth century, as directed by the 'Malleus Maleficarum'. The witch hunter's bible, essentially. A few witches have survived the branding but were unable to remove it. I don't understand that," I say, stopping to take another bite. "My mom has cured the worst burns I've ever seen. And not just from us girls, but her patients. Why can't it be cured?"

Blue stretches out his back, rolling his neck. *"What are you saying? You think the brands might be magical? Perhaps the Nefari are behind this?"*

I lean back on my pillows, mulling this over. "That was a leap. But now that you say this, I don't know. You said Elspeth has a connection to all of this and she's Nefari. But that tattoo," I say, picturing Nick's wrist tattoo with that frightened rabbit running under that pyramid. "Nick has to be involved. I mean, that tattoo is too weird, too specific."

*"He can't just have a rabbit tattoo?"*

I roll my eyes. "No, not in Salem. Not when witches are dying."

*"Witches disguised themselves as rabbits for their own protection. If the outside world knew, then it wouldn't be so safe now, would it?"*

I shrug. "Well, the secret is out. What are you trying to argue?" I ask.

*"Perhaps what we're dealing with isn't human. And I find it troubling you're so defensive of Nefari. You should hope it's them. If they are behind these murders, then we can seek retribution."*

*And if they're human?*

*"Not much we can do, then."*

I gather up my research and fly it over to my desk. "I feel like no matter how close I get to uncovering the truth, I'm still impossibly far away." I roll my lips in thinking, realizing that I can no longer avoid this. If I want answers, I have to go to the source. "Blue, I need to go back to Purgatory."

Blue jerks his head in my direction. *"I beg your pardon?"*

"I need to speak to Elspeth."

# Chapter Forty-Six
## I Shine, Not Burn

*"I emphatically disagree, Miss. This can't be the only possible way."*

I roll on my knee-high socks, getting ready for school. "Blue, Trixie's research has only gotten me so far. If Elspeth knows something, I don't have a choice. And you confirmed she's somehow involved."

Blue pounces on my schoolbag on the floor just as I reach for it. *"Why don't you go back to the archives and—"*

No, it's too risky.

*"And Purgatory isn't!?"* he screeches in my head.

I brush him off my bag, as we continue the same argument we had last night since my announcement. "Blue, I'm running out of time. I can feel it. Whoever is doing this is about to make a move, and…I think I know who they'll target next." My brain conjures up images of my family, or even Trixie's family. They've already taken Trixie. They'd know she isn't the only witch in the family. Or perhaps Winston. That avuncular man with his elbow patches, waxed mustache, and pipe. His crime was just protecting me. I sling my bag over my shoulder. "It's happening, Blue. You can either help me or I'll go somewhere and attempt it on my own."

Blue sighs, making his aggravation clear. *"Fine. After school. But I promise you. It won't be pleasant."*

I pass Nick in the parking lot hanging out with his friends next to his truck, his arm in a sling today. I roll my eyes and park as far away from him as possible.

I race into Mr. Edwards's classroom, eager to share my discovery of the omega symbol. I spin, closing the door behind me, knowing we only have about ten minutes until kids arrive, but what I see next stops me in my tracks.

Winston is hunched over his desk, filling up a cardboard box of belongings while Headmaster Archibald watches shrewdly, with his arms crossed over his narrow chest. His face is screwed into a petulant scowl.

"What's going on?" I question my eyes sliding from the headmaster to Mr. Edwards.

Mr. Edwards straightens, adjusting his tweed coat. "It appears my services at this institution will no longer be needed."

Mr. Archibald shakes his head. "You are not to answer any student's questions regarding your termination. Miss O'Reilly, I ask that you leave the classroom until the first bell. I'll be taking over your class for today. There will be a new instructor tomorrow. And you don't have to worry, this won't affect your finals," he assures, still watching Mr. Edwards from the corner of his eyes with pure malice. "Go now."

"I wasn't worried about that—I don't understand. Why is he being let go?" I question. There's a knock on the door, then two officers file in, peering over to Headmaster Archibald.

"Mr. Edwards, these gentlemen will escort you off campus and to your car." The headmaster waves the officers over.

I shuffle around the marching officers and sprint down the hall, dodging students and curious glances from teachers. There's a shortcut to the faculty parking lot through the back courtyard and around the chapel. I pant for air as I hide behind a car with embarrassing bumper stickers. The two burley officers walk a few feet behind Mr. Edwards as he hauls his sad little box through the parking lot. As soon as he reaches his car, the officers turn and leave. One gives into a yawn and stretches his arms over his head.

"Mr. Edwards!" I shout, racing out from behind the car.

Winston, not appearing surprised whatsoever, opens the back door of his Cadillac and slides his box in. "Eleanor," he greets morosely.

I rush to his side. "Why are they doing this? Is this because of Nick?" I ask, my hands curling into furious fists.

Winston opens his driver's side door. "No, sadly, it's much worse than that. Just don't believe what you hear. If you think it's poppycock, you're right." He bends down, stepping into his car.

"Wait, I found out about the omega symbols. Trixie was only the latest victim; there are lots more. The witch brandings are straight out of this creepy book called the Malleus Maleficarum—"

"The Hammer of Witches," he interrupts. "I've read that. In fact, I've read every update, every edition. There's never been mention of what you're saying," he states with a muddled look.

"But it's mentioned in The Committee's digitized documents. There must be a copy that has it. In all your studies, have you ever come across a group working from that book? Because whoever is hunting, branding, and killing witches, they're using the book as their instruction manual," I say, almost out of breath.

"Heinrich Kramer is the author of the aforementioned book, but as for his dedicated followers, I cannot say. He was declared a heretic and disavowed. His most devout believers have been long forgotten by history," Winston says. "To fully understand these matters, you would need to speak to someone who was there," he says, dismayed.

I take a step closer. "I am. I'm going to speak to Elspeth, she's connected to this. My familiar—"

"Pyewacket," he murmurs.

"I call him Blue now," I correct. "He confirmed that she's connected to all of this, everything that's happening," I feel a strange desperation to convince him, like he's given up.

Mr. Edwards's eyes drift up to the school, turning his face ashen. "Whatever you do, be careful, Eleanor. That woman is the essence of evil."

I nod hastily. "I know but we can't give up. We need to stop who's doing this. Mr. Edwards, we don't know who is going to be next."

"MacKenzie," he utters quietly.

"What?"

His sad hazel eyes drift over to me. "My real name is Winston Balthazar, Leopold MacKenzie. I am the last of the MacKenzie witch line as my family has been hunted and snuffed out by hunters. I changed my name to Edwards after my mother's family."

I hold my elbows feeling an icy chill from more than just the oncoming storm. "I'm so sorry."

He gives me a sullen nod. "Luceo Non Uro," he mutters, looking up to the grey sky with crumpling storm clouds.

"What's that?" I ask.

"My Clan's motto, I shine, not burn." He shakes his head at himself. "But I must away. Take care and we'll speak soon," he says, giving my head a little pat like a good little pupil. He slides into his seat and shuts the car door.

My nerves percolate to the surface, and I start to hiccup. The school is slowly purging itself of witches, leaving me alone to fend for myself. *I can't. I'm not ready. I'm too scared.* I rap my knuckles on his window.

His engine purrs and he cranks the window open. "Yes?"

Hic. "Um, you and Aunt Marie," hic, "are still eloping tomorrow," hic, "right?" I suddenly realize I'm desperate for him to assure me that things will be alright, that we have nothing to fear.

Winston combs his bushy mustache with his fingers. "If she'll still have me. Why don't you come to the house tomorrow? I have something that might be of interest to you. Now watch your toes," he says, his face holds a smile weighed down by melancholy. "Pip, pip," he says, tipping his head towards me before putting the car in drive.

I feel the storm clouds gather overhead, physically and metaphorically. A water droplet smacks the crown of my head, then rolls down the back of my neck. Another heavy drop hits my collar, and sleeve, then thumps on car hoods and roofs in heavy staccato. I glance back at the school, blurred faces behind stained glass windows. Gripping the strap of my bag, I duck my head and hurry to the student parking lot. *Hopefully, mom will understand my need to ditch.*

I whip my car into reverse and peel out of the lot. I catch a glimpse of my reflection in the rearview mirror, not recognizing myself. Not in appearance, but in action. Eleanor O'Reilly would never skip school, especially with finals looming. My life revolved around getting into a renowned university, putting me on a perfectly calculated track for med school. Nothing could have deterred me from my plan. Now, I'm reaching into Purgatory to speak to the woman who created me with magic, hoping to solve my friend's murder and prevent another. *There's my college essay.*

I slow my speed to a crawl, approaching the house. My windshield wipers furiously swipe away streams of water. *Is there a way I can sneak into the house and past my mother?* I think to myself.

"Eleanor? What are you doing home?"

I crane my neck, spotting Blue in my tower window. *Hey! You can help me. I ditched school. Winston has been sacked and I need to communicate with Elspeth, but if my mom sees me she's going—*

"She's not here. She's headed to Winstons with your aunts. Apparently, there has been a very disturbing development."

My stomach twists, wondering if it's more than just his firing. *Do you know what it is?*

"No, I didn't pry. But I'm sure Priscilla or Pyre will share; they love a good story. Persephone, however, keeps things close to the chest."

I dash into the house, hoping to avoid getting more soaked than I already am, and climb the staircases to my bedroom. I pause in the doorway, confused and a little frightened. In a four-foot column on the floor is a pile of broken glass. Like someone has smashed three or four mason jars onto my floor. "What the hell happened?"

"Not Hell, Purgatory. You still want to go, don't you?" He challenges, as if he knows I'm going to chicken out.

I frown. "What does that have to do with the broken glass?" I question, dropping my bag and carefully walking around the sharp mess.

Blue pounces onto my bed. *"The glass will keep you tethered to this plane. You need pain. Last time I clawed you to bring you back. But I don't know when you'll be ready to come back. If we are going to risk you going at all, we might as well get all the information we need. Hence the glass. You lay on it, and when you're ready to come home, put your body in more discomfort to pull you back."*

*So, you finally see I have no choice? You're on board with me going?*

*"Absolutely not! I don't like this one bit. I'm hoping laying on glass will be enough of a deterrent to keep you from attempting this ridiculous stunt."*

My eyes survey the sharp shards on the floor. I start unbuttoning my blouse. "I have to do this. For Trixie, and for my family, who could very well be at stake." I toss my shirt onto my bed and unzip my skirt.

*"Do you even have a plan for convincing Elspeth to assist you?"*

I sigh, my finger hesitating on the zipper of my skirt. "No. I'm not clever enough to trick her. I'll have to bargain with her or something." My eyes drop to the glass, a cold panic sweat breaks out across my brow. *I can't back out. I have to convince Elspeth to help me. What if my family is hurt because I was too scared to go? I can do this. I need to prove to Winston that we can get through this.*

*"Winston?"* Blue questions, interrupting my pep talk to myself.

I release a nervous breath, dropping my skirt to the floor. "I don't know. But I can feel him giving up." I think back on his defeated demeanor. He was more than just down in the mouth. He was resigning himself to something, accepting an ominous fate. *My family has lost too much already. My coven has lost too much.*

I stop moving for a moment, caught off guard by my own fierce protective feelings referring to the coven. My family's coven. *My* coven.

Standing in my bra and underwear, I grip my hips, staring down at the glass. "So…how do I do this?"

Blue appraises the floor nervously. *"I still don't like this. She shouldn't be doing this. She could get stuck. What if the glass isn't enough to save her? She could become trapped in a coma. There's a better chance of that than Elspeth actually helping her.*

"Blue? Who are you talking to?"

His eyes flick over to me. *"That dark blue candle on the shelf has Wolfsbane in it. Light it. Then light the Hyacinth next to it. That white candle with the red specs on the bottom are rose hips with witch blood. There are two wicks; light both of them."*

While staying put, I motion with my finger to light the three candles.

*"Very good. Now, take the selenite from your dresser and place it at whichever*

*end of the glass you'll place your head. Then take the hematite from the bottom of your wardrobe and place it down where your feet will be."*

I pick up the clear white selenite from my dresser and the black hematite from the wardrobe and do exactly as Blue instructed. "Okay," I say, looking over the setup. "Now what?"

*"Lay down on the glass,"* Blue says, his tail sweeping back and forth.

*Oh my gosh, I can't do this.* I panic, looking over the razor-sharp shards, the reality of what I'm about to do only now sinking in. *I can't just lay down on glass. What the hell am I thinking? Not to mention, once I wake up, I'll be covered in glass.* I start pacing next to my window. *Oh yeah, don't mind me. I'm just going to pop on over to Purgatory. I'll be in mental anguish there and physical anguish here...score!*

My eyes gloss over. I march over to my bed, snatching my phone. It's only ten-fifteen. *Second hour is still happening. If I get dressed now, I can get back in time to make it to orchestra.* The back of my mind recalls images of Trixie's burnt flesh. The pain she must have endured. *I can't abandon her now.* I look at Blue, grateful he let me have my little nervous breakdown without interruption. "How should I," I look down at the glass and grimace, "get on the floor."

*"Magic. Have you seen this wonderful silent film Nosferatu? A true cinematic masterpiece."*

Warmth spills in my chest. Dad loved anything black and white. "Yeah, I have."

*"Do the reverse vampire. Use your magic to slowly descend until you are on the floor. Now Eleanor, this is going to be the most difficult part. You need to open yourself up to Elspeth. Call to her. She won't be able to help herself. She'll answer, and you'll be invited in."*

Rain streams down my windows, and a flash of lightning lights up the murky sky. Fitting weather to visit Purgatory.

"I don't know how to open myself to Elspeth," I say nervously. Hic!

*"You do. Concentrate on lowering yourself down. Envision, incantation, keep the magic flowing, and call to Elspeth."* Blue slinks onto the trunk at the foot of my bed and gives me a simple nod to proceed.

I wiggle my shoulders, take a breath, and shut my eyes. I cross my arms over my chest. Blue scoffs, but I ignore him. I imagine lowering myself stiff and ramrod straight, down towards the ground just like Count Orlok rising from his coffin. Steady, even. *La Caeli.* I feel myself tilt back like a board, easing myself lower and lower. *Elspeth.* I picture her narrow face, dark eyes, and wild, unkempt auburn hair. *Elspeth.* I feel something jagged and sharp dig into my calves. *Elspeth.* I imagine my body and mind like a small white house with open windows and billowing curtains floating in a breeze. Open, serene. Easy to enter. *Elspeth.* I instinctively flex my behind as my thighs crunch on the glass, wincing as a narrow piece of glass punctures my skin. My heart rate soars as my body registers the pain. *Elspeth. Where are you?* My lower back is now receiving the needle like shards. *My creator. I'm coming to you.*

My shoulder blades settle on a thick down comforter. It smells strongly of detergent. My head lulls back on a fluffy pillow that's a little too soft to be comfortable, a strong contrast to the bed I'm lying on that's just a little too rigid. I inhale citrus candles, cello rosin, and chili. My dad's homemade chili.

*I'm home.*

I open my eyes, seeing my old childhood bedroom with its yellow walls, band posters, and short carpeting with a small root beer stain in the corner. A spider about the size of a dime crawls across the window next to my bed. The light flicks on from the ceiling just as the sky outside darkens.

"Elspeth?" I call out, rising from my bed. I hurry down the hall, checking all the bedroom doors. "Elspeth?" I shout, coming down the stairs and sliding on the last step that's a little loose. An old jazz album plays from back in the kitchen. I walk through the living room where Elspeth is dropping silverware into the garbage disposal. But as I pass through the living room, I notice the framed family pictures are all a little off. My mom's wedding dress is short with no veil. In Shannyn's graduation picture, her robe isn't maroon like it was that day. Her eyes seem almost runny, like eggs in a frying pan. And in our family portrait, our smiles are all a little queasy, crooked, and curled.

"Eleanor McEwen," she says, without turning around when I enter the room.

I bite my tongue, deciding not to challenge her. I pull out a chair at the oval table and take a seat. "Elspeth."

She twirls around, still wearing that black airy dress. "I'm surprised you've come back. Miss the beach?" She drops a fork and fills the room with discordant grinding. She flicks the switch, turning off the disposal just before I was about to beg her to stop.

"I'm not going to lie, and I'm not going to try to trick you," I say, hoping my transparency will make her more compliant. Besides, I'm in her domain. I doubt I could outwit her.

She smiles condescendingly. "You can always try." She cocks her head to the side, staring at me.

I don't have much time. Soon I'll forget why I'm here, then who I am entirely. "Witches are being hunted. I need to know who's hunting them."

She sighs, pushing off from the counter and slips into a chair at the table. "And why would you think I'd know? Or would tell you if I did?"

I interlace my fingers, resting them on the table. "I know you are connected, somehow."

"Says who?" she says with a skeptical, challenging brow.

"Pyewacket."

She chuckles darkly, hanging her head back. "Oh, that silly little cat."

"Was he wrong?"

She shrugs her narrow, boney shoulders. "No. But here we are at the negotiation table. What do you have to offer me?"

I brace myself for whatever she's going to say. "What is that you want?"

"To begin with, unbind me," she says, her mouth in a tight line.

I shake my head. "No. I need information to keep my family safe. With you on the loose, it makes the negotiation void. There's no point to any of this."

She smiles, her eyes twinkling insidiously. "I'd promise not to hurt them, but I can't."

*"She can't hurt them,"* Blue interrupts, *"She could only hurt us. But unbinding her will allow her to travel between Purgatory and our realm easier. She—"*

She claps her hand together like smashing a bug. "No Pyewacket during private arbitration. Now, where were we?"

"Unbinding," I say, fear and anger bubbles inside the pit of my stomach.

She grins. "Yes, that's right. For every question, you fulfill my request. Including to be unbound."

I have to lie. I have no choice. *Who knows if there even is a spell to unbind her.* "Deal," I agree, knowing if she overplays her hand, I'll refuse the other requests. "To be unbound, I want to know who's murdering witches?"

She leans back in her chair, rolling her head from shoulder to shoulder. "They were called The Disciples. They followed Matthew Hopkins, a devout student of Heinrich Kramer. They held pseudo trials where the accused would always be found guilty. He would brand them, torture them, then kill them. But the church disavowed them. The Hammer of Witches was edited and republished. Mr. Hopkins kept the branding a secret for those in The Disciples' order."

I nod along, listening. "Okay, but that doesn't tell me who is doing it now, which was what I asked," I say pointedly.

Elspeth sighs, bored. "I don't know what he calls himself these days, nor what he's calling his group that follows him. But I do know that it's Matthew Hopkins's heir, and his reach spans the globe," she prattles, drilling her nails onto the tabletop. She snaps to attention, grinning. "Now, unbind me from this place," she orders.

"I can't, but I will as soon as I'm back on my own plane. But I will, I promise," I lie, worried she can detect my dishonesty.

Her eyes narrow on me, turning hard and cold, before an icy, terrifying smile plays across her lips. "All I need is your promise, thank you. So, know what daughter, I'm going to trust you. In fact, I'll give you a free one. No quid pro quo."

My skin crawls hearing her call me "daughter". She continues grinning wickedly at me, making me shiver in my seat, and shrink back just a little.

"Okay, this is a two parter," I warn.

She chuckles. "Greedy, greedy."

"How are you connected to the hunters and how are the hunters then connected to Salem?"

She pushes up from the table and circles the room aimlessly. "Matthew Hopkins had a young widow. She took their son to the new world for a better life. He was a young man when the trials were occurring. He heavily advised the accusers." She lifts her brow with a halfcocked grin, as if impressed. "Even at his young pubescent age he had a thirst to watch those witches die. Although despite his encouragements, they opted to hang instead of a burning. He preached from his father's book, *The Witches Apocalypse*, but quickly realized it was written as a distraction. To muddy the waters from their work as divine disciples. So, he spent his afternoon preaching his father's work and at night recruiting the devout under the direction of the Malleus Maleficarum."

"And your involvement?" I question. I'm taken aback at just how forthcoming she's been. There's a sick twisting feeling in my gut, *there's an angle here I don't see. She'd only give me this information if it will play to her advantage. But I can't see how this would help her.*

She smiles, enjoying some private joke. "I gave Matthew Hopkins his branding prods. Seventeen long ones," she says, as if stating something deliciously vulgar. "They would take two men to operate. He wanted them shortened, because of course he had limited vision. But I explained that he'd need to break them down throughout the centuries, using specks of the originals to make new ones. They would need just a miniscule amount from just one of the original seventeen to make a lasting brand."

"That's why they couldn't remove the brand. You used the mind spell enchanting them. You must be exceptionally powerful to pull that off. But why would he take them from you? He was killing witches," I say, confused, while also subtlety padding her ego.

She shrugs simply, leaning against the fridge. "He was easily manipulated by the power lust. It was insatiably strong with him. The thirst he had for us was voracious," she says with a catlike smile.

*Translation: they were lovers.* I internally gag.

"But why would you help him?" I ask, struggling to bury my judgmental tone. "He was killing your coven, your fellow brothers and sisters."

Her jaw clicks tightly, she dips her chin low. "Yes, those same brothers and sisters who turned me over to the inquisition. The ones who held me in the tower, torturing me endlessly. I lost track of time. I couldn't even recite the incantations to destroy them all because of the pain. Your little familiar, my Pyewacket, he knows exactly what I endured. He should want them dead just as much as I do. If I could, I'd aid them now. I'd wipe as many witches from this earth as possible. It's what they deserve."

I hear glass shatter and I shudder. I glance about frantically trying to place it but sounds almost muted as if something broke far away. "What was that?"

"It's your gift calling. Maybe you should check on your neighbor," she says, nodding her head towards the cupboards.

"The Garcias?" I ask, getting to my feet. I sprint into my parents' bedroom and huddle in their window that overlooks our neighbors' house. I cup my fingers around my eyes, pressing into the glass. *This isn't right...* Where I should be seeing the Garcia's mansion, instead I see East Coast-looking home. The windows of the house glow brightly, a stark contrast against the dark.

I squint, trying to figure out what I'm seeing. There's a long-haired cat with a patch on his eyes in the window, staring directly at me. Mortimer. *This is Winston's house.* I spot Winston tied to a chair on the second story in what looks like a home library. His face is battered, bruised, and bleeding. Six cloaked figures gather around him. More glass breaks. There's angry yelling, none of it from Winston.

I bang on the window. "Stop! Stop!"

There's a chuckle, weak, pained, and clearly Winston's that rings in my head as if he's opened a telepathic line for me. "You may kill me but by doing so, you seal your fate as well. Luceo Non Uro."

Mortimer falls off the windowsill. Dead.

The lights go out.

*I need to get back. I need to stop this.*

"Stop what?" Elspeth appears in the doorway.

"Stop…" I trail off. It's at the tip of my tongue. I know I need to stop something. Something bad. Someone I care about is in danger. I point to the window, but the lights in the house are off and the entire place is sheathed in darkness.

"You know, Eleanor, I think I enjoy having you here, if only I didn't need you to unbind me," she laughs darkly.

My back and legs prickle in pain. *Why does my body hurt? The glass!* I drop to the floor, grinding myself into the carpet, wriggling against the fibers. I can feel my legs and back become wet. *I want to wake up! I want to wake up! Please! Help me!*

I hear a sickening voice, like a snake hissing as it slithers around in my head. *"Pyewacket can't reach you. I'm not letting him. Not this time, I will to speak to you without disruption."* The woman walks over and kneels over my writhing body. *"Know this my daughter your number will be called, and I will be there. You will full fill my wish by your own volition."*

The pinching and slicing against my body is worsening, and I'm starting to wonder why. Like a trapdoor being opened, I'm falling through the carpet and land in a thud on my current bedroom floor.

Blue is leaning over me, inches from my face. *"Oh, thank Brighid! You're back. You've grounded the glass beneath you into powder."*

My body shrieks in pain but I have no time. "It's Mr. Edwards!" I cry. "They've got him!"

# Chapter Forty-Seven
## Vacations and Murder

The grandfather clock chimes 9:00 p.m as I pass it on the landing. I must have been in Purgatory for longer than I thought. The stairs moan with each painstaking step. Every breath is like knives pressing into my back. My entire backside is sickeningly wet with blood. I drag my feet down the hall, wanting to rush to my family in the kitchen, but the pain is making me dizzy.

"Eleanor?" Mom calls from the kitchen, probably hearing the floor shift beneath. My mom and her sisters are sipping tea, leaning against the counters talking. There is no sneaking in this house. "Are you feeling any better? Your familiar let the other know you came home sick. But Ell—" All the color drains from her face when I enter the kitchen.

"You're not dressed. Eleanor, you're bleeding!" Mom practically lunges at me. Her hands clasp my shoulders only to immediately release me, examining her fingers covered in blood. She whips me around and gasps. "What happened!?"

"You need to—" I pause, taking small breaths, "go back to Winston's. He's in danger. You need to go now. They know about him," I say, staring at my confused and mortified aunts.

"Marie, let's go. I'll take you," Sally says, snapping to attention. She tugs on her sister's arm. Marie gapes at me waddling past, only to release a gasp of her own seeing the carnage on my back.

"What happened?" Mom questions me irate the moment the aunts are out the door.

I fill my mother in about Mercy, Purgatory, Elspeth's connection, what the omega symbol means, Matthew Hopkins, Malleus Maleficarum, the heir, and the vision I had of Winston while in Purgatory.

Mom has me on my stomach, laid out on a towel on the dining room table. She's quiet, silently fuming as she examines my back. I feel her hair trail as she gets mere inches from my lacerations. "I can either do this piece by piece with tweezers or I can remove it all at once with my magic. Either way, it's going to hurt," she says without an ounce of mercy.

"All at once," I mumble, then bite the corner of the towel. "But wait, can't we use the mind spell, and I don't know, numb me up or something?"

"No. I need to make sure we get all the glass out. If you're immune to the pain, you won't detect any slivers left over," she says.

I wince and lay my head back down.

Mom waves her hands over my back, making small concentric circles. The air in the room changes, everything becomes stagnant. There's a soft sucking sound, then an unimaginable pain, like I'm having my entire back, butt, and legs all flayed open at once. I release a piercing scream that rips at my throat. Within seconds, bloodied glass clinks into a jar.

"Move around, adjust. Do you feel any glass left behind me?"

I roll my shoulders a little, scared of that sharp pain returning. I inhale deeply and release. Nothing. "No, I think you got it all."

"Go wash up in the shower and come back down when you're done. I've got a healing balm I'll rub on it. You're going to be sore for a few days but there shouldn't be any scaring," she assures gruffly.

"Mom," I say, easing myself off the table. "I'm sorry. I had no choice, and I knew if I came to you first, you wouldn't have let me go."

She has her arms folded over her chest, peering away from me, shaking her head while a glassy tide of tears rise in her eyes. "I forbid you from going back to The Old Town Hall. If Mercy had suspected you, you would have just disappeared from our lives. We would have had no idea what happened to you. And don't get me started on going to Purgatory. It shouldn't have even been possible for you to go," she says, angrily wiping away tears from the corners of her eyes.

I nod, deciding it's best not to explain that it's possible because of my connection to someone stuck there. She knew Elspeth helped create me, and that idea was unbearable enough. For both of us.

Her face softens, but she's still unable to look at me. "Trixie's funeral was today. It was a private gathering. Just her family. I thought you'd like to know." Her eyes finally slide over to me.

It doesn't hit me the way it did with my dad, but it's still unreal. It still feels like I'll see her tomorrow at school, stowing away different enchanted plants for my benefit.

When the water hits my back, I suck in air through clenched teeth and quiver in pain. I can barely take the stinging but I'm sure Mom is listening, making sure I give the water enough chance to rinse the wounds out. The water runs red, then pink down the drain.

*"I admit I was hoping for more of a flogging."*
*Says the cat who helped me get there.*
*"I do your bidding, doesn't mean I agree with it."*
*Do you think it was a mistake?*
*"Hard to say. We have more to work with now, however Elspeth will seek vengeance for double crossing her."*
*We'll see. One problem at a time.*

When the water starts running clear, I turn off the water and hop out. I wrap a towel around myself, leaving it loose on my back. My mind drifts back to Winston. *Sally and Marie will make it in time. They'll get him out.*

*Blue, I think I know who the heir is.*

*"Who?"*

I waddle up to my room to grab a baggy shirt and shorts for after my mom treats my back, then I shove my feet into my fuzzy slippers. "Nick Andersen."

Blue chuckles in my head. *"You think that knuckle dragging troglodyte has organized an international witch hunting organization that has evaded detection for centuries?"*

I open my bedroom door, eager to get back downstairs for some of my mother's healing balm. "Then his father or grandfather then. Some parent runs it, but he's the future. That tattoo was too on the nose to be a coincidence."

I trek down the stairs, but come to a halt on the second story landing. My aunts have returned. I stay in the shadows, leaning forward to listen.

"The house was partially ransacked," Sally says, her voice strained with grief.

My heart clenches.

"But Winston?" Mom questions.

There's a pause, a choke of emotion and the air is static with tension.

"He wasn't there. He was gone," Sally answers quietly.

I settle back on my heels, releasing air through pursed lips. *Winston got out. He either saw them coming and vanished or he refused to be a lamb to the slaughter and fought his way out.* I place a hand on my thumping heart.

"Eleanor..."

"But Mortimer is dead," Marie squeaks through tears. "Wherever they took him, Winston has passed."

I crumple to the floor. Fresh blood beads across my cuts. *They're wrong, right? They're eloping tomorrow.*

Blue curls up in my lap, rubbing his head against my abdomen. I can hear his thoughts, wondering if he was doing it right.

"Oh Marie, I'm so sorry. What do you want to do?" my mother asks. Marie sniffs. "I need to speak to Eleanor."

"Eleanor?" my mom asks.

I give myself a moment to compose myself before pushing to my feet and tiptoeing downstairs. I clutch my towel closed, trying to be as modest as possible.

All three of them, huddled in the entryway, turn as I descend the staircase.

Marie dabs at her eyes with her hanky. Her round little nose is red and inflamed. "Eleanor, I want you to leave it alone," she orders. For a moment, she's no longer her usual Minnie-Mouse-meets-Betty-Crocker. Instead, her voice rings with authority, despite the waves of grief wafting from her very being.

I open my mouth to question her, only for her to cut me off.

"We know you're investigating. Stop. No more. We need to lie low, keep our heads down. For Winnie, for Trixie, for this family." The devastated look on Marie's face forbids any further discussion.

Sally wraps her long, spindly arm around Marie's trembling shoulders. "Tonight, we drink, cry, and toast to that wonderful man. And tomorrow, we embrace Brighid's light where he's basking right now," Sally says to her, towing her back to the kitchen.

Mom watches them go before turning to me. "Come, let's take care of your back." Mom hauls me into Marie's sewing room for more privacy and I drop my towel. She sprays homebrewed witch hazel on my back, which sizzles on my punctures and cuts. "Don't tell Margaret about Winston, okay? She's been through too much death. You both have. Maybe we could get away for a few days? What do you think? We can go see Shannyn in Boston, we could go to New York, Maine, heck we could do a week in Florida. We could go to that little resort we love in Key West," she suggests while rubbing in a soothing, cooling balm.

"I can't. I have finals coming up, but maybe you should take Maggie away for a bit. She's sensitive," I reply.

"So are you, even if you pretend not to be. Just because you can't cry, Ella, doesn't mean I don't know you're hurting deeply."

Mom uses the air spell to dry off my back, then applies a second coat. "I second Marie, by the way. No more looking into the culprit. It's dangerous, Eleanor. I mean, look at you, I'm healing your back because you laid down on glass to keep yourself from crossing over to Purgatory," she says incredulously.

"Yeah," I lie. *I can't stop*. Not when I've come this far. Burying our heads in the sand won't save us from anything. If anything, that will put them on the chopping block sooner. I can't give into grief; I need to find who did this.

The moment my mother finishes I sprint up to my bedroom. Throwing on the baggy top and bottoms, I sit cross-legged on my bed at my laptop. I sip the rosemary chicken soup my mother sends up that she made earlier, thinking I was ill.

I scroll through Nick's social media profile. He was in town to commit Trixie's murder, but he had a Lacrosse game where he was photographed when River and Doris died. But he isn't working alone. I flick through his posted videos of his workouts, lacrosse practice, pranks pulled on his friends at his family cabin. Him ribbing his mom on her way to work, dressed in scrubs. Videos of his pet Beagles. Lots of videos of his dogs.

*"Do you think he recorded himself committing atrocities and posted them on the interweb for all to see, authorities included, and what, has evaded arrest?"* Blue sends sarcastically, peering at the screen.

A robotic female voice states over the video, *People think I look like my dad. What do you think?* Side by side baby pictures, childhood photos and then high school pictures. I nearly spill my soup onto my lap. "Oh my gosh, how did I not realize that? Mr. Andersen, my history teacher, is his dad." *How did I miss that? It's a common last name, and I just didn't put it together.*

*"Does that matter?"*

*Yeah. He's been able to observe us. He probably had Trixie's trust as her teacher. He could be orchestrating this.*

I start searching for his family's ties to the city, but I don't come up with anything substantial. His dad, James Andersen, was born and raised in Boston. His mother Stacey Jones Andersen was originally from Alexandria, Minnesota, but moved to Danvers Massachusetts when she was twelve. *So, Stacey is not Salem legacy but maybe his dad has a connection.* After searching for what feels like hours, there seems to be no definitive tie between the famous trials and James Andersen. I click on important dates that link me to names of the major players of the historic trials and just before I close out, I see a name next to a sketch drawing of a gentleman with a rather large powdery white wig. Cotton Mather. *Mather.* Vivienne Mather. *No way.*

Information on the Mather family is far more extensive and readily available. Cotton Mather, Pastor, infamous for laying the groundwork for the witch trials with his book *Memorable Providences.* Thankfully, because his legacy is so illustrious, it's easy to track. Vivienne's father, the Massachusetts Supreme Court Justice, Walden Mather, has been investigated multiples times, questioning his shockingly high net worth with a suspicious paper trail but as soon as it's been reported in the New York Post, the Times, Boston Herald, there's no follow up, it simply disappears.

*"Friends in high places..."* Blue notes looking over my shoulder.

I roll my lips in between my teeth, thinking. *Sure, Walden seems dirty, and his daughter is the freaking devil, but does that translate to witch killers?* Something clicks inside my brain. I rush over to my dresser, snatching up the printed research from the archives. On my phone, I pull up Vivienne's social media. Her vacations from the time she started documenting them at age eleven, all correspond with dates and locations of murdered witches. I read her caption below the photo. *Myspace pic from my new digital camera! What do u guys think?!*

"She seems so young and innocent," I say, feeling a bizarre surge of sympathy.

*"Vivienne and Nick may be members, but they aren't the heir..."*

I sigh, the rush of realization leaving me drained. I glance back at her smiling face, hair braided in pigtails as she's sitting in a hammock with her mom. Her first post was in San Diego where six witches were murdered. The dates overlap completely. "No way it's a fluke, right?" *Did I just find another member of the Disciples, or do I just want her to be because she's cruel and enjoys human misery?*

Suddenly I feel this strange pull, a flutter in my heart. *Jack.* He's close, I can feel it. *But how is that possible? He isn't supposed to be home until tomorrow.* However, at the same time, I feel another internal tug in the complete opposite direction. *Winston. Is it just grief I feel at his loss?* I close my eyes, leaning my head back, letting myself experience and wade through this strange tide of emotion. I recall something Winston said to me earlier today, *"...I have something of interest for you."* I sit up. "Blue, I need to go to Mr. Edwards's house."

*"Absolutely not. It's a crime scene,"* he objects shrilly, in my head.

I shake my head, sliding off my bed. "No, not yet, it isn't. Now is my only time." I pull on my sweatshirt and tug on my converse shoes.

My phone rings. The screen reads: Jack Woods.

"Hello?" I quickly answer.

"Hey," he says, his voice is warm, like a velvety blanket.

"Are you back in town?" I ask, hopeful, momentarily forgetting my task.

He chuckles. "Yeah, I am. I know it's really late, but would your mother mind terribly if I stopped by? It's just, what I have to say should be in person."

My skin breaks out in goosebumps from my scalp to my toes, like someone has doused me in ice water. "Are you breaking up with me?" I ask, my stupid voice cracking a little. *You can't. We're meant to be,* I want to argue.

"No," he shoots back, "no chance of that. I'm nearby. Can I see you? Tell your mom I won't stay long, promise."

"Actually, I have a better idea..."

# Chapter Forty-Eight
## Witch Finder General

After the house is asleep, I fetch my broom and use the air spell to help me float to the ground outside my window while Blue balances on the bristles, insisting on coming. *My aunts are right, it really does help with direction.*

As requested, Jack has parked his car several yards away with the lights off. Still on my broom I zip over to his vehicle and climb in, wedging my broom between me and the door.

He grins at me, shaking his head. "I missed you so much." His hands cradle my jaw as he draws me in for a kiss. We take a breath before diving back in for more, dragging my teeth on his bottom lip, feeling him smiling against me. He rests his forehead against mine. "The moment I got on that plane, I regretted it. I was so close to running off that tarmac and coming back here. I had to convince myself every day to stay and speak to Allen, but I just wanted to be back with you," he admits, his voice dips sheepishly. "I'm aware of how hopelessly pathetic I am."

I close my eyes, taking in his comforting scent. The aroma alone is enough to make me swoon. "I'm so glad you're back. I love you," I whisper in the car.

Jack gives me one more peck on the lips before putting the car in reverse. He turns around and coasts down the gravel path, waiting until we're sheathed by the woods before turning on his headlights. "Who's that little guy?" he asks, peering at Blue resting at my feet. He squints. "That's the cat from the party."

"Yes," I say, bucking my seatbelt. "He's my familiar."

"Familiars work as your guardian angels, right?" Jack says, recalling our conversation at the cemetery. He eyes Blue as the cat hops onto my lap, then stares back at him.

I nod. "Yeah, pretty much. Did you put in the address I gave you?" I ask, motioning to his phone he's using as GPS.

"Yes, we're going to Mr. Edwards, does he know we're coming?" he questions.

Blue scoffs in my head.

"Yeah...so, you never told me what needed to be said in person," I say, dreading telling Jack about our beloved teacher.

"Yes," he says, his eyebrows lifting on his face as if just remembering, "I was able to successfully sequester him for dinner. I thought I'd be more nervous, but it was weird. I felt more...sad, like I resigned myself to being cut off from my family. We aren't the Dunphys or anything, but at the end of the day, they're still my family."

I reach over, gripping his knee.

"I knew that after our drink order I would need to just be direct, don't lay groundwork, no clever segues, just blunt, unapologetic honesty. So, I began with what is most important to me. I explained that I wouldn't be resuming any kind of courtship with Vivienne. I told him I had full intention of pursuing a relationship with you. Now," he looks at me from the corner of his eye, a smile growing on his handsome face as he slows at a light, "I didn't explain the nature of our relationship. I gave him just the basics I thought he needed to know, that you make me happy, and I want to be with you." He kisses my hand.

"Okay, from your smile, I can guess it went...well?" I ask in disbelief.

Jack continues, all the while massaging my hand with his thumb, nearly making me purr. "Better than I could have expected. I told him my plans for RISD, I even volunteered to forfeit my trust fund, which he refused but I've already divested myself of it. I've paid back what I used and closed my account linked to it. He didn't seem all that bothered about Vivienne, but he was...irritated by my school choice. So, he wasn't happy with me, but in the end, he accepted my decision. Then we turned the conversation over to NASDAQ, the Ukrainian heavyweight champion, and how awkward it was going to be to see Doreen Rockefeller in Gstaad after that really disastrous breakup with Marshall a year ago."

My chest swells with joy. Finally, a bit of good news; I think I might cry.

"I'm worried there's another angle he's working, so I'm treading lightly, not quite ready to celebrate. But still, it's good news for us." He smiles over at me, his face glowing in the dashboard light. His face turns somber, his eyes soft. "I'm sorry again about Trixie. I still can't believe it. Do they know what happened? I read it was suicide. I admit I didn't know her all that well, but she didn't seem the type."

I shake my head, turning to the window. "They're lying. She didn't kill herself."

Jack eases us through the roundabout before turning onto Winston's street. "It's the blue one there on the corner," I say, pointing.

He peers though this windshield surprised. Jack pulls around back and parks in the alley behind his house. "I didn't see his car; I didn't want to take his space. Are you sure he's home? There aren't any lights on."

"He's not home. He...the same thing that happened to Trixie has happened to Winston," I say, taking off my seatbelt.

Jack's eyes bulge and his mouth hangs open. He drops his hand from his ignition, having turned off the car. "I can't believe it. Are you okay? Wait, what are we doing here then?" He glances back at the house behind him.

"I understand if you want to stay here. But there's something inside that house for me, something that I have a feeling will help me figure out who is doing this." I step out of the car and Blue hops out with me. As I sneak in between the houses to get to Winston's front door, Jack intercepts, going first.

We hurry up his front steps and freeze, seeing the front door a jar. Jack puts his arm out in front of me. "Let me go in first. We should probably keep the lights off," he advises. He flicks on his flashlight from his phone and steps inside. The door moans as it swings open. Jack walks farther into the hall, flashing the light up the stairs and into rooms. He peeks his head into the kitchen, then into the parlor. "Stay here, let me check upstairs," he whispers before tiptoeing up the steps, his flashlight held high, and his other arm is in a protective stance.

"Okay, it's clear," he calls down to me in a hush tone.

I peek into the front sitting room, not a pin out of place. The cracked leather furniture breathed a legendary, antique feel into the room. He even had a stag's head above the fireplace. There was a worn, crinkled map in a frame on the wall. A modest bar with glass decanters below a shelf of scotch glasses. This was an adventurer's room. It smelt like mint and pipe tobacco. The room spoke of war and glory. Of blood, piss, and vinegar, and all the rest. If a room ever defined a person, this was it. This was Winston Edwards, or moreover Winston MacKenzie.

I stride over to the little table next to the armchair where his pipe laid on its side next to a fringed lamp. I slip it into my sweatshirt pocket for Marie.

"Eleanor?" Jack calls over the railing.

"Coming." I rush up the stairs where oil portraits and sepia-toned photographs are preserved in bubbled glass. They all hang crooked, like someone took their hand running it up the wall. I grip his pipe in my pocket, feeling his loss grow greater with every step.

We pass a bathroom at the top of the stairs. The medicine cabinet has been ripped from the wall and smashed on the ground. His mustache accoutrements scattered across the black and white tiling. In his bedroom, his bed has been tipped over onto its side. His two art deco dressers have all had their drawers ripped out.

Jack steps out into the hall from the last room to the left at the top of the stairs. "You should come in here."

My thumb rubs against the basin of the pipe. *I'm so sorry I didn't stop this sooner.*

Jack stands in the middle of the study, looking about. Two of the four walls are floor-to-ceiling bookshelves, their contents litter the floor. Above the rolltop desk is a narrow window looking out onto the street. Its blinds are bent and broken. An antique globe is poised next to the desk, but is dented and cracked.

Jack frowns, his flashlight aimed at the floor. "This all seems very... strange."

"What is it?" I ask, walking over to his desk chair and sitting down. The need to grieve is mounting, making my investigation lose wind.

"Doesn't this seem horribly staged? Like it was overkill? He has expensive antiquities in here, none of them have been taken. He has a sword mounted on his wall in his bedroom that if someone turned over his bed in a fit, they would have knocked it down. This seems calculated," he concluded.

*"I'm inclined to agree with the boy."* Blue creeps into the room, startling me. *"Some things have been destroyed, others have not. It appears so abundantly obvious that there's no mistaking it. Whoever did this wants it to look like Winston set up a burglary gone wrong."*

*Blue do you have any clue what Winston might have left me?*

Blue nods. *"Yes, I think Mortimer is pointing to it."*

I leap up from my seat, spotting Mortimer's lifeless body sprawled on the floor, his paw outstretched, as if reaching for something that's fallen behind the desk.

Blue tiptoes over to him and solemnly nods. *"He was a good friend. Those are hard to find."*

*I'm sorry, Blue.*

"Jack, there's something behind this desk. Can you help me?" I ask, too exhausted to move it with my magic. Jack crosses the room to me and with a good hard shove, moves the desk over a foot. Glass crunches as the desk slides. Jack stops, bending over to pick up whatever slipped behind the desk. His flashlight reflects off the shattered glass. He removes the picture from the frame. It's an old field hockey team photograph. There are two lines of boys ranging from fourteen to sixteen. From the haircuts of the boys and the fuzziness of the picture, I'd guess it was taken forty, maybe fifty years ago.

I sit back down at the desk, disheartened, allowing Jack to keep the photograph. *No way it's that picture he thought I'd be interested in. Wait, maybe he was pointing at the drawers...*

I swivel around and pull out the bottom drawer. Inside are polaroids, hundreds of them. Blonde hair. My shaking hand drops my phone into the drawer. I snatch it back up, pointing the light downward. "Oh my gosh." The open drawer is filled with pictures of Trixie. Her hair fanned out on a pillow. Her asleep. A lot of her sleeping in bed. Pictures of her dancing in her room, the angle is from the tree branch outside her window. Pictures of her walking the school grounds. Trixie tending her garden. Trixie reading outside. Trixie driving. Trixie eating at Dotty and Ray's. Trixie curled up on a window seat, asleep with her cat. I dig through pictures, refusing to believe Winston took any of these voyeuristic, pervy pics. My finger scrapes against a book underneath all the pictures. I unearth it, sending a few polaroids fluttering to the floor. I hold my light steady, placing the item in my lap. Trixie's diary.

There are a few pictures pasted to the inside. I flip it open. Only to slam it close at the first sight of a salacious photograph. I take a deep breath and crack it back open and then sigh, relieved. Trixie's long hair is draped down her chest. She's wearing a terracotta-colored one piece swimsuit sitting on a rocky shore. She's blowing the camera a kiss. I read the entry that details a fun day at the beach, away from Salem, of course. As she put it, he only takes her out in public if they are out of town. Skipping forward, her entries become more drastic, erratic, and desperate as she's burning with an all-consuming love for her teacher, Mr. Winston Edwards. *That's bull crap! This is garbage! Someone put this in here! They're trying to destroy Winston. Death wasn't enough for them. No! I won't let them do this.*

I gather all the pictures from the drawer and put them inside the metal globe, diary included. *Ne Feerah.* I use the globe as a crucible, watching the pictures blacken and curl. *La Caeli.* I disperse the smoke throughout the house and out the broken window in Winston's room.

"What was that?" Jack asks, turning away from the photograph.

"Burning their lies," I utter darkly. My head whips up as bright red and blue lights flash in the window and the front door swings open.

In a split-second decision, Jack takes my hand, hauls me to the guest room next door, and drops to the floor. He scurries under the bed, waving for me to do the same. The moment I'm on my stomach Jack pulls me back under the bed beside.

The front door closes and feet can be heard walking beneath us. There are grunts and garbled voices.

*Blue, where are you?*

*"I'm keeping an eye on things. I'm rather good at being unseen…"*

The hall light flashes on and lumbering footsteps can be heard hauling up the stairs. "Winston Edwards?" a gruff voice calls. "This is the Salem police department. Your neighbors complained about the noises coming from here."

The hall creaks as he stands right outside the room. He stops, and I stop breathing. I squeeze my eyes shut like a child. If I can't see them, they can't see me. Jack is stiff and alert next to me, his breathing light and slow. As if sensing my fear, he grips my hand. My body quivers, shaking the bed.

He turns on his heel, heading to the study. At least two more officers join the first cop upstairs, calling out for Mr. Edwards.

From under the bed, I can see a pair of feet stride in from the hall, pulling on a cord and illuminating the room. From the size of the feet and choice of loafers, it's clearly a man. He walks about, almost in a casual stroll.

*Blue, someone is in the room with us.*

*"Where are you?"*

*Guest room. Under the bed.*

Someone hovers in the doorway. "Excuse me, sir, you really can't be in here," he says in that penal code authority.

They exchange something in silence and the officer walks back down the hall.

The expensive loafers continue to meander about the room. He pops open the closet door, then pivots on his heel, heading for the door. He stops. His feet turn, his toes pointing towards the bed.

Jack sees it first. His jaw flexes and his nostrils flare. I follow his line of sight, spotting the half-burnt corner of a polaroid.

Knees crack as he bends down to pick it up, and I cup my nose and mouth with my hand. A large mitt of a hand plucks the burned remnant off the floor. The cuff of his shirt lifts just slightly, exposing the all-seeing eye on top of a pyramid. He swiftly marches out of the room and straight into the study. A door slams shut, and things start crashing about the room.

*We need to get out of here. Blue, what can I do? Should I use my magic?*

*"No."*

Jack turns his head to me, desperate to escape.

There's a loud shattering. A gun goes off. There's yelling. Whoever is in the study flings the door open and sprints down the hall until he's down the stairs.

*"Go now! Out the bedroom window, fly down. I'll meet you at the car."*

*Was that a gunshot!?*

"*Go!*"

Jack and I scramble out from under the bed, gripping each other's hands as we dash as silently as possible down the hall until we are in Winston's bedroom.

"To the window," I whisper.

Jack carefully slides the window up and crouches in. He peers down into the dark alley. "I think I can jump, then maybe I can help you down, or catch you," he says, raking his brain for the safest escape possible.

"No need," I say, squeezing past him so my back is to his chest, our hips tight. "Now hold on to me." He wraps his arms around my waist, gripping his forearms. I close my eyes, imagining us safely levitating to the ground. *La Caeli.* I take a breath and like a sky diver push us from the windowsill. We slowly fall, wobbly and ungraceful. When we land, Jack is on his feet and I fall to my butt. Jack yanks me up and we make a run for his car.

Blue leaps from the darkness. Gliding through the closed car door and landing lithely on my lap.

"Wait, did I just…yeah okay," Jack says, turning his car on and driving at a leisurely pace as to not attract attention.

"He was one of them," I say not feeling brave enough to speak until we are further from the Winston's house crawling with cops and a witch hunter.

"What?" he questions.

"That man who was in the room with us, when he picked up part of the polaroid, I saw a tattoo on his wrist. I saw something just like it on Nick," I say.

"Nick? Nick Andersen?"

"Yes. Okay, I'm going to tell you something that happened, but you can't get angry," I warn.

His eyes drift over to me then back to the road. His jaw is tight, and he's breathing only through his nose. "Okay," he agrees reluctantly.

I hurriedly explain about our history project and Nick coming over. I shared that I went into my bedroom for something, and he followed. Jack's hands tightened on the wheel, his knuckles straining white, and he takes another breath, bracing himself. I express that Nick was at first friendly, but when he kissed me and tried to do more, he became violent in a rage; I don't think he even understood it himself. I described his tattoo in great detail, then the knife and Winston possibly breaking his wrist.

"Are you okay?" I ask when Jack's mouth forms a hard line.

"If I had been there, I might have broken his neck. Are you okay, though? You aren't hurt?" he asked, his icy demeanor melting away into concern.

I nod, finishing my story by relating all I learned in my research while he was away.

"But Vivienne doesn't have a tattoo," he says flatly. Not defensive of Vivienne, more unconvinced by it, yet there was a detached coolness to his tone.

By the time I finish explaining everything, we are pulling back up my driveway.

*"Something is off with him…"* Blue notes.

I reach over, gently touching his forearm. "Is everything okay?"

He parks, turning off his car, and runs his hands down his face, releasing a pent-up breath. "No."

"Jack?" I ask. My insides twitch nervously as I watch different emotions play across his features.

He reaches into his pocket, retrieving a folded-up paper. He turns on the light in his car, unfolding what turns out to be the field hockey team picture. He points to the last boy on the left, second row, standing in front of what I realize is a slightly younger Winston in a very coach-like stance. "That boy is my father."

I stare closer at the picture now seeing the square jaw but soft, boyish features. His dark set eyes outlined by thick black lashes, and that broad grin that lacked the masculine confidence adult Allen commanded.

Jack takes the picture, flipping to the back where the boys' names are listed in order. Under the words *Top Left* reads: Allen Hopkins.

My mouth dries and my ears ring. *Did I really just find Matthew Hopkins's heir?* Despite the hours of research, visiting Purgatory, and the very real danger we were just in, finding his name clearly printed feels too easy.

*"You know what they say about the simplest answers."*

*No, it can't be. That can't be him.*

*"You just don't want Allen to be Hopkins heir, which would mean Jack is also to inherit…"*

"I saw that name listed, and that's clearly my father. But when you brought up Matthew Hopkins, and I don't know, something in me snapped." Jack turns to me, his brow furrowed in despair.

"It could be a misprint. Or you know, Hopkins isn't a rare, unheard-of name," I suggest.

Jack shakes his head. "My sophomore year at Griggs we had a DNA project in advanced bio. My mother's family tree can be traced back to the mayflower. I found what settlement the Godspeeds established, which colony, the noble blood in England all the way back to Charlamagne. But Allen Marshall Jackson Woods didn't exist until three years prior to my

parents' marriage. Nothing. No medical history. Dental records. Diplomas."
He shrugs. "He was a ghost. I told this to Marshall, and he hired two or three
P.I.'s to investigate, and they dug and dug until they insisted that Allen was
an illusion then quit. I moved on. No big deal. Perhaps my dad changed his
name. People do that all the time. And then tonight," he looks back down
at the picture in his hands, "you tell me that the heir of the Witch Finder
General, Matthew Hopkins, is a serial killer and here's a picture of my father
with the last name of Hopkins." He tosses the photo onto the dash.

My heart breaks watching him grapple with the revelation. "What if I'm
wrong?" I ask, trying to ease the blow. "Does your father have a tattoo on his
wrist, like the one I described?" I question.

He shakes his head. "No, not that've seen. But he's usually wearing a
watch. So, I don't know."

"Jack, I'm—I'm," I try to find the words, but I struggle and stammer.
My soulmate's father ordered, perhaps even carried out the murder of my
fellow witches, my would-be-uncle, and my friends. "I'm really sorry. I don't
want to be right about this."

Jack pulls me into him, tucking me into his chest, holding me fiercely.
His cheek is securely pressed against my head. Blue leaps into the footwell,
thankfully giving us at least a minute of space. My hand rests on his sculpted
pec, feeling his heart pounding in his chest. "I'm so sorry," he whispers
against me. "I'm so, so sorry."

"Jack," I say, pulling away, so I can peer into those stormy sea-green eyes.
I cup his face; he places a hand on top of mine. "We don't know any of this
with absolute certainty, but we need to," I say fervently.

He nods in my hands. "What do we need to do?"

I take a deep breath, summoning the courage I'm gravely lacking. "You
need to join them. You need to become a witch hunter."

# Chapter Forty-Nine
## Broken Up

Mom perches on the corner of Margaret's bed just as Margaret starts getting ready for school. Mom reaches for her hand, easing her back down onto the bed next to her.

I tiptoe past, knowing exactly what my mother is explaining. She'll express her love for her, make sure my sister feels safe, then delicately inform her that there will be no elopement today.

I grind my teeth, starting my car. I feel sick to my stomach. I want to break down and cry, crawl back into bed, but I can't. Winston's and Trixie's killer is on the loose. My brain conjures the image of Mr. Woods from when I attended their family dinner. *I just wish it wasn't him.*

Despite the gut wrenching plan I have for the day, the silk screen sky above is bright and clear, goading for an early summer. Jack's gleaming white mustang is parked dead center of the student parking lot, and as planned, I drive past, parking in the row behind him eight stalls away.

I glance around to see if anyone is watching, but there seems to be no one. I sprint over to Jack's car and slide in.

"I should have kissed you longer last night," he says, passing me a blueberry muffin and apple juice. "For the girl who doesn't like bagels."

"Thank you," I say, peeling off the sticky wrapper around my muffin that's still warm and smells heavenly. "We'll kiss again very soon," I reassure, refusing to believe otherwise.

"Will we make up for lost time?" His finger grazes my bare knee, tracing the outline of my scar, drawing invisible shapes and sending a pleasurable shiver up my spine. For a moment, I forget how to swallow.

*Where were my nerve endings before Jack?* My skin, body, lips, they all seemed useless before he came along.

With the tip of his finger, he draws a figure eight on the outside of my leg, dipping just beneath the edge of my skirt hem. My head lowers back against the headrest, my body feels like it's coming undone, unspooling from my skeleton. I release a strange almost whimper as I yearn for more. *Wait, no, we can't do this.*

"Stop, this isn't fair. We're supposed to be broken up," I chastise, mostly at myself.

He sighs. "You're right. Couldn't you have worn, I don't know, a parka or something?"

I look down at my unsightly school uniform. The skirt is scratchy and hangs awkwardly at my knees, my blouse bags in all the wrong places, and don't get me started on this weird ascot-bowtie thing we have to wear. "You mean the awful school issued uniform?"

He stares at me longingly. "Yes. Although you'd look adorable in a parka too, so it's a loss for me either way."

I blush, turning away so I don't start giggling like the silly schoolgirl that I am. "Did you set everything up?"

He digs his phone out of his pocket. "Yes, I now have a presence on three different social media platforms. I'm marked single here, then on these I've uploaded a bunch of pics of Vivienne and I, and a few others." He shows me, scrolling through innocuous group photos, proms, cotillions, obligatory sibling pics, then the more salacious beach photos of girls in bikinis playing volleyball with him at the beach, cuddling with a scantily clad Vivienne under a cabana. Already he has over three thousand followers.

"How long have these been up?"

"A few hours," he says nonchalantly. "I want to delete these the moment we "get back together"."

For Jack to infiltrate his father's group, we had to have the pretense of a breakup. To really sell the breakup, it needed to be official online. This presented a problem at first, as neither of us had much of a social media presence.

Jack gazes at my lips. With one hand on the steering wheel, he leans forward, tilting his head to the side. His eyes flick past me. He sighs and settles back down in his seat as students begin trickling into the lot. "I'll see if I can text you tonight. I love you," he says, his voice dropping low, his eyes downcast.

"I love you too," I mumble before stepping out of his car.

Jack waited a few minutes, giving us space so we wouldn't walk in together. I peek over my shoulder at him. His head is back on the headrest, staring up at the ceiling of his car. I duck my head, turning my gaze to my shoes when I walk past Vivienne and her cohorts just walking up to the courtyard, their blouses undone low enough to get just the hint of cleavage.

On nice days, they typically held audience in the courtyard, sunning themselves on the stone benches. I hate that I'm getting jealous knowing Jack is going to probably linger, maybe even stop to talk to the girls. *Don't be an idiot. This was your bright idea. It'd better work.*

I consider skipping Mr. Edwards's class and going straight to the library to study but decide against. I don't need that kind of attention right now. The substitute, Mr. Delaney, is an arrogant jerk straight out of his master's program. He trashes Mr. Edwards's syllabus, lamenting how Shakespeare didn't write his own plays, then pulls out his list of books we should have been reading.

In history, every glance Mr. Andersen gives me makes me instinctively flinch and recoil. Nick acknowledges me for the first time since Saturday night. His eyes slide from his dad at the front of the class to me, back and forth.

"Your papers are due Friday, that gives you forty-eight hours to stress, panic, rethink your life's plan, make peace with your God, and go through the stages of grief," he jokes to a smattering of giggles, mostly from smitten female students. "Nickolas and Eleanor have already turned their paper in. So, tick tock ladies and gentlemen."

Mr. Andersen trails his finger across my table as he passes me on his way to his desk. "Nice work, I was very impressed," he whispers.

My eyes search his wrists for the tattoo, but the cuffs of his shirt conveniently shield them.

The moment the bell rings, I spring from my seat and I'm out the door despite hearing Nick call after me. The rest of the day is both pointless and endless. Girls glance at me, checking their phones then looking back at me giggling, trying to force eye contact with me to ensure I saw their slight. The orchestra is a buzz with our breakup, although none of them claim to be all that surprised. Who was Eleanor O'Reilly to steal their golden boy? At least people are believing the lie.

At lunch, Jack sits with his typical crew, laughing at whatever Hale is saying to the group. Sitting alone by myself at my table makes it easy to eavesdrop, that and the fact each of them are braying for Jack's attention now that he has returned to them. Callum pretends to hang himself by his tie, Vivienne snaps pictures, and Poppy complains about the school's outdated air conditioning. And Jack, to his credit, looked captivated. Vivienne, however, keeps glancing at me skeptically.

"Hey," Nick says, approaching me with caution.

I lift my gaze from my lunch tray.

"I heard about you and Jack." He glances back at his friends waiting for him at their table, scratching his neck as he searches for the right words.

I peer at his miraculously healed wrist that's wrapped in athletic tape. I walk around him and dump my tray before marching out of the lunchroom, stealing one more glance at Jack.

By Friday, I've usurped Trixie's position as the invisible girl. The giggling has stopped, the gossip run dry. Even Nick takes the hint I will never speak to him again.

I'm eager for the weekend, knowing I have my family who will not only acknowledge me, but even speak to me. Saturday is spent at Margaret's soccer game, which I actually attend this time. Marie sticks out like the grim reaper in her long black skirt and sweater. Mom and I occasionally lean over our folding chairs, giving her hand a squeeze. Sally, however, can't be bothered as she is busy pacing the sidelines and yelling at the refs.

"I swear, if she's betting on these games…" Mom says, shaking her head at her sister yelling at the coach.

I impulsively check my phone, hoping for a message from Jack that never comes. After the game, we meet up with Shannyn and Lennox to celebrate Margaret's win and continue our attempts to comfort Marie.

By Sunday, I'm going stir crazy. I pace the house, only falling on the couch to obsess over Jack's new pics taken on Friday with his arms around Vivienne and Caroline Chen. They're all grinning in Jack's hot tub. *His smile seems genuine. Have we taken this too far? Has he gone native? Maybe he actually misses his old life…*

*"I swear if you don't call this off tomorrow, I'm going to take the lead brick and bury myself."* It's far from the first threat Blue has made this weekend.

*I thought he'd at least call me. Or text me.*

Mom questions if Jack and I are okay. I tell her not really and that I don't want to talk about it. Mom sighs with a knowing smile and a condescending look.

I toss and turn all Sunday night in anticipation for Monday. Blue gives up around 3:00 a.m. and finds a different room to sleep in.

But Monday comes and goes in the same fashion as the previous days. Jack is followed by an adoring crowd, leaving girls whispering on the fringes, batting their eyes.

By Friday, I have adjusted to my new life. Isolation, invisibility, homework, practicing spells, dinner, more spells, lectures from Blue, then bed. Rinse and repeat. The emptiness inside is spreading. I lie in my bed, peering down at my body, wondering if I will actually disappear. *Did Jack even remember the plan? Perhaps he joined them for real.*

*"I want a lobotomy. I'll go get the spoon, you dig,"* Blue grumbles. He then

walks through the closed door and doesn't return until morning.

The following Monday, I'm stuck with the other plebs lugging our belongings from class to class as we were late to sign up for a coveted study space in the library.

"It's unfair that prom is in the middle of finals. Then next weekend is graduation. It blows," Ana Cortez complains to Pippa Winslowe, two rows behind me.

With everything going on, I had completely forgotten about prom. My heart sinks. That silly, girly, romantic part of me reveled in the idea of going with Jack dressed in a tailored suit, looking like a dashing rogue picking me up in his mustang. I stare at the cursor blinking on my screen. *I doubt we'll go now.* I shouldn't feel so disappointed given what Jack is trying to do for us, but I do.

As I study morphological and syntactic structure for my French final, my phone buzzes in my bag. I ignore it and put on my headphones, preparing for the oral portion of my final. My phone continues to buzz at my feet.

I hit pause and snatch my phone ready to set it to Do Not Disturb. Then I see a text from an unknown number. I glance about, as if I'm going to see the sender busily typing into their phone.

> It's me. I'm using a burner. Long story.
> I'm in. I have induction tonight.
> Noble Hunting.

I tuck my phone close to my face, my eyes dart about paranoid someone else is reading my message. I swiftly type in my reply, asking where they're meeting.

> Below The Algonquin Club. DO NOT COME.

My stomach drops when I read those last three words. *There's nothing to panic over,* I assure myself. *He just wants to protect me. But then, why is my heart pounding?*

I finish in the library with less dedication than before and escape as soon as the end of the day bell chimes our grateful release.

*Blue, they're called Noble Hunters.* I send to him while I drive home from school. *They've accepted him. He's going to be inducted tonight, whatever that means.*

*"Now the real danger begins."*

*What do you mean?* I linger too long at a stop sign, causing someone to blast their horn at me.

*"Haven't you thought about what they'll do to him if they find him false?"*

*Yes, but it's his father. His father wouldn't hurt him.*

*"He wouldn't? One of the most powerful men in the world and he would allow mere flesh and blood to go unchecked?"*

I gulp, suddenly gripped by dizzying panic. I idle where I'm supposed to take the turnoff through the woods to my house. I tap my fingers anxiously. A pulse resonates deep inside me. A tug, like a line being pulled. There's a pinching in my chest and an unmistakable force trying to propel me. *Something is going to go wrong tonight. Jack is going to be found out. Jack is in danger. Did they see through our ruse?*

I fetch my phone out of my bag, messaging my mom that I'm going to a study group tonight with other students from my physics class. Be back late.

I whip a U-turn and look up directions to The Algonquin Club in Boston.

*"Eleanor...what are you doing?"*

*I've got to go help Jack. He might be walking into a trap.*

*"What are you thinking!? You're a lamb walking into a den of lions! Turn your car around now!"*

*Blue, I can't let anything happen to Jack. I'm sorry.*

*"The farther you are from me the weaker our connection. I may not be able to reach you..."*

I hit the freeway and merge onto my exit for Boston. The urgency that pulsated in tandem with my heart slows the closer I get to the club. I keep glancing in the rearview mirror. *What if I'm being followed? No, that's crazy.*

My phone announces that I've arrived at my destination. I slow down, approaching an imposing grey stone building with roman pillars and a valet parking sports cars. I circle around the block, looking for street parking before squeezing into a parallel spot six blocks away.

I tuck my school bag under my front seat still formulating my plan, but I can barely think. I flip down my visor mirror and imagine my brain like a car stereo, turning down the volume to my anxiety over Jack. I imagine a woman with a square jaw, brown eyes, and amber-colored hair with tawny skin. Not too beautiful to stand out in a crowd and not too ugly and plain to be mocked. *Oculi Tempe.* My oval face immediately shifts, shortening and widening. Like flipping through a color template, my lavender eyes darken and darken until they're a warm brown. I shake out my cropped amber locks. I can't help but smile, noticing the early signs of crow's feet and smile lines. I keep running my hands through my hair, admiring the texture and detail of a few stray grays at my temples. I look like a mother in a teenage soap opera; the kind of person who loathes my age and is overly critical of their daughter. In spite of myself, I chuckle, a little creeped out by the stranger staring at me from the mirror.

I unbuckle my seatbelt and blanch at my outfit. *Crap. I can't be a forty-six-year-old woman in a private school girl uniform.* I've never used a glamour on my clothes before. I take my anxiety and shove it as far down as I can, forcing the stormy seas to calm. What would a woman at my pretend age wear to a place like this? *Evelyn.* I think of her cream cashmere sweater the way it perfectly hugged and tucked around her form. Her luxurious pants that laid pin straight, not a wrinkle, not a stitch out of place. Her jewelry was conservative but expensive, genuine diamonds and pearls. High heels with pointed toes. *Oculi Tempe.*

I feel cashmere caress my arms. My skirt rippling away into pants that feel more expensive than the Mercedes. My toes feel pinched and crowded in the uncomfortable high-end shoes. I flip the visor up and step out of the car, tucking the keys into my bra.

Into the lion's den I go…

# Chapter Fifty
## Heaven

I groan when I realize I left my ID in the car with the rest of my stuff. I read it's easier to do the mind spell transforming something than whip something out of thin air. I linger on the periphery of the club, watching people trickle in. Men in casual sports coats and slacks in the six-figure range, women in "casual" cocktail dresses that cost more than the average rent in Boston.

An older gentleman, dignified in manner and short in stature, greets the doorman as he sweeps the door open.

The man guarding the door smiles warmly at the gentleman while adjusting his earpiece. "Bernie," the doorman says, with a slight bow of his head. He exudes all the snobbery one would expect from this type of establishment.

*Well, this always works in the movies.* "Bernie?" I shout, marching up the steps towards him. My voice still sounds like myself. *Crap.*

His thick brows furrow as he stares at me, probably trying to place me from a charity gala or wedding he was stuck attending. "Hello?" he says confused.

I press my powdered cheek to his papery one. "How are you?" I glance at his left hand spotting a gaudy, thick diamond ring on his left hand. "How's the wife?"

He glances at the doorman, bewildered. "She's fine, ah…"

The doorman appraises me skeptically, cocking a brow, his eyes sweeping from my shoes to my hairline.

I link arms with Bernie, trying to force us to take a step forward, but Bernie wriggles his arm out from my grasp, taking a few steps back. "I'm sorry, I think you've mistaken me for someone else." He turns to the man still holding the gilded glass door open for us. "I don't know her. Excuse me," he says, shaking his head irked that he's being held up.

The doorman forcibly closes the door behind him. "Your membership card, ma'am?" He states dryly, chin in the air, haughty with authority.

My chest shudders with a hiccup and I can feel my toes are slowly expanding, the high heels are slowly disappearing back to my converse. I adjust my wide pants leg, tucking my feet in. "Of course, of course," I say. I envision a card, no bigger than a driver's license, which again is difficult to do without actually holding an object in my hand. Then comes the even harder part, trying to trick his mind into seeing what he has seen before with membership cards. According to the grimoire I studied, my magic would need to mess with an entirely different part of the brain, the temporal lobe where memories are stored while manipulating the occipital lobe so he actually see's that specific memory. Before self-doubt and more hiccups can throw me off course, I recite the mind spell, commanding my magic. I hold out my hand as if I'm holding out a card.

He leans forward, examining my empty hand. "I don't understand. Do you have a membership?"

I swallow a hiccup. "Of course, it's right here." I hold my hand out more, trying to hand him the invisible card.

His eyes roll to the sky. "Ma'am there's nothing in your hand. Please step aside for actual members," he says, waving through a group he recognizes. The man snaps a gracious smile into place and calls each person by name as they breeze through, throwing me curious glances.

*Crap. I knew this wasn't going to work.* I snap my fingers in an "awe, shucks" gesture. "I was only teasing," I say, retreating down the stone steps. "I left it in my car. Be right back."

"I'll get the valet ma'am," he says, motioning to the man waiting at the booth full of car keys.

I shake my head and wave him off. "No need. I parked around the corner."

"Of course, you did." He steps back under the awning, turning his head away from me.

I speed walk around the corner and once I'm safely out of sight I lean against the wall, catching my breath. *Okay, new disguise.* I conjure up long tan legs, maybe a woman of five-ten, model height. Long slender arms that have been sculpted by a private trainer six days a week. An amble chest that protrudes and bounces with every step, cinched in waist, curved reality show hips, movie star lips giving me a sexy pout, smoldering eyes yearning for a bedroom, and a face that you would believe you've seen saucily splashed about Times Square, Paris Fashion week, and other less reputable publications. My back immediately aches, and I feel like I'm about to fall forward onto my face, my chest having exploded from petite A-cup to double D on a small frame not built to handle such a load. I wrap this sexpot in a tight but tasteful red bodycon dress.

I nearly faceplant on the sidewalk in my eight-inch heels.

A man drops his Maserati keys into the open palm of the valet without looking at him. The valet then eyes the car with mouth dripping envy. The man, who's wearing a little too much hair gel, then finishes putting on his coat and tugs on his lapels. He glances at me then does a double take, his lips parting and his eyes bulging. His eyes slide from side to side as I approach him. He hastily snaps up, rights his shoulders, and plays with his cufflink, playing it cool with an easy smile.

"Hi," I say, my voice this time is deep and sultry almost like a purr. I smile demurely and tuck my blonde hair behind one ear. "I'm supposed to be meeting someone, but of course, he forgot to put me on the list, any way you could help me out?" I ask with a little pout, pushing my chest out like I've seen in films. *Although, the movies have been failing me tonight.*

His gaze conspicuously falls to my chest, inappropriately lingering there, unabashedly making me feel cheap.

I fight the urge to cover myself up. My eyes drift about awkwardly as he stares. The sky is shifting from light pink to blazing oranges and reds; it'll be dark by the time the man is done gawking at me. I glance down at my fingers realizing my chipped and chewed-on nails are still the same, so I ball my fists to hide them.

The man takes a step closer to me. "You know, "wives" usually go in through the back. And if I make an exception for you, and trust me, I really want to, I'd have to make one for everyone. Just go through the back. The lady in the kitchen will let you in," he assures, scoping my body out once more. "Once you get in, come find me inside. You'll find me in Scotties." He winks before strolling away with an arrogant master-of-the-universe gait.

*Damnit.* I hadn't anticipated getting in would be the hardest part of the evening. I exhale frustratedly and wonder if I should shimmy up to the doorman, if I could possibly persuade him. Suddenly, I feel a strange light flicker, like a little glowing flame in my chest. *This isn't my magic, it's something new yet familiar.* I place a hand on my chest. *Jack.*

"Miss, can I help you?" the valet asks with an eager smile.

I take a step back on the sidewalk as three shiny black town cars pull up to the curb. Almost in synchronized movements, the drivers stride around

# Burned

their cars then swing the doors open, taking a step back allowing the occupants to exit.

Allen Woods is the first to step out, brushing out his suit pants and strolls up to the door not even giving me a cursory glance. He speaks to the doorman, who cowers just nodding along to whatever Allen is saying.

I take several steps back, pretending to be interested in the architecture of the building while watching the passengers pour out of the cars laughing and jesting with each other.

Vivienne, clad in a backless bodysuit and trousers, is swarmed by her usual posse dressed equally expensive and chic. Vivienne sucks on her silver vape pen giggling to her friends. Poppy Simonsen, Caroline Wong, Hazel Bartlett, Sienna Prescott, and Margot Ruiz are all accounted for. All Noble Hunters.

Jack steps out, looking dashing in a black sweater and jeans. He reaches into the car pulling out a blazer that he slips on while listening to his friends prattle about something. Another car pulls up, a bright yellow Porche. Marshall hops out and practically pelts his keys at the valet who fails to catch them.

He jovially rushes over to Jack, jumping on his back. Six more members, all around Marshall's age, join the ruckus crowd gathering.

Allen frowns, his posture remaining rigid. "Let's go," he says, motioning impatiently for everyone to join him.

Knowing I have to act, I close my eyes picturing a teenage girl my own age, with a similar skin tone and shape to Jack's sister, Honor.

"Excuse me, but have we met?"

My spell is interrupted. I open my eyes, Marshall stands so close my chest is nearly pressed against his. "Excuse me?" I ask panicked, but I can see I'm still in my form fitting dress with an ample chest.

He places a lecherous hand around my waist, tucking me into him. "Yeah, don't you remember at Henry's gig. It was great," he says grinning, trying to pull the same slick move I had played and failed at earlier.

*Here's my in.* I nod my head, feigning recognition. "Yeah, sorry I was so…hammered that night. I barely remember," I say, rolling my eyes at myself.

He laughs, his fingers draped dangerously low on my hipbone. "Yep, that's the night," he says with a laugh. His eyes keep straying from my face.

I gaze past his head, watching Jack and his friends disappear through the doors, past Allen who's glaring at Marshall and me.

"Shall we?" I say, nodding my head towards the club, looping my arm around his back.

Marshall's grin falls and his eyes grow. "Absolutely," he agrees with a slobbery hunger. As we walk up the steps, his hand slides up my ribcage, so his thumb grazes my bust. He winks at the doorman as we pass and his father grumbles trudging in behind us.

The lobby is a cathedral of old-world taste with stylish excess. Its checkered marble flooring, granite pillars, chestnut tables are each adorned with a fresh bouquet of flowers lending their sweet aroma to the area.

Marshall pulls me into him so our hips are crushed together. "I've got a meeting I need to get to but go to the front desk there, tell them you're a Woods guest and they'll take you to my room." He leans in close, his lips tickling my ear uncomfortably. "I expect that dress to be on the floor and your heels still on."

My skin crawls when he kisses my cheek.

"Marshall," Allen calls with a stoney glare.

Marshall spins on his heel and joins his father and the rest of their sizable group to the small elevator in the corner. Allen appears to be chastising Marshall until the elevator doors slide open. Allen, Jack, Vivienne and two others climb aboard. Marshall waits with everyone else, hands shoved in his pockets, unbothered by his father's finger wagging.

I sneak away to a small alcove, making sure Marshall and his small assembly are still waiting for the elevator. I lean my back against the cool wall. My stomach knots and wobbles; getting in was supposed to be the easy part. *No time for self-doubt.* My eyes fall gently shut, imagining I'm one with the room, my entire body disappearing, invisible, every hair, every freckle, every pore transparent, allowing you to see right through me to the other side. I'm able to run, skip, jump, float, sit, spin, dance, tip toe, all the while being perfectly transparent. *Oculi Tempe.* I open my eyes and peer down, seeing my school uniform and gangly body. *Well great, this is just perfect.*

A couple stumbles into the alcove, nearly crashing into me. I quickly step aside.

The elevators open, half occupied. Marshall shakes his head, probably telling them they'll take the next one. The doors close.

"I told you your wife suspected something, she's upstairs right now!" the young woman complains, crossing her arms in a sulky frown.

"Bunny, she means nothing to me, you're everything. Please don't be mad. Just wait in the pub for me, get whatever you want. Put it on my tab," he begs pathetically.

I look away, embarrassed.

"Of course, it's going on your tab. Ugh this was a mistake, I think I'm just going to go home," she threatens halfheartedly.

*Why are they doing this in front of me? Wait…*

I stick my hand between their faces while he grovels, wholly expecting them to snap at me, but they don't. *Oh my gosh, I did it. I'm invisible.*

The elevator doors slide open, Marshall and everyone left piles in. I sprint, dodging people as I slide in just before the elevators close. I hold my breath squeezing in against the door.

Marshall pulls out a key, turning a lock inside a box in the elevator sending us down into the basement.

Margot plays with her cigarette case as we descend. "We need to get our own building. This is ridiculous. Is Allen paying a premium for this?" she questions, staring at the numbers dropping.

"They have no idea that we meet below the building," he replies with a roll of his eyes. "Our section isn't even in the blueprints. Why should we move when this is so convenient? Don't fix what isn't broken," Marshall drawls, bored.

The elevator opens to a dark, musty smelling basement. I leap out of the way so I can trail behind them, passing laundry rooms, a boiler room, janitor supplies, and broken furniture discarded to the side. Maids, janitors and various staff pass us suspiciously, constantly throwing up strange looks.

We stop at a door at the end of the hall. Marshall punches in a keycode on the wall. "Okay, you know the drill, one at a time. Don't linger, just go." A lock turns and the door becomes available to open.

Margot is the first to push her way through, pulling the door open and closing it behind her. One by one everyone follows suit. I slip in with Hazel Barlett who is last besides Marshall. The closet is narrow and dark, scarcely larger than a coffin. Hazel draws a sharp breath, startled as I've bumped into her twice now.

*If only I had gone invisible from the start.*

"Hazel Maurine Bartlett," she announces in the box. A flash camera illuminates the room for a split second. I feel the wonky sensation of movement as I realize this room is basically a dumbwaiter, taking us down to the Noble Hunter's club, where the *actual* elite meet. A doorman and a card are a piece of cake compared to the hoops one needs to jump through to get to the Noble Hunters' domain.

The door slides up from bottom to top and we both quickly leap out. Hazel quickly strolls away, tucking her strawberry blonde hair behind her ears and glancing back at the dumbwaiter with an eerie expression.

Wait staff in tight button ups and paisley bowties circulate the room offering flutes of champagne. I'm not sure what I was expecting after squeezing into that dank dumbwaiter, but it certainly wasn't this. Soft jazz trickles from speakers. The room has barrel ceilings with alabaster columns, dark matte walls with chestnut board and batten panel wainscoting, gilded chandeliers dripping in filigree, with tuft couches positioned throughout. Jack is lounging on one of those couches with Vivienne curled up beside him.

Jack's arm rests on the back of the couch, appearing disinterested while everyone else mingles, enjoying champagne and specialty cocktails at the bar. His sports coat is folded over the arm of the sofa.

Marshall exits the dumbwaiter and makes a beeline for the bar waving away the waiter who rushed to him with champagne. Margot blows smoke into the air, grinning saucily at an older man who has her cornered next to a Rembrandt style painting of a witch burning at the stake.

I perch on the ottoman near Jack's feet and take in the scene around me. I quickly retract my hand when I catch myself reaching out to caress his leg.

Vivienne pushes up his sweater sleeve revealing a black pyramid topped with an eye and a running rabbit at the base. She purses her lips planting a kiss there. Then licks where her lips just were. "So sexy," she whispers.

He gives her condescending, placating smile.

My heart hammers. *He got a tattoo? Is that permanent? Just how deep is he willing to go? Maybe they didn't give him a choice.*

A man strolls up with a bit of a belly leaking over his belt, grins at Jack and Vivienne. From the pictures I've seen online, he's the Honorable Walden Mather, Vivienne's father. "The prodigal son finally joins us. When your father said you were coming, I was in disbelief," he says with an astonished chuckle, holding his hand out to Jack. "I am curious as to the cause of this awakening."

Jack hoists himself up off the couch and claps his hand in Walden's. "Let's just say I've become more cognizant of my life choices."

Walden nods suspiciously. "And this revelation hit you...when?"

"Daddy, stop grilling him. Seriously," Vivienne orders, momentarily pausing from examining her possible split ends.

Jack chuckles with a nonchalant roll of his eyes. "It was when we were in Gstaad. I realized what I'd be giving up and what I was giving it up for wasn't worth it."

"*She* wasn't worth it," Vivienne mumbles, from the sofa.

Marshall saunters over carrying two scotch glasses, shoving one into Jack's hand. "So, what do you think of Heaven?" he asks, motioning to the room. "It's our best facility, in my humble opinion. Though the one in Paris is pretty impressive. But this location is by far the biggest. We've got a pool, hot tub, sauna, thirty different bedrooms, gun range, gym, theater. You name it, we've got it. Hungry?" he says, slinging an arm around his brother's shoulders.

Jack nods. "Yeah, actually. I'm starving."

"No time for that now," Allen marches over, clapping his sons on their shoulders.

The calming piano and upright base fade out, replaced by a crackling tune. "On the farm, ev'ry Friday, on the farm, it's rabbit pie day…run rabbit, run rabbit, run, run, run…" plays on the overhead speakers.

"It's time," Allen says, steering Jack down a opaque hall. The crowd follows them, giddy with little quiet claps as they parade down the hall.

I silently follow, but something catches my eye. Displayed on a wooden stand, poised under a spotlight is a book opened inside a glass case. I quickly tiptoe over, hoping to not be locked out wherever they're headed.

The book is opened to a page titled: Branding. It has a large drawing of a red omega symbol on ancient, yellowing paper with frayed edges. It described the sacred act of branding the witch, sealing her fate into the eternities of damnation and hellfire. The Malleus Maleficarum, the secret edition, detailing the consecrated ritual branding.

I shiver, running my hands up my arms despite not being cold. Voices laugh and carry down the hallway, pulling my attention. I hurry past an IT room with about thirty monitors, a security room with hundreds of TVs and security guards watching the footage, and step into a movie theater. Everyone is talking throwing around the words "de-sensitivity training".

I hover in the back where most of the adults are drinking and chatting.

The lights dim and the projection flickers on. Trixie's frozen, terrified face fills the screen and the crowd cheers from their seats below.

"Let the hunt begin!" Vivienne shouts. A thunderous applause fills the room.

# Chapter Fifty-One
## Save the Boy

I'm going to be sick. Everything in my stomach churns at the sight of Trixie screaming, running away from the braying mob. A drone camera deftly swerves and bobs capturing the fever excitement of the running crowd and Trixie's horror. Kids laugh watching when she trips, skinning her knees and hands, while the adults socialize on the edges of the theater whisper casually.

I turn away, running towards the door, but they're closed, and I can't draw attention by having them breeze open by themselves. Leaning against the wall, I slide down to my backside, tucking my head away on my knees and crossed arms. Her screams rattle my ears as they brand her. A voice I think I recognize can be heard from the screen, darkly volunteering to hold her down while they slice her arms open. Intermingled with her screams is run rabbit, run rabbit, run, run, run that someone places from portable speakers in the video.

I shove my fingers in my ears, painfully, trying to block out her screams as they slowly fade out, her life slipping away. The audience cheers as a new victim lights up the screen and I say a prayer it isn't Winston. A waiter, holding a silver tray with an envelope strolls through the doors and I scramble on my hands and knees crawling out into the hall, the door hitting my foot. I quickly roll out of way when the waiter breezes back out of the theater humming the run rabbit song to himself.

I lay on my back, staring up at the textured ceiling. *I can't do this, Blue. I made a mistake. I want to go home…* I clutch my arms to my chest quivering in a dry sob knowing Blue can't hear me. *Trixie…I'm so sorry. I tried to save you. I swear I tried. I'm so sorry.* I ponder what Marie said about halted correspondence, about paradise and Brighid, about the feeling of contentment and happiness unknown. I wish knowing Trixie reached the destination we all strive for made this easier. I just hope one day, she can forgive me. Perhaps if I had cared earlier, she'd still be here.

I roll onto my side realizing I'm falling asleep. The training has gone on well over an hour and I'm not sure how much longer I have. The invisibility spell is almost as draining as being forced to watch Trixie's murder. I worry my spell will start to wear off. *Perhaps I need to find a way out of here. But what if Jack needs me? I can't just leave him.*

The theater doors burst open and I lean against the wall as much as possible to make room for the mass exodus. After they clear, I push myself to my feet and follow them down a corner leading to another seemingly endless hallway. *This place is a labyrinth. If I'm not careful, I'm going to get lost.*

The crowd pours into a room, and I squeeze past the few stragglers huddled in the doorway of what looks like a collegiate space for wrestlers. The floors are covered in blue mats and the walls are encased in black foam pads. Allen and Jack take center stage standing in the middle of the mats.

Allen squares his shoulders with a smile so arrogant it's nearly blinding to look at. "It's an auspicious day when a son follows in his father's footsteps. Tonight, Jack takes the next step in becoming one of the chosen, a Noble Hunter, a calling set forth by God himself."

Everyone raises a glass. "A Noble Hunter," they chant before taking a sip.

Allen turns, addressing his son, placing a heavy hand on his shoulder. "There isn't a person in this room that hasn't had to take a similar step in their progression." Still gazing at his son, he bends his hand, waving someone in.

In the corner across from where I'm standing, a hidden door opens up.

But before I can see who is coming inside something catches my attention. A boy hoots and cheers, another boy next to him laughs. My head snaps in that direction, I step forward turning knowing exactly who that belonged to. Standing with a brown bottle in his hand with a freshly shaved head, having forgone his manbun, is Nick Andersen, complete with Pete Martin laughing beside him. Pete grins, shaking his head watching the scene behind me. It was Pete who volunteered to hold Trixie down.

*I knew Nick was part of this. But why him? His father is a teacher, not exactly the most elite in the country. And Pete Martin, he was teased for being a transfer from public school. So why them?*

There's a stillness in the room, all eyes are drawn to Jack and Allen standing behind me. I swivel and clasp my hand over my mouth to keep me from crying aloud. A boy, no older than twelve years old, is lying on his side, his hands bound behind him as he's been stripped down to his boxershorts. He cries, whimpering to himself asking for his mother.

*This can't be happening. This isn't happening. I won't let this happen.* My stomach clenches in horror and my magic surges inside me, begging to be used. My breathing is getting heavy, almost noticeably so. I step away from the gawkers lining the walls. Like a dam opening my magic floods my veins, pulsing so powerfully I feel like my skin my tear. I glance down, unable to see my feet, legs, or middle. I hold up my hands to my face put there's nothing there. I'm more invisible that even before. I feel light, almost weightless.

Jack's eyes are glassy, but his face remains an impenetrable mask. His nostrils flare as he breathes.

Marshall strolls over holding out a branding iron, much shorter than what Elspeth described, but then again she did say they were broken down over the centuries so more could be made. He bows to Jack, the prod lay across both hands as he holds it out to his brother.

Jack's head whips to his father.

Allen tightens his hold on Jack's shoulder, giving it a good, menacing squeeze. "You must do the honor."

Jack stares at the branding iron, his mask fracturing. He reaches for it then drops his hand. His eyes dart about the crowd, possibly wondering how many he could take down. He glances at the cameras fastened to the ceiling in each corner of the room. He's plotting, it's obvious the wheels in his head are turning and he's grappling for an exit strategy. He glances at the boy then the door.

"Jack," Allen says threateningly.

"Does the wittle pansy need a dwink?" Nick mocks, from the wall.

Pete laughs. "I'll do it if Jack is too chicken shit."

"Stop!" Vivienne steps forward. "Of course, Jack doesn't need a drink. Right, babe?" she says, quickly stepping across the mat towards them. "Just do it," she hisses through clenched teeth at him when she's closer.

Allen chuckles shaking his head. "Does your fiancé really have more balls than you, son?"

My footsteps down make a sound when I circle around them until I'm a foot from the boy. "Don't move, it's going to be okay. Pretend you don't hear me," I whisper to him.

Tears stream down his dirty and bruised face as he looks about.

"Dad," Marshall says, "I was wasted the first time I branded someone. That stench of burning flesh is enough to make you gag. A stiff drink might actually help."

Jack glances at his brother grateful and relieved, color slowly returns to his face.

Marshall turns on his heel and quickly crosses the room to the nearest door. I push to my feet, sprinting after him. Marshall rolls his shoulders and exhales seemingly tired of this whole charade especially with some woman waiting in a suite for him.

I pause, Marshall continues to the main hall towards the bar. My brain races as I try to come up with a plan. *I can't risk using my magic, I'm already doing everything I can to remain invisible.* I sniff the air inhaling a decadent aroma of butter, sautéing meat and rosemary. Theres a clattering and commotion coming from a kitchen a few doors down. An idea occurs to me. I turn from Marshall and run in the opposite direction towards the kitchen.

I bump the swinging doors open hoping the busy chefs won't notice. Eight sous chefs are bent over plating delicate meat next to three roasted carrots on oversized square plates. They carefully drip sauce across the plate turning the dinner into an artful masterpiece.

I stride over to the sixteen-burner stove top and ignite three burners. I peek over my shoulder making sure not to be noticed, then smash a bottle of cooking oil across the stovetop. I leap back as the entire stainless-steel stove is engulfed in orange and red flames that lick up the walls and nip at the ceiling.

The sprinkler system activates. I knock over two more bottles of oil helping fan the flames. *What if this isn't enough? What if the water puts the fire out?* Alarms sound off and the lights go out, replaced by flashing emergency lights. Chefs flee the kitchen as smoke engulfs the room. Before following them, I close my eyes. *I have to do this, it's worth the risk.* I imagine a Michael Bay-worthy explosion, one that isn't so easily extinguished. *Ne Feerah.* The glass windows in the kitchen doors explode out of their frame and I rush to join the flood into the main hall with everyone.

Everyone huddles together tittering nervously about the fire. Vivienne clings to Jack, but he forgets to protectively wrap his arms around her. He peels her hands away from his sweater, quickly pacing over to his father speaking to his security crew.

"Dad, we're in an underground bunker, what are we going to do?" Jack questions.

Allen sighs with very little care. "My men are on it. The fire will be put out momentarily. We have jugs of blessed water for emergencies," he informs cryptically.

Jack frowns. "What?"

I blanch recognizing the term. *Are Noble Hunters working with Nefari witches? But why, I read that Nefari believe humans are so far beneath them. Elspeth only helped because of a personal vendetta.*

"What about the boy?" Jack inquires.

Smoke now billows from the hall but with much less ferocity now.

Allen shakes his head aggravatedly as a security team member whispers something in his ear. "Damnit. Everything will need to be reupholstered. The refurbishment will be a nightmare. Damnit!" he yells, balling his fists until his knuckles strain white.

"And the boy?" Jack asks louder.

Allen's head whips in Jack direction, his face a deadly scowl. "He'll be drugged and returned, to be taken at a later date. Everything we do is precisely timed. He should have already been branded and gone by this point. You risk everything when you don't keep to the plan. But mark my word, you will brand him. If you don't, you'll be the one on that mat. Believe that."

"Wait," Vivienne says, stomping over to them.

Allen closes his eyes, his mouth a hard line as he searches for patience.

"We aren't going to kill him?" Vivienne questions incredulously.

Allen sighs, opening and closing his fists. "No. When a witch has yet to ascend, we only brand them. Once he starts practicing magic, then we kill."

Vivienne scoffs. "Why are we giving the abomination a chance? This is ridiculous. What happened to branding then killing?"

Four towering men in ash covered suits reeking of smoke asks to have a word with Allen who grunts in response and marches away with them.

Jack stares after his dad while Vivienne pouts at his side. The commotion in the great hall begins to settle, the wait staff flutters about offering cocktails and appetizers that have been saved from the fire as they were already waiting in the dining room.

Nick and Pete worm their way through the anxious crowd, making their way to Jack and Vivienne.

Nick's dark eyes narrow on Jack. "You're gonna have to do it you know. Your dad won't let you get away with punking out." Nick's smile is a slash across his face, a madman enjoying the thought of watching the "golden boy" get his hands dirty. "I had to gut an old man for my initiation. I didn't get off on some simple branding," Nick sneers.

"Back off, creatin," Vivienne snaps, stepping in front of Jack.

Nick glares down at her, posturing inches from her. "What? You can't do shit. I'm part of this club. I've seen video of you burning Mr. Edwards. And I was there when you shot that River kid. If you try to mess with me, remember you'll go down."

Color drains from her face, her jaw falls. "Are you threatening me, you ape!? You took an oath. Besides, did you miss the videos we just watched of you and your dad holding down Doris, Trixie, Frank, Ennis, just to name a few."

Nick fans his arms out like he's about to shove her, but Pete jumps between them.

"Dude, mutual destruction. That's why those tapes exist. She can't expose you without exposing herself. Let's just go over there. I heard from Marshall and Sampson that the entertainment is still coming," Pete says, soothingly. He successfully nudges Nick away from Jack and Vivienne.

Vivienne shakes her head then snatches a champagne flute from a hovering waiter. "Your father should have them killed. They're too reckless. I know he needs bottom feeders to manipulate, but Nick Andersen and Pete Martin? It's pathetic." She throws the glass back in a single gulp.

Jack holds a shrewd scowl on his face, glaring at everyone in the room. "That's not why those videos exist…" He mutters.

"What are you talking about baby?" Vivienne frowns then looks for more alcohol.

"Did you notice who is never on those tapes? Allen. It isn't about mutually assured destruction, it's about control. He pulls the strings because at any moment he could turn his minions in, destroy their lives," he sneers.

"Jack," she says, glancing about, "What are you saying?" she takes a step closer, their faces only inches apart. "Stop talking right now. This is why no one believes you're serious. That's why your dad gave you a shit initiation. He was calling your bluff. Don't you get it? Jack, if you don't knock this off, he will end you." She finishes another glass. "So, smile like a good little boy, then brand the witch, and kill it. Cause if you fail your first assignment," she stops, her lower jaw trembling, "just don't, okay?"

Jack peers down at Vivienne, listening to her plead. The anger blazing behind his eyes simmers down. A serene mask slips into place and he tilts Vivienne's face up to him and he kisses her lips gingerly.

She throws her arms around his neck, deepening the intimacy.

I turn away, desperate to leave, feeling my magic continue to flow I don't want to continue this gamble. My heart doesn't ache in betrayal, it's too broken for that, mortified over the grizzly snuff film and the kidnapped boy. My eyes fill with tears only to quickly sink back down. *How can there be so much evil?* You hear things, you see the news, police cams, war footage, but to witness it, to behold the pleading screams of someone you know and the deranged gleeful response is something else entirely. My magic throbs inside me, desperate to be unleashed once again. My palms prickle with sweat. I don't know how to rein my power back in without turning visible.

Allen comes strolling down the hall and claps his hands together trying to attract everyone's attention. "I apologize everyone for that disastrous interruption. The fire was in the kitchen, but it has since been extinguished. The west wing hasn't been affected, if we could all congregate there, we can let the celebration of our newest member begin."

He leads the way to a ballroom where a DJ is set up and a laser light show is set on dazzling display. All the teens convene in the center, jumping up and down with their hands in the air, shouting along to the current earworm on the radio.

Marshall huddles next to Jack, "When dad is ready to retire and I take over, we're going to streamline things. No more going out in teams, I like playing things solo. Quick easy kills, no trophies from the victims, no attempts to destroy their lives beyond their death. I promise, it gets easier," he assures. Caroline Chen in a barely there dress strolls by, catching Marshall's eye. "She's eighteen, right?" he says, partly joking before strutting behind her, snatching her waist.

Jack idles on the edge of the dance floor, his hands shoved into the pocket of his pants while Vivienne grinds against Margot dancing for him despite his eyes fixed on the floor.

I drift from the dance filled with reckless abandon as girls undress, boys grind against them and liquor sloshes out of cups soaking their bodies. Marshall sloppily dances with two wait staff in a manner of undress making many of the adults blush and look away, marching out of the door.

I meander to the billiard room listening to Allen discussing his flight in the morning to Belarus where a burning had been made public.

Jack strides into the room, causing my heart to lift in my chest. He marches past me, but pauses, his eyes sliding towards me, then back to the floor before continuing his stride to the tuft lounger where his dad is scowling. "I apologize about tonight. I would like another opportunity. And if the place nearly burns down to the ground again," he jokes darkly, Walden chuckles, Allen raises a brow, "I'll act faster. Let me know when, I'm ready." He bows his head before sweeping from the room. I carefully follow him down the hall, striding past the rowdy party.

Heat radiates from his body when he steps onto the dumbwaiter and I slip in beside him. He squeezes his eyes shut, his hands shake, balled at his sides.

I struggle to keep up with him to the elevator and through the club entry.

The valet must sense Jack's simmering rage, because he says nothing and instead hastily fetches the car. Jack peels away from the curb, flips a dangerously close U-turn, and speeds down the street.

I peer down at my feet, seeing a faint ghostly outline of my shoes. I brush past people on the sidewalk rushing to my car, but then I spot Jack's car parked in an alleyway. I look around before silently approaching.

Jack pounds his steering wheel screaming. He grips the wheel nearly ripping his throat as he releases another heart-breaking, ear-piercing scream. He rests his head on his steering wheel, his shoulders trembling.

I want to reach in and comfort him, hold and cradle him in my arms. I lay my back against the brick wall and shut my eyes, trying to call my magic to cease and let me be seen. I feel my magic drain, the flow becoming a tepid stream, until it's just the barely noticeable hum I've grown accustomed to.

I open my eyes, seeing the phantom outline of my hands. I bend and stretch my fingers. Just as my legs are becoming more solidified Jack starts his car and pulls out of the alley, going a safer speed back down the street.

I trudge to my car, seeing a ticket under the windshield wiper. Just a cherry atop one of the worst nights of my life.

By the time I'm pulling into the driveway, it's well after 10:00 and I'm finally visible. I kick off my shoes in the entry and announce I'm home.

"Why don't you come into the kitchen, Eleanor," Mom shouts, the kitchen doors breeze open from her magic.

I try to decipher her tone, unsure if it's angry or not. Coming down the hall, I can see my mom leaning against the sink, teacup in hand, her elbow resting on her arm folded across her body. She gazes at me, bemused, the kind of expression she makes when I've been caught in a lie.

*Great.*

"I'm sorry I didn't call. My phone was dead. Honest," I say, holding up my dead cellphone.

Blue sits on the island next to a bowl of fruit, his tail swishing back and forth. Sally sits cross-legged on the countertop smiling, and standing next to the hearth is Jack, his eyes red and his face drained of color.

My heart lifts, then beats nervously at the sight of him.

*"It appears you survived. Don't ever do that to me again."*

"We were all worried," Mom chastises. Her eyes narrow on me, her mouth forms a facetious grin, "even Jack was concerned as there are witches going missing and you're out late without so much as a phone call to check in."

Jack gives me an apologetic look. "I told your mother—"

"Helen," she corrects, gently.

"I explained to Helen," he amends with a smile, "that neither of us view this as a casual relationship, given I've dreamt about you and have the evidence in art form to prove it." Even with his exhausted tone, he still manages to sound teasing.

"Ell, I want to see that painting he made for you. Is it pretty yummy?" Sally questions behind her hand.

"Jack said he needs to speak to you in private, but he gives you permission to share everything he is about to tell you, with us," mom says, tipping her head to the side. "You two can speak in your room. But Eleanor, you're grounded as soon as he leaves, so if you would like to attend prom with him, I advise you don't push it," she says with sharp eyes and a biting smile in a way only a mother can.

*Blue, please stay here. You're going to be listening anyway. So just stay put.*

Shockingly, Blue actually listens. He rests on the island, turning away from me.

Jack remains silent as we climb the stairs to my bedroom. The moment I close my bedroom door behind him he pulls me into his arms, holding me there in silence. I can feel the emotional exhaustion roll off him in heavy waves. His arms tremble around me as he rests his forehead against mine. I tighten my grip on him, only now realizing the toll that infiltrating The Noble Hunters took on him.

"I'm sorry we haven't spoken," he whispers, his eyes still closed. "There were so many nights I considered throwing in the towel, ditching the plan and rushing over here."

"You got the tattoo," I note.

He nods, our foreheads still touching. "I had to. It was the only way. But it's not like a *magic* tattoo, it can be removed."

"How did you get here? I didn't see your car?" I ask.

"I wasn't sure if I was being followed, I parked a mile up the road and walked." He steps back from me, his hand sliding from my waist to my hand. "I need to ask you something, were you there tonight?"

I let go of his hand and go sit on my bed. "Yeah. I'm sorry, my magic was warning me you were in danger, I had no choice. I had to come."

He nods again, then sits next to me on my bed. "I thought I felt you. Were...were you...gosh I wish there was a way to ask this that didn't sound so stupid," he says bashfully, rolling his eyes at himself.

"Yeah, I was invisible," I answer him, finishing his question. "It was really hard. My entire body feels sunburned now, and my head feels like I have a brain freeze, so it'll be a long time before I do that again, if ever."

He takes my hand in his. "Then you saw me kiss Vivienne? I hope you know that didn't mean anything. Less than nothing, if that's possible." He stops, his face falls, mortified, having just realized something, "Eleanor, were you there during the...videos?"

Flashes of Trixie playing in my mind, her scream ringing in my ears. "Yes," I whimper.

He wraps me in his arms, tucking my head under his chin. "There aren't words to convey a proper apology. I-I—I am so sorry, Eleanor. I..." he stops, his voice cracking, his arms quiver around me. "We've got them. I promise we've got them."

I lean back so that I may see his face, as if that will help give me clarity. "What do you mean?"

He runs his hands through his hair, releasing a big gust of air. "Allen kept meticulous files on every Noble Hunter. They're supposedly a nonprofit organization with the most exclusive membership. A member's personal wealth quintuples under my father, assisted in back room deals, and he promises you a high that you could never experience anywhere else, all you had to do was give up your darkest secrets and let Allen film you committing murder." Jack reaches into his pocket and fishes out a bone white business card, elegant in simplicity. It merely reads: Noble Hunting, 1644. "If you're one of the "lucky" chosen, this card will find its way into your hands and Allen's people will contact you."

I can barely sit still as Jack details the files he found and copies of divorce filings, bank transfers, wiring tapping, insider trading, legislation drafted at Allen's request, trade deals falling through, shifting seats in the senate, congress, parliament. And if that wasn't enough, there are photographs of men in the club with younger women, clearly not their wives. Things like red district clubs, kinks, and creepy rituals that would make even Stanley Kubrick blush.

"That's just the tipping point; we haven't even got to the murders yet," His hands shudder at different times. He swallows unable to continue when he gets to the de-sensitivity training. "I have it all on film. And some clips I've taken off Allen's hard drive before he could have it cleaned. We need to release them, send them to the police but not just the department here in Salem. My dad has friends in the CIA, FBI, DEA, ATF, I don't know who can be trusted there. And we need to release it online, to independent journalists, mainstream media, *everyone*," he says, his face looks hollow as he speaks like he's been beaten down and every bit of hope and happiness carved out. "I can't go home until it's done," Jack says. "I'm watched, recorded, followed, my phone, computer, scanned. I have the thumb drive with all the files, photos, video, including what I recorded on the camera I wore tonight. If I don't send this out tonight, I won't get the chance to," Jack insists, staring into my eyes pleadingly.

I exhale, knowing he's right. Even if they're his family, things need to be brought to light. And if we don't do it now, who knows what will happen. "Why don't I go brew us some tea, I think we have a long night ahead of us."

Jack reaches up, kissing me before I go.

With my magic, I toss him my computer, leaving him grinning as I head downstairs. I brew us a specific batch intended to give us energy to work. My mother was skeptical of allowing Jack to stay past midnight, but thankfully, she took me at my word that there was something that couldn't wait.

I watch Jack type away at my computer, consulting his burner phone, his regular phone, then an iPad that he swiped from the club. I begin to nod off listening to the grandfather clock in the hall chime 3:00 a.m.

Jack gently nudges me awake. "Eleanor, it's done," he says.

I open my eyes, groggy and struggling to sit up. "What is it?"

He smiles sweetly at me, tucking my hair behind my ear. "Everything has been sent and I sent it out to everyone CNN, Fox, ABC, CBS, TMZ, eighteen different crime watch podcasters, thirteen different political podcasters that constantly search for this type of corruption. Even to different state agencies. I'm sorry it took me so long; I was consulting with a kid in Singapore about using encryptions and ghost servers. I'm totally clueless when it comes to that sort of stuff."

I pull him onto the bed with me, enveloping him in a tight, loving hug. "I'm so proud of you. That couldn't have been easy," I whisper against his cheek. I lean back against the pillow as he hovers over me, staring at me tenderly and with great relief. "What do we do now?" I ask.

Jack smile turns glum, almost bleak. "Now we wait for the world to fall apart."

# Chapter Fifty-Two
## As the World Falls Down

Jack and I agreed we need to keep the charade going until the news breaks. Thankfully, Jack was able to convince Allen to delay finishing his initiation until after finals. Communicating only through Jack's burner, we both comb every news source desperately waiting for a pronouncement, a leak, anything. But there's nothing, not even a whisper. Jack is starting to lose hope. If he doesn't brand that child, Allen will end him. I wasn't even sure what that meant. *Would Allen truly kill his own son?*

On the first day of finals, I text Jack asking if we should just run away together. He responds that no matter where we go, Allen will find us.

"Eyes on your own screen," Mr. Delaney snaps at no one in particular as he and two other proctors stalk up and down the aisle, glowering at every student.

I struggle with my essay portion of Mr. Edwards' final. A part of me yearns to smash my laptop over the desk and scream. My jaw trembles and the words on my screen blur. *How can they get away with everything?* How do you find justice when the scales are tipped so heavily in the elite's favor? *It is the hubris of youth,* Winston would have said, *to believe that justice could be served in such an unjust world.*

The door bangs against the wall. Everyone jumps in their seats.

Headmaster Archibald waves out his arms trying to block four police officers charging into the room, while a short stout man in an expensive suit and oversized glasses squeeze by them.

The headmaster keeps trying to run interference, trying to cut off the officers. "You can't do this! These are students! We are in the middle of finals!" he yells.

A burly cop with hairy knuckles nearly bulldozes him over, retrieving his cuffs from his belt. "Poppy Simonsen, you have the right to remain silent…"

The pipsqueak in the bowtie shouts, "Poppy, don't say anything!"

The tallest officer marches to Vivienne's desk, grabs her arm, and tugs her out of her seat. "Vivienne Mather, you have the right to remain silent, anything you say can and will be used against you in the court of law."

The entire room gives a collective gasp as the insanity unfolds.

"Are you kidding me?" Vivienne screams. "Do you even know who my father is? Hello? You will all regret this. I swear. Your jobs, pension, gone!"

Everyone whips out their phones recording.

A thin, overly tanned man rushes into the room, heaving out of breath. He glances at all the students gawking and straightens his tie. "Vivienne don't speak. I represent Miss Mather, I'm her attorney."

"But I didn't do anything!" Poppy cries as she's escorted from the room.

Headmaster Archibald hurries after them, threatening lawsuits against each of the officers. "You're trespassing on private property!" he hollers over their warrants.

Everyone rushes to the door and trickles into the hallway to witness Poppy and Vivienne perp walked down the hall, abandoning our English final. The girls' cries echo and reverberate against the terrazzo floors and stone walls.

"Dad! Dad, what's going on!?"

All of our heads snap in the other direction, now seeing more kids flood out of classrooms as Nick Andersen is towed out of class by two police officers, his father, also in cuffs follows suit, staring at the ground refusing to meet the eyes of the gaping students, all rubbernecking to get the perfect shot on their phone. The excitement is palpable.

"They've got Sienna Hastings!" someone shouts from down the corridor.

High pitch shrieks sound from the second floor. Next there's a slam of the side door on the first floor as someone makes a run for it. A female officer chases after him, eventually tasing him as he tries to climb the gate.

"Students, we are still in the middle of testing, now everyone back into the classrooms," teachers urge, trying to usher the students back in. But it's too late, the entire school has broken into pure pandemonium.

Students rush at each other, sharing their phones and showing the different videos they'd taken. News reports pour in like tidal waves. Different news anchors and podcasters can be heard echoing up and down the halls as kids, and even a few teachers now, play the different news segments from phones in a deafening cacophony.

I gaze up and down the hall and catch a Fox News report showing a video of the FBI filtering in and out of the Mather mansion, carrying out box after box of files. On another phone next to me, CNN shows a member of parliament being escorted out of office.

Huddles of students giggle and gasp over their luminated screens. It doesn't matter if you admire or fear the Griggs Academy royalty. If you love them or hate them. Befriend them or were bullied by them. The entire student body is electrified with titillation, because regardless of your feelings for them, *everyone* loves a scandal even more. And this is one for the books.

I jump when two hands land gingerly on my hips. Jack twirls me around to face him. "We did it. Look." He turns his phone to me, scrolling through endless article suggestions on his news feed. D.C., L.A., Chicago, Seattle, San Fransisco, Paris, Berlin, London, Shanghai, Tokyo, have videos of CEOs, CFOs, COOs, politicians, brokers, celebrities, captains of industry dodging flashing cameras, their attorneys insisting they have nothing to say, several articles included mug shots and even one or two attempted suicides while trying to evade capture.

I search for words, but my brain is still reeling just from Vivienne's arrest. *Is this it? Are Noble Hunters truly facing justice?* "No, Jack, you did it. Thank you! Thank you!" I cry, leaping into his arms.

Jack tilts his head so his lips are close to my ear. "I'd be dead if you hadn't come that night. You saved me, again. *We* did this," he whispers holding me tight.

"What does this mean for you?" I ask glancing up and down the gossiping hallway.

Jack shrugs. "I don't know. I haven't seen anything about my dad yet. He's kept himself extremely well-insulated. But the files we sent exposed him as well."

I feel his phone buzz in his pocket against my leg, we reluctantly break apart as he snags his phone from his pocket. He sighs, staring at the screen.

"It's my family's attorney," he says, showing me the phone. "I'll be right back," he says, picking up my hand, giving it a kiss before turning into a quiet classroom to take the call.

The headmaster comes jogging back down the hall. "Shows over, everyone! Everyone!?" Slowly kids lift their heads from their phones. "Everybody, we will be meeting in the chapel. Head there now or finals will be canceled, and you'll all fail," he threatens, struggling to shout over the excitement. "Seniors, remember acceptances can be rescinded!"

Students grumble and mutter complaints under their breath, shoving their phones back into their pockets and purses while they collectively trudge down the hall and out the side door.

I linger waiting for Jack to come back.

"You too, Miss O'Reilly," Headmaster Archibald chides. He places his hand on my back, nudging me forward. I peek over my shoulder at the classroom that Jack disappeared into, worried that perhaps Jack implicated himself in all this as well.

The classroom door creaks open and Jack steps out, his face ashen and haggard, having aged ten years behind that door. His sea green eyes peer over at me.

I shrug off the headmaster's hand and stride back over to Jack. I can feel Mr. Archibald's glare burning on my back. "Hey, everything okay?" I question anxiously.

"O'Reilly, Woods, get to the chapel. Now!" Headmaster snaps before marching away.

We stay rooted in our spot in the hall.

Jack takes a step closer to me. "We are having a family meeting. My father has flown to Brussels and Marshall has fled to Argentina for an "extended vacation". Honor and my mother weren't on any of the tapes. Honor was a member but didn't have the stomach for it. I don't know how she got away with that, but okay. And my mother seems just as ignorant as ever. But we've added extra security, given how the press has our house under siege right now. We are to stay put, united front and all that. I'm being ordered home."

I reach up, brushing his hair from his forehead. "Do you think they suspect you?" I whisper, then look about the hall, making sure no one is around.

Jack shakes his head. "Nah, I had some help leaving a bit of a trail pointing to several different members. Basically, if you were in any way involved with Trixie or Mr. Edwards, you've been implicated as the rat," he answers. "Sorry I can't attend that riveting meeting with you, though."

I shrug, forcing a smile through my worry. "Don't worry, I'll take notes for you."

Jack gives me a small kiss before turning down the hall to the parking lot.

Fighting the urge to follow him, I join the last few students and teachers straggling out to the chapel.

"We are suspending finals for the rest of the day," our headmaster announces to roaring applause and cheers. He scowls in response. "We will also be canceling school tomorrow—"

More cheers erupt. Students jump to their feet in a standing ovation. I stay in my seat in the last pew, clicking on article after article looking for anything that hints toward the entire Woods family facing charges.

After a moment of celebration, a few girls' faces fall as something dawns on them. CeCe Johnston waves her hands trying to stop the high fiving, fist bumping jubilation. "What about prom on Saturday?" she questions. Everyone's heads turn towards our Headmaster.

Mr. Archibald's eyes roll to the ceiling, his mouth forms a tight quivering line as if he's using all his self-control not to spew his unfiltered thoughts on the student body. "Prom will still be held at the Hawthorne this Saturday night, but—" he stops short, interrupted by relief-filled cheers by the female students, "finals will be concluded next week, with extended school hours. You have been warned, so make the necessary accommodations. Now, for those ready for their fifteen minutes of fame excitedly waiting to speak to the press and share the salacious videos they filmed, think again."

He goes onto threaten expulsion, failing finals, permanent record, college rejection and anything else he can think to throw at us. All the students hear though is *blah, blah, blah*, as the girls titter about prom and the boys whisper what this meant for state championships for lacrosse with their captain behind bars.

I peer up and down the pews, listening to the girls describe their dresses and hair and the boys formulating a plan now that their coach and several members of their varsity team are gone. I marvel how quickly everyone has moved on. *Well, at least their priorities are in order,* I think sarcastically.

On the way home from school, I tune into the local radio station covering the arrests. Judge Mather has been indicted on four counts of fraud, bribery, and racketeering. *But not murder?* I keep listening hoping that will be listed. "Vivienne, the mega influencer," as they put it, "has lost all endorsements deals, including her collaboration with Adidas, as she has been charged with murder in the first degree in connection with missing local girl, Trixie Caldwell… Nickolas and James Andersen have been charged in connection to private school teacher Winston Edwards."

I flick off the radio. *I did it Winston.* I think back on the vision I had while in Purgatory, Winston assured the Noble Hunters that if they killed him they would seal their fate too. I think he knew that with his death, I wouldn't stop. I would keep searching until I discovered their identities and put an end to them. He had more faith in me than I. My heart sags in my chest. *I'm going to really miss you.*

As the trees part and my house comes into view, I see a sheriff's car parked in the driveway. *Oh crap. Oh crap. Oh crap. Oh crap.* My knees rattle under my skirt, and I feel like I might hurl. *Blue, do you know what this is about?*

*"I don't have the faintest idea. He just pulled up. He hasn't even stepped out of his cruiser yet. Normally, I'd guess Sally has done something, but seeing how the pillars of the community are being arrested today, perhaps you're receiving a medal. Or a rail on which to drive you out of town."*

I creep up behind his car and put it in park, unsure if I should get out or wait. *No one knows I'm involved. I would have been wacked before leaving campus if anyone even suspected anything,* I assure him, and partly myself. Jack would have made certain nothing could be traced back to me. Hopefully, not at the expense of himself.

The sheriff's car door pops open and a middle-aged man with a little tire around his middle and curly blonde hair steps out. He snuggly places a brown hat on top of his head, eyeing me in my car through narrow slits. He adjusts his belt before marching over and rapping his knuckles on my window.

I roll down my window, my body becoming slick with perspiration. "Hi." Hic! "Everything—" Hic! "Okay?"

"I'm Sheriff Abe Fuller, are you Eleanor O'Reilly?" he inquires.

I nod slowly. *Blue! Blue, what am I going to do?! Does he work with Noble Hunting? Is he here for me? Do they want me to testify or something? Blue!? What am I going to do!?*

*"Stay calm. Let's hear why he's here before you have stroke."*

"Do you have a parent or guardian inside?" he points his thumb to the house.

I nod, too frightened to speak. My shoulders leap with hiccups.

"Why don't we head inside," he suggests.

Each step with him is filled with dread. I keep glancing around us waiting for federal agents to pop out with guns. Sheriff Fuller frowns at the cats gathered in the front window.

I ring the doorbell unsure if we should just step inside or not.

"Is this not your house?" He questions with a raised brow.

Before I can respond Marie swings the door open. "Eleanor, my dear!" she says, sounding breathy with excitement and bewilderment. "The news today, have you…" She stops, as if just noticing the police officer hovering at my side. "Oh ah, hello, can I help you?"

He sticks his thumbs in his belt like some old cowboy in a western. "I need to speak to this young lady's parent or guardian," he says dryly.

"Oh dear," she says, her hand flutters to her chest, "Won't you come in, I'm her aunt. Her mother is in the front room here." She sweeps out of the way, pointing with her arm where to go.

The sheriff tips his hat before removing it completely. I numbly follow behind him. The news can be heard blasting from the television in the living room.

"What's this about, sweetie?" Marie whispers to me after the officer strolls past.

I shrug with a shake of my head.

My mother is perched on the edge of the sofa, her eyes glued to the television screen. She glances at me and the sheriff before doing a double take. She leaps to her feet, turning off the TV. "Eleanor, what's going on?"

"Ma'am, why don't you and your daughter take a seat," he recommends, motioning towards the couch where my mom was sitting.

I sit down, obeying orders as my mind reels with all the horrible possibilities for him being here. Mom lowers to the cushion next to me and Marie rushes into the room.

"What is this regarding?" my mother questions impatiently.

Blue tiptoes down the stairs, watching everyone as he takes a seat on the last stair.

Sheriff Fuller clears his throat before speaking. "Ma'am, I'm not sure if you are aware, but we've made an arrest in connection to the death of a young woman, a classmate of your daughter's," he says.

"Trixie Caldwell. Yes, I'm aware," she says, nodding her head for him to continue to his point.

He again clears his throat. "Well, we've come across disturbing text messages between the five arrested female minors that indicate that your daughter was a possible target. Do you have any reason to suspect they would want to cause your daughter or Miss Caldwell harm?" he inquires.

My head snaps to my mother, almost pleadingly, not sure what I'm supposed to say. *Yes, sir. We're witches, but the real kind.*

My mother stares into my eyes, as if reading something there. She turns back to the officer. "They began harassing my daughter once she began dating a boy in their circle," she answers calmly, confidently.

I reach over, shakily taking her hand, finding immediate comfort there.

Sheriff Fuller takes out a small device and an electronic pen. "That boy's name?"

"Jack Woods," I answer, feeling safer with my mom clasping my hand.

His pen stops. He hesitates, and lifts his eyes to me. "Jack Woods. As in Allen Woods's son?"

I nod.

"Oh damn, what's with the cop car? I swear it wasn't me this time," Sally calls, stomping down the stairs.

"When did—" the officer's eyes bulge, watching Sally come marching into the room.

I look over, curious if she'd come down naked or something, but she's wearing her usual attire. A dark floral, velvet dress with a deep V-neck, buttons down the front with bell sleeves, and thigh-high boots.

My aunt cranes her head, squinting. "Abe?"

"Sally?" he gapes. His round apple cheeks bloom a deep red. "What are you doing here?"

Aunt Sally blanches, glancing at everyone in the room. "I, um, live here…
now," she answers.

"Since she was pubescent," Marie mutters.

"I thought you moved to Canada?" he says confused.

Sally smiles uncomfortably. "I didn't like maple syrup, it turns out." She
shrugs. "I still have the ring," she says, pointing upstairs. "We could go get it."

"Excuse me," mom interrupts, crossly, "you were saying my daughter
was a target in a murder plot?"

The sheriff clamps his jaw closed. He blinks several times, clearly trying
to regain control of his faculties. "Ah, hem," he coughs into his fist. "Yes,
she was. They believed they were speaking over encrypted text when they
expressed their desire to go after your daughter, Eleanor." He glances over at
Sally uneasy. "Would you and your daughter come to the station tomorrow?"

"Yes, that's fine," my mother says sharply, giving Sally a disgruntled look
while the sheriff hands her his card.

Sally follows him out to his patrol car.

We all gather by the window watching them talk.

Mom closes the curtains, then swivels around. "Okay, you have some
serious explaining to do. These arrests, does any of it have to do with what
you and Jack were working on that night?"

I glance at Marie, who's staring at me intently.

"Yeah, I do have some things to tell you, but you might want to sit
down," I begin.

Mom shakes her head. "No, no one is telling me to sit down anymore. I
want some explanations."

I explain that Winston had pieced together that Allen Woods was
Matthew Hopkin's descendant and ordered the latest murdered witches.
Mom and Marie stumble into seats, carefully processing every word. They
both yell at Sally to hush when she came waltzing back into the house, giggling about how embarrassing that was.

"Geez, what's going on?" she asks, puzzled. She plops down in the
nearest armchair.

I continue on, describing Jack infiltrating their group, piling evidence
against them. Much to my mother's horror, I share that I followed him into
their meeting house, witnessed the beginning of Trixie's filmed murder, how
they were about to brand a young witch that hadn't even turned yet.

Mom holds her head, her elbows resting on her knees, overwhelmed by
the risks I took. Marie sniffs as tears gathered in her eyes.

I step closer to my aunt. "I'm sorry I continued to dig even though you
asked me not to. But those involved in Winston's murder have been charged.

He's getting justice."

Marie peers down at her quivering hands folded in her lap. "You put his pipe in my room," she whispers tepidly.

I nod. "Yeah. I think he'd want you to have it."

"I thought maybe he, I don't know, brought it to me or..."

I kneel down in front of my kind, kooky aunt who now I can't imagine my life without her. "He's with Brighid now. He and his family are reunited and getting the place ready for the one day you join them," I say, feeling a strange turning of the tables. "It's exciting when we get welcomed back."

Marie pulls me into a hug, her whole body vibrating as she blubbers on my shoulder, tears soaking through my school blouse. I pat her back, giving her a little loving squeeze.

"Thank you," she breathes in my ear.

Still embraced by my aunt, I feel a hand on my shoulder. I look up to see my mom accepting what I've done, and she gives me a little nudge.

We all turn as there is a loud panicked knock at the door.

# Chapter Fifty-Three
## Prom Night

Shannyn stampedes into the room and tosses a long rectangular white box onto the coffee table. "Is it true? Noble Hunting? That's the witch hunting clan?" Shannyn's eyes bounce from person to person as we all nod. She collapses onto the ottoman, hyperventilating. Tears spring to her eyes and trickle down her cheeks, rolling over her chin. "It's over…"

Mom perches on the edge of the sofa, reaching out for her.

Shannyn's jaw trembles. "My gift, it isn't a gift at all. I have the grim reaper's curse."

Mom's jaw drops, her eyes staring off into the distance. "Like your grandma Colleen."

"I've seen hundreds of witch's deaths. All over the world. I never saw who did it. Just… just their deaths. Sometimes I take belladonna just to sleep through the night with their screams echoing in my head," Shannyn cries, holding her head in her hands.

I look to my aunts for answers as Mom gathers my sister in a comforting hug.

Sally leans close to me. "A gift of the mind spell. I won't bore you with the science of it, but with the grim reaper's curse, you see when a witch or human dies. Often just the moment of death itself. Doesn't have to be murder, their passing could be natural, random, even unconnected. Many witches have lost their minds due to the gift'.'"

Shannyn gasps as Mom fills her in on everything that's happened. Her eyes dart to me after Mom finishes, then surprises me by rising from the ottoman and gathering me in her arms.

Margaret comes home from school and announces that three students had their parents arrested, but everyone is too emotionally exhausted to react. We all dig into pints of ice cream, including the cats who each have their own scoop served inside a teacup. The delivery boy who dropped off the ice cream was nearly shaking when he rang the doorbell to Salem's oldest urban legend.

We light all the candles in the living room, then place Winston's tobacco pipe and Trixie's pressed flowers in the center of the coffee table with a rose quartz between them. Leaving our spoons resting in our melting pints, we say a witch's prayer and send our love and thoughts to them in the land beyond, finally ready to say goodbye.

With "Bewitched" playing in the background, we snack and laugh for what feels like the first time in ages.

"So, Abe Fuller is the one you left at the alter?" Mom questions.

"One of the many," Marie chides with a mouth full of mint chip.

Pyer sits defensively at Sally's feet, glaring at all who laugh at her ward. Sally just acts like she didn't hear us.

My eyes flick over to the forgotten white box. "What's in there?" I ask curiously.

Shannyn's eyes bulge. She pushes her Triple Chocolate Chunk to the side and retrieves the box. "This is actually for you. Mom asked me to pick something up for you at Esmerelda's since I'm probably her best customer," she says, handing the box across the table to me. "You're still going to prom, aren't you?"

My brows leap up my face. "You bought me a prom dress?" I ask, shocked. I push myself up out of the love seat I share with Margaret and lift the lid, not sure what to expect. My taste differs greatly from Shannyn's.

I unfold the tissue paper, revealing a midnight blue gown with a sweetheart neckline. I lift the gown out of the box, my eyes sweeping the A-line skirt and the off -the-shoulder chiffon sleeves that bubble out and gather at the wrist. The dark blue fabric shimmers in the light.

I hold the dress up to myself, unsure.

"You can't wear a chunky sweater to prom," Shannyn chastises. "When you twirl, you'll see a ghostly outline of the moon and stars. It's so faint, you'll only catch it if you're looking for it."

I smile glumly with a roll of my eyes at her sweater jibe, nestling the dress back in the tissue paper. "I don't even know if I'm going. Jack's got a lot going on with his family," I say. My stomach twitches with unease as I haven't heard from him since school. "But I still really appreciate the dress. It's gorgeous."

"Well, let's not write it off entirely," Mom suggests.

I nod, peering down at my phone, wishing it would ring with Jack on the other end.

Shannyn stays the night suggesting that us sisters have an old fashion sleep over, so mom agrees to let Margaret skip school tomorrow. We laugh, gossip, and feel like kids again. For lunch on Friday, I suggest we go to Ray and Dotty's in honor of Trixie.

After lunch, my sisters somehow convince me to go shoe shopping. Maggie, of course, finds several perfect pairs, as does Shannyn, while I meander the store feeling lost and constantly checking my phone for a missed call from Jack. *It's starting to feel like two weeks ago when we weren't talking.* I place a hand on my heart, not feeling any kind of pressure, not any kind of pull. *He must be safe. But why isn't he calling? Should I call him? But what if there's a reason he's not speaking…*

Before I slip into my pajamas, I try on my dress, turning and gazing at myself in my oval mirror. The bodice is tight but still allows me to breath, and the voluminous layers make me feel like the main character of a romance novel. I brush my cheek against my bare shoulder, missing Jack. I twirl, making my skirt whoosh around me, causing constellations to sparkle across the skirt. Shannyn is right, Esmerelda is a genius. I peer down at my arms, sheathed in see-through billowy fabric, unable to hide my smile. This is a dress the princess in the tower wears. The kind of dress whose wearer deserves to be serenaded. To dance and twirl and kiss. I glance at my silent phone. *But probably not. Prom is the least of Jack's concerns at the moment. And it should be the least of mine.* But as I place the dress back on a hanger, hooking it on the door of the wardrobe, I can't help but sigh. *I really want this. Even more than that, I need this. So does Jack. We need a night that can belong to us.*

I crawl into bed, disheartened, and reach over to flick off the light, too tired to use my magic. Blue's sitting at the window, anxiously kneading the pillow seat.

"Blue?" I call.

He doesn't turn away from the window.

"Blue?" I try again.

*"Don't you find it suspect that Elspeth gave up all that information and has remained silent despite you haven't unbound her?"*

I drop my hand from the lamp, rolling over on my side to better face him. "To be honest, I was so grateful for the revelation, I haven't really given it much thought. I've been a little busy."

*"She's planning something. I can feel it."*

I sit up. "But she has limited power. She's still stuck in Purgatory," I state feigning courage.

Blue nods, peering over at me now. *"True. But I can feel her. We need to be careful."*

I flick my light off with an exhausted exhale. "That's good because I was worried things would start getting a little boring."

My body relaxes, practically melting into a deep, visionless sleep.

Blue's tail whispers across my face and I brush it away, rolling over to my other side just as my phone rings. The morning light fills my room making it hard to sleep. I moan as I reach for my phone still ringing.

I shoot up in bed seeing Jack's name on my screen. "Hello?" I answer.

"Hey," he says, his voice warm and deep. "I'm sorry I didn't call you yesterday. Things have been a bit crazy around here. Lawyers, financial advisers, PR agents, it's been a circus."

I pull my blankets up to my chin. "I'm sorry. Is there anything I can do?"

He lightly chuckles. "Go to prom with me tonight?" he asks. I can hear the smile in his voice.

"Really?" I ask, sitting up a little more. "You aren't under house arrest? I thought they had to keep you guys under lockdown."

"I've earned time off for good behavior," he jokes.

"Ha! If only they knew," I tease.

"Sshhh… Yeah, but they don't, and I intend on keeping it that way," Jack replies. "Now," he asks seriously, "are you a limo kind of girl?"

I chuckle. "I prefer to be carried off on a white steed."

He laughs. "I love you, Eleanor. And I don't regret what we did."

"Neither do I."

The room continues to brighten with the rising sun. Blue mumbles something and moves down on my bed by my feet.

We say goodbye and I spring out of bed with newfound energy. As I spoon a mouthful of soggy cereal along with my family, we listen to the news streaming from my mom's phone. More arrests are announced, questions of informants arise, accusations are flung, and more leaks seep out. A senator and two congressmen announced their resignation in shame.

Mom shakes her head. "I don't think a nuclear war would make the news right now. It's going to be a long summer of trials and plea deals," she says, clearing the table.

A small shiver of fear trickles down my spine. I feel silly now, realizing I never considered they might still get away with their crimes. I naively thought with all the evidence they'd be convicted, but even with every picture taken of them, every film crew stalking them, they're still insulated by an arsenal of attorneys and friends in high places.

"Do you really think they'll get off?" I ask.

Mom frowns, standing in the kitchen doorway. "Possibly. I mean, more evidence is still mounting against them, fortunes are being destroyed, but they're still powerful families."

I further slump in my chair, crestfallen, picturing Vivienne marching out of the court in brand new stilettos, grinning from ear to ear. With the right PR spin, she might even earn more followers than before.

"But," my mom adds, trying to rein in my despair, "the public is demanding blood. They want to see these elite get the justice they deserve. Not everyone has been bought and paid for, so don't start losing hope yet." A warm smile brightens her face. "Besides, those grisly videos are damning, and experts are already weighing in confirming their authenticity. Trust me, no one is just walking away from this."

Shannyn strides into the kitchen from the back door, returning from her run, glistening in a hot pink sports bra and itty-bitty shorts. She grabs a water bottle from the fridge. "So, what's the word, are we getting ready for prom?" she questions, raising her eyebrows. She takes several large gulps, peering over at me.

A small smile curls on my lips, allowing my mother's hope to protectively coat me. "Yeah, we're on for tonight."

Sally hoots and my mother smiles.

"Okay, let me go shower and we'll go get manicures!" Shannyn squeals.

The next several hours are spent with my family trying to primp and pamper. I veto the long glued on nails as they're forbidden in orchestra. Which I'm not too disappointed with, honestly.

"Ouch!" I yelp when Sally lets the curling iron dip too close to my scalp.

"Hold still," Shannyn orders, plucking at my brow.

Margaret and my mom hover over my dress laid out across my bed comparing different shoes and clutches.

"Nah, I don't like that one. It's got to be the silver clutch with the crystal beading," Maggie insists, exchanging the white satin purse with a silver chain.

Blue continues to pace about my room, muttering things about Elspeth and broken promises. I do my best to block him out. I'm asking for one night. Tonight belongs to Jack and me. Not to the coven. Not to the Committee. Not to The Noble Hunters. For tonight, I'm just a seventeen-year-old girl going to prom with her boyfriend. Purgatory and my evil third parent can wait. *Remember, she can't do anything, Blue.*

He scoffs and continues to pace.

"Sally, Marie," mom says, nodding her head towards the door. My aunts frown as they follow her out of the room.

Shannyn finishes my makeup, plastering on more than I'm used to. Margaret joins her in pinning up my curls, insisting that off-the-shoulder gowns demand hair to styled up to elongate the neck and compliment the shoulders. Then they help me zip up the back and fluff out the skirt.

"Eleanor," mom says, walking back in, flanked by her sisters. "I want you to wear this." In her hands is a narrow wooden box, about the length of my hand, that creaks as she opens it. Nestled against the dark velvet interior is a delicate silver chain with an antique looking silver star, with four long points and two thin points in between each long point. "The north star. My mother made it. It belonged to me a long time ago, and now it belongs to you."

I peer over, noticing Shannyn receiving a golden sun on a thin chain from Sally, and Marie fastening a golden crescent moon around Margaret's neck.

"Each of us girls had one. We thought we lost them, but Persephone stumbled upon them in the sewing room this morning," Marie informs. She glances over lovingly at my mom's familiar sitting poised in the doorway.

Mom plants a light kiss on my forehead. "You look beautiful, darling."

Sally claps like she's at the theater. "Now, stay up here in your room so you can make a grand entrance down the staircase when Jack arrives."

Mom gives me a wink before following everyone downstairs.

I gather my skirt and tiptoe over to the window seat overlooking the driveway.

*"There is something wrong, I can sense it."* Blue sends.

I reach over, scratching his head. His fur is scraggly and rough, like astro-turf. *I promise, tonight when I return, we'll figure out a plan for dealing with Elspeth.* I gaze at him curiously. "Blue, is there something you're not telling me about Elspeth? Has her power grown?"

Blue shakes his head, still dismayed. *"But Eleanor, she's only ever been out for herself, so why would she deign to help you?"*

I recall reneging on her quid pro quo deal. At the time, I was too eager to really question it, and now I'm too desperate to leave it in the past. "What can you feel from her?" I ask, glancing at the time on my phone. Jack should arrive any minute.

Blue pensively turns his head, peering out the window. His eyes glow against the light of the setting sun. The blood red and bright orange sky makes the forest appear on fire.

*"I feel her... joy,"* he sends. *"It's a dark joy. She's enjoying some kind of secret. But I have yet to figure it out. You can't feel joy in Purgatory, but she is. Or at least she wants me to believe she is. But why would she do that? What is the end goal? But you mark my words, there's a quid pro quo to be sure."* His head slowly turns to me. *"She plans on making you pay."*

Blue protectively lays across my lap and I glide my fingers over the ridges of his ribs, my thumb running the length of his protruding spine. He quivers against my legs fearfully as we watch the sun dip below the horizon.

Swallowing my worry, I pick up my phone and call Jack. It rings three times before he answers.

"Hey, I'm so sorry," he says in a rush of words. "We've run into a problem and I'm still trying to solve it," he explains, repentantly.

My heart stops. "What is it, what's going on?"

"My car is totaled. I think someone took a baseball bat to it," he says in frustration. "But I've been on the phone trying to find a car for the evening. Of course, every limo company is fully booked, but even local car rentals are apparently all unavailable."

"But you're okay?" I question.

He sighs. "Yeah, I'm okay. My car's not salvageable, unfortunately."

I lean against the window. "I don't understand, I thought you had extra security."

"Yeah, they're completely dumbfounded. I don't know if it was someone from my old group, or maybe Vivienne's. Perhaps the security team recognized them and let them through. But everyone is denying they saw anything."

I say the air spell in my mind and motion for my purse and car keys to fly to me. "Jack why don't I come pick you up," I suggest.

Another sigh but this time resigned. "Yeah, I think that's the only way we'll get there. I'm sorry, I had this whole thing planned. I wanted it to be romantic."

I chuckle. "I don't know, rescuing you has kind of become our thing," I tease.

Blue springs off my lap, soundlessly landing on the floor. *"Be careful,"* Blue sends before sauntering out of the room.

I pick up my skirt and hurry down the stairs, I shout to my family in the living room as they argue about what movie to watch, that Jack is experiencing car trouble before dashing to my car.

I smoosh my skirt out of the way before I shut the car door without snagging the fabric. I flick off the news, refusing to listen to any more coverage tonight. After pulling out of the driveway, I play my favorite Foo Fighters song that now reminds me of Jack. Despite Jack's car trouble, and despite Blue's incessant worrying, I can't stop smiling. Even with road closures and detours, I find myself eager for Jack to see me in this gorgeous gown. It's a strange, unfamiliar sensation.

I turn up the radio, getting lost in Dave Grohl's hypnotic voice. The forest trees are a black encompassing wall on either side of my car.

Red and blue lights flash in my rearview mirror.

*Crap.* I groan to myself, coasting to a stop as I pull to the side of the road.

*I wasn't even going that fast.* A thought occurs to me, causing me to roll my eyes. *My mom called Abe Fuller to escort me, I guarantee. Ugh! Mom! Or he's upset that we didn't make it to the station like we were supposed to.*

The officer taps my window.

I quickly roll it down. "I'm really sorry if my mom—"

The officer doesn't bend down to meet me. Instead, he raps the roof of my car with his hand. "Can you step out of your vehicle, miss?"

My eyes slide to my dashboard; prom started twenty minutes ago. I know it's fashionable to be late, but I don't want to lose a single minute of the night. I leave the keys in the ignition and carefully step out of the car. I hold my skirt up, worried about mud in my silver high heels.

"Both hands on your car Miss," the officer orders, standing back by his car.

I glance over at his cruiser, blinded by his headlights. *This isn't right.*

The trees are still, the night is silent. I can't even hear crickets' chirp.

"Hello?" I call, trying to peer at the car but seeing nothing but bright light.

Bows draw back on fiddle strings and piano keys plunk down in a plucky tune. Blood drains from my face and my mouth goes dry. "On the farm, ev'ry Friday, on the farm, it's rabbit pie day…"

I drop my hands from the car. "Wait! Wait!" I shout, holding my hands out defensively as a dark figure approach. A firm hand clamps down on my mouth. My nose is filled with a burning chemical smell as a cloth is pressed against my face. I lose my footing and tumble to the ground. The hand drives me into the dirt, pressing my skull backward forcing me to inhale.

I try to hold my breath as I claw at his hands to no avail. My eyelids are closing, and I've already breathed in so much my lungs are on fire. I go limp in his arms and drift into the dark.

# Chapter Fifty-Four
## Too Late

I flutter in and out of consciousness, my head lulls from side to side, and my feet drag on the ground like a rag doll. My eyes are sandbags demanding an insurmountable strength to open them. There's a gurgling of voices, but it's like my ears are underwater. A strong commanding voice speaks, but I can't make out what it says. The same authoritative voice rings out again, repeating himself over and over, becoming clearer and clearer until finally...

"Eleanor O'Reilly!"

"Y-y-yes?" My tongue weighs a hundred pounds. Arms on each side keep me hoisted up. An angry slap stings my face. I blink several times, finally able to open my eyes, but everything is still hazy. Orange and yellow waves hover in the air, slowly taking shape. They're flames. Torches, to be precise, on long wooden poles about eight feet high. Maroon headstones tower over me. *No, not headstones.* They're people dressed in robes with their hoods up, sheathing their faces in shadow. My stomach roils inside me.

"You're... Noble Hunters...aren't you?" I ask. I slowly feel my body tightening up, like it's piecing itself back together. I'm becoming more aware of the throb on my cheek and the tight pinching of my arms.

"Yes," the strong voice answers.

Colors, lines, and depth all snap into place. I now see a man on a white horse behind the crowd, watching me and holding an open book.

*Death rides a pale horse,* I think groggily.

"Do you know why you are here, Eleanor O'Reilly?" he says as if my name leaves a foul taste on his tongue. "I warn you, lying will not help you here."

It's strange, but I can't think of a lie. "Yes."

"Eleanor O'Reilly, you have been found guilty in the devil's work committing the gravest sin of witchcraft," he declares loudly, fervently, upon his steed.

This is no trial. They have already convened as judge, jury, and executioner. The Noble Hunters aren't here to hear me out, listen to me beg for my life. They are here for one reason only: to kill me.

Bang, bang, bang goes the farmers gun...so run rabbit, run, run, run... The song continues to play.

I try to scan their faces, narrowing my eyes on each of them, but I can't make anything out under their hoods. *Who could possibly be left? The highest-ranking members have all been arrested. Who did we leave out?*

As if hearing my thoughts, the leader perched on his horse pulls down his hood, exposing his face to the firelight.

Allen Woods.

"The body of a witch must be purified through blood, breaking down the flesh to be offered up to the Holy One," he says pompously, as if speaking about himself. Maybe he is. Perhaps he's a God unto himself. His eyes are like stone, meeting mine with such malice I feel my body wither under his glare.

Nine members encircle me, including the ones that were hoisting me up. I wobble, uneasy on my feet, only now realizing that my shoes are gone. I hold my shaking arms up to protect me.

"Daughter," he says, glancing to a girl beside him. "You have been chosen to draw first blood. Let it begin."

A girl too short to be honor steps forward. She winds her fist back, then plows into my face splitting my lips and sending me flying into the followers behind me. The metallic taste of blood spills into my mouth, dribbles out of the open wound, and down my chin.

The circle closes in around me, their shoulders pressed tightly together. Another punch deftly connects between my eyes. My head flings back, straining my neck with whiplash. My ears ring. A hard kick meets my knee sending me sprawling to the ground where more feet swing, meeting my abdomen in a harsh punt.

I gasp for air and try to cry out, but I can't breathe. I can't catch my breath. Someone grinds my face into the dirt, causing pine needles, dirt, and other forest debris to fill my mouth and nostrils. A foot stomps on my spine as another collides with my head. My right eye swells shut, and something warm and wet trickles down the side of my face. The crowd laughs in a bloodthirsty frenzy.

My entire body screams in pain, but I can't cry out. I can't even get enough oxygen inside me to plead. There's a pop as the bridge of my nose shatters against the steel toes of a boot. Rivulets of warm blood spill down my face, coating my lips, chin, and neck. I try to form words, but my broken jaw doesn't respond My body shudders, barely registering the pain anymore as it begins to shut down. .

"Enough!" Allen screams. "We need her alive and aware for the branding." His voice sounds like it's getting closer, but it's hard to tell with the ringing and sound of blood pumping behind my ears.

My eyes are swollen, rendering me blind. My breath wheezes in and out of my gaping mouth, my ribs struggle trying to expand.

There's one more kick to my shoulder.

"Eleanor, answer me."

There's an inhuman moan and a gurgling of blood. If it weren't for the pain trying to speak, I wouldn't have known those bizarre sounds were coming from me.

"And so, in this twilight and evening of the world, when sin is flourishing on every side and in every place… the evil of witches and their iniquities superabound…."

I sputter, desperate to breathe, but finding only a faint, narrow stream of gasps in and out.

There's murmuring and giggling. Voices pipe up but are too quiet for my bruised, bloodied ears to pick up.

"Silence! Now, roll her onto her stomach."

I grunt as I'm turned on my side; excruciating pain ripples throughout my body with every movement. Panic rings through me when I land facedown. My blood-coated mouth is dry and cracked, my tongue feels scaley with residue and my lungs feel ablaze, shrieking for air. *I can't breathe! Someone help me! Please! Mom, I'm scared! I can't breathe!* I feel myself drifting in the dark.

There's a rough tug on the back of my dress then a tearing of fabric.

"Eleanor O'Reilly, you will be branded with the omega, marking the end of your witchcraft and the end of your life. Let this symbol testify of your guilt to the world and to your demonic coven."

There's a searing between my shoulder blades. My body, too exhausted to move, stays deadly still beneath the poker.

"Can we hurry? I'm technically under house arrest, and these cheap robes irritate my skin…"

The ringing in my head becomes unbearable. *Mom, I'm so sorry I couldn't stop this. I thought you were safe, I thought all of you were safe. Jack, I love you.*

# Chapter Fifty-Five
## Lifeless

An ethereal melody resonates from a harp. The delicate notes shimmer and ripple out like a silken stream. *It's so beautiful. I must be dead. I'm dead, and I made it to Heaven. Right? How else am I able to breath? Or smell such sweet aroma? There's even a heavenly harp. But if I'm dead, though, why am I still so sore?*

I find lifting my eye lids suspiciously easy. I feel a slight tug across one eyelid, but I'm able to blink and look around without much trouble. The light surrounding me is bright, but not supernal white; more yellow like lightbulbs. I peer about the space, my eyes taking a moment to adjust. Surrounding me are hundreds, no, *thousands* of flowers of every variety.

For a moment, I think I'm in a garden. *Wait, is Heaven like a garden?* But then I notice my canopy bed, and in the corner, I can see the top of my wardrobe behind a tiered stack of marigolds. Next to my pentagon window is a water barrel, filled to the brim with water lilies floating across.

I sit up more in my bed, wincing as a slashing pain strikes across my chest and abdomen. *I'm still in pain, so I'm alive?*

"You're alive."

The flowers on the floor tremble as something darts through them. Blue pounces on the bed, careful not to land on me. He glances at me, then quickly looks away.

"How am I alive? I remember taking a last breath, then everything went black." My head feels heavy so I lean back against my pillows.

Last night is a hazy blur. All I can recall is the horrific pain and a crowd of burgundy robes. Noble Hunters. The searing pain of being branded. I move my hand to feel my back, but I cry out in pain, unable to bend that way.

*"Yes. It's there. You were branded. You'll carry that mark for the rest of your life. Try not to move, you're still healing. But it wasn't last night that you were branded, you've been unconscious for four days."*

Mom appears in the doorway, her eyes filled with tears. "Persephone said you'd woken up." She carefully makes her way over to the very edge of my doughy bed. Her hands reach for me, then stop, unsure of where she can touch without hurting me. She blinks away her tears and sniffs. "How are you feeling? Do you need anything for pain?"

I nod. "Yes, please," I answer.

Mom closes her eyes, probably saying a spell to gather some elixir from the greenhouse.

"Why are there so many flowers in my room?" I ask, my voice is rough, gravelly. I glance about, wondering if my room is now the new greenhouse.

Mom smiles sweetly at me. "The healing powers of plants go far beyond ingestion. Have you ever wondered why people bring flowers to coma patients?" She lets out a tired, gentle chuckle when I stiffly shake my head. she reaches down and plucks a pansy from a flourishing pot. "It's a tradition passed down by witches. They just don't know it. When the world was young and people were new, witches were sent to guide them, as you know. Floral aroma can help heal." She places the pansy in my palm and closes my hand.

"How did I get here? And how am I...alive right now?" I touch my head, feeling a bandage tautly wrapped.

Mom clears her throat and looks away, wiping a glassy tear escaping from the corner of her eye. "Thankfully, you have a skilled nurse as a mother, and a neurosurgeon, a pediatrician, and an ER doctor in our coven who came to your aid. They performed surgery right here in your room. You had two dislocated shoulders, three broken ribs, a dislocated jaw, broken nose, broken collarbone, a fractured skull, an eyelid laceration, torn cartilage in your knee, and a broken back," she lists, sounding almost clinical. "The only reason you're able to move is because our medical procedures are somewhat unique, as you are well aware." She tries to push a cheerful smile onto her grim face. Only now do I notice the circles under her eyes and the scarlet nostrils from crying. It's exactly the way she looked the day after my dad passed away.

Where I was branded, the burn itches and stings. "And there's absolutely nothing you can do for the brand?" I question.

She sniffs, peering down at her lap. "No. Unfortunately. I can help ease your pain but you'll always carry that scar."

I nod, disappointed but figuring as much. "How did you find me?" I ask.

A teacup and saucer float into the room with a spoon swirling around inside the cup. It lands gently in my lap.

"Sip it slowly," Mom orders. "It's quite powerful." She tentatively watches me take a sip. Despite the steam rising from the cup, it feels and tastes...cold, like a frozen mint.

As the liquid slowly trickles down my throat, it coats my raw insides, soothing as it goes. The muscles in my neck feel looser and the pounding that was starting to build in the back of my head quiets.

"Jack found you," she says. "He called me, asking what to do and I ordered him to bring you here. I called members of our coven, and I assessed the damage when you arrived. He stayed by your side the entire time. Even slept in that window seat over there until this morning when I *forced* him to go home. He needed to shower, eat, and rest. It took some cajoling, but I was finally able to convince him."

I snuggle deeper into my pillows and pull the covers up to my chin. *Jack. We never made it to prom.* There's a sudden flash of Allen Woods in my mind, reading from an ancient book. I think Vivienne may have also been there. I take a large gulp from my tea as my heart starts to pound.

*"You're safe, Eleanor. No harm will come to you here. I'm sure you no longer feel you can trust me, but I vow to you, you are safe within these walls."*

*What? Why would you think I couldn't trust you?* I try to adjust my pillow, but my mother springs into action, insisting she can do that for me and that I shouldn't exert myself.

Blue's eyes slide to mine before down casting in shame. *"So fixated was I on Elspeth that I couldn't see the danger right before you. I was angry at you for dangerously penetrating their organization."*

*Ew. Could you have used a different word?*

Blue chuckles, finding just enough courage to peer back up at me. *"I'm sorry I wasn't there to protect you."*

Mom busies herself with adjusting the flowers, making room by my bed if I feel like standing. She instructs me to ring the bell next to my bed if I need anything.

I stare back at Blue. *I'm not mad at you.*

*"Your feelings are irrelevant."*

*There's the cat I know and love.*

*"I served you poorly. If you think of a proper punishment, I will submit to it."*

I roll my eyes at him. *Sure, I'll let you know,* I send sardonically.

"Now," Mom settles me back down at the edge of my bed, taking the empty teacup from my hands. "Rest. That's the best thing you can do right now." Mom delicately kisses my bandaged forehead, then looks over at my windows. The shades begin to lower. She flicks her finger at an old CD player with a label that reads "Property of Marie, not Sally", and the glimmering harp music ceases. "I love you. Sleep well. Remember, if you need anything, ring that bell."

Blue nestles into my side. I nestle into the doughy folds of my bed lulling my broken, healing body to sleep. I close my eyes, and embrace the darkness, still holding the pansy in my palm.

Jack is driving a silver Lexus and his hands shake as he grips the steering wheel. The high beams cut through the darkness with the precision of a scalpel, illuminating everything in its wake. "Where are you," he utters to himself. His eyes dart about and he keeps placing his hands strangely over his heart. "You're close, I know you're close. Eleanor, I don't know how this works, but if you can hear me, please give me a sign."

I peer about as if I'm sitting in the passenger seat. He's driving through the woods and just around the bend his headlights catch billowy smoke and flames. Jack speeds up, whipping around the corner only to slam on his brakes. Parked on the side of the road is my Mercedes engulfed in flames. Jack throws his car in park and jumps out.

"Eleanor!" he shouts. He tears at his bowtie and tosses his tuxedo coat into the car before taking off into the woods. As if I'm merely a member of an audience watching a movie, I'm able to follow him running and shouting, aiming his flashlight all about.

"Eleanor!" he screams. He circles about, running his hands through his golden hair. His jaw trembles. He closes his eyes, places his hand over his heart once more, and steadies his breathing. For about a minute, he stands there, still and silent. Doubt and despair ebbs away at him as tears streak his cheeks. He continues hiking for what seems like hours, sweeping his flashlight in wide arcs across the forest floor.

His light shines on something white, like a mannequin discarded on the ground. He takes several staggering steps forward, his flashlight poised at the object a few yards away. It's not a mannequin, it's my body. It lays at an unnatural angle on the ground, twisted. My curls are matted in clots of blood and dirt. He sprints, hurdling over a fallen tree until he reaches where I lie.

He falls to his knees, his hands quiver reaching out for me. "No, no, please, no!"

My bruised and battered face is unrecognizable. My nose is bent awkwardly, my eyes are nothing but swollen, bloodied slits. The top of my dress is torn away, exposing my strapless bra covered in dark, dried blood.

He cradles me in his arms. "Please, Eleanor. Please come back to me. Eleanor, please," he cries. "Please!" He carefully places his fingers on my neck and closes his eyes. His eyes spring open detecting a pulse. He looks about and hoists me into the air carrying me the entire way back to the car. He delicately places me in the back seat and swiftly rushes to the driver's seat. "Helen," he calls my mother on the Bluetooth. "I've found her. I-I-I don't know if she's breathing. She's badly hurt. I can bring her to the hosp—" my mother interrupts him with firm instructions to bring me to the house.

His face is in agony as he races down the road dodging cars with near expertise. He glances at me from the rearview mirror.

"Allen. He did this. I knew he was in town. My mother must have been hiding him in the house. He didn't flee. He must be stopped. I have to do something," he mutters to himself, the grief in his voice eclipses into anger and hate.

The vision becomes fuzzy around the edges until fading out into black.

"Eleanor…" Jack's voice rings clearly in my head. "I need your help."

My eyes burst open, and I'm filled with panic. "Blue," I call. I can feel his movement in the dark. Using the air spell, I flick on the lights. I squint and blink as my eyes adjust to the sudden light.

Blue sits next to me.

"Something's wrong," I say.

*"Jack?"* He sends.

I nod. "I need to go." I carefully inch off the bed.

*"Forgive me, I understand I'm from a rather different time, but don't you have these marvelous inventions known as the mobile phone? You can't just call him?"* he sends sarcastically, sounding more like himself.

I glance about my room, wincing. A thought dawns on me. "I don't have a phone. It was in my car and they torched it." I swing my legs off my bed and immediately fall back onto the mattress. My right knee is bandaged and doesn't bend very well.

*"Eleanor, you can't do this. You need to stay and rest!"* Blue lunges to the floor, knocking over two daisy pots.

There's a rising tide of panic inside me that feels almost separate from me, as if it's being sent by another person. "Blue, this isn't me being irrationally worried. I can feel Jack is in trouble. I have to go."

*"Then get Helen, or Sally, or Marie. Shannyn's still here, too. Hell, bring all of them if you insist on leaving."*

There's a struggle, a thumping in my chest almost like a warning. "I can't risk their lives too. And if I tell them, they won't allow me to come. I don't have a choice," I say, feeling the weight and truth of my words. Whatever is happening with Jack, my family can't be involved.

*"Fine. But I'm coming with you."*

I slide into loose cotton pants with a drawstring waist and tug on a lightweight pullover, wincing with every movement. I then follow the tiny path between all the flowerpots to my bedroom door. The hallway seems menacing in the dark. The grandfather clock chimes the midnight hour. I carefully creep past the landing, holding my sides in. All the bedroom doors are open, probably to hear the bell from my room. A stab of guilt jabs my heart; this feels like a betrayal. I snag a cloth bag from under the bathroom sink and stash every healing balm and elixir from the medicine cabinet before tiptoeing back into the hall.

The floorboards moan beneath my feet. I whip my head around, then grimace at the pain. Worried someone might stir, I close my eyes and imagine gracefully levitating down the staircase like a phantom. *La Caeli*. Both feet lift off the ground and I float down the steps with all the grace of a one-eyed pigeon. I land at the bottom of the stairs and grip the rail just as the clock finishes chiming the hour. I brace for any sound of my family waking, but the house stays silent.

Blue grumbles following me out into the garage, snatching my mother's car keys. I forgo the seatbelt and drive into the night. *I'm coming, Jack.*

*"We'll see if he's alright, then it's straight back to the house."* Blue hisses in my head. *If there is any sign of trouble, Eleanor, you turn around and go home. Understand?"*

"Sure, I'll call Sheriff Fuller and get the hell out of dodge. Happy?"

*"I don't even remotely believe you."*

I slow down, pulling up to the community gate that's strangely left open. I peer into the little brick booth in the center of the lane. Empty. I drive through. Panic churns inside me. *Jack, please be okay.* The private security at the second gate is also curiously gone.

*"I don't like this."*

"For all we know, they quit. They didn't want to work for a murdering psychopath. Or they were all fired." I silently cruise up the drive. The spurting fountains have been shut off. Their immense topiaries loom like sinister, watchful figures in the dark. The lights that dotted either side of the blacktop are strangely turned off. The Woods residence that generally glowed like a glorious beacon is unusually dim, like the house itself is in mourning.

I leave my car mere feet from the front door. No valet greets me. Blue slinks beside me as we creep into the house. I squint nervously in the dark, climbing the stairs and trying to retrace my steps the night of the family dinner. After trying a few doors and failing, I find Jack's bedroom.

"Jack?" I croak, my throat is starting to feel raw again. I step inside, everything looks in order, nothing seems out of the ordinary. The closet doors are open, the light shines brightly, and the shoe rack in the middle is pulled to the side exposing the staircase into his studio. "Jack?" I call again as I drag my hands down the wall and carefully taking each step. The stairwell brightens the closer I get to the bottom.

I step into his studio and release a choking, strangled scream. Jack's lifeless body lies bloodied across the Persian rug.

# Chapter Fifty-Six
## Eternal consequences

"Jack!" I cry, taking a stumbling step forward.

"Don't!" Allen orders, his back to me as he cleans his bloodied hands in the sink at the bar. "Stay where you are." His white button up shirt is splattered with blood, his sleeves are rolled to his elbows.

My heart hammers in my chest as fear seizes me. My eyes dart back to Jack. "Jack!" I yell to him, still frozen to my spot by the stairs.

"You witches, truly astonishing." He dries his hands and forearms on a rag. He tosses it carelessly to the side. "We had a certified coroner declare your death. Yet," he smiles, spreading out his arms, "here you are."

My eyes slide from Allen to Jack and back.

*You're no match for my mother,* I think. My body shudders recalling the pain from our last meeting.

*"Say nothing."* Blue slinks over to Jack, sniffing him. *"He's breathing…"*

*Oh gosh! Thank Brighid.* I gasp and gulp back air, relieved.

Allen stares over at Blue with a cocked brow. "Your familiar looks *odd.*"

"He died a few centuries ago," I answer, staring at Jack watching him stir. I take a step forward only for Allen to wag his finger at me.

"Ah uh, I believe I told you not to move."

Blue circles Jack, examining him. *"He's badly hurt. He needs medical attention."*

"I knew you'd come. Witches seem to have an unnatural pull on their lovers." He stares disdainfully at his son motionless on the floor. "Look what you've brought him to. He had so much potential. So much promise. Wasted." He shakes his head, strolling past us.

With his back to us, I limp over to Jack and crumble to the floor next to him. I dig through my bag for a little tin filled with herbal tablets the size of a pea. I pop one into his open mouth. His clef chin is blue with fresh bruises, his right eye is black, and there is a small slit at the corner of his forehead.

Allen tugs a painting off the wall and smashes it on the ground, destroying

Jack's magnificent work. He tears down the sheet separating his studio from his sacred little corner that he dedicated to me.

Jack's eyes fly open. He gasps and his eyes roll about, landing on me with surprise and love, only to be overcome by terror.

"What are you doing here?" He reaches up, caressing my cheek. Blood is dried and cracked at his wrist, missing a chunk of skin where his tattoo has been flayed off.

I recoil from pain sitting in this position. My body feels disjointed, like jigsaw pieces that have been glued back together.

Jack shakes his head, pushing himself up. "We need to get you out of here." He helps me to my feet.

"You called for me, you needed me to come," I say.

Jack frowns at me. "I didn't call for you. I pushed you from my mind so you wouldn't—feel me, or whatever this is," he says, motioning between us. "You barely survived before. I would never put you in harm's way."

Although Allen doesn't turn around, he's keenly aware of us. He shakes his head, picking up a small square canvas of me standing at the edge of a cliff under a full moon. "Stay on the floor, Jackie boy. You belong there. Such a disappointment." He places the work of art under his shoe and stomps on it, fracturing the wooden frame.

Jack and I hobble towards the staircase as Blue trails behind us.

"*Look out!*"

A gunshot blasts. We instinctually duck out of the way. Jack tucks me behind him, and we turn to see a bullet hole in the cement wall behind us.

My ears ring from the discharge.

"That was a warning. Why don't you both take a seat," Allen says. His voice is light, almost cordial, savoring his torment. He waves his gun towards the short leather sofa in the far corner adjacent from him. He knocks another painting off the wall, an abstract of me and Jack embracing.

Jack clenches his jaw, keeping his face as neutral as possible. He reaches over to my lap, taking my hand, then releases a slow breath through his nostrils as his father rampages through years of work.

For the larger paintings, Allen retrieves a knife from his pocket and flicks out a blade. He silently stabs my naked spine in the skyline painting, then drags the knife down, only to abruptly stop. He pulls his knife back and takes a closer examination of the painting. His fingers trace a marking between my shoulder blades, an oddly wide and stout horseshoe. *An omega.*

In one of Jack's dreams, he saw that symbol on my back. I was always going to be branded. There was no escaping it. *But why? Am I supposed to end this once and for all?* We tried to terminate their hunting club through lawful means, but what if that wasn't the coarse, I was to follow…

*"Don't go down that road. We will find a way out of this."*

"I was unaware of your immense talent, Jack. Here you are, painting the future. Have you become one of them, then? Signed your name in the book?" Allen jabs his knife back in the painting and slashes down.

"There are more things in Heaven and Earth, Horatio, than are dreamt of in your philosophy," Jack answers, surprisingly glib.

Allen laughs a grunting, humorless laugh. "A waste of time, a spectacular waste of time." He knocks more paintings off the wall. "But you," he points his gun at me, "you have been rather extraordinary. A lifetime of meticulous work toppled by some wicked whore that's bewitched my son."

Jack flexes his hand into a tight fist, cracking his knuckles.

"Truly, no one has ever made a bigger mess of things," he says, slashing artwork as he speaks. "But I'm not worried. Are you familiar with the Lernaean Hydra, Eleanor?" he asks. He snaps the blade closed and tucks it in his pocket. "You cut off one head and another grows in its place. You'll never get rid of us. I'm just one man, but there are thousands of us, all with the same goal and gusto to rid the world of witches." He strides across the room in an undulating, cavalier stroll, like he's already won.

Allen stops a foot from the couch, cocking his head to the side, surveying me with careful consideration. He reaches forward, snagging my arm and roughly wrenching me off the couch. Jack leaps to his feet, cocking his arm back, but Allen slides the muzzle of the pistol across my ribs, stopping at my sternum. "Why don't you take a seat, son."

Jack lowers himself back on the couch, his breathing quick as he watches Allen slowly inch me against the wall. "You overplayed your hand, Allen. Hunters are being arrested all over the world. You won't recover from this."

Allen's boxy hand curls around my throat, tight enough to keep me in place while still allowing me to breathe. Everything, every word, every moment is weighed. He's just toying with us before he goes in for the kill.

He presses the gun deeper into me as he gazes over at Jack in utter disbelief. "It was you that copied the files, released the tape, called in the tips."

Jack glowers at his father. "Of course, it was me. Walden warned you I couldn't be trusted. But you couldn't be proven wrong. You decided no matter what I said in Ibiza, that I would be a Noble Hunter. You just never thought *you'd* be hunted."

Allen's eyes dart about, his entire paradigm crumbling. His hand slowly tightens. His head snaps in my direction. His smile is carved into his face, as if whittled there by a crude knife. His expression is wild, manic. With his gun shoved painfully into my ribs, he uses his free hand to grope my waist.

"At least my son hasn't chosen an ugly witch to spend his evenings with. Just a dumb one." With his hand gripping my throat, he runs his thumb over my lips. I try to wretch my face away, but I'm too sore, and he's too strong. "Looks like the innocent flower," he says, "but I know better. You were the serpent all along." He moves closer, throwing his son a lascivious smile.

I whimper against him, trying to jerk my head away.

Blue curses in my head. I can hear him struggle for a plan but coming up short. Can anything stop the rich and powerful? We did everything we could to stop him while following the rules, and he's still going to kill us. *He's going to kill Jack. Can I do what it takes to stop him?* My mind races with my heart. *What does that even mean? Would I have to hurt him, maybe even kill him? I can't, I won't! I'll become a Nefari for certain. I won't be with my family in the life to come. I'd give up ever seeing my father again.*

Allen presses his lips close to my bruised ear and chuckles softly. "You're a filthy, disgusting *witch*. The very thought of taking you that way makes me physically ill. And knowing you seduced my son away," he says, shoving the gun so hard into me I gasp and fall forward, leaning on his chest, "I need you to know before I pull this righteous trigger that it will be Jack next, then that little sister of yours, Margaret. Then Shannyn, your mother, your entire coven burned, and snuffed out for eternity."

Spiders crawl across Allen's face, in and out of his nose and mouth, clawing down his neck and arms. He flinches and twitches as they scurry about but stays rooted in front of me. "I know they aren't real. I know your tricks."

*Blue are you doing that? I'm not.*

"*Elspeth.*"

In a blur of movement, Jack lunges from the couch and tackles his father to the floor. The gun goes off, shooting a hole in the ceiling. Plaster dust explodes above us.

Jack wrestles his father as they both grapple for the gun. I hold my hand out, then hesitate. *If I use my magic, will I be able to control it?* My magic wants to rule over me. Allen throws a hard right hook to Jack's face. Jack's head snaps back taking the full brunt of the hit on his jaw.

I don't have time to deliberate, I have to think fast. Jack doesn't have time. I have to do something. I think of my family, my dad.

Allen crawls for the gun, but Jack leaps onto his back and struggles to put him into a sleeper hold. I watch in horror as Allen's hand finds the knife on the ground and he plunges it into Jack's side.

"NO!" I scream, rushing to Jack as Allen is released and scrambles for the gun and onto his feet. He aims the gun at Jack, bleeding out.

Jack gasps for air. His eyes bulge and his body falls limp to the floor. *I need to stop the bleeding.* I remove my top and press it into his side. I feel the gun's heavy glare. I lean over Jack, covering him with my body but carefully not placing any weight on him. I won't let Jack die, no matter the cost.

A malevolent giggle echoes out from the crevice of my mind. A voice, decadent and dark as night, whispers, *"Do it, Eleanor. It's either him or your beloved...you've made the decision, now act."*

I squeeze my eyes shut, envisioning exactly what I want my magic to do. I have to do this. Allen will keep coming and it'll never end. I will protect Jack even if it costs me...

*"Eleanor!"* Blue screeches.

The gun fires. The bullet slows, rotating in midair, arching back towards Allen. Before he can scream, the bullet burrows itself into the middle of Allen's forehead and he crashes onto the cement floor. The heir is dead.

Like a switch being flicked, the flow of my magic instantly ceases. I hurry and tend to Jack's wound, dress the bleed with the herbs and blessed wrapping I packed. "Jack, stay with me!" My top is soaked in his blood.

His face is waxen and slick. His eyes flutter open and close.

*I can't be too late!*

Something dark, something evil smiles inside me. *"Well done, Eleanor. Well done..."* Elspeth congratulates.

*Why?* I question, my chest heaving, exhausted from working the spell.

*"I needed you to spill the blood of a son or daughter. Now your power has grown as has mine..."* Her voice trails off as she fades away, leaving me for now.

I shake my head, banishing her from my thoughts as Jack needs my attention. I quickly retrieve his phone and call my mother, explaining where I am, and that Jack desperately needs her help. I lovingly caress Jack's cheek as his head rests in my lap. "It'll be okay," I whisper.

Allen forgot how that Greek story ended. Hercules burned each wound, cauterizing it so they wouldn't grow back. Allen can't curry any favors, train anymore foot soldiers. The head of the snake has been cut.

"Is it actually over?" Jack asks weakly, his eyes gently closed.

I delicately kiss his forehead. "Yes, it is."

Jack's bleeding has slowed, and his breathing is steady, albeit weak. I cradle him close.

*Blue,* I call out with my mind. *Elspeth is no longer bound. How did that happen?*

*"Eleanor."* Blue tip toes over to me and stares at me stoically. *"No test will be needed now. You took a human life. No matter how noble or right you believed it to be. Your magic will crave more blood, more carnage. You are now, and forever will be, a Nefarious witch..."*

I peer down at Jack's sallow face. I had no choice. And I would do it again.

# Epilogue
## To Heal, to Love, to Run

The sun was almost too bright as it shone down on the Academy's courtyard. The air was a cloud of Chanel number five. Contoured cheeks pressed to contoured cheeks, all self-congratulatory at their children's glorious graduation day while their husband's stepped away to answer calls from the office.

Evelyn Godspeed, as she's known these days, kept to herself wearing a carefully curated outfit to dispel any rumors about a dwindling fortune. Allen kept it carefully stowed away in offshore accounts and shell companies. Supposedly, Honor checks in with their accountants daily to make sure it's all there and accounted for.

He had to use a cane, but Jack was able to walk across the stage and accept his diploma. His mother and sister sat grim faced in the back of the audience, hiding behind oversized designer sunglasses. Sally leapt to her feet, cheering and hooting, making a spectacle while the rest of us blushed and cheered Jack on from our seats.

Allen Woods' funeral was a desolate gathering. The only one's present were Evelyn, Honor, Jack, and, at his request, me. Marshall is still "missing", evading authorities somewhere in South America.

I gave Jack's hand an affectionate squeeze as I bent my head, peering over at his eyes. I thought of that day, running into him in the hallways at Griggs, those eyes, once a virgin spring full of hope and innocence, now smoldering ashes.

It was ruled that Allen took his own life. My mother and the aunts assisted in making the wound look self-inflicted, moving the bullet hole from the center of his forehead to the temple. Eventually it will switch back, wearing off like a temporary tattoo, but by then Allen's body will be decaying beneath the earth.

With the head of Noble Hunting gone, the club was scattered to the wind, unorganized, desperate to keep their fortunes rather than continue their pernicious practices.

Sentences for the local members are still pending, but the legal analysts, talking heads on TV, and endless podcasters all predict certain doom for anyone involved. The grisly videos keep cropping up online only to be taken down, then popping back up on different channels, causing their defense attorneys to reconsider plea deals.

In the middle of July, my mother flipped off the television and forbade each of us from watching anymore coverage, saying it was time to move on. All summer long, Jack and I spent every moment together. My mother worked tirelessly to help ease my magic from attacking me whenever I experienced happiness, but my mother slowed down her efforts when she recognized the attacks occurred usually late at night when Jack and I would be alone, my magic grounding us to first base.

Elspeth is no longer bound in Purgatory. All she needed to sever the binding was my vow to release her. Apparently, vows made in Purgatory are iron clad. Since then, she has remained oddly quiet. Blue believes she is passing through different planes seeking further help in her quest to return as spilling the blood of a human has made her more powerful, enough she believes she can be reborn.

"So, will I get a sibling or will she murder my family?" I questioned darkly one night after wedding cake tasting with my mom and sisters.

Blue shook his head, beset with me. *"You haven't studied any of the readings I've given you. You made a promise which unbound her, so she'll be able to contact us much easier. You took a human life so now she's powerful enough that she may pass through the different circles of Hell and Purgatory but she's still a disembodied spirit, she can't harm anyone. Other than possibly us..."*

"Why would she want to go to Hell?" I asked.

*"She's a witch, they are regarded like royalty there, obsequious demons will be eager to assist her quest in finding a body for herself."*

That was weeks ago, and still no word from Elspeth.

I shake and fluff out my hair, ready to tour the RISD campus with Jack. And, of course, check out his off-campus apartment. I finger the north star my mother gave me, resting against my fully healed collarbone. I know it saved me the night of the branding, a mother's protection.

As I snag my Converse high tops from my wardrobe, my bedroom door swings open. Maggie, wearing a swimsuit and cutoffs, is licking a popsicle. Of course, my baby sister is the one redhead in the world that can tan with little to no effort. "Mom told me to come tell you to stay in your room," she says, before hastily licking a red syrupy drip.

I roll my eyes groaning. "What? No, I'm not grounded anymore, she said I could go," I complain hoisting myself to my feet. After sneaking out of the house to rescue Jack, my mother grounded me for two solid months for not seeking help. I wasn't allowed to leave the house, but Jack was at least allowed to come over. My mother felt his house was more akin to a prison after his father's passing and decided he should be allowed to spend his time with us.

I march down my tower steps to the second landing, but Blue pounces in front of me.

*"Don't!"* He warns.

I frown at him, then my ears perk up, hearing my mother and aunts entertaining someone downstairs.

"That's very troubling, are you sure?" my mother asks.

Maggie and I crane our heads, peering through the spindles of the spiral staircase.

Mom sits, perched on the edge of the sofa with her sisters as Mercy Wicklow, head of the North American Witches Committee stands, addressing them, commanding the room.

"Yes," Mercy insists. "We are detecting high levels of Nefari activity in the city. Which is why Helen, we would like to induct you into The Committee. You're a powerful witch and I believe you can help us bring the Nefari to their knees once and for all..."

Maggie's head slowly turns, gazing over at me. "Aren't you a Nefari?" she asks nervously.

I guess my days of running aren't over...

# THE END

# ABOUT THE AUTHOR

Kellie O'Neill originally wrote the Daughters of Salem series when she was sixteen years old, and the first edition of Burned was published while she was in high school.

This updated version was published ahead of the next of the three books in the series which Kellie is looking forward to publishing soon.

In her spare time, Kellie haunts her local bookstore and takes classes on neuropsychology. She currently resides in Texas where she enjoys life as a wife and mother.

## A WORD FROM THE AUTHOR

"Thank you so much for reading *Burned*. The Daughters of Salem story is very dear to me, and I am beyond excited to be able to share it with the world. Life for Eleanor and Jack is about to become infinitely more complex, and I hope you'll continue that journey with us to the end."

– *Kellie O'Neill*

For more information about Kellie's beloved characters and the future of the Daughters of Salem series, visit:

# www.kellieoneillbooks.com

Made in the USA
Las Vegas, NV
14 January 2024